The Wine of Angels

Tears are the Wine of Angels . . .
the best . . . to quench the devil's fires.

from a seventeenth-century meditation
attributed to Thomas Traherne

Phil Rickman

THE WINE OF ANGELS & CANDLELIGHT

PAN BOOKS

The Wine of Angels first published 1998 by Macmillan
Candlelight first published 1991 by Gerald Duckworth & Co. Ltd

This omnibus edition published 2002 by Pan Books
an imprint of Pan Macmillan Ltd
Pan Macmillan, 20 New Wharf Road, London N1 9RR
Basingstoke and Oxford
Associated companies throughout the world
www.panmacmillan.com

ISBN 0 330 41514 X

1 3 5 7 9 8 6 4 2

A CIP catalogue record for this book is available from
the British Library.

Printed and bound in Great Britain by
Mackays of Chatham plc, Chatham, Kent

The Wine of Angels
&
Candlelight

Phil Rickman was born in Lancashire. He has won awards for his TV and radio journalism, and his highly acclaimed novels *Candlelight, Crybbe, The Man in the Moss, December* and *The Chalice* are also available from Pan Books in paperback, as is *Midwinter of the Spirit,* which charts Merrily Watkins's eventful debut as diocesan exorcist. He is married and lives on the Welsh Border.

Visit the Phil Rickman Web site at
http://www.geocities.com/philrickman

Also by Phil Rickman

CRYBBE
THE MAN IN THE MOSS
DECEMBER
THE CHALICE
THE WINE OF ANGELS

Prologue

Old Winter's frost and hoary hair
With garland's crowned . . .

Thomas Traherne,
Poems of Felicity

Prologue

Twelfth Night

Twisty old devil.

Looked as if it held a grudge in every scabby branch, and if you touched it there'd be sharp, pointy bits, like thorns. And it wouldn't give you any fruit, on principle, wassail or no wassail, because, left to rot, apple trees . . .

. . . *they grows resentful.*

Merrily's grandad had told her that once, when she was a little girl. Frightening her, because you always thought of apples as cheerful and wholesome. Oaks could be gnarled and forbidding, pines scraggy and cruel. But apple trees were essentially good-natured, weren't they? All the same, every evening for weeks afterwards, Merrily would go down to the orchard and wish the trees a wary goodnight, assuring them they could always count on being looked after as long as she was around.

This was Merrily's problem. Always felt responsible.

Perhaps, to get Grandad Watkins's point, you had to see a tree as old as this one on a night this cold, the orchard glittering grimly in bilious lamplight.

Merrily shivered like a little rabbit inside her tired, old, fake Barbour, stamping her boots on the stone-hard earth in the clearing.

There'd be about thirty of them, strangers now, but people she'd have to get to know very well if she decided to go for it. They didn't look over-friendly at the moment, all hunched up in a hand-rubbing, steam-breathing circle, like tramps around a brazier.

Except there wasn't a brazier. Just this frosted, naked apple tree, the biggest one remaining in an orchard left to rot for years. But no ordinary apple tree – according to Mrs Caroline Cassidy, of the famous Cassidy's Country Kitchen, this was the Apple Tree *Man*.

The very spirit of the orchard.

So now we all know. Merrily turned away and sighed, and the sigh recorded itself on the frigid air as a tiny white cloud. Uncle Ted, who'd excused himself because of a cold, thought it might be an interesting experience for her. To observe a cross-section of the parish. Go undercover, armed with Ted's word-portraits of the major players. All of them at least occasional churchgoers. But wasn't this ritual just a bit . . .?

'Barbaric,' Miss Lucy Devenish muttered, more loudly than she needed to. 'Utterly barbaric. Isn't seemly. Isn't local. Isn't *right*.'

Actually *pagan* had been the word Merrily had in mind, but barbaric would do. According to Uncle Ted, Miss Devenish had been muttering about this for most of the past week. Been along to a meeting of the parish council to demand they get it stopped. Which, of course, was beyond the powers of the parish council to do even if they'd wanted to offend Councillor Powell, who owned the orchard. She'd also have known better than to petition the vicar. *Lesson one*, Uncle Ted said: *keep your nose out where you can.*

'Isn't traditional to the area,' Miss Devenish said. 'And so it *can't* be right. Do you see my point?'

She wore a big, wide-brimmed hat and a camel-hair poncho. Looked like an old Red Indian scout, talked like a headmistress. *Delightful old girl*, Uncle Ted had said. *May,*

4

however, be some sort of witch. Don't be tempted to get too close.
But Miss Devenish was talking to her.

'Well . . . picturesque though,' Merrily said feebly. 'In a Christmas card sort of way.'

Some folk were holding up hurricane lamps, throwing oily light on frosty bark, bringing up a dull lustre on the barrels of the shotguns.

Which were *not* very Christmas card.

Seven of them. Carried by local farmers and landowners and patrons of the Cassidy restaurant who happened to be country-sports enthusiasts or clay-shooters. *Lesson seventeen: where bloodsports are concerned, sit on the fence and hope for the best.*

'Oh hell,' said Lucy Devenish. 'Here it comes.'

Smiling a troublemaker's smile at the arrival of the organizer, Mr Terrence – *Not* Terry, If You Don't Mind – Cassidy. Long, herringbone-tweed overcoat, Russian-style furry hat. Learned-looking, in half-glasses.

'Right. Are we all here? Good, good.' Mr Cassidy positioned himself under a lamp on a stick. 'But do we all know *why* we're here?'

Like a teacher addressing an infants' class. According to Uncle Ted, who'd lived here most of his adult life, the secret of being accepted in the village was to keep your head well down for two years' minimum. But the Cassidys clearly weren't keeping-your-head-down people. While her husband was lecturing the poor primitive yokels about the importance of their traditions, Mrs Caroline Cassidy, all kitted-out for skiing in the Alps, was arranging plastic beermugs on a wooden picnic table beside the frost-rimed cask of cider. Occasionally flicking a glance towards Miss Devenish, who was Trouble.

Through the hoary trees behind her, Merrily could see

the village lights: yellow, amber and red behind drawn curtains: very cosy, but strangely far away. By day, you would have seen the church through the naked trees. At night, the orchard was a separate place.

'. . . and so, people, we revive a very ancient custom.'

Mr Cassidy had a high, nasal voice, like the wind down a drainpipe. He reminded them that next May would see the start of the first Ledwardine Festival: a summer-long smorgasbord of music, poetry, drama, houses and gardens open to the public, guided tours. A major exhibition of Our Heritage.

Lucy Devenish snorted.

Mr Cassidy raised his voice. 'And as fine local cider *was* that heritage, we intend . . . that it should be revived.'

Pause for gasps that didn't come. Nice enough idea, Merrily thought, but it was never going to be any more than a gimmick. The cider trade in Herefordshire was pretty well sewn up, most growers in these parts selling their apples in bulk to Bulmers or Dunkertons. Anyway, most of the orchards hereabouts had been grubbed up during the great Victorian cider-slump.

'We shall be recommending local cider at our own restaurant. The Black Swan, will also, I trust, promote it. But, of course, the creation of this venerable beverage depends upon obtaining a significant crop of the famous Pharisees Red. As grown for centuries, in this very orchard, by . . .'

Cassidy extended an arm, like a variety-show compère.

'. . . the Powell family.'

Everybody stared across at Garrod, farmer and county councillor, and his son Lloyd. And Grandad – Edgar, was it? – gripping the stock of the family shotgun with fingers like knotty little roots and staring directly at Merrily. But not seeing her, she was sure. He wasn't here at all, wasn't old Edgar.

Everybody else merely didn't *want* to be here. Because, of course, it was pointless, it was artificial, it had been put on mainly for the Press who hadn't bothered to turn up. And it was *so . . . bloody . . . cold.*

Merrily pulled up the hood of her fake Barbour. This wasn't the right attitude, was it? She should be cheerful, hearty. Joining in. But this . . . this facsimile of rural life as it was thought to have been lived, this 'traditional' gathering involving, for the most part, incomers, while the members of the old, yeoman families sat at home watching the late movies with cans of lager and the remains of a tandoori . . . well, this also left her cold.

Lucy Devenish was breathing like a bull over a gate as Mr Cassidy explained how the Powells had graciously agreed to let them have last year's crop for the festival cider.

'However, as the apple harvest in recent years has been somewhat limited, my ever-resourceful wife proposed that we might resort to the time-honoured method of arousing the, ah, temporarily dormant fecundity of the orchard.'

'Pompous arsehole,' Miss Devenish growled.

'The happy tradition of wassailing' – Mr Cassidy, looking as happy as the night and his thin, pale face would allow – 'dates back, presumably, to pagan times, it being necessary to petition the gods in good time for spring. I am not myself *particularly* moved to call upon the services of those ancient deities, but I *do* believe that the good wishes of neighbours – symbolically expressed here tonight – will have a strongly beneficial effect on this once-supreme orchard, and on the festival . . . and, indeed, on the fortunes of our village.'

'Do you know how long they've lived here?' Miss Devenish muttered. 'One and a half years. *Our* village.'

'Gerronwithit.' A small, wiry man in a flat cap and a muffler bit down on his cigarette. Gomer Parry, Merrily remembered. Former digger-driver and contractor. Frost had turned his little round glasses into communion wafers. 'All bloody hot air,' Gomer mumbled. His plump wife – pink earmuffs – nudged him in the ribs.

Merrily glimpsed a smirk on the taut, patrician face of James Bull-Davies, of Upper Hall. He was passing a chromium flask to a blonde woman next to him. Very *much* next to him. She had a swig and giggled as she helped him stow the flask inside his sheepskin bomber-jacket, hungrily kneading his chest through his sweater.

Hence the smirk. Merrily pretended not to notice. *Lesson five: Don't offend anyone called Bull-Davies; the church would be rubble but for them.*

'With all this talk of paganism,' Cassidy was saying, 'it's a pity we don't at present have a parish priest to balance things up, but I'm assured a number of candidates for the living are being interviewed. And, indeed, the word is that one of them may even be in the village tonight.'

Oh no. Merrily shrank behind a lesser apple tree.

'I don't think I should say any more than that.'

Good.

'And so, without further ado, I call upon James and his colleagues to check their cartridges or whatever they need to do. And let the wassailing—'

'*One moment!*'

Miss Lucy Devenish had swept back her poncho like a veteran warrior from the Dark Ages and marched into the centre of the clearing.

'You really don't know what the hell you're doing, do you? This has always been a peaceful place, a place of seclusion. It is also virtually adjacent to the churchyard and is itself a burial place . . .'

'Miss Devenish—'

'And there is absolutely no way at all that you can justify these frightful *guns*.'

8

'Miss Devenish, we've been into all this before—'

'And I'll prove that. I'll *prove* it to you. Because, you see, I have with me – ' Miss Devenish paused dramatically and held up the large book she'd been concealing under her poncho ' – *Mrs Leather*!'

Ella Leather. *The Folklore of Herefordshire*, published 1912.

'This . . .' Mr Cassidy rose up in the lamplight '. . . is inexcusable.'

'Now. According to Mrs Leather, the custom of wassailing on Twelfth Night involved lighting fires in the fields – usually wheatfields, *not* apple orchards, for obvious reasons, but I shall let that pass – and there is *no mention at all* . . . of the use of firearms.'

A few people started murmuring. Miss Devenish glared defiantly at Cassidy in the lamplight, clasping the old book to her chest.

'Now just a minute!' Mrs Caroline Cassidy had appeared behind an impatient frown. 'Terrence . . . torch!' She had a large book as well.

Mr Cassidy directed the flashlight beam as his wife riffled through the pages.

'OK, right,' Caroline trilled. '*Collected Folk Customs of the British Isles*, page one hundred and five. I quote: "It was customary for such members of the local yeomanry as possessed guns to assemble around the largest tree in the orchard, referred to as the Apple Tree Man, and to discharge their weapons into its topmost branches in the belief that this would drive away evil spirits and stimulate fertility." *There*.'

'Where?' demanded Miss Devenish.

'I've just told you, *Collected Folk Customs of the British Isles*, by C. Alfred Churchman—'

'I mean where*abouts* in the British Isles is this nonsense supposed to have been enacted?'

9

'In the West of England, of course. Are we not—?'

'*Precisely?*' Miss Devenish tilted her head under its enormous cowboy hat. '*May* one ask?'

'Oh, this is utterly nonsensical.' Mrs Cassidy getting increasingly shrill. 'Everyone knew what we'd agreed.'

'What *we'd* agreed? My dear Mrs Cassidy, if we *had* to do this, some of us might have preferred an innocent singalong over the wassail cup. As distinct from a remake of the Gunfight at the OK Corral.'

'Oh, a *singalong*.' Mrs Cassidy threw up her hands, appealing to the crowd. 'How very spectacular.'

'Certainly less insulting to the poor trees. Now, are you going to tell us where this dubious business with guns was last recorded, or not?'

Mrs Cassidy looked sulky and brushed at her designer ski-jacket. 'Devonshire. But I don't see that it matters.'

'Well, you wouldn't, would you?'

'Now, look here—'

'Ladies!' James Bull-Davies had stepped forward now, shotgun casually broken over an arm. 'Look. Mindful as one must be of old customs, it really is awfully cold. Why don't we proceed with the aspect we're all agreed on and pour out this excellent cider 'fore the damn stuff freezes over? Discuss it over a drink is what I'm suggesting.'

Recognizing the semi-military tone of the Old Squire-archy, even the Cassidys shut up. Bull-Davies bent over the cask and started filling the plastic tumblers himself. Merrily smelled the cider, sour and musty. She wondered where they'd got it from.

She found herself glancing at old Edgar Powell. His face like an old tobacco pouch and his eyes wide open, still looking her way. He wasn't here tonight, old Edgar, wasn't here at all.

Perhaps, wherever he was, that was a better place to be tonight.

*

'Of course, we all know what all this is about,' Miss Devenish told her in a very loud whisper. 'These awful people – these Cassidys – they think the Powells could be terribly quaint and old-fashioned, with their ancient cider press and their old recipe, and they just want to turn them into a tourist sideshow. And Garrod Powell's going along with it to keep the peace and just in case there's a few quid to be made without too much work, and—'

'Is that so bad for the village?'

'Bad?' Miss Devenish snorted. 'The Cassidys'll just turn honest cider into some horrible fizz in champagne bottles and sell it for a quite ridiculous price in their ghastly restaurant to awful people like themselves. When I was a gel, the farm labourers still used to receive gallons of Pharisee Red as part of their wages. It was the People's drink. Do you see?'

'My grandad used to say it was just a way of keeping them grossly underpaid and too drunk to notice,' said Merrily.

'Your grandad?' Miss Devenish observing her shrewdly from under that hat, possibly putting two and two together. 'Are you local, my dear?'

'Sort of. My grandfather had a farm about six miles away. Mansell Lacy.'

'Jolly good. Who was your grandfather?'

'Charlie Watkins?'

'Didn't know him personally, but there are many Watkinses in the area. My God . . .' Miss Devenish was gazing over Merrily's left shoulder. 'Just look at that little whore with Bull-Davies. She'll have his cock out in a minute.'

'Huh?'

'Alison Kinnersley. A destroyer, I suspect.'

Merrily risked a glance. Bull-Davies was talking to some of the other guys with guns. Alison Kinnersley was standing behind him, keeping her hands warm in his trouser pockets.

'That poor boy.'

'James Bull-Davies?'

'Good heavens, no. Kinnersley's boyfriend. Former boyfriend. Not the Bull. The Bulls can look after themselves. Trouble is, they want to look after everyone else. But it goes wrong. Never trust the Bulls, my dear. Remember that. Remember poor Will.'

'Sorry?'

'OK! Listen, everybody!'

James Bull-Davies had disentangled himself from Alison. He reached up, snapped a lump of brittle, dead branch from the Apple Tree Man and banged it on the cider cask, like a chairman's gavel.

'We're going to do it. Had a brief chat with the chaps here. Seven of us brought shotguns along, and if we're talking about old traditions, well, I rather suspect there must be one about it being bad luck to take one's weapon home without loosing orf a single shot. Miss Devenish – apologies, but we're going to do it.'

Miss Devenish stiffened as the shotgun men gathered in a semicircle around the tree, shuffling cartridges from their pockets.

'Something we have to sing or something, is there, Terrence?' boomed Bull-Davies.

'I have it here, James. It's a sort of chant. If you say it after me . . .'

'OK. Orf you go then. Stand back, everybody. Well back.'

There was silence, everyone waiting.

Miss Devenish said loudly, 'Well, I've done all I can. If you wish to disturb the dead, go ahead.'

Her voice still rang in the hard air as she turned away. Bull-Davies shrugged as he accepted the folklore book, cleared his throat and began to read.

'Hail to thee, old apple tree!'

'*Hail to thee, old apple tree,*' the shooters chanted, gruffly self-conscious.

'And let thy branches fruitful be . . .'

'*And let thy branches . . .*'

'Going to cause offence.' Miss Devenish had a prominent hooked nose; it twitched. 'Can't anyone see that? Deep offence.'

Merrily shook her head, tired of all this. It wasn't as if they were going to shoot any animals; just blast a few pounds of shot into the air through branches that were probably mostly already dead.

'Why did he have to break off that branch? Showing his contempt, you see. For the tree and all that dwells there.'

'Well,' said Merrily, 'there's nothing dwelling in there now, is there?'

Miss Devenish pulled the wide brim of her hat down over her ears as the gunmen chanted.

'. . . *armsful, hatsful, cartsful of apples . . .*

Huzzah!

Huzzah!

Huzzah!'

And shouldered their shotguns. Merrily thought, unnerved for a second, of a firing squad, as Miss Devenish turned away and the night went *whump, whump, whump, whump-ump-ump,* and the air was full of cordite farts.

Merrily was aware of a fine spray on her face. Probably particles of ice from the shocked branches, but it felt warm, like the poor old Apple Tree Man was weeping.

When the shooting stopped, there was a touch of anti-climax. Obviously the book didn't say what you did afterwards.

'Er ... well done, chaps,' James Bull-Davies said half-heartedly.

A few villagers clapped in a desultory sort of way. Caroline Cassidy came out from behind a tree and sniffed.

'We haven't got a single picture of this, have we? As for the BBC ... I shall write and complain.'

Merrily was aware of a silence growing in the clearing, the sort of silence that was like a balloon being blown up, and up and up, until ...

The half-scream, half-retch from only yards away was more penetrating than any bang, and it came as Caroline Cassidy's features went as flaccid as a rubber clown-mask, lips sagging, eyes staring, and she cried, 'What's that on your *face*?'

In the middle of the scream – it had come from Alison Kinnersley – Merrily had put a hand to her face and felt wetness, and now she held up her hand to the light and it was smeared dark red.

'I say, look, get ... get back ...' The voice of James Bull-Davies pitched schoolboy-high.

'Bloody Nora,' Gomer Parry said hoarsely.

Merrily saw black drips on Garrod Powell's cap-shaded cheeks. A smear around Lloyd's mouth like badly applied lipstick. Spots on Gomer's glasses. Blotches on his wife's earmuffs, hanging around her neck like headphones.

Caroline Cassidy teetered back in her thigh-boots, making an ugly snuffling noise, and Merrily saw the worst and went stiff with the shock.

Between the Powells, at the foot of the stricken old tree, what looked like a milk churn in an overcoat was pumping out dark fluid, black milk.

A scarf of cold tightened around Merrily's throat.

'What's the matter?' Terrence Cassidy's cultured tones rising ludicrously out of the clearing, like something out of Noël Coward. 'What's happened? I don't understand. For heaven's sake, all we wanted to . . .'

Gomer Parry looked up at Cassidy through his red glasses and spat out his cigarette. 'Somebody better call the police, I reckon.'

Merrily had found a handkerchief and was numbly wiping the blood from her face. Unable to pull her gaze away from the horror inside the collar of Edgar's overcoat, knowing that most of his head would be in the tree, hanging like some garish leftover Christmas bauble amid tinselly, frosted twigs.

She crumpled the handkerchief. Her face was still wet. It felt like some horrific baptism.

And, hearing Miss Devenish whispering, '*I knew it, I knew it*,' she knew she would have to look up into the tree.

Part One

Can closed eyes even in the darkest night
See through their lids and be inform'd with sight?

Thomas Traherne,
Poems of Felicity

ONE

Third Floor

Merrily had a recurring dream. She'd read somewhere that it was really quite a common dream, with obvious symbolism.

By recurring . . . well, she'd have it maybe once every few months, or the gaps might be even longer nowadays.

There *was* a period, not long before Sean died, when it came almost nightly. Or even, in that intense and suffocating period, twice or three times the same night – she'd close her eyes and the dream would be waiting there like an empty train by a deserted platform. Sometimes it was merely puzzling, sometimes it seemed to open up exciting possibilities. Occasionally, it was very frightening and she awoke shredded with dread.

What happened . . . she was in a house. Not always the same house, but it was her own house, and she'd lived there quite some time without realizing. Or sometimes she'd just forgotten, she'd gone on living there, possibly for years, without registering that the house had . . . a third floor.

It was clear that she'd lived quite comfortably in this house, which was often bright and pleasant, and that she must have passed the extra staircase thousands of times, either unaware of it or because there was simply no reason to go up there.

In the dream, however, she *had* to go up. With varying

amounts of anticipation or cold dread. Because something up there had made its presence known to her.

She'd nearly always awaken before she made it to the top of the stairs. Either disappointed or trembling with relief. Just occasionally, before her eyes opened, she would glimpse a gloomy, airless landing with a row of grey doors.

In reality, if you excluded flats, she had never lived in a three-storey house.

Now, however . . .

*

'Jesus,' Merrily said. 'We can't live in *this*.'

'Yes, I suppose it is big,' Uncle Ted conceded. 'Didn't think about that. Never a problem for Alf Hayden. Six kids, endless grandchildren . . .'

It was big, all right. Seventeenth century, timber-framed, black and white. Seven bedrooms. Absolutely bloody huge if there was just the two of you. Very quaint, but also unexpectedly, depressingly grotty; nothing seemed to have altered since about the 1950s.

'Of course, it's church policy these days to flog off these draughty old vicarages,' Uncle Ted said. 'Replace them with nice, modern boxes. Worth a lot of money, your old black and whites. Well . . . not this one, at present, not in the state it's in after thirty-odd years of Alf and Betty.'

There was quaint, Merrily thought, and there was horribly old-fashioned. Like the steel-grey four-bar electric fire blocking up the inglenook. Like a kitchen the size of a small abattoir with no real cupboards but endless open shelves and all the pipes coiled under the sink like a nest of cobras.

'Besides,' Ted said, 'we haven't got any nice, modern boxes to spare. Three applications for housing estates've been turned down in as many years. Not in keeping.' He frowned.

'Conservation's a fine idea, but not when it turns a nice, old village into an enclave of the elite.'

In his habitual cardigan and slippers, Ted Clowes, two years retired, didn't look at all like a lawyer any more. His face had gone ruddy, like a farmer's, and his body had thickened. He looked as seasoned and solid as one of the oak pillars holding up the vicarage walls.

As senior church warden, Ted had made himself responsible for getting the vicarage into some kind of shape. Negotiating with builders and plumbers and decorators. But, well into April, the work had hardly begun; it looked as though Merrily was going to have to spend the first month of her ministry in a bed-and-breakfast.

She was relieved, in a way. A place this size – it was ridiculous. And an unoccupied third floor, full of dust and echoes.

*

She stood on the first-floor landing, miserably looking up. 'All these staircases.'

'Yeah,' Jane said thoughtfully. 'This puts a whole new perspective on the entire scenario.'

'It does?'

Merrily watched warily as the kid took off up the stairs to the third storey. She'd been sulking, on and off, for three days. She'd quite enjoyed the two years in Birmingham while Merrily was at college, loved the time in Liverpool when Merrily was a curate. Big-city woman now. On the way here, she'd said that if Cheltenham was an old people's home, rural Herefordshire looked like premature burial.

'*Yes*.' Jane paused halfway up, looking around.

'You *like* this?'

'At least we've cleared all those rooms now,' Ted said.

21

'Alf and Betty were generous enough to leave us a quarter of a century's worth of junk. Yellowing newspapers with pictures of the first moon-landing.'

Jane had a forefinger placed pensively on her chin. 'Far more rooms than you'd need, Mum, right?'

'Mmm . . . yes.'

'Even for all your Bible classes and parish meetings and visiting evangelists from Nigeria.'

'Ye . . . es. Unless, of course, they're travelling with their extended families.'

'So this whole storey is, in effect, going spare.'

'Conceivably.'

Her daughter was starting to operate like a slick barrister. (The barrister Merrily might have become had it not been for God's unexpected little blessing. Would she still eventually have wound up in the Church if Jane hadn't come along?)

'Don't look at me like that, Mum. All I'm saying is I could have a kind of group of rooms up here. Like a suite. Because . . . be*cause* . . . if you think about it, those back stairs come off a separate entrance . . . a third door, right?'

Ted chuckled. He knew all about daughters.

'Right,' Merrily said. 'And?'

'So it would be kind of my own entrance. It would be . . . in fact . . . like *my own flat.*'

'Oh. I see.'

The third door with its own illuminated bell and a card under perspex: *Flat One. Ms Jane Watkins.* She was fifteen.

'And you'd pay the heating bills for this, er, suite, would you?'

'Oh God.' Jane glared down over the oak banister. 'Here we go. Mrs bloody Negative.'

'Or maybe you could sub-let a couple of rooms.'

Jane scowled and flounced off along the short passage. Oak floorboards creaked, a door rattled open. That empty sound.

'Could be a double-bluff.' Merrily said, her daughter pacing bare boards overhead, probably working out where to put her stereo speakers for optimum sound. 'The picture she's feeding me is that she's going to be so bored here she'll have to invite half the young farmers' club over for wild parties. All these rural Romeos popping pills on the back stairs.'

Ted laughed. 'Young farmers aren't pill-popping yet. Well . . . none that I know of. Pressure job, now, though. Diminishing returns, EC on your back, quotas for this, quotas for that, a hundred forms to fill in, mad cow disease. Suicide figures are already . . . Sorry. Bad memories.'

'What? Oh.'

'I seem to remember saying, "If you want an informal picture of village life, why not pop along to this wassailing thing?" Not quite what I had in mind. Awfully sorry, Merrily.'

She looked through the landing window, down into a small, square rose garden, where the pink and orange of the soil seemed more exotic than the flowers. Over a hedge lay the churchyard with its cosy, sandstone graves.

Oddly, that awful, public death hadn't given her a single nightmare. In her memory it was all too surreal. As though violent death had been an optional climax to the wassailing and, as the oldest shooter in the pack, Edgar Powell had felt obliged to take it.

'You know, standing in that orchard, covered with that poor old bloke's blood, that was when I decided to go for it. I clearly remember thinking that nothing so immediate and so utterly shocking ever happened quite that close to me in

Liverpool. That maybe, in some ways, this village could actually be the sharp end. I thought, am I going to wash off his blood and walk away?'

'It always affects you more in the country.' Ted came to stand beside her at the window. 'Everything that happens. Because you know everybody. *Every*body. And you'll find, as minister, that you're regarded as more of a . . . a *key person*. Births and deaths, you really have to *be* there. Even if nobody from the family's been to a church service since the war.'

'That's fair enough. Far as I'm concerned, belonging to the Church doesn't have to involve coming to services.'

'And you'll find that hills and meadows are far more claustrophobic than housing estates. You see somebody coming across a twelve-acre field towards you, you can't dodge into a bus shelter.'

'Fine.'

Ted raised a dubious eyebrow. 'And everybody gossips,' he said. 'For instance, they'll all tell you Edgar Powell'd been handling that shotgun since for ever.'

'Making it suicide?'

'What it looks like, but they haven't got a motive. Money worries? No more than the average farmer. Isolation? Hardly – not living on the edge of the village. Depression? Hard to say. Perhaps he'd just had enough. Or perhaps he simply wanted to ruin the Cassidys' olde English soirée. Been a spiteful old bugger in his time.'

'You *are* kidding, aren't you?'

'Anyway, Garrod Powell's insisting it was an accident. Came to consult me about it. He'll be telling the coroner the old chap was simply going soft in the head. Can't blame him. Who wants a family suicide? I suggested he have a word with young Asprey, get something medical. But it could even be an open verdict.'

'What's that mean exactly, Uncle Ted?'

Merrily turned to find Jane sitting on the top stair, elbows on knees, chin cupped in her hands.

'Means they can't be entirely sure what happened, Jane,' Ted said.

'Wish I'd been there.'

Merrily rolled her eyes. Having made a point of leaving Jane at her mother's when she'd come to do her bit of undercover surveillance prior to applying – or not – for the post. The kid would've given them away in no time.

'Do you get many suicides in the village?' Jane asked.

'Not with audience-participation,' Ted said dryly.

Merrily was thinking, half-guiltily, how she'd scrubbed and scrubbed at her face that night and had to throw away the old fake Barbour.

*

They stayed the night at the Black Swan, sharing a room. On the third floor, as it happened, but it was different in a hotel. The Black Swan, like all the major buildings in Ledwardine – with the obvious exception of the vicarage – had been sensitively modernized; the room was ancient but luxurious.

Jane was asleep about thirty seconds after sliding into her bed. Jane could slip into untroubled sleep anywhere. She'd accepted her father's death with an equanimity that was almost worrying. A blip. Sean had lived in the fast lane and that was precisely where he died. Bang. Gone.

Sadder about the girl in the car with him. She could have been Jane in a few years' time. Or Merrily herself, ten years or so earlier.

Too many thoughts crowding in, Merrily upended the pillow behind her, leaned into it and lit the last cigarette of the day. Through the deep, oak-sunk window, the crooked, picture-book roofs of the village snuggled into a soft and woolly pale night sky.

Perfect. Too perfect, perhaps. If you actually lived here, with roses round the door, what was there left to dream of?

*

'How are things financially, now?' Ted had asked in the lounge bar, after dinner.

Jane had mooched off into the untypically warm April evening to check out the village. And the local totty, she'd added provocatively.

'Oh – ' Merrily drank some lager ' – we get by. Sean's debts weren't as awesome as we'd been led to believe. And a few of the debtors seem less eager to collect than they were at first. I think it was meeting me. In the dog collar. It was like . . . you know . . . dangling a sprig of garlic in front of Dracula. I'm glad I met them. I don't feel so bad about it now I know what kind of semi-criminal creeps they are. Jesus, what am I saying, *semi*?'

'I won't ask. But I did think he was being a little over-ambitious setting up on his own. Why didn't you both come to me for some advice?'

'You know Sean. Knew. Anyway, I blame myself. If I hadn't got pregnant instead of a degree, it was going to be Super-lawyer and Lois-thing, defending the poor, serving the cause of real justice. Zap. Pow. But . . . there you go. He was on his own, and with the responsibility of a kid and every-thing, he was floundering, and he got a little careless about the clients he took on. It's a slippery slope. I wasn't aware of the way things were going. Too busy being mummy.'

'You blame yourself for letting him get you pregnant?' Ted raised helpless eyes to the ceiling. 'Blame yourself for anything, won't you, Merrily? Dangerous that, in a vicar.'

'Priest-in-charge.'

'Only a matter of time. Now Alf Hayden . . . he never accepted the blame for anything. Act of God. Providence.

His favourite words. Had us tearing our hair. But you can't get rid of a vicar, can you? Once they're in, they're in and that's that.'

'Not any more. My contract's for five years.'

'Red tape,' Ted said. 'Don't worry about it.'

'Please, Uncle Ted. Don't do anything . . . . anything else.'

'You're not feeling manipulated, are you?'

'Of course not. Well . . . . maybe. A little.'

As if having a woman priest in the family wasn't enough, her mother, from the safety of suburban Cheltenham, had been out of her mind when Merrily had gone as a curate to inner-city Liverpool, all concrete and drugs and domestic violence. Running youth clubs and refuges for prozzies and rent boys. Terrific, Jane had thought. Cathartic, Merrily had found.

While her mother was putting out feelers.

Good old Ted had come up with the goods inside a year. The vicar of Ledwardine was retiring. Beautiful Ledwardine, only an hour or so's drive from Cheltenham. And Ted was not only senior church warden but used to be the bishop's solicitor. No string-pulling, of course; she'd only get the job if she was considered up to it and the other candidates were weak . . . which, at less than fifteen grand a year, they almost certainly would be.

'You've had a stressful time,' Ted said. He'd never asked her why she'd abandoned the law for the Church. It was evidently taken for granted that this was some kind of reaction against Sean going bent. 'But you do feel right about this place now?'

'I think so. And listen, don't imagine I'll be giving you an easy time.'

'Ha. Alf was always far too apathetic to sustain a decent dispute. What did you have in mind?'

'Well, you need toilets in that church for a start. I don't

care if it *is* Grade One listed with five stars, a lot of people won't come to a place where they're scared of being taken short. Especially on winter mornings.'

'Shouldn't be too much of a problem. If you can raise the money.'

'I'm also into more streamlined services. No, streamlined's not the word exactly. Shorter and more . . . intense. Fewer hymns. Less *meaningless* ritual. I mean, we won't be kicking people out afterwards. There'll be tea and biscuits and all that, though I won't ask for the espresso machine until I've been around for a while.'

'What about the prayer book?'

'Oh, strictly Book of Common Prayer. And no happy-clappy. Well, not much, anyway. Not for the grown-ups.'

Ted Clowes twisted his brandy glass around, as if contemplating something. 'I shouldn't really be saying this, but a few people were a little wary about you at first. Big parish for . . . for . . .'

'For a woman?'

'Well, yes.' He looked uncomfortable. 'But there were other considerations. It's a mightily useful church, you see. Big. And with quite remarkable acoustics. Best concert hall for a good many miles.'

'So I gather.'

'And no shortage of people who recognize its qualities. People who've moved into the area. Dermot Child, the composer and early-music expert and your organist, of course. And Richard Coffey, the playwright.'

'*He* lives here?'

'Well, some of the time. With his young friend. An actor, not one you'd have heard of. And the Cassidys are very, er, cultured. Well, that's just the core of it, but there are lesser figures and acolytes and followers. And you have to take notice of these people because they bring bodies – and

28

money – into the church. Into the diocese. And a certain . . . cultural cachet. Can't be cynical about this sort of thing, Merrily.'

'Has the Church ever been?'

'Perhaps not. And most of us realize the Church needs a kick up the backside, and if it's delivered by a more prettily shod foot, fair enough. Alf was always a bit of an old woman, time for a young one. But, naturally, we have our traditionalists. People who may have tried to block the way.'

'Ah,' Merrily said. 'Would it help if I knew who they were?'

Ted didn't hesitate. 'Well, James Bull-Davies. He's the only one counts for anything. Funny sort of chap, James. Career army officer. Then his marriage breaks up and his father dies quite unexpectedly from some sort of embolism following a routine op. James has to give up his career, come back and take over the estate. Catapulted into the situation really.'

'What situation's that?'

'Weight of tradition, I suppose. Had to sell land and property to cover death duties and what have you, in addition to whatever it cost him to pay Sarah off. Left him with Upper Hall. And the burden of tradition. Soldier mentality, you see. Taken on the role of the squire in a way his father never did. Feels it's his function to stop the slide of country values. Keep the modern world at arm's length.'

'I see,' Merrily said. 'And that includes . . . what's her name? Alison?'

'Oh, well, nobody knows what goes on there. Power of the flesh, I'm afraid. Anyway, women in the boudoir, that's one thing. Women in the pulpit of the church housing the bones of one's ancestors is something else entirely.'

Merrily slowly shook her head.

'It isn't you, my dear,' Ted assured her. 'It's the principle.

The tradition. However, to his chagrin, he's found that, in what was once a little world where the squire was a demi-god, there are now other influential parties. Notably the affluent, articulate incomers, most of whom were rather keen on the idea of a lady cleric. Question of image, you see.'

'Image? Somebody *said* that?'

'They tolerated Alf, of course. Fat, scruffy old cove. Not very ambitious, not terribly bright. Always a bit of egg-yolk on the old cassock. But what the parish needs at this stage of the village's development is someone more sophisticated, more attuned to the, ah . . . is Zeitgeist the word I'm looking for?'

'They'd prefer a woman priest because it's cool and state-of-the-art? Jesus.'

'Not *merely* a woman.' Ted shuffled about a bit. 'I mean, when they saw you at the wassailing and somebody put two and two together . . .'

'What?'

'Oh, Merrily, don't make me spell it out. You're young and you rather, as someone said, would rather smoulder . . . in black.'

'Oh no. Oh, hell. Who said that?'

'Not going to say. Told you I shouldn't have said anything.'

'Bloody hell, Ted.'

*

Merrily awoke just as it was growing light. Above the timbered gables, a wooded hill had formed.

She was brightening with the sky. What had been outrageous last night seemed quite funny now. *Smoulder*. Who'd said that? And where? Hopefully, not at the bishop's palace. Things really had changed, hadn't they? Used to be school-girls falling for the new curate.

Merrily smiled, feeling younger than she had in quite a while. She looked across at Jane, who was still asleep. Hey, what the hell? If she wanted to set up some kind of apartment under the eaves, why not? The kid had given up enough these past years: two changes of school, becoming single-parented, coping with a mother who spent whole nights fuming about some of the crap they threw at you in theological college.

And, for Merrily – she glanced at the thick-beamed ceiling – it would take away the irrational, background stress connected with an empty third storey.

She went to the window which was set into a wall divided into irregular, white rectangles by huge varicose veins of Tudor oak. Jane, who was into fine art these days, said those white areas were just crying out for something interesting with acrylics. Oh dear.

Merrily gazed out over the inn-sign, across to the intimate market square with the squat, crablike, oak-legged shelter they called the market hall or cross. Overhung with shape-shifting black and white houses, every crooked beam and truss preserved and presented with pride.

The village wore its past like a row of glittering horse-brasses over an inglenook fireplace. Defined by its past, shaped by invaders. The Norman church with Saxon origins at the end of a Roman road. The cramped, cobbled alleyway where the gutters had once overflowed with pig-blood and piss, now a bijou arcade, soon to be scented with fountains of flowers from a score of hanging baskets.

For the new invaders, the Cassidys of this world, were here not to pillage or desecrate or change, but only to preserve, preserve, preserve. And wallow. Preserve and wallow.

Merrily looked down into the still-shadowed street, saw Dr Kent Asprey, heart-throb GP and fitness-freak leading his jogging party of sweating matrons past the new tourist information office. Saw Gomer Parry, the retired digger-driver, kick a stone into the road and stand on the kerb, hands rammed deep into his pockets, cigarette jammed between his lips. He looked aimless. What, after all, was there to do in this village but stand and stare, appreciate, absorb, be enriched?

Ideal, her mother had said. *After what you've been through, you need somewhere quiet with no stress and no drug addicts and homeless people to make you feel guilty. Somewhere you can sit back a bit and take stock.*

Merrily knelt before the window to pray. She thought, No need for homeless people to make *me* feel guilty.

According to dream analysts, the one about the realization of a third storey was an indication of a whole new area of yourself which remained unexplored. A higher consciousness.

'Dear God,' Merrily whispered, her palms together, angled on the rising sun.

From behind her, she heard the squeak of Jane's bed as the kid sat up.

'Oh shit,' her daughter muttered, sleepy and cross. 'Do you really *have* to do that in here?'

Black-eyed Dog

Lol planned his suicide with all the precision missing from his life.

He drew curtains across the small, leaded windows facing the lane and the orchard. The curtains were cheap and thin but they took away the brightness of the morning. And also meant that Alison would not be able to look through the windows for his body.

On the turntable, Lol placed his third, already-worn copy of Nick Drake's first album, *Five Leaves Left*. The lush arrangements, the soft and ghostly vocals of a man with only five years to live. All his adult life, he'd identified with Nick Drake, even though Nick had been taller and posher and dead – by his own hand – since 1974.

The album hissed and clicked into 'Time Has Told Me', veined through with Richard Thompson's serene guitar. Lol went outside to check on the milk. With the bright mornings, the milkman had been arriving earlier of late. So the bottle was already on the step.

OK. He went back for another bottle from the fridge – yesterday's, unopened – and set it down next to the new one. Then he shut the door and went to explain to Ethel, kneeling down on the carpet, looking into the unmoving green-gold eyes.

'I'm going to have to shut you in. It won't be for long. Don't want you looking for me, OK?'

Ethel looked unconvinced, licked red mud from a paw. She was technically a stray, or maybe dumped. He'd heard this piteous mewling two nights running in the middle of January and finally found this thing in the hedge, about five inches long and not much thicker than a piece of black hosepipe. At first, Alison had not been pleased, displaying that hard edge he used to think would eventually wear away in the country. But on the morning she left, she said she was glad Lol had Ethel. Something for him to feel responsible for.

Lol went into the kitchen and didn't put the toaster on; the smell of hot toast was one of the great scents of life. It would be hard to die with the smell of hot toast in the air. He didn't switch on the radio either. He didn't rake out the woodstove. He sat down at the table, facing the pot of Women's Institute plum jam. He pulled off the rubber band and the parchment top, smelling the sweetness.

'You should've told me,' he said to the jam.

Meaning he should have realized. This was the last of the three pots Alison had brought back from the Women's Institute. The day after she brought it, she'd told him herself and he'd just broken down into tears, here at this table, with the shock.

He'd always been naive. As a kid. As a songwriter. But naivety was something you were supposed to grow out of, like spots.

At the time, the idea of Alison joining all the farmers' wives at the WI had seemed, OK, a little bizarre. But also kind of quaint and homely. It showed that coming here had really worked. It made him want to become part of the community too, a bellringer or something. Keep chickens, grow tomatoes for the chutney Alison would learn to make . . . at the WI.

Just off to the WI. It had been a while before he'd realized that all those times she'd said she was off to the WI and returned a few hours later with a pot of jam, she'd really been with James Bull-Davies in the big bed at the big farmhouse called Upper Hall.

How had it begun? He didn't know. Everyone else in the village seemed to know – the new woman in the life of the Squire of Upper Hall, that was bound to be a talking point. But there was nobody who'd have told Lol. He was a stranger, even to all the village newcomers. Lucy Devenish might have broken it to him, but he hadn't known her then, in those long, hazy days of trying to get vegetables to grow and watching Alison's easy smile slowly stiffen in her beautiful face.

Lol's chin dropped into the crumbs on the kitchen table. All he wanted was to know why.

He closed his eyes and saw Alison riding, as she did almost every day, down the bridleway from Upper Hall, along the edge of the orchard and out into Blackberry Lane just before the cottage gate.

She was on her chestnut stallion. Alison knew a lot about horses and rode this one with something like contempt. It looked muscular and spectacularly masculine, a thoroughbred beast she could make a gesture out of being able to handle with no particular effort. Like Bull-Davies himself, who was the horse's owner but would never, Lol was sure, be Alison's.

He'd kept watching out for her, convinced she'd come back. For several weeks he'd really thought she would. Then he'd thought that one day she would at least dismount, lead the horse to the door, explain what had happened between them. But the morning ride always ended with an apparently casual glance towards the cottage, to see the smoke from the chimney, signs of life, signs of Lol's survival . . . before Alison and the stallion turned, both heads high, back into the bridleway.

Today there would be no smoke.

*

'You all right, mate?'

Lol's eyes had shuddered open when the knock came at the front door.

'Oh.' He didn't know how long he must have been staring at the postman. 'Sorry. Do I have to sign for it?'

'No, I just couldn't get it through the letter box, could I?'

'Oh,' Lol said. 'Right. Sorry. Thanks very much.'

'Your milk's come.'

'Oh . . . I'll come back for it. Thanks.'

'Cheers,' said the postman.

Lol carried the parcel into the kitchen, laid it down on the table. Ethel jumped on it, whiskers twitching.

The parcel was about fifteen inches square and an inch thick. It was postmarked Wiltshire. His name was on the front, typed on a label. Did he know anybody in Wiltshire? Lol lifted the cat to the floor and slit the brown paper with the butter knife.

Inside, under some stiff cardboard, was an LP record. Nick Drake. *Time of No Reply*.

Lol stared at it. He didn't understand. He was afraid to touch it.

This was the posthumous album. The one with 'Black-eyed Dog', the bleak and eerie little song of depression and impending death. The one where Nick said he was feeling old and he wanted to go home. He was twenty-five years old. At barely twenty-six, he'd taken one anti-depressant too many and his mother had found him lying dead across his single bed.

Lol began to shake. Out of the speakers, from slightly happier days, Nick sang 'Way to Blue'.

What kind of omen was this? He looked up at the curtained window facing the orchard. Suddenly had the overpowering feeling that posh, languid Nick was standing out there among the trees, waiting for him. A bass player he'd once met said he'd been to this party once at someone's flat and Nick Drake, six months before he died, had been there and had stood leaning in a corner next to a candle for two and a half hours, spoken to nobody and then slipped silently away, like a ghost.

There was a letter with the album. Neat and official and word-processed and signed . . .

. . . Dennis Clarke.

Oh. Lol sat down. Oh, yeah. It was, in fact, his own album, the one he'd left with Dennis when he went into the hospital.

Dear Lol,

I found this record when Gill and I were sorting everything out for the move. Sorry, I've been meaning to send it for months. To be honest, Gill kept putting me off, saying it might make you depressed again. But now we know you're over it and settled with a nice lady, well, here it is.

As you can see, we're in Chippenham now, where I am a partner in a new accountancy firm. A couple of us decided to break away from the old outfit and set up on our own, and I think it's paying off.

Gill and I have got three kids now, and we live in a four-bedroomed, neo-Georgian villa, extremely suburban. I do think about the old days quite a lot, how things might have been. Disastrous, probably. On reflection I'm always glad it ended when it did. We still get our royalties, don't we?

Anyway, the real reason I'm writing is that I had a visit yesterday evening. From Karl.

Lol let the letter fall to the table. He didn't want to read any more, and he didn't need to, did he? Karl was over. Karl was gone. Karl was in . . .

If you remember, he was in Seattle, managing a band and doing very well. However, it seems they split quite suddenly (musical differences, of course!!) and Karl was left with quite a few pieces to pick up. Anyway, he's back in this country now because this is now Where the Future Is. He says.

I was a bit thrown when he went on to say he was convinced WE were part of that future. I never read the music papers these days, don't have the time or, to be quite honest, the interest. However, according to Karl, the first two albums are now considered Seminal. That is, they have been discovered by a couple of the major bands – one of them might have been The Verve, no less – who list them among their influences, and sales are picking up again (expect to see this reflected in the next royalties, or I'll want to know why!!).

Needless to say, I'd be happy to see those albums get the recognition they never really had in their day (with whatever resulting remuneration might be forthcoming!!) but I've been out of the business for a considerable time now and that's what I told Karl when he said we should be thinking seriously about re-forming the band. Look, I said, I shall be forty-five next year, I have lost most of my hair, I have got three kids to support and I am very happy to be a chartered accountant in a nice part of the country. Also I have had a periodic problem with my elbow and have not lifted a drumstick in about three years.

Well, he didn't push too hard, because, let's face it, he can manage without me. I never wrote a song. I wasn't even a very good drummer. It's you he needs – not only the major talent in the band but nearly ten years younger than the rest of us and so less likely to seem like an old fart.

I don't know how you feel about this. I did wonder, with you being in a stable relationship now and perhaps better able to hold your own with Karl, whether you might not be ready for something like this. However, when he asked me where you were living now, I decided on caution. I said, Look, Lol's had his problems, you had better go easy. I think he got the message. Naturally, I said I didn't know where you were living now, and I rang that guy Chris in A and R at TMM and warned them not to give your address to him either, but somebody's bound to leak it, and that's why I'm writing. I would have phoned, but I find you are ex-directory.

Anyway, I thought I had better let you know. Karl has changed . . . well, a little. All the same, Gill didn't take to him and was not at all happy when he took out what I would swear is the SAME TIN and rolled himself a joint, which, as you can imagine, is not exactly the drug of choice in our part of Chippenham.

Let me know if you hear anything. Give my best wishes to – Alison, is it? We were both so delighted to hear things are working out for you at last on a personal level and once again, sorry for keeping the album so long.

With very best wishes,

Denmis

Dennis Clarke

Dear old Dennis Clarke

Methodical, play-it-safe Dennis. *If you work it out for yourselves, lads, you'll see that if we do these two gigs in Banbury, we'll be twenty-seven pounds better off than if we go up to Sheffield, taking into consideration at least three Little Chef meals, eleven gallons of petrol and tyre-wear . . .*

Dear old stupid, bloody Dennis. *Put it behind you, Lol, it's not the end of the world. Make a new start. In a couple of years you'll be laughing about it.*

Lol slumped into the old blue armchair.

Nick Drake sang 'Cello Song'. Calm, upper-class English accent. And yet the black-eyed dog had been at Nick Drake's door, as sure as the Hellhound had pursued Robert Johnson, the poor bluesman, over half a century ago. Both of them dead before the age of twenty-seven.

The thought of the hellhound who was Karl Windling back on *his* trail made Lol's mouth go dry.

He thought, Where will I go?

The days were growing longer. Living in the country, you could really feel the earth turning, and it made you dizzy.

He would do it. He'd go. Now. In the springtime, when the sun was beginning to linger over the village with its ancient black and white cottages and inns, its old and mellowed church, its narrow, brown river.

In a similar village, not two hours' drive from here, sometime in the night, Nick Drake had opened his door to the black-eyed dog.

Now, out there in the orchard, Nick was waiting for Lol.

THREE

Local History

Actually, Jane thought, it was excellent living at the pub.

Even though they had to share a bedroom: her at one end knocking off her homework, Mum at the other agonizing over a sermon. Even though you had to be up and into the bathroom pretty early to avoid having to watch Mum saying – oh my *God* – her morning prayers.

You tried not to be embarrassed, you really did try. But a grown woman, who actually wasn't bad-looking for her age, down on her knees under the window, whispering sweet nothings to some invisible old bloke in the sky . . .

What a psychologist would have said, how a *counsellor* would have put it, was that Jane was actually *jealous* of God. This single-parent only child, OK, a semi-orphan, and here's her widowed mother taking up with Another Guy and this time it's much more intense, this time it's the Big Guy, the Real Thing.

This was what a psychologist would say. And was, in fact, more or less what a counsellor *had* said. The counsellor forced on her by Mum's bloody theological college the time she *ran away*, as they insisted on putting it. Or *took a night off*, as she tried to explain it to them.

Anyway, the night off had involved putting on some serious make-up and going to a pub and getting chatted up by a computer salesman from Edgbaston before being spotted by one of the prissy bloody trainee vicars who fancied Mum and took great pleasure in grassing up the delinquent daughter. Jesus, how ironic.

*

'All right, what's on your mind, flower?'

Mum plonked two Diet Cokes on the pub table, the one near the toilets that was always the last to be taken – except, of course, when good old humble Mum was around.

'Oh,' Jane said. 'You know. I mean, nothing really. As such.'

'As such.' Mum nodded solemnly.

'Just wondering if I can put up with that bloody school for another two years before I wind up doing drugs and self-mutilation.'

Third new school in as many years. Though, frankly, when you'd done it once, it got easier. The kids were always more curious about you than you were about them, everybody wanted to hang out with the new girl, and the teachers would give you the benefit of the doubt for months before proclaiming you Public Enemy Number One.

'Mmm,' Mum said. 'Is it that particular school or just any school desperate enough to take you?'

Jane wrinkled her nose. 'I just sometimes think I'm too old for it.'

'Too old for school?'

'Older than everybody else my age, anyway. Do you really *have* to wear that thing in here?'

Saturday lunchtime. With the post-Easter tourist season starting up, the bar was pretty full. Being seen lunching with your mother was one thing, sharing a table with the Vicar was something else.

'Yes, I really think I do.' Mum patted her ridiculous collar with something Jane was horribly afraid could be pride.

She lowered her eyes. Hell, even a *real* dog collar would look better, one of those with coloured-glass jewels or brass spikes. People of Mum's generation apparently used to wear them quite a lot during the punk era. She remembered Dad telling her once that Mum, as a teenager, had been a sort of punk. Not exactly the full safety-pin-through-the-nose bit, but certainly cropped hair and black lipstick. Dad talking in a way that suggested he'd been quite turned on by it. Pretty revolting, really. And the music was embarrassingly awful.

'Going undercover was never a good idea,' Mum said. 'Not in the parish. It only leads to embarrassment later.'

Possibly meaning the guy who'd tried to pick her up in this very bar and had turned out to be head of English at Jane's new school, the smarmball who could be teaching her A-level next year. Which – him being married to the girls' PE teacher – Jane would not hesitate to use to stitch him up if the oily git should give *her* any hassle.

It was OK staying at the pub, because you learned things about people. Things you might not find out for ages if you were banged up in the vicarage. Like that TV-playwright guy, Richard Coffey, moving this youngish actor into his house on a fairly permanent basis. The actor was called Stefan Alder and was really succulent totty. Apart from being gay, of course. Or maybe he just hadn't met the right woman.

So, yeah, it was good at the Black Swan. Swinging off the school bus and strolling coolly into the bar. On the other hand, there was the question of her apartment. Mustn't let that one slide.

'So, how long before they finish de-Alfing the rectory?'

'That's what I was about to tell you.'

Mum was taking delivery of a couple of ploughmans-with-cheddar from the waitress. *Don't do it*, Jane pleaded silently. *Please don't say fucking grace* . . .

'I meant to say last night.' Mum speared a piece of celery.

(Thank Christ for that.) 'The rewiring's complete, they've nearly finished work on the kitchen. And yesterday, apparently, they took out that huge electric fire which is so old it breaks every known regulation. According to Uncle Ted, Alf Hayden must have been getting divine protection to have avoided being fried. Anyway the bottom line is, we could be in by next weekend. Good?'

'Yeah. Could be OK.'

Give her the whole of the summer holidays to get things together, apartment-wise. She had in mind this kind of Mondrian effect for the main room; you could paint the squares inside the timbers in different colours. Ingenious, huh?

It was Uncle Ted, of course, who'd fixed it for them to stay on at the Black Swan, persuading the diocese to fork out for the Woolhope Suite, a bedroom, bathroom and small sitting room with a decent-sized TV. It was still off-season, so Roland, the proprietor, had been amenable to the kind of deal that people like Uncle Ted prided themselves on making.

Uncle Ted was widowed and seemed to have an arrangement with a widowed lady in Church Street. Ledwardine was really quite liberal and sophisticated. Perhaps the country had always been like that.

To Jane's horror, the local paper had been along, to get a picture of her and Mum outside the pub. Mum had insisted on wearing the clerical clobber, and the photographer had made them both sit on the pub steps, smiling like idiots. *B and B Vicar Holds the Fort*, it said. Yuk!

Mum's only objection was to the word vicar. Priest-in-charge was the correct term. It was a temporary thing; apparently there was going to be this big reorganization and Mum could wind up with about four extra churches, making her a kind of flying minister. That was when they'd give her the official title; meantime it was just the one church, which should have been a piece of cake. Would have been to anyone but Mum, who seemed determined to become some kind of spiritual doormat: people cornering her in the pub all the time, emergency meetings of the Church Council, articles to write for the parish magazine (*Dear Friends . . . yuk!*), four trips to Hereford to see parishioners in hospital.

And three funerals inside a fortnight: mega-depressing, or what?

Well, obviously you'd get used to that – be like planting bulbs after a while. Except, if you were Mum, you felt obliged to spend most of a day and a night quizzing relatives and neighbours about what kind of person the prospective interee was prior to being dead. *It's a life, Jane. You can't just dismiss a life with a handful of clichés and a couple of jam scones in the village hall.*

She wasn't even getting bloody overtime. And she was starting to look seriously knackered.

*

'Ah. Merrily. Might one perhaps have a word?'

Jane looked up from her lunch. Yeah, she thought. The word is *tosser*.

'Sure,' Mum said. 'Take a pew.'

'Thank you.'

Mr Cassidy, of Cassidy's Country Kitchen – naff, twee, or what? – parked his tight arse, in pristine stonewashed jeans, on the edge of a stool. He held a glass of white wine. He smiled indulgently down.

'And how are you, Jane?'

'Getting by.'

'We really must arrange for you to meet Colette.'

His snotty daughter, who went to the Cathedral School in Hereford. You saw her posing around the square in the evenings. Sixteen (nearly) and sultry. Jane kept her distance.

'Super,' she said.

'Got a problem, Terrence?' Mum said briskly.

Mrs Fixit. Why didn't she just tell him to sod off until she'd finished her lunch?

'No . . . No . . .' Cassidy said airily. 'It's simply . . . Are you doing anything special tonight?'

Is she ever?

'Depends which part of the night, really, Terrence.'

'Mum hates to miss *Homicide, Life on the Street*.'

The vicar frowned at her daughter. Mr Cassidy smiled thinly. Everything about him was thin, which told you all you needed to know about his bloody awful restaurant.

'This would be about eight,' he said. 'It's an impromptu meeting of the Festival Committee.'

'Am I *on* the Festival Committee?' Mum wondered.

'Well, Alf Hayden wasn't. But we rather thought you should have a say. Especially as we were hoping this year to make more use of the church itself in other than musical areas. To be specific: drama.'

'Oh, I'm sure it's seen plenty of that in its time.'

'Quite. In fact, it's about that . . . You see, Richard's over from London for the weekend . . . Richard Coffey.'

'With his boyfriend?'

'Shut up, Jane,' Mum said.

'As you may have heard,' Cassidy said, 'Richard has agreed to write a short play especially for the festival, to illustrate a lesser known aspect of local history.'

'Gosh,' Mum said. 'There's prestigious.'

'We originally had in mind something *social*. Perhaps showing how the trade in high-quality cider was almost irrevocably damaged in the eighteenth century by the growing fashion for French wines.'

'Yeah, you could invite the Euro-MP—'

'*Jane* . . .'

Jane retired behind a smirk.

'However,' said Cassidy, 'Richard's apparently become fascinated by the story of Wil Williams. Which I suppose also has a social aspect, in its way.'

'Mmm,' Mum said.

'Obviously, it's not something the village nowadays is particularly proud of.'

'No,' Mum said. 'Quite.'

'Although I suppose it has its tourist possibilities, in a lurid sort of way. Point is, Richard's drawn certain conclusions which appear to have quite excited him. The case itself is not well documented, as you know – probably some sort of kangaroo court. But this, of course, gives Richard considerable artistic licence.'

'Right.' Mum nodded.

'And as he's even talking about bringing in some professional actors, which would be wonderful, especially if the play went on to London. Be rather super, wouldn't it? Premiered in Ledwardine Church, and then conquers the capital.'

Mum nodded again. Her eyes had acquired a guarded look.

'I'd have to talk to the bishop.'

'Of course.'

'And, er, Richard's going to be revealing his plans at tonight's meeting, is he?'

'We hope so.'

'Eight o'clock, you said.'

'At the village hall. We normally meet in the restaurant, but Saturday is our busy night. You'll be there?'

'Well . . . all right.'

'You haven't met Richard, have you?'

'We've seen him in the bar, though,' Jane said. 'With his b—'

'Look forward to it, Terrence.'

Mum laid her knife and fork neatly down the middle of her half-full plate. Another aborted lunch. You could get quite worried about Mum sometimes. She wasn't getting any younger. Past the age when you should be eating like a supermodel.

'Splendid.' Cassidy wove off through the crush, holding up his wine like some sort of sacrament.

*

Jane grinned.

'I thought you didn't.'

Mum tossed her bag on her bed.

'How the hell should I be expected to know who Wil Williams was. I've been too busy to even think about local history.'

'Never mind, you've got hours yet.'

'No, I haven't. I've got to meet Gomer Parry at four. The digger man. Wasn't for him and the gardening club, the churchyard'd be some kind of nature reserve.'

'What a great idea.'

'Don't start!'

Mum flopped back on the bed, covered her eyes. The sun blared in through the old leaded window and turned her into a tableau: the exhausted saint.

'And it's Saturday afternoon, so the libraries are closed in Hereford and Leominster.'

'Mum, this is ridiculous, nobody expects you to know absolutely *everything*.'

'Yes, they do! That's the whole point. Jane, I'm the bloody priest-in-charge. I'm supposed to have done my homework. I suppose I could go round and see . . . who's that old bloke who does the all-our-yesterdays bit for the parish mag?'

48

'God, no. I heard him in the post office once. Great queue of people and he was on about how you could send a three-piece suite through the post for less than a shilling in 1938. You'd be lucky to get away in time for the meeting. Look, OK . . . *I'll* find out who he was.'

Mum took her hands away from her eyes.

'How?'

'Don't look at me like I've never done anything for you *ever*!'

'I mean . . . properly?'

'No, I'll make it all up. Of course properly. *And* I'll keep you out of it. I'll say it's for a school project.'

'Where will you go?'

'Ledwardine Lore.'

'But that's—'

'Miss Devenish.'

Mum sat up. 'Oh no. You said *properly*. You'll just get the Miss Devenish version, which may not . . . And anyway . . .'

'Yes?'

Mum did one of her heavy sighs. She'd had this thing about Miss Devenish ever since the great Powell suicide. The old girl had made a scene about this wassailing scenario being all wrong and no good would come of it and . . . *bang!* . . . no good came of it. Spooky, yeah? *Right.* Jane was never going to forgive herself for missing all that. Of course, that was in her Ledwardine Denial Period; she was over that now.

'Mum, look, that's the only shop in the village where you can get real local history books. We're going to have to get one *some*time.'

'All right, just pop in and grab a book.'

'I won't know which one it's in, will I? You can't stand there in a shop that size, going through all the indexes. I'll have to ask her about it.'

Jane sat on a corner of the bed, searching out her mother's eyes. People said they had the same eyes, dark and curious.

'Got you,' she said. 'You don't like me going in there, do you? Because people say she's a bit of an old witch. Daughter of the priest-in-charge mustn't be seen consorting with satanic forces, right?'

'That's cobblers, Jane. However, until we've got our feet under the table we're going to have to tread carefully, walk on a few eggshells. Is that a mixed metaphor?'

'No, spot on, actually. In an accidental sort of way. So. How do you want to play it? Do you want me to find out who Wil Williams was, or do you want to busk it with Coffey and Cassidy? Hey, you think *Stefan* might be there tonight?'

'I have no idea.'

'Can I come?'

'Absolutely not. God forbid. Neither will you hang around the bar. You can stay up here and watch TV.'

'It's Saturday night.'

'Look, flower, we'll have a home in a week or so. We can start shipping all your clothes and your albums and books and stuff over from Cheltenham.'

'Yeah.' She supposed there *had* been cultural withdrawal symptoms, from the music especially. Weeks since she'd lain on a bed with her eyes closed in a room full of Radiohead.

'You won't have to be bored any more,' Mum said. 'We'll be settled, for the first time in years.'

'You think so?'

'Actually, I don't know. I don't really know what I'm doing.' Mum sighed. 'Sod it, flower,' she said wearily. 'I suppose I could consult Ted, but I've been bothering him too much lately. Go on. Go and ask Miss Devenish who on earth Wil Williams is.'

FOUR

Straight Shooter

This frenzied *slam, slam slam*, flat of a hand on the door panels, someone who'd given up with the bell, given up with the knocker.

Lol flailed out of unconsciousness. Must've fallen asleep. Did that so easily now in the daytime, result of spending evenings dozing in front of the stove, staggering miserably to bed and lying awake until it was light. Yet there was something different about today . . . wasn't there?

Now the door handle was being rattled, the letter-flap pushed in and out, his name being screamed.

Oh my God. The black cat sailed from his knees. He rolled out of the chair. *Alison. She's here.*

Go carefully. Go slowly. You only get one chance. Be cool.

Yeah, I'm fine. I just needed to talk to you. No weeping, no pleading. Just the truth. Because I can't believe it was some fast-flowering infatuation did this to us, nor a sudden realization that he was what you'd always wanted. I can't believe you saw him in his tweeds and his gumboots and you thought, that's what I need to give my life direction, a genuine old-style landowner in a damp old seven-bedroomed farmhouse with cowshit on the lino and—

'Laurence! Are you there? Laurence!'

Close to the door, Lol sagged.

It was not Alison. No indeed. He opened up, and there she was under the big hat, elbows making batwings out of the poncho.

'You dismal tripehound! What the *fuck* are you playing at?' Striding into the living room, flinging back curtains. 'Do you know what time it is?'

He looked at the travel alarm on the mantelpiece. It said 14.15. This had to be wrong; maybe it had stopped.

Christ, six *hours*?

Lol looked sheepishly into Lucy's hot, glaring face. 'I . . . fell asleep.'

He remembered that this was Saturday afternoon. He'd promised to mind her shop.

The Nick Drake album was still revolving on the turntable, the needle grinding it up. It would be ruined now. Like everything he touched.

'Don't know what happened, Luce. It was just like . . . I got up this morning . . . then like fell asleep in the chair. Just completely—'

'You're lying.' She was advancing on him like a big policewoman. 'Come on, hand them over.'

'Huh?'

'Pills.' She held out a big, pink palm. 'Don't fart about with me, Laurence, I'm not in the mood. *Pills*. Want to see what they are.'

'I haven't got any pills.' He spread his hands. 'Honestly.'

'People with a background like yours,' Lucy said, '*always* have pills.'

'Oh God.' He was far too ashamed to explain. 'Doesn't everything go pear-shaped?'

'What you mean by that?' Her eyes nail-gunned him to the wall. 'Two days' milk outside? All the curtains drawn? I won't ask you again . . . . How many did you take?'

'Lucy,' Lol said, 'would I leave a little cat to starve?'

She loomed over him. 'Answer my question, damn you, or I'll box your bloody ears.'

He stood back, both hands up. 'I didn't take any. No pills. All right?'

'The milk? The curtains?'

'See, I was lying awake all night. I'm thinking, you know, you've got to get your shit together, you can't be a little wimp all your life, you've got to talk to her. And that . . . I mean, that isn't easy. I can't go up to her in the street, I'm not ready to do that.'

'Why can't you simply phone her up?'

'Because either he answers and I hang up, or she answers and *she* hangs up. She doesn't want to talk to me. But she likes to know I'm all right, that I haven't done anything really stupid. Like, what she really wants is for me to move out, but in the meantime she rides past the house every couple of mornings, presumably hoping she'll see a For Sale sign but, failing that, some reassurance that I haven't set fire to the place, cut my wrists in the bath, you know?'

'How thoughtful,' Lucy said.

'I find that . . . comforting.'

'That she's worried she might have driven you to take your own life? Ah . . .' Lucy took off her hat, tossed it on the chair. 'One begins to see. You really are a sick, twisted little person, aren't you, Laurence?'

He said nothing.

'A silly charade. This was a silly, stupid charade. You wanted her to think you'd done it. You drew the curtains, made it seem as if you hadn't collected the milk for two days, put on some mournful record. And then what? She sees you're alive and falls into your arms?'

'We just talk,' Lol said. 'Finally, we talk. See, I tried calling to her. She won't get off the horse. She just turns around, trots away. You run after her. She—'

'Pshaw!' Lucy said. She was the only person he'd ever encountered who actually said this. 'If attempted suicide is a cry for help, Laurence, this is, at best, a feeble squeak.'

'Mmm.' He nodded miserably.

'Laurence!' Lucy held his eyes like a hypnotist. 'You're letting me bully you! You aren't even putting up a fight against an old woman with no business interfering in your affairs. We can't have that, can we? Can we, Laurence?'

'No,' he said humbly, and she threw up her arms.

'Aaagh! You can have what the hell you like, you clown. It's your *life*. My God, but those hospital shrinks have a lot to answer for. Keep 'em drugged up to the eyeballs and then send 'em out like zombies.'

'Actually, I was a bit like that before I went in.'

Lucy shook her head. 'Come on,' she said. 'Have a pee, splash some water on your face, and then we'll go.'

Through the window, he saw her moped parked behind his muddied Astra in the short drive.

'All right,' Lol said.

*

She let him push the moped down Blackberry Lane, across the square and into the mews enclosing Ledwardine Lore.

Lucy insisted she needed somebody to look after the shop occasionally. When was she to do her own shopping otherwise? Used to be a girl came in two afternoons a week, but she'd had a baby and left the area.

'Everything's priced,' Lucy told Lol, unlocking the door. 'And if it's not, you can always make one up.'

She was doing this to bring him out, bring him into the village. He hated coming into Ledwardine on his own. They still smirked at him in shops. Been smirking at him for months. He'd thought it was because he was such an obvious townie and maybe he should grow sideburns below his ears, buy a rusty pick-up truck. Not realizing they all knew what he didn't, that the entire bloody village knew.

'And you won't have to face any of the locals,' she said, identifying his fears, gathering them up. 'Only tourists on a Saturday.'

He relaxed. Lucy's tiny, overcrowded shop had in it the essence of what he liked about this place, what he'd miss when he sold the cottage and cleared out: the red soil and the long, wooded hills and the twisted houses with old bones of blackened oak. And the apples. Why were apples so cheerful and wholesome, while the orchard was so oppressive?

'Bad for you,' Lucy was saying. 'Wrong type of woman entirely. Not that she won't be bad for *him*. But that's his lookout. And he's stronger than you are.'

'Thanks.'

'I never dress things up. Woman's a destroyer. What you need is a preserver.'

'We had something,' Lol said. 'I know I'm naive, I know I don't see things. But you don't set up a home with someone in a new place unless you feel there's something worth having.'

Lucy shook her head at his short-sightedness. Lol thought of the day he'd come home to find Bull-Davies's big Land Rover outside the cottage, filled up to the canvas with Alison's stuff. How cool she'd been, how matter-of-fact about it, sitting him down at the kitchen table and telling him simply and concisely. Apologizing, in an almost formal way. Kissing him calmly, like she was just going off to London or somewhere for the day.

'If you'd seen her at that Twelfth Night debacle,' Lucy said, 'you wouldn't be so damned charitable. Where *were* you on Twelfth Night, anyway?'

'Oxford. With a bloke I'd done some lyrics for.'

'A cruel woman. And yet curiously shallow. Horse-riding, point-to-point, driving around in muddy Land Rovers, racing up the sweeping drive, being lady of the manor . . .'

'You're making her sound starry-eyed,' Lol said. 'She's not.'

'No, indeed. She's cunning. Manipulative. Knows how to use her looks. And the Bull's a male-menopausal stooge who's known only two kinds of women, garrison-town whores and county-set heifers. She's got his balls in the palm of her hand and she's not going to let go. And if you think a passing concern that little Laurence might top himself is any sign she may come back when she tires of the Bull's body then, my boy, you're even less bright than you look.'

'Thanks.'

'I'm a straight shooter, Laurence. You were just a stepping stone to the mansion on the hill. Poor James.'

'Poor James?' Lol sat down on the stool behind the counter. 'He's *got* the mansion on the hill, even if it is crumbling around him. Now he's got the girl, too, no strings. Yeah, poor old James.'

'I'm sorry. It's just that I knew his father. Or at least I knew Patricia Young, who, I suppose, was one of the old man's Alisons.'

'Family tradition, huh?'

'A tradition in most old country families. I say one of the old man's Alisons, but she wasn't at all like that. Patricia was bright, but a little naive. Like you. Stablegirl at the Hall who hadn't realized that part of a stablegirl's job was to lie down in the hay with her breeches off, as required. For John Bull-Davies.'

Lucy frowned. She took a paperback book down from a shelf, laid it on the counter.

'Dissolute old bastard, John Bull-Davies. Slave to the flesh, and let everything else slip through his fingers: money, land, public esteem. If he hadn't died when he did, there'd've been nothing left for James. Perhaps that would have been no bad thing, boy seemed to have been on the straight and narrow in the army. Now he's been forced to pick up the pieces. And seems, unfortunately, to have slipped further into the family mould than I'd have expected.'

'What happened to the stablegirl?'

'I warned her to get out and she did. She left. I'm sure he must have found a replacement – or two, or three – before he died. Time that family faded out of the picture, I say. Turn Upper Hall into a nursing home. And that's coming from an old conservationist. No, I hope your Alison takes him for everything he's got, forces him to sell up and move away. It isn't healthy for him here, because James has some sort of conscience. But that's not your problem.'

He no longer understood what she was on about. She looked down at him, pushed towards him the paperback book she'd taken down.

'I shall be back by five-thirty,' she said. 'Read this between customers. If you don't get any customers, you'll be able to read the lot.'

Lol picked up the book. A Penguin Classic. *Thomas Traherne: Selected Poems and Prose.*

'This is the man you need,' Lucy said. 'Sitting there playing your mournful, wistful records. Do you no damn good at all. It's spring. Let Traherne into your life. Open your heart to the Eternal.'

Lol had heard of the guy. Seventeenth-century visionary poet, born in Hereford, lived in Credenhill, about seven miles from here, where he was . . .

'He was a priest, wasn't he? Vicar?'

'Rector of Credenhill. I know what you're thinking, but Traherne's spirituality and your parents' so-called Christianity are poles apart. That's the whole point of this. *You never*

*enjoy the world aright till the sea itself floweth in your veins,
till you are clothed with the heavens and crown'd with the
stars.'*

'That was him?'

'You have to learn to open up. Let the world flow into
you again. Go into the village on your own and go in smiling.
That's what Traherne did. Happiest man in the county.
Discovered *felicity*. His great realization was that God wants
us to enjoy life and nature. That if we don't, we're throwing
it all back in His face. Traherne walked the fields and was
truly happy.'

'Maybe he'd just discovered magic mushrooms,' Lol said.

Lucy snorted, pulled down her big hat and left him to it.

Buds

The truth of it was that, from that first solo stroll around the village, Jane had been looking for an excuse to go into Ledwardine Lore.

She'd been up to it several times, but you could see through the window that the place was too small to browse around and escape without buying something. Maybe that was why so few local people seemed to go in – made more sense than all this stuff about Miss Devenish being weird. Like weirdness was something *new* in the countryside.

Emerging from the lustrous oakiness of the Black Swan, Jane skipped down the five steps to the cobbles. These were mainly new cobbles, the original ones being so worn away by horses' hoofs that they'd apparently been considered too dangerous; smart ladies en route to Cassidy's Country Kitchen might fracture their stiletto heels.

The alleyway was just yards from the bottom of the steps. It was *très bijou*, the most terminally *bijou* part of the village, all bulging walls and lamp-brackets. In the days when the Black Swan was a coaching inn, it was probably a mews, with stables. Now the stables and an attached barn had become Cassidy's Country Kitchen, with its deli and its restaurant, specializing in game and salmon and things served in nouvelle-cuisine-size portions at silly prices. Jane thought she'd have

preferred it in the old days when the best you could expect
was a nosebag full of oats.

There were a few early tourists about. Also the famous
Colette Cassidy, shrugged into the Country Kitchen doorway, looking like a high-class hooker in a short, white dress.
She raised an eyebrow at Jane but didn't smile. Jane, in jeans
and an old blue Pulp T-shirt, breezed past with a non-
committal 'Hi'.

Ledwardine Lore was at the very end of the mews,
crunched into a corner by the flatulent spread of the Country
Kitchen. The sign over the window was uptilted so that
'Lore' was almost pointing at the twisted chimney; if it had
been horizontal they'd never have squeezed all the letters in.
As she pushed open the door, Jane could have sworn she
heard an amused snort from Colette and was disgusted with
herself for blushing.

Inside the shop, there was more standing room than you
found in a phone box, but not a lot more. Jane felt suddenly
nervous, like when you went into a fortune-teller's tent and
it was just you and her. When she closed the door behind
her, this smell went straight to the back of her throat: not
the usual horrible incense, but a piercing fruity scent.

She looked around and, at first, it seemed like just the
usual tourist bric-a-brac: pottery ornaments and those little
stained-glass panels you put over your windows. Cellophane-
covered jugs of pot-pourri and gift packs of local wine. And
books. Jane's eyes went in search of history and found the
usual paperbacks: *Herefordshire Curiosities*, *Herefordshire
Castles*, *The Folklore of Herefordshire*, *The Old Straight Track*,
The Old Golden Land.

Plus dozens of other books about apples. *Apples for
Growing*. *Apples for Health*. *Identifying Apples*. Books of
apple-legends, apple-customs, superstitions, games, even a
book of poems called *Ripest Apples*.

And then she saw that most of the tourist stuff was apple-shaped and apple-coloured. The pottery was little apple jugs and mugs. The pot-pourri was orchard-scented, which accounted for the pervading smell. The stained-glass panels featured Eve and what looked like an oversized Cox's Orange Pippin. The local wine was in fact cider, twin green bottles labelled Bittersweet and Bittersharp. There were also rosy apples in small oil paintings, crudely framed. Russet apples glazed on kitchen tiles. Wax apples, apple-shaped notepads and address books and naff fluffy apples, like the dice people hung in their cars, dangling in bunches from the ceiling beams.

And clinging to the fluffy apples and the jugs and the mugs and the frames of the paintings were scores of what looked like butterflies, but on closer inspection proved to be . . .

'Fairies!' Jane said in surprise. They were tiny and delicate with little matchstick bodies and wings of soft red and yellow and green. Apple colours.

'Lucy makes them. Two pounds each or three for a fiver.'

'Oh!' She jumped. She hadn't seen him behind the counter. Well, until he stood up you couldn't see anything at all behind the counter because of a pile of big green and red apple-shaped candles promising to give your living room an exquisite orchard ambience.

He peered out between the candles. He had long hair tied up in a ponytail and small, brass-rimmed, tinted glasses. He didn't seem very tall.

'Sorry,' Jane said. 'It didn't look as if there was anybody here. Just . . . apples.'

'Pick-your-own?' He plucked a fairy from a candle wick. 'Spend over ten quid, we throw one of these in for nothing. They're very lucky. Apparently.'

'I didn't really come in for a fairy. I was looking for a book on local history.'

'Right,' he said uncertainly. 'Well, they're around. They *are* around. You just have to keep moving things until you find what you're after.'

She turned to look around and everything started to rustle and jingle.

'I'm scared to touch anything. You never know what you might bring down.'

He smiled, indicating a small sign in a wooden frame between the candles on the counter. It said,

> **Lovely to look at**
> **Delightful to hold**
> **But if you break it . . .**
> **don't worry, it's my own**
> **bloody fault for daring to**
> **run a business in such a**
> **grotty little hovel.**

'Cool,' Jane said, impressed.

'Lucy's got a bit of a thing about these really precious gift shops that have all this delicate stuff in precarious places then make you pay through the nose when you dislodge one with your elbow. You said local history . . . How local?'

'*Very* local.'

'Try up there.'

He didn't seem to want to come out from behind the counter. A Roswell-style alien face stared impassively from his black sweatshirt. She reached up to a stack of volumes between stone book-ends featuring a sort of Gothic Rotweiler with an apple in its mouth.

'There,' he said. 'That one.'

Pulling down a soft-backed book, she knocked over a stack of greeting cards displaying appley watercolours.

'Chaos, here.' But he didn't come round the counter to help her pick them up. 'It's OK. I'll do it later.'

The book she held was not very thick. *The Black and White Villages: A short history.* Jane flicked through it; it seemed to be mainly photographs.

'I'm trying to find some information about a guy called Wil Williams.'

'Ah,' he said. 'Mmm. Right.'

'You know who I mean?'

'You won't find much in there.'

'So where *would* I find something?'

He shrugged. 'Difficult.'

'This is my only hope. I need it. School essay.'

'Well . . .' His accent wasn't local, but there was an accent there, a vaguely rural one. 'It's difficult.'

'You keep on saying that.' What was it with this guy? He seemed harmless but he was definitely weird. Almost like he was scared of her.

'Problem is,' he said, 'Lucy's not happy about the way the story's been handled. Doesn't think they've got it right. Lucy has very definite ideas about things.'

You'll just get the Miss Devenish version . . . Yeah, OK, Mum.

'Look,' Jane said. 'I don't need anything in any great depth. I mean, just who *was* Wil Williams?'

'I thought you were doing a school essay on him.'

'I . . .' Her mind went fuzzy.

He smiled, took off his glasses. He wasn't as young as she'd first thought. That is, he had a young face, but there were deep little lines around his eyes. He'd be more like Mum's age, really. Pity.

'He was the vicar. '

'Oh, really? When?'

'In the seventeenth century. About 1670, something like that. I'm not sure whether they actually called them vicars in those days, but that was what he was. See, Lucy'd give you the whole bit, but she takes Saturday afternoons off when she can. I don't know that much about it. Keep meaning to find out, but at the end of the day, I don't really think there's much known for certain. It's like one of those murky areas of history. All kinds of atrocities in those days, weren't there?'

Atrocities?

'But he was the minister of . . . this church?'

He didn't reply. He seemed suddenly to have forgotten she was here. He was staring through the window, into the mews, where Colette Cassidy still stood in her doorway and a bearded man was strolling by. The man looked at Colette's legs.

'This church,' Jane said. 'You mean the village church? Excuse me?'

'Oh, shit.'

The shop guy folded his fingers together and squeezed hard. It was difficult to be sure in this light, but Jane thought he'd gone pale. He looked at her.

'Look . . . You on your own?'

'Well . . .'

She felt uncomfortable, found herself backing instinctively towards the door.

'What I mean . . . you're not with that bloke out there?'

'What?'

The bearded man was standing in the middle of the mews, about fifteen feet away. He wore jeans and a denim shirt and those dark glasses that went all the way round. He had his hands in his pockets and was gazing at the shop window. He seemed a quite ordinary tourist-type, perhaps waiting for his wife.

'Why would you think I should know *him*? I've never even seen him before.'

The shop man had his glasses back on. He didn't look cool any more. He sort of . . . *jittered*. He bit his lip.

'Yeah. Right. OK. Do me a favour, er . . .?'

'Jane.'

'Jane.' He shook his head, in a wry you-have-to-laugh kind of way. Then the hunted look was back. 'Jane, could I ask you to mind the store?'

*

'Right,' said little Gomer Parry through his cigarette. 'That bit, that's all yours, Vicar, see.'

She'd given up correcting people when they called her vicar. You couldn't really have people calling you Priest-in-Charge anyway, could you?

Gomer was pointing to a small meadow, about two acres, Merrily reckoned, sloping gently from one end of the church-yard down to the river.

'Now, what we done the past couple o' years,' Gomer said, 'is we mowed 'im, end of July roundabout, then we sells the bales to Powell. We could sell the ole grass standing, let Powell cut it 'isself, but bein' as how I got the gear, where's the point in loppin' off the profits? Plus, Gomer Parry Agricultural and Plant Hire, we does a tidy job.'

'And what do you charge, Gomer?'

'Aye, well,' Gomer Parry said. 'Bloody retired, en't I? Can't charge nothing no more, see.'

As Minnie, his wife of four years, never neglected to remind people, Gomer Parry Plant Hire, in the literal sense, was no more. Which Merrily reckoned accounted for Gomer's general air of depression.

'But the running costs,' she said. 'The maintenance of all that machinery . . .'

'Ah, does it good to get the ole things up and turnin'. All it is now is just a – ' Gomer struggled to cough up the contemptible word. ' – *hobby*.'

She felt sorry for him. Apparently, Minnie had refused to marry him unless he promised to pass on the operational side of the business to his nephew, Nev, and move these twenty miles back over the English border. But as he kept on telling you, he was only sixty-eight. What was sixty-eight in the Age of Power Steering?

Could it really be that Minnie hadn't realized that Plant Hire was part of his name, part of who he was?

'Mebbe you could mention me to the Ole Feller sometime,' Gomer said. 'In passing, like.'

'Old . . .? Oh. Right.' Merrily nodded. 'I'm sure He does notice these things.'

'All respect, see, but the way I sees it, it's a better thing all round if I'm out yere getting to grips with God's good earth than inside that ole church throwing everybody off key with my deplorable bloody singing.'

'Mmm,' Merrily said dubiously. 'We'll, er, maybe go into that argument in more detail sometime.'

'I never argues with the clergy.' Gomer said, putting the lid on that one. 'Now, your ditches. As I kept pointin' out to the Reverend Hayden, them ditches is in a mess. En't been cleared in my time back yere, which is four years come October, and there's all kinds o' shit down there.'

Gomer led Merrily along a crooked avenue of eighteenth-century graves to where the churchyard met the Powell orchard. It was a raised, circular churchyard, partly bordered by a bramble-covered ditch about four feet deep.

'Get rid o' this lot, no big problem, Vicar. However, wise not to widen the ditch this side, on account some of these ole graves've slipped and slid a bit over the centuries like, and you goes into that bit o' bank you never quite knows what's gonner tumble out, you get my meaning.'

'Oh.'

Merrily imagined ancient bones rattling into the shovel of Gomer's JCB.

'As for the other side . . . Well, who knows, Vicar, who knows?'

'Who knows what?'

She hitched up her cassock to bend down and peer into the ditch. A rich, musty smell rose up. She looked across to the other side; the nearest apple tree was a good twenty yards away. Further into the tangly orchard, she was sure she recognized the twisted boughs of the Apple Tree Man and couldn't suppress a shudder.

Gomer followed her gaze.

'They won't do that again, Vicar.'

'The wassailing? No, I suppose not.'

'Funny thing, though . . . You wanner see the buds on 'im now.'

'On the . . .?'

Merrily looked at Gomer. Those ridiculous, little round glasses and the often-unlit cigarette, like a baby's dummy, made it hard to take him seriously.

'Gonner be ablaze with blossom in a week or two, that ole bugger. You'd've sworn he'd given up. Makes you think, don't it?'

She was chilled.

'I think I'd rather *not* think. What did you mean just now when you said *who knows*? About the other side of the ditch.'

'Ah. Well. You gotter ask yourself why the ole orchard's still there, see. Rod Powell, he en't a man to keep a worthless bit o' scrub without there's a reason for it. Well, a cider apple's no use for nothin' but cider, specially them stunted little buggers, and the Powells en't made but their own in half a century. Rest of the farm's beef and' – Gomer growled – 'battery chickens.'

Merrily, who also disapproved of battery chickens, kept quiet.

'So you gotter ask yourself, Vicar, why's he keep that ole orchard?'

'Sentiment?' Before the word was out, Merrily felt embarrassed.

'Superstition.' Gomer tapped his nose. 'Them as don't believe superstition counts for much in the countryside no more en't never lived yere. Powells put in a bunch of new trees down the bottom end, to please that Cassidy, but Edgar wouldn't grub up this bit, nor even scrat around too much in there, on account of he knows and all his family knows that there's . . .'

Gomer paused, took off his flat cap. Wild white hair erected itself.

'. . . the First Unhallowed Ground.'

Merrily thought she understood, but she wasn't sure.

'You dig up decently buried bones, see, well, that's one thing. You just puts 'em straight back. But any bones the *other* side o' that ditch . . . Now don't get me wrong, Vicar, I'm not saying I goes for this ole toffee, I'm just telling you the kind of superstition you'll encounter if you sticks around these parts . . . But the bones t'other side, them's the ones you don't wanner be diggin' up, you get my meaning.'

*

On the other side of a curtain behind the counter was an iron spiral staircase leading up into what seemed like complete darkness, apparently a loft without a window. Jane stuck her head through the curtain.

'OK, Lol. He's gone.'

'You sure?'

The voice was hollow with – Jane was amazed and thrilled – actual, real *fear*. It made her think again about the little crunch before the man had left.

'Jane?'

'Yeah, honest. I'm certain. Gave him two minutes, then I went to the end of the mews and he was talking to Colette Cassidy, then he was getting into this pretty smart yellow sports car. Toyota.'

'He didn't see you following him?'

'Not a chance.'

His face appeared at the top of the spiral, blinking from the dark, full of suspicion and . . . yeah, anxiety. Definitely that. The lines around his eyes deeper.

'You know the Cassidy girl?'

'Only by sight.'

He came down. 'That means you're local?' He looked dismayed.

'I am now,' Jane said. 'For my sins.'

She was still feeling rather electrified. This could be the most utterly bloody brilliant place she'd ever lived. Best of all, she felt in control. She'd saved this man from God knows what. He owed her one.

'So what exactly are we looking at here?' Jane said loftily. 'Drugs?'

'Huh?' He slumped back on the stool behind the counter, shaking his head. He looked drained, as though he'd spent the last few minutes on the lavatory.

Pretty heavy.

'Listen.' Putting on her cynical smile. 'I might be local now, *Mr Robinson*, but I've been around. Like you're into that guy for some amount you can't afford, and he wants his money. What are we talking? Coke? Smack?'

'What?'

Jane said, 'Es? Whizz?'

'Huh?'

'You can tell me.'

'Oh . . . *God*.' It was probably the last thing he felt like, but he started to laugh. 'Who the hell *are* you?'

'Don't change the subject. My general feeling is, that wasn't a very nice guy. Underneath all the charm and the Florida tan and the really white teeth. I can sense these things.'

'He buy anything?'

'He said he was looking for an old friend. He described you. Puny little guy, long hair, glasses. He said he'd been to your house and asked around and somebody said they'd seen you with Miss Devenish, and this is her shop, so . . .'

'And you said?'

'I said I didn't know anybody called Robinson, which was true. I said I couldn't think who he meant. So he's like . . . Oh, well, he might've changed, got fatter, lost his hair. And I'm saying, Well, in that case he could be any one of a dozen people.'

'Thank you.'

'Like, I don't think he believed me that you weren't here. He said – in this kind of *knowing* way – that if I should just happen to come across you, tell you he'd be back. And he kept like looking at the curtain. As if he was wondering whether to thrust me aside and go in and drag you out.'

God, this was fun. If not so much for Mr Robinson.

'He say *when* he'd be back?'

'Nn-nn.'

'What was his attitude?'

'Like I said, charming. Lovely white teeth. Capped, I suppose. He imports the stuff, does he?'

'Look . . .' Mr Robinson pulled hair out of his glasses. 'He may be into drugs, I wouldn't know. We are not business associates. He's what he said he was. An old . . . friend. Sort of.'

'If you think I'm that dumb,' Jane said loftily, 'you're spending too much time with the fairies.'

'He's just hard to get rid of. You must've had friends like that. That's all it was. No drugs. Sorry. Oh—' Alarm doubled back across his face. 'You say he talked to the Cassidy girl?'

'Briefly. Like he was asking her the way or something.'

'Look. Seriously. Jane? You listening? If you see him again, keep out of his way, yeah? Will you promise me that, Jane?'

'You want me to come and tell you if I see him again?'

'No! Just stay out of his way. Tell Colette, too . . . No, don't, it'd just get her interested. Leave it. Please. Forget it happened.'

Fatal instruction. 'Bit bloody one-way, this, if you ask me,' Jane said.

'Suppose I give you the dirt on Wil Williams.'

'Oh, sure,' Jane said. 'Change the subject.'

'It's one L, by the way,' Lol said. 'If you didn't know. W–I–L. The Welsh way.'

'All right then,' Jane said. 'Wil Williams. One L. And it better be good.'

'It wasn't that good for him. But I expect you'll find it good. It's spooky. Here, have a notebook to write it down.'

Lol reached up, flipped one from a rack behind him. A quick, nervous thing, as though he was giving his hands something to do to stop them shaking. He laid the notebook on the counter; it had an apple on the front.

'I'll pay for it,' Jane said primly. 'And what should I do about *this*?'

Opening her left hand over the counter. A tiny fairy looked up, stricken, from her palm, its apple-streaked gossamer wings in shreds, its matchstick spine snapped.

'Your . . . old friend . . . knocked it off its perch. Crunched it under his shoe on his way out. Pretended not to notice, but I think he did.'

Both Lol's hands were behind his back now. He bit his lip.

*

After the lady vicar had gone, Gomer Parry was down the ditch dragging some of the brambles away, sizing up the job, when the shadow fell across him.

'What d'you think of her, Gomer?'

The hooked nose under the hat. Like some old eagle, she was.

'The vicar? 'Er's all right, Lucy. Nice little girl. Don't throw the Ole Feller in your face the whole time.'

'*Nice little girl.* Pshaw! You know what I'm asking, Gomer. Is she strong?'

''Er gonner need t'be, Lucy?'

'She's a woman.'

'Never thought to hear that comin' from you.'

'Because you don't know what I mean, do you?'

Gomer tried to climb out of the ditch, slipped back, and she offered him a hand and pulled him out easy as this hydraulic winch he used to have.

'What did you talk about? When you were looking out to the orchard?'

Ah, watching them, was she? 'This an' that,' Gomer said. 'Number of buds in the Apple Tree Man kind of thing.'

'The Apple Tree Man?' Face near black against the light. 'Heaven save us, there's no such damn thing as the Apple Tree Man! Not *here*. That's Somersetshire lore. Ours is a different tradition altogether. You should know that. No apple tree man, no guns.'

'Well, pardon me,' Gomer said, 'for bein' just a humble plant-hire operative.'

'It's *important*, Gomer. These clowns move in with their twisted interpretations, and we wake up one day and we're living in a different place – a fantasy village. It's what happens when you get too much change too quickly. This was a terribly poor place when I was a child – miserable farm wages, children still in rags. Now it's damn near the richest village in the county. Looks beautifully authentic, but it's a sham. And do they care, the locals, what's left of them? Do they hell.'

'Money's money,' Gomer said, winding her up, see where this was heading. 'Shops doin' well. Plenty jobs for plumbers, builders, carpenters, the ole rural craftsmen. Why should they care?'

'It's false wealth, you know that. *Cider* was Ledwardine's wealth, and it dried up long ago.'

'But hang on yere, Lucy, if this Mr Cassidy's out to *revive* it—'

'In his dilettante, touristy fashion.'

Gomer studied her. She'd never been what you'd call pretty, but there was a time when she could've had her pick of men. And, from what he'd heard, she'd picked a fair few in her time and thrown them back a bit more out-of-breath than they might've reckoned on. But time passed.

'Well.' He fished out his ciggy. 'I wouldn't know what that means, dilly-whatever . . . me bein' just an ill-educated plant-hire man, like. But it do strike me, Lucy, as you're bein' a bit of a wosname in the manger. Cause you din't think of it yourself, you don't wannit to work. Same with the festival. You feels . . . what the word? Sidelined.'

Lucy Devenish blinked and brought a hand to her face, and for one terrible moment, Gomer feared she had a tear coming. But she used the hand to straighten her hat.

'What I feel, Gomer,' she said, 'especially when I stand on this side of the churchyard, is a certain fear for your nice little girl.'

Cold in the House of God

Merrily walked softly into the darkening church, still hesitant, still unsure.

'Do you know what I couldn't do?' her mother had said a couple of years ago. 'I couldn't go into one of those old churches alone at night. Spooky. Anybody could be in there: tramps, rapists. That's another reason why it isn't a job for a woman, in my view.'

Least of my problems, Merrily thought, still half-afraid that she would be met by a chill of hostility, a cavernous yawn of disapproval.

It had all been too easy, so far. Respectable congregations (all right, curiosity, novelty value). Sermons which seemed to write themselves, even in the hotel room at midnight. No dark looks in the street, no suspicious stares.

And not even inducted yet. Apart from reducing the number of hymns, she hadn't even started on what she planned. Although she didn't, to be honest, know what form it was going to take yet.

It still didn't feel quite real, this was the problem. Staying in a hotel – even when you had to drive into Hereford at night to use the launderette – created this illusion of a holiday. Perhaps when they moved into the vicarage, reality would set in.

She wasn't looking forward to that; the vicarage was

too big to be a home; it scared her far more than the church.

It was a dull evening now, the stained glass fading to opaque. Her hand slid over the stone, up to the light switches. Even the air in here was temperate. The brass-bracketed lamps came on. In the soft amber, the walls themselves glistened with antiquity, yet not in an austere, forbidding way. The stones were mellow and softly encrusted, like country honey.

The evening visit had become a kind of ritual. Her trainers pattered on the flagged floor of the nave. Her footsteps made no echoes; the acoustics, as Alf had said, were warm and tight.

Walking on bones. Several of the flags were memorial stones, dating back three, four centuries. Francis Mott, d. 1713. John Jenkyn, whose dates were worn away into the sandstone like the lower half of the indented skull in the centre of Jenkyn's flag – they didn't dress it up in those days.

Couldn't be more different from the last place, in Liverpool: a warehouse: scuffed, kicked about, a city church of smutted brick, with no graveyard, only rusty railings. The building couldn't have been less important; it was what you did there, what you brought to it.

This church *was* important – medieval, Grade One Listed. Beautiful beyond price, even to people with no faith. And it felt friendly. Even to a woman. It enfolded you.

Hey, don't knock it.

Merrily faced the altar through the rood-screen out of which row upon row of apple shapes were carved. Closed her eyes and saw a deep, dark velvety blue. Feeling at once guilty about this habitual need for reassurance.

'Mum? That you?'

Merrily's eyes opened. 'In here!'

Jane's head appeared round the door, hair as dark as the oak. 'You're not doing anything . . . private?'

'Like what, for heaven's sake?'

'You *know* . . .'

'Like doing the rounds? Locking up?'

Merrily stood with hands on hips. Getting a bit fed up with this attitude, the kid treating God like a stepfather. Was it always going to be like this until she left home and old mum in the dog collar became a figure of affectionate amusement?

'Got him, Mum.'

'Well, don't leave him on the mat. Who are we talking about?'

'Wil. Wil Williams.'

'Oh.'

'One L. He was Welsh.'

'Anything wrong with that in the seventeenth century?'

'A lot wrong with *him*,' Jane said. 'In the seventeenth century. Though I don't think it would've worried me.'

*

'Well, that's wonderful,' Merrily said glumly. 'That's all we need, isn't it?'

They sat side by side in the front pew.

'There's no evidence he *was*.' Jane picked at the thick varnish on the prayer-book ledge. 'Not what you'd call *real* evidence. I mean, people were always getting stitched up in those days.'

'But not vicars. Believe me, there's very little history of this kind of thing inside the Anglican Church.'

'Very little of interest has *ever* gone on inside the Anglican Church.' Jane grinned. 'Still, they haven't had you very long yet, have they?'

'Ha.' Merrily looked up at the Norman arch, so plain, so

curiously modern-looking. 'All right, why hadn't we heard about this, Jane? Why isn't it a celebrated case, like Salem, Massachusetts?'

'Because he was only one bloke, I suppose. Besides, it never came to a trial, according to Lol.'

'Lol?'

'Guy in the shop. Very nervous.'

'You make everyone nervous. Where was Miss Devenish?'

'Day off. Look, it's all straight up.' Jane pulled a little notepad from her jacket. 'Date: 1670. That makes it after the Reformation, right?'

'Restoration.'

'Whatever. After Cromwell. Was that Charles the Second's time, guy in the curly wig? Anyway, in rural areas, they were still very reactionary and always on the lookout for witches to persecute. Poor old Wil put himself well in the frame.'

'Meaning?'

'I'll tell it in sequence, so I get it right. He'd been vicar a couple of years, OK? Got the job possibly on the recommendation of the Rector of Credenhill, the poet guy . . .?'

'Thomas Traherne.'

'Yeah. They were mates. Went for long nature rambles together, Lol reckons, discussing ethics and stuff. Only then Traherne gets a new job near London, and when he leaves there's nobody to stick up for little Wil and somebody like dropped him in it, big-time.'

Merrily smiled. Jane's style of historical narration wasn't exactly textbook, but it did confer a certain immediacy.

'See, from what I can make out, Wil Williams was serious, *serious* totty. Like really great-looking, in a poetic, ethereal, unworldly sort of way. Strawberry-blond, unblemished, lovely smile. Women swooning in the aisle kind of scenario.'

Merrily frowned. 'You're not embellishing this by any chance? Because if you drop me in it at this meeting . . .'

'Swear to God. And it's significant because this could be one reason he wasn't all that popular with the men. I mean the macho, hunting types who ran things. Lol reckons parsons in those days were expected to ride with the hunt, drink too much port, get gout . . .'

'Sure. Go on.'

Jane turned over a page in her notebook, following the lines with a forefinger; she'd never quite outgrown that.

'Very superstitious times, OK? So when you get reports of strange phenomena, I mean, you know . . . Sounds like complete rubbish, total crap, today. But people didn't take too much convincing back then. Everything was an omen. You only had to start a rumour and they'd all be screaming for blood.'

'What sort of phenomena?'

'I'm coming to it. Most of it was centred on the orchard . . . just over the wall? Powell's orchard? Mum, you shivered . . .'

'I didn't!'

'You bloody did. And now you've lied in the House of God!'

Merrily growled. 'It gets cold in the House of God after a while. Just shut up and get on with it.'

Jane peered at her notes. 'Something about . . . hogs? Oh. Yeah. The orchard belonged to the Church back then. They produced quite a lot of cider in those days, apparently, and the vicar's stipend included what he could make out of it. Which was expected to be about fifty hogsheads of cider every year. Is that a lot?'

'I have no idea. What happened in the orchard?'

'Lights,' Jane said. 'Lights and music.'

'Parish barbecue?'

'Strains of eerie music in the night.' Jane's voice dropped to a sepulchral whisper, which wasn't actually all that funny in the vast, lamplit church. 'Fiddle music, like for dancing. Little, glowing, bobbing lights among the apple trees. Wil Williams . . . dancing with demons.'

'I see.'

'One guy actually *did* see. Or claimed to. Lol couldn't remember his name, but he was a local miller or tanner, one of these quaint, rustic professions. One dark night, he was coming back from the pub – probably well pissed – and he strayed from the track and wound up in the orchard. Or was kind of lured towards the lights and the music, couldn't help himself. What's that noise, Mum?'

'Bats, probably. Vampire bats. Don't try it on, Jane, I've got approximately an hour before the meeting. What happened to the miller?'

'Private screening of the seventeenth-century equivalent of a dirty video. Wil Williams stark naked, dancing around an unearthly light with these silvery, shapely . . . demons. Or sprites, as he called them.'

'How very tawdry.'

'Obviously gave the miller a hell of a hard-on.'

'Jane!'

'Sorry. Sorry, God. No, naturally, the miller claimed to have been shocked and terrified and he spread it all round the village, and word reached the Sheriff of Hereford and the Bishop of Hereford, and eventually a bunch of them went round to the vicarage, all official—'

'*Our* vicarage?'

'Presumably. It's old enough, isn't it? So all these sanctimonious gits arrive on Wil's doorstep to ask for an explanation or arrest him for devil-worship or whatever the charge was. But there was no answer when they knocked on the door. So they came . . . here. '

Merrily didn't move. Resisted the urge to look around. It was only a story, it was all in the past, and yet . . . she was

79

apprehensive. She didn't want there to have been some sort of Thomas à Becket death scene at the altar, the honeyed stones stained with innocent blood ... some set-piece slaughter she'd have to try not to think about when she arrived to take communion on drab winter mornings.

'Somebody kicked open the door,' Jane said.

This time Merrily did look – towards the main oak door, imagining the group of po-faced guardians of the law striding righteously past the font, bearded men with swords half-drawn.

'But the church was empty,' Jane whispered. 'Wil Williams wasn't here.'

Merrily sighed. The kid really knew how to spin out a story.

'He was outside,' Jane said. 'In the orchard. All dressed up for them, in his full vestments and things.'

'He was expecting them?'

'Presumably,' Jane said.

'This is the suspense bit, is it?'

'You could say that.' Jane gave half a smile. 'He was hanging from an apple tree.'

'Oh God.'

'In his richest vestments,' Jane said dreamily. 'Poor Wil, dangling there, all aglow on a bright, sunny morning.'

Jane nodded to signify The End and closed the notebook with a snap, raising her gaze to the vaulted ceiling so that the amber lights were reflected in her big, dark eyes.

'Terrific.' Merrily blacked out a flash-image of the half-head of old Edgar Powell hanging like a left-over Christmas bauble on the Apple Tree Man. 'I hate that bloody orchard.'

Funny thing, though, Gomer Parry had said ... *You wanner see the buds on 'im now.*

So the orchard used to belong to the Church, although it

was not, of course, holy ground. And yet close. The First Unhallowed Ground, Gomer had called it. Suicides were invariably buried in unhallowed ground.

'He knew they'd be coming for him,' Jane said. 'And he couldn't face it. The trial, the abuse and everything. Poor, sensitive soul. He was only about twenty-five.'

Obviously, Terrence Cassidy had said, *it's not something the village nowadays is particularly proud of. Although I suppose it has its tourist possibilities, in a lurid sort of way.*

'So they buried him where he died – in the orchard. With only an apple tree to mark his grave. And, as apple trees don't live very long, nobody knows where it is now.'

Merrily recalled what Gomer had had to say about the reasons the Powells had never grubbed up their unproductive orchard.

. . . the bones t'other side, them's the ones you don't wanner be diggin' up, you get my meaning.

Unless you were a distinguished playwright, for whom no bones could be buried too deep.

She watched Jane's gaze travelling around the church with a new interest. The first time, in fact, that the kid had displayed *any* interest. It would have a history now, a mystery, a romance. In that age-blackened pulpit had stood the doomed Wil Williams, serious totty, with the sunlight in his strawberry-blond hair.

'Heavy stuff, huh?' Jane said, well satisfied.

Nothing unhealthy about this. Wil Williams was as remote and unreachable as the lead singer of some boy band in *Sugar* magazine. Merrily remembered the stage when *she* would fall in love with the ludicrous heroes of fantasy novels, princes with magic swords. It was a phase. A safe phase which wouldn't last long. Not long enough. Real boys, real men would be in the picture all too soon.

'Sure,' Merrily said. 'Heavy stuff.'

And felt a pang of impending loss. The sandstone walls still had an old-gold glaze in the lamplight but, when she stood up, she was sensing an end to the honeymoon period.

'Well,' she said. 'Thanks, flower.'

Dirty Video

'I beg your pardon,' Terrence Cassidy said, irritated.

'*Old Cider!*' Dermot Child, the musician, thumped the table. 'That's what we should call it!'

'I don't understand.'

'The entire event. The festival. Old *Ciderrrrr*! Resonates.'

Everything Dermot Child said seemed to resonate. He was a plump friar of a man, who, without being obviously Irish, Scottish or Welsh – indeed, his accent was closer to Oxford – vibrated with an emotional fervour you could only describe as *Celtic*. Merrily quite liked him.

In the absence of the parish secretary, who was also the treasurer of the Women's Institute (as distinct from the Women's *Group*, formed by newcomers) and was attending some sort of WI convention, she'd agreed to take the minutes of this hastily called meeting. She wrote down, *Old Cider*?

'Explain, shall I . . . Mr Chairman?' Child leaned over onto an elbow, making a determined fist, as if prepared to arm-wrestle Cassidy into submission.

'Please do,' Cassidy said, resignation soaked in acid. It was, after all, *his* festival, Merrily thought. His idea, his *concept*. Eccentrics like Child should content themselves with being occasionally amusing.

Merrily smiled. Child caught her eye, winked. Outside, a small motorcycle was being expertly skidded on the cinders under the open window. Councillor Garrod Powell moved swiftly to the door. 'Give it a rest, Kirk,' they heard him shout mildly. 'Else I'll be round to see your dad, boy.'

It was getting rather dim in the village hall, screened from the sunset by two huge oaks. On the way back to his chair, Councillor Powell lifted a hand over the panel of metal switches to the left of the T'ai Chi group noticeboard. 'Leave it a moment, would you, Rod?' Child said.

Powell, tall and trim and oddly dignified, shrugged and went back to his seat between Cassidy and a moody-looking James Bull-Davies.

'It begins with "Crying the Mare",' said Child. 'You'd know all about that, Rod. They used to do that on your farm?'

'Sure to,' Powell said uncertainly.

'Harvest custom. They'd leave the last of the corn standing, separating it out into four bundles, sticking up like legs. The Mare, you see? Then they'd tie these together at the top to make a single sheaf, step a few paces back and *hurl* their hooks and sickles at it, to try and cut off the ears of corn.'

'Sounds rather pointless to me,' observed Terrence Cassidy, apparently failing to recall his role as principal organizer of the infamous Twelfth Night event in which shotguns were discharged into an apple tree.

Dermot Child ignored him. 'Be interesting to arrange a contest in one of the fields, see how many chaps can still do it.'

Somehow, Merrily couldn't quite imagine Lloyd and Garrod Powell, plus sundry seasonal labourers, abandoning the combine harvester to waste a valuable daylight hour attempting to shave a sheaf with tossed sickles.

'However,' Child said, 'this was really a preamble. On this and other occasions, the ritual would invariably conclude

with mugs of cider all round. Now. This would be preceded
by all the chaps gathering into a circle and intoning—'

Abruptly, he pushed back his chair, stood up, filled his
lungs. And with his fingertips pressed into the tabletop,
bellowed in a lugubrious bass, '*Auld . . . ciderrrrrrrrrrrr.*'

Rolling and dragging out the word on a single note, in a
deep, rumbling drone, a Herefordshire mantra. Merrily was
startled. How eerily primeval it seemed in the purply gloom.
You felt that if several of them were doing it, the walls would
start to peel and crumble.

No one spoke again until Child sat down.

'Aye,' Rod Powell said then, into the silence. 'I remember.' He moved to the switches again, and bluish fluorescent
tubes began to flicker.

Merrily recalled, as the lights revealed the sickly, 'sixties,
pink-brick interior of Ledwardine's only real architectural
embarrassment, what Gomer Parry had said about even the
mercenary Powells being far from immune from superstition.

Dermot Child was patting his chest.

'Don't know about the rest of you, but I find that
absolutely *thrilling.* Bunch of working men using their lungs
and their throats to make contact with the earth itself. Setting
up this marvellously powerful vibration . . . *Ciderrrrr.* The
very *roots* of music.'

'Sort of vibration we need for this festival,' said James
Bull-Davies. 'That's what you're saying?'

Bull-Davies was wearing a tan gilet over a checked shirt
with a cravat. Until you actually lived in a place like this,
Merrily thought, the idea of there still being a kind of
uniform for local squires would strike you as a joke. But
it was a fact that people like James did not wear jeans, they
did not wear T-shirts, and they would *never*, under any
circumstances, be seen in a baseball cap, even the right way
round.

'You know . . .' Child leaned across the table. 'You'd be absolutely perfect for it, James. Your voice has the *timbre*.'

Cassidy scowled but said nothing. Probably not caring to emphasize his own reedy *lack* of timbre. Merrily wanted to giggle. James Bull-Davies caught her eye and looked away at once. Merrily stifled a sigh. How long would it take for this guy to come to terms with a woman priest? Answer: he never would; it wasn't the *thing*.

'I'm planning, you see,' Child announced, 'a new choral work, for which this will be the focus. *Old Cider*. I'm looking for voices. Local voices. I want to work *with* the voices. I want the composition to arise *from* those voices. From the earth, the red earth of Ledwardine. Any thoughts, Rod?'

'We did have a male voice choir, Mr Child, some years back. Folded through lack of support. A few of the ole boys still around, though, sure to be.'

Child beamed. 'Vicar?'

'I could put the word around the church choir,' Merrily said. 'See if we can get a few volunteers.'

'Good girl.' Child reached over and patted her hand, lingering perhaps a little too long on her fingers. 'So what's the committee's view on using "Old Cider" as the name of the festival. Terry?'

'*Terrence*,' Cassidy said tightly. 'Well, we obviously can't make a decision tonight—'

'Who says we can't?'

'Look, I suggest you submit a paper on the proposal and we'll circulate it before the next meeting.'

'Hell fire!' boomed Bull-Davies. 'Only a question of a bloody title. I propose, Chairman, that we take a vote on whether to decide it here and now. In fact, not to prolong the issue, I formally propose the Ledwardine Festival be known hereafter as the Old Cider festival.'

'Seconded,' Child said quickly.

'Now just a minute . . .' Terrence Cassidy's thin face was flushed. 'What this means is that the entire festival would effectively be promoting your as yet unwritten choral work.'

'Or my choral work, for heaven's sake' – Child threw up his arms – 'would be supporting the concept of the *festival*.'

'Proposition on the table, gentlemen.' Bull-Davies made a grimace of a smile. 'And, ah . . . lady. Chairman, my understanding of the rules of the committee game is that what you do next is ask if there are any amendments.'

Cassidy folded his arms obstinately. 'I think we should wait until Richard Coffey arrives. His play's going to be the thing that gets us national publicity, and he might—'

'Chap knew it was eight pm, didn't he?' Bull-Davies rumbled. 'Can't wait all night. Move progress.'

'All right.' Cassidy very red now. 'Very well. If that's what you want. So be it.'

Looking around for an amendment. In vain. Even to Merrily, the idea sounded simple and unpretentious, reflected the identity of the village and would look good on posters. Why waste time?

'Old Cider' was passed by three votes to one. Councillor Garrod Powell, as the only official local politician there, did what local politicians did best and abstained. Hostile looks were exchanged.

Oh God, Merrily thought, it's going to be *that* sort of committee.

She was suddenly depressed. Was this how Alf Hayden had started out: dutifully attending all the bitchy little meetings, wondering how God wanted him to vote? Wondering, after a while, if God was really concerned one way or the other? Village life: the cradle of society, or just a shallow pond across which Jesus surely would never have bothered to walk?

Tyres crunched the cinders under the window.

'Richard, I imagine,' Cassidy said, as if it didn't matter any more, as if he'd washed his hands of them all.

Merrily had hoped Coffey wouldn't show. After what Jane had told her, she needed a bit of time to think about Wil Williams, minister of this parish 1668 to 1670. She needed to consult a few people. If James Bull-Davies was in a decision-making mood tonight, she might be pushed into a corner on the issue of whether the local Church should be actively involved and allow its premises to be used for the resurrection of a seventeenth-century minister apparently hounded to death by his own parishioners.

Her first dicey decision. Sitting directly beneath the *No Smoking* sign, Merrily ached for a cigarette.

*

Back at the Black Swan, Jane watched *National Lottery Live* on TV, alone in the tiny, half-panelled residents' lounge, and almost began to understand why her mother had gone into the Church.

The bloody lottery. Look at them all, whooping and squealing with every number drawn. Was this what the human race had come to – naked lust for money, mob greed?

Greed. Well, of course, Dad had been greedy. No getting around that.

Poor bloody stupid Dad.

For nearly two years, she'd kept a secret picture of the wreckage. Secret from Mum, that is. Mum having tried to shield Jane, at eleven, from the worst of it. No local papers had been allowed into the house that week.

But Dad's car was such a horrific mess, like a screwed-up ball of newspaper, you could hardly tell it had ever *been* a car, that the picture had made it to a couple of the nationals. She'd cut it out, hid it under her mattress.

The picture froze her up inside, but she'd forced herself to bring it out every night before she went to bed and she'd stare at it and stare at it, knowing he was still *in* there when the photo was taken, like shreds of meat in a burger.

Dadburger.

With added Karen. Fragments of Dad and Karen all mixed up, intermingled: flesh around flesh, bone to bone, tissue on tissue, sinews intertwined. More together than they could ever have been in life. More intimate than Sean Barrow had ever been with Mum. Karen had him totally at the end and for ever and ever, and it would be convenient to think that this was what had driven Mum into the arms of God. Only it wasn't that easy, it had been coming on for quite a while before that. The impenetrable paperbacks, the long walks, the tedium of evensong, the voluntary work at the Christian Youth Centre. Creepy.

'Ah, here you are.'

A powerful whiff of musk made Jane spin round in her chair, and there, in the doorway, was the glamorous Ms Colette Cassidy in her teenage-hooker dress. Glancing at the TV, smirking.

'Yeah, they said you were an intellectual.'

'Stick around,' Jane said coolly. 'You might even see me watching *Gladiators*.'

'*Gladiators* isn't even on—'

Jane grinned triumphantly. They'd passed each other a few times, sidelong glances, vague acknowledgements, but this was the first time actual sentences had been exchanged.

'Anyway,' Colette said, regaining the high ground, '*Gladiators* is different. *Gladiators* is serious, heavy-duty.'

'If you like that kind of thing.'

'You don't know what you like.' Colette ran her tongue around the inside of her wide, sensuous lips. 'Until you've shopped around.'

OK, you win. You win this round. But there will be others, Ms Cool.

Colette smiled graciously. 'Want to come for a drink?'

'More than my life's worth,' Jane said frankly. She hadn't been Mum-less in a bar since the infamous running-away incident in Birmingham, since the creepy counselling session.

'I didn't mean *here*,' Colette said. 'We could go down the Ox.'

Jane was reluctantly impressed. The Ox was this tiny, seedy pub, flickering with gaming machines on the corner of the alleyway leading to the public toilets.

This was a test, wasn't it?

'Your mother isn't going to get away from that meeting this side of eleven,' Colette said. 'My old man'll see to that. Gives you a couple of hours, at least.'

'I don't know.' Jane was thinking fast, too fast, feeling flustered. Street cred on the line in a big way here.

Colette tossed back her dark-brown hair like an impatient, thoroughbred pony. She had this scintillating diamond nose-stud. Could you get away with that at the Cathedral School, or was it a weekend thing? Must be a pain to keep taking it in and out. Worthwhile pain, though.

'And if you're worrying about word getting back to the Reverend Mummy,' Colette said smoothly, 'I think it's fair to say that the clientele of the Ox aren't known for religion.'

'Especially on the morning after Saturday night, I suppose.'

'You got it.' Colette smiled her sophisticated smile, fifteen going on thirty-five.

'It's a bit close to the village hall.'

'Live dangerously,' Colette said.

Jane stood up, no option.

*

'Am I late?'

Not actually sounding as if he cared one way or the other, the playwright slid his briefcase across the table, shed his jacket, spidered into a seat. A single motion. Richard Coffey was all motion.

'Not at all.' Terrence Cassidy gathered his papers, and his dignity, to his chest.

'Yes,' James Bull-Davies snapped.

This was unnecessary, Merrily thought. Uncalled for. But nobody appeared to have heard him. The lord of the manor had been eclipsed. There was a powerful new energy in the meeting.

'Er, Richard . . .' Cassidy half-rose '. . . I'd like to introduce our new vicar, Merrily Watkins.'

'Charming name,' Richard Coffey drawled.

Merrily had never seen him up close before. He was, she thought, almost shocking. Had the taut, muscular body of an ageing ballet-dancer, at the stage where staying fit was becoming painfully obsessive. His lean, pocked face vibrated with colours and textures, divided into pulsing segments like a portrait by Lucien Freud or Francis Bacon, full of life and personal history, a history, you would have to conclude – even if you hadn't heard the stories – of sensual excess.

She was fascinated and wasn't aware of how long she'd been staring at him until the vacuum of silence around them was popped by a discreet chairman's cough.

'What it is' – she heard herself burbling – '. . . I was born on Christmas Eve, but my mother didn't like the name Noelle, and Dad's favourite carol was Ding Dong Merrily on High, so . . .'

Coffey smiled easily through fleshy, wine-coloured lips.

'Stupid, really,' Merrily said. And certainly felt it.

'Well. We mustn't waste time.' Terrence Cassidy tapped his pen on the table. 'You all know Richard as one of our most celebrated contemporary writers for both the stage and television. He's now living, part of the time, at Upper Hall Lodge, and naturally we're glad he chose our village as his weekend retreat.'

'My feeling now is that it chose me,' Coffey purred diffidently.

Merrily saw James Bull-Davies gazing at the ceiling. Envisaged words in a bubble above his head. *Tiresome bloody poofter*, something like that. He'd be seeing rather more of Coffey than any of them; Upper Hall Lodge was, of course, at the bottom of his drive and used to be occupied by generations of Bull-Davies gamekeepers.

Cassidy nodded. 'I'm sure that's true. And we're all delighted at Richard's plan to use the Ledwardine Festival to premiere a major new drama illuminating a rather . . . rather unfortunate episode in our history. Unfortunate, but . . . but fascinating. Ah, at the moment, apart from its general theme, I know no more than any of you about the project. Which is why I asked Richard along tonight to tell us as much as he feels able to divulge at this stage of the, ah, creative process.'

'Thank you, Mr Chairman.' Coffey fluidly opening his briefcase and extracting a file of papers. 'I should, however, say from the outset that the prospect of staging a complete production, with a full cast, here in late summer, early autumn, is not really a viable one.'

'But, I . . .' Cassidy fought for balance, the rug sliding from under him. Merrily saw Dermot Child perk up.

'However – calm yourself, Terrence – what I do have in mind will be very much an event in itself. A re-creation, in the original setting, which I think could be absolutely electric. Will not only, I believe, lay a ghost, clear the name of a good man, but effectively solve a three-hundred-year-old mystery.'

'Oh. Is *that* all?' Bull-Davies said sourly.

Yes, it *would* upset him, having his village's history mined for nuggets of controversy by the celebrated interloper who'd turned his one-time gamekeeper's lodge into a less-than-discreet second home. Had he, Merrily wondered, seen *The Crystal Dungeon*, Richard Coffey's controversial TV play about a reclusive earl's incestuous relationship with his sister and their persecution by an evil butler?

Coffey didn't even seem to recognize the big, tweedy person as the owner of the rundown heap at the top of the drive.

'Anyway,' he said smoothly, 'I propose to outline my idea and then leave you to discuss it amongst yourselves. If it bothers any of you, I'm sure one of the other villages . . .'

'No!' Cassidy looked helpless. 'I mean, tell us, Richard. Tell us.'

*

'Wil Williams.' Coffey slid on half-glasses, spoke with precision. A man with nothing to prove and no time to waste on dissent. 'I take it we're all conversant with the brief facts.'

Merrily was able to nod. Thank God for Jane.

'Williams became rector here in the late 1660s. We don't know how old he was when he arrived. We think late twenties. His friend and neighbouring cleric, the poet Traherne, in a letter to his brother Philip, describes Williams as fair-haired, youthful in appearance and exuding a kind of perpetual joy.'

'Traherne.' James Bull-Davies was scornful. 'Chap never had a bad word for anybody. Walked around in bloody cloud-cuckoo-land half the time. Wrote as if he was *on* something.'

'One could argue at some length with you there. But this is not the occasion. I think no one would deny Williams was a man who loved the area and exulted in his ministry.'

Bull-Davies shrugged impatiently. Merrily wrote down, *Traherne*, feeling a bit ignorant. Traherne had been mentioned briefly at college as a major literary precursor of Wordsworth and Blake and one of the greatest Christian mystical poets, but she actually didn't know that much about him or his work. Fairly reprehensible, really, considering he'd been rector of a parish not ten miles away.

'As I understand it,' Dermot Child said, 'it was Traherne who more or less secured the Ledwardine post for Williams. Then buggered off.'

'It's never been proved that Traherne had a hand in the appointment of Williams,' said Coffey. 'Although, as you say, it is a theory. Certainly the two knew each other before Williams came here, possibly at Oxford. You say "buggered off" . . . Traherne certainly appears to have lost touch with Williams when he left the area in 1669. We know of no correspondence, and it seems unlikely that Traherne knew of the subsequent persecution. Perhaps because Williams made a point of not telling him.'

'Not telling him he'd been accused of bloody witchcraft?' Child leaned over the table, hands clasped together. 'Man's life was on the line. Surely, he needed all the support he could get. Traherne had good contacts by then – chaplain to this fellow, er . . .'

'Sir Orlando Bridgeman, one-time Lord Keeper of the Great Seal for Charles the Second. Yes, Traherne could perhaps have helped him, had the charges quashed. But Williams didn't seek Traherne's help. Why? I see that question as crucial.'

Merrily said tentatively, 'It seems incredible to me that a minister of the Church could find himself accused of witchcraft, even then. I know that was a fairly paranoid period, but . . .'

Coffey glanced at her, twitched a smile.

94

Merrily said, 'You're going to say he was fitted up, aren't you, Mr Coffey?'

'Absolutely.'

'On what basis?' Bull-Davies said sullenly.

'Well.' Coffey eased from his case a photocopied document. 'Let's look at the evidence. In September 1670, Williams was accused of "consorting with sprites". What do we mean by "sprites"?'

Silence.

'Spirits of the dead?' Child offered finally. 'Evil spirits?'

'I think not,' Coffey said. 'The only specific evidence handed down to us is a statement by one Silas Monks, a tanner . . .'

'The only evidence that *remains*,' Bull-Davies said. His eyes were hard.

'. . . who tells us that, while returning to his holding from the inn one night, he saw Williams in the orchard next to the churchyard, cavorting under the fruit-laden trees with an unspecified number of "vague and slender persons . . . whose forms shone palely in the moonlight".'

He paused, presumably to allow everyone to draw individual conclusions about this. Merrily thought of what Jane had said about the seventeenth-century equivalent of a dirty video, and a slippery, silvery image floated into her mind. She felt herself blush.

'Well, good for him.' Dermot Child laughed lightly, as if to dispel what Merrily sensed was a thickening fog of discomfort around the table.

'But it wasn't, was it?' Coffey said. 'On the alleged evidence of this presumably drunken tanner, and the resulting rumours, Wil Williams was visited and formally accused of witchcraft by a delegation including a Justice of the Peace, the local schoolmaster and, ah . . .'

A chair's metal legs scraped on the wooden floor. James

Bull-Davies stood up, eyes reduced to black slits in a big, darkened face.

'I'm leaving. I'll be in the pub. Call me back when you've heard enough of this shit.'

'James . . .' Cassidy coming to his feet in a panic.

Bull-Davies didn't look back.

The After-hours Social Club

'It's like I've walked in on her and she's having sex or something, you know? I'm like, *Ooops, sorry*. Backing out of the room, kind of all gooeyed-up inside. And then she tries to talk to me about it, which makes it worse.'

Jane was sweating. She drank some more cider to cool herself down. The cider was quite sweet and very soft. Never had it before. Amazing. You could actually taste apples.

'Can't handle it,' she said. 'Talk about a cross to bear. Just embarrasses me to bits.'

It was really dark in the Ox. Dark like a church. And hazy, so that the red and green and orange lights in the old slot-machines hung in the gloom like the small panes in the corners of stained-glass windows. Which was what had reminded her, brought up the awful image of Mum wearing out the knees of her tights.

Colette was unimpressed. 'At least praying's quiet. My mother shouts a lot now. Shouts at my old man, shouts at the cleaner and the cook and the waitresses. I don't mean bollocking them, just being loud. Asserting herself. It's one of her new words. Assertive. She went on this course for it. Kind of menopause training – when you start to lose your looks, make sure you get on top in bed kind of stuff.'

Jane didn't contest the issue. Everybody knew Colette's parents were a first-division pain.

'You just have to accept,' Colette said, 'that one way or the other they're going to embarrass the piss out of you. It's what they're for. At least yours is youngish.'

'And paranoid. She's convinced I'm gonna make the same mistake. Like get pregnant before I'm twenty. Doesn't realize how everything's changed. Like with condoms. Her day, you had to sneak into chemist shops wearing a false beard or something. Now they're hanging on Christmas trees. Anyway, I'm *never* going to get pregnant. Nobody with any sense of responsibility these days wants to dump another kid on the heap.'

'You should get her to put a condom machine in the church porch,' Colette said. 'That's where it all happens.'

'Yeah. And have them handed out with the prayer books!'

And they both broke up laughing and clutched at each other, and Jane thought, Hey, this woman is really OK, you should never judge people by their parents.

'Another one.' Colette stood up. 'You got any more money?'

Jane found the last fiver in her jacket pocket. Colette was getting the drinks because she looked the older, at least twenty-five, although she was only a few months older than Jane, coming up to sixteen and able to do It legally – be no fun any more, she reckoned. Woman of the world.

And one day . . . Jane leaned back against the scratched oak settle, which was kind of like a pew. Feeling pretty dreamy actually.

But aware that some of the guys at the bar were sneaking little glances at her. Even if one of them was this oozing gumboil, Dean Wall, a year over her at the high school. Dean and his mates played three-card-brag on the bus, big men. When they'd sidled over once tonight, Colette had taken no crap at all, told them to piss off back to their homework, and they'd slunk off, laughing, although you could tell they were really feeling stupid. One of them said something to Colette now, as she turned away from the bar with the drinks, white dress rucked up to her thighs, and she turned and raised a contemptuous middle finger and the boy laughed, but he was blushing too, under the sweat.

'Virgins.' Colette put down their ciders. 'Got virgin written all over them.'

Jane instinctively looked down at her own T-shirt, but all it said there was PULP.

'Except for the ones who've done it with sheep,' Colette said.

'That's not really true, is it?' Jane drank some cider. 'I mean you hear all these jokes—'

'Of *course* it's true! This is *the country*. You only have to look at that Dean Wall, his eyes all wide apart. Even looks like a sheep.'

'Maybe his *mother* was a sheep.'

Jane looked over at Dean Wall, and his eyes were actually quite a long way apart and also his upper lip seemed to overhang the other one, like a sheep's did. She spluttered helplessly over her drink. Couldn't remember how many they'd had; must be the fourth, good job it was only sweet cider. She mopped her mouth and then the table with her handkerchief. The table seemed quite a long way below her and wobbling, and she kept missing the puddles.

She remembered something important. 'Hey, what did that bloke say to you this afternoon?'

'What bloke?'

'In the sports car?'

'Oh, yeah, right. Not bad, was he? Bit old. He just said was it too late to get some lunch, and I said it was and he said maybe he'd come back for dinner, would I be there, the way guys do. What were you doing with little Lol?'

'Oh. Just, like . . . . checking out the shop. Weird.'

'Sad. Lol's *mega*-sad. Lucy doesn't need anybody to look after the shop on a Saturday, she's just trying to bring him out, introduce him into the community. Gives him nice poetry to read.'

'Huh?'

'Like with mental patients. They don't lock them away any more, they let them out on the streets. The way there used to be village idiots.'

'You're saying he's mental?'

'Sort of. He had a breakdown. Actually, he used to be a sort of pop star, way back. Well, very minor. I mean, like, *tiny*.'

'*Pop star . . .?*'

'Well, sort of. Like, he was in this band and he wrote songs for other people.'

'Like what?'

'I don't know, do I? It's *way* back. I'm not interested. I only listen to dance music.'

'Why'd he have a breakdown?'

'*I* don't know. He lost his girlfriend, but I'm not sure whether that was before or after or maybe the *reason* she walked out on him. They never looked right together, she was taller than Lol for a start. And then she left him for . . . Oh . . . in fact, for *him*.'

Colette nodded towards a big guy in a tweed jacket, with leather patches, and khaki-coloured trousers. Jane recognized him at once, course she did. Why, it was . . . it was . . . Jesus, what was up with her?

'James,' Colette said. 'The anachronism. Hey, *anachronism*. Not bad after six glasses.'

Six? 'What?'

'Bull-Davies. He's this kind of throwback. Family used to be lords of the manor. They say he's got a seventeen-inch . . .'

'*What?*'

'Maybe it was seven. Oh, shit. He's on the bloody festival committee, isn't he?'

Jane blinked blankly.

'Means they're out, Jane. Yes? Got it? Committee-meeting over? Reverend Mumsie on the loose?'

'God, wazza time?' Where was the clock? Didn't seem to have one at the Ox. Hadn't been here that long, had they? Then again, it seemed like hours, days . . . 'Oh, shit. This is the problem when you have to share a suite with your mother. Can't sneak in, can't sneak out. We'd berrer go.'

'Finish your drink first. You paid for it.'

Jane didn't really feel like it, but at least it was only cider and went down quite easily. Trouble was that when she stood up, she couldn't. Well, couldn't *stay* up. Sank back into the settle and didn't want to move again. All the little red and green and orange lights dancing like the fairies on wires in Ledwardine Lore.

'Oh no,' Colette said. 'I can't believe it.'

'Wassup?' Over the other side of the bar she saw Dean Wall and his mates nudging each other in a kind of soupy haze.

Colette wore a big, ice-cream grin. 'You are completely *pissed*.'

'I'm *not*! You can't get pished on cider.'

'I can't believe it. You poor little sod. Come on, Janey, we'll make a discreet exit. Just like hold on to my arm.'

Jane raised herself up again and Colette threw a surprisingly capable arm around her waist. She was already a good mate, Colette. You needed a good mate in a new place.

'Don't look at Jimmy Bull, Jane. Don't look at anybody. And for Christ's sake don't throw up on me.'

*

Silence hung over the four of them for quite a while. The festival chairman, the musician, the councillor, the new vicar.

'Well,' Garrod Powell said slowly. 'If he wasn't a witch, what was he?'

He looked genuinely puzzled.

Richard Coffey opened out his hands. 'I shall let you deliberate at your leisure. Suspect I'm overdue for an early night. Country air rather hits one after a couple of weeks in town. I'd ask you, of course, to keep the details to yourselves until we're ready for the publicity.'

'Of course. Thank you for coming, Richard.' Cassidy's face was glazed. 'I'll call you tomorrow, if I may.'

'Make it Monday.'

'Of course.'

'Well,' Dermot Child said when they heard Coffey's tyres spinning brusquely on the gravel. 'It's quite funny, really.'

'Is it?' Cassidy said weakly, covering his eyes with the fingers of both hands. '*Is* it funny, Dermot? I don't think it is. I think it's going to cause a lot of trouble. I think it's going to split the village and I don't see what we can do about it.'

James Bull-Davies had not returned. Perhaps, Merrily thought, that was as well.

'He could, of course, be right,' she said hesitantly. 'About Wil Williams. It makes a lot of sense.'

'It makes perfect sense,' Dermot said. 'But it doesn't make it into a happier story with which to climax the festival and put Ledwardine on the national tourism map.'

'I suppose it might become more of a . . . a sort of shrine. To a certain kind of martyr. If you see what I mean.'

'And how would the Church take that, Vicar?'

Merrily shrugged uncertainly. 'These days, no problem. I suppose. It's politically correct. Plus, it removes the ancient stain of Satanism or whatever.'

'Just, just . . .' Councillor Garrod Powell beat a small, agitated tattoo on the tabletop '. . . just let me get this absolutely right. What our friend Mr Coffey is suggesting is that he uses the church for a performance featuring his . . . companion . . . Mr Stephen . . .'

'Stefan Alder, Rod,' Cassidy said through his fingers. 'Alder, as Williams, will appear in the pulpit before a capacity congregation to formally defend himself against the charges of witchcraft levelled by his parishioners.'

'The delegation of local bigwigs will lay out the various charges, one by one,' Dermot Child said. 'Witnesses will be called, including the drunken tanner, Silas . . . Monk? Monks? And Williams will reject all the accusations of consorting with sprites, giving the simple explanation that, although he is a fully committed Christian and renounces the devil and all his works, he is also . . .'

'A homosexual,' said Councillor Powell. His voice was flat. 'That's right, is it?'

Child sighed with mischievous pleasure. 'Yes, it is, Rod.'

Councillor Powell thought about this for nearly half a minute before he said, 'So what this play's gonner be implying is that the people of our village – that's our ancestors . . . *our* ancestors, not Mr Coffey's ancestors – drove this young man to his death . . .'

'. . . in a frenzy of post-Restoration queer-bashing,' Child said. 'Also – I wasn't entirely sure about this, but the impression I gathered was that the slender persons shining palely in the moonlight will turn out to have been not necessarily local youths corrupted by Williams, as much as—'

'Careful,' Cassidy said.

'Sorry, did I mean converted? Not so much having been *converted* by Williams, as having conspired together to display their bodies in his churchyard, thus tormenting the poor bloke beyond the point of human endurance, until he chased them into what is now your orchard, Rod, and—'

'What I thought.' Powell's face had closed right up. 'I think I've heard enough.'

Taking a stand at last, from which he'd not be swayed. Of course, Merrily realized, he was a magistrate. If it was happening today he'd be in that stern delegation of local bigwigs.

'And I would have to say, as your elected local government representative, that, in my view, this is a very sick idea. Gonner rake up stuff as shouldn't be raked up.'

'*Idea* being the operative word, Rod,' Child said. 'Coffey's using the Williams story to make a political point. In *The Crucible*, Arthur Miller employed the Salem witch trials as a parable reflecting McCarthyism. Coffey's turning Wil Williams into a gay icon. There's really no evidence at all that Williams was gay.'

Merrily's liberal instincts began to nudge her. 'You'd rather he was a devil-worshipper?'

Dermot Child regarded her with a lopsided smile. 'I do believe you're starting to smoulder, Vicar.'

Merrily scowled.

'What *I* would rather . . .' Rod Powell was on his feet. He made quite a distinguished figure, the only one of them in a suit and tie. '. . . is that this whole damn business went away.'

'Well, it won't,' Cassidy said. 'So let's not get it out of proportion. At the end of the day, we're being given the opportunity to present a significant work of art by a distinguished writer.'

'With an axe to grind, Mr Chairman.' Rod Powell thumped the table. 'An axe to grind.'

'Well, perhaps . . . But isn't that what worthwhile art is all about?'

'Then let him grind it somewhere else, sir. Not in our church.'

'I rather think that's up to the Church itself to decide, don't you?'

They all turned to Merrily.

'Hey, don't look at me, I'm only the vicar. I'll have to consult . . . somebody.'

'And your conscience, Mrs Watkins.' Rod Powell's voice was low and quiet but somehow carried all the resonant menace of Dermot's *auld ciderrrrr*.

The village hall went ominously quiet after this. Until Terrence Cassidy said gently, 'Merrily, I rather think you may find, at the end of the day, that this *will* be your decision.'

Well, thank *you*, Mr Chairman. How was she supposed to react? Come over all spiritual and lofty, tell them she'd pray for guidance and hope they'd all do the same?

Garrod Powell looked distant, Terrence Cassidy anguished. Dermot Child gave his vicar a sympathetic smile, but his eyes were bright with anarchic glee.

'Er . . .' Merrily reached for her bag. 'Anybody mind if I have a cigarette?'

*

Before Colette pushed her out of the pub door, Jane glanced over her shoulder and saw the slug Dean Wall and his mates frantically gulping down their lagers.

'Shit,' Colette said. 'Move, you silly cow. Listen. When we get outside, we go *right*. Got that?'

Jane's legs felt like somebody else's legs.

'Jane . . . You listening to me? I'm not dragging you up the street, past all the houses. Those low-lifes'll be trailing after us, making smart remarks, and it'll be all round the village before breakfast, and you'll never get out at night again.'

'Legless.'

'What?'

'Leg . . .' All the times she'd heard the term and never once thought about what it really meant, and now she knew. '. . . less. I'm *leglesh*!'

It was suddenly the funniest expression she'd ever heard.

'Jesus wept,' said Colette.

The spring night air was lovely and warm. Softly lit by a wrought-iron lamp over the pub entrance and overlooked by crooked black and white gable-ends, the cobbled alley was intimate and story-book romantic. Ledwardine by night: wonderful. Jane stood there, gazing up at the stars, feeling suddenly, amazingly, more absolutely *at home* than she'd felt anywhere they'd ever lived and that was a lot of places. Another lantern hung across the entrance of the alleyway, orangey, alluring, and she glided towards it.

'Not that way. *Right*.' Colette tugging her back across the cobbles. 'Follow your nose.'

Meaning the horrible, acidy pong from the public toilets at the end of the alleyway. The proximity of the dirty-brick toilet-block spoiled the idyll, and the smell killed the atmosphere stone dead. Obstinately, Jane turned her back on it.

'Why can't we go—?'

'Shut up!' Colette's hand came down over Jane's mouth with a slap. 'They're coming out.'

Jane was shocked into silence. She swallowed, feeling unsteady inside. Colette took the hand away from her mouth and used it to haul her past the cracked GENTS sign, up some steps, on which Jane stumbled, and then it was soft underfoot and suddenly really dark.

'The old bowling green, all right?' Colette said. 'We cut across here, over to the footpath, round by the churchyard, out of the church close and we're back on the square.'

'Ingeniush,' Jane said thickly. She looked up. The sky was

brilliant, the stars huge and blotchy like Van Gogh stars. Actually, everything was bigger and blotchier.

'All right?' Cocky voice from just a few yards behind them. 'Need any help, do we, ladies?'

'Shit.' Colette pulled Jane across the grass. 'Duck.' Branches grazing her head. 'Not a word.' Colette tugged her down behind the trees. She fell back into the grass, lovely and soft at first. Closed her eyes and everything turned into a big, waltzing fairground ride, which wasn't so pleasant, so she opened her eyes and sat up, feeling kind of damp and clammy and wishing she was in bed in the Black Swan.

'You all right, girls?'

'Danny Gittoes,' Colette hissed into her ear. 'If he knew where we were he wouldn't keep shouting.'

'He's not so bad.' Jane recalled a lanky, slow-moving character who played the trombone in the school orchestra.

'Keep your bloody voice down. Not so bad *sober*. Not so bad on his *own*. Bunch of them at closing time, you don't get involved. Bad news. I got caught once, never again.'

'Thought you were a woman of the world.'

'You do it on *your* terms, Jane. Not theirs. Never theirs. Besides, if Gittoes was mine, you'd get Wall. Up against the back of the toilets. Fancy that, do you?'

'Yuk.'

'Right. So shut up. Come on, on your feet. There's a path. We get to the churchyard we're all right.'

'You wanner come to a party, girls?' Danny Gittoes called out, further away now.

Colette sniffed. 'Very *small* party, I reckon. Hold on to my arm, Jane, this bit's muddy.'

Danny Gittoes bawled out, 'Bring your mother, you wanner.'

The ground was harder underfoot; they'd found the path.

Danny Gittoes was lumbering about, a good twenty-five yards behind.

'Give 'er some holy communion, I would. Any day o' the bloody week.'

'I rest my case,' Colette murmured. 'Scumbag?'

'Scumbag. Least he's on his own.'

'Yeah, but that worries me a bit.'

Jane felt cold now. She was glad to see the big, black hulk of the church thrusting through the trees and bushes like a liner on a dark ocean, stars drifting around the steeple. Another hundred yards and they'd be out on the square and the only problem then would be slipping quietly into the Black Swan and looking like she'd just been for a meditative stroll. Best thing, before going up to the suite, would be to pop into the downstairs Ladies, slap some cold water on her face. Although the chances were Mum would be too stressed up over tomorrow's sermon to notice much.

'Wow.' Jane leaned into the rough stones of the church wall. She felt like they'd walked miles. 'I think I got cider a bit wrong.' When she closed her eyes it felt like she was falling *through* the wall. 'Jesus.'

'Yeah, well, we all have to learn.' Colette patted her shoulder. 'Come on, Janey.'

'Sorry.' Jane blinked a few times and straightened up. 'I . . . you know . . . I just . . .'

Becoming aware that Colette's hand hadn't left her shoulder. In fact it had gone into a grip.

'Shit,' Colette said. Jane turned quickly; the sudden motion made her queasy.

'Evening, girls.'

He was leaning up against the wooden lych-gate. Dean Wall. The sheep-shagger.

'Very clever,' Colette said in a bored voice. 'Do they call that a pincer movement?'

'Told 'em about the party.' Danny Gittoes came up behind. 'At the club.'

'What you on about?' Dean said. 'Oh. Right. The ole after-hours social club.'

The only good light was pooled around one lamp on the corner of the close, where it met the square. She saw two other boys skirting the light. There was nobody else about, no cars. The olde worlde, time-warped magic of Ledwardine late at night.

The two other boys slouched into the close to join Danny and Dean, the four of them forming a rough circle around Colette and Jane. God. Big boys. Men, really. In the same way that Colette was a woman.

So why did Jane feel like a little girl? Wanting to be up in the big, safe hotel suite, warm in the glow from two bedside lamps, Mum bent over her sermon pad.

Another figure walked over from the square. 'What's all this, then?'

It was Lloyd Powell, the councillor's son. He was a few years older than the others, a working farmer. Lloyd was good-looking, drove a white American truck and was considered intensely cool by some of the girls at school, possibly because he was always so aloof.

'What you got yere, Dean?'

'No problem, Lloyd.'

'You girls all right? This lot bothering you?' Like his old man, Lloyd was an old-fashioned gentleman. Pretty boring, in some ways.

Colette said lazily, 'Like he said, no problem.' Jane, who was starting to feel sick, was annoyed with her. Lloyd Powell could've stopped this, let them get home.

'You sure?' Lloyd said.

'Yeah,' said Colette. 'The day I can't handle hairballs like this is the day I enter a fucking closed order.'

Lloyd shrugged and strolled back to the market place. Jane suspected there were going to be times when she wished Colette's sass-quotient was not so far off the local scale.

Still, she did her best to sound cool.

'So like where's the After-hours Social Club?'

Colette Cassidy sighed. Dean Wall grinned. He really was huge and had big muscles. You saw him heaving around great sacks of potatoes and stuff at his father's farm shop on the edge of the village.

'I think he means the church porch,' Colette said.

A Night in Suicide Orchard

'Poor Merrily.' Like a white, woolly terrier, Dermot Child followed her into the lobby of the village hall. 'Can I walk you back to the Swan?'

Merrily unhooked her coat from the peg. 'You can walk *with* me. If you're going that way.'

'Well . . . yes.' Child held open the metal door for her. 'I thought I'd have a nightcap.'

Merrily locked up the hall. Double lock, big key. She had quite a bunch of these things in her bag; the vicar seemed to be responsible for the security of half the public buildings in the village. Maybe she *could* use a minder.

But not Mr Child. Oh no. He'd nearly become Dermot, but he was Child again now. Quite blatantly fancied her, but was not necessarily on her side. Bad combination.

'Rod and Terry cleared off pretty rapidly, Vicar.' Wry smile as they crossed the car park.

True enough. Rod Powell heading for the Ox, round the corner, Cassidy striding rapidly up towards the lights of the square and his restaurant, to regale Caroline with the juicy details of their dilemma.

'A lot to talk about, I suppose,' Merrily said.

'Oh yes.' Dermot Child fairly bounced along, his springy, white hair flopping. One of those volatile characters who thrives on discord, was energized by controversy. Fun to have around, but you wouldn't trust him to the end of the street.

'All right.' Plunging her hands down the pockets of her new but even cheaper fake Barbour. 'What did you mean, *poor Merrily*?'

'Well . . .' He gazed up the dark street, into the future. 'Going to get the blame, aren't you?'

'For what?'

'For whatever you decide. Yes or no to a witch trial in the church. You'll be either the trendy, radical priest who cares nothing for local sensibilities or just another reactionary who doesn't want to muddy the waters or offend the nobs. Either way, your congregation suffers. Must be hell, being a vicar.'

'Hang on. What makes you all so sure it's going to be me who makes the decision?'

'Oh, really!' Dermot Child stopped, leaned back against the railings of a white, Georgian village house, base of Kent Asprey, the jogging doc. 'You were there when they *decided*!'

'I don't understand.'

'Well, Bull-Davies buggered off – for reasons which will soon become very apparent. Then Rod Powell advised you to examine your conscience. And finally the appalling Cassidy told you very politely and sympathetically that he rather *thought* it was going to be your decision. How firm d'you want it? They've all officially copped out! Tossed the hot potato into your lap and run like hell. When it makes the papers – which it surely will – it'll be *Vicar Bans Top Writer*.'

'And if I don't? If I don't block it?'

'Then you'll get – I don't know – *Vicar Backs Poof Playwright Against Local Protests* . . . Well, not that, obviously, but you get the idea.'

'I see,' Merrily said. 'You're saying that, whatever happens, I'm stuffed.'

'Burden of village life, my dear. This was some suburban

112

parish in London or Birmingham, you'd have a small flurry of controversy and then it would all be forgotten. Here . . . Well, don't be fooled by appearances. All right, post-modern . . . state of the art . . . the New Countryside of rich commuters, hi-tech home business people, oak beams and the Internet . . .'

He motioned to a half-lit shop window. MARCHES MEDIA: *Fax, photocopying, computer supplies.*

'Illusion. Surface glitter, Merrily. And only the *surface* changes. Underneath, the structure's as rigid as an old iron bedframe.'

'You seem to like it here, all the same.' She knew he'd been a music teacher at some London college, had links with a small record label specializing in modern choral works. Suspected he'd left at least one ex-wife somewhere.

'I know my way around, Vicar. May not sound like it, but I'm a local boy. We go back three generations. Not many, compared to your Powells and your Bull-Davieses, but it'll do. Born here, and I suppose I'll die here, sooner or later. As for that big, sloppy lump of life in the middle, skipping round London, Paris, Milan . . . that was just time spent finding out that, in the end, it's really better the hell you know . . .'

'Hell?'

He didn't respond. There were eight or nine cars parked on the square, clustered under a black-stemmed electrified gas lamp. The cars included two BMWs, a Jaguar and a Range Rover. People dining at Cassidy's or the Black Swan. The village centre, also quietly lit by uncurtained windows and the stars, looked, if not exactly smug, quite settled in its prosperity.

'When d'you move into the vicarage, Merrily?'

'Could be next week.'

'Terrific. Mind you . . . big old place.'

They could see, on the edge of the church close, the end

gable of the vicarage and its chimneys, rising above most of the others.

'I think I'd rather have a bungalow,' Merrily said.

'Oh no. God, no. That would never do. Has to be the official residence. Nice, roomy lawn for garden parties. Vicar – all right, priest-in-charge, but still an important figure in Ledwardine. Mind you, you do need a husband.'

'Oh, really?'

'Oh yes. Decent local man. Solid foundation. The WI will have it at the top of their agenda.'

'Bloody nerve,' Merrily said. 'What is this, Jane Austen?'

'Like I told you, the framework doesn't change. What do you expect? You're a very lovely young woman.'

'Oh, *please*. Anyway, I'm an old widow.'

'Ah yes.' They'd stopped at the steps of the Black Swan. 'Which rather got you out of a hole, I gather.'

Merrily froze.

Dermot Child dropped a hand on her shoulder. 'Sorry, my dear. Am I being indiscreet?'

Merrily gazed across the square towards the vicarage.

'Ted Clowes is a dead man,' she said.

*

Of course, it was Colette they really wanted. The squashy lips, the provocative breasts in the white frock. Colette was the Spice Girl, the nymph, the real thing. Grown up.

This was very clear to Jane, if nothing else was. She could smell their sweat, and the heat source that brought it out was Colette.

Jane was feeling more and more queasy, and strangely separated from it all. Like they were the players and she was merely the audience. And she couldn't alter what was happening because she was just . . . well, just a kid. If she spoke, nobody would hear her. *Bring your mother . . . give* 'er *some holy communion . . .*

Her stomach felt horribly tight and distended. Something like liquid gas welled up in her throat and she gulped it back, clinging to the church wall. The stones felt damp and gritty. Slimy. The sweat smell was a disgusting haze.

'Come *on*,' one of them said. 'We got a few bottles. And Mark's brought some sweeties.'

'Oh yeah?' Colette said.

'Es,' this Mark said. 'No rubbish, mind. Got 'em in Leominster.'

Colette looked at them, hands on her white-sheathed hips, shoulders against the church wall.

'Oh, for fuck's sake, doesn't that just about show the mentality of you seed-suckers? Like we're all going to get hyped-up in the church porch and put on our Walkmans and pretend it's a major rave. Come back when you're older, yeah?'

'How old you like us to be?' said the fourth boy, who'd come along with Mark who had the pills.

'Old enough that you don't have to hang around with kids any more,' Colette said.

Jane was in awe of her. The boys were quiet for a moment. She could smell the beer on them, through the hot sweat. Their senses were surely too fuddled for clever repartee; maybe they'd slink off, spit a few insults from across the street then melt into the night like foxes.

But then Dean Wall said, all the humour gone, 'Think we're kids, is it?'

Danny Gittoes put a hand on his arm. 'Let it go, Dean.'

Dean shook him off. 'Fucked if I will.'

'Please.' Colette smiled thinly. 'Don't use words till you know what they mean.'

Dean took a couple of seconds to work this out, then he gave out a kind of strangled sob.

'Right. Got some'ing to prove, do you?'

'Not now, Dean,' Danny said. 'You blown it, I reckon.'

'Come yere . . .' Dean moved apelike towards Colette. 'Come yere, you fuckin' clever bitch.' Big hands clawing for Colette's breasts. She sprang back like a cat, reared and spat.

'Touch me *once*, mucus-sac, and I'll tear your balls off!'

'Wooooh!' Danny Gittoes and Mark backed off in not-quite-mock terror.

But Dean didn't. It was personal now. It had history.

'Cathedral fucking School fucking snob,' Dean snarled. 'Not puttin' out for the likes of us, eh? You're just a slag, Cassidy. Stand outside your shitty café, tongue hangin' out. You're panting for it, you are.'

'Well, may*be*.' Colette didn't blink. 'But unless you've brought along one of your old man's best carrots—'

Like a sack of potatoes falling over, Dean Wall tumbled at Colette, who was spinning and hissing, too fast for him, but there were four of them, and in a second it had become a soggy blur and although Jane thought she heard a distant man's voice shouting, 'What's going on down there?' there was no sound of footsteps behind the squeals and grunts.

And so, feeling very ill, Jane went in scratching, nails raking the back of a leather jacket.

'Nnnnnooooo!' she screamed.

Aware, though, before it was half out, that it was going to be rather more than a scream.

That she was being sick.

Boy, was she being sick . . .

'Oh! Oh, *shit*! Oh, you fuckin' little cow!' Dean Wall was on his feet, flailing about, dripping. He no longer stank of sweat. 'Oh, you fuckin' disgustin' little . . .'

Dean had his jacket off and he was shaking it, gobbets of vomit flying through the air. Then he started slapping it against the church wall, screeching outrage, Danny and Mark laughing at him from a safe distance.

'I'm sorry,' Jane gasped, wiping her lips on her sleeve, mouth full of sourness. 'Oh God, I—'

Then her left hand was snatched, her arm jerked savagely out in front of her and she had to start running to avoid falling over. All she could hear behind her, as she was dragged over something shin-scrapingly hard and wooden, were curses and oaths and the sound of the leather jacket being slapped repeatedly against the church wall.

'No escape that way, you bitches.' From a distance.

'Up yours, slimeball!' Colette shrieked, triumphant.

*

Halfway up the steps of the Black Swan, Merrily tensed.

'What was that?'

'Kids, I expect.'

'In the churchyard?' Happened every night in Liverpool; you didn't expect it here.

'They don't have many places to go,' Dermot Child said. 'There was a plan for a big youth centre a couple of years ago. On the derelict bowling green behind the Ox. An influential lobby of local people – i.e. newcomers – managed to get it squashed. Not in keeping, you understand.'

'Look, I think I'd better pop down to the church and see what's happening.'

'Merrily, look, if you were supposed to police the place, the bishop would've supplied you with a truncheon.' Dermot elbowed open the double doors at the top of the steps. 'Come and have a drink.'

'I don't think I will, thanks. Got a sermon to go over. Dermot—'

He raised an eyebrow. She joined him on the top step, pulled the doors closed again.

'What did Ted say about my marriage?'

He was unembarrassed. 'Not a great deal. Don't be too hard on Ted. I think he had your best interests at heart. Wanted us to know you weren't just some new-broom, feminist theologian. That you'd had a bad time. Been through the mill.'

'So what, precisely, did he say?'

'Oh, he . . . he said your husband was unfaithful. That a reconciliation was out of the question. That this unfortunately coincided with your decision to apply for theological college. When it must have occurred to you that ordination and divorce were still quite some way from being entirely compatible. And then, just when all seemed lost, your husband and his, er . . .'

'Secretary,' Merrily said. 'As corny as that.'

'Piled into a viaduct on . . . the M5, was it? Very quick, apparently. No one suffered.'

'No.'

'Except you, of course. Perverse kind of guilt.'

'Ted *was* talkative,' Merrily said grimly.

'Agonizing over whether you'd wished it on him, to clear the way for your Calling. Ridiculous of course.'

'Sean was a lawyer,' Merrily said. 'I was going to be one too. A barrister. We met at university. We were very idealistic. We were going to work for people who'd been dumped on but couldn't afford proper representation. Batman and Robin in wigs.'

'Very commendable.'

'Sure, but most young lawyers start out like that. It doesn't last. Certainly didn't for Sean. He changed his mind, became a solicitor, joined a practice I didn't care for, then went solo. As for me, I hadn't even finished the first year before he got me pregnant. Sorry. Unchristian. Before *I* got pregnant.'

'You could have resumed, though, couldn't you? Something happened to turn you away from the law and, er, towards the Lord?'

'Ted didn't tell you about that?'

'He didn't tell me any of this. Look, let's go in the lounge bar, get a couple of single malts, and—'

Merrily smiled and moved delicately past him through the double doors. 'Goodnight, Dermot.'

*

Jane was aware of sitting in grass, in absolute darkness, wiping her mouth on a tissue she'd found in her jacket, her brain about six miles away and still travelling.

'Oh God. Oh God. I'm dying.'

'You ain't felt nothin' yet, honeychile.' Colette's smokey tone drifted comfortably out of the blackness at her side. 'You wait till tomorrow.'

'Where are we?' Jane sat up.

'Hey, nice one, Janey. Men these days are so particular about their clothing.'

'I couldn't help it.'

'Don't spoil it. Jesus, that was so *funny*.'

'You could have been raped.'

'Those hairballs couldn't summon a decent hard-on with a year's supply of *Playboy*s and a splint.'

'Well, messed about then. Oh yuk.' Her mouth and throat felt rank.

'Yeah,' Colette conceded. 'Maybe messed about.' She sounded very high, not fully in control.

'Where are we?'

'Where they won't come.'

Jane put out a hand. Touched something cold and knobbly. 'Come on, where are we?'

'Relax. It's a good place.'

'It's Powells' orchard, isn't it?

Orchard . . . apples . . . *cider*. She felt sick and closed her eyes, leaning back against the scabby tree trunk. Never again, never, never, never.

'Yeah,' Colette said. 'It's the Powell orchard.'

Jane took a gulp of clean night air. 'Why's this a good place? Why won't they come here?'

'They won't come in. They're shit scared, Janey.' Colette raised her voice. 'Scared of . . . *old Edgar*.'

A swish of bushes. Jane opened her eyes, looked up and couldn't see any stars. She could make out the shape of Colette's white dress now. Just the dress.

'You see? They're there, all right. Four brave country boys. You there, slimeball? But they won't come any further. Because' – her voice rising to a kind of whoop – '*we* . . . are under Edgar Powell's tree!'

Jane sat up rapidly, inched forward on her bottom, away from the tree trunk.

'The Apple Tree Man,' Colette said. 'The old king of the orchard. I often come here.'

'On your *own*?'

'No, with the Cricket Club. *Of course* on my own!'

'Aren't you scared?'

'You mean of the ghost of Edgar Powell? Well, actually— Hey, listen, all of you, listen – He's been seen, OK? He *has* been seen. I heard some people whispering about it in the restaurant. Old Edgar Powell, the headless farmer. All aglow and hovering about nine inches off the ground.'

'No. Stop it.' Jane giggled and shuddered simultaneously. 'You're making that up.'

'Sort of a grey light around him, from his feet to his neck. Situation is that his mind was going before it happened and he doesn't know why he did it to himself. Doesn't know he's dead, probably. So he just walks around the orchard. He Walks. *Plod. Plod. Plod.*'

'Colette,' Jane said. 'Shut up. Would you mind?'

'You believe in ghosts, Janey?'

'No.'

'Does the Reverend Mummy?'

'I don't know. But I do know the Reverend Mummy'll be out of her mind with worry if she gets back and I'm not there, so I think we should get moving.'

Colette laughed.

'It's not funny,' Jane said. 'It's her big working day tomorrow, up at five-thirty. She's going to kill me.'

Colette said, 'This grey light, it's from his feet to his neck, did I just say that? Just his neck. No head. Now where could his head be? *I* know. Look up. Look up, Janey!'

Jane looked down. She didn't want to think about Edgar Powell. Instead, she found herself thinking of Wil Williams, poor dishy Wil, coming out here on a lovely spring morning to hang himself. Oh God . . . a night in Suicide Orchard. Goosebumps started forming on her arms.

Colette said slowly, 'You look up . . . into the branches . . . and maybe there's this wizened old face. Grinning. Gappy old grin. Eyes like grey holes. Most of his chin blown away, though. In these very branches, just over where we are.'

'Shut *up*!'

'Go on . . . have a look.'

'Sod off.'

'Just a little glance, Janey.'

'Don't be stupid.'

'You can look through your fingers if you want.'

'I *don't* want. I want to go home.'

'I thought you didn't believe in ghosts.'

'Leave me alone.'

'Don't go all fractious on me, Jane. This is fun.'

'It's not.' Jane hugged herself and tried to see the shapes of apple trees. Or anybody behind one. 'They're not here at all, are they? Dean Wall and Gittoes. They never followed us. They've gone to get cleaned up.'

'I don't know,' Colette said. 'Why don't you take a chance on it? Get up and just walk away, and pray they don't . . . grab you!'

Jane screamed. Colette had seized her from behind. Her arms were very cold.

'Go on, Janey! Edgar will protect you. He'll put his old mac around your shoulders. Squeeze you tight.'

'*Stop it!*' Jane felt tears coming.

'Look up. For me. Just look up, once. And then we'll go.'

'OK. There. Now can we—?'

'You didn't look up.'

'I did!'

'You didn't, Janey,' Colette said lightly.

'All right!'

With Colette's cold arms around her, Jane looked up.

Mistress

The knocking on the door had Lol rolling on to his side on the rug, where he'd been reading Traherne's *Centuries*. Bringing his knees up, like an embryo in the womb – he was aware of that and ashamed, but he didn't move all the same.

But what about his breathing? If you put your ear right up to the thinly curtained glass you'd surely be able to hear the ragged, terrified pumping of Lol's lungs. He tried to slow his breathing; it nearly threw him into a coughing fit. He choked weakly.

At least you couldn't see much through the curtains. He'd been outside and tested it out, creeping like a burglar through his tangled front garden. All you could see was the glow of the lamp, and that was OK, because people often left lamps on when they were out, for security. So he could be out, could be down the pub drinking with his mates. Except that if you knew Lol, you'd know he wouldn't have any mates and was too shy to go in a pub on his own . . . full of people he didn't know . . . but they all knew who *he* was. People laughing.

Thump. Rattle. Batter.

He didn't move. Reciting Traherne in his head. *You never enjoy the world aright till you so love the beauty of enjoying it that you are covetous and earnest to persuade others to enjoy it . . .*

If he let Karl in . . .

Karl would have a bottle with him, maybe two, and they'd still be drinking when the sun came up on a new and ominous day.

. . . and so perfectly hate the abominable corruption of men in despising it, that you had rather suffer the flames of Hell than willingly be guilty of their error. There is so much blindness and ingratitude and damned folly . . .

Batter, batter batter. Almost frantic. Someone losing it.

Karl wouldn't do that. Not at this stage. Karl stoked his rages slowly, with finesse. Karl laid detonators, timed his explosions.

Not Karl? A cautious relief began to seep like warm oil into Lol's clenched-up muscles.

'Lol! For Christ's sake!' A woman's voice, and *batter, batter, crash*.

He stood up shakily, shuffling into his sandals. In the hall, he switched on the bulkhead light on the outside wall before he opened the front door and Ethel the cat streaked in between his legs as though she'd absorbed some of the agitation radiating from . . .

. . . Colette Cassidy.

'For fuck's *sake* . . .' Colette's face was full of fury and reminded him of Alison. Except Colette was fifteen years old and she was on her own, in a skimpy white frock, and it was late at night. 'What were you bloody doing, Lol?'

'Sorry. I fell asleep on the rug. Is there something wrong?'

She stared at him in despair, a bit like the way Alison used to stare at him. Disappointed that he was all there was. He found that look, under the circumstances, almost comforting, but he didn't want her here at night. He had to get rid of her.

'You've got to help me,' Colette said, and it was an

instruction, not a plea. 'She's going on about little lights in the tree.'

*

Within five minutes, Merrily was back downstairs, edging into the lounge bar, peering over heads and into every corner. The low-beamed room was mellow with buttery lamplight and soft laughter. Well-dressed, well-off couples relaxing after dinner, not many locals.

Except, of course, for Dermot Child, on his own on a stool at the bar, accepting what must be his second Scotch from the morose manager, Roland, and brightening visibly when he spotted Merrily. She went right up to him, wasn't going to tell the entire room.

'Dermot, you haven't seen Jane?'

'Is she supposed to be here?'

'Certainly not. She's supposed to be in our suite, watching TV.'

'Perhaps she's just popped out for a walk.'

Merrily shook her head. 'We have this agreement that she never goes out alone at night without I know precisely where and when.'

'But this is Ledwardine, Merrily.'

'That's a pretty stupid thing to say. Didn't a teenage girl go missing from Kingsland last year? Oh, look, I'm sorry, I'm just getting . . .'

'No, no.' Dermot put down his glass. 'You're right, of course. No one can be too careful these days. Let's go and find her.'

'Sorry. Hysterical mother. It's just that she knows I have to get to bed at a reasonable time on a Saturday night. She's rarely *intentionally* thoughtless, if you see what—'

'We'll *find* her.' He took her left hand in both of his, pressed it. 'Hold on to that malt for me, would you, Roland?'

'I'll be closing in twenty minutes, Mr Child.'

'You drink it then.' Dermot was on his feet. 'Come along, Merrily.' Steering her into the oak-panelled passageway. 'Now, have you checked the residents' lounge?'

'And the public bar. And the snooker room. She's definitely not in the building.'

'Can't be far away. Not into badger-spotting or anything like that, I take it.' Hustling her out into the porch.

'Nor bats, nor owls. I don't *think*.'

Down in the square, a couple got into a Range Rover and four youths played drunken football with a beer can on the cobbles. Dermot said, 'She have a boyfriend?'

'No one since we came here. Been a couple in the past. Nothing too intense. As far as you can ever tell.'

'Must be a difficult age.'

'Every age is a difficult age.'

'Including yours? Sorry!' Dermot clapped a hand to his head. 'I'm sorry, Merrily. And please believe me, I didn't mean to pry earlier. We just want you to be happy here. We know how lucky we are to have you. Old Alf . . . I mean, he'd just been going through the motions for years. Just being there. Church is like the Royal Family. Needs more to survive these days than just being there. Needs motion.'

'Motion?' From the double-doorway of the porch, Merrily was scouring the square. *Please, Jane* . . . 'Don't know about motion. Sometimes I think I'm struggling just to stay upright.'

'You're doing fine,' Dermot Child whispered. 'You have absolutely nothing to worry about.'

And she felt his arm around her waist.

'We'll keep you on your feet,' he said.

She didn't speak. She didn't freeze. She was the vicar. He was the organist.

He was the best organist in the county, the presumptuous

little bastard. She contemplated moving towards him, looking deep into his eyes. Then bringing up her right knee and turning his balls to paste.

Instead, she said, 'Who's that, Dermot?' And walked steadily out on to the steps.

Dermot followed her but didn't touch her again. 'Wouldn't you know it?' he said.

James Bull-Davies walked out of Church Street on to the square. He walked almost delicately, like a wading bird, long legs rigid, neck extended.

'Been in the Ox,' Dermot said. 'Drinks socially in the Swan, but when he's serious about it, he'll go to the Ox. He'll stand at a corner of the bar, by himself, and he'll sink one after another, cheapest whisky they've got, until his eyes glaze. Happens two or three times a year. He isn't an alcoholic. Just needs to do it sometimes, to keep going.'

'Keep going?'

'He hates it here,' Dermot murmured out of the side of his mouth. 'Haven't you realized that? Hates what he is. Or what he feels he has to be. Would've stayed in the army, the old man hadn't keeled over. Probably be a brigadier by now, but like poor bloody Prince Charles, he's got to keep going.'

Bull-Davies was in the centre of the square, looking over the parked cars, peering at each one individually, like a crazed traffic warden.

'Coffey's play brought this on?' Merrily wished James would just go away; whatever his problems were, they weren't as immediate as hers.

Dermot lowered his voice. 'I don't know many details of the Williams affair – mostly pure legend, anyway, I'd guess. But I'd be very surprised if, among that long-ago lynch mob at the vicarage, there wasn't a Bull or a Davies.'

Oh God. Merrily stiffened. *Remember poor . . .*

'Never trust the Bulls,' she whispered.

'Who says that?'

'Miss Devenish. On the night of the . . . wassailing. Just after she had that row with the Cassidys.'

'Didn't go to that thing. Couldn't face it. Too cold. What did Miss Devenish say?'

'"Never trust the Bulls. Remember poor . . . poor . . . Wil." Of course.'

'Old gypsy's warning, eh?'

'Never thought about it from that moment to this. I suppose what happened a few minutes later rather . . .'

'Woman's insane, of course,' he said. 'Never forget that.'

'Oh?'

'Bonkers. And embittered. Used to write children's books, but nobody'll publish them any more. Roald Dahl, she wasn't.'

Enjoying himself again. Trying to work his way up to another arm around the waist. She'd have to do something, couldn't put up with months, years of this. She could deal with it. Would deal with it. If she could just *find Jane*.

'Also feels threatened,' Dermot said. 'Mostly by the Cassidys because they want her shop to extend their restaurant. Well, partly that and partly because Caroline feels the Devenish emporium's cheap and tacky and not in keeping with the sophisticated image they're after. Every so often they'll make the old girl an offer. How she can afford to keep refusing is beyond me, because that little shop's doing next to nothing.'

'That's sad.' Merrily moved as far away from him as she could get without falling off the damned step. 'Jane went in there today, she—'

She stopped because she didn't want to explain why Jane had gone to the shop and also because James Bull-Davies had kicked over a litterbin.

'Fuckers!' he roared. 'Bloody *fuckers*!'

He slipped and went down on one knee.

'Fuckers,' he said in a normal voice. Then laughed, picking himself up.

Evidently unaware of Merrily and Dermot Child, he leaned against the metal lamp-post beside the market cross and peered down Church Street, where the lights of a vehicle had appeared. The litterbin was still rolling along the cobbles.

'Perhaps I should go down and talk to him,' Merrily said. 'This is my job, isn't it?'

'For what my opinion's worth, Vicar, I'd seriously advise against it. He won't be terribly civil, even if he recognizes you, and he won't thank you for it in the morning.'

The vehicle stopped on the square, engine rattling. It was an old and muddy blue Land Rover. Alison Kinnersley jumped down. She wore tight jeans and a black shirt; her blonde hair shone like a brass helmet in the fake gaslight.

'Come on then, my lord.' She stood relaxed, legs apart, on the cobbles, the Land Rover snorting behind her like the stallion she rode around the village. 'Let's go home.'

Bull-Davies didn't move from his lamp-post. 'You whore. Who told you?'

'Powell called.'

'Good old saintly bloody Powell. Thought I saw his head come round the pub door.'

'Let's go home, Squire.'

'Do you demand it?' Bull-Davies grinned savagely. 'D'you demand it, mistress?'

God, Merrily thought, she's got him locked into some pathetic Brontë-esque sex play.

Alison seemed to shrug. Her breasts rather than her shoulders. Merrily felt Dermot Child quiver, and she shuddered and wanted to be almost anywhere else. But she also wanted to find Jane, and if Alison and James didn't take their games home, she was going down there anyway.

'Do it here, hey, my slinky, slinky whore?' Bull-Davies

rasped hoarsely. 'Shag ourselves senseless on the bloody cobbles? Give the prissy bastards a show? Dent someone's shiny Merc with your lovely arse?'

'James, you're pretty senseless already,' Alison said coolly. 'You've got ten seconds to get in before I leave you to sleep it off in the gutter.'

'Whore.' Bull-Davies detached himself from the lamp-post.

'Get in the truck, James. There's a good boy. We have your reputation to look after.' Alison sounding as if she knew they had an audience, of which James remained oblivious.

'Reputation? Wassat going to be worth when that scented arse-bandit shafts me? You tell me, mistress. You bloody tell me.'

He walked unsteadily towards the Land Rover, mumbling morosely to the cobbles about the little, shirt-lifting, socialist scum, squatting at the bottom of the drive with his odious catamite.

'You sold it, darling,' Alison said wearily, as though they'd gone through all this many times before. 'It isn't yours any more.'

'Man's a piece of shit.'

'Whatever. Do get in, Jamie.'

The Land Rover door was slammed. The chassis groaned, the engine spluttered and gagged and the battered vehicle was reversed, illegally, into the alley leading to Cassidy's Country Kitchen and Ledwardine Lore.

'Well,' Dermot said after a moment. 'I did warn you, didn't I? The way it would go.'

But Merrily wasn't listening; she was already stumbling down the steps.

Through the dirty wool of exhaust in the diesel-stinking air, she could see them bringing Jane along Church Street.

ELEVEN

Pious Cow

'And it's a really terrifying situation to be in. I mean, you know, what on earth do we *do*? How can *we* – ordinary, fallible human beings – even *contemplate* making a decision which we know is going – whichever way we turn – to offend somebody?'

Pause. Merrily took a step back from the edge of the pulpit. She felt awful. The light sizzled harshly in the stained-glass windows, yellows and reds glaring out, florid and sickly. Something they never told you at college: you needed to be fit for this job.

'What's the first thing we usually do? We panic, of course. We just want to run away. That's always the first instinct, isn't it? Why me? What have *I* done to get landed with this one?'

You always asked them questions. You were conversational about it. Just having a chat. OK, I'm up here, you're down there, but we're all in the same boat really. Sometimes, you found yourself hoping one of them would stand up, join in, help you out a bit. *Yeah, I take your point, Vicar, but the way I see it* ... God knew, she could use some help from the punters: maybe she should hold a parish referendum: Wil Williams – Yes or No?

Coward's way out. She swallowed. Her mouth felt like a sandpit. It was a warm, sunny, good-to-be-alive morning. She felt cold in her stomach. She hadn't eaten, hardly slept.

'But you know, in your heart of hearts, that running away isn't the answer to anything . . . ever. Sooner or later you're going to have to face up to it.'

Pitching her voice at the rafters; she knew what they meant about the warm acoustic. She'd never needed it more.

Packed house, of course. Well, it would be, wouldn't it? Sod's Law. They were all here this morning. The twenty or so regulars, including Councillor Garrod Powell and his son Lloyd, both of them sober, dark-suited, expressionless, deeply *local*. Plus the occasionals – a resentful-looking Gomer Parry with his comfortable wife, Minnie. And Miss Lucy Devenish, who, according to Alf, would often walk out if the hymns were tuneless or the sermon insufficiently compelling.

Also the *very* occasionals, like Terrence and Caroline Cassidy ('Sunday's *such* a busy day, now – lunches *and* dinners, which effectively rules out both services, but we do often pop in during the week for a few minutes of *quiet time*').

In addition, the never-seen-here-befores: Richard Coffey in a light brown velvet suit, with his wafery friend Stefan Alder, flop-haired and sulky-eyed, in jeans.

And the totally unexpected-under-the-circumstances: James Bull-Davies, frozen-faced and solitary in the old family pew. Well. Merrily leaned over the pulpit, hands clasped. This one's for you . . . *Jamie*.

'So what *do* you do? The pressure's building up. You're starting to feel a bit beleaguered.'

Two messages had been on the answering machine she'd fixed up in the room; must have come in while she was out there trying to locate Jane. Terrence Cassidy: 'Perhaps we could arrange a small chat, Merrily. Would you call me?' Councillor Garrod Powell: 'A word or two might be in order, Vicar, if you can spare the time. I'll be in church as usual tomorrow.'

Bull-Davies wasn't looking at her. He had his arms folded and his legs stretched out as far as they would go in the confining space between pews. He faced the door which led to the belfry. Just about the last place he'd want to go if the inside of his head was in the condition it deserved to be after last night.

'Rule One: don't give in to pressure. Rule Two: collect all the information you can get, listen to all the arguments, seek out independent people who might have an opinion or a point of view you hadn't thought about. Try to step back and see it from a different angle.'

Dermot Child, thankfully, was out of view from the pulpit. He'd be smiling to himself on the organ-stool, half-concealed from the congregation, the only one of them who knew just how little time she must have had to put this one together.

'And then . . .' Merrily said. 'Well, you know what I'm going to say next, don't you? You're thinking what else *can* she say, in her position?'

She focused on Miss Devenish, who fearlessly met her eyes.

'Because of what I am, I'm going to tell you there's only one place you can go for help. But I'm also saying it because, to me, it makes perfect sense. You could take your dilemma to the United Nations, the House of Lords, the European Court of Human Rights, wherever . . . and all you'd wind up with is a whole stack of reports and lists of precedents and Green Papers and White Papers. Bumph, in other words. Take you a couple of months to wade through it, and you'd be no wiser at all, just a whole lot more confused. And the decision would *still* be yours.'

Miss Devenish smiled, the old witch doctor's face crinkling, the side of the mouth tilting wryly up to the eagle nose.

'So why not put it all on Him. That's what He's there for.

133

The best advice it's possible to get. And absolutely free. Go into a quiet place . . . the middle of a field, your bathroom – or come in here, if you like. Sit down, you don't have to kneel, or you can walk about if you want to. However you feel relaxed. But *put that question*. Tell Him it's urgent. Tell Him you'd like an answer as quickly as possible.'

Merrily gathered her props together: Bible, Prayer Book, clipboard, felt-tip pen.

'And I'm prepared to guarantee,' she said crisply, 'that you'll get one.'

*

Outside, when it was all over, nobody mentioned the sermon. To most of them it would have been routine stuff. But, during the ritual shaking of hands by the porch, there were discreet approaches from those who ought to know what it was about.

Councillor Garrod Powell mumbled, 'Got my message, did you, Vicar?'

James Bull-Davies coughed. 'Need to talk, Mrs Watkins. Problem is, never know where to find you.'

Caroline Cassidy, dark-suited and pearled, turned imploring eyes on Merrily, took both her hands, whispered, 'I'm so, *so* sorry about what happened last night. Girls of that age . . . We must talk this over, as parents. Soon.'

Merrily put them all off. Explaining that it would be a bit chaotic this week because they were moving, at last, into the vicarage. So if whatever it was could possibly wait, she'd be delighted to offer them coffee there – once she had a table to put the cups on.

Buying time.

But not from Miss Devenish, thoughtful enough to make sure she was the last to emerge from the church. She wore a wide-brimmed straw hat and her summer poncho, Aztec zigzags.

'So what are you doing this afternoon?' Merrily murmured.

'Go for a walk, shall we, Mrs Watkins?'

'Whatever suits you.'

'Two stiles on the edge of the churchyard, yes? Not the orchard one, the other one. Three o'clock?'

'Fine,' Merrily said. It would give her a couple of hours for that long, meaningful mother–daughter discussion.

'Oh, and don't bring the child, will you?' Miss Devenish said. From behind her, Richard Coffey honoured Merrily with a distant smile and a minimal nod.

*

Jane looked up.

'I was just a bit tired.'

'You bloody well deserve it. And the headache. And the nausea.'

Rising abruptly from the corner of the bed, staring angrily out of the window at the sun-splashed square.

'Did I say I had a headache? Did I say I felt sick?'

'You threw up enough last night. I could smell it.'

'That's not fair.'

'Jane,' Merrily said, 'do me the courtesy of *not* trying to bluff it out.'

It wasn't meant to be like this. Returning from morning service, Merrily had made a point of changing out of her cassock, dispensing with the collar, putting on jeans. It was going to be one-to-one. Mother and daughter. Friends, even. The long, meaningful chat dealing frankly with important, practical subjects.

Like (i) cider. A few facts: it was unexpectedly cheap, went down very easily but was also usually over seven per cent proof, which was approximately twice the alcohol content of beer. Bottom line: cider gets you pissed before you know it.

And like (ii) Colette Cassidy: a difficult, spoiled girl, with a weak father and a neurotic mother. Appeared sophisticated – probably been wearing make-up since the age of ten – but it was all superficial. According to Ted, who had a friend who taught at the Hereford Cathedral School, Colette's worldliness was not balanced by any great intellect.

So the message to Jane, who only yesterday had loftily professed herself more mature than her contemporaries at the high school, was: don't think you can learn anything from Colette Cassidy. Be your own woman.

And don't get pissed again.

She'd left Jane to sleep through the morning undisturbed, asking Roland, the manager, to hold off the chambermaid until tomorrow because the poor kid was ill. No, nothing to worry about, just a mild stomach upset.

And what should have been a shattering hangover.

So where was the damned hangover?

Christ, she *needed* Jane to feel bloody awful for the whole of Sunday. It was part of the lesson: you got drunk, you went through hell next day, you were chastened. Time-honoured pattern.

The great, wonderful pang of anger and relief last night, when she'd discovered what had happened. When Jane had appeared in Church Street, supported by Miss Devenish and a smallish, long-haired guy she hadn't seen before, with the guilty party, Colette Cassidy, trailing sullenly behind. All right, it wasn't convenient, it had lost Merrily most of a night's sleep, but it was one of those things which had to happen one day. God – *her* first time with excess alcohol had been *much* worse; it had involved *boys*, and she'd been lucky not to . . .

Anyway. Calm yourself, woman. People react differently, that's all.

She turned back to the bed. 'What about some lunch?'

'I'm not hungry,' Jane said tonelessly.

Well, fair enough. Merrily could remember a whole day of hugging the pillow, between Paracetamols.

But it wasn't like that, was it? The kid was lying on her bed quite relaxed, almost serene in her white nightdress. Which she must have changed into this morning, because she'd gone to bed in that old Pulp T-shirt.

'Cup of tea?' Merrily offered desperately.

'No, thanks. I might get myself one later.'

'Jane . . .' She sat down again on a corner of the bed. 'I'm sorry to labour the point, but you're sure there were no men . . . no boys . . . with you?'

'I told you, we got rid of them.'

'They didn't follow you? They weren't around when you . . . lost consciousness?'

'Oh, Mother . . .' Jane closed her eyes. 'Your generation thinks everything has to do with sex. I had too much to drink, I went to sleep—'

'You passed out!'

'Yeah, all right. But when I woke up I felt . . . well, good, actually. Yeah, good. But nobody touched me. They couldn't . . . get near.'

Jane looked faintly puzzled, then it passed.

'I'm fine,' she said. 'I'm sorry about this, but I'm really OK.'

Merrily breathed in, counted slowly, lips tight. One . . . two . . . three . . . four . . . five.

'I have to go out again,' she said.

*

Jane stood at the window, watching bloody Mum cross the bloody square, heading towards the bloody church, where bloody else, the pious cow?

She walked experimentally around the room. She didn't fall down. Legs felt like her own legs again. She felt good. She hadn't been bluffing, hadn't been taking the piss. She'd had a good night's sleep.

She shrugged.

She had a swift shower, towelled her hair and got dressed.

She still felt fine.

She padded down the oak staircase and out into the square without, thank God, meeting anyone who might accuse her of having a drink problem. The only problem was she couldn't recall very much of what had happened. The last she remembered with any clarity was being on the right track for losing her virginity to bloody Dean Wall or one of his spotty mates in the church porch.

Colette had got them out of that, although she couldn't quite remember how.

Good old Colette.

Jane slipped into the cobbled alley. Cassidy's Country Kitchen was closed after the Sunday lunch crowd. There was no sign of Colette. Jane wandered down to Ledwardine Lore, which was also closed. She stood at the window, looking in at all the apple curios. It seemed like months since she'd gone in there and the very odd but quite nice Lol Robinson had asked her to mind the store because of the guy he wanted to avoid. Weird. And then there was the story of Wil Williams who'd hanged himself and was buried in the

orchard

The orchard! Jane pressed her forehead into the cool glass, Colette's voice drawling in her head.

Old Edgar Powell, the headless farmer. All aglow and hovering about nine inches off the ground.

Oh God, yes. She remembered running away from the Wall gang and then she was lying in some grass under branches and

. . . gappy old grin. Eyes like grey holes . . . these very branches . . . Look up, Janey . . .

Colette was taunting her, just like she'd taunted the boys. Colette's voice harsh and sly. Sassy, superior Colette.

Look up.

And had she? Had she looked up, with Colette and then Dean Wall and Danny Gittoes and somebody called Mark coming out of the bushes to stand around and laugh themselves sick?

Good old Colette? Bollocks.

Feeling really hot and embarrassed now, she glared resentfully at the shuttered façade of Cassidy's Country Kitchen, seriously bloody glad now that Colette wasn't there. In fact, she never, never, *never* wanted to see that bitch again.

She turned and ran out of the alley and into the square and stood there panting, confusion giving way to a sense of being horribly stupid and, worst of all, really, really *young*.

Luckily it was Sunday. Soporific Sunday afternoon, and nobody to laugh at her humiliation. Even the Black Swan closed its bars on Sunday afternoons, and there were only a couple of cars parked on the square. Jane stood in the middle of the road, at the top of Church Street, staring at her shadow on the cobbles.

Wondering how she could *ever* have felt at home here.

The yellow Toyota sports car came out of nowhere – well, in fact, out of Great Barn Street, which linked Church Street to the B-road to Hereford – and had to swerve to avoid splattering Jane all over the market cross.

Brakes went on, a window glided down. 'Tired of life, are we, darlin'?'

Jane sniffed, put on a smile. 'Sorry.'

'Ah . . .' She saw a beard enclosing a very white smile. 'It's you again.'

It was the man from the shop. The man who was not dealing drugs, who accidentally crushed fairies and frightened Lol. Yellow Toyota – of course.

He said, 'So you don't know anyone called Lol Robinson, huh?'

'Oh,' Jane said. 'Well, I do *now*. I just didn't know his name at the time. I'm quite new around here. I know who he is now.'

'I described him to you, sweetheart, and it still meant nothing. How do you . . .? Oh, never mind. Would I be chancing my arm if I were to ask you where Blackberry Lane is?'

'It's up there. See that funny little building in the square? Just go up the side, to the left, and it's this really narrow little lane. You'll have to go a lot slower than you did when you came round that corner or you'll wind up under a tractor or something.'

'Thanks.'

The window went up; Jane watched the car move off. She hadn't really wanted to help him, but he would have found out anyway. She supposed Lol lived up there, and now he'd get a nasty surprise.

He had a breakdown. Actually, he used to be a sort of pop star, way back. Well, very minor. I mean, like, tiny.

She'd forgotten that. And Colette saying Lol was megasad. And . . . and . . .

And she'd seen him again. She'd been in his arms. *Carried* in his arms. Oh God, he'd brought her home last night!

And now she'd shopped him to this bastard.

The Reverend Mum was right, as usual. She'd got pissed and left a trail of disaster. She had a lot of apologizing to do.

TWELVE

Sympathetic Magic

A wispy breeze plucking at her poncho, Miss Devenish climbed, without much effort, to the top of the knoll. With her back to the sun, the big hat pulled down, she loomed over Merrily like some ancient warrior chieftain.

'You're never alone in the countryside, Mrs Watkins. It's *the* most intimate place. The poet Traherne knew that. When he walked out here, Traherne knew he was inside the mind of God.'

Below them, nearly a mile away down the long, wooded valley, the village of Ledwardine lay like an antique sundial in an old and luxuriant garden.

'The core of the apple,' Miss Devenish said. 'The orb. Traherne was always talking about orbs and spheres. Understanding that he was at the very centre of creation.'

'Suppose he'd lived in some filthy city.' Merrily looked down on the lushness of it all. 'Or a desert somewhere.'

'Wouldn't have mattered. The man was a natural visionary. He instinctively picked up the pattern, the design. Before Wordsworth, before Blake, he stood here and he *saw*.'

Merrily sat down on the edge of the green knoll, her legs dangling over a mini-cliff of rich, red soil. 'How do you know he stood precisely here?'

'I don't.' Miss Devenish smiled enigmatically. 'And yet I

do. He would've walked here with his friend Williams, to see the best view of the village.'

Because of the hedges, freshly greened, you couldn't see the roads; you couldn't see the cars and vans and tractors, only hear their buzzing.

'So much country,' Merrily mused. 'Even inside the village.'

'Still, thank God, an organic community. In spite of the best efforts of those who'd turn it into a museum full of horse-brasses and warming pans. And supposedly authentic ceremonies – ' darkness entered Miss Devenish's voice ' – which belong elsewhere.'

Merrily looked towards the church. The sandstone steeple stood proud, like the gnomon of the sundial, but the graves were all hidden by trees and bushes. The churchyard, more egg-shaped than circular, was partly enclosed by the orchard which, from here, had a deceptive density. Had the church once been entirely surrounded by apple trees?

'Indeed. The heart, Mrs Watkins. And the blood it pumped was cider.'

Along the hidden road, a heavy lorry rumbled, the landscape seemed to tremble and her mind replayed the deepened voice of Dermot Child. *Auld ciderrrrrrrrrr* . . .

'Yes.' Merrily pulled herself together. 'And talking of cider . . .'

'I can't tell you what happened to the child.' The old girl scrambled gracelessly down from the top of the knoll and came to sit beside Merrily. 'And if I tell you what I *think* might have happened, I'm afraid our embryonic relationship might well be aborted.'

'Don't like the sound of that.'

'Laurence phoned me,' Miss Devenish said. 'The Cassidy girl had arrived at his door.'

'That's . . . Lol?'

'I do so hate slovenly abbreviations. Gaz. Chuck. Appalling. Laurence Robinson helps me in the shop. His is the nearest cottage to that end of the orchard. The Cassidy girl was somewhat distressed – well, as close to distress as that madam's capable of getting. Told Laurence your daughter had drunk too much and passed out in the orchard. The two of them brought her back to the cottage. Which was where I first saw her.'

'She was conscious by then?'

'I wonder,' said Miss Devenish, 'if she had ever been, in the strictest sense, *un*conscious.'

'Meaning?'

'She'd apparently been sick. *Before* she apparently passed out. My distant memories of such things tell me it's usually the other way about.'

'Was she coherent?'

'Perhaps.'

Merrily took a deep breath. 'Miss Devenish, she's fifteen years old. She has no father, she's had to change schools rather a lot, and . . . well, she's very intelligent, but rather less sophisticated than she thinks she is. Last night she was with a girl who seems to me to have been . . .'

'Been around. Yes.'

'They seem to have been . . . pursued . . . by some boys. What I'm trying to get at is, when you found them, did you see any suggestion of . . . of . . .?'

'Hanky-panky? No, Mrs Watkins. I don't think you need worry on that score.'

'Thank you. Next question. I don't know how much cider she drank, but it was enough to knock her over. The first time I got drunk – not that much older than Jane – I spent most of the following day wanting to die. Jane slept like a baby and woke up with absolutely no trace of a hangover. So I wondered . . . I mean, the word is, Miss Devenish, that you know a thing or two about herbal medicines. And things. I just wanted—'

'My assessment of the situation tells me,' said Miss Devenish, 'that you wanted her to suffer.'

'Well . . .' Merrily averted her eyes. 'Let's say I wanted her to regret it.'

'Well, of course,' said Miss Devenish, 'you're a Christian, and Christians are reluctant to believe that any significant lesson can be learned without suffering.'

'And what are *you*, Miss Devenish?'

'Labels!' The old girl glared at her. 'Why should one always have to be a *something*? Traherne was a Christian, but with the perceptions . . . the *antennae* . . . of a pagan. But I'll not be drawn into that sort of argument. I'd prefer us to remain on speaking terms. You want to know how your daughter could get horribly inebriated on copious draughts of rough cider and come out of it without a king-size hangover, and I'm trying to give you a possible explanation without offending your religious sensibilities.'

'I'm sorry.' Merrily lay back against the knoll. 'I'm not some fundamentalist bigot, honestly. Go on.'

'What we used to call sympathetic magic. You'll probably think this whimsical.'

'I'll try not to.'

'All right. Like cures like. If you're drunk on cider, what better place to sleep it off than an apple orchard? Crawl into the centre of the orb and curl up. Let nature do the rest.'

'You're right. That *is* whimsical.'

'Wouldn't work for everyone. The orchard's a risky place, an entity in itself, a sphere. And this is a very old orchard. So it tells you – or rather it tells *me* – something about your daughter.'

'I'm sorry, but what does it tell *you* about my daughter?'

'I really don't want us to fall out,' Miss Devenish said. 'But you would do well to trust the child.'

*

Wearily, Lol opened his front door.

In the brightness of the afternoon, the willow tree in the front garden dusted with gold, it was almost a relief to see Karl Windling there on the step. In person, in his denims, beaming through his beard. A moment of ridiculous anti-climax. No surprise; Karl would know Dennis would have warned Lol.

'How the hell *are* you, son?'

'I'm all right,' Lol said tentatively. 'How are you?'

'Pretty good,' Karl said seriously. 'Pretty . . . fucking . . . good.'

And looked it. It was nine years since they'd last been face-to-face. Karl's beard was evenly clipped like a hair-brush. It was probably concealing a double chin; he'd put on some weight, but only the kind of weight you needed to make work-out sessions worthwhile. He looked fitter, in fact, than he had fifteen years ago when he used to remind Lol of Bluto in the old Popeye cartoons. The difference being, course, that there was never any real, lasting harm in Bluto.

'Hey, this is cute.' Karl stepped back on to the lawn. He wasn't actually that big, when you saw him. Only huge in the memory. 'This is picture postcard. How long you been here now, son?'

'A year. Something like that.' Lol felt numb, anaesthetized by the new acceptance that no matter where he went, how he lived, he was never going to have the balls to control his own life.

'Quaint.' Karl fingered the rotting trellis. 'Sweet little

cottage at the end of a country lane. Little garden, little porch. Retirement home. Lovely.'

Lol nodded. He didn't have to rise to it, or hide. Only let Karl see him as he really was: a small, spent force, a loser. And then Karl would leave him alone.

'But you're writing a bit, I hear. Few lyrics for Gary Kennedy?'

Lol shrugged. 'He sends me tapes.'

'You can do better than that, son. Gary's long gone.'

'Still writes good tunes.'

'He's *gone*, son. Washed up.' Karl prodded a cracked plantpot with his desert boot; they must be back in fashion. 'Look, we just enjoying the lovely country air, or are you gonna invite me in to meet your lady?'

'There *is* no lady,' Lol said.

Karl grinned in disbelief. In the old days, one of his more socially dubious pastimes had been poaching women from his friends and colleagues. He'd screw them once, rarely more than that, then give them back. To varying degrees, the friends and colleagues had found this irritating, but there was no record of retaliation.

'You're shitting me, son. You were always so popular with ladies. That air of helplessness brings out the universal mothering instinct. Made us all very, very jealous.'

'That was then,' Lol said.

'So Dennis got it wrong.'

'There was somebody,' Lol said. 'She left.'

'Ah.' Karl peered over Lol's shoulder into the hall. 'So you're on your own.'

Lol stepped back to let Karl into the cottage. It felt like holding out your wrists for the handcuffs, baring your belly for the knife.

*

'I don't want to fall out with anyone.' Merrily nibbled a stem of grass. She was finding Miss Devenish disturbingly easy to talk to. 'I'm the new kid on the block, trying not to put my foot in it. But something tells me I'm on the edge of a minefield.'

'Ah,' said Miss Devenish. 'Methinks the Reverend Wil Williams rears his pretty head.'

'Perhaps, under the present circumstances, we ought to avoid words like "pretty". Who told you about it?'

'Anyone residing within a few hundred yards of Cassidy's restaurant this morning would have heard the appalling Terrence beating his sunken breast. But I got the full details from Colette, as no one else seemed to be talking to her after last night. Don't agonize about it, my dear. That's my advice, for what it's worth.'

'It's my job to agonize.' Merrily sat up, reached for her bag. 'Would you mind if I had a cigarette?'

'Feel free to be human.'

'Thanks.' Merrily gratefully extracted the Silk Cut.

'Agonizing.' Miss Devenish regarded her intently as she lit up. 'The need to agonize. That's very interesting. I wonder, would your predecessor have said the same?'

'Alf Hayden?'

'Faced with any moral challenge, the dreadful Hayden would simply erect the screen of buffoonery and vacuous twittering that's sustained the Anglican clerical tradition for the past fifty years.'

Merrily laughed, the smoke softening her up, the sun warm on her face and arms. 'You're a cynic, Miss Devenish.'

'So perhaps the ordination of women *will* be the salvation of the Church. Women listen. Women worry. Call me Lucy. Listen, my advice, for what it's worth, is to let it happen. Let the awful Coffey have his play.'

The face was shaded by the big hat and the eyes were

invisible. The hands lay placidly where the hem of the poncho met a baggy frock splattered with sunflowers.

Merrily was cautious. 'Why do you say that? I mean, Cassidy, for one, would be glad to hear you say it, but—'

'Good heavens, whichever way it goes, Cassidy's screwed, isn't he? The festival needs Coffey for artistic credibility, but it needs Bull-Davies . . . well, not for money any more, obviously, but certainly for the use of land for marquees and car parking. And also, more importantly, because Bull-Davies is the voice of the county set, and those buggers still stick together – more than ever, in adversity. Cause offence in that quarter and all kinds of barriers are erected. No, I shall enjoy watching Cassidy squirm. May even poke him with the occasional twig.'

Under the shadow of the hat, the lips twisted with a happy malice.

Merrily sighed. 'So you think the play's going to be valid.'

'What?' The hat came off to reveal a steel-grey plait in a tight coil and a fierce cobalt glare. 'Valid? I think the whole concept is absolute cock.'

'Then I don't understand.'

'Frolicking in the orchard with naked youths? Utter tosh. And yet the poor man *was* misjudged, I'm sure of that. Friend of Traherne's, you see. Not a poet, unfortunately, but were his perceptions any less keen for that?'

'So what are you saying? *Was* Williams a witch?'

'Was *Traherne* a witch?'

'Of course he wasn't.'

'Really? You're sure of that?'

This was getting silly. 'I wouldn't claim to know much about him, but people who do tell me he saw God in everything.'

'Quite.' Lucy Devenish stood up, jammed on her hat.

Merrily followed her as she stalked down the footpath,

across the sloping field towards the village. 'You still haven't explained . . .'

Lucy carried on walking, with long strides.

'. . . why you think the play should go ahead in the church,' Merrily said, out of breath now.

'Why? For the truth, of course. Nobody cares about truth any more. Coffey doesn't care – he just wants to mangle history for his own purposes. Cassidy doesn't care – he sees the past as a marketing tool. Bull-Davies cares, of course, but only about his personal heritage, his reputation. His family have doubtless been distorting the truth for generations.'

'But we don't know what the truth *is*.'

'No.' The old girl stopped. They were on low ground now. Ledwardine had sunk into the trees so that only the steeple was visible, like a rocket waiting to be launched. 'But when the ditchwaters are stirred, the turds often surface.'

*

'Just don't tell me', Karl said, 'that you don't miss it.'

A pigeon, disturbed, battered its way out of the hedge and flew up past the open window.

Lol was silent. Sitting in the blue chair with the cat on his knees. Being himself. A sad person.

'Well, then?' Karl looked around the room again, at the few cheap things in it. 'Well?'

'I'm doing what you said,' Lol said desperately. 'Not telling you I don't miss it.'

'Nah. You're not being honest with yourself, son.'

Karl was leaning back in Ethel the cat's chair, with one of the three cans of half-frozen lager Lol had found at the back of the fridge. He had his tobacco tin on the arm of the chair, the tin which had upset Dennis Clarke because it was not the drug of choice in his part of Chippenham. As he relaxed, another drug – California – had drifted into Karl's accent.

'This guy in LA, right? I hadn't been there very long, and he was another Brit. Ex-para. Bodyguard to the stars now. Big bucks. We get pissed one night. I'm saying, So this is living, right? He gives me a funny look. Sour. He says, This is cruisin', man, living it ain't. He says, You wanna know the last time I was really alive? Port Stanley, he says. Or it might've been Goose Green. Back in the Falklands War, anyway. The last time his senses were really buzzing. I didn't believe it. But like I say, I hadn't been in Hollywood very long.'

Karl drained the can, crushed it with feeling.

'What am I saying, son? I'll tell you. His time in the Falklands was like our times on the road, gigging. The buzz, right? On stage, a little pissed, high on your own music, and the thought of—'

'No! Bollocks.'

'Listen, a year ago, I played bass for two nights with a band called APB, from Santa Monica. I was older than any of those guys, by a good twelve years. But it was still there, son. By Christ, it was *there*. Afterwards . . .'

Afterwards. Was that what Dennis Clarke's letter was saying in its cautious, accountantly way? Was that what had really offended the neat, suburban Mrs Gillian Clarke – Karl going on about the good old days of hot nights and tender young flesh? Lol tried to switch off Karl's voice, summoning Traherne. *Your enjoyment of the world is never right till you awake in heaven, till you . . . till you look upon the earth . . . no . . . till you look upon the skies, the earth and the air as celestial joys . . .*

'. . . tell you, I coulda gone on all night. Incredible. Left my brains all over the bedroom ceiling, yeah?'

Lol's fingers tightening on Ethel's scruff; Ethel purred. *You never enjoy the world aright till the sea itself floweth in your veins, till you are clothed with the heavens and crowned*

*with the stars . . . and . . . and perceive yourself to be the sole
heir of the whole world . . . and . . .*

'. . . stayed in Hereford last night. This morning, I'm in
Andy's, browsing through the albums, and – I'm not kidding, son, this was like a mystical experience – these two
young girls, sixteen, seventeen, black stockings, skirts up to
here. Combing the racks – obviously not got a bundle to
spend – pick one up, study it, put it back, have arguments.
Finally, they come up with one CD. One says, *Look, it's mid-
price, too.* Guess what it was . . . *Guess—*'

*The world . . . the world is a mirror of infinite beauty yet no
man sees it. It is a Temple of Majesty, yet no man . . . no man
regards it. It is a region of Light and Peace . . . it is . . . it is
. . . it is . . .*

'The '96 reissue. I just wanted to kiss their little feet.
Christ, if this wasn't a sign . . . They probably weren't even
born when we did that album. Their mothers had safety pins
through their nipples and thought we were soft shit. Now,
after all these years, we are becoming *warm.* Our time has
come, son. It's all turned around. Our . . . time . . . has . . .
fucking *come.* And I will not be deprived of it by someone
whose balls are made of blancmange. You follow?'

*

Jane moved a little closer to the open window. Thanks to
Lol's inactivity in the garden, she was sure she wasn't visible
from the lane, but, Jesus, she'd nearly fainted when that
pigeon crashed out of the hedge.

Her left leg had gone numb from crouching between the
hedge and the window, but you couldn't have prised her out
of there now.

*

'Just listen to me,' Lol said. 'Please. I can't do it any more. I can write lyrics for other people, but I have to have that degree of separation. I can't write them for me. I can't marry up the tunes. I start to imagine being on stage again, I start shaking. I wasn't any good even then. All I ever did was try and be Nick Drake.'

'But he wasn't appreciated then, was he? Plus he was dead anyway. Now he's a bleedin' icon. And you could be. *We* could be. Don't even have to die.'

Karl was laughing. Lol had a distinct memory of Karl kicking his guitar over. *Can't you write anything but this wimpy shit? When're your fucking balls gonna drop?*

'All I'm saying' – Karl giving the crushed can an extra squeeze until it was the shape of an apple core – 'is you give it some thought. We don't have to go on the road. I know how that messed you up. I know we had problems.'

Problems? *Problems?* Oh Jesus, he was losing it. The cat, alarmed, jumping off his knee. 'My parents didn't speak to me after that. Ever again. My devout, God-fearing parents. Three years later, my mum died not having spoken a word to me, and my dad . . . at the funeral, my dad turned his back.'

'Listen.' Karl didn't want to hear this shit. 'We're looking at *real money*. And we're older. We know how it works. *I* know how it works. I'll see you don't get shafted. Look, we do an album first. Give me six new songs, and we'll recycle some of the old stuff. Maybe even do a couple of Drake's.'

Lol was shaking his head so hard his ponytail was banging his nose.

'What you got to lose?' Karl waving a hand around the room, at the two old chairs, the table, the woodstove and the guitar. 'The bitch obviously took you to the cleaners. Left you with the rubbish and the cat.'

'No. She only took her clothes and a few other things. The rest I . . . just got rid of.'

'Why you do that?'

Lol shook his head. How could he explain about Traherne, the need for simplicity, the need to appreciate the real moon, the actual stars?

'Old people do that.' Karl's face was an open sneer. 'When they know they don't have long. Tidying up. Unloading all their junk, giving away their prized possessions. Finally having to admit they can't take it with them. Bad sign, when you start tidying up. Ominous.'

Prodding Lol, like he used to do physically when they couldn't agree about a song or what to do after the gig. Using the word *ominous*. Talking earlier about *a sign*. No coincidence; he'd remembered that these were always Lol's words, that Lol was deeply superstitious. *Little Mr Ominous*, they called him.

'You have something in mind, son?'

Lol shook his head, too quickly.

'Shit.' Karl's eyes lit up. 'You've thought about it, haven't you?'

'Hasn't everybody?'

'Only you. Only you would say that. Look . . .'

Karl stood up. Lol shrank back into his chair.

'. . . I'll go, all right? I'll leave you to think about it, and I'll try not to worry, 'cause if you were gonna do it you'd've done it by now. Kurt Cobain, fair enough, he was mega, now he's a legend. But Drake, he did it too soon. And you – you're just . . . I mean, who'd notice? Who'd give a shit? Who'd put flowers on *your* grave?'

A short while later, Jane crept away, wrapped in a clammy confusion of emotions.

*

'There's something I've been meaning to ask you,' Merrily said, as they walked back into the village, the footpath fringing the orchard. 'It goes back to, you know, *that* night.'

'Ah,' Lucy Devenish said. 'Twelfth Night. What a disturbing introduction that must have been to our little community.'

'After it happened, when we were all deeply shocked and uncomprehending, I heard you whispering, *I knew it, I knew it.*'

'You have good ears.'

'Not specially. *What* did you know?'

'Only that someone was going to die.'

'On that particular night?'

'I thought it might have been sooner, but when autumn turned into winter and it didn't happen, I began to suspect it might be something rather extraordinary. The orchard had told me, you see.'

'Right,' Merrily said calmly. 'I see.'

'Of course you don't, and who could expect you to? I've been close to apples and orchards, and particularly that orchard, all my life. The apple's the fruit of Herefordshire, its colours glow from the earth, its spirit shines out of the land. And the apples are terribly sensitive, the apples know.'

'Know when someone's going to die?'

'Oh yes.'

'I see.'

Miss Devenish threw her a glance.

'Sorry.'

'What you have to watch out for, Merrily, is uncharacteristic behaviour. Unseasonal phenomena.'

Several apple trees were overhanging the path, although not in a graceful way, Merrily thought. The apple was an ungainly little tree, spiky and irregular.

'They're going to be laden with blossom this year,' Lucy observed.

'That a good sign?'

Lucy sniffed. 'Implies a big crop, but nothing's certain about the apple. Especially this particular species, the Pharisees Red.'

'Why do they call it that?'

Lucy smiled. 'You asked me how I knew there was death in the wind. It's because last autumn there was blossom. Out of season.'

'Ah,' Merrily said. 'An old country omen.'

'*A bloom on the tree when the apples are ripe / is a sure termination of somebody's life,*' pronounced Miss Lucy Devenish.

'Classy piece of rhyming,' Merrily said. 'So there was blossom in the orchard last autumn.'

'As late as November,' Lucy said. 'But only on one tree.'

Merrily turned away from the orchard, annoyed with herself, as a minister of God, for shuddering.

'Before we part, my dear . . .'

'Yes?'

'I want you to know, whatever you may have heard about me, that I have your best interests close to my heart. And if anything disturbs you . . . anything frightens you . . .'

'Like what?' Merrily saw that the old girl was no longer smiling.

'Oh, I think I'll wait for your specific questions. I don't want to . . .'

'Quarrel, huh?' Merrily said.

'And don't dismiss the orchard. It still surrounds the village.'

Part Two

As in the house I sate
Alone and desolate
. . . I lift mine eye
Up to the wall
And in the silent hall
Saw nothing mine.

Thomas Traherne,
Poems of Felicity

Part Two

The Feudalist

Early Monday evening, Uncle Ted took them back to the vicarage. Apart from the new sink and cupboards in the kitchen, square-pin sockets everywhere and a black hole where the monster electric fire had been stuffed into the inglenook, it wasn't a lot different.

'It's still huge,' Merrily said hopelessly.

'Don't worry, girl!' Ted squeezed her arm. 'You'll grow into it in no time. You and Jane'll fill this place in no time. In fact' – he beamed – 'the way you've held things together, you've already grown a hell of a lot over the past few weeks. In everyone's estimation.'

'That's very nice of you, but it was just the honeymoon period.'

'Nonsense.' Ted chuckled. 'Dermot dropped in last night to deplete my Scotch. He says you're holding your own better than he'd imagined. Your Own Woman, he says. That's good.'

Bloody Dermot. Bloody Ted. She wondered what else they'd discussed. Her delinquent daughter, product of a disastrous marriage to a crook?

She felt the vicarage looming behind her, huge and ancient and forbidding like someone else's family seat.

'Merrily,' Ted said, 'you'll come to love it. I've been in some really awful, draughty old mausoleums, but this place has such a lovely, warm, enclosing sort of atmosphere that you'll simply forget how big it is after a while. Especially when Jane has her Own Apartment. Eh?'

Jane grinned. Merrily said, 'We'll see.'

*

Ted vanished into Church Street, Merrily wondering when she would get to meet his widow. Jane disappeared eagerly into the vicarage. Merrily was about to follow her, somewhat less eagerly, when Gomer Parry appeared in the drive, blinking through his glasses, unlit cigarette wagging in his teeth. For a pensioner, Gomer had a surprising amount of half-suppressed energy.

'Removals, Vicar. What you got planned?'

'Erm . . .' She'd given more thought to how they were going to spread the stuff around to make the vicarage look less like a derelict sixteenth-century warehouse than the method of actually getting it here.

'Only, if you en't made arrangements, see, you don't wanner go botherin' with no expensive removals firm when I got a very clean truck entirely at your disposal.'

When you thought about it, it *was* going to be a bit complicated. 'It's all around Cheltenham, you see. All over the place. Some bits in store, some at my mother's house, some at—'

'No problem, Vicar. Couple hours' round trip. Piece o' piss—cake. 'Sides which – ' Gomer leaned closer, taking out his cigarette, confidential ' – keeps the ole truck in business, know what I mean? Minnie, her says the place looks like a bloody scrapyard, I says you never know what you're gonner need in life.'

'How many vehicles have you got there, Gomer?'

'Oh, no more'n four now. And Gwynneth, the digger.'

The mind boggled; it was only a bungalow with a garden.

'Her's given me three months to get 'em out, see. But Minnie's a bit more, like, you know, religious than what I am. So I tells her, if this yere plant-hire equipment is in the service of the Lord . . . Get my point?'

'Understood. Bless, you, Gomer. Look, I'll pay you in advance—'

Gomer backed off, outraged.

'All right, the petrol, at least the petrol. Diesel. Whatever. How many gallons – ten, twelve?'

'Full tank in there already, Vicar.' He looked up at the house. 'Three floors, eh? Gonner take a bit o' manoeuvring about. What I'll do, I'll get my nephew, Nev. Big lad. What day you want us? Any day but Thursday, which is Nev's day for the cesspits. Oh, and tomorrow. Inquest tomorrow, see.'

'Inquest?'

'Edgar Powell. Opened back in January then adjourned. Took 'em long enough to get it sorted. Ole Edgar'll be compost by now.'

'You're a witness, Gomer?'

'Oh hell, aye. Me and about half a dozen others. Prob'ly drag on till flamin' teatime. 'Specially if it's true Rod's gonner get Doc Asprey to stand in the box and tell 'em his dad was halfway round the twist.'

'Why would Rod want him to do that?'

'Stigma, Vicar. No way do he want his ole man put down as a suicide. So if they got evidence of Edgar bein' three bales short of a full stack, it's more likely he done it by accident, see?'

'Right.' She did, come to think of it, remember Alf saying Garrod Powell was insisting his father hadn't taken his own life. 'And what are *you* going to tell the coroner, Gomer?'

''Pends what they ask me. All I can say is what I seen. Which is not a lot, on account my glasses got all bloodied up. But before that, I do recall as when the others put up

161

their guns, Edgar, he just *didn't*. Now make of that what you like.'

'I suppose it'll be a question of whether he just had a funny turn and got all confused, or . . .'

'Or he had it all worked out. Gotter say that don't ring true to me. He wasn't no kind of show-off, farmers en't, as a rule. You'd think if he wanted to do away with hisself, he'd do it in the barn. Yet . . . I dunno . . . He weren't daft in any respect, ole Edgar. How 'bout Wednesday?'

'That would be brilliant. This is above and beyond, Gomer.'

Gomer slipped his cigarette into his grin. 'You don't owe me nothing, Vicar, never think that. But there may be one small thing one day, just one . . . How's the kiddie, now?'

'Oh God, does *everybody* know?'

'Hell, Vicar, don't go worryin' about that. They all knows what that Cassidy girl's like. Too promiscuous by half, Minnie reckons.'

'I just hope she means precocious,' Merrily said.

'Aye,' Gomer said. 'That was prob'ly it.'

*

Jane stood on the first landing, looking up.

'Hey, listen. Why don't we just move in? Like tonight.'

Her voice echoing in the emptiness. She was still in her school uniform, the dark blue blazer, the pleated skirt. Merrily, at the foot of the stairs, felt a heart-pang of love and fear that she wouldn't have been able to explain.

'How can we do that? Even with Gomer's help, it'll be nearly the weekend before we can get all the stuff in and sorted out. Besides, with the Diocese paying for the hotel, it means we can get everything right, for once. Instead of being in the usual chaos.'

Going to be a disaster, she was thinking. You could get

all their stuff, beds included, into two rooms; they'd be rattling around like two peas in a coffee tin.

'We've got sleeping bags, Mum. We could spread them out in the drawing room. Get the feel of the place. Go on. It'd be fun.'

'On those flags? Jane, you are joking.'

Jane stared down the stairs at her. 'You don't really want to move in at all, do you?'

'That's stupid,' Merrily said uncomfortably.

All around her, doors. Above her, doors. All of them half open, to signify empty rooms. She wanted to rush from door to door, shepherding Jane before her, banging each one shut and then finally the front door, behind them, as they ran into the square and the sanctuary of the Black Swan.

'I can tell by the way you talk about it,' Jane said. 'Always going on about how big it is. At the Swan it's kind of temporary, like a holiday. In here you've got to face what you're taking on. Like the full burden.'

God, the perceptiveness of this kid was frightening.

'Come on, Mum, there's no shame in admitting it.'

'I just want to do it efficiently, I . . .'

Did it remind her of moving from the flat into the four-bedroomed – it seemed enormous at the time – suburban villa that Sean had suddenly acquired, at an amazingly modest price, from A Client? Somewhere for her to organize, decorate. Somewhere to keep her occupied while . . .

'. . . I just want it all to be, you know, *right*,' Merrily said.

Which, right now, seemed an impossible dream.

'For a major-league Christian,' Jane said, 'you don't half lie a lot.'

Merrily felt her face darken. The doorbell saved them both.

*

'Heard you were finally taking up occupancy. Called to see if I could be of any help.'

No, you didn't.

'That's kind,' Merrily said. 'But we're just giving the place the once-over. We won't be actually moving in for a couple of days yet.'

James Bull-Davies looked around the empty, dusty hall. Sniffed once, like a pointer on a heath. He'd obviously waited until Gomer Parry had gone. Damn. She'd as good as told him to leave it for a while; he was either dense or simply didn't believe his family was obliged to bow to the wishes of anyone in Ledwardine.

'Interesting sermon of yours, yesterday, Mrs Watkins. Wrote that after the meeting, I suppose.'

'Didn't write it at all,' Merrily said brusquely. 'Came off the top of my head, more or less. Sometimes you have to busk it.'

'Really. Don't recall Hayden "busking".'

'Perhaps he was just better at it than me,' she said sweetly. 'Er, I think I can cobble together a mug of tea, if you have the time. Can't do any better than that at the moment.'

He looked down at her with suspicion. Perhaps wondering if she'd heard about him being rolling drunk in the square on Saturday night, offering to lay his concubine on the cobbles. She walked through to the kitchen, which had fitted units now but still some of the old formicaed shelves and white tiles. She wrinkled her nose. Not yet her kind of kitchen.

James Bull-Davies shuffled awkwardly in the middle of the flagged floor. She was clearly not his kind of vicar. He didn't know what to do with her. He wasn't even happy looking at her, preferred the ceiling.

'Used to be two rooms, this, as I recall. When I was a

boy. That section over there used to be a pantry or buttery or something.'

'Did you come here often?' Someone had left a tiny kettle for the Aga; Merrily filled it over the open sink, with all the pipework visible underneath. 'I mean recently.'

'Only when there was business to deal with. Parish business.'

Don't offend anyone called Bull-Davies, Ted had said. *The church would be rubble but for them.* Strange how things changed; from what she'd heard, Upper Hall was closer to rubble these days. Not a great deal left from the old days. His divorce, presumably, had not helped. Were there children, or was that another source of pressure, the inheritance factor?

Perhaps, after the parish business had been dealt with, he'd have discussed some of his problems with Alf. As his priest, his *padre*. The way a man like James would never be able to do with a woman because women were mothers or aunts or sisters or you fucked them.

Merrily set the kettle on the stove. Perhaps she was wrong. 'Sorry, there's nowhere to sit. We'll have to lean on the Aga.'

It occurred to her that this was the first time they'd been alone together, the squire and the *parsoness* he didn't want in his village. She hoped Jane would stay out.

James Bull-Davies propped himself stiffly against one end of the big stove's chromium bar, leaving a good two feet between them. A woman in a cassock? Perverse, surely.

Or did it secretly turn him on, like, say, the matron at his public school? Merrily suspected she would never know.

'That sermon . . .' She squeezed the warm bar. 'I suppose I was just stalling for time.'

'Message seemed to be that you were going to lay the whole vexed issue before the Almighty, let him sort it out.'

'If you want to look at it that way, yes, I suppose that's what I'm going to do. In the end.'

'Way I look at it,' he said, 'it has bugger-all to do with God. Question of honour. And responsibility.'

'Meaning your honour, my responsibility?'

Merrily looked sideways at him, but he wouldn't meet her eyes, stared across the kitchen, his full lips in a kind of pout. A surprisingly powerful shaft of evening sunlight brutally exposed his bald patch and put a shine on his tightly shaven jaw – he'd shaved again, before coming here?

'Why did you walk out the other night, Mr Davies? I'd've thought you'd have wanted to stay and confront the enemy.'

He lowered his gaze to the stained flags. 'Perhaps I couldn't trust myself not to smash his smug face in.'

'Oh, I think you could. Disciplined, military chap like you.'

He exhaled a short laugh.

'I mean, I can see your point,' Merrily said. 'If he's got to make a statement about the treatment of gay people, why use a real character who might not, in fact, have been—'

'It's personal. It's political.'

'Yes. Obviously.'

'Oh, I don't mean *poof* politics. Though obviously that's the other chip on his shoulder. Coffey fell in love, if you like, with the village, the area. Wanted the keeper's lodge, bottom of my drive. Wasn't for sale, but it *was* empty – had to dispense with the keeper's services year or two ago, matter of cash flow. But that's the nearest dwelling to Upper Hall and I wasn't letting it go for peanuts. Made him pay. Made him *pay.*'

'And he resents that, does he?'

'Look . . .' Bull-Davies levered himself from the stove. '*He* wanted the lodge. I wasn't touting. Never told him he wouldn't have to spend a substantial amount of money on the place.'

'Oh.'

'Didn't need that much to make it perfectly habitable. Of course, to turn it into the kind of perfumed brothel *he* wanted – I mean, the water supply was perfectly fine – nobody has to have a . . . a *whirlpool bath*.'

Merrily tried not to smile. His father would probably have said the same about hot water. 'So it's a personal vendetta because of what you've cost him. That's what you're saying?'

'I think it's a probability you should consider.'

'That he's written a whole play to get back at you?'

'Hardly a *whole* play . . . Vicar.'

'I'm a bit lost here,' Merrily said. 'I don't even know for sure why this would hurt you so much. I know your family's well-embedded in the village, but, I mean, *was* one of your ancestors seriously involved in the persecution of Williams?'

Bull-Davies didn't answer. He looked down at the flag-stones and bit his upper lip with his lower teeth, which made him look momentarily feral, and it was at that moment that dear little Jane decided to stroll airily in.

'Mum, I . . .' As if she hadn't been listening outside the door. As if she'd had no idea there was a visitor. 'Oh, hello.'

Bull-Davies looked at the kid and nodded. Merrily said, thinking fast, 'Jane, if we're going to spend the evening here, we need to eat. Why don't you get some money out of my bag and pop over to the chip shop?'

'They won't be open.'

'Yes,' Merrily said grimly. 'They will.'

Jane's eyes had the mutinous look of one who'd been stitched up; she shrugged. 'OK, then. Can I have a pickled egg?'

'Get two.'

When the front door slammed, with a vaultlike echo, Merrily turned and faced the Squire. 'I think we have enough time before she gets back for you to tell me what all this is *really* about.'

*

The wooden clock in the fish-and-chip shop window indicated that it wouldn't be open for another quarter of an hour, so she'd lied again. Mum lied all the time. Like vicars had some kind of special dispensation.

The chip shop was on the corner of Old Barn Street and the Hereford road. On the edge of the village and therefore outside the main conservation area, which probably explained why it was allowed to exist. It was still a dull-looking joint, denied the brilliantly greasy illuminated signs you found on chippies in Liverpool. Jane turned away and strolled back towards the village centre, wondering if there'd be time to nip into the Black Swan and ditch the uniform.

Circumstances dictated otherwise. As she emerged into Church Street, Colette Cassidy was walking down from the square.

Colette seemed to be studying the texture of the cobbles, and neither of them acknowledged the other until they were about to collide.

'Hi,' Jane said, kind of throwaway.

'How's it going?' Colette wore jeans and a black scoop-necked top under a studded leather jacket. But no make-up, no nose-stud. She carried a small brown-paper bag.

'OK,' Jane said. 'I suppose.'

'Get much hassle?'

'Bit. You?'

'They do the motions. Uh . . .' Colette proffered the bag. 'I got you this.'

'Oh.' She took the bag, surprised. It felt like a CD.

'You were asking about Lol Robinson. That's his last album, reissued. Well, his band, from way back. One of the guys at school bought one after she read in some magazine how this guy out of Radiohead likes them. When I saw what it was called, I thought you'd . . . Anyway, it was the last copy.'

'Oh. Wow.' This was unexpectedly touching. 'That's amazing. I mean . . . thanks.'

'It was only mid-price,' Colette said. 'Don't take it out of the bag, or people'll think we're really sad. Listen, I'm having this kind of a birthday party. My sixteenth. Friday after next. Just guys from school and one or two marginally cool people. And Dr Samedi – this DJ, who's like *really* cool. Dr Samedi's Mojomix? Heavy voodoo, Janey.'

'Sounds excellent,' Jane said. 'Where's it going to be?'

'They're letting me have the restaurant. Big gesture. They've promised to go out and *stay* out.'

'Are they mad?'

'Well, Barry the manager'll be in charge, but he's relatively OK. Also, it's got to be invitation only, no riffraff, no low-life.' Colette smiled cynically.

'Cool,' Jane said. 'If I tell Mum it's at the Country Kitchen, *no* problem.'

'Good,' Colette said. 'Listen. I mean, thanks for not grassing me up about what happened. Like, it was pretty shitty of me, all that Edgar Powell stuff. I was feeling moderately pissed off by then, with those tossers and every-thing. So, like, thanks.'

'No problem.'

'So you gonna tell me?'

'Huh?'

'What happened. Weird scenes, Janey. I thought you'd gone.'

'Gone where?'

'Like dead. Then suddenly opening your eyes, rambling about these kind of little lights. And then you've like gone again. Coma-stuff.'

Jane felt strange. She looked behind Colette and along Old Barn Street. There was a couple of women with a pram heading down from the Market Cross, no one else in sight. She felt strange, like she wasn't here at all.

Colette's eyes flashed. 'Oh, come on, Janey. Don't tell me you don't remember. Don't shit me.'

'I don't.'

'What did Devenish say then?'

'She just brought me back. She was just like . . . cool about it. I don't even know how she came to be there.'

'Lol phoned her. Any crisis, he calls Lucy. She's like his therapist, poor little sod. He was really shit scared. Wouldn't go in that big, old orchard in the dark without Lucy to protect him. Well, he wouldn't go in with me. I think he's even scared of me. You imagine that?'

Jane didn't say anything. Colette was trying to recapture ground, saying Lol was scared of her. She decided not to tell Colette about what she'd heard under Lol's window. Maybe the person to tell was Miss Devenish. Really needed to see the old girl, like soon.

'I don't know why the fuck I bothered,' Colette said bitterly.

On the way back to the chip shop, Jane took the CD out of its paper bag. When she saw what it was called, she gasped.

*

'People don't understand. Think we're simply stuff-shirted shits. Hunting, shooting and fishing, lording it over the peasants.'

James Bull-Davies stood up straight and still very much the army officer.

'We merely serve,' he said. 'We serve our country. We serve the countryside. Wasn't for us, the traditional land-owners, place just wouldn't look the same, wouldn't have the same atmosphere, the same beauty, the same harmony. We're the stewards. The custodians. We don't have power. We have responsibility.'

It sounded very noble. It didn't, however, sound like the man who liked to call his mistress a slinky whore while she called him My Lord. Unless, of course, that was all down to Alison and her feminine wiles, bringing out the feudalist in him.

'I'm an army man. Understand the army. Well-oiled ma-chine. Puts human relations, dealing with people, into some form of order. You know who you are, what you are. Most chaps like me, when they come out, go on calling themselves Colonel, as though they still have some sort of authority, as though the commoners should salute. Look in the local phone book: Colonel this, Colonel that. Pointless. Meaning-less affectation. No time for it. I'm *Mr* Bull-Davies, now. James, to chaps I wish I'd had in the army, knock off some of the damn pretentions.'

Like Terrence Cassidy, presumably. Merrily smiled to herself.

'I've no illusions.' James paced the kitchen. 'Wasn't ex-pecting it to happen when it did, wasn't expecting the old man to keel over for another twenty years. But no getting out of it. When the time comes, you have to shoulder the responsibility and that's that. No arguments. And you become someone else. In the army you're what you are. No complications. Here – no getting away from it – you're what your *family* is. What your family *was*. You have a responsibility not only to the living – the living people, the living countryside – but also to the dead. You see where I'm heading, Mrs Watkins?'

Merrily stirred the tea in the pot. 'Army-strength?'

'Not too strong. Civilian now. Do you know what Cassidy said to me? Came to see me yesterday. Dithering. "But, James," he said, "this was *a long time ago.*" You credit that? Man's an arsehole. Shows the state of Britain that the rural economy's now increasingly reliant on specimens like this – bloody caterers.'

His eyes met Merrily's for the first time. They were pale blue and showed a surprising insecurity.

'I'm sorry if I speak crudely. You're . . . Well. Never minced words with Hayden.'

'My last parish was in a rundown part of Liverpool,' Merrily said. 'The only soldiers were squaddies back from Belfast. They tended to be the more refined parishioners.'

James barked a laugh.

'I do understand', Merrily said, 'that three centuries, in the history of a rural family like yours, is not so very long.'

'I said to him – ' James's lower lip jutted and curled – 'Cassidy, I said, you've been here about *two minutes.* In the past three centuries, your family – what anyone can trace of it – has probably lived in a couple of dozen different houses in God knows how many different towns. However many generations it goes back, whatever the rights and wrongs of the situation, this is *my family.* In *my village.* How could I possibly condone some fatuous little *pageant*' – he spat out the word like a pip – 'which seeks to demean and ridicule my heritage? Yes, the local magistrate was Thomas Bull. Yes, he was one of the party who confronted Wil Williams. Yes, he was there when they found the body. And *yes*, he believed the evidence. *Yes*, he was convinced Williams was in league with the devil and should die for it. He was a man of his time. Homosexuality doesn't come into it, and I won't have his memory soiled by some sordid little queer in the name of so-called *art* and a few dozen visiting trendies paying London prices for fancy fodder at Cassidy's Country bloody Kitchen.'

He came up to Merrily. The stove was hot against her bottom, but she didn't move.

'Went along with the wassailing fiasco last winter because that was at least an attempt at reinstating a tradition. But this festival's in danger of going the wrong way and dragging my village along with it. Realize there's going to be some change. Even if I disagree with it. Recognize that your presence here's part of that change.'

'And naturally you're opposed to the ordination of women.'

James backed off a little. 'There are some who say it's going to strengthen the Church. Have my doubts about that, but there's nothing I can do now. You're here, and you at least seem like a reasonable sort of woman, head screwed on.'

'Thank you very much,' Merrily said acidly.

'But you must understand my position, Mrs Watkins. Where my family stands. We have a role. That role, regardless of how we may feel as individuals, is to resist change. It's what we do. We defend. And so I opposed your appointment, made no secret of it. Well, all right, that battle's lost, it's over. You're here. Generally speaking, under most circumstances, you can now count on my support.'

Merrily said nothing.

'So long,' he said, 'as you remain sensitive to the best interests of this village.'

'I see. And if –' Merrily prised herself painfully from the Aga ' – on some significant and controversial issue, we don't agree on what those best interests might be?'

'I really don't think', said James Bull-Davies, 'that you would ever be so short-sighted.'

'But say there *was*. Say there was an issue on which your idea of what was in the best interests of the village was in conflict with what I considered to be morally and spiritually right.'

He sighed. 'You make it hard for me, Mrs Watkins. And perhaps for yourself.'

Merrily took a deep breath. 'You haven't answered my question. How would you react in a situation where we found it impossible to work out our differences?'

'All right. Depending on the seriousness of the, er, matter under discussion, I should be obliged to use what influence I have. To get you out of the parish.'

Like your wretched ancestor did with Wil Williams? Merrily didn't say it.

She didn't say it.

'Thank you for your honesty,' she said.

He nodded to her and left before she could pour his tea.

*

When Jane came back with the fish and chips, she found her mother white-faced and furious, hands wrapped around the chrome bar of the Aga and twisting.

'Mum . . .?' Jane stood in the doorway, holding the hot paper package. 'What . . .?'

'Put them in the warming oven.' Mum's voice was a small, curled-up thing. 'We'll go and get the car.'

'Car?'

'And the sleeping bags, if you want.'

'We're staying the night?'

'Yeah. We bloody are.'

'Oh. What changed your mind? Something he said?'

'We're getting our feet under the bloody table. We're letting the good folk of Ledwardine know we've arrived.'

Mum's hands had stopped twisting on the bar. She was very, very still now.

'No more shit.' She'd never used that word to Jane before. 'No more *shit*.'

FOURTEEN

Grown Women, or What?

Trust nobody.

OK, not a very Christian maxim, but . . .

Merrily dragged a bulging suitcase through the Black Swan's porch and out on to the steps.

Remembering being in this very spot on Saturday night, in the frozen moments before the James Bull-Davies drama, when Dermot Child had so confidently slipped an arm around her waist, shortly after explaining to her how Cassidy and Powell, politicians both, had nominated her for the role of parish scapegoat.

Stitched up, sexually patronized . . . and now, openly threatened.

Stuff them all.

Even less Christian. What was this place doing to her? Were all rural parishes this stifling?

Jane had already carried down a bag full of toiletries and overnight stuff, a few clothes. Merrily had stopped at reception to leave a message for Roland, the manager, who, with the approach of the real tourist season, had been mildly indicating that he could use their rooms more profitably. As a tourist venue, Ledwardine was finally taking off.

Just at the moment, and for the first time, Merrily felt like taking off too. They'd been in Ledwardine over a month, and the only resident she'd felt entirely relaxed with had been Miss Devenish. Of whom the cautious Ted Clowes had once said, *Delightful old girl, may be some sort of witch. Don't be tempted to get too close.*

Plaintive music drifted across the residents' car park, in the yard behind the inn. It was coming from the Volvo, their one-time 'family' car later spurned by Sean for something smaller and faster and, as it turned out, less resistant to impact. The Volvo still had the eight-speaker stereo with built-in CD-autochanger presented to Sean, as such items often had been, by A Client. As Merrily got in, a wispy male voice sang low and breathy over an acoustic wash.

> *Walked her up and down the garden in the rain.*
> *I called her name.*
> *She didn't know it . . .*

'Turn it down, huh, Jane.'

'Isn't it great? It's like really moving. His girlfriend's a junkie and he doesn't—'

'It's OK. Sounds like, what's his name? He killed himself – Nick Drake?'

'Nick Drake killed himself?'

'We had all his albums when I was a kid, courtesy of your Uncle Jonathan in his morose phase. Listen, I said we wouldn't be back tonight, but we'd get the rooms cleaned out by tomorrow night, so that Roland can charge twice as much for them. So don't make any other arrangements, all right?'

'Would I?'

'No, flower,' Merrily said. 'You wouldn't. You're my very best friend.'

'Oh please!' Jane made a vomiting sound. 'You can't be *that* sad!'

Merrily turned on the engine for the first time in days. All she had to do was drive out of the yard, across the square and about thirty yards down Church Street to where the vicarage drive was overhung by a weeping birch. Although she didn't even get out of second gear, it felt like driving across some distant frontier into another country. A foreign country where no one could be trusted.

'Oh, I can, flower,' Merrily said.

Through the eight speakers – on the dashboard, the rear parcel shelf and all four doors – the same voice sang another song, its muted chorus concluding,

> *. . . and it's sometimes on the sunny days*
> *you feel you can't go on.*

Jane picked up the CD box from the dash, running her finger down the track list as the Volvo wobbled over the cobbles. She looked up, the plastic box between limp fingers. When she spoke she sounded subdued, a little worried.

'It's called *Song for Nick*,' she said.

*

By nightfall, they must have walked all over the vicarage about four times, trying to make it seem smaller. And failing, as Merrily always knew they would.

Yeah, sure, it was a big mistake, coming to camp here – a futile gesture of defiance from Merrily, a silly adventure for Jane.

They were both overwhelmed. Even small houses looked enormous without furniture. Even small, *new* houses. This place – without a TV set, a microwave, even a bookcase full of paperbacks – was oppressive with age. In the light of naked bulbs, the walls looked grey and damp. Upstairs, where wardrobes had stood, there were great meshes of cobwebs, big as fishermen's nets.

'Before . . .' Jane said. 'Before . . . it just looked big. You know what I mean?'

Merrily nodded. Freshly vacated, the house was huge and naked and dead, its skeleton of woodwormed oak exposed – the shrunken remains of trees, killed half a millennium ago, embalmed and mummified in the walls. How, with their minimal furniture, their token pots and pans, could they possibly get its blood flowing again?

'I wonder if I'm allowed to take in lodgers,' Merrily said gloomily. 'Maybe one of those guys who sit in the middle of Hereford with a penny whistle and a dog.'

'Or four of them,' Jane said. 'All with dogs. Barking.'

Because it was so quiet. Whether it was the trees all around or whatever, you wouldn't know you were near the centre of the village.

After Sean's death, before she'd gone to college, she'd sold all the fancy new furniture, the rich-lawyer toys. *This is tragic*, her mother had said, *all these nice things . . . you may find you regret it one day when you have a big house again.*

I'm never going to have a big house again, Merrily had said very calmly.

'Still,' Jane said. 'We're seeing it at its very worst. It can only get better and better, can't it?'

'It can, flower. And it will. Look, let's forget this idea. Mrs Peat's coming tomorrow, the cleaner. Why don't we let her have a go at it first? Come on, let's go back to the pub.'

Jane hesitated. She was standing by the window in the drawing room made mauve by dull twilight through the surrounding trees. Across the room the inglenook yawned like an open tomb, its lintel two feet thick. There'd been an archaic, coal-effect electric fire in there when the Haydens were here; now it was just blackened stone, and you couldn't light a fire because the wide chimney had been sealed off for insulation.

179

'Buy you dinner, OK?' Merrily said. 'We could extend to that. Not in the bar. I mean in the restaurant. Those chips'll be all stuck together by now, anyway.'

It was just stone flags underfoot, like the ones in the church but without the memorials and carved-out skulls. You could spend a year's stipend just carpeting the downstairs.

'What do you say, flower?'

'No.' Jane stamped a foot on the stone. 'We should stay. It's stupid to be scared of your house. Are we grown women, or what?'

*

In the end, they slept in the bedroom Merrily had used that first night. At least it had a wooden floor. They spread out the red and blue sleeping bags bought for a camping holiday in the Lake District, a holiday which never happened, the summer after Sean died.

It was still cold at night, especially in here. The sleeping bags were a couple of feet apart, up against the wall with the door in it. Two kids in a haunted house.

'Isn't it funny', Jane said into the darkness, 'how, when you finally get to bed on a cold night, you always want to go to the loo?'

'All in the mind. Which means I'm not going with you.'

'Did I ask you to?'

'Think of something else,' Merrily said. 'It'll go away.'

'OK.'

Silence. Odd, really; a place this old, you expected creaks and groans. Didn't timber-frame houses kind of settle down for the night?

'Mum . . .'

'Mm-mm.'

'You ever know anybody who committed suicide?'

The kid had always been good at choosing her moments.

'I can't think,' Merrily said. 'Nobody close, anyway.'

There was Edgar Powell, of course, whose inquest was to be concluded tomorrow. But she hadn't really known him, only seen him. In the last hour of the last night of his life. *Go to sleep, Jane.*

'What happened to Nick Drake?'

Merrily sighed. 'I don't know if that was suicide or not.'

'You said he killed himself.'

'Well, he died of an overdose of antidepressants, so he must have *taken* them himself. Whether he actually intended to take an overdose seems to be questionable. He was just a sad, withdrawn young guy whose career wasn't taking off, that's all. It was before you were born, anyway.'

Before you were born. Another lifetime. Before Jane was born, Merrily had been almost a child. In a few years' time, Jane would be older than Merrily had been then. Was probably already, in some ways, more mature. Over the congealed chips, she'd explained how James Bull-Davies had made her so angry, and Jane had said, *If he's so sensitive to the best interests of the village, what's he doing shacking up with that woman?*

What indeed? Merrily rolled on to her side.

'Mum.'

'What?'

'If Dad hadn't been killed, would he have gone to jail?'

God almighty. Dark Night of the Soul, or what?

'I don't know. It's possible. He might just have been struck off. Wasn't a criminal. As such. He was just frustrated and he could see people around him making lots of money in unorthodox ways. And they became his clients. You know all this.'

'When did you find out?'

'When it was too late to stop him.'

'Why didn't you leave him then?'

'I expect I would have.'

'And would you have still got into theological college?'

'Sure.'

'But would you still have been acceptable as a vicar?'

'I don't know.'

'Did you feel sort of . . . soiled? Because we'd benefited from dirty money.'

'Yeah.'

'Did that make you all the keener to get into the Church? To throw yourself into it?'

'You make it sound like a canal.'

'Did you love him? Even when you found out he was bent?'

'You don't stop loving people just like . . .?'

'What about when you found out about his affair?'

'I don't know. I hated him then, I suppose. I thought I hated him. I mean, I'm not Jesus, am I?'

'You forgiven him now?'

'I like to think so.'

'If he hadn't been killed, would you have?'

'*I* don't know. Would have depended on what he did next.'

'If he was sorry.'

'Yeah. If he was sorry. Jane, what's all this about?'

Jane's thin, white arm came out of the sleeping bag. 'I just keep going back over things. Everything seems . . . not real. Like a dream. I have to keep working out how we got here. Just in case this *is* a dream. I don't really like it.'

Merrily didn't know how to respond.

'Is it because I got drunk? Is it the cider? Does it go on affecting you for days?'

Merrily had to smile. 'No.' She reached out and took the small, cold hand. 'And I'm afraid this is not a dream. Janey, love, is all this anything to do with that record? The CD you had in the car. Where'd it come from?'

'Oh. A friend gave it to me.'

'Right.'

Merrily closed her eyes. She was determined they weren't going to do this again tomorrow. She'd make a deal with Roland for another couple of nights, until they had their own beds in here.

'I told you about Lol,' Jane said. 'It's his old band. He was apparently very influenced by Nick Drake.'

'Only musically, one hopes.'

Jane didn't reply. Merrily opened her eyes and lay on her back, gazing through the long window, pondering on this Lol, about whom Jane seemed to know a little too much. A small, yellow light, as from a candle or a child's nightlight, shone between the thickening trees from a window across the street.

*

Later, much later, when she awoke to a tugging on her hand, the only light through the window was from a misty quarter moon, which turned the room grey.

Damn. Why can't she hold out till morning?

Merrily squirmed, not half-awake, out of the warm sleeping bag into the damp air. The bedroom door was already ajar and she slid cautiously through the gap. She didn't need to do this, of course; but she knew that Jane, for all her bravado, would not like wandering alone around the not even half-known rooms of the big, empty house.

Outside, there was the passage with doors and doors and doors, and one must be the bathroom, she couldn't remember which, only that it was a stark, 'sixties bathroom with a black, plastic lavatory seat and cracked tiles everywhere.

She'd left her dressing gown at the Black Swan, and it was pre-dawn cold out here in just a short nightdress, bare feet on oak boards. Across the stairs, the landing window was an oblong of flat aluminium.

'Jane?'

The house was absolutely still. *Why can't you creak? Have you no personality?*

'Ja—ane?'

Which one *was* the bathroom? She opened a door; space and silence sucked at her and she shut it quickly.

A pace along the passage and she lost the moonlight. Now, there was only the faint, green spot of a smoke-alarm on a ceiling beam and the deeper darkness of doorways. She put a hand into a recess, found a cold doorknob and then drew back.

'Jane!'

Shouting this time, but the passage swallowed it; she could almost see the short, bright name narrowing like a light down a tunnel, vanishing in no time. She was aware of a slow panic, like a dark train coming, and she grabbed the handle and turned it and the door didn't open; perhaps this was the bathroom and the kid had locked it. '*Jane* . . .'

A sudden yielding, and she stumbled, the oak door rolling away into the vastness of a long, long bedroom, empty as an open field, and Merrily grabbed at the handle and hauled the door closed, turning away and finding herself facing another door and she opened that, and there was the lavatory with its seat up and caught in a frail moonbeam, making an apologetic O.

As in NO. No Jane . . .

No, no, no, no, no . . . She fled along the passage, all the doors closed and blank. She felt she'd been out here for hours, trying door after door, and in that time Jane must have finished in the bathroom and gone back to bed, so which one was the bedroom?

Which one was the bloody bedroom?

All the doors were closed, and she'd surely left the bedroom door open, hadn't she? But maybe Jane had closed it, shut her out. Jane had shut her out. '*Jane!!!*' she screamed, and ran wildly from door to door, all the same, all black oak and all shut.

And spun round and round and found herself facing stairs. Where was she now? Had she gone downstairs? Had she gone down to the dreadful kitchen or the drawing room with its chimney blocked; she couldn't have.

No. These were the other stairs. The *next* stairs. Oh, Jesus, there were more stairs.

The extra floor. A third and empty floor of doors and doors and doors.

She stood at the bottom of the stairs and couldn't look up. She hugged herself, and felt sweat cold on her shoulders.

She knew, of course, that she would have to go up there.

In all her dreams of being in a house and suddenly discovering it had a third storey, she had accepted that, sooner or later, she was going to have to climb those final stairs. Because of the presence. Because there was someone up there waiting for her. In the best dreams, it was herself; if she climbed the stairs, she would find her true self, discover her hidden potential. This, said the analysts she had read over the years, was the true meaning of this dream. It was about reaching for the higher dimension. Or, in a spiritual sense, carrying the lantern of faith along the dark corridors to the foot of the last stairs, at the top of which was the greater light.

But in the worst dreams, the presence at the top of the stairs, along the final passage, behind the final doors, was neither her higher self nor the light of lights. For a while, after his death, it had been Sean, still greedily grinning through the torn metal, through his blood.

So, which one was this: the good dream or the bad dream?

No.

It wasn't a dream. This was the promised reality, the culmination. She had obeyed her calling, given herself up to the Holy Spirit. And moved at last into the house with three floors. Oh God, the tugging on the hand . . .

Jane?

No.

All right. So be it. Merrily relaxed the grip on her cold shoulders, let her arms fall to her side.

She looked up.

*

Couldn't breathe.

'Mum?'

Oh my God, my God, my God, my God, my God, I can't breathe.

'Mum!'

Her chest was rigid, as though there was a tourniquet around it, winding tighter and tighter, squashing her breasts. She rolled over, gasping.

'Mummy!' Her eyes blinked open and the breath gushed into her, and she sat up, coughing. Jane had hold of her shoulders. Big, frightened eyes, dark hair fluffed up and haloed by the pinky-orange light of dawn.

'You're back,' Merrily croaked.

'Mum, I haven't been anywhere.'

'You went to the bathroom.'

'No . . .'

Merrily turned to the door. It was closed.

'You were having a dream,' Jane said.

'It couldn't have been a dream. I followed you out.'

Jane shook her head wryly and skipped to the window. 'Oh, look, you can see the hills. You can see right over the houses across the road. I bet it's brilliant from upstairs, on the top floor. In my apartment.'

She turned back to Merrily and grinned.

'I'll go and make some tea.'

Merrily closed her eyes. When she opened them, Jane was gone, the door slamming behind her. Merrily's hair felt cold and damp around the numbness of her face, and her chest felt like it had been sat on. She was exhausted.

FIFTEEN

Hazey Jane

Of course, she'd had this kind of nightmare before. Everybody had. The point about dreams was that your reactions were often intensified because you were so helpless. Apprehension, mild fear, turned very quickly into terror; small, disquieting things were sometimes loaded with a bloated menace, which gradually deflated when you awoke.

Well. Usually.

Very occasionally, the essence of it remained draped over you like dusty, moth-eaten rags, for most of the day. Merrily knelt under the pink-washed window, hoping to rinse her spirits with prayer. But it was mechanical, she couldn't find the level. It was as though the nightmare had blocked her spiritual pores.

And something else was blocked. *What did I see?* she kept asking herself. *What did I see when I looked up those stairs?* And something cold crept up her vertebrae and left behind it a formless, drifting dread.

She stood up and shook herself. Found a towel and some shampoo in the overnight bag, went for a bath but nearly chickened out: the sight of the cold, tiled bathroom made clammy skin and sweat-stiffened hair seem rather less offensive, and she had to dismiss sinful images of the warm, creamy comforts of the en-suite at the Black Swan, the urge to slip back there for one last, glorious soak.

Anyway, it was only about five-thirty. Too early even to get into the Swan. Oh, come on. *Are we grown women, or what?* She helped a big spider to freedom and turned on the flaking, chromium taps, noticing that the oak floorboards had been concealed, probably for the past thirty years, under well-worn, well-cracked black and white lino tiles.

During Alf Hayden's lengthy tenure, the nouveau riche village of Ledwardine had managed to leave its vicarage a long way behind.

*

'You', her daughter said, looking thoughtful, 'are looking pretty rough.'

They'd bought a loaf last night from the Late store, and Jane was trying to make the Aga make toast.

'Why don't you just go back to bed?'

'*What* bloody bed?' Merrily leaned over the stove with a cigarette in her mouth, wondering if there was somewhere to ignite it; evidently there wasn't.

'I'm quite sure,' Jane said primly, 'that your God wouldn't want you to smoke like a chimney.'

'Listen, flower, if you can find the bit in the Bible where it says *that* . . .'

'All right, sorry. Just because I had a decent night's sleep and you didn't.'

'That's because you're a child. An innocent. Look, I don't suppose, if I were to mind your toast, you could run upstairs and fetch my Zippo from the bathroom?'

Jane raised her eyes cynically to the ceiling and trotted off. Merrily stood resting her forehead on folded arms on the plate rack over the stove.

Stress? Hell, she'd only been here a month. It hadn't started yet. She wasn't even official until the end of the week, and people were still not sure where to find her. There were communion classes to organize, visits to the primary school, the senior citizens' social club, an invitation to address the WI . . .

And there'd be more, much more. Domestic situations where, as she'd learned in Liverpool, a clergy*man* would never have been approached. Failing marriages. Problem kids. Spiteful, invalid mothers who declined to die. Any one of which would make something like the Wil Williams controversy seem precious and fatuous.

She needed to get it all into perspective. She'd wander over to the church after breakfast, when Jane had gone to school, and she wouldn't come out until she felt purged.

*

Although it was more than an hour before the school bus was due, Jane didn't see much point in hanging around an empty house with a grouchy parent. Besides, it was good walking about the village before most people were up and about. It sparkled, as though the air itself were alive. Strange.

And she might see Miss Devenish.

The need to see Miss Devenish was, in fact, pretty urgent. Firstly, she had to thank her for whatever she did on Saturday night. Secondly, there was the question of Lol Robinson. The way that guy Karl had been winding him up, the talk of suicide and Kurt Cobain and Nick Drake . . . and then Colette implying that Lol was already wound so tight he couldn't go out in the dark without Miss Devenish to hold his hand.

Karl was obviously the Karl Windling (*bass, backing vocals*) mentioned on the back of the CD. Karl was offering to kick-start Lol's career again. And on the evidence of the album, for which Lol had written all the songs, Lol was good, Lol was brilliant. But for some reason he didn't want to go back, and it wasn't just a case of playing hard to get. He hadn't even wanted to see Karl; he'd been *afraid* to see Karl. So why was he in this state? Why was he hiding himself away in Ledwardine? Why was he alone? Why had the cool, beautiful Alison left him for the horrible and grotesquely *old* James Bull-Davies?

Money and status probably. Actually, what was even more strange was how someone as sensitive as Lol had ever got involved with someone as glossy and superficial as Alison.

It all made Jane feel anxious, in a rather thrilling way. And protective, because Karl Windling was such a bully. She tried to feel the state of mind you'd have to be in to want to just end your life. Where you didn't want to do anything else in the world ever again, or go anywhere, or love anyone. Or write another sad song.

She couldn't imagine it. She was probably emotionally backward. Though, perhaps, in some cases, it was just kind of an impulse thing. Especially if you were already more than a bit unstable.

She wondered where Miss Devenish lived. No point in going to the shop this early. But Miss Devenish and Jane, they needed to talk.

It was going to be another warm day. She walked up to the square, school books in a canvas airline bag over one shoulder, school blazer over the other. Nearly forty-five minutes to kill before the bus was due. School: French and economics and maths, then double games. She looked up into a tide of flawless blue coming in over a smooth sandbank of early cloud. What, really, was the point of going to sodding school today when there was so much she needed to learn here in the village? Schoolwork, essays and stuff, you could always get over that with a bit of effort. Real life . . . not so easy.

A snatch of one of Lol's songs kept coming back to her.

*. . . and it's sometimes on the sunny days
you feel you can't go on.*

That album was sending her signals. She just knew that the girls Karl Windling had seen in Andy's Records in Hereford had been the friends of Colette's who'd bought the album.

It was all fated: Jane Watkins was somehow destined to rescue the tragic Lol Robinson. The cobbles glittered in affirmation. Strange.

It wasn't a schoolgirl crush, of course. Nothing so immature. Anyway, he was old enough to be her father. No, this was on an altogether higher level.

She'd known last night, when she'd first opened the brown-paper bag and seen the name of the band on the front of the CD. The band formed by Lol Robinson over fifteen years ago, before she was born. Or perhaps . . . perhaps exactly at the time she was born.

Some kind of omen; it had to be. The name so exactly summing up the way she was feeling. Had been feeling since . . . well, Saturday night.

Lol's old band had been called – eerily – *Hazey Jane*.

Hardly even thinking about what she was doing, Jane wandered past the market cross and into the cool, secretive shade of Blackberry Lane, the trees overhead throbbing and pulsing with spring. Spring like she'd never felt it before.

*

A grey van was parked outside the church. Who could that be? The main door was still shut, so Merrily went round the back with her fat bunch of jailer's keys.

However, the small, south-east door, leading in by the Bull Chapel, was already ajar. As she slipped inside, there was a vast discordant wail from the organ, and she jumped, alarmed. An organ in an empty church was a spooky sound.

'See?' Dermot Child's voice called out. 'It's sticking. I've tried working it up and down.'

'Hmm. May need replacing. You can't keep on bodging these things for ever.'

Midlands accent. Obviously Mr Gerald Watts, the organ repair man from Bromsgrove. Ted had mentioned him; his phone number was in the book of essential parish contacts. And Dermot had remarked the other week that the organ would soon need some attention.

'Problem is, Dermot, I'd have to make one to fit. Can you manage like this for a couple of weeks?'

'Sounds like I haven't got a choice.'

Merrily slid into the Bull Chapel. It was separated from the organ by an eighteenth-century wooden screen, so they couldn't see each other, she and Dermot and Mr Watts, the organ man. She stood with her back to the screen, didn't want to interrupt them.

'So what's the damage, Gerry? Roughly. If it's over fifty, I'll need to check it with the vicar.'

Sunlight fanned in through the chapel's leaded window and pooled in the eyes of Thomas Bull. They were fully open. She hadn't really noticed that before. It was disturbing, abnormal. His lids surely should be lowered, displaying for eternity the familiar and usually false humility of the wealthy dead.

'All right, what I'll do, Dermot, if it's looking a bit heavy I'll send a copy of the estimate to Hayden, but I'll give you a ring first, so you'll know.'

'It isn't Hayden any more.'

'Lord, no, I'd forgotten. Saw her picture in the *Hereford Times*. Looked like a pretty fair swap to me, unless it was an unusually flattering photo.'

'Didn't do her justice, Gerry. Didn't do her justice. Absolute little cracker. I tell you, it's bloody hard to concentrate on your playing sometimes.'

Merrily was aware of smiling. What, in the end, could you say?

'Must be a new experience for you,' Mr Watts said. 'Fancying the vicar. Least, I hope it is.'

'It's a funny thing, Gerry. It's a bit like nurses. The uniform gives it an added *something*. She's being very traditional – I suppose she's a bit insecure – and she wears this long, supposedly shapeless black cassock. Only on her it's not shapeless at all. You get bumps in all the right places. And it's got about a hundred buttons down the front, and you imagine yourself undoing them all, very slowly, one by one. Oh God.'

Merrily's face began to burn.

Mr Watts said, 'What d'you reckon they wear underneath?'

'Exactly. What *do* they wear underneath? You could go mad thinking about it. Could be nothing, couldn't it? I mean, it could be *nothing at all*.'

'In your dreams.'

'In my dreams, Gerald, she's wearing nothing but the bloody dog collar. Imagine that: white collar, pink body, brown nipples.'

Merrily wasn't smiling any more. Her eyes found the wide-open dead eyes of Thomas Bull. He was clothed in what, for those frilly Cavalier times, must have been a rather severe jacket, with a high collar. A sword, unsheathed, was lying by his side. Thomas was carved out of local stone, worn smooth now, his eyes wide open to face his God without fear, without excuses, in the year 1696 – a quarter of a century after his pivotal role in the hounding of Wil Williams. Bull's face was stern, but, as she watched, the angle of the sun created the illusion of a supercilious smirk on the full, beard-fringed lips.

Mr Watts said, 'You'll go to hell, Dermot.'

'Yes,' said Dermot Child. 'And it might even be worth it. Don't forget your cap.'

They were coming out and there wasn't time for her to reach the door without being seen.

*

Lol's cottage was really rather lonely, the last one in the lane before it narrowed into a cart track. On each side, the Powell Orchard was starting to shimmer with new blossom.

Jane walked up the path between the front lawn that needed mowing and the fence bordering the orchard, and found herself knocking on the white-painted door around which red and orange early roses grew.

There was no answer. A small black cat watched her from a fence post.

She peered through the window into the room where Lol had talked with Karl Windling. It was so sparsely furnished it gave you the impression the cottage was not really occupied. As though someone had dumped a few things there in advance of moving in.

What if I'm too late? In her mind was an image of Lol lying limply across his bed, one arm outstretched, the fingers just parted from a small brown pill bottle. A variation, she realized, of a famous painting about a dead, young poet. But oh God . . . She had to stop herself banging on the window. When she stepped away from it, she could hear faint music from the rear of the cottage.

There was a small gate hanging from one rusty hinge, and the path continued round the back. Jane carefully lifted open the gate and went, half-fearfully, through. In the small back garden were about four apple trees, all of them bending away from the cottage, as if the garden were trying to join the orchard. Or the orchard was trying to draw in the garden. Sunlight was sprinkled through the fragile white blossom.

> *. . . and it's sometimes on the sunny days*
> *you feel you can't go on.*

Trembling a little, Jane went to the back door and was about to knock gently when she became aware of the music again. It was behind her now and so not coming from inside the cottage but from the garden itself, or the orchard, separated from it by the narrow path she knew was a bridle-way.

She wandered among the apple trees, and the music came and went in snatches. It sounded a little like the music on the album, *Hazey Jane*, far away and melancholy.

There was another old garden gate, leading to the bridle-way and the orchard. Jane drifted towards it.

*

The side of the tomb was cold on her face. She crouched there in her cassock, furious – hiding in her own church! – as Dermot Child and Mr Watts walked out. The cassock felt soiled, as though Child's fingers had already been up and down the buttons. She wanted to have another bath, to scrub herself like she'd done once, late at night, to remove the blood of Edgar Powell.

Dermot's key turned in the lock, but she didn't move from behind the tomb, in case they came back.

Silence in the chapel. Only inches between her and Tom Bull's bones. She saw, with a twinge of unease, that part of the tomb, below the feet of the effigy, had been repaired, as though Tom Bull had stretched out in death and pushed out a couple of the sandstone bricks to make more room for himself. You could feel quite resentful at the way influential local families thought they could buy into Paradise with a fancy tomb.

Traherne had a lot to say about that. Tom Bull must have known Traherne. But Traherne had left for London by the time they were laying their accusations at the door of his friend, Wil Williams.

How did James know about his ancestor's role in the persecution and his feelings at the time? Were there family documents?

How, in fact, had the Williams story been passed down? She was reluctant to ask the old guy who did the All Our Yesterdays bit for the parish mag. He was sentimental and unreliable, and he'd keep her talking all day. And, anyway, he would never have been given access to the Bull-Davies family records.

Merrily stood up, brushed herself down. 'Smug bastards,' she muttered to Tom Bull and his absent descendant. 'Nothing changes, does it?'

'Well, that's true,' a woman murmured behind her. 'In this family, anyway.'

Merrily spun round.

She wore an ankle-length skirt, the colour of Ledwardine soil, and possibly the same black, cotton shirt she'd worn on the square that night, open to the gold pendant in the cleft of her breasts. She also wore a knowing smile.

'You drop something?'

'Just a key,' Merrily lied. She hadn't heard the porch door open, or footsteps. 'Sorry. Have you been here long?'

'Just this minute walked in.' She had glazed, Marilyn Monroe lips, but the resemblance ended there, before the steep, regal nose, before the slanting, dark blue eyes. 'Alison Kinnersley. I don't think we've been formally introduced.'

'Probably because I've never seen you here before. Merrily Watkins.'

'I do come here sometimes,' Alison said. 'To look around. And think. But never with James.' Her voice dropped into the Bull-Davies bark. 'Not seemly, you know.'

Merrily raised an eyebrow. 'Anyone care about seemly any more?'

Twenty-five, even fifteen years ago, Alison Kinnersley would have been a scarlet woman. Today, the villagers still gossiped, but not many would be scandalized.

'James cares,' Alison said.

'Yes.' Merrily walked away from the tomb. 'I expect he would.'

Then why? she wanted to ask. Remembering Alison's hands inside James's sheepskin on the night of the wassailing. *Why does he let you flaunt him in public and yet, when you're not there, behave as if you don't exist?*

'Poor guy . . .' Alison moved into Merrily's place at the tombside. 'Poor guy came home in a bit of a state last night. He's convinced you're going to shaft him over that play.'

'That's rich. He threatened to shaft *me*.'

Alison laughed. 'James is full of shit. OK? I just thought I should tell you that.' She looked down dispassionately at the effigy. 'He's gone to Hereford today. For the Powell inquest. Gone to do his duty and help Rod Powell convince the coroner his old man didn't top himself. He'll be gone most of the day. And so, I . . .'

The dark blue eyes focused directly on Merrily, as though this was very important.

'. . . I just got the feeling you'd had this horrendous scene with him and you might be feeling intimidated. So I thought I'd tell you he was full of shit and whatever he said you should disregard. I'm relying, of course, on your discretion. As a woman of the cloth.'

Merrily didn't know how to react. As a woman of the cloth or, indeed, as a woman.

'I really wouldn't mind seeing that play,' Alison said. 'I think it could be quite interesting.'

There was the faint hint of a rural vowel there – *quoit* interesting – which showed she didn't exactly share James's background.

'I'll tell you one thing.' She touched, with a pink, ovalled fingernail, the sandstone lips of Tom Bull. 'There was more to this old bastard than James is prepared to admit.'

'Like what?'

'Frankly, I don't know.' Alison's lips turned down. 'If I knew that . . .' She pulled her hand away from the effigy. 'Anyway.'

'Excuse me,' Merrily said. 'I'm a bit baffled. You're James's . . .'

'Mistress,' Alison said softly. 'Mistress. Old-fashioned word, old-fashioned guy.'

'I had that impression.'

'So why would I want to do this to him?'

'Something like that.'

'Hmm.' Alison nodded. 'Well, you've met him. You've been exposed to the archaic, paternalistic balls.'

'I'm still baffled,' Merrily said.

'Well, fine,' Alison said lightly. 'That's all right. So long as you're not unsettled about it.'

She began to walk away, half turned, wryly raised a hand and brought the fingers down twice, like a bird pecking.

'See you, Vicar.'

*

Merrily went directly to the Black Swan. She had some pleading to do; couldn't face another night in a sleeping bag.

'Well, I'm sorry, Mrs Watkins,' Roland said. 'I was only

going by your instructions. I've got a theatre director and his partner arriving for lunch tomorrow, and they'll be taking the Woolhope Suite until the weekend.'

'One more night?'

'I'm *so* sorry. No reflection on you, of course, but it'll require the full works tonight. We were allowing for you having all your things out by . . . seven? Oh, and this came for you. Somebody dropped it through the letterbox.'

A white envelope addressed to The Vicar, The Black Swan.

'OK,' Merrily said wearily. 'I'll go up and get everything sorted out and when Jane comes home we'll get it all moved.'

Up in the suite, she thought, sod it, and ran a bath in the creamy bathroom. Got out of the cassock, rolled it into a ball and threw it into a corner. So much for tradition. As the bath filled up, she went to the wardrobe and found a plain black sweater and a charcoal-grey jersey skirt. Too hot but probably less appealing to the fetishist. Pity about the cassock; it was comfortable, like a kaftan, but it wasn't coming back.

After her last, luxurious bath, Merrily lay down on the bed and tore open the letter. Looked like an invitation, a mixed blessing for vicars.

It was a card. A funeral card, with a black border. It said,

**WIL WILLIAMS
WAS THE DEVIL'S MINISTER.**

**LET HIM LIE.
BE WARNED.**

Merrily let it fall to the floor.

She should take it to the police. It was a threat, wasn't it?

And what would the police do? Fingerprint it? Then fingerprint the entire village?

She sat up and looked again at the card. The message had been printed on a slip of paper, which had been pasted inside the black rectangle. Anyone with access to a computer could have done it. And anyone could have access to a computer; for a very small fee you could use the one in Marches Media.

Waste of time. Some crank. On impulse, she took the card to the window, set light to it with her Zippo and let the air take the ashes.

Crank, maybe, but someone had spent some time on it. Another indication that something in this Wil Williams business went very deep in Ledwardine. Alison Kinnersley and Lucy Devenish both thought Coffey's play would open up the can of worms and that would be no bad thing. But here was proof that Bull-Davies was clearly not alone in wanting to keep the lid on.

She shut the window and went back and lay on the bed, her whole body shaking with anger and what she suspected, after last night, was nervous exhaustion.

SIXTEEN

Like Lace

This was a secret place, an old place.

To begin with, it existed only as warmth and a sense-sapping humidity. Then she was aware of lustrous, wet stone walls on every side, like some Middle Eastern dungeon. But the atmosphere was dense and dark and syrupy with a sour-sweet aroma, fruitier and earthier than wine: a heavy drenching of deepest rural England.

His face went in and out of focus, sweat rippling down his cheeks like wax down a candle. His eyes were sly, his hands were busy. The lower half of him was lost in steam but it was moving. Squirming.

She, however, was lying helplessly still in what felt like damp hay. She couldn't move at all; her muscles were heavy and sagging, like balloons full of water. She kept trying to concentrate, make out details, but her vision was all fuzzy and her self-control just drifted away into the thick, cloying, musted air.

She didn't know where this was; it might be underground, at England's core, it was hot enough. Above her, no sun, only oaken rafters, pickled in centuries of juice.

Hot enough to be hell. And his face . . .

His mad, moist face had split into a wide grin, the way a crisp apple splits. But it was rotten inside, oozing brown pulp, and the pips dropped from his stained teeth and, behind, she saw his fat buttocks rising out of the vapour, glossy orbs, rosy apples.

He took in a slow, wheezing breath. Eyes popping in his friar's face as his buttocks tensed, and she realized, with terror tightening inside, that he was fully on top of her.

And she was wearing the tattered remnants of the black cassock, ripped down the front and stained with stinking apple pulp. And her collar was tightening like a shackle, like a stiff, white noose.

White collar. He began to gasp. *Pink body. Brown nipples. Absolute little cracker.*

There was the squeak and grind of an ancient mechanism, the sense of an enormous, waiting weight, before a lunge and a squeezing and a second of silence like a crack in the universe until – accompanied by a long, liquid gush – Dermot Child snarled out, his enormous voice echoing through caverns of time as her own throat constricted.

'*Auld . . . ciderrrrrrrrrrrrrrrrrrrrrr . . .*'

*

Bastards!

Merrily hurled clothes, unfolded, into the open suitcase. The cassock last, but the lid wouldn't close, and in a rage she seized the cassock and tore it down the back and threw it into the bin liner with the rubbish.

Look at the time, look at the *time*. Four-fifteen! She'd slept for nearly five hours. God al*mighty*.

Calm down.

She sat on a corner of the bed, settled her breathing, gave herself a good talking-to. Alf Hayden would have chuckled and let it all pass over him – Child, Bull-Davies and his mistress, the funeral card. Nothing would intrude into Alf's placid dreams.

But would any of it have happened to Alf? Merrily didn't somehow think it would.

When she'd awakened – the dream-Child's ghastly orgasmic cry biting into her brain like an alarm clock – she'd stripped at once in front of the bathroom washbasin, throwing angry handfuls of cold tap water at herself and then drinking half a pint of tepid spring water from a plastic bottle and brushing her teeth with a violence that made her gums bleed.

Just calm down. Jane'll be getting off the bus in about ten minutes; you can't let her see you like this.

In the bedroom, she dressed in the quietly secular black jumper and skirt, slotted her clerical collar under her dark-brown curls. *Pink skin, brown nipples, white—*

Stop it!

Before the open window overlooking the mellowed, red-cobbled village square, she knelt to pray. Pressing her palms flat together, sandwiching the heat between them. Stilling her mind, entering the inner temple, before whispering into the Silence.

O God, I know you're testing me. As you will, no doubt, test all women who dare to don the cloth . . .

Stop. You're sounding resentful. You're whingeing.

She knelt in silence for several minutes, waiting for the right tone, the right level. Waiting for the calm. But, to her anguish, her senses began to fill up with the pulpy essence of the foetid cider cellar, the organist's sweating face. Sweat and rotting apples; how was she ever going to bring herself to talk to that bloody man again?

You pompous cow. He's just a normal guy. If you're not responsible for your dreams, Dermot Child certainly isn't!

Sure. Reluctantly, she stood up. The odd thing was, she'd never seen a cider mill at work, only the static exhibits at the Bulmer's Museum in Hereford. She'd never smelt the powerful aroma, although she'd read about it. Never experienced the moment when the press came down on the cloth-rolled pulp and the first juice burst out like—

A bus juddered to a stop on the edge of the square; through the open window she heard chattering and laughter.

Jane's bus.

Merrily stood the suitcase in the centre of the room together with the bin liner and three cardboard wine boxes from Sainsbury's to put the rest of the stuff in. She dashed into the bathroom, started to drag a comb through her tangled hair, but it snagged and she gave up and ran out of the Woolhope Suite, down the stairs and into the square, to grab hold of Jane before she tramped back to an empty vicarage.

And what have you been doing today, Mum? Well, I slept most of it, actually, flower, then I had a pornographic dream.

Help!

The kids on the square were separating slowly, school shirts and blouses pulled out of waistbands, gestures of slovenly cool. No sign of Jane. One of the older boys spotted Merrily and nudged his mate and they smiled slyly, and Merrily thought, Jesus, is there no end to this?

When she walked up to them, retrieving her breath, the tall, thin one went gratifyingly red. Merrily didn't smile at him.

'You seen Jane Watkins anywhere?'

'Yeah,' the other boy said. 'I seen her a few times. Nice-looking. Bit like you.' Smothering a giggle with his hand, cocky little sod.

'And do you know', Merrily said patiently, 'where she is?'

'Hang on,' the tall one said, 'I never seen her on the bus. You see her, Dean?'

'She weren't on the bus. She weren't on the bus this morning neither, I'm pretty sure.'

Merrily frowned.

'No, honestly.' Dean was overweight and beady-eyed. 'There's six of us gets on at this stop, right? And she's always there when I gets yere. Last minute, me. Matter of pride. Jane wasn't there, Vicar.' He grinned in her face. 'Swear to God.'

'Thanks,' Merrily said tightly.

'Looks like 'er bunked off, dunnit? Naughty, naughty.'

The square swam before her. She couldn't believe it. Not for one minute. Whatever she said about school, most of it disparaging, Jane did not *bunk off*. Jane had never missed a day except through illness and family tragedy. The youth was lying. Why was he lying to her?

Dean nonchalantly pulled from his schoolbag a can of Woodpecker cider, ripped off the tab. Merrily was sure she could smell it. Sweat and apples. She turned away in disgust. The kids were separating, going off in different directions. Maybe Jane had missed the bus. But if she wasn't there this morning?

Merrily went cold. She turned round and round, the square blurring into the Black Swan, the Country Kitchen alleyway, the Late Shop, Church Street, the vicarage behind its trees. *Not again. Jane, please God, not again, don't do this to me.*

Calm down. It's broad daylight. She's fifteen years old, she's smart, she's been around. She's probably at the vicarage. Up in her Apartment with a tape-measure.

I'll kill her.

*

In his last, morose months, Nick Drake, aged twenty-six, would get into his car and drive and drive until he ran out of petrol, because he hadn't the confidence to stop at a garage.

Often, his father would have to travel about seventy miles to bring him home.

When he was not out in his car, Nick would sit with his guitar in his room at his parents' home and play the same chord sequence over and over again, like some sad mantra. There had been a time, not so many years ago, when all this had made terrifying sense to Lol.

He sat on the chair arm with the dented Washburn on his knee. His fingers found A-minor and then F and then E-minor, stroking the strings with nails ruined by a winter of collecting and chopping logs for the stove. Conceding that Nick's chord-sequence, even in those faded days, was probably a good deal more complex. Never could work out his tunings.

On the table was a letter which had arrived this morning from the record company, TMM. It was pleased to inform Lol Robinson that the compilers of a new mass-market collection, to be called Acoustic Echoes, would be interested in including his song 'Dandelion Dreams' from the third and last Hazey Jane album.

Money for nothing. Backed by TV-advertising, these compilation albums sold by the vanload and also generated new interest in your old records. This was the fourth in two years to include one of his songs; it was how he lived. And it *was* a living; it paid the mortgage on the cottage, it put food on Lol's table and Ethel's dish. It was enough. Wasn't it?

He struck the doleful E-minor. He wanted to write again, sure he did, but when you lost it you lost it. You were supposed to be more inspired when you were unhappy, when your woman had gone and left you all alone. How come he could just about cobble lyrics together for Gary Kennedy's adequate tunes and that was it?

The phone rang. It would be Karl. Karl had rung twice

since the weekend. The second time, he'd said, *I'm going to come and see you again. I've got some ideas for songs.* As if Lol had never said, No way, no I'm not doing it, I can't do it. *Got some ideas for songs*, Karl had said, voice absolutely bland, no hint of menace. *I'm going to come and see you again.*

He put down the guitar, picked up the phone.

'Lol? It's, er, it's Dennis. Dennis Clarke.'

'Hello,' Lol said, relieved. 'How are you doing? Thanks for the album.'

'No, er, no problem.' Dennis coughed. 'So you saw Karl, then.'

'He came over.'

'Yeah,' Dennis said. 'Right. He came back to see me again. We had a talk.'

'He tell you about this gig he did with this band in America and all the girls afterwards and how he could've gone on all night despite being twice their age?'

'No,' Dennis said. 'Gillian was there. He told me about how much money we could make if we did another album.'

'And were you impressed?'

Dennis went quiet.

Lol said, 'Was *Gillian* impressed?'

'Lol, OK, look, I . . . Well, I said . . . I said yes. I said I would.'

'Would what?'

'Do another album.'

This time Lol went quiet.

'It's just a record, Lol. It won't mean touring. I mean . . . I can fit it in. Karl says they'll organize a studio at Chipping Camden or somewhere, so I travel up, come home at night. Gillian's . . . Gill says she doesn't mind.'

'What about your wrist?'

'Elbow. I suppose, if I take a couple of pain-killers . . .'

'Right,' Lol said. 'Well, good luck. I'll look out for it.'

'No, hang on. I mean . . . I mean, you have to be in the band, obviously.'

'That's funny, Dennis, because I told Karl I wasn't going to do it.'

'Lol, you've *got* to do it.'

'Oh. I see,' Lol said. 'He kind of threatened you, did he? What was it, plain violence, or something Gillian doesn't know about? I have to say, it was the violence used to work with me. But that was nearly twenty years ago. Not now, I don't think. What he did finally was worse.'

'Lol, listen—'

'He says, Dennis, you persuade that little bastard, or—?'

'No! No, he didn't! It was nothing like that.'

Lol felt sorry for him. He felt sorry for himself too, but maybe Dennis, the safe, Chippenham accountant, was more vulnerable right now.

'Dennis, if he ever asks, I'll tell him you did your best.'

'Lol, for Christ's sake . . .' He sensed Dennis was near to tears. 'Oh, come on, man, you know it's you he needs. You know he can't write a fucking song to save his life.'

'Dennis.' Lol was surprised how firm his own voice sounded. 'Just tell him to leave me alone. Tell him not to come near me.'

Outside the window, there was white blossom on the apple trees. Why did white blossom depress him so much? Maybe the memory of white flowers on his mother's coffin. His father turning his back on Lol at the graveside. On a luminously still May afternoon much like this one.

'I won't tell him that,' Dennis said. 'Not yet. Jesus Christ, it's only an album, Lol. Just the one.'

*

'Vicar!'

She turned impatiently at the vicarage gate. 'Oh. Gomer. Oh dear, I'm sorry, I'm—'

'You got some addresses for me, Vicar?' He was wearing a dark suit and a black tie with what had to be a twenty-year-old knot.

'Sorry?'

'In Cheltenham. Figured I'd set off early, like.'

'Oh. Of course. I'm really sorry, Gomer, things have been . . . Would you mind if I were to call you with the stuff tonight? It's just—'

'Whenever you like, Vicar. The ole inquest's over and done now.'

'Oh.' She'd have to ask. 'How did it go?'

'Death – ' Gomer snatched out his cigarette in disgust ' – by misadventure.'

'Accident, then. Councillor Powell must be pleased.'

'Ah. Bloody ole whitewash, Vicar. Bull-Davies, he give evidence of how he couldn't get no sense out of Edgar all night and how he was a bit worried about the ole feller havin' charge of a shotgun and how he wishes he'd taken some action when he had the chance. Well, load of ole sheepshit, sure t' be, 'scuse my language. But you puts a Bull-Davies in the witness box they all thinks it's bloody gospel. Something botherin' you, Vicar?'

'Sorry, I was just looking out for Jane. So you think he really did kill himself deliberately?'

'Ah . . .' Gomer rubbed at his glasses, as though this would clarify things. 'Call me a cynic, but it was the way they was all tryin' to convince the whats-his-name, the judge . . .'

'Coroner.'

'Aye. The way they was all bangin' on about Edgar not bein' his ole self, acting confused-like all day, like. Doc Asprey – wouldn't trust that young bugger to the end o' the yard – he says Edgar had a bit o' trouble comin' in the arteries as could give 'im funny turns. Well, see, I could understand Rod not wantin' his ole feller buried the wrong side o' the churchyard—'

'We don't actually do that any more, Gomer.'

'I was speaking metaphysically, Vicar. It's still the stigma, see. You don't want a reputation as a suicide family. So you could understand Rod perjurin' his bollocks off, but Bull-Davies . . . Big guns, Vicar. Big guns. Course, the Bulls, they been relyin' on the Powells for generations.'

'You think Edgar wasn't actually confused? I wasn't really taking much notice.'

'He weren't confused in the Ox earlier on, is all I can say. And he weren't drunk neither, though he'd had a few, all paid for by other folk as usual. Crafty ole bugger, Edgar Powell. I been thinkin' a lot about this, see – got plenty bloody time to think nowadays, more's the pity – and I reckon, whether he done isself by accident or deliberate, summat put the wind up Edgar that night. If you gets time to think back on it, Vicar, I'd be interested in your opinion. As an outsider like.'

'I think I was just trying to keep warm at the time. But perhaps we could discuss it tomorrow over a cup of—'

'I'm delayin' you, Vicar.' Gomer threw up his hands. 'Gettin' an ole woman, see. What bloody retirement does for you. Useless bastard of a thing retirement, 'scuse my language . . .'

*

It was only when she was halfway up the vicarage drive that Merrily realized Jane couldn't possibly be inside. Because she hadn't yet got a key.

She looked up in despair at the beautiful, old, oak-framed pile, the oldest three-storey house in Ledwardine, and felt it repelling her. The highest, smallest windows seemed remote; even the trees didn't reach them. The unwindowed oak door looked like the door of some old jail.

She didn't go in. 'Jane . . .' She hurried around the side of the house, under a wooden arch and on to the big, square lawn overhung with willow and birch. 'Jane!'

She walked right round the house. The Volvo was still parked under the trees. She'd had it nicked four times in Liverpool, and she was always ridiculously grateful to see it. Why couldn't they have stayed in cosy old Liverpool, where you only worried about your car getting nicked?

Jane's CD case was still on the dash, with its photo of four men in a forest clearing watching a blurred girl-shape, and the words *Hazey Jane*. Merrily smiled. No wonder the kid was infatuated. Tears pricking. 'Jane!'

Brushing at her eyes, she found her face was glazed with sweat. She ran back to the gate. No schoolkids left on the square now. Just two women with prams and toddlers. It was nearly five o'clock. Oh my *God*.

No. Stop. Think.

All right . . . She wasn't on the bus tonight, she probably didn't catch it this morning. She'd made a point of leaving early. To take a stroll around the village. Well, OK. Merrily hadn't questioned that; Jane was a curious kid, liked to get to know places. On the other hand, Ledwardine wasn't a place that took that much getting to know, not when you'd already lived here for several weeks.

She'd arranged to meet someone? A boyfriend? Merrily thought of the overweight youth slurping his cider. Please not.

Cider.

Her mouth tightened. She strode across the square towards Cassidy's Country Kitchen.

I'll kill her.

Oh God, please let her be out with that little bitch on some unholy binge.

*

Lol walked out into the garden. White blossom. Spring. Always the most depressing time of year. All those long, empty summer days ahead. In winter, on your own, you could spend whole hours of dwindling daylight chopping logs to stay warm through the evenings.

Blossom all over the orchard. Even though it began at the bottom of his garden, Lol had hardly ever been in there. It was someone else's property. It was also unwelcoming, overgrown and gloomy – nothing picturesque about neglected apple trees.

It was Alison who'd really liked this place. Alison who'd said how much she would love it here, watching Lol rebuild himself. Turned to him with that look of longing and then the coy smile, with eyes downcast that always worked for the late Princess of Wales. Turning Lol like the right key in a rusted lock.

Scattered with clusters of tiny flowers the orchard was no longer clawed and sinister. But still eerie, the old, gnarled fingers white-gloved.

He wondered if it would have made a difference if he'd been here with Alison at the wassailing on Twelfth Night. The truth was he hadn't wanted to go, be among all those strangers. Partly why he'd agreed to go over to Oxford to work on the songs with the fading legend Gary Kennedy. (Lol felt safer with people who were fading.) Thinking Alison would go with him, but she'd said she was sure she had a cold coming on and it was better if she stayed here, kept warm.

There'd been no cold, but she'd kept warm. Perhaps she and Bull-Davies had come back to the cottage afterwards to shower away bits of the old man.

Old man Powell. This made it two suicides, if you included the hanged minister, Wil Williams. At least two. A place to stay out of, if you were that way inclined. He'd been amazed to find himself following Colette Cassidy into the heart of it last Saturday night. He hadn't had time to think.

But he was thinking now. Thinking hard. Thinking, *You have to do this. You have to keep fighting back.*

Against Karl. Dennis behind him now – reluctantly, of course. Dennis was a nice guy. Karl Windling wasn't. Karl wouldn't give up. He'd come again to the cottage. And when Karl had finally exhausted his limited powers of persuasion, when he realized there was nothing else to be done, nothing to lose, nothing to gain, he would become destructive. His pride would demand it.

Lol walked on, becoming increasingly depressed. All this blossom, promising apples. The only harvest last year had been logs from dead and dying trees. Last winter, he and Alison had bought a trailer-load of apple logs from the Powells. On the wood-burner, with the doors open, it had perfumed the whole room. No logs like apple logs for perfume; if traditional Christmas cards were scented, this was how they'd smell.

Lol had wanted to make love with Alison on the rug beside the stove at Christmas, but it had never happened.

How she'd changed. How classy she looked in her dark-blue riding gear, very point-to-point. Classy, but not sexy. Too militaristic.

When he turned round, the cottage had vanished into a tangle of white-dusted trees. Soon, he'd reach the so-called Apple Tree Man, where he and Colette had found Jane. It would be today's test to get that far on his own, to touch the Man's scabby bark. And then he'd turn and go back.

Clouds had gathered and the sky was nearly white, with holes of wet sunlight and veins like cheese mould. The trees closer packed, their blossom exploding around him, like a flour bomb; whichever way he turned it was the same, and even though there was no breeze, the whiteness seemed to swirl. He felt disoriented, but he wouldn't stop. A battle against himself. He moved on through the warm, windless snowstorm. When he looked up, the blossom and sky absorbed each other and floated down around him like a crinkling shroud; he didn't like that, looked down at the ground.

Where he saw, God help him, the girl lying across the path. Apple blossom around her face, like lace.

Whiteout

'Oh, hi,' Colette Cassidy said without enthusiasm. 'You want to talk to my father?'

Merrily's heart plunged. The girl shouldn't be here. She should be somewhere – anywhere – forbidden. With Jane Watkins.

'Because he's out,' Colette said.

She had a luscious, sulky mouth, which seemed to be all there was under heavy, mid-brown hair. She had in abundance what you could only call Attitude. Merrily saw in Colette a lot of things she'd never seen in Jane. Yet.

The girl leaned inside the doorway of Cassidy's Country Kitchen, arms folded, long denim legs straight. It was a wide doorway, built into what had evidently been the bay of a barn. Colette hardly barred the way, but there was a certain type of customer her presence would deter. And probably another type it would attract.

'Colette, where's Jane?'

Colette shrugged. 'I should know?'

'I hoped you would, yeah.'

'Well, I don't,' Colette said. 'Sorry.'

Through the flower transfers on the high, glass doors, Merrily saw Caroline Cassidy scurrying across the delicatessen. Caroline spotted her and changed direction.

'You're sure?' Merrily said.

'I wouldn't lie to *you*, Vicar,' Colette gave her a Nutra-sweet smile as Caroline came out. Tipping a glance at her mother that said, At least, not like I lie to *her*.

'Merrily!' Caroline wore a kind of milkmaid dress with gingham sleeves; only true townies dressed like this. 'We've been dying for you to come . . .'

'Hello, Caroline.'

'. . . but I said to Terrence, for God's sake don't pressure the girl, she's far too much on her plate to worry about our little festival.'

Throwing her all into a smile of sympathy and true compassion. Right now, it almost helped.

'I was just asking your daughter if she'd seen Jane.'

Caroline's face hardened. 'Colette?'

'No, I haven't.' Colette levered herself upright. 'I really haven't, OK? I mean, like, what *is* this, for Christ's sake? Just because we went out *once* and got a tiny bit pissed, everybody thinks we're on some kind of permanent pub crawl. I saw Jane for a few minutes last night and I haven't seen her since, OK?'

'Colette, two coffees. Go.' Caroline pushed her daughter through the doors, turned back to Merrily. 'Is there a problem here? When did you last see her?'

'This morning. When she left for school.'

'Oh, yes, she goes to that . . . comprehensive. Isn't there a special bus?'

'She wasn't on it.'

Caroline shook her head with a jingle of earrings. 'Teenage girls are so utterly thoughtless. She's probably stayed behind to play tennis or something.'

'You think so?' For a moment, Merrily clutched at it. Caroline Cassidy was perhaps twelve years older, she had a very difficult daughter; this must have taught her something. She took Merrily by an arm.

'Come and have that coffee. You've been very lucky with Jane if this is the first time she's done this to you. Look, why don't you ring the school from here? There's always someone around these places for hours.'

'No, it . . .' It came down on Merrily that, according to the cider-swigging youth, Jane hadn't even taken the bus this morning. How long, she wondered despairingly, were you supposed to wait before you called the police?

Caroline Cassidy propelled her inside, sat her at one of three empty tables in the deli, went back to the door and turned over the laminated CLOSED sign.

'You know, teenagers, much more than children, have a problem moving to a new place.'

'She's done it several times,' Merrily said. 'OK, she was unhappy about it at first, but lately she's been fine. More or less.'

'Is there anyone she knows, locally, apart from Colette?'

'Nobody . . .' She thought of this man, Lol. She'd been remiss; she ought to have checked him out. 'Nobody special. Look, I'm sorry, I'm probably worrying about nothing, but didn't a girl go missing from Kingsland or somewhere a few months ago: Petra . . .?'

'Good, I think. Petra Good. But that was back in the winter. Look, Merrily . . .'

'And they haven't found her, have they?'

'My dear, you won't find many parts of the country where there isn't a girl missing. That doesn't mean— Colette, isn't that coffee ready yet?'

Merrily said, 'Do you know Lol Robinson?'

Caroline sniffed. 'Works for *her*, sometimes. Miss Devenish. Odd little man. Alison Kinnersley, James Bull-Davies's . . . partner . . . she used to live with Robinson. They bought the Timlins' cottage in Blackberry Lane – old couple, he died, she went into a home. Hadn't been there more than a few months and Alison'd taken up with James. One suspects there could be a drug problem.'

'*What?*' Merrily's fingers tightened on the seat of the rustic, wooden chair.

Caroline's look was penetrating. 'Jane knows him?'

'She had one of his records, that's all.'

'Aw, look . . .' Colette dumped two coffees, with cartons of cream. 'He's harmless. He's just screwed up is all.'

Her mother looked up sharply.

'Look,' Colette said, 'we've all been round there. At first, you think like, wow, a rock musician, and you're expecting him to have his own studio and cool people around, but he's like . . . like he could be a bank clerk or something. One old guitar. Anyway, he's all messed up over Alison. He won't stay around here. Or, if he does, he'll like OD or something.'

'I have to go.'

Merrily stood up. She was thinking of that album. The track called 'Song for Nick'. Jane asking her, as they lay in their sleeping bags, *You ever know anybody who committed suicide?*

'You've been very kind. But what if she's come back to the vicarage or the inn? I'm sorry—'

'Drink your coffee, Merrily, please. Colette, go to the vicarage, go to the Black Swan, ask around and *be discreet.*'

Colette went without a word and Caroline gently pressed Merrily back into her chair, sat down opposite her.

'I can assure you she'll leave no stone unturned. My daughter is being ultra co-operative – at least until after the party.'

'Sorry. Party?'

'Didn't Jane tell you? She's certainly invited.'

'Well, I—' There was obviously a whole lot Jane hadn't

told her. Merrily drank some coffee, although she was starting to feel sick. 'She probably mentioned it and I forgot. Things have been . . . you know.'

Caroline slid a hand over Merrily's, squeezed it. 'You're taking on too much. You really ought to let us help. Alfred delegated. He'd learned, you see. No, the party . . . Oh dear, it's her sixteenth. People say we must be absolutely mad to let her have it in the restaurant. But what I say is, better our own premises here in the village than some awful disco-club in Hereford. We've promised to go out, but Barry will be in charge. Our restaurant manager. Barry's awfully capable.'

Merrily was only half-listening. She was thinking of suicide. Mass suicides of once-rational people, like the Heaven's Gate thing. Suicide was contagious. God, you really thought you knew your own child. You thought your generation was going to be different. There was going to be nothing you wouldn't be able to talk about, that you couldn't iron out between you. But every generation, there was something new growing in their heads, something terrifying.

'Terrence has gone to see Richard Coffey,' Caroline said brightly. 'They were hoping to catch up with you over the weekend. Richard's got some friends down from London, a theatre director whose name I ought to know but I've forgotten. They were hoping to put their proposals to you . . . for the church?'

Maybe it was the Church. God. God had come between them, made Merrily into a remote figure. Or even an embarrassment. The way Jane looked at her when she went to pray. She'd thought that was just going to be a phase.

Caroline said, 'They want to show you they can present *Wil* in a way that would cause absolutely minimal disruption to normal services and things. Hasn't Richard been to see you yet? With his friend? One has to say he totes that young man around like a trophy wife.'

'I . . . I've been putting people off. Until we got settled into the vicarage. Well, not settled, exactly, that could take years. But, you know, *in*. Oh my God, we're supposed to be moving tomorrow.'

'We'll help. Of course we will. Everything will be absolutely fine, you'll see.' Caroline paused, eyes narrowing. 'We, er, we heard James came to see you.'

'Yes.'

'I don't know what's got into that man. He was always so enthusiastic about developing the village economy and restoring a degree of self-sufficiency. Suddenly, he's become a positive millstone, and Terrence is terribly scared that Richard will simply turn his back on us and the whole festival will be a disaster. It's all so worrying.'

'You seem to be . . . treading on old corns.' Merrily drank some more coffee; most of her mind was out on the square with Colette.

Caroline scowled. 'That illustrates precisely what we have to overcome if we're going to get this place buzzing. The past is over. It can't harm us. But we can use it. Do you see? We're lucky enough to have these wonderful old buildings, set in such beautiful countryside, and an absolute wealth of traditions. But, Lord, we mustn't let them hold us back.'

Merrily suspected Caroline Cassidy had just said something deeply flawed, but her anxiety wouldn't let her concentrate.

There was a tapping on the glass.

'We're closed!' Caroline called out. Then she said, 'Oh, no.' Pushed her coffee cup aside. 'Bloody woman. Now *she* really does make you think you're trapped in some ghastly timewarp.'

Caroline opened one of the double glass doors.

'Is that the vicar I see with you, Mrs Cassidy?'

Merrily stood up, heart thumping.

Miss Devenish was hatless. She wore a shapeless dress with a geranium pattern. Her hair was in two plaits which looked as strong as anchor chains. Her face was grave.

'Ah. Mrs Watkins. Yes. Could I talk to you, please? In my shop?'

*

Lol was shivering in the dark. Hunched into a corner of the loft, hugging his knees; he felt like a priest in a priest's hole. Hunted.

Filtered through a tiny, mossed-over skylight, the only light in here was green. It was unearthly, it made his fingers look like corpse fingers; he shuffled to squeeze himself into shadow.

Although his eyes were fixed on the green skylight, the pictures rolling in were all white. The warm blizzard of blossom in the orchard. The disorientation.

The whiteout. And the girl. Her features indistinct, a corpse under a pale catafalque of blossom.

Oh God, the girl.

*

The mews was deserted. The shops had closed, the afternoon clouded over. Lucy Devenish didn't speak until the double doors were between them and the face of Caroline Cassidy, puckered with resentment.

'Appalling woman. Never tell her anything you don't want the entire county to know.'

Merrily said, 'Lucy, unless this is really important, could we perhaps talk tomorrow? I'm honestly not thinking too well at the moment.'

But it clearly was important. 'Come to the shop.' Lucy Devenish took her arm and led her into the mews. 'Please.'

From even a few yards away, Ledwardine Lore looked like

an old-fashioned fruit shop. Then you saw that none of the apples in the window were real and small butterfly creatures were all over them. Merrily experienced a momentary illusion of being outside herself, as though nothing at all here was real, as though this was an enchanted village in a child's dream. It was a moment of strange relief.

'Come in, Merrily.'

The door was unlocked, but the shop had closed, the lights were out. It was dim inside. The smell of apples was overwhelming.

'Hello, Mum,' Jane said softly.

*

Lucy Devenish didn't put on the lights. As though she didn't want Merrily to see Jane too clearly.

The kid was on a stool up against the counter. Her features were indistinct. There was a couple of yards between them, so Merrily couldn't tell whether she was smiling or serious. All around her, things shaped like apples. Mugs, candles, ornaments. Pot fruit, wax fruit, fluffy fruits.

Breath bolted into Merrily. Her anxiety swelled for an instant and then burst, like a boil. Relief, but a discoloured relief.

'Oh Jesus,' she croaked finally. 'Where the hell have you been?'

Jane said nothing. Merrily saw that she was holding an apple-shaped mug, faintly steaming, between her hands, as if for warmth.

Lucy Devenish shut the door.

'She's been with me,' she said.

Merrily turned on her angrily. 'For how long?'

'Oh,' Lucy said. 'All . . . all day.'

'I don't understand.' Her vision adjusting to the dimness, she saw that Jane still wore her school uniform, even the

223

blazer, even the tie. 'She should have been at school, for heaven's sake. What's going on? What's happened to her?'

'It was me,' Lucy said quickly. 'I went for my early-morning walk and I'm afraid I collapsed. In Blackberry Lane. Stupid of me, I thought the fresh air would make me feel better.'

She had her back to the door, her face almost entirely in shadow.

'It's . . . it's a blood pressure problem. One forgets one's age. All I can say is thank God for Jane. I was lying in the hedge when she found me. Somehow, she got me home. And then she made me some tea. And she insisted on staying with me. I kept telling her to leave, but she wouldn't. Of course, she missed the bus.'

Jane didn't move, her hands still clasping the steaming orb of the apple mug.

'I wanted to drive her to school, but she said I wasn't fit to drive in my condition. A bossy child.'

'You could have sent her to find me,' Merrily said cautiously. 'I could've taken her.'

'Oh. Well. If I'm being truthful – I'm sorry, Jane – that was why she didn't *want* to find you. Because she said you would only have insisted on taking her to school and she told me she didn't want to have to explain to everybody.'

Merrily sighed. 'I've been worried sick. When she didn't get off the school bus . . .'

'She's been helping me in the shop. We rather lost track of time. I'm so sorry, Merrily.'

'I just wish somebody had told me. How are you feeling now, Miss Devenish?'

'Much better, thank you.'

'Have you seen the doctor?'

'That twerp Asprey? No, thank you. And indeed, Merrily,

I'd be very grateful if you wouldn't mention this to anybody. Tell the Cassidy woman to mind her own damn business.'

'Is there anything *I* can do for you?'

'Your daughter's done everything. Take her home.'

*

Caroline Cassidy's gossip-greedy gaze alighted on them as soon as they emerged into the mews.

'Oh, Merrily, I'm so glad!'

Perhaps she noticed Jane's vacant eyes, because she backed off a little, with a meaningful glance towards the door of Ledwardine Lore.

'She, er, she was helping Miss Devenish,' Merrily said.

'All *day*?'

'No, that was . . . a mistake on my part. I got a little confused. Everything got kind of criss-crossed. I'm sorry to have caused such a fuss.'

Caroline's tilted smile showed she believed not a word, and who could blame her.

Jane was silent. Crossing the market place. Merrily kept glancing at her, sure she was a little pale. In curious contrast, as it happened, to Miss Lucy Devenish, who'd looked as ripe and ruddy as one of the apples in her damned shop window. Blood-pressure – balls.

They crossed the square to the church and the vicarage shoulder to shoulder, but there was distance between them.

Into the silence came a long, low rumble from the church. Merrily could see through the lych-gate that the porch doors were wide open, like amplifying hands. The sound was like the rising drone of an enormous vacuum cleaner.

'Again!' sang a man's voice. 'Come on, again! Fill those lungs!'

Dermot Child, rehearsing his choral work, the male voices like mud in the bottom of a deep pond.

Aullllllld ciderrrrrrrr.

Jane didn't look up, but Merrily thought she saw the kid shiver.

*

Lol came down from the loft. He stumbled.

'This is a nightmare, Lucy.'

'Perhaps.' Lucy's face was gaunt in the gloom. 'If her mother doesn't start to realize a few things soon, I'm going to have to talk to the child in greater depth.'

All the apple colours and the translucence in the wings of the fairies had dulled like a stained-glass window at night. The shop seemed heavy around Lucy. It seemed to be not so much a diversion for her as a symbol of responsibility. For the first time it occurred to him that she was probably quite an old woman.

'I'm sorry,' he said. 'She was just lying there. She was all white. At first, I thought she was dead. When she moved, it . . . I just wanted to run away from it. But I couldn't. You know? I couldn't move. What was she *doing* there, Lucy? Again.'

'Laurence,' Lucy said, 'you're living on your own, too near the orchard. At the wrong time. If you have a weakness, some things will play to that weakness. When you're prepared to tell me what the weakness is, we can take it from there.'

'I'm all weakness,' Lol said.

'You're not helping yourself.' Lucy's face darkened. 'I can't help you if I don't know the root of the problem.'

'Can I think about this?'

'It seems to me', Lucy said severely, 'that you've already been thinking about it rather too long.'

EIGHTEEN

The Little Green Orchard

It was, Merrily thought in dismay, like still living in a hotel. One without any guests or staff. A hotel in winter.

'Sure this is the lot, Vicar?' Gomer Parry had asked her, about three times.

'I'm afraid it is.'

This is awful, she was still thinking, after two days of moving things around. She'd forgotten quite how much furniture she'd sold or given away over the past three years. What it meant was that they had about enough for a decent-sized flat with one living room and a couple of bedrooms.

Gomer Parry had done it in one trip. Bloody sight easier, he said, than when he and Minnie moved in from the Radnor Valley, with all Minnie's clutter from nearly forty years of marriage to the late Frank. Gomer and his nephew, Nev, took no more than half an hour to get all the stuff in. But, until such time as the property market improved to a point where the Diocese could make a killing on Ledwardine Vicarage, Merrily was stuck with it.

Behind the door, she'd found a letter from the North Herefordshire Gay and Lesbian Collective expressing support for Richard Coffey's 'brave re-appraisal of an historic injustice' and urging her to 'do the right thing'. She filed it for a future non-committal reply and returned to practical problems.

So. OK. There were two ways they could handle this situation. They could scatter the bits and pieces around, so that the whole place had the air of somewhere partly moved-into. Or they could furnish a couple of rooms reasonably well, which made it seem as though you were the live-in caretakers in some kind of hostel.

'I'm told there's a couple of reasonable secondhand shops in Hereford. If we spent say two hundred pounds fairly wisely, we might make a bit of a difference.'

'Yeah,' Jane said. 'Whatever.'

It didn't help that the kid was still into the idea of this third-floor flat arrangement. More into it than ever, in fact. She'd charmed Gomer and Nev into taking her bed to the top floor, into one of the smaller bedrooms, while the biggest one up there, which she insisted on keeping locked until she'd finished painting the walls, had her stereo, her albums, her books.

Merrily felt guilty as well as intimidated. Acres – literally, probably – of wasted space.

'But, my dear, virtually all country vicarages are like this,' Caroline Cassidy said, when she and Terrence arrived to assist. 'That's why so many vicars end up having enormous families. Of course, you'll marry again one day. Oh yes, you will!'

'Perhaps I could offer a home to some refugees,' Merrily had said, and Caroline had looked quite appalled. Almost as appalled as she'd been when she first saw their miserable collection of worthless furniture, making Merrily scared that they were going to be regarded as a charity case and all kinds of appalling junk would get dumped on them. 'Actually,' she'd lied, 'there's quite a bit more over in Cheltenham, but we wanted to do a bit of decorating first.' Caroline had looked sceptical.

As, in fact, she had over the issue of Jane's disappearance, which Merrily had tried to gloss over. Fairly sure she hadn't mentioned to Caroline that the kid had failed to catch the bus in the morning, she'd said Jane had simply missed the one home and had to get a lift from a friend's father.

All right then, flower, what *really* happened?

She never seemed to get a chance to ask the question – one for a long night in front of a log fire. But it was getting too close to summer for log fires and they never seemed to get a full night in together. Now people knew where to find the vicar, the doorbell and the phone rarely stopped.

Which was good. In a way. It was good to deal with day-to-day stuff: planning weddings and christenings, agonizing over whether to buy new prayer books. And putting off decisions on more contentious issues.

*

On Friday night, Richard Coffey invited her to dinner at the Black Swan. He had with him a man called Martin Creighton, a theatre director, and Creighton's earnest girlfriend Mira Wickham, a set designer.

'I happened to run into the bishop,' Coffey said.

'Oh.' Merrily fingered her napkin. 'I wondered if you might.'

'He's thrilled, of course, about our idea for staging *Wil* in the church. He's very keen to encourage the wider use of ecclesiastical premises. For the church to be the centre of the community again.'

'Well, me too, obviously, it's just . . . Well, I'd like to have some time to look into the Wil Williams story. I feel it's important we get him right.'

'Get him *right*?' Coffey's map-like face pulsed in the candlelight. Merrily blinked wearily; she was too tired for all this.

'If you were doing it in a theatre, that would be one

thing. But in the church where he . . . preached . . . I just think we all have a responsibility to get as close to the truth as we can.'

'Ah, the *truth*. What an adaptable little word that is. *The* truth. *A* truth. The literal truth. A universal truth. Where do we begin?'

Martin Creighton laughed. Mira Wickham smiled.

'I think we have to begin', Merrily said, 'with whether Wil Williams really was a witch.' She took a quick sip of wine. 'And whether he really was gay.'

Coffey leaned back. He wore a black leather jacket and a white shirt and a sort of chamois-leather bow tie. He was not accompanied by Stefan Alder, his partner. There was no humour in his smile.

'Mrs Watkins, if you were to substitute the word "heterosexual" – as in "whether he was heterosexual" – you would perhaps appreciate the degree of offence implicit in the line you're taking.'

'Oh, now, look, obviously I intended no offence at all. I have absolutely nothing against—'

'Woofters? Queers?' Tilting his head, playing with her.

'All I'm saying, Mr Coffey' – Merrily gripped her napkin – 'is that if we're talking about causing offence—'

'I *know* what you're saying. I gather you've already had a state visit from a certain descendant of the tyrannical Thomas Bull. Who thinks I've developed a grudge against his entire lineage because the bastard capitalized so ruthlessly on my friend Stefan's desire to live in his lodge.'

'Something like that,' Merrily admitted.

'All right, let me explain something to you. I'm an exhaustive researcher. I like to know every minute detail of the background against which I am working. Correct, Martin?'

'Richard's compulsion to *know* is legendary,' Creighton said obsequiously.

'I have read, therefore, everything extant on the Williams case. Which, I have to say, is not a tremendous amount. It's very sparse. But perhaps my use of the word extant is a *mis*use. Available would be a better word. Because there *are* other documents in existence. Several sources, for instance, make mention of the Journal of Thomas Bull, parts of which have been published – the ones relating to the Civil War, for instance, and the Siege of Hereford. Bull's interesting to historians because, although a supporter of the Crown, he was, in his private life, a puritan.'

Merrily thought of Bull's effigy in the church, the rustic simplicity of his clothing.

'Now. As Justice of the Peace, it was Bull's job to initiate a prosecution of Williams, if he was· convinced there was sufficient evidence. Do you know how this began, Mrs Watkins?'

'You mean, the chap who saw him dancing with devilish sprites?'

'No, no, before that; the poor man was accused by one John Rudge, a wealthy, independent farmer, of bringing down a blight on his orchard and destroying his crop of cider apples. Williams, it seems, had good reason to be opposed to the ready availability of cider, having been assaulted by a drunk who wandered into his church. Now . . .'

Coffey angled forward, the tabletop candles reflected in his eyes.

'. . . we know that, as a puritan – with, if you like, a small p – Thomas Bull also was very much opposed to drink and drunkenness and would not allow cider apples to be grown by any of his tenants. Therefore, he might have been expected, might he not, to take the side of Wil Williams in his crusade for sobriety?'

Merrily nodded slowly.

'Instead of which,' Coffey said, 'Bull appears to have

seized on the accusation with a kind of sorrowful glee. This suggests he was already harbouring a certain prejudice against Wil Williams?'

'I suppose it might. But how will we ever know?'

'Only' – Coffey spread his hand delicately – 'by obtaining access to the unpublished journals of Thomas Bull. Which our friend James Bull-Davies keeps, no doubt, in the deepest of bank vaults. So, the next time he tries to lean on you, Mrs Watkins, I suggest you invite him to resolve the issue by producing them.'

'Do you have any proof that he's got them?'

'I'd be astonished if he hadn't. And, given his recent, ah, cash-flow difficulty, do you not think he wouldn't have attempted to sell the journals for publication? I'm not suggesting Tom Bull was any kind of rural Pepys. But his Civil War memoirs are surprisingly erudite. Be worth a good few thousand, I suspect. Certainly well worth putting on the market. Unless of course they contained material which, in the current climate, might be considered highly damaging to the family's reputation.'

All this made a certain sense.

'Oh dear,' Merrily said. 'It gets complicated, doesn't it?'

'So . . .' Coffey said, 'would you object if Martin and Mira were to have a look at the church over the weekend?'

Of course they already would have done. He was just testing her.

'Sure,' Merrily said, resignedly. 'Go ahead.'

*

The next day, Jane announced that she was to be manager of Ledwardine Lore for the afternoon. Lol Robinson, who usually conquered his shyness to take care of things while Lucy had a half-day off, had gone to a place near Oxford for a few days, to work on some new songs with Gary Kennedy, leaving Lucy to feed his cat, so . . .

'*The* Gary Kennedy?'

'Oh, Mum, how unutterably sad. *The* Gary Kennedy!'

'Listen, when I was your age—'

'Yeah, yeah, he was huge. Personally, I find it unbelievable that someone like Lol should be reduced to writing lyrics for someone as tragically awful as Gary Kennedy but there you are.'

Merrily watched from the window as Jane crossed the square and entered the mews, to make sure she really was going to Ledwardine Lore. It was wrong to be so suspicious, but she couldn't dispel the feeling that the kid and Lucy Devenish had come to some kind of arrangement.

When Jane had not emerged from the mews after five minutes, Merrily went into the hall, where Alf had left a few books of local interest on a shelf under the cupboard housing the electric meters. She pulled out a well-thumbed soft-covered book entitled *The Black and White Villages of Herefordshire: A short history* and carried it into the kitchen, where they'd temporarily placed two easy chairs and the TV, neither of them feeling quite up to the drawing room.

OK. Index. *Williams, Wil. p 98.*

Merrily pushed the chair on its castors to a spot side-on to the Aga and threw herself down. She wasn't going to get much out of this, but it would be a start.

*

'You've been avoiding me.'

Colette was standing right in the centre of the mews, so no chance of avoiding her this time. Short, red plastic windcheater with probably nothing underneath.

'No, I haven't.'

'You fucking have, Janey. I get sent off to scour the village for the vicar's precious child – and believe me the Reverend Mumsy was in a big, big fret – and the next thing I hear is you've turned up in Devenish's den in like seriously mysterious circumstances.'

'That's bollocks. There was nothing mysterious at all, there—'

She stopped talking, spotting the slow-growing smile and knowing she'd blown it, because if there was genuinely nothing to hide then she'd have played along, pretending there *was*, wouldn't she?

'Oh, Janey, what *are* we getting into? I mean, are we like talking, erm . . . we talking orchard?'

'No way.'

'See, like, there's two possibles where that orchard's concerned. One is that you've actually got a secret *guy*.'

'Bitch,' said Jane. 'How did you find out?'

'Or it goes back to that night when the cider did things for you it ain't never done for me, and you know how I really hate it when that happens.'

'Well, obviously it did things to me it didn't do to you, on account of you've been getting regularly pissed out of your mind for years.'

'Not good enough. Plus there's the Devenish angle. That creepy, tacky little shop you can't turn round in without horrible little fairies dropping down your front. You're going there now, yeah? Again?'

'So? It's a weekend job, all right? We're not all seriously rich, like on the Cassidy scale.'

'I'll find out,' Colette said menacingly. 'You can frigging count on it.'

*

By the mid-1600s, prosecutions for witchcraft were rare in the western half of the country. A notable exception was the case of Wil Williams, of Ledwardine, the second English vicar in this period to be accused of consorting with the devil. About twenty-five years earlier, the Reverend John Lowes, vicar of Brandeston in Suffolk, had been brought to justice by the notorious Witch-finder General, Matthew Hopkins. Lowes, who was over eighty when he was ducked in the moat of Framlingham Castle, was alleged to have caused the death of a child and a number of cattle by witchcraft as well as employing a familiar spirit to sink a ship off Harwich.

By comparison, Williams's alleged crime was minor: he was accused by a local farmer of ruining his crop of cider apples. However, other witnesses were said to be ready to testify that the vicar had been seen dancing with shining spirits in the orchard which, at that time, almost surrounded the church.

Whether these charges would have been proved in court will ever remain a mystery as, when warned of his impending arrest, Williams hanged himself in the very orchard he had been accused of bewitching. This was naturally taken as proof of his guilt, and he was buried in unhallowed ground, with only an apple tree to mark his resting place. It was said that neither this tree nor any others planted on the spot ever yielded an apple. The farmer who had laid the charge died soon afterwards and his family was quick to dispose of the orchard, dividing it into sections which were sold off separately. Ledwardine would never again be quite true to its reputation as The Village in the Orchard.

Merrily laid the book on the pine table – which looked like a footstool in this barn of a kitchen – and made herself some tea. Certainly this account backed up Coffey's argument that Williams had been framed, and this surely could only have been done with the approval of the local JP, Thomas Bull. But it was still a big leap to the idea that Wil was gay.

There was something missing.

*

Jane was embarrassed. She thought hurting anyone's feelings was the worst thing you could do to them. Sticks and stones might break your bones, but bones usually healed.

'I feel awful,' she said. 'I didn't know.'

'Nonsense,' said Lucy Devenish. 'I wouldn't have expected you to. You're not old enough.'

The book before Jane on the counter in Ledwardine Lore was quite slim and clearly for children. Its cover was this splodgy watercolour, all green. A small girl, done in pen and ink, was sitting in a clearing in a wood surrounded by trees which were not big but, with their tangled branches making the vague shapes of faces, were very sinister. The girl was looking, half-fearfully, over her shoulder.

The book was called *The Little Green Orchard*.

It was by Lucy Devenish.

'Title came from Walter de la Mare's poem,' Lucy said. 'Do you know it?'

Oh yes, Jane remembered that poem from way back in primary school, when it had frightened her a lot. It was about someone you couldn't see but who was always waiting there in this little green orchard. Always watching you.

'It used to scare me.'

'Good,' Lucy snapped. 'Children today are not scared nearly often enough. A child that grows up without fear grows up to be a danger to us all.'

Jane opened the book. Its dust jacket was quite dry and brittle and its price was seven shillings and sixpence.

'Nineteen sixty-four,' Lucy said. 'They stopped wanting

to publish me about seven years later. Fairy stories? Oh dear me, no. They wanted tales about robots and space ships. Old Dahl kept getting away with it, the bastard, and Blyton lives for ever. But I accept I wasn't such a wonderful writer that I could do what I wanted, so I stopped doing it. Jumble-sale fodder before you were born, so it's hardly surprising you'd never heard of me.'

There was another book underneath the first. This one was larger format and had a more cheerful cover, with a happy-looking landscape of smiley flowers, friendly-looking shady trees and sunny hills. And another small girl, this one wandering down a long path and looking kind of blissed-out. In fact the whole package looked a bit like one of those album-covers from the sixties, when bands first discovered mind-altering drugs. Lucy seemed a bit old to have been involved in all that; perhaps it was just the artist. This book was called *The Other Voices*.

'Did you never think of reprinting them and selling them here in the shop?'

'Heavens,' Lucy said. 'That *would* have been desperate, wouldn't it? Oh, one might do a spot of squirming at the efforts of the dreadful Duchess of York, but at the end of the day . . . well, at the end of the day, it's the end of the bloody day, isn't it?'

'Don't say that!'

'Jane.' Lucy leaned over her folded arms. 'Watch my lips. I *don't care*. Don't give a flying fart. I got the book out because I wanted you to read it. Now. At once. Look, I brought you a stool. Be a good girl, sit down over there and read the books. Take you about twenty minutes each. They're only children's stories, but they might make some things clearer. Read *The Other Voices* first, then ask any questions you like.'

At which point, Lucy seemed to lose all interest in Jane,

took down a row of apple mugs and set about them with a duster.

Jane had no alternative but to sit down and get into *The Other Voices*, which was probably intended for nine-year-olds, max.

It was about a little girl called Rosemary whose mother was ill, and so she went to stay with her grandparents in Herefordshire, natch, on a farm so remote that there were no other children to play with for miles. For a while, Rosemary was very sad, and wandered the fields and paths talking to the flowers and the trees because there was no one else. Pretty soon, she was imagining that the flowers and trees were talking back (which seemed, psychologically, reasonable enough to Jane), each with a distinctive voice. Like the dandelions had these high, pealing *yellow* voices. The bluebells, because there were so many of them so close together, spoke in a soft, blue harmonious chorus, watched over by the oak trees who, of course, had very deep, powerful brown voices. Soon, in the background, Rosemary could hear other sounds and realized that the hills themselves were breathing. In fact, if she looked hard, she could even *see* them breathing, their misty sides going in and out, very slowly, far more slowly than human breathing.

This went on for some days, Rosemary waking earlier and earlier because she couldn't wait to get outside to be with her friends. One morning, she awoke especially early, for this was midsummer, and her friends were putting on a special concert. The birds started them off, the dawn chorus activating everything. And then, as the sun rose, the flowers began to open and as they opened they started to sing, and the trees joined in with their bass notes and the hills amplified their heartbeats like drums and by the time the sun was fully up, Rosemary could no longer hear separate voices, but only musical tones, which blended together until the whole of nature became one huge, magnificent orchestra.

And Rosemary started to wonder about the orchestra's conductor. Who had composed the music, who had arranged it.

Of course, Rosemary's mother came out of hospital, which she was very glad about, except that she had to go home to the city, which kind of mortified her. She at once caught a cold which turned into flu, and she was very miserable. One day, when she was a little better, to give her some air, her mother took her out to the dreary old park she'd been to a thousand times . . . and, on the way there, Rosemary spotted a single dandelion growing out of a patch of earth around a street lamp, and the dandelion beamed up at her in recognition and she looked up over the rooftops to distant hills and could feel them . . . breathing, *inside her*, and by the time they got to the park, well . . .

And Rosemary realized everything had changed, for ever.

Jane looked up. '*She'd* changed, of course. But you never say that.'

'First rule of writing for children. Never lecture. Never let them think it's a parable. Which of course' – Lucy put down her duster – '*you* know it isn't.'

'Shame there aren't books like that for adults.'

'Adults', said Lucy, 'can read Traherne.'

'Oh,' Jane said. 'Right.' Not a single customer had been in while she was reading; she wondered how Lucy kept this place going.

'The story you've just read is, of course, an introduction to Traherne's world. Traherne showed how higher consciousness is there for us all. I'll give you some of his work to take home. Leave it lying about and hope your mother reads it. There's so much she needs to know, if she's going to surv— succeed here.' Lucy snatched up her duster. 'Now read the other one.'

*

In the little green orchard, there was an awesome hush.

In the little green orchard, it all became serious.

Rosemary again. A little older.

Her grandfather had died and she was spending the holidays with her grandmother, helping out on the farm, where it would soon be time to harvest the apples.

Rosemary had never been into the orchard before.

She was to discover that the orchard was the heart of everything.

NINETEEN

The Nighthouse

Lucy sent Jane to the village stores to buy a pound of apples. Any apples would do. Jane returned with three large Bramleys. The apples lay on the counter, the only living fruit in a shop devoted to artificial representations of it.

Lucy talked about apples. As the highest and purest and most magical of fruits. She talked of the golden apples of Greek myth. Of the mystical Avalon, the orchard where King Arthur had passed over. Of Eve.

And of the apple as the mystic heart of Herefordshire. The seventeenth-century diarist, John Evelyn, had written that 'all Herefordshire has become, in a manner, but one entire orchard', praising Lord Scudamore, who had improved and refined the cider apple, developing the famous Redstreak, from which the Ledwardine apple, the Pharisees Red, had been, in turn, created.

'Why's it called that?' Jane asked.

Lucy smiled. When she did that, her cheeks seemed to take on the ruddier colours of the apples on the counter. She was wearing a long, green dress, her hair in this complicated bun. She must have really quite long hair, Jane realized. You could imagine her, in years gone by, striding the land with her hair blowing out parallel to the ground. Listening to the hills breathe. Believing everything was possible. Like some ancient, Celtic enchantress.

Jane was just blown away. Lucy was just, like, *the* coolest person she'd ever met.

'Pay *attention*, Jane!' Lucy snapped.

'Sorry.'

'Now.' Lucy plucked a souvenir penknife from a rack. She selected an apple, laid it on a square of plain wrapping paper. 'I'm going to cut it sideways. Have you ever done this before?'

Jane shook her head and Lucy pushed the point of the knife into the apple and sliced it in half.

'There.' She held out a half in the palm of each hand. 'What do you see?'

Jane leaned over the counter. The green-white pulp was veined with thin green lines and dots which made a kind of wheel.

'Count the spokes,' Lucy said.

'Five.'

'It makes a five-pointed star, you see? Inside a circle. A pentagram.'

'Oh, wow.' Jane had read enough weird books involving pentagrams in her time.

'Forget all this black magic nonsense. The pentagram's a very ancient symbol of purification and of protection. And there's one at the heart of every apple. That says something, doesn't it?'

'That's like really amazing.' She couldn't stop looking at the little green veins. 'Something really ordinary, like an apple.'

'*Nothing* is ordinary! Read Traherne.'

'I'm going to.'

'Least of all the apple,' Lucy said sternly. 'Let no one talk of the humble apple to *me*.'

Jane looked around the shop and saw it with different eyes, like the storybook child, Rosemary, in the park. It was more than a little souvenir shop, it was a shrine. A temple. A temple to the apple.

'You were going to tell me why it was called the Pharisees Red.'

'No, I wasn't,' Lucy said.

'All right, well, I asked you, didn't I?'

'That's not the same thing.'

'*Will* you tell me? Like in the scribes and pharisees, all that stuff?'

'Jane, you're so ill-read.' Lucy came out from behind the counter, pulled down a large, fat, soft-backed book. 'Here, find out for yourself. Page forty-three.'

It was *The Folklore of Herefordshire* by Ella Mary Leather.

'Published in 1912,' Lucy said. 'A formidable work of research and scholarship.'

On page forty-three, Jane found a sub-heading.

> **(5) Fairies.**
> Although there are now but few persons living in Herefordshire who believe in fairies, faith in their existence must have been common enough with the folk of the last generation. All the old people who can tell anything about fairies do not call them fairies at all, but 'farises'; the word is pronounced almost like Pharisees.

'So you see, Jane, nothing too biblical about that.'

'Oh, wow.'

'Don't keep *saying* that. It's most annoying. Of course, people deny today that it's anything to do with fairies, but people always deny fairies because the word itself has become such a term of ridicule.'

Jane looked at the matchstick-limbed, gossamer-winged

things clinging to the rims of cups and plaques, perched on the tops of shelves, the edges of picture frames.

'Nothing like those, Jane, I'm afraid. Those are the traditional forms that everybody knows, and if one is to create an impression of the spirit in nature, that's the one people are normally prepared to accept, even as a joke. If one were to create an effigy of a *real* tree spirit, as they're more often perceived by those able to, the customers would be disturbed and I'd have a reputation as something a good deal worse than a lunatic crone.'

'Tree spirits?'

'For want of a more credible term. Essences, whatever you want to call them. They are, in fact, more perceptible in and around fruit-bearing trees. The female trees. That's why I was so outraged by all this nonsensical talk of the oldest tree in the orchard as the Apple Tree *Man*. Not a feminist thing, simply the way it is.'

'But I still don't understand why the apples were called Farises Red. Were they supposed to belong to the fairies?'

'What you have', said Lucy, 'is a belief in some supernatural intervention in the creation of this particular apple. It's a not-so-rare blending of paganism, as we're forced to call it, and Christianity. The church being, for much of its history, in the very centre of the orchard. Which came first, I wouldn't like to say, though I suspect the orchard. Perhaps there was a pre-Christian shrine where the church now stands, we can't say, we can but speculate.'

'Oh, w—' Jane swallowed. Waited. Lucy detached one of the tiny fairies from a shelf edge, held it up to the light.

'Translucence, you see. That's the essence of it. As fine as air. Spirits of the air. The spirits of the earth, goblins and things, are denser. The tree elves are brown and green. They're the protective and motivating forces in nature. Some of them are of limited intelligence but, like us, they evolve. I find it impossible to explain the phenomenon of life without them.'

'Mum might not be sympathetic.'

Lucy thought for a moment, her lips becoming a tight bud.

After a while she said, 'The great mystery of life can be approached in terms of pure physics – the electronic soup of atoms and particles. And also in religious terms. Terms, that's all it is, Jane. Traherne never speaks of elves or devas, but he refers all the time to angels. Cherubim and seraphim and cupids who pass through the air bringing love. Traherne is full of coded references – we know of his interest in the ancient occult philosophy of Hermes Trismegistus, we know from the writings of John Aubrey that Traherne was psychic. But in those days, as you know, one had to be extremely cautious.'

'Or you ended up like Wil Williams?'

'Precisely, Jane. Williams, we know, was Traherne's protégé as well as his neighbour. I think Wil was a little too incautious in his attempts to walk with the angels.'

Jane said, 'Mum doesn't have much to say about angels. Angels are not cool in today's streetwise Church. I mean . . .'

'Angelic forces correspond to what are called devic presences. The devas are the prime movers, if you like, in the structure. A deva may control a whole area, a whole sphere of activity, or an ecosystem.'

'Like an orchard?' Jane said automatically.

Lucy positively purred with pleasure. 'You're making the leaps. You're receiving help. The channel was opened – you know when.'

'I thought it was just the cider.'

'Oh, the cider's very much a part of it. The cider's the blood of the orchard. It's in your blood now. I felt at once that it had to be one or both of you.'

'Us?'

'You and Merrily.'

'She won't want to know,' Jane said.

*

Jane returned just before six. She said trade had not been exactly brisk, but a nice Brummie couple with a corgi had bought a set of four hand-painted apple-shaped cups and saucers for sixty-four pounds.

'Thank heavens for people with no taste,' Jane said.

Merrily noticed she had with her a copy of the Penguin edition of selected poems and prose by Thomas Traherne.

'You bought that with your wages?'

'Lucy gave it to me. I refused to take any wages. It's fun playing shop.'

'You going to actually read it?'

'Of course I'm going to read it. Traherne's cool.'

'Oh. Right. Should've realized. Why is he cool?'

'Because he could see that we were surrounded by all this beauty, but we didn't appreciate it, and we were quite likely to destroy it. Which was pretty prophetic thinking back in the mid-seventeenth century, when there was no industry and no insecticides and things.'

'Fair enough,' Merrily said.

'And he said we should enjoy the world. Get a buzz out of it. Get high on nature. Like, God wanted us to be happy.'

'Like have parties and things?' Merrily said provocatively.

'You know,' Jane said, 'you kind of make me sick sometimes. You're so smug.'

Merrily said nothing. Oh, dear. One of *those* moods.

And yet – thinking about it – she hadn't been at all sullen or sulky of late. Just distant, more self-contained. As if there was something going on inside her. Which, of course, there would be at her age, all kinds of volatile chemicals sloshing about.

A boy?

Possibly. But why would she hide that? She'd never hidden it in the past. No, this was something to do with Miss Devenish. Twice Jane had disappeared, twice she'd turned up with Lucy Devenish.

But I rather *like* Lucy Devenish.

Merrily lit a cigarette. Should she go and talk to the old girl?

Jane went up to her apartment to work on her Mondrian walls. This apparently involved painting the irregular rectangles between the oak beams in blue, black, red and white. The Listed Buildings inspector would probably come out in the same colours if he ever saw it. Still, as even Merrily wasn't allowed to see it . . .

What the hell . . . Sometimes kids should be allowed – even encouraged – to behave bizarrely. Merrily finished her cigarette then went to put some supper together.

When Jane came down to eat, she dropped the big one.

'I'll probably go to church tomorrow.'

'Sorry?' Merrily turned from the Aga, dropping a slice of hot focaccia in shock. 'What did you just say?'

'I think you heard.'

'All right, flower,' Merrily said calmly, 'you go and lie down, I'll call the doctor.'

'Very funny.'

Jane walked over to the kitchen window. There was a sunset blush on the lawn. Merrily gazed out, a little bewildered, unsure how to handle this development. She'd made a point of never exerting any pressure to get the kid into a service. Admittedly, it would be politic for the minister's daughter to be present at her mother's official installation ceremony with the bishop next Friday, and to persuade Jane to come, she'd planned a small deal – after the service, she could go on to Colette Cassidy's birthday party, no restrictions.

It looked as if no deal would be needed. Who was the influence? Thomas Traherne? Miss Devenish, more like. She should be delighted, but somehow she felt rather offended.

She took in a big breath. 'Jane.'

'Huh?'

'What happened the day you didn't go to school?'

Jane looked at her, almost through her. The dark blue eyes were completely blank. She'd seen eyes like that on kids a year or two older than Jane, up in Liverpool; they were usually on drugs.

Merrily tried not to panic. 'Tell me what happened, Jane.'

'She told you,' Jane said almost wildly. 'Lucy told you.'

'I want to hear it from you.'

'You don't believe me.'

'You haven't told me anything not to believe.'

A shadow seemed to pass between them. She remembered how, as a small child, Jane would conceal small things – an old tennis ball, once, that she'd found in the garden – for fear they would be taken away from her if her mother found out. At the age of ten, she'd got hold of a thick paperback by Jilly Cooper, hiding it under a panel in the floor of her wardrobe like it was real hard porn.

'You're all the same.' The kid's face suddenly crumpled like a tissue. 'You think you know everything.'

'What . . .' Merrily moved towards her. 'What's wrong, flower?'

'You . . .' Jane backed away, something inflamed about her eyes. 'You stand up there in your pulpit, Mrs sodding Holier-than-thou, and you drivel on about the Virgin Birth and the Holy bloody Ghost, the same stuff, over and over and over again, and—'

'Jane? What's all this about?'

'What's the fucking use? I don't think I'll bother with any supper. I'll just go to bed.'

'You're not making a word of sense, do you know that? What's brought this on? Can we talk about it?'

Jane just stamped past her, gripping the copy of Traherne.

*

It must be . . . what? Three a.m.?

The alarm clock ticking, very loud in the big bedroom with hardly any furniture. The clock – an old-fashioned one with twin bells, none of your cell-battery bleepers in this house – set for five-thirty because there was Holy Communion at eight. Only about half a dozen people last week, mainly pensioners, including Uncle Ted out of familial loyalty.

She thought about Jane, then, and her mind flooded with anxiety. Once again, the kid had a secret she was afraid might be taken away from her. This time it would not be so innocuous.

She drifted away again, with the ticking of the alarm clock. A night breeze ruffled the trees. And the sounds overhead. Footsteps. Very soft. Bare feet, slithering.

Merrily was icily awake.

The room – one pine wardrobe, one small table, one bed – was grey-washed by the moon behind clouds like smoke. She lifted up an arm, and that also was grey, as though her skin was transparent and her body was filled with moon gases which made it very light, and so she didn't even remember getting out of bed and moving to the door. *I'm dreaming*, she told herself. *This is a dream*. But she didn't wake up.

Outside were the doors, concealing mournful, derelict rooms that would never be filled. Rooms where even the memories were stale. She was alone on the first floor of Ledwardine Vicarage. A bathroom, a toilet and four bedrooms, only one slept in. She was alone on this level, while Jane paced overhead, angrily painting her walls by night. Was this part of her secret? Was the secret simply that she had to have secrets, a private life?

Merrily shivered; it would soon be summer and the nighthouse was November-cold.

The nighthouse. A different place, a colder place.

The noises overhead had stopped. Well, all right, if Jane wanted to paint in the night, that was up to her. It was the weekend; she could keep her own hours in her own apartment. Merrily, on the other hand, needed her sleep if she was going to be up and bathed and breakfasted in time for Holy Communion.

She found herself standing by the stairs, a hand on the oak rail, a foot on the first step to the third storey. She looked up quickly and thought she saw a light glowing, and then she turned away, took a step back. It was Jane's storey, Jane's apartment, none of her business. But in the moment she turned away, she felt an aching sense of impending loss.

She would go back to bed, try for two more hours' sleep. She turned to her door and realized she didn't know which it was.

She trembled, hugged herself, arms bubbled with goosebumps. Doors. Moonlight turning their brass knobs into silver balls. She lunged at the nearest, grabbed it, turned it. Stumbled in with her eyes closed, slammed the door behind her. In dreams, you could make as much noise as you liked. *When I open my eyes, I'll awaken in my own bed. It will be nearly morning.*

Cold moonlight soaked an empty room, a room she hardly

recognized, been inside it no more than a couple of times. A long, narrow room, uncarpeted, its floorboards black and bumpy and ending in a long and leaded window, unseasonally running with condensation.

A figure stood by the window, its back to her.

'Jane? What are you doing down here?'

There was a vibration in the room, running like a mouse along the floorboard from the window to where she stood; she could feel it through the soles of her bare feet, and it ran up the backs of her legs, under her nightdress to her spine.

It wasn't Jane.

She backed up to the door, her fingers feeling behind her for the knob and gripping it and turning it. The brass knob turned and turned again, but the door did not open.

Merrily turned it harder and faster, in a panic now. The figure at the window began to shift, and she saw the head in profile and the face was a man's.

The knob loosened, began to spin in the lock until it just came out in her hand in the very instant that the figure turned from the window to face her, and it needed no moon, it carried its own pale light.

'Oh, please,' Merrily whispered. 'Please, not here.'

Sean glided towards her. He could not speak for the blood in his mouth.

*

Jane didn't make it to church after all. There was no explanation. After the morning service, two parishioners commented on there being only two hymns, and Uncle Ted had told Merrily she wasn't looking at all well. It must have been a wearing few weeks, getting used to everything and now moving into a new house. She ought to think about having a few days away. Perhaps after her installation service, when she felt more secure, more bound to the parish.

Merrily asked, in a steady voice, if her predecessor, Alf Hayden, would be at the service. There were some things she wanted to ask him. About the vicarage.

'Ah, yes,' Ted said. 'Alf.'

No, he said, Alf would not be coming, as he was rather unwilling to embarrass his successor at this difficult time.

'I don't understand.'

'This is difficult,' Ted said. 'Alf's received a letter signed by a number of parishioners urging him to use his influence to keep Richard Coffey's play out of the village.'

She was dismayed. 'Why've they written to *him*?'

Ted cleared his throat, embarrassed. 'Well, they, ah . . . because they don't feel they know you well enough yet to approach you on such a . . . contentious issue.'

'And because they think that as a trendy woman priest, I'm bound to support it! Is that right? Which of my parishioners are we talking about here, Ted?'

'It's causing considerable anxiety in certain areas,' Ted said. 'It's only a few people, of course.'

'But influential people, right? I suppose they know the bishop's supporting Coffey?'

'I shall attempt to acquaint the bishop with the way local opinion seems to be moving,' Ted said, 'during a dinner party to which I understand we are both invited.'

Merrily was beginning to be aware of the levels of local society she was unlikely to penetrate. Even if she wanted to. She found she was shaking with anger. It was marginally more acceptable than fear.

*

When she got home, Jane wasn't there. This was no surprise.

She searched her conscience, as a parent. Then, as a parent, she walked up two flights to Jane's apartment. Stood outside the doors on the third floor.

Went into Jane's bedroom, where she found the bed neatly made and clothes neatly on hangers in the wardrobe. The copy of the collected poems of Thomas Traherne was on the floor beside the bed, opened spine-up. She turned it over. It was open to a poem entitled 'The Vision', which began,

> *Flight is but the preparative: the sight*
> *Is deep and infinite.*

She put the book down where she'd found it, went out and closed the door. The next door was to the so-called sitting-room/study, where Jane had been painting the Mondrian walls.

It was locked. She turned away, not entirely surprised, and went down the stairs to the first floor. A weak sun sent half-hearted beams through the landing window and through the oak balusters.

Merrily went into her own room to change into a skirt and jumper. The thought struck her that Jane, on the third floor, had risen above her. As if the third floor represented something Merrily couldn't reach. She was on the halfway floor with her anxieties and trepidations, her earthly ties, her clinging past, her sick dreams of Sean.

She came out of the bedroom and, instead of going directly to the stairs, turned left, trying to remember which had been the door in her dream. The passage didn't look the same at all. She opened a door at random, into a square, bare room with two small, irregular windows. Would they ever be familiar, these rooms? She tried another. The bathroom, of course. God, this was so stupid. You couldn't control your dreams, but you must never give into them, let yourself be ruled by a runaway subconscious. Angrily, almost absently, she threw open another door.

Found herself in a long, narrow room with black bumpy floorboards and a long, leaded window.

It all came back at her then. The vague, sun-stroked morning was kicked aside by jagged memories of the night. She couldn't stand it. With a tiny cry, she sprang back out of the room, pulling the door behind her.

As it slammed shut, she heard the handle fall out on the other side.

Hysterical Women

Much of the time, over the next week, Jane was fine.

She'd do nice things, like get up early, have Merrily's breakfast made. Bring her a mug of tea when she was working on the admin stuff or her piece for the parish mag. Be very pleasant to the parishioners and church wardens who turned up in the middle of *Friends* or something. Be sympathetic when Merrily got letters like,

Dear Mrs Watkins,

As you may have noticed, my wife is an excellent singer who used to perform regularly at concerts. Sadly, the village concert as we used to know it is no longer a part of community life and as church is her only opportunity to exercise her undoubted vocal talents in public, both my wife and I have been dismayed by the recent unexplained reduction in the number of hymns at our Sunday services. I trust this is only a temporary aberration and that we can expect a return to the three or four hymns we were used to during the ministry of the Reverend Hayden . . .

'Don't back down,' Jane said, efficiently clearing away the breakfast things. 'From what I've heard, old Hayden only had lots of hymns so there'd be less for him to do. His sermons were notoriously crap, apparently.'

'And who've you heard that from, flower?'

'Oh, you know . . . people.'

'Miss Devenish?'

'People.'

'I see. Jane, what do you think of *modern* hymns?'

'They're still hymns, aren't they? People don't actually *think* about them. It's like being at primary school. Like that alternative prayer book. It's not really alternative at all, is it? You might as well stick to the old one, it's more . . .'

'Resonant?'

'Yeah. How far have you got with that idea for getting the punters to talk back?'

'I'm kind of working up to it. I don't know. Maybe I'd just be doing an Alf Hayden because I'm insecure about preaching and can't accept that my views can be more significant than theirs.'

'But you're the middleman, Mum. God speaks through you.'

'You don't have to be sarcastic.'

'I'm not sure I was,' Jane said.

Merrily had not told her about the six letters she'd received, four of them anonymous, urging her to not on any account allow the church to be used for the performance of a play variously described as 'blasphemous', 'satanic', 'obscene' and, most amusingly, 'typical of a man who writes plays for Channel Four'.

*

On Wednesday, her mother phoned from Cheltenham to say she'd developed flu and seemed unlikely to make it to this induction service or whatever it was called.

Oh, sure. Nothing to do with her finding the idea of Merrily being a priest a little embarrassing. *I just don't*

understand. We've never had one of those *in the family before.
I mean, you never showed any interest in religion as a child.*

She'd never been able to talk in any kind of depth to her
mother, and she never saw her father, who'd moved to
Canada after the divorce. Oh yes, had a few of those in the
family, haven't we, Mummy?

'I gather Ted will be involved in this installation business,'
her mother said. 'I suppose he'll look after you.'

**Service for the licensing and installation of
THE REVEREND MERRILY WATKINS
as Priest-in-Charge of the parish of Ledwardine.
7.30 pm.**

ALL WELCOME.

'Expect a full house,' Ted said when he turned up with the
printed leaflets. 'We haven't had one of these for over thirty
years . . . and a woman, too. You'll enjoy it. You'll sparkle, I
know you will.'

Merrily rubbed tired eyes. 'How about if I just smoulder?'

Ted smiled. 'By the way, was it something important you
wanted to ask Alf? Because the old bugger won't be coming.
He's in the Algarve. Timeshare villa.'

'Easier to maintain than this place.' Merrily noticed that
the kitchen's smallest window had been reduced, by a ramp-
ant Russian vine, to the size of one of those arrow-slits you
found in castles.

'Ah,' Ted said. 'It's this house, isn't it? You really
shouldn't have to tire yourself out trying to make the place
habitable.' He paused. 'Look, I've been making a few enquir-
ies. If you can hang on for a year, I think we'll be able to
find you something more manageable. Plans've gone in for a

small development down by the Hereford road. Executive housing, aimed at the kind of people who'd eat at Cassidy's, so he won't be objecting, for once.'

Merrily said carefully, 'Was Alf Hayden glad to get away?'

'He was glad to *retire*. Even more time for golf and fishing. I don't know about get away from the village.'

'I meant from this house.'

'Well, it was different for him, as I say, with that big family. He always seemed fond of this pile, even if he didn't take care of it.'

'He actually found it a good . . . atmosphere?'

'Atmosphere?' The lawyer's eyes narrowing in the florid farmer's face.

Drop it, Merrily thought. Let it go.

'Sorry.' She carried his cup and saucer to the sink. 'It's just a bit dreary, that's all.'

'You'll brighten it up. And Jane. How's her apartment coming along?'

'I don't really know. She's keeping it under wraps.'

Jane had bought her own paints and brushes to do her Mondrian thing. Coming out once to meet Merrily halfway up the second stairs, arms spread wide. 'No – stay out. You'll only say I'm making a mess.' Knowing her mum was far too honourable to sneak up there while she was at school.

Separate lives. My God, Merrily thought, we're starting to lead separate lives, meeting at mealtimes like hotel guests.

*

On Thursday night, the night before the installation service, she was awoken by a sound from above.

A single, tentative footstep. As though someone was testing the floor, to be sure the boards were firm between the joists. Like one of those ball-bearings in a gaming machine, the sound must have been rolling around her head for an inordinately long time.

Wake up. Come on. Don't rise to this. Wake up *now*.

Because she wasn't really awake at all, was she? Every time something like this happened, she dreamed she was waking up and she got out of bed . . . and there were always more doors than there really were in that passage. Doors which should never be opened. Doors to the past. The image of Sean formed again behind her eyes. Sean turning from the window, eyes full of blood, hands feeling the air like the hands of someone newly blind. Merrily remembered shrinking back against the door, knowing that if his hands had found her, he wouldn't let go and he would always be in that room. She couldn't remember getting out of there, only awakening, in this bed, in her terror, to the morning.

Merrily opened one eye, with some difficulty. It had been a sticky, sucking sleep, like treacle. She pulled her head from the pillow, looking for the window. A strange, terracotta moon hung low and sultry between the trees. She sat up, blinking. Pushed her hands through her hair. It was damp with sweat. Her nightdress was pasted to her skin. There was a tightness around her chest.

Another footfall. And then another, closer. And then a flurry of them before two final, emphatic steps, like someone taking up a position directly over her bed.

And then silence. *What the hell's she doing up there?*

*

'No. I slept really well, thank you. Didn't get up once.' Wrapped in her yellow towelling robe, Jane spread sunflower marg on crispbread. 'I don't get up in the night unless I'm ill, you know that. What time was this?'

'I don't know.' Merrily carried bread to the toaster; she

didn't want any toast, just a night's sleep. 'After midnight, before dawn.'

'Oh, Mum, do you remember me *ever* getting up in the night?'

'Well yes, as a matter of fact, the first night we spent here you got up to go to the loo.'

'I didn't.'

'Jane, I'm trying to be patient. You did.'

'No, I said I wanted to go when I first got into the sleeping bag, and you said forget about it, it'll go away and so I did and it did.'

'You got up in the night, flower,' Merrily said through her teeth. 'You wanted me to go with you. You were tugging on my hand.'

'Bloody hell!' Jane threw down the butter knife. 'Where do you get this crap from? You were dreaming, for God's sake! All right. Look. I should've told you. I was throwing this wild party last night. Yeah, we had this all-night binge with masses of booze and hard drugs. I'd've invited you, but I knew you wanted a good night's sleep before your initiation ceremony. Christ, Mother!'

'So you're saying you didn't hear anything at all last night,' Merrily said in a small voice, bent over the toaster, her back to Jane. There was a dull ache far behind her eyes.

Jane made a clicking noise, beyond exasperation. 'I sleep, as you used to keep pointing out, the sleep of the innocent. Perhaps it was a ghost.'

Merrily dropped hot toast.

Jane grinned slyly. 'Place is old enough. Yeah, bound to have ghosts. Maybe you should do an exorcism. We have the book, we have the candles, don't know about the bell, would a bicycle bell do? Hey, did you have, like, mock-hauntings at college to practise your technique?'

'We didn't do exorcism. The only ghost that ever got a mention was the Holy Ghost.'

'I can't believe it. They didn't teach you anything useful at that college, did they?' Jane crunched her crispbread thoughtfully. 'Er, do you think it's *him*?'

'What?' Merrily shovelled her toast on to a plate and brought it to the table. She didn't want to talk about this any more. One of them was going a little mad. What did it mean when half your night seemed to be spent in some ungodly no man's land between reality and dreams? How could you be suffocated by a house this big?

'Wil.' Jane smiled wistfully.

'Don't be silly.'

'Hey, if I'd known I could've invited him to my party. There's no decent totty in Ledwardine these days.'

'All *right*. Let it go. And talking of parties, will you be coming to mine?'

'The initiation? That's what you call a party, is it?'

'I know, very sad. But the Cassidys are laying on a buffet afterwards in the church itself. Should be over by about half-nine or ten. But perhaps you could slip away, get changed and drift over to Colette's thing, up in the restaurant?'

Jane met her eyes. The kid could always recognize a deal.

'What makes you think I want to go to Colette's party?'

'Don't you?'

Jane shrugged. 'What time would I have to be home?'

Merrily shrugged.

'Really?'

'I trust you to be careful. And to remember that *you're* not sixteen yet.'

'So don't get shagged is what you mean.'

Merrily held the kid's brazen gaze. 'Something like that.'

261

'Well. Like I said – ' Jane smiled ruefully, looking suddenly and disturbingly older ' – there's no worthwhile totty around here these days, is there?'

*

When Jane had left for school, Merrily sat for a while, staring at the cold, uneaten toast, and then she dragged the phone over to the table.

An admission of defeat, but what could she do? Jane, as usual, had touched a nerve. Merrily tapped out the college number from memory.

'Is it possible to speak to Dr Campbell?'

The switchboard said David Campbell was on the phone; Merrily said she'd wait. David was the only one of her old tutors she figured would be any help. He was a liberal, but he'd also been High Church in his time, an incense-burner.

We didn't do exorcism. The only ghost that ever got a mention was the Holy Ghost.

She felt more than a little stupid about this. Once, in Liverpool, one of her prozzies had asked Merrily what she could do about her flat, which was haunted. The flat had been supplied by the woman's pimp, who owned the building; Merrily had interpreted this as a cry for help, found her a room in a shelter, but she'd gone back to the flat and the pimp after a week, never made contact again.

'Putting you through,' the switchboard said.

'Merrily Watkins! How are you, love?'

'Hello, David.'

'Installation day, right?'

'Tonight. How did you know?'

'Word gets around. You won't mind if I don't come, I hate bloody parishes, as you know.'

'I remember. David, are you alone?'

'One always hopes not.'

He meant God. Merrily pondered the get-out option: asking him about some aspect of installation-night protocol. But she let the silence hang too long.

'What's the problem, love?' David said quietly.

'OK. I think ... Oh, Jesus, it sounds so—' Her head thumping away.

'Go on.'

'All right. I think my vicarage is haunted, and I don't know how to handle that.'

David said, 'I see.' She imagined him in his office, his metal-stemmed pipe sticking out of the pen-pot on the desk.

'I'm glad you see,' she said, 'because I don't. According to my Uncle Ted, churchwarden and oracle, the last incumbent had no problems in that department. And that was over about thirty-five years.'

'What makes you think it's haunted?'

Was she imagining a shift in his voice, a reserve setting in?

'Oh,' she said, 'usual stuff. Or what I understand is usual. Footsteps in the night. Seeing things that ... that can't be there. It isn't imagination, although the experiences do seem to be interwoven with dreams. What I mean ... some of it happens in actual dreams – sometimes I think I'm awake when I'm really dreaming and maybe the other way around, too. And I ... Look, I know what you're thinking, and I *have* been overworking a bit and things have been very fraught, what with living out of a pub and then moving into an old house that's far too big and ... What?'

'Hold on. Steady.'

'I'm perfectly steady. I mean, this morning, my daughter's saying to me, didn't they teach you how to do an exorcism in college, and I have to say no, we didn't even touch on it. Why didn't we touch on it, David?'

'How *is* Jane?'

'She's fine.'

'She'd be . . . what? Fourteen?'

'Fifteen. What are you saying? That most poltergeist activity is caused by adolescent children? That it's Jane who's doing it?'

'I'm not qualified to say anything.'

'But why?' Merrily demanded. 'Why *didn't* we go into this stuff? We're supposed to be at the cutting edge, aren't we? We're supposed to be dealing with the supernatural on a day-to-day basis, and yet we never talked about ghosts.'

'True,' David said. 'We never once discussed the area of parapsychology, and perhaps we should have, if only to examine the demarcation lines.'

'You've lost me.'

'All right . . .' She envisaged him shifting in his old captain's chair, leaning an elbow on the cushion over an arm, establishing a position. 'Let me say, first of all, that I accept entirely that certain unexplained events occur. All the time.'

'So you're not saying I'm nuts.'

'Certainly not. There's far too much evidence. What I am saying, however – and I say it as a question to which I don't really have an answer – is, do these phenomena really fit inside our field of operation?'

'Good or evil, they're spiritual matters.'

'But are they? Are we not simply talking about, say, forms of energy, which are, as yet, unknown to science? Yes, certainly, this sphere of activity was absolutely central to the work of the medieval Church. Much of what priests were up to in those days would constitute what we now dismiss as magic; illusion. They'd find it expedient to produce the odd miracle out of their back pockets to maintain their . . . what you might call their street cred. What we know to be perfectly natural electrical phenomena would, then, have been seen as the work of either God or Satan. Yes, I do believe in haunted houses.'

'But you think – let me get this right – you think there's a scientific explanation that has nothing to do with religion and therefore nothing to do with us. So all the official diocesan exorcists are just remnants of the Middle Ages.'

'Dangerous ground, here, Merrily. Yes, some clergy feel drawn to that kind of work. But even they are increasingly seeing what they do as a form of psychology. The Church is guarded about ghosts and demons and alleged appearances of the Mother of God as damp stains in kitchen walls, and rightly so in my view. But that doesn't mean there isn't something happening.'

Dangerous ground indeed, Merrily thought. How far was he from saying that one day science would explain God, and then they'd all be redundant?

'So you think I should see a scientist. Or a shrink.'

'Certainly not.'

'Or take Jane to one?'

David Campbell sighed. 'You're a sensible person, Merrily. That's why you're in a responsible position.'

'Even though I'm a woman.'

'It's still sensitive,' David said. Now there was an unmistakable coldness in his voice.

'You're saying I should keep my mouth shut,' Merrily said. 'Or I'll have the diocesan chauvinists twittering to the bishop – told you what happens when you let hysterical women take over. That sort of thing.'

'I think you should give it a few more weeks. It isn't . . . harmful in any way, is it?'

She thought of Sean peering and groping through the mist of blood. The dream-Sean. That definitely was a dream. Wasn't it? The phone felt slippery in her hand.

'And I wouldn't have thought,' David said, 'that after all the emotional traumas you've come through, you would find these minor paranormal fluctuations at all frightening.'

'No.' She paused to bring her voice down. 'Oh no.'

'You say you don't know how to handle it, as if there's a secret technique we didn't bother to tell you about. There isn't, I'm afraid. Sorry, love, but you have to search your own faith, your own belief system. Look, call me again in a week or two, if it's still worrying you.'

But he was telling her not to. He was telling her that, as far as the Church was concerned, she was on her own.

Tears

She hauled her headache off to the church. Was it because she didn't like being alone in the vicarage? Because the even older church, with its tombs and the fractured skulls grinning up at you from stone flags, was actually homelier?

Frightened? Frightened of a *paranormal fluctuation*? Frightened for her daughter's emotional condition, her own mental state? The Priest-in-Charge? God's handmaiden? Good God, no. Perish the thought.

Her head felt like a foundry; she'd never ring David Campbell or anyone else at that bloody college again.

She gripped the cold ring-handle of the door into the porch. Pausing there, as she tended to these days. If Dermot Child was slowly undressing her for the benefit of the bell-ringers she didn't want to be a captive audience. She opened the church door just a crack. Through it echoed a torn and stricken howl.

'. . . you!'

She stopped, head pulsing.

'. . . you, Liza Howells . . . the night you came to me with your bruises, your torn lip, mouth smashed and teeth gone . . . that night your husband beat you for your dalliance with Joseph Pritchard . . .'

Her first thought was that this was something to do with the pageant the Women's Institute was organizing for the festival, a parade of Ledwardine society through the ages.

'OK.' Footsteps. 'Leave it there a minute.'

But this voice she'd heard before. Martin Creighton, the theatre director.

'So, OK, if we had this Liza sitting somewhere in the middle, and she's wearing . . . what?'

'A fairly simple black dress.' Mira Wickham, the designer. 'Nothing obvious until she's on her feet. It's important that the members of the audience sitting all around her don't realize she isn't one of them until she starts to react.'

Merrily walked in, stood by the Norman font.

'In fact, you know, I think what would be really good', Mira said, 'is if Liza and one or two of the others have been chatting to people – in character – before the lights go down. A merging of present-day villagers with their ancestors. So that it seems to several people that they know Liza and the others as individuals. And this communicates itself. We get a blur. A timeslip.'

'Spooky,' Creighton said. 'But that only works if you have real locals in the audience every night.'

'So we offer free seats to regular churchgoers. Let the vicar sort that out.'

'You might find it just a bit more complicated than that,' Merrily said, and there was silence.

Stefan Alder spotted her from the pulpit. 'Oh . . . Hi!' He bounded down, loped along the aisle, grabbed her hand. 'You're . . . Merrily Watkins, right?'

'Mr Alder.'

Creighton and Wickham came to stand either side of him. They looked uncomfortable.

'Look,' Creighton said. 'I hope you don't think we're being presumptuous. Obviously, we've got to plan as if the thing is going to happen here, but if you say no . . .' He wiped the air, both hands flat. 'That's it. We'll understand.'

'And where would you go then?'

'Oh.' Stefan Alder flicked back his ash-blond fringe. 'I'm sure the bishop would fix Richard up with something. Although, personally, if we couldn't do it here I'd be inclined to knock it on the head. You see—'

Creighton was glaring at him.

'—no, really, Martin, I want to be up-front about this whole thing. It was my idea after all. I . . . Look, are you doing anything absolutely vital, Merrily? I mean, can we talk about this? The two of us?'

*

Really succulent totty, Jane had described him once, being provocative. Maybe this was what she saw when she thought of Wil Williams. It was understandable. In a cream-coloured sweat-top and light blue jeans, he looked as fresh and innocent as Richard Coffey seemed seasoned and corrupt. He looked like the singer with one of those boy bands Jane claimed she'd grown out of.

Down past the last of the graves, where the church bordered the orchard on one side and the vicarage garden on the other, there was an apple tree in the hedge.

'It could have been this one,' Stefan said. 'Well, I mean, obviously not this particular tree, but its ancestor. I was talking to your Mr Parry, and he said this particular spot could well have been orchard in Wil's time. You notice how all the graves at this end are relatively modern, showing where they had to extend the churchyard.'

It was true. There was even a grave of black marble, put in before the conservationists got them banned.

'Couldn't be this particular tree, though, could it?'

Merrily said. 'According to the legend, no actual apples would ever grow over the place where he lay.'

Whereas the tree in the hedge was heavily talcumed with blossom.

'They would say that, though, wouldn't they? All these stories are supposed to have an eerie postscript.' Stefan plucked off a sprig. 'I remember the first time I came here I'd read an account of it and I'd thought, you know, Poor sod. There was no emotional involvement at that stage, not until I actually came here. I just thought what a bloody shame. I mean, even if he *was* a witch . . . damaging an apple crop? Really!'

'Perhaps, if it had gone to court, it would've been thrown out. That was happening, increasingly. It's my understanding that, by 1670, people were getting a bit wise to all these witchcraft accusations. You had a neighbour you couldn't get on with, you'd just accuse him of making your prize bull impotent or something.'

'You're right. There had to be more. They wanted him dead, otherwise what was the point?'

'They wanted him dead because he was gay?'

'Thomas Bull wanted him dead. And James Bull-Davies knows that.'

His eyes, the colour of his jeans, were shining with a very innocent kind of fervour. He looked on the edge of tears. He looked too frail and vulnerable to be living with someone as coldly manipulative as Richard Coffey. But that was none of her business.

They walked to the churchyard wall – yes, this part was newer, some of the stone wasn't even local – and stood leaning against it, looking back at the church whose stones, if they could speak, would be able to answer all their questions.

'Let's look at it objectively,' Merrily said. 'You're saying,

I think, that because Bull was a puritan he'd be absolutely shattered to discover his parish priest was homosexual. Now I can't quite remember what percentage of today's Anglican ministers are gay, but it's a substantial one, and if they all got fired a few hundred churches would have to close overnight. Now, how different was it then, in a country area where people's attitude to all matters sexual would have been . . . well . . . tolerant. Down-to-earth, shall we say?'

'Look, I don't know . . .' He fingered his fringe. 'I don't know where *you* stand. As a woman.'

'For what it's worth,' Merrily said, 'I think gays have always been drawn to the priesthood because it's something they do rather well. It being a job that often calls for feminine qualities. I suppose, as we weren't allowed in for so long, gay men have helped to hold it all together. They've given the Church a breadth of compassion without which it might not even have survived. That make any sense?'

Stefan Alder stepped back, striking an unselfconsciously camp pose, with one hand on a hip. She was sure she'd seen him before, not just in the village. Must have been on television, maybe a victim in *The Bill* or a casualty in *Casualty*.

'That's beautiful.' He smiled radiantly and handed her the sprig of apple blossom. 'That's a really beautiful thing to say, you know? I feel I can trust you now, I really do.'

'Oh, well . . . It was just Richard seemed to think I was prejudiced in some way. And I'm not. That's all.'

'Look,' he said. 'Look, I want to explain to you . . . At first – I mean, he's committed to it, it's his project – but at first, Richard was only doing this for me. He wasn't especially struck by the story, or the village. We were having a few days' break and Richard was half-looking for a holiday cottage, and we spent a night at the Black Swan. After dinner, he was tired, and he had a headache, so he went up to bed and I sat in the lounge with some coffee, idly reading some local guidebooks. It seemed odd, coming across a mention of Ledwardine Church and looking up and seeing the steeple through the lounge window. And then I saw a brief mention of Wil . . . I mean, I'd read the story but I hadn't remembered the name of the village and it was such a shock realizing I was sitting just a short walk away from where he . . . died. The next thing I knew, I was just sort of . . . here.'

He looked very ethereal against the apple trees which themselves, with their heavy blossom, were like the ghosts of trees. It was a cloudy morning, a fine spring drizzle beginning.

'It's incredible in autumn, isn't it?' Stefan said. 'The air around Hereford is so full of apple scent. It seems in the evening as if the whole county's heavy and drunk on it. And even though this orchard was looking rather sad and neglected, I felt the way it was, back then. Huge and bountiful. The absolute core of the county. The very centre of what Traherne called the Orb.'

Merrily remembered, with an unsettling feeling, what Gomer Parry had said about the Apple Tree Man. So gnarled and barren-looking in the ice, now full of thrusting buds.

'I just knew that Wil, even if he'd had the power, would never destroy an orchard,' Stefan said. 'Not the biggest orchard in Hereford. It would be like poisoning the country. More than that, it . . . I mean, he was a friend of Traherne. Nature was an aspect of God. It would have been blasphemy. He wasn't a witch at all. I suddenly felt very, *very* close to him. He was in the air, in the scent, the whole apple-aura of this place. And then . . .'

He was close to whispering. Merrily was still holding the sprig of blossom he'd given her. She was aware of being set up, dropped into a little cameo scene, but the snowy numinescence had settled on her senses; she was softened.

'I could suddenly see him. I could see that poor, perse-cuted boy hanging here. All alone. All alone among the apple trees. It was spring then, like today. I could see the blossom which had fallen on his hair like stars . . .'

There were big, theatrical tears in his eyes now, but it didn't seem like a performance; she didn't feel, somehow, that he was that good an actor. Did he really think he'd seen Wil hanging here or was he describing an exercise in imagina-tion? Perhaps it didn't matter.

'Merrily, it was the most spiritual moment of my life. I just knew I'd been brought here. Just me. But why me? Who was I? Was I him? Had I been him in a previous life? No.' He shook his head. 'You don't fall in love with yourself, do you? Not like that.'

God. She didn't know how she felt about this at all.

'I just knew in that moment what Wil was. Why *I* had to be here. To be near to him. To convey the truth about him. That it could be the most important thing I would ever do. I couldn't sleep, I was tortured. I awoke early, walked all around the village – there was nothing for sale. Not a single For Sale sign. And then I saw the lodge, empty and derelict-looking and I just knew that whatever it cost . . .'

He stopped speaking, looking for some reaction.

Merrily said, 'Did Richard know why you were so anxious to live here?'

'Oh yes,' Stefan said. 'If you've seen some of Richard's plays you'll know he's fascinated by obsession. I suppose, at that time, I'd become sort of . . . his. Obsession. So he bought the lodge.'

At a price. Merrily could hear James Bull-Davies. *Made him pay. Made him* pay.

'I have to play him,' Stefan Alder said very quietly. 'I have to feel him inside me – in the purest sense. I mean, I have to *be* Wil. I have to *be Wil here*. You do understand that, don't you, Merrily?'

*

After they parted, Merrily walked around the churchyard for some time, alone.

Decision time?

Well, he was a nice guy, an honest guy. But he was in love with a dead man, with a ghost, and there'd been a certain madness in those tear-glazed eyes.

Coffey? He was in love with Stefan. He'd bought a house in the village because of it. But he hated the vendor, Bull-Davies; he had a score to settle there and he would use Stefan's desire.

Coffey and Bull-Davies were both, in their separate ways, powerful and influential men. Stefan Alder was neither and so was vulnerable. But he was also the catalyst.

Merrily sighed and thought back to her famous Wil Williams sermon.

Collect all the information you can get, listen to all the arguments.

Yes, done that.

Seek out independent people who might have an opinion or a point of view you hadn't thought about.

Nobody here is entirely independent. Not Lucy Devenish, nor Alison Kinnersley. They each have their own hidden agenda.

So why not put it all on Him? That's what He's there for. Go into a quiet place . . .

'Yes. I'm here.'

In a cushion of soft, white petals.

Put that question. Tell Him it's urgent. Tell Him you'd like an answer as quickly as possible.

'I wouldn't mind an answer now, actually. If that's all right with You.'

She looked up to where the church steeple was fingering Heaven. Focusing on the gilded weathercock on top of the steeple as if it could point her in the right direction.

Perhaps only the weathercock had changed since Williams's day. The steeples and towers were still the tallest structures in the countryside. The churches were powerful places.

Merrily bit her lip. Was this the answer? Freedom of expression was one thing, multiple obsession and the taint of necrophilia something else?

You let obsession into a church at your peril?

*

When she went back into the building, the theatricals had gone, replaced by Uncle Ted, Caroline Cassidy and her restaurant manager, Barry Bloom. They were setting up tables in the space behind the pews.

'I really don't know about this,' Ted was saying. 'It *is* a church.'

'Oh, but the very name of the cider, Ted!' Caroline sang. 'And if as many people as you say turn up, they'll get about half a paper cupful each. Ah, Merrily! Merrily will decide.'

'Thanks a lot,' Merrily said without thinking. 'What is it this time?'

Ted and Caroline both stared at her. Oh God.

'Sorry. I'm a bit on edge. Big night.'

'Coffee, Vicar?' Barry Bloom said. He was squat, wide-shouldered, frizz-haired. Ex-SAS, it was rumoured, like, for some reason, quite a few people in the catering business around Hereford. Barry already had a coffee machine set up next to the font.

'Oh, thanks. Caffeine. Wonderful.' She hadn't had any breakfast, wasn't likely to get any lunch. She was dying for a smoke, but maybe not. 'So, what's the problem?'

'Well, as you know,' Caroline said, 'the Ledwardine festival officially opens on Saturday.'

'Does it? God.' Wrapping her hands around the hot, polystyrene coffee cup. This meant she'd be expected to announce her decision about the play.

Caroline said, 'The idea is we open in a small way, with a ceremony in the square in the afternoon – Terrence has hired a town-crier. We'll hold some of the lesser events and exhibitions in the first weeks, and then gradually build up to the major concerts and the pl— and whatever else we arrange. But, you see, my dear, we wanted, before the opening, to introduce our new cider, produced by the Powells to their old recipe – with a little help from Barry, of course . . .'

'I just organized the bottles,' Barry said. 'I gather they had to get in some extra apples to supplement the Pharisees Reds. The orchard wasn't over-productive last year. Hadn't been pruned hardly in years. Be a good crop this year, though, by the looks of it.'

'We have an absolutely terrific label,' Caroline said, 'designed by the young man at Marches Media on his computers. It has a drawing of the church on it – Alfred approved that, before he left.'

'How many bottles?' Merrily asked.

'How many, Barry, three hundred?'

'Nearer five.'

'It's going to be frightfully exclusive and rather expensive. Proper champagne bottles, naturally. There was a time when good cider was valued higher than champagne, and this is an *awfully* good cider, isn't it, Barry? *Not* the kind of beverage likely to be on sale to the village louts at the Ox. So we wondered if we might use the occasion of your induction . . .'

'Installation.'

'Makes you sound rather like a household appliance, my dear.' Caroline squeezed Merrily's arm. 'No, we wondered if we might uncork the first bottle at your reception.'

'And give everyone a drink?'

'Perhaps just a teensy one. The cider, you see – this was Dermot Child's idea – will have an ecclesiastical connection, because the church was itself once in the very centre of the orchard, wasn't it? And the name we chose – I gather this originated from—'

'Lucy Devenish,' said Barry.

'Quite.' Caroline tossed him a disapproving glance. 'I *was* going to say the poet Traherne.'

'The poet Traherne, via Miss Devenish,' Barry said stolidly. 'Being as none of us were that conversant with his work. It comes from a prayer Traherne's supposed to have written with a woman over at Kington, but nobody's quite certain about that.'

'Well,' Merrily said. 'It sounds fair enough to me. As you've probably gathered, I'm trying to make the church less formal, more accessible, and while it might be a bit early to set up an actual bar, with beer pumps and optics and things—'

Caroline tittered shrilly.

'—I can't see any problem over a few glasses of cider. Do you want me to kind of bless the stuff or something?'

Caroline looked thrilled. 'Would that be in order?'

'I don't know, really. Ted?'

Didn't know why she was asking him. She was, after all, entirely on her own.

'Merrily,' Ted said, 'in his time, Alf Hayden blessed

everything from tractors to the microwave oven in the village hall.'

Didn't seem to be a problem, then, even if the mention of Dermot Child in connection with cider had sent a bad ripple down her spine.

'OK then,' she said. 'What's it called?'

'The cider?' Barry Bloom said. 'The Wine of Angels. You like that?'

'That's Traherne?'

'The line goes "Tears are the Wine of Angels and the Delight of God, which falling from . . ." what is it, Mrs Cassidy? The whole verse is printed on a label on the back.'

'Something about them being, sweet, precious and whole-some.'

'That's the bit. "Sweet, precious and wholesome . . . and delicious indeed." And then there's a bit of a duff line about them being the best water works to quench the Devil's Fires, but we've stopped it before that. Sweet, precious and whole-some and delicious indeed. You couldn't get an ad agency to do a better one than that, could you, Vicar?'

'But, I mean, he wasn't actually talking about cider, he was talking about tears.'

'Well . . .' Barry spread his hands. 'If it ends in tears, at least we can all get drunk.'

*

Leaving the church, Merrily met James Bull-Davies coming in.

'Ah. Mrs Watkins.'

As if the meeting was a surprise.

It was the first time they'd been face-to-face since the exchange in the vicarage kitchen.

'Look.' Bull-Davies shuffled slightly. 'Glad I caught you.

Fact of the matter is . . . bit of a pig the other night. Tried to pressure you. Wrong of me. Want to apologize.'

Merrily said nothing. She walked out of the porch. He followed her into the churchyard.

'Gets on top of one, the old family heritage thing. Narrows the outlook. Can't focus. Sorry.'

'So.' Merrily stopped before the first grave, turned to look up at him. 'You've had a think about it.'

His eyes narrowed.

'And perhaps come to the conclusion that the idea of your family's stature being toppled by a polemical play with an axe to grind about gay rights is something of an overreaction?'

His long face began to redden. He had not, of course, concluded any such thing.

'Anyway,' Merrily said, 'on the question of the church being used, I've come to a decision, and I'll probably slip it in when I say a few words at the reception tonight, OK?'

The silence lasted all of three seconds. Merrily didn't move.

'You have made a decision,' Bull-Davies said heavily.

'Yeah. Just this afternoon, actually.'

He scowled. 'Heard you'd been talking to the actor. Alder.'

'Sure. We had a chat.'

She wondered how he knew, who his informant was. Or perhaps he'd seen them himself.

'Suppose he won you over. Cried on your shoulder.'

'We had a private conversation.'

'I don't cry myself,' James Bull-Davies said.

'Well,' Merrily said, 'real men don't, do they?'

'You're mocking me.'

Merrily thought about him in the vicarage kitchen. *You make it hard for me, Mrs Watkins. And perhaps for yourself.*

She thought of the funeral card delivered to the Black Swan – *Wil Williams was the Devil's Minister*. She thought her decision was the right decision, but, by God, some people were making it bloody hard and all her human reactions were still urging her to go the other way.

But she had to say something. So she thought what Jane would say and said that.

'You know, James, you really are a sad bastard.'

He blinked.

'I gave it a lot of thought. And the only decision that seemed ethically and spiritually right, in the end, was to offer Richard Coffey and Stefan Alder the village hall for their play. If that's all right with the parish council.'

'Oh,' he said.

'I'm not going to explain how I decided. But I can say it had nothing to do with anything you said about the need to protect your illustrious family. And in fact . . .'

She went right up to him. Looked up, a full foot, into his narrow, autocrat's face.

'. . . if you ever . . . *ever* . . . try to put the arm on me again, over anything – anything at all – I'll . . . I'll have your balls.'

She stepped back. There was no reaction on James Bull-Davies's face, but his back stiffened and she saw his feet come instinctively together. His eyes were focused over her right shoulder.

'Understood,' he said.

TWENTY-TWO

I, Merrily . . .

The first person Jane saw when she got off the school bus was Colette, wearing her leather jacket and a black chiffon scarf. She was with a black guy, maybe in his thirties, unloading some gear from a dirty, white Transit van.

Unfortunately, Dean Wall and Danny Gittoes and a couple of their mates had spotted them too.

'I'm telling you, it *is*,' Danny Gittoes said. 'I seen him in Shrewsbury. He looks different, nat'rally, with all the stuff on.'

'Yeah, yeah,' Dean said. 'Mr Cosmopolitan. You hear that, men? Gittoes's been to Shrewsbury. Hang on, I'll find out. I'll ask the slag.'

It was a dull afternoon, a slow drizzle starting. Dean Wall waddled across the square to Colette, Jane following at an angle.

'Party then, is it?' Dean trying to peer into the van.

Colette didn't look at him. 'Might be.'

'This a mate o' yours?'

Dean looked down at the black guy, who was short and lithe, wore a black T-shirt and white leather trousers, Dean looking like a Land Rover next to a Porsche.

Colette still didn't look at him.

'This is Dr Samedi,' she said.

'No shit,' Dean said, reluctantly awed.

Dr Samedi lifted a big, square vinyl case out of the van and pushed it into Dean's barrel stomach.

'Carry dis into de restaurant fuh me, mon?' Dr Samedi said.

'Right,' Dean said. 'Sure.'

'Don' drop it.'

Danny Gittoes had arched over, with his big, stupid grin, and Dr Samedi allowed him to carry an even bigger black vinyl case into Cassidy's Country Kitchen.

'Seen you in Shrewsbury last year,' Danny called over his shoulder. 'Shit hot. Man.'

'Up de stairs,' Dr Samedi said. 'Leave 'im by de restaurant door. An' no peakin'.'

When they'd gone, Colette looked at Jane and shook her head and grinned. 'This is Jeff. Jeff, this is Janey. Her mother's a priest.'

'Brilliant. Yow bringing her along, too?' His accent was now closer to Kidderminster than Kingston, Jamaica.

'I don't somehow think so,' Jane said. 'Er . . . you *are* Dr Samedi?'

He fixed lazy eyes on Jane's. He growled, a low, seismic rumble.

'*Long night, moonbright, burnin' on a low light, everythin' you wearin', honey, just a liddle too tight . . .*'

'Oh, wow,' Jane said, impressed. She'd always found rap and drum 'n bass stuff quite tedious after a while, but the idea of it happening in Ledwardine was something else.

'*. . . and de drummin' begin, feel de drummin' inside, fingers dancin', dancin', dancin' up an' down yo' spine . . .*'

Jeff killed the rap, yawned and stretched. 'Excuse me, ladies, I better go make sure them sheep-shaggers don't put that gear the wrong way up.'

Colette watched the little guy sashay towards the glass doors. 'Isn't he just like magnetic?'

'I guess.'

'He will blow you away, Janey. I promise. Heavy magic.'

'Seems a bit cheeky, getting Wall and Gittoes to carry all the stuff in when they aren't invited,' Jane said. 'I mean, you know, cool. But . . .'

'I want them like really desperate to get in.' Colette lightly tongued her upper lip. 'And all their mates. I want them wetting themselves to be in there.'

Jane looked at her. There was this perverse side to Colette she didn't quite understand.

'They might cause trouble.'

'Mmm-hmm,' Colette agreed. 'They just might. If they can find their balls.'

'You *want* that?'

'Sure.'

'I don't understand.'

'Oh, Janey . . .' Colette sighed in despair. 'When they *do* get in, I want them to feel like gatecrashers. Unwanted. Resentful, you know? My dipshit parents have naturally gone over the guest list, so we have a lot of *nice* boys from *good* families, that kind of thing, plus a few like Lloyd Powell on account of his old man's a *councillor*. I mean, you tell me, where is the tension in that?'

'Tension?'

'A party,' Colette said with heavy patience. 'Ain't a party. Without tension.'

*

The evening was still and heavy with the scent of apple blossom, which clung to the orchard trees like hoar frost. Made Lol shudder as he got out of the rusting Astra in the drive.

As he let himself into the cottage, the phone began to ring, and his spirits collapsed like a card-house. It's Lucy, he thought. Something's wrong.

Around his trainers, on the doormat, he saw a pale confetti.

On the mat *inside*. Oh Jesus, oh Jesus. Examining the soles of his shoes to make sure he hadn't brought them in himself. The orchard was coming in on him. There'd be petals all over the carpets, on the table, over the bed, in the bath. *Jesus.* Calling out, in his panic, to the stern, unforgiving God of his parents, collecting the usual stab of guilt – he'd once, aged sixteen, dropped a cup washing up and muttered *Jesus Christ*, and his mother had slapped his face with some ferocity, wouldn't speak to him for two days.

The phone kept on ringing and Lol kept staring at the petals on the mat.

Maybe they just came in through the cat door. Maybe Ethel brought them in. That was it: Ethel had been hunting in the orchard and returned with her fur full of apple blossom. That made sense, didn't it?

The phone went on ringing. Who would know he was back, except Lucy?

Lucy. Who had sent him away after the thing with Jane Watkins. Seeing at once that he was in no fit state to go back to the cottage. *Go off somewhere for a few days. I'll feed the cat. Go to a city. Somewhere not like this, do you understand, Laurence? We'll talk when you return. When you're in a more receptive state.*

In Oxford, over four days, he hadn't even seen Gary Kennedy. Just walked the touristy streets and the parks and gardens and the riverside, dipping into bookshops and record shops and pubs.

And reading Thomas Traherne and getting as much sleep as he could take and reading more Traherne – the poet who'd found the whole universe in the fields and woods and hills within a few miles of Lol's cottage and was completely knocked out by everything he experienced out there.

He has drowned our understanding in a multitude of wonders. Lucy had underlined this in his copy of Traherne's *Centuries*, and written in pencil in the margin. *Just because it's something you can't explain, it doesn't have to be bad. It doesn't have to be ominous. It might just be wonderful.*

But the old strength, the conviction, had been missing. It was a worried Lucy who'd waved him off in the rusting Astra. When he'd come down from the loft and said this was a nightmare she hadn't contradicted him. It had a fuzzy dreamlike quality when it happened, when he saw Jane Watkins lying in the orchard, but the implications were nightmarish.

The living-room door was always left ajar for Ethel, and when Lol went in, she was weaving in and out of his ankles. He picked her up and she purred into his chest as he grabbed the phone.

'Hello?'

'You little fuck.' The rasp distorting in the earpiece. 'What you trying to do to me?'

Karl Windling, the *old* Karl Windling sounding cracklingly close. He'd spoken to Dennis; it had made him angry. Lol felt cold sweat on his forehead. Windling could be at the Black Swan. He could be in his car, in the lane.

'Don't shit me, son. Do *not* shit me.'

Lol said, 'Where are you?'

'Close enough. Now you fucking stay there. You understand? You go anywhere, I'll find you. You don't move the rest of the night. I'm coming over. I'll have a nice, simple contract with me. Which you are signing, son. You won't—'

Very gently, Lol put down the phone. Thought for a moment then unplugged the wire from the wall. Went to the window: just the Astra in the drive. And blossom in the orchard.

He carried Ethel into the kitchen where he put out a bowl

of wet food, a bowl of dry food and more water. He got out the litter tray, filled it and laid it by the door. He stroked the little black cat and put her down.

Not knowing how long he would have to be away before Karl Windling gave up.

*

When the kid walked in, Merrily was at the kitchen table with a pot of tea and an ashtray full of butts.

Jane dumped her schoolbag. 'You have to be at the church by seven, don't you?'

'Yeah,' Merrily said glumly. 'Sure do.'

Jane sat down opposite her. 'Second thoughts? Bit late for that, isn't it?

Merrily lit another cigarette. When Jane was away at school, she couldn't wait for the kid to come back. Fooling herself that her daughter was entirely on her wavelength. But looking at her now . . . there was a distance. In her eyes. This was not paranoia, not isolation. Whether she knew it herself or not, part of Jane was somewhere else.

'I had a chat with Stefan Alder today.'

'Cool,' Jane said non-committally. Even a couple of weeks ago, her eyes would have lit up and she'd have wanted to know all about it because, even if he *was* gay, Stefan was really heavy-duty totty.

'He was telling me about the play and how they came up with—'

Merrily paused. She'd have to explain this sometime, because there was going to be a fuss about it, but she wondered if Jane was really mature enough to understand.

She put down her cigarette. 'It's because of Stefan that Richard Coffey wrote the play. Stefan's gay, right? Stefan's a homosexual.'

'I do know what gay means,' Jane said sullenly. 'And I

know they think Wil Williams was persecuted because of that. Even if he wasn't.'

'Right.' Merrily was encouraged by the last bit. 'Stefan is . . . I don't know if his relationship with Coffey's going through a bad patch or if he only stays with Coffey because of his career—'

'That's a bit cynical.'

'I said I don't *know*, Jane. What I do know, what I strongly *feel*, is that Stefan Alder believes that he's been – I don't want to use the word possessed, because he didn't use it – chosen, by the spirit of Wil Williams, to recreate the circumstances of his death, to reveal the truth.'

'Wow,' Jane said.

'It's become an obsession.'

'Yeah.'

'Stefan's in love with . . . a ghost.'

'It's a bit beautiful, isn't it?' Jane said.

'No! It isn't beautiful! It's unnatural and it's dangerous, and Coffey's only going along with it because he's a very warped individual. And I think it would be very wrong for me to let it happen in the church.'

'What?'

Merrily picked up the cigarette and drew on it. 'I'm going to suggest they put it on in the village hall. I'll tell everybody tonight. I thought I'd tell you first.'

'You can't,' Jane said.

'I have to, flower.'

'Jesus!' Jane stood up; the chair clattered to the floor behind her. 'You sad cow. And I really thought you were smart.'

*

Lol drove twice around the village, looking for somewhere discreet to park the Astra. There were far more cars in the village than usual; the square was packed, a few dozen people walking about. Something on in the church?

Arriving at the square a second time, he panicked – suppose Karl's car appeared in the mirror, a car which could go twice as fast, driven by a man ten times as hungry. He swung down Church Street and left the Astra by the kerb, at the bottom end, near the Ox, getting out and crossing to the shadowed side of the street.

Lucy Devenish lived in the middle of a small black and white terrace halfway up Church Street, doors opening to the street. He had reservations about going there for sanctuary. Visions of Windling finding out, busting in drunk, smashing things. But what could he do? No other options. He slid across the road, lifted the small, brass goblin knocker and rapped twice. It sounded very loud in the street, too loud.

No answer. Shit, what if Windling was to drive past now? He rapped again. Please, Lucy.

She wasn't in. It occurred to him that, whatever was happening in the church, she might be there. He ran back across the road, sweating now. On the noticeboard was a small poster.

Service for the licensing and installation of
THE REVEREND MERRILY WATKINS
as Priest-in-Charge of the Parish of Ledwardine.

And a couple of dozen cars on the square. Yeah, Lucy would be in there, along with anybody who was anybody. Including – he spotted a familiar old blue Land Rover – James Bull-Davies. He stood on the cobbles staring at the Land Rover, recognizing the repairs in the canvas, each one stitched into his mind from the day it had been parked outside the cottage with all of Alison's stuff inside.

**. . . at 7.30 p.m. followed by refreshments in the church, courtesy of Cassidy's Country Kitchen.
ALL WELCOME.**

Should he go in there and try to attract her attention. Hadn't been inside a church since his mother's funeral. The thought of it created a ball of cold in his stomach. Ominous. Wouldn't help his state of mind going into a church, especially tonight. Besides, James Bull-Davies would be in there, and probably Alison.

No. Not Alison.

A small tremor went through him. Bull-Davies and Alison rarely appeared in the village together. Bull-Davies, with his sense of what was proper, would never bring her to church.

Lol looked up at the church clock. It was not yet seven-fifteen. How long did these things take? Couple of hours, at least.

Chances were, Alison would be alone at Upper Hall.

*

She felt completely wrong. She felt overdressed and under-qualified for the white surplice and the clerical scarf and the academic hood from theological college.

She should have been barefoot, in sackcloth. She was here to serve, and she wasn't up to it. She was going to be a disaster. She looked out at all the pious, formal faces, fronting for the inveterate village gossips who'd always known she wasn't going to fit in.

She'd fasted, at least – if unintentionally. A whole day on tea and coffee and cigs. Her head felt like it was somewhere in the rafters. She didn't much care.

The bishop was ritually explaining a few basics to the congregation, as if they needed to know.

'The Church of England is part of the One, Holy Catholic

289

and Apostolic Church worshipping the one true God –
Father, Son and Holy Spirit. It professes the faith uniquely
revealed in the Holy Scriptures and set forth in the catholic
creeds, which faith the Church is called upon to proclaim
afresh in each generation.'

The word *generation* making her think at once of her
daughter.

Oh, Jane.

The kid had stalked out and Merrily had sat there for
another twenty minutes and smoked another two cigarettes.
Was she being weak, uncool, pathetic? Even *homophobic*, for
heaven's sake, in spite of everything she'd said to Stefan Alder?
And now Jane – even if, with her famous sense of honour, she
wouldn't tell anyone why – would boycott the service.

And then, just as Merrily was rising wearily from the table
to go and change into her vestments, Jane had appeared in
the kitchen doorway, dressed demurely in a high-necked
jumper and skirt. *I said I'd go and I'll go, Mother. I'll go on
my own. I'll see you afterwards.*

A long time afterwards. They'd agreed that the kid would
leave after the service, come back and change into her party
gear, all laid out, presumably, in her bedroom, in her apartment, her separate life.

Meanwhile, in public, Jane would do the honourable
thing, play the dutiful daughter. Oh God.

Half an hour later, while making her lonely, sorrowful,
self-conscious way to the church, the fake Barbour flung over
her clerical finery, Merrily had met Lucy Devenish. Or rather
Lucy had blocked her path, just short of the lych-gate, the
poncho spread wide like a bullfighter's blanket.

'I was hoping, Merrily,' she'd said without preamble, 'that
you would have come to me. But it's not too late. We have
to talk, you and I.'

'Oh, you really think we should talk, do you, Miss Devenish? That's you and me rather than you and Jane.'

'You're angry.'

'Just sad.'

'My fault. I was arrogant, as usual. I truly thought that you would come to me.'

'You said we'd quarrel,' Merrily reminded her.

'Pshaw!' – she'd actually produced that archaic sound – 'A ploy. A challenge to which I was sure you'd rise. I suppose you've been too busy. But we can't put it off. I need your help. The village needs your help. And, of course, your daughter.'

Merrily had glared at the old bat for presuming to know what her own daughter needed.

'Meanwhile, all I would say to you tonight – directly, a personal plea – is that you should announce, without delay, your decision to permit this man Coffey to stage his play in the church. Do it now. Do it tonight. Believe me, it will clear the air and alter the focus and make your life so much less complicated.'

Merrily had felt the smoke beginning to rise between her ears. She'd made herself take a long breath before reacting, even though about a dozen parishioners were converging on them.

'Miss Devenish, I don't have time to discuss this right now, but you can take it that I will not be announcing my decision to let Coffey's play go ahead in the church. Not tonight, not any night.'

Fury and anxiety nudging each other as she went in to make her vows to the bishop and to God and to blessed Ledwardine.

*

'Oh shit,' Alison said.

Standing just inside the crumbling Georgian doorway, mistress of the house.

He'd come on foot, figuring that if she saw his car wheezing up the drive, she just wouldn't answer the door. He'd followed, with some trepidation, the route Alison took in the mornings on her horse, the old bridleway alongside the orchard. Trying not to look at the apple trees, but the image of Jane Watkins going in and out of focus in his head, the smell of spring orchard powerfully everywhere and full of a mustiness that made him think of old sepia photographs.

The bridleway had come out near a pair of huge stone gateposts topped with the blurred stumps of what might once have been lions or eagles. He'd let his anger propel him between them. It had been a long time coming, this anger, and it felt strange and cumbersome, like a stiff, new overcoat. He knew he'd always been one of life's accepters. Like when Alison had walked out, he'd accepted it must be his fault, there must some deficiency in his character, his sexual ability, his social behaviour . . .

Well, all right, there was, he knew that for a fact, he was screwed up, and yet . . .

'Don't do this to me, Lol,' Alison said, expressionless. Echoing Karl Windling. It was always *him* doing it to *them*.

Lol looked over his shoulder, down the hill to where the spire sprang up between the trees with the big red sun almost on its tip, like a needle about to burst a balloon. Like he wanted to burst the smug bubble around Alison.

'Figured the colonel'd be in church, doing his squire bit. I thought this would be a good time.'

'Lol,' Alison said gently. 'The good times are over.'

She looked dramatically sultry in black silk trousers, a black shirt open to the unexpected freckles between her breasts. After all this time he wanted her very badly and that made him angry and sad and . . .

'Don't I even get to come in?'

'I don't think that's very wise, do you?'

This was where he was supposed to lose his temper, break down, start asking her if Bull-Davies had a much bigger dick, that kind of hysteria.

'When I saw his Land Rover on the square, I thought maybe I could go into the church, sit next to him, ask him a few things.'

'That would have been embarrassing for you both.'

'But only one of us would have anything to lose.'

Alison started to close the door. He put his foot in it. Knowing this rarely worked, that if she wanted to, with a door this size, she could probably just break his ankle. It would depend on whether she wanted to hurt him any more.

She drew the door back, for momentum. He left his puny trainer in the gap.

'Fuck you.' Alison let the door fall open and walked away into the house, and he followed her.

*

The bishop said, 'In the declaration that you are about to make, will you affirm your loyalty . . .'

When they'd met before the service, the bishop had enthused about Richard Coffey's exciting plans. A parish church should be a Happening Environment, the bishop said. He was so glad that this beautiful, vibrant village, so full of creative people, should have a priest who was young and energetic and sensitive and, yes, dare he say it . . .?

Female.

It's still sensitive, David Campbell, at the college, had said. Sensitive. James Bull-Davies was out there, alone in his family pew. James, who had said he would support her *so long as you remain sensitive to the best interests of this village.*

She hadn't said a word to the bishop about Bull-Davies's threat. It didn't matter now. Bull-Davies had sworn allegiance, would be her friend for life. Coffey and Alder – and maybe the bishop himself – her enemies.

She felt dangerously light-headed. She should have eaten. She shouldn't have drunk so much coffee.

The bishop intoned, '. . . in bringing the grace and truth of Christ to this generation and making him known to those in your care?'

A question? Oh God, it must be her bit now. *I Merrily Rose Watkins do so affirm and accordingly declare my belief . . .*

The bishop waited, the bright red evening sun burnishing his high forehead and the apple in the hand of Eve in the great, west-facing stained-glass window, the one so often reproduced on postcards. A congregation of over a hundred men, women and children waiting for their new minister to speak. In a woman's voice.

Her face lifted slowly to the light. In the vivid sunset, the sandstone walls looked redder than she'd ever known them. The red of arterial blood. The red of hellfire. The red of the Pharisees Red, the traditional cider apple of Ledwardine, the Village in the Orchard.

They waited. The congregation . . . the bishop . . .

. . . God.

And Merrily shivered as, for wild, glowing moments, the walls of the church seemed to curve together, the pews warping, the congregation coalescing, faces blending into pink pulp.

As the church itself became a swelling apple, and she found she was caressing it in her hands, and its rigid stalk was the steeple, and she heard a roaring in her head and tumbled away from it, losing all sense of where she was or why.

. . . an acidic smell. Breath on her face.

'Merrily?'

The bishop leaning over her, disturbed at her silence. A heavy, very earthly, pragmatic presence, the bishop: the Administrator, the Chief Executive. She could hear his breathing, faintly puffy, smell his vaguely vinegary breath. Her own body felt very light, as though she could raise her arms in her surplice and float away like a bat among the cobwebbed, oaken rafters.

I'm sorry. She couldn't even say that.

Someone coughed. She saw the congregation below her. Caroline Cassidy in her light blue jersey suit, the sun putting a sheen on Terrence's pointed head. At the other end of the pew, Richard Coffey – here because of the bishop, his supporter – and Stefan Alder. A respectable distance between them and the Cassidys, but the fact that they were on the same pew showing how the battle lines had been drawn.

Stefan's eyes were shining, reflecting some erotic Wil Williams fantasy and the conviction that the priest was on his side.

But you couldn't trust a woman could you? He'd be there at the reception afterwards, with his glass of the Wine of Angels. How was she going to face him? What was she going to say to him?

I, Merrily . . .

Come *on.* She'd learned all the replies, practised them, testing herself, but the words wouldn't come and a part of her didn't care, because they wouldn't, Oh God, be coming from the heart.

Why not? And did it matter?

She heard whispers washing through the congregation. A

spreading awareness of something wrong. And it was her. *She* was wrong. The Reverend Merrily Rose Watkins. A mistake. They were all realizing their terrible mistake. She saw Jane for the first time, right at the back, on the end of the pew, gripping the prayer-book shelf. White-knuckled. You could sense the tension in that grip.

A tension, too, under Merrily's arms, a friction on the skin, a burning sensation and then that sudden tightening around the chest, as though someone had grabbed her from behind, grasping both breasts, squeezing and pulling them back into her ribcage. She thought of Child, felt physically sick, rocked backwards, all the breath forced out of her.

She saw James Bull-Davies's left arm stretched along the back of the pew, no concern on his face. Priests came, priests went; the rock on which this church was founded had *Bull* inscribed upon it.

She saw Jane, half out of her pew now.

I, Merrily . . .

But the priest could not move. Her chest was as tight and rigid as a wooden board.

A shockingly cold thrill passed from pew to pew. *The vicar can't go through with it!*

The priest saw Eve in the window, holding out the apple to her. The apple which she knew instinctively was a Pharisees Red.

No.

Try. Try to speak. Draw a breath. Let it out. *I . . .*

'I . . . Merrily Rose Watkins, do so affirm and acc—'

The breath caught in her throat like phlegm. The dregs of her voice drifted away into an empty church.

The pressure was abruptly released from her chest. She swayed, taking rapid, shallow breaths. She looked around.

She was on her own. The bishop was gone, the congregation had vanished. The church was empty. The soaring red walls had faded. There were no colours in the windows. The air was chill.

Something crawled, on hands and knees, up the aisle towards her. It was naked, pale and stark as a cold candle.

Her mouth opened as it slid towards her, its head bowed, its body racked and twisted. Its anguish crawled into Merrily's raw and empty stomach and unravelled a dark ribbon of bile. She tried to scream but her throat filled up.

*

The congregation rose in horror as the priest-in-charge fell forward into her own thin vomit.

TWENTY-THREE

Black-eyed Dog II

Almost sulkily, Alison said, 'It really isn't complicated. I give him what he needs, he gives me what I want.'

She was sprawled in an ancient, shapeless chintzy chair, stretching out her legs, inspecting her bare toes. Finding them more interesting than Lol.

The room was lofty and colourless, with a high, tiled fireplace, and no way could he believe this was what she wanted.

None of it sounded right. He'd sat here nearly an hour and she'd talked, and it was all superficial crap. How she'd always had this fantasy of living in the country since she was a kid in Swindon and helped out at this riding school. How she'd thought that, when she and Lol got here, meaningful things to do would suggest themselves: ways of making money, finding fulfilment. But when you were living, as they had, in a little cottage with a little garden you might just as well be in some suburban villa. Whereas this, *this* was the real thing. Country life as it was meant to be lived.

What she was saying was profound like *Hello!* magazine was profound. For once, Lol couldn't let himself accept it.

'Hang on . . .' He moved to the corner of a sagging settee, leaned towards her. '. . . You chose the cottage. You said it was perfect.'

'So I was wrong. It was small, it was shut-in. It was worse than the city. Nothing suggested itself.'

'Except Bull-Davies, apparently.'

Alison still didn't look at him.

'Look,' she said, 'that may not be precisely what you think, OK?'

'What do you think I think?'

The sun was sinking below the sills of the deep Georgian windows, the room fading to dusty sepia.

'Well,' she said. 'I imagine you're hurt. Wounded. You think I never really cared for you. That I just used you until someone more interesting came along.'

Took the words out of his head. It was still killing him to think she might have been this superficial all along.

'I really didn't want you to get hurt, Lol. I wanted you to be, you know . . . angry. As in hating me. I didn't want any of this honourable, shaking hands, let's-still-be-friends shit.'

He stared at her.

'I mean, that was the very last thing you needed. Aggression. You needed aggression. Bitterness. You were never bitter. I couldn't understand that. Why were you never bitter? Dumped by your family, messed around by the system . . . Where was the resentment? I wanted you to hate me, rather than . . . I mean I couldn't bear to see you just crawling away and crying into the bloody cat.'

'How do you know I did that?'

It was not too dark to see her looking pained. He remembered how, when people started smirking at him in the shops, he thought it was because he was this really obvious townie and maybe he needed to wear a flat cap, buy a beat-up truck. Grow sideburns below the jawline.

She curled her toes at him in exasperation.

'Somebody really should have told you. I put on a hell of a show for Miss Devenish at that Twelfth Night thing. Poor

James was dreadfully embarrassed. And even she didn't take you on one side. Jesus. Little harmless-looking guy like you and nobody has the consideration or even the bottle to tell him his woman's screwing around.'

Lol winced. 'Little harmless guy. Thirty-seven years old and the best I ever managed was Little Harmless Guy.'

'And endearingly messed up. Women love men to be messed up. I really was going to sort you out. But, you know, you get a . . . an opportunity . . . you have to take it. I didn't imagine it was going to come so quickly. I'm sorry.'

He felt cold. There were no visible central-heating radiators and although paper and logs were built up in the dog grate, she hadn't attempted to light them. The message here, at least, was clear.

'For what it's worth,' Alison said, 'it was that day I went into the village and got a puncture. James was parking his Land Rover on the square. He changed the wheel for me, I said I'd buy him a drink, so we went across to the Black Swan. We talked. For ages. At one point, I said I liked riding, and he said he had horses, didn't know why he kept them on. Just that the family always had, for hunting and things. James hates to let go of a tradition. That's sort of admirable, isn't it?'

'From what I heard,' Lol said, 'his father seems to have kept horses so there'd always be a steady supply of stable girls.'

There was a heartbeat's silence.

'Where'd you hear that?' Her voice stayed casual, he couldn't see her expression, but he was sure he saw her toes tense.

'A friend mentioned it.'

'Lol, you only have one friend. What exactly did Devenish say about the old man?'

'Does it matter? He's dead, isn't he?'

'Humour me.'

'You'll just tell bloody James.'

'James . . .' Alison said in a measured kind of way '. . . is the last person I'll tell.'

'She said disregard for the finer feelings of women was a family trait. Lucy had a friend who was one of the stable girls. Patricia somebody?'

The windows lit up.

'Shit,' Alison said.

Land Rover lights.

'Get your head down,' Alison said.

Lol didn't move. 'But she did suggest James was different,' he said, more out of fairness to Lucy than consideration for Bull-Davies. 'On account of having a conscience. Like he was the first in the family to have one, and he ought to get out of this house before—'

'What the hell's he doing back? He said it'd be at least half-ten.'

Maybe this was meant, Lol thought. Face-to-face in a cold triangle.

'Listen,' Alison hissed. 'He finds you here, he'll kill you. Listen to me. He'll come in the back way, so *listen* . . . Wait in the hall until you hear his key and then leave quietly by the front door. Just pull it to behind you.'

'And there was me,' Lol murmured, 'getting all hyped up for a fight.'

'Go!' Alison was on her feet. 'Piss off!'

He stood up, disoriented in the gloom.

'Please.' Alison's eyes glowing urgently.

'All right.'

In the hall, he stood next to a coat stand smelling of Barbour-wax and manure. He heard a key jingling in a distant lock, but he didn't move.

'Utterly unbelievable,' Bull-Davies bawled.

'Darling?' Her voice was pitched up the social scale. 'Are you OK?'

'Silly bloody bitch *threw up*! In the damn church!'

'Who did?'

'Ten minutes into the service, loses her bloody lunch. I ask you, does a real priest *ever* lose control of himself like that? I've seen Hayden in that pulpit with streaming eyes, two boxes of Kleenex for Men . . .'

'James, what *are* you talking about?'

'The damn *vicar*. Physically sick in front of half the village. Perhaps they'll realize their mistake when we get a notice outside the church saying All Services Postponed due to Menstrual fucking Cycle.'

Lol hung on, half-fascinated. Alison was a committed feminist; if he'd said half of that she'd be into his throat.

'Well, darling,' Alison said soothingly, 'you did tell them, didn't you?'

Lol let himself out. Stumbled down the steep drive, between the broken gateposts, the last of the sunset spread out before him like a long beach, the church spire a lighthouse without a light. Nothing left that seemed real.

*

They'd brought her into the vestry. She must have fainted. There was a couch in there and they'd laid her on it and someone had put a rug over her. Faces came into focus, like a surgical team around an operating table, stern and concerned and . . . triumphant?

She must have passed out again and when she came round she didn't remember whose faces those had been.

'Stressed out, I'd say,' Dr Kent Asprey said. 'Overworked, neglecting herself. Mrs Watkins? Can you hear me? Merrily?'

'I'm so sorry,' Merrily whispered. 'I don't know what . . . Is the bishop . . .?'

'He's out there taking charge,' Uncle Ted said. 'Don't worry about that.'

'Where's Jane?'

'I'm here, Mum.' Kid hanging back, sounding scared.

'Oh God.' A white, naked figure, pale as veined marble still crawled amongst her wildly flickering thoughts. 'What have I done?'

'You were taken ill,' Uncle Ted said. She sensed a reserve in his voice. Not the churchwarden, now, but the old, wary lawyer.

The pale figure was inside her now, like a white worm. She tasted bile, sat up at once, clutching at her throat. Someone had removed her dog collar.

She hadn't completed her vows.

In the church, organ chords swelled. Pause. Singing began.

Haven't made my vows!

'All right, Merrily,' Dr Kent Asprey said. 'Just relax.'

'I've got to go back. I haven't made—'

'Someone's going to bring you a cup of tea, and then you're going home.'

'No . . . Please . . .' The thought of going back to the huge, empty, haunted vicarage suddenly terrified her. 'This is my home.'

'Just relax,' Asprey said.

'What am I going to do? What am I going to *do*?'

'You're going home to bed and I'm going to come and see you in the morning.'

She stared at him, all crinkly eyed and caring, the stupid, fatuous sod.

'Just get a good night's sleep, Merrily.'

In Ledwardine vicarage? She wanted to laugh in his face. To scream in his face. To scream and scream.

Scream herself sick.

*

The small shadow became detached from the hedge in Blackberry Lane. Lol thought it was a rat, until it rolled on to his shoe.

When he bent down, it produced a tiny cry.

He went down on his knees, but when he touched her she hissed and slashed at him and rolled over and tried to stand up and couldn't. He felt wet in his fingers. Blood.

'Oh God.'

He'd left her shut in the kitchen, with food and water and a full litter tray. Hadn't he?

She squealed when he picked her up and when he tucked her under his jacket he could feel her trembling. When he reached the gate and heard the music, she was purring, but he knew there were two kinds of purr and one was a sign of pain.

All the lights were on in the cottage. He saw the front downstairs window had been thrown open, and the music shivered out into the lane, the late Nick Drake singing 'Black-eyed Dog', the death song, the stereo cranked up beyond distortion level, fracturing the already tight, brittle splinters of guitar.

He could see Karl Windling's wide-shouldered silhouette in the chair under the open window. Facing into the room. Facing the open kitchen door.

Nick sang that there was a black-eyed dog calling at his door and it was calling for more. It called for more and it knew his name. Nick's voice was cut up and broken by the volume. Under Lol's jacket, Ethel, the little black cat, quaked with pain. Beyond the kitchen door there was cat-litter all over the carpet, fragments of food dish.

In a high, scared, doomed voice, Nick Drake, at twenty-six, sang that he was growing old and he wanted to go home.

There was apple blossom all over the lawn, and the white petals were huge now. The song ended and Karl Windling's shadow filled the window for a moment before the stylus was ripped across the record with a jagged whizz of puckered vinyl.

Lol saw that the white petals on the lawn were the torn and scattered pages of a book. He bent and picked one up and held it into the light from the window.

. . . to love all persons in all ages, all angels, all worlds, is divine and heavenly . . . To love all . . .

The house invaded, the book torn down the spine, the album ruined, the cat kicked half to death. Lol's life smashed and the fragments scattered.

And there was me, getting all hyped up for a fight.

Karl would be well-stoned by now; that was his style – a satisfying surge of violence and then a nice, fat joint to make it feel doubly all right. Lol thought, I should go straight in there – it's my house, for Christ's sake, my own home – and . . . and . . .

I wanted you to hate, Alison had said, not half an hour ago.

But Karl knew Lol Robinson from way back. Knew he didn't fight and lacked the nerve to hate. Knew that Lol's speciality was fear.

All the lights on, the window open. Karl Windling standing in the centre of the room now, staring directly at the window, but he couldn't see Lol in the darkness. Karl's bearded face unsmiling.

Lol glanced at the empty drive, wondering for a second

what Karl had done to the Astra before remembering he'd parked it in the village.

Under his jacket, Ethel had gone still.

He heard his own thin whimper on the air, as he turned and walked away from his home into the darkness of Blackberry Lane.

*

She felt like some child molester leaving court.

As the remaining congregation sang, watched over by the bishop, Merrily Watkins was escorted from the church wrapped in the rug, surrounded by Kent Asprey and Uncle Ted and Jane and Caroline Cassidy and Councillor Garrod Powell, their bodies hiding hers.

Hiding her from the eyes of villagers who'd left the congregation before the bishop had restored order but were still bunched in the darkness, like sightseers on the scene of a fatal road accident.

'En't a good sign,' an old woman whispered too loudly.

Across the square, Merrily saw the softly illuminated hanging sign of the Black Swan, a beacon of stability in what was turning into an alien world. They'd been happy there. Now she was cold and confused and frightened and she didn't know why, and none of the people with her said a word, not even Jane; it was like a funeral procession.

They took her into the vicarage. Ted still had keys, as if he'd known she was only on probation and it might not work out.

'I'll make some tea.' Caroline Cassidy looked with distaste around the grim kitchen, still partly lit by unshaded, underpowered bulbs. 'Where's your kettle, my dear?'

'No,' Jane said. 'I'll do it.'

'Look.' Merrily struggled to keep her voice level. 'You've

306

done so much already and I've ruined it, but if you leave now you can still go ahead with your cider launch.'

'Merrily, I wouldn't dream—'

'Yes, you would. You have to. Village life goes on. Anyway, I'd be less embarrassed if I thought it wasn't all a total disaster.'

'Well, if you're sure . . .'

'Yes.' She sat down at the table. 'All of you. Please.'

'You go to bed.' Dr Kent Asprey gave her a shrewdly caring look. 'I'll call tomorrow.'

'I'll call you,' Merrily said. 'If it's necessary. Thank you.'

'I'll tell the bishop you'll be in touch,' Ted said ponderously. 'When you're well.'

'I'll call him tomorrow.'

Thank God Dermot Child had been detained at the organ; he'd have been less easy to get rid of. Merrily let her head fall briefly into her hands as the door closed behind them and Jane came back alone. Peered through her fingers at the kid's face, flushed with concern, or it might have been humiliation.

'Go and change, flower. Get off to the party.'

'You are joking,' Jane said.

'I need to do some thinking.' Merrily raised her head. 'All right?'

'Mum, you're ill. If you go to bed, I'll bring you whatever you need . . . hot-water bottle.'

'I don't need anything, and I'm not going to bed.'

'Well, you can't stay in here, it's dismal. I'll light the fire in the parlour.'

'Just leave me, Jane.'

Jane hung on.

'What was it? Something you ate?'

'I didn't eat anything all day, did I? I expect that was the

307

problem. And getting uptight. Anyway, I feel terrible about everything, and I'm always better feeling terrible on my own.'

'I'm going to stay,' Jane said.

'All right, you light a fire and we'll sit and have a good old discussion. We'll talk about Miss Devenish and what happened when you went to her aid that day instead of going to school and what you talk about together. All those things we've been meaning to discuss.'

'I'll get changed then,' Jane said.

*

But she wasn't too happy about it. Throwing up in church, when you were in Mum's line of work, was not exactly a really brilliant thing to do, and since coming to Ledwardine Mum had been, for the first time, quite hot on keeping up appearances. This was going to damage her. Maybe, in the years to come, she'd be quite affectionately known as the vicar who tossed her cookies down the nave. But maybe there wouldn't be years to come, not now.

How did she feel about that? Bad. Because coming here had put her on to like a whole new level of life. What Lucy called a new depth of *Being*. Whatever this meant, it wasn't in the Bible, which was why it was unwise to even approach the subject with Mum. Particularly tonight.

In the solitude of her apartment, Jane looked up.

At what were supposed to have been the Mondrian walls. And the sloping ceiling between the beams. Into the blue and gold. Into the *otherness*. It was all so strange. Made her feel . . . ooooh. She shook herself.

Clothes-wise, she didn't overdo it. Black velvet trousers and silky purple top. Not a good night for making a spectacle of herself. Plus, if it turned out to be the kind of party Colette had in mind, a quick getaway might just be called for.

She'd gone ahead and lit the fire in the drawing room. Not so much because it was cold as because it might look halfway homely in there with a few flames. Before changing, she'd brought in some logs and filled up a bucket with coal. Kind of wishing she was staying in. But that invitation to a serious discussion left her no option. Jesus, Mum, she wanted to say, I don't *know* what happened that day. Or that night under the apple tree. I'm not *clear* on it.

But I'm getting help.

Before she left, she stoked up the fire. Mum was down on the rug in a thick bottle-green polo-neck jumper and jeans, hugging her knees. It was a May night out there, but the vicarage remained in January. Except for the top floor.

'I won't be too late.'

'I'll wait up.'

'You mustn't. I'll be annoyed if you do.'

'OK, flower,' Mum said.

With her face washed clean of make-up and her hair pushed behind her ears, she looked awfully young and vulnerable. Younger than me in some ways, Jane thought. And feeling there's so much she doesn't know.

Uh-oh . . .

At the core of a bedlam of bodies, Colette Cassidy was mouthing at her.

'What?'

'. . . you *been*, Janey? It's nearly midnight.'

Jane stayed where she was and let Colette come stammering towards her through the strobe storm, through a foundry of sound. The restaurant at Cassidy's Country Kitchen was this square, attic space with irregular beams and white, bumpy walls. There was a stage area, where the Cassidys sometimes had a pianist, but tonight the piano, like most of the tables, had been taken away and the stage had become Dr Samedi's spectacular sound-lab.

'Sorry. Had problems.'

'So I heard.' Colette's grin was lifted by the lights and put back intact. 'Cool.'

'What?'

'Give the Reverend Mummy my compliments. Bet the bloody bishop wasn't expecting that.'

Gossip seemed to spread at more than the speed of sound in this village. Jane didn't bother to explain that it hadn't actually been all that funny at the time.

There must be eighty or ninety people here, mostly imports, Colette's age and a year or two older. The flashing lights were reflected in a lot of sweat on faces. Jane recognized hardly anybody, suspecting she was the youngest here. Some of the dancers looked . . . well . . . out of it. There was nothing stronger than Coke and Dr Pepper on the tables pushed up against the walls, but she thought she'd seen the boy from her school called Mark, who seemed to be the fourth-form's principal dealer in Es and speed.

'All the same, Janey,' Colette was saying, 'you didn't have to spend half the night with the old girl.'

'Sorry. Something else came up.'

Colette didn't seem to hear. Dr Samedi was squealing something over the industrial drum 'n' bass on tapes. He wore a top hat, with ribbons, and a black bow tie. No shirt. Jacket open to his shiny chest with a white necklace showing. It was a jacket from a morning suit, black, with tails, and strategically torn in several places like the jackets the punks used to wear in Mum's day. It was a scarecrow's jacket, and that was what Dr Samedi looked like, a scarecrow animated by lightning.

'I *said*,' Jane shouted, 'something came up!'

'You should be so lucky. Listen—'

Colette was wearing something black and shiny and daring, naturally. A gangly guy in a white shirt was hanging around behind her. Colette moved close to Jane.

'OK, listen, that's Quentin the Suitable.'

'Who?'

'Like, the parents always have to make sure there's a Suitable One, you know what I mean? His old man's some kind of exalted surgeon at the General. I just wish somebody would surgically remove *him*.'

Quentin was tall and looked about seventeen.

'He's not bad,' Jane said.

'Especially if you're into vintage tractors. His *hobby*. He also dances like one.'

Jane smiled. Quentin strobed unhappily about six feet away. Colette put her squashy lips against Jane's ear.

'Janey, I can't unload the dim bastard. I go for a tinkle, he waits outside the fucking door.'

'. . . you want *me* to do?'

'Take him off my hands?'

'You are joking . . .'

'Oh, come on, your night's ruined anyway. You don't have to snog him or anything, just keep him for two minutes while I melt away. The guy's so sad if you tell him you have fantasies about having sex on a tractor, he'll just ask you what make. Please, Janey . . .'

Colette looked desperate, like life was running out on her. But then it *was* her party. On the stage, Dr Samedi hovered demonically over his mixers, moving in a vibrating swirl of lights, as though he was turning himself into light, into pure, bright energy. And Jane understood – hated the heartless music, understood perfectly about Dr Samedi's need to become light. Dr Samedi was in his element. In his orb.

She felt suddenly half-separated from it all, as though the dance floor represented all human life and she was flickering on the edge of it. For an instant, she felt weightless, as though she might vanish into one of the cracks of darkness between strobes. She felt like this quite often now, but never inside a building before. Well, except for the church, for a moment, earlier on.

'Janey?' Colette clutched at her. 'Christ, I thought you'd . . .'

'Sorry.'

'Please, Janey . . .'

'Sure,' Jane said, squeezing her hands together to bring herself down. 'Whatever.'

*

When Merrily awoke on the sofa in front of the dying fire, she was happy for a moment. Frozen and stiff, but she'd been asleep for two, three hours and hadn't dreamed about anything she could recall. A small miracle.

But this time, reality was the curse. The priest-in-charge had tonight been physically sick in her own beautiful and historic church in front of the biggest congregation she'd ever pulled.

How could she have just let that happen? *Children* did that, just threw up without warning. The priest-in-charge was not even in charge of her own metabolism.

Merrily rolled down from the sofa to the rough, industrial carpet. After a while, she sat up, shivering, and threw more lumps of coal onto the embers in the dog grate, thrusting in the poker, levering up some heat, inching closer, on this balmy May evening, to the miniature medieval hell of smoking cliffs and molten canyons.

Medieval hell. She was part of a medieval institution. Just that the modern Church refused to connect with its roots. Which was why the modern Church was losing it.

If you'd said that to her six months ago, she'd have flared up a whole lot faster than this coal, but there was no denying it any more: in a world where huge numbers of people were begging for spiritual sustenance from exotic gurus and mediums and clairvoyants and healers, the Church was getting sidelined.

David Campbell had actually asked the question, *Do these phenomena really fit inside our field of operation?* The Church still asking everyone to put their faith in a huge all-powerful supernatural being while loftily backing away from lesser phenomena.

Like a pale, naked figure, cold as a slug, crawling towards you up the aisle of your church. Obviously, a representation of her own perceived isolation as the first woman minister of Ledwardine?

Ha.

From far up in the soaring hollows of the house came a sudden, resonant bump.

*

There was a break in the music, the strobes were off. On the stage, Dr Samedi was guardedly allowing some of the boys to examine his mixers and tape decks and things. At a table near the door, Jane sat with Quentin the Suitable in his baggy cricket shirt.

It had been hard going at first, but so far he hadn't mentioned tractors.

'Actually,' he said, 'I didn't really want to come tonight at all.'

'No kidding.'

'It's just that my parents come for dinner here quite regularly, and they've become fairly friendly with Colette's parents.'

'They must be really sad, lonely people,' Jane said.

Quentin didn't get it.

Jane smiled at him. 'So tonight's the first time you've actually met Colette?'

'I tend to be away at school a lot. Only this weekend, our half-term's started, so . . . No, I've never actually met her before.'

Jane said airily, 'Some bitch, huh?'

'Pardon?'

'Take my advice, Quentin, don't get involved. She's, you know, she's kind of been around.'

Quentin looked puzzled. 'You mean abroad?'

Jane rolled her eyes. 'I mean been around as in eat-you-for-breakfast kind of been around.'

'Oh,' Quentin said. 'I see. Well, she did seem a bit disconcerted when her father asked her to sort of . . . look after me. I think she had other plans.'

'Colette always has plans.'

'No, I mean someone she was interested in.'

'Oh?' Jane sat up.

'I may be wrong.'

'No, go on.' Jane looked into his soupy eyes, but he quickly averted them. 'This is interesting. What made you think that, Quentin?'

But she didn't find out because this quivering shadow fell across the table and she looked up into the face of a grossly sweating Dean Wall.

'This'll do.' Dean pulled out a chair opposite Jane and sank into it and beamed at Jane and then at Quentin. Danny Gittoes was with him and Mark, the reputed dealer. 'All right, are we?'

Jesus, Jane thought, who let these bozos in? She'd forgotten about Colette's professed need for 'tension'. Silly cow. She looked around for Barry, the manager, locating him behind the bar where a waitress was putting out things to nibble, apparently on the instructions of Colette's mother who didn't realize that the only things that got nibbled at parties like this were ears. To begin with.

Mark the Dealer stood by the door, hands in his pockets. Danny Gittoes sat down opposite Quentin, who seemed to be urgently wishing he was somewhere else. Like the dentist's.

'So, go on . . .' Dean nodded towards Dr Samedi and looked at Danny. 'Voodoo, eh?'

'Kind of thing,' Danny said.

'Where's this then, Gittoes? Jamaica?'

'Haiti. He was this voodoo God in Haiti. Only he was called *Baron* Samedi, see. God of the dead. Hung around graves. Led these tribes of zombies. And he wore that same gear – coat with tails and a top hat. Maybe a stick. Like a cane. I read this book. So that's where he gets it from, see?'

Dean winked at Quentin, who smiled stiffly. 'And this was, like, devil worship, right?'

'Yeah. Well, more or less.'

''Cause Jane's well into that, see,' Dean said, not looking at Jane.

'You on about?'

'Got her ma into it now, too, from what they says.'

'OK.' Jane half rose. 'Watch it.'

She saw Quentin's hand tightening around his can of Dr Pepper's.

'What they're saying', Dean said, 'is that Jane's mother, the vicar, she chucked her load in church tonight.'

Danny Gittoes said, 'Eh?'

'You en't yeard? All over the village, man. 'Er chucked up. Splatted all over the bloody bishop.'

'Geddoff!' Danny said theatrically. Jane smelled set-up.

'Runs in the family, see.' Dean's little eyes glinting. 'Can't keep nothin' down. Throws up right in the middle of 'er ordination service, whatever they calls it.'

'Never!'

Dean cackled. 'Er'd prob'ly been on the cider!'

'Shut your fat face!' Jane was out of her seat. But Dean went on as if he hadn't heard her.

'Well, what's that but a sign of Satanism, see. A devil-worshipper, witch, whatever you wanner call 'em, they can't go into a Christian church without they vomits. I seen it in a film. Ole black and white job. *Mark o' the Witch*, some shit like that. Chucks her—'

'Stop it!' Jane screamed. 'You bastard!'

'You year some'ing then, Gittoes?' Dean leaned back smugly. 'Makes you think, though, dunnit? Why don't Jane Watkins ever go to church of a Sunday? You ever see Jane in church?'

'Don't go, do I?'

'Well me neither, but my gran does and 'er says to me the other day, 'er says, You never sees the vicar's daughter at no services, do you? En't right, that. En't right *at all*.'

'She was there tonight,' Danny Gittoes said. 'I seen 'er goin' in. School uniform an' all.'

'Ec . . . *sacly*,' Dean said. 'Exacly, boy. Special occasion, so 'er'd need to be there, bring down the forces of darkness, innit? Now . . . No, listen, this is interestin' . . . You remember that night Jane threw up on us. Where'd that happen exacly? *Right outside the bloody church!* In fact . . . in *fact* . . . it was up agin' the ole church wall, right? So that's holy ground, innit? An' *we* said, we said we was all gonner go in the church porch, open a coupler cans, and that was when she done it. You think about that, Gittoes . . .'

'Fuckin' hell, Dean—'

Danny Gittoes broke off because the lights began to fade and the strobing began from the stage, Dr Samedi demonstrating something. Dean's voice rose placidly out of the flashes.

'She only got to think about goin' in the church porch, see, an' up it comes. Splat. Well, all right, Jane never threw up tonight, see, but her *evil presence* in that church was enough to—'

Jane threw herself at him, knocking the glass out of his hand, seeing alarm on his fat, porous face, but, because of the strobe, when she saw it again it was wearing a grin and he was on his feet, around her side of the table and his arms were around her.

'Wanner dance with me, is it . . . devil woman?'

'Get your filthy—'

Dean gripped her tightly; she felt something hard against her stomach. She realized that in the strobe it might look as though they were actually snogging. She couldn't kick him because of the chair legs in the way. She wondered where she could bite him without encountering great pools of sweat.

'All right.' Quentin was on his feet. 'Now let's stop this.'

'Hey,' Dean said over Jane's shoulder. 'It fuckin' talks. I 'ad it figured for one 'o Doc Samedi's zombies.'

'You just . . . just let her go,' Quentin said uncertainly.

'*Let her geeeow!* What you gonner do about it, sunshine? Phone up your dad on the mobile, is it?'

Through the flashes, Jane saw that Danny Gittoes had pushed his chair back but was still sitting on it. The third boy, Mark, however, had moved in from the door. His hands were out of his pockets, something gleaming in one of them.

Jane screamed, '*He's got a knife!*'

And the room went quiet.

'Lights,' someone snapped. Dean Wall's arms went slack and Jane stepped away as the strobe stopped and the main lights came up.

Barry, the manager, ex-SAS, came across the room like a small tank. Behind him, Lloyd Powell.

'Who shouted?' Barry demanded.

Jane looked across at Mark. He was a slight, quiet-looking, mousy-haired boy. You tended not to notice him. Both arms hung by his side, the hands empty. Could she have been mistaken?

She looked away from Mark and across at Barry. 'Sorry. I thought someone had a knife.'

'One of these boys?' Lloyd Powell wandered over, hooked out a chair with his foot to see if anything had been kicked under it. Lloyd looked pretty cool in a timeless sort of way; he was the only guy here who could get away with wearing a patched tweed jacket over his jeans and denim workshirt.

'I didn't really see,' Jane said. 'There was just a sort of flash. But with the strobelights . . . Sorry.'

'All right,' Barry said. 'You.' Stabbing a finger at Dean Wall then Danny Gittoes, then Mark. 'Out.'

'Aw, come on, man.' Dean stepped away from Jane. 'We was only havin' a laugh. Tell 'im, Lloyd.'

'You're outer line, boy,' Lloyd said sternly. He folded his arms, stood shoulder-to-shoulder with Barry.

'Out,' Barry said. 'Now.'

Danny Gittoes stood up and edged towards the door. Some of the kids began to move back towards the walls. Dr Samedi stood protectively in front of his main console. Dean Wall didn't move.

'You've got five seconds,' Barry said, like they were terrorists or something. 'And that includes the door closing behind you.'

It was starting to look nasty. Then Colette was there.

'Ease up, Barry.'

There was silence. Jane reckoned that every man in the room must be looking at Colette, including Barry and Lloyd. She looked like she'd stepped out of one of those moody, sexy, Sunday-supplement fashion spreads, one of the thread-like straps of her tight, black dress just parted from the shoulder, a perfect dab of perspiration in the little cleft over her top lip. She looked about twenty-seven and drop-dead gorgeous.

'I'd be prepared to bet these lads are not on the guest list,' Barry said stiffly. 'You know your parents' rules.'

'One of *my* rules, Barry,' Colette said, 'was that the word *parents* would not be mentioned in here tonight, yeah?'

'Sorry, Colette, but they pay my wages. We have a guest list, nobody comes in they're not on it.'

'These are local guys,' Colette said. 'We don't want to be seen as snobbish, do we?'

Dean Wall leered at Colette. 'Tell the bastard, darlin'.

These ex-SAS guys, they en't got it out their system, see. They're jus' lookin' for innocent people to beat up.'

'Shut it, lad.' Barry's lips barely moved.

'What you gonner do? You got a Hechler and Koch down your trousers, is it?'

Danny Gittoes laughed feebly.

'Don't push it, boy,' Lloyd Powell said.

Dean turned on him. 'Shit, Powell, I thought you were a mate.'

'You're outer line, boy.'

'Colette, look . . .' Barry lowered his voice. 'It's getting late.'

'So it is . . .'

Colette's eyes were shining with a steady, steely light that didn't seem quite natural to Jane. Had she taken something? Well, of course she had. The eyes turned on Barry.

'I mean, I know you army guys like your early nights, but you're in the catering trade now, Baz.'

'Just there's a little ceremony planned,' Barry said uncomfortably.

Colette gave him a hard stare. 'What did you say?'

'It's your birthday party.' Barry blushed. 'We've got this . . . cake.'

'For fuck's sake!' Colette looked appalled. 'Who's idea was *that*?'

'Your mother's.'

'Jesus wept!' Jane saw Colette's fists clench. 'How old they think I am? Six?'

'Please,' Barry said. 'It was supposed to be a surprise.'

'Jesus *Christ*!' Colette's whole body went rigid and Jane saw tears of outrage and betrayal spring into her eyes. 'They're not *coming*?'

Barry gritted his teeth. 'Just for a few minutes.'

Colette began to breathe rapidly, her breasts rising half

out of the shiny, black dress, bringing a half-suppressed whimper out of Dean Wall.

'I'm sorry,' Barry said.

'You little toad, Barry,' Colette spat. 'You little fucking *toad*. You lied to me! *They* lied to me. What time?'

'It's after midnight.'

'I mean what time are they *coming*, shithead?'

'Just before one,' Barry said. 'Look, Colette, you're their daughter – you can't blame them for wanting to share just a few minutes of your party.'

'Balls. They just want to wind things up while the place is still intact and embarrass the piss out of me at the same time.'

'Come on, love, you'd be winding up by then, anyway.'

'Like fuck we would.'

Colette strode away, the tips of two fingers to her mouth, thinking hard, that cold light in her eyes. A rock slide of emotions came down on Jane, a giddying combination of nervousness and extreme excitement.

She watched Colette approach Dr Samedi, the whole room in a hush. Everybody looking for the first time tonight, Jane thought, like kids, unsure of how they were supposed to react to the hostess throwing a wobbly. Colette was speaking quickly to Dr Samedi, who started to back away, making sweeping motions with his hands, Colette pursuing him, her voice rising.

'. . . getting half a fucking grand for this, Jeff, remember?'

Dr Samedi glanced wildly from side to side, at the spread of his equipment, and Colette carried on advancing and talking ferociously at him, until he had his back against one of the big speakers, his top hat fallen off, and he seemed to concede, submit, whatever, his head nodding wearily. Colette smiled grimly, walked back to the centre of the room.

'All right. Everybody listen up. Seems some of you are not, like, considered suitable.'

Dean Wall whooped.

'Yeah, yeah.' Colette waved a dismissive hand. 'Wall's first taste of fame, very sad. OK ... So if some of us are not welcome, I think we should all go, yeah?'

'Thank God for that,' Quentin sighed. But Jane suspected he was being seriously premature.

'It's not a bad night out there, right?' Colette said.

'Could be better,' a boy shouted bravely.

'It will be. I reckon we get out of this shithole, take the action into the streets, yeah?'

There was half a second of hesitation before the roars of enthusiasm started gathering their meaningless momentum.

'Struth.' Barry rammed his hands into his jacket pockets, glared at the floor. Jane was standing quite close to him now and she heard him mutter to Lloyd Powell out of the side of his mouth, 'You better tag along with them, mate. I'll make an anonymous call to the police.'

Jane thought, *Uh-oh*.

Carnival

Merrily moved into the dark kitchen, carrying the poker.

The Aga chuntered smugly in its insulated world. She laid a palm flat on one of its hotplate covers, held it there until it felt uncomfortably warm.

What else could she do? Pinch herself? Did that really work? In the event, as she pulled away, she tripped on the edge of the rug and ... 'Oh *shit*!' dropped the poker, bumped her knee violently on a hard corner of the Aga, sending a bullet of pain spinning to the top of her head.

She staggered to the switches, slammed on all the lights, bent down, rubbing hard at her knee. Apart from severe pain, what other proof could you give yourself that you were, in fact, fully awake, not dreaming?

No, it was all real. It was quiet up there now, but the noise she'd heard from the drawing room had been real. And it wasn't a mouse, it wasn't a squirrel, it wasn't a bird in the eaves, it wasn't . . .

Real. What was real? Was a minister of the Church obliged to consult a psychiatrist these days to find out?

Another small bump.

Slowly, holding back her breath, Merrily picked up the poker.

Closer, this time. Certainly not at the top of the house. She looked at the scullery door, which was never opened.

The so-called scullery was a narrow room, probably something connected with the dairy in centuries past. They'd found no use for it as yet, never went in.

She lifted the metal latch and went through, wrinkling her nose as her hair mingled with greasy cobwebs. At the far end, another door opened on to a small, square hall. She found a switch and a dangling economy bulb sputtered on, curled-up white tubes like some frozen bodily organ sending shadows up walls already going black with damp. The absence of oak beams in here suggested it was a Victorian addition. Opposite her was the second back door, still boarded up.

Except it wasn't. The boards had been prised away; they were leaning against a wall, rusty nails sticking out of them. This was recent. *Very* recent. Jane. The separate door to the Apartment, soon to have an illuminated bell and a dinky little nameplate: *Ms Jane Watkins*. The door leading up, via the disused back stairs that you would forget were even here.

The stairs came out at a black, wooden door. Her fingers found a hole to lift the latch. Of course, she knew where the stairs came out, but it seemed strange seeing it from this angle, the dim, first-floor passage with all the doors, all of them locked now, since the Sean dream, and the keys taken out and thrown into an ashtray in the kitchen.

Padding past the locked doors, she arrived at the top of the main stairs, the oak-ballustraded landing with its window full of pale, night sky. She stood at the foot of the second stairway to Jane's apartment. Why was she doing this? Despite the unsealing of the second back door, she knew there was nobody up there. Nobody *real*. Why was she putting herself through this?

Because I'm a priest, and priests are not supposed to be scared because they know that the strength and certainty of their faith protects them from the evil that walks by night . . . don't they just?

Oh *really* . . . Jane came up here all the time, for heaven's sake. Jane skipped up here, never a thought, with books and boxes and cans of variously coloured paint and brushes and CDs, to be locked away in her secret study.

It's me. It only happens to me.

I'm a sick woman.

She thought.

Before registering that one of the doors on the landing was already half-open and a shadow-figure was watching her from the threshold.

*

Jane knew it was going wrong when she saw Mark and this unknown older guy in the unlit doorway of the computer shop, Marches Media.

Or maybe wrong was the way it was supposed to go. *A party ain't a party without tension.*

Maybe this party was going exactly the way Colette had planned . . . the plan hardening up when she learned she was being double-crossed by her parents. Actually, Jane didn't see what was so wrong with having a sixteenth birthday cake. And if the Cassidys wanted to share the moment – well, they *had* paid for everything. *And* let her use their precious restaurant.

Maybe Colette was going just a bit over the top.

Jane watched from the cobbles, leaning against one of the oaken uprights of the market cross. With a low-burning excitement, because it was obvious what was going on down there in the shadowed doorway of Marches Media: the mousy Mark and the older guy were busy dealing drugs.

And no shortage of customers. The *nice* boys from *good* families. Going in one after another, schoolkids at the tuck-shop. Not all the guests, but enough of them to put the market square well into orbit. This would be a good, safe pitch – rich kids at a posh party in a select restaurant in a picture-postcard village encircled by hills and woodland and with no resident police. Profitable, too. Most of these guys would have no idea of current street prices.

Not that Jane did. It was just cool to watch from the shadows and speculate about these things.

She was on her own now. The craven Quentin had made a swift escape, car keys in hand, a couple of other vehicles also puttering pusillanimously away from the square. She saw Dean Wall and Danny Gittoes watching Colette, keeping a respectful distance. A heavy chick.

She and Dr Samedi were at the back of his Transit van, one rear door open. Dr Samedi backing out, arms full of something black, the size and shape of a child's coffin. 'Oh yes!' Colette cried. 'Yes, yes yes!'

Dr Samedi was still unhappy and wouldn't let go of whatever it was. But tonight you didn't argue with Colette; she wrapped her arms around the black thing, wrestling with poor Jeff, until they both sprang back and the black box was in Colette's arms now.

Lloyd Powell was watching from the foot of the Black Swan steps. Mr Responsible, Jane thought. He might seem cool now, with that rangy Paul Weller look and his white pick-up truck, but Lloyd would turn, as the years went by, into his father, get elected on to the council. By which time Rod would have shrunken into Edgar, half-baked and not to be trusted with a shotgun. It was the depressing side of country life; they all seemed to know their place in the Pattern and the Pattern didn't change.

People like Colette fascinated them because they were part of a different pattern, Jane thought. But there was no meaningful overlap. She was thinking what a really profound philosophical concept this was, when it all began.

'All right!'

A voice crackling into the night. Dr Samedi had materialized under swathes of bunting put up for tomorrow's festival
launch. He held an old-fashioned trumpet loud hailer. His
top hat was back on.

'How you doin'? Sweatin'? Yeah!'

A few cheers. Dean Wall's familiar whoop.

'All right!' Dr Samedi raised the white loud hailer up over
his head. A signal, obviously. Because, at that moment, the
perfectly preserved medieval market square of rural Ledwardine just . . . well, just erupted.

The black thing, like a small coffin, had proclaimed itself,
in the way it knew best, as a huge ghetto-blaster with about
eight speakers. It was sitting on the roof of the van now,
pumping tumultuous drum and bass into the square at this
unbelievable volume, and Colette Cassidy was bouncing up
and down beside the van and screaming, 'Yes, yes, yes, yes,
yes!'

A circle of people rapidly formed around her, everybody
moving in a way it was hard not to when the big, black beat
was everywhere and loud enough to pop up all the cobbles
on the square. Oh my God, Jane thought, they'll hear this in
the centre of Hereford.

'Welcome, ma friends . . .'

Dr Samedi's phoney West Indian drawl had been processed by the primitive megaphone into a deep and eerie
croak.

'*Wel-come . . . to . . . de . . . carn-i-val!*'

*

The ceiling light was blurred and swirling.

She was waking up. She'd been asleep. Dreamed it all.
Again. Oh my God.

It was not *possible*. Hadn't she heated her hands on the
Aga, gripped the poker until it hurt, bashed her knee so hard

the pain had given her a headache? Proving beyond all doubt that she was awake?

The light above her was in a warm, orange shade. Jane's shade. Taken with her from Birmingham to Liverpool to Ledwardine . . .

To the third floor.

She was in Jane's bedroom, in the Apartment. Lying on Jane's bed. She didn't remember coming here. Why would she come in here, lie down on Jane's bed? Fear streaked through her and she struggled to sit up and looked into a blank, grey, oval face with dark slits for eyes.

Merrily screamed and squirmed away. Hurled herself back against the headboard, slamming it into the wall behind.

'It's OK!'

The grey face was printed on a jumper, a sweatshirt. Over it was a real face behind glasses. The real face looked scared.

'No . . . look . . . hey . . .' he said. 'I'm harmless.'

She looked down, registering that she was fully dressed, the bed unrumpled.

'Mrs Watkins . . . I'm really, really sorry.'

'Christ.'

'I thought you might need a cup of tea . . .'

One of her cups coming at her, on one of her saucers. She didn't move.

'What are you doing? What are you doing in . . . '

Aware that, even in her fear, she couldn't say, What are you doing in my house? It wasn't. It was the vicarage. It was huge and alien and maybe this man lived here, too, in some derelict attic room, coming and going by the forgotten back stairs. Part of the mad, sporadic nightmare. Oh God, get me out of here.

'I'm a kind of . . . friend of Jane's.' He was very unto-gether; big, unsteady eyes behind the glasses. Like a scared version of the alien on his sweater.

'Where is she?'

'She went to a party. See, what happened, we met in the street, I needed to take a look at my cat, and she just like brought me up here, you know? Jane says, you know, Bring her inside, we'll have a look at her. Obviously I didn't realize she meant . . . her room. Believe me, there is no way I'd've come up here.'

'Cat,' Merrily said.

'Somebody gave her a kicking. We brought her up here and then she got away. We must've touched her in the wrong place. I'm sorry. I don't *do* things like this.'

She accepted the tea with numb relief. 'You've got an injured cat somewhere in the house? Wandering around, making bumping noises maybe.'

'Probably.'

Merrily could hear heavy music coming through the trees from the square, insistent as a road drill. This wasn't going to endear the Cassidys to their neighbours. 'Let's go downstairs,' she said. 'I need a cigarette.'

*

It wasn't long before they started coming out of their homes, gathering in small groups. You could see pyjama bottoms sticking out of trouser turn-ups, one woman in an actual hairnet. Big torches, walking sticks.

'Who's in charge here?' a man shouted. Not a local voice. A sort of retired colonel voice.

The music was turned up even higher. Maybe fifty people dancing. Someone grabbed hold of Jane's arm, tried to pull her into the crush of quivering bodies.

It was Colette. 'Aw, come on, Janey. Get your shit together. Stuff the Reverend Mumsy. Like *she's* in any position to complain.'

'You're disturbing the peace!' The man's voice rose again.

'This is noise pollution. If you don't turn that racket off and go away now, at once, I'm going to call the police! Do you hear me?'

Jane let herself be dragged in, knowing they were all on borrowed time. If Barry hadn't rung the police already, quite a few people were surely doing it right now; you looked up and you could see small, furious faces peering out of dark windows, could imagine outraged fingers stiffly prodding out 999. Anticipating it, Mark and his friend had already disappeared from the Marches Media doorway. But whatever they'd been selling was taking effect: all around her, open mouths and too-bright eyes.

'We comin' out,' rapped Dr Samedi. 'We comin' back. We gonna turn, gonna turn de whole sky *black*.' But he no longer sounded in control.

A boy pushed past Jane, having come out of the antique shop doorway, zipping up his jeans. 'Did you *see* that?' a woman yelped. 'That yob's just urinated in there!'

'You hear me?' the man shouted. 'I'm calling the police!'

'Oh, do fuck off, grandad!' replied a girl with an equally posh voice, and there were wild peals of laughter and somebody turned the music up even higher, so that even Dr Samedi was drowned out.

But they were on borrowed time and Jane wasn't unhappy about that because she needed to get back and find out about Lol. Lol who'd come over very weird when she'd taken him up the back stairs and he'd found himself in her room. Backing off, shaking his head, saying this was a mistake. His agitation picked up by Ethel, the cat, squirming out of his arms and disappearing into the bowels of the vicarage.

Lol was in trouble. He couldn't go home because Karl was in there and Lol, for reasons Jane still couldn't quite put together, was scared of Karl. And was also – for reasons even more obscure – scared of *her*. He'd seemed relieved to pack her off to the party, to hide out there alone in the part of the house where Mum was banned. He wouldn't be there when she got home, he said. He'd wait until Ethel reappeared and then he'd go. She'd left him her secret key to lock the small back door behind him; he'd leave it, he said, with Lucy.

But what if Karl was still in the cottage when he got back? Where would Lol go then?

One idea had occurred to Jane. Maybe she could get a few of the guys from the party – rugby-player types – to go over to Lol's place and force that bastard out of there. But the state they were in now, how could you even explain to them what was needed? By the time they made it to Blackberry Lane they'd have forgotten why they were going.

Chaos. Nothing more unstable than well-brought-up kids on the loose in some place they and their parents weren't known.

The music stopped.

The silence was deafening. Beyond the hollow roaring in her ears, Jane heard the sound of car engines.

'OK.' Colette's voice over the loud hailer. 'Listen up. It's probably the filth, yeah? We're moving on. Don't worry, no cars required. Follow me . . . or Janey. Where's Janey? She knows.'

It wasn't the police. The car that turned on to the edge of the square was a Volvo like Mum's, only about ten years younger. Both front doors opened at once.

The Cassidys.

'Janey,' Colette called out. 'OK?' And then the loud hailer was silent.

Jane didn't move. What was Colette saying to her? *She knows.* What? She slipped back under the market cross as

Terrence Cassidy appeared on the cobbles, panting. 'Colette! Where are you? Please—' and was almost pulled off his feet by the stampede from the square.

'Colette!'

Mrs Cassidy was less circumspect. 'The unutterable little *bitch*. I *knew* something like this would—'

'Colette,' Terrence implored. 'Where are you. Why are you *doing* this to us?'

'It's 'cause you're such a wanker, mate,' Dean Wall confided chattily over his shoulder and cackled and followed the others.

The music had resumed, from the top of Church Street, booming off into the churchyard. Jane's shoulder brushed against a poster tacked to one of the pillars of the market cross, bold black and yellow lettering inside a big red apple. LEDWARDINE SUMMER FESTIVAL: OFFICIAL OPENING, SATURDAY, MAY 23. MARKET SQUARE 2.00 p.m. BE THERE!

'Bloody hell!'

Jane found Dr Samedi next to her, the loud hailer dangling limply from his hand. Back in Midlands mode.

'Can y' believe it? She's buggered off with my flamin' box. Bloody rich kids. I hate bloody rich kids, I do. Gimme ghetto any day of the week.'

'Sorry, Jeff. She's hard to stop when she gets going.'

'That don't help me, does it?'

And suddenly, Jane knew where Colette was taking them.

'Oh no.' She looked around for help, but the Cassidys had rushed into their restaurant, presumably to assess the damage and take it out on Barry. Even the locals were melting away – wherever the mob was heading, it was at least out of their earshot, away from their backyards, so what did they care?

'Thing is,' Dr Samedi was moaning, 'I don't know if my insurance covers this.'

Jane saw a tall figure strolling towards the churchyard. 'Lloyd!'

Lloyd Powell turned and waited for her under the fake gaslight, Jane found herself clutching at his sleeve.

'You've got to stop them.'

'I think we'll wait for the police, don't you, Miss Watkins?'

'No!' You could never tell with people like Lloyd whether they called you Miss out of politeness or because they were laughing at you. 'They're going to the orchard. You can stop them. It's your land. You can go in there and turn them out.'

'On my own?'

He *was* laughing at her. Everybody knew the Powells didn't really care about their orchard.

But they should. They *should*.

'Please. It's not safe. It's not respectful. You've got to get them out. Please, Lloyd.'

'Hey.' He put his big, rugged hands on her shoulders, peered at her from under his Paul Weller fringe. 'Don't get into a state about this. They're just daft kids.'

'Please.' She was crying now.

'All right,' Lloyd said. 'I'll go and see what I can do.' He smiled wryly, hunching his shoulders. 'You wanner come?'

'Oh no,' Jane said. 'I couldn't.'

She stood on the edge of the cobbles, hopelessly confused, awfully apprehensive for reasons she couldn't explain.

The Mondrian Walls

'Bleeding from the mouth,' Merrily said.

Lol Robinson held Ethel on the kitchen table. 'That means internal injuries?' He looked shattered.

They'd found the little black cat cowering into the side of the Aga.

'Who did this?'

He didn't reply, which meant he knew. In the hall Merrily found an old quilted body-warmer she'd kept for gardening.

'You know what to do with this?'

'I've never actually had a cat before.'

'You wrap her up tight, so there's just her head sticking out. So there's plenty between you and the claws?'

'Er . . . right.'

'Never mind. Just grab her by the scruff and don't let go. No . . . You have to be *firm*, Lol.'

'I'm not really a firm person,' Lol said.

Merrily rolled up the sleeves of her sweater. She opened out the jacket, swept it swiftly around the cat. She tucked the ends around Ethel's claws.

'Anybody I might know? Anybody whose soiled soul I should be praying for?'

'Any spare prayers,' he said quietly, 'I would hang on to them.'

'No prayers are wasted.' Handing him a bundle with a

small black head sticking out. 'Hold her very tightly. God, these lights are crap.'

He glanced up at her.

'Yeah, I know, some people would call that taking the Lord's name in vain.' Trying to prise the jaws apart. 'No, *tight*, Lol, you've got a leg coming out. The way I see it, it helps keep the holy names in circulation. Especially when used in times of stress.'

Ethel's mouth snapped open; Merrily gritted her teeth, slipped a forefinger inside.

'Not entirely sure whether I should've used it in the same sentence as *crap*, mind . . . See there? Lost a tooth. Possibly a couple. Where the blood's coming from.'

'Not internal?'

'Don't think so.' She touched the spot; Ethel writhed. 'Good.'

'God,' said Lol. 'Thank you.'

'One of my uncles used to be a vet. In Cheltenham.'

'I wanted to be a vet when I was a kid, then I found out you had to put things down a lot. She'll be OK?'

'If you're still worried, you can pop her over to a real vet in the morning. You can let her go now.'

They watched the liberated Ethel make like a bullet for the door to the scullery. Merrily held up her finger with blood and a tiny, white splinter on the end.

'That's probably the last bit of it. So . . .' Merrily sat down and lit a cigarette. 'Talk to me, Mr Robinson. I'm a priest.'

*

It was fairly quiet on the square now, but she could hear music coming from somewhere else, fainter. It didn't seem a problem but it didn't make sense.

Ethel had re-appeared in the doorway, looking miffed but not distressed. Merrily wished Jane would also show.

She smoked in silence while he told her about this guy, now occupying his cottage, who'd been in the band, Hazey Jane, with him years ago and had come back from the States with ambitions involving Lol and some new songs and an album. Which sounded reasonable.

'Just I have problems with this guy,' Lol said.

'He knows that?'

'He doesn't seem to realize how deep it goes.'

'Not a sensitive person, then.'

'That would be about right,' Lol said. 'And he drinks. And when he drinks he gets over-emotional.'

'Violent temper.'

'As you saw.'

'And he's in your house. He's broken in.'

'Right.'

'So – pardon me if this is incredibly naive – but why don't you just call the police?'

Almost immediately she regretted asking that. He looked like he'd rather throw himself in the river.

*

The police arrived, just the two of them in a car. No hurry, no panic – except on the part of the Cassidys, who came out of the alley to meet them, with Barry the manager.

Jane crept back under the market hall to listen, blending into the mingled shadows of the oak pillars.

'Certainly seems quiet enough now,' one of the cops said.

'That' – Caroline Cassidy was in tears – 'is because they've gone on some sort of drug-crazed rampage. Everything was perfectly under control, all decent, well-behaved young people from good families, no strong drink. And then it was gatecrashed by some ghastly local thugs. Barry . . . Barry, you tell them.'

'Exactly as Mrs Cassidy says,' Barry said, the crawling sod.

'It was all fine until these lads came in. Somebody must've *let* them in, because we had the doors bolted. Well, with the flashing lights and things I didn't notice them for a while. But they brought the drugs in, no question.'

'Kind of drugs, Mr Bloom?'

'Oh, well, Ecstasy, I reckon. Probably some amphetamines. Crack, maybe, I wouldn't rule it out. They target parties, don't they?'

'You know them?'

'Seen 'em around. There's a thin lad, about seventeen. Mark . . . Putley? Dad's got the garage on the Leominster Road. Then the fat one, Dean . . . Dean . . . I can find out.'

'Where are they now?'

'It's what I've been trying to tell you!' Mrs Cassidy was close to hysteria. 'They've gone into the woods. *They've taken my daughter!*'

Unbelievable. Jane longed to step out there and tell them it was the other way round, that if they pulled in Colette, it would all be sorted out. Tonight, Colette was overstepping even Jane's mark. On the other hand, she didn't want to get involved. She just wanted the police to get them out of the orchard.

'And where were you while this was going on, Mrs Cassidy?'

'My wife and I', said Terrence, 'were having discussions with Mr Richard Coffey, the playwright, at his home. Earlier, we'd been to an event at the church.'

'All right. And you think the kids've gone into some woods?'

'The orchard. Down there, through the churchyard. The Powells' land.'

'I don't think we're going to get too excited about trespass at the moment, sir. You think they've got drugs with them, that's going to be our main interest.'

'And my daughter . . .'

'Quite.'

*

Lol was cleaning his glasses on the hem of his sweatshirt. Without them, he looked bewildered and innocent, an ageing teenager. She was supposed to turn him out now, with his injured cat in his arms?

'You obviously can't go home tonight.' Teapot and cigarettes between them on the kitchen table. 'You need to give this guy a chance to sober up and realize what he's done. So if you don't mind a sleeping bag, you could stay here. We've got masses of bedrooms, no beds.'

Lol said that was really nice of her, but it was OK, really, he'd got a car down the road. Merrily thought the state he was in he'd probably pile it into a tree.

'Look at it this way. One of the oldest traditions of the Church is offering sanctuary. I've always liked to do that. I'm not good at much else. I write lousy sermons, my voice is too tuneless to lead the hymns, I get upset at funerals and I've had a really bad night. So just give me a break, huh?'

'I heard about that,' Lol said.

'Heard what?'

'That you . . . weren't well.'

Merrily felt for another cigarette. 'Who told you that?'

'I . . . overheard somebody talking about it.'

'Saying what?' She bit on the cigarette, fumbled for her lighter.

'That you were ill. At your inauguration service.'

'Word travels fast in a village.' By tomorrow half the county would know. She stood up. 'Let's get this sleeping bag sorted out.'

'You're still not well, are you, Mrs Watkins?'

'I'm Merrily. And I'm fine. Just need to eat sometime, but it's a little early for breakfast. I'm trying to think where we put the sleeping bags. I think Jane's room. Jane's *apartment*.'

He followed her upstairs, the main stairs this time.

'It's a big house, isn't it?'

'You could say that.'

'Would it be OK if I slept downstairs?'

'Wherever you like.' She waited for him on the upper landing. Glad he'd said that, she didn't quite like the idea of a stranger up here with Jane.

The sleeping bags weren't in the kid's bedroom. Which left the sitting room/study, into which Merrily had been forbidden to go until the completion of the famous Mondrian walls. Well, this was an emergency, and it was Jane's fault, so she'd have to slip in there, grab one of the bags and just not look at the walls.

But the door was locked. 'Damn. The kid is so exasperating sometimes. I like to think I've never been the kind of mother who spies, you know?'

Lol said tentatively, 'I think there was a key on the bedside table. In Jane's room.'

'Makes sense. She'd hardly take it to Colette's party.'

Feeling a need to explain, she said, 'Jane's had this long-term plan to paint the plaster squares and rectangles between the wall-beams in different colours, so it'd be like sitting inside this huge Mondrian painting. You know Mondrian. Dutch painter? We had a couple of days in London last year and we went to this exhibition of his stuff, and when we came here she got this ambitious idea. It probably looks terrible.'

The key fitted. The sleeping bags were rolled up behind the door. Merrily could have gathered one up, brought it out with barely a glance at the Mondrian walls. Maybe she'd have done that. If they'd been Mondrian walls, nice plain squares of colour.

'What . . .?' She froze in the doorway.

'You OK?'

'No.' Merrily put on the lights.

The walls had been painted all one colour. Blue. Midnight blue, divided by the timber-framing. But the timbers were part of it. Painted branches were made to protrude from them, thicker ones closer to the floor, becoming more plentiful as they neared the ceiling where they all joined together in a mesh.

As though she'd tried to bring the timbers in the wall alive, turn them back into trees.

'I don't understand.' Merrily fought to keep her voice level.

'Must have taken her a long time,' Lol said.

'Must have taken her whole nights. Why? What does it mean?'

He didn't reply. He was looking at the ceiling. Among the beams and the intertwining branches were many small orbs of yellow and white, meticulously painted. Lights in the trees.

'Little golden lanterns,' Lol said. 'Hanging in the night.'

She thought he must be quoting some line of half-remembered poetry.

*

The police left their car on the square and walked towards the church gates. Jane followed them, about thirty yards behind.

'Some back-up, you reckon, Kirk?' one said.

'In bloody Ledwardine, in the early hours? Let's take a

look around first. It turns out they've just gone in there for a smoke and a shag, we're gonner look like prats.'

The first two people to come out of the orchard walked straight into the two policemen. They were Danny Gittoes and Dean Wall. They were both drunk.

'Aw shit.' Dean put up his hands. 'I never done it, officer.'

'Over by the wall, lads. Let's have your names.'

Dean and Danny were having their pockets turned out when Jane slipped behind a row of graves and past them into the orchard. Moving not stealthily but with great care, excusing herself as she passed between the trees. *Respect is the important thing*, Lucy Devenish said. *Individual trees can be trimmed and pruned and chopped down when they are dying, but you must always show respect for the orchard as an entity. Never take an apple after the harvest. Never touch the trees in spring. Never take the blossom. Never* ever *bring any into the house.*

Spending hours with Lucy and Lucy's books, there wasn't much she didn't know now about apples and orchards. Knowledge was the best defence, Lucy said. Knowledge or felicity. Thomas Traherne had learned felicity. Had discovered, against all the odds, the secret of happiness through oneness with nature, with the orb.

Sometimes over the past week, usually in the daytime, Jane's worldly self had told her other self that this was all absolute, total bollocks.

But now, with the white-clothed apple trees all around her, the blossom hanging from them like robes, it was Lucy's world that seemed like the real world.

The moon had come out, and its milky light bathed the Powell orchard, and Jane felt she was on the threshold of a great mystery.

If Dean Walls and Danny Gittoes were refusing to come quietly, Jane wasn't aware of it. If the bassy music was still booming from Dr Samedi's black box, she could no longer hear it. If the guests at Colette's party were making their stoned, confused way among the tangle of trees, she couldn't see them.

Although there *were* figures here, she was sure. Pale and glistening, moonbeam shapes interweaving amid the blossom branches, as though each blanched petal had a ghost, and all these spirit petals had coalesced into translucent, dancing figurines.

And you wanted to join them in the dance, far finer and more fluid than the grossness on the square. The further into the orchard you went, the lighter you felt. As though you too were made of petals and could be fragmented and blown away by a breeze, dissolving and separating, a snow of molecules, until you were absorbed into the moonbeams, disappearing from the mortal sight.

A bump. A bump stopped her.

A bump and a bouncing.

Jane bent down as it rolled almost to her feet. She picked it up. It was small and its skin was soft and puckered and withered like the cheeks of a very old woman.

She held it in the palm of her hand. It was no bigger than a billiard ball, though only a fraction as heavy. It must have been up on the tree all winter. Perhaps the only one. All winter through, and the birds had left it alone.

In most parts of Britain, according to Lucy's books, a single apple that remained on a tree all winter was a harbinger of death.

A bloom on the tree when the apples are ripe
is a sure termination of somebody's life.

(The fact that it didn't really rhyme, Lucy said, was a sure sign of the truth in it.)

What did it mean when an overripe apple survived the winter to tumble from a tree in full blossom?

Jane thought back over everything that had happened tonight. The images stammering through her mind like a videotape in fast-reverse. The tape stopped at a moment in the church, Mum on her knees, bent over, then looking up, threads of vomit on her lips.

Looking up.

Jane's arm jerked back in a spasm and she threw the mummified apple so far into the orchard she didn't hear it land, and she turned and ran all the way to the vicarage.

Part Three

Airy things thy soul beguile . . .

Thomas Traherne,
The Instruction

Part Three

High Flier

Six a.m. and fully light, if overcast and cool. A thin, sharp breeze blew apple blossom over the churchyard wall from which the church noticeboard projected.

On it, a printed poster for the festival opening – the old, prosaic title, Ledwardine Summer Festival having pushed out Dermot's Old Cider suggestion precisely because most of the posters had already been printed. But over this poster another smaller one, A4 size, had been drawing-pinned, giving notice of a

---

Special midnight service

THE REVEREND MERILLY WATKINS
will be holding a

BLACK MASS

(Bring your own sickbags)

Merrily stared at it for several seconds, quite shocked, before understanding dawned. Being sick in church was allegedly one way of identifying yourself as a Satanist – some old Dennis Wheatley line.

This was probably one of the high-school kids with a computer. Things could be difficult for Jane on Monday, with the story all round the school. She tore down the notice and crumpled it up, forcing a smile, even though there was no one to observe it. If you didn't smile you would go completely out of your mind. If anyone could handle this it was Jane.

But the smile wandered when she thought about the funeral card with *Wil Williams, the Devil's Minister* on it. Could be the same person, couldn't it? In which case, a schoolkid was less likely; it would be another move in the campaign, if such it was, to persuade her to keep the Coffey play out of church.

Which, of course, disinclined to feed Stefan's obsession, she'd already decided to do, with a formal, public announcement of her decision at the buffet reception following her installation.

But that was yesterday. Before something she was insisting to herself was beyond her control had prevented her making her vows and established her as a weak, unstable woman entirely unfit to replace the stolid, long-serving Alfred Hayden.

Perhaps the parish really didn't want her. Were ministers of the Church supposed to have regard to omens, or was that only for anthropologists and social historians, just as hauntings were the preserve of psychologists?

Something else not dealt with at theological college.

She was shivering inside the fake Barbour, feeling starved. She hadn't really slept. It was well after 2 a.m. when she'd heard Jane come in, using her front-door key. Merrily lying on her bed, fully clothed, for over an hour in case the kid should drift into the drawing room and stumble over the refugee in his sleeping bag. In the event, Jane had come directly up to the third-floor bedroom next to the sitting room/study with its decidedly non-Mondrian walls.

About which Lol Robinson – rich coming from a manifest paranoiac – had told her not to worry too much. Something, possibly, that Miss Devenish would be able to explain.

She thought angrily that if she did leave this village it would not be because of her own humiliation but because of what Ledwardine – or something, or even Miss Devenish – was doing to Jane.

She dug her hands into her coat pockets and walked, head down, into the market place. It didn't feel like a spring morning. The glorious, false summer was in suspension, the blossom on the churchyard apple trees looking grey, like ice.

A few cars were still parked on the square, and she saw that one was a police car. Some damage during or after the party? Vandalism? A break-in?

A compact figure in a flat cap and muffler waved at her and crossed over from Church Street. 'Cold mornin', Vicar.'

'It sure is.'

He came and stood companionably beside her, unlit cigarette stub between his teeth. Had he been in last night's congregation? She couldn't remember. Either way, she felt absurdly pleased that Gomer Parry was still speaking to her.

'En't found her yet then, Vicar.'

'Sorry?'

Gomer dipped his cigarette towards the mews enclosing Cassidy's Country Kitchen. 'Could be anywhere, see, flighty piece like that.'

Merrily looked from Gomer to the police car and back. 'Colette Cassidy?'

'You en't yeard? Missing, she is.'

'My God. Since the party? Jane didn't say anything.'

'Ah well,' Gomer said, 'mabbe 'er'd left, see, 'fore they knowed this girl wasn't around n' more. Far's I can make out, what happened, she'd brought in a few undesirables, and this din't go down too well with that SAS bloke runs the restaurant, and there's a bit of a row like and the next thing she's walked out an' they've all followed her and everybody's dancin' about the square an' raisin' Cain, half of 'em doped up to the eyeballs, an' then the law rolls up and they're off like buggery an' . . .'

'Merrily!'

An urgent clacking of heels on the cobbles and Caroline Cassidy appeared in the entrance to the mews. Caroline as Merrily – and probably Ledwardine – had never seen her before, her eyes hot and glowing like small torchbulbs out of a Hallowe'en mask of ruined make-up.

Gomer Parry took one look and stepped hurriedly aside.

'Oh, Merrily, I was going to send the police to you. Where's Jane? Did Jane come home?'

'Jane's still in bed. I hope. Caroline, I've just heard.'

'We should never, never, never have let it happen, but Terrence said, in Ledwardine, what could possibly go wrong? What has *ever* happened in Ledwardine? Merrily, I'm frantic. I keep thinking of that girl over in Kingsland who just disappeared, fourteen years old.'

'I'm sure there's nothing like that to worry about. Probably a bunch of them went off in a car to some club in Hereford and she's just a bit sheepish about coming home. Colette's very . . . mature.'

'She's a *child*.' Caroline's mouth slack with fear. 'You don't know her. Everybody thinks she's so precocious, but it's all an act.'

'I'm sorry.' Merrily put an arm around her. 'But I know that, with so many other people about, she'll be OK. What actually happened?'

Caroline sniffed. 'Come in and have . . . have some coffee?'

Merrily thought of Jane back at the vicarage. She *was* still there, wasn't she? And Lol Robinson, to whom she was giving sanctuary. A priest's job was to help people in trouble.

'OK.'

*

Lol awoke on the drawing-room rug to a dead fire and Ethel peering down at him from the sofa. He knew at once where he was and conflicting emotions crowded in on him, scaring him at first, like hungry fans after a gig.

The vicarage. Church property. His old enemy, the Church. This big, damp house: soulless. Why did all church buildings seem cold and forbidding and soulless?

Ethel nuzzled him and purred. It wasn't the pain-purr this time. Cats could always put the past behind them, no matter how bad the past was.

He stroked Ethel and thought about Merrily Watkins, who was nothing like the Church, and felt a strange sense of lightness. In one night, he'd lost everything, his last hope of Alison coming back and then his house. He lay and almost luxuriated in the simplicity of it, knowing that as soon as he climbed out of this sleeping bag, responsibilities would tighten around him.

You never enjoy the world aright, till the sea itself floweth in your veins and you are clothed in the heavens and crowned with the stars.

Wild.

He was filling the kettle when Jane appeared, in jeans and an orange cotton top. The skin around her dark eyes looked pink and swollen. She peered at Lol, recollecting slowly.

'Oh, hell, she knows, right? I thought she was going to be like out cold for the entire night.'

Lol told her sincerely that her mother had been incredible. He told her about Ethel. 'Lost a tooth, but she's not vain.'

Jane smiled, but her eyes had a distant, haunted look. 'Where *is* Mum?'

'I think she went out.' Lol adjusted the rubber band around his ponytail. He'd washed at the sink, but obviously couldn't shave. 'When she comes back, I'll clear off. Sort things out.'

Jane sat down at the kitchen table. 'This was the best thing. You can't reason with people like that.'

'No.' He sat down opposite her. 'It was the pathetic thing.'

Jane shook her head slowly. 'Where did you sleep?'

'In the parlour. On the rug. In a sleeping bag.'

'Right,' Jane said. And then he saw her face tense. 'Where did you get the sleeping bag?'

'From the room . . . next to your bedroom.'

There was a moment of stillness in the kitchen before the kettle started to whistle.

'Oh, great,' Jane said tonelessly. 'Oh, terrific.'

*

Once inside the Country Kitchen, Merrily realized there must be at least one more police car on the square, but unmarked. Terrence Cassidy was at a central table with a man and a woman, the man taking notes, the woman asking questions.

'Just try and calm down and think, Mr Cassidy. Think if there's anyone you've missed out.'

Terrence, unshaven, raised a hand to Merrily. Caroline went across.

'Anything?'

'What we're trying to do, Mrs Cassidy,' the woman said, 'is to compile a list of everyone who was at the party, invited or uninvited, and check; first of all, if anyone else is missing. That's going to take time.'

'What about the actual *search*?' Caroline's voice was frayed and jagged. 'The woods . . . the orchard. The orchard's huge.'

'We've still got some people out there, but it begins to look as if we need to extend the area of operation.' The woman looked enquiringly at Merrily.

'This is Merrily Watkins, our Priest-in-Charge,' Terrence said. 'Also the mother of a close friend of Colette's.'

'Ah.' The woman stood up. 'Good morning. I'm Detective Inspector Annie Howe, this is DC Mumford. Take a seat, Ms Watkins.'

DI Howe had a surgical look. Tall. Fine, light hair, thin lips. If she'd worn glasses they would have been rimless, Merrily thought. But she wasn't a surgeon; she had a law degree. It had been in the *Hereford Times*. Annie Howe was new to the Division, a high-flier from Sussex, thirty-one years old.

'So your daughter was at the party? And her name would be . . .?'

'Jane. She's fifteen.'

DC Mumford wrote it down. He was thickset and older than his boss by a good ten years.

'And although she was a close friend of Colette,' Howe said, 'she clearly didn't spend the whole evening with her.'

'Don't say *was* like that!' Caroline shrieked.

'I'm very sorry, Mrs Cassidy. Nothing negative was implied. Just that by the end of the evening, they weren't quite so close, as they appear to have gone off in different directions. What time did your daughter get home, Ms Watkins?'

'I don't remember exactly. Perhaps around two . . . two-thirty.'

'Were you worried?'

Merrily smiled stiffly. 'You're always a bit worried, aren't you? Even though you know they're not far away.'

'Were you aware of the disturbance on the square?'

'Not really. There are several big trees between the vicarage and the road. Plus, I might have fallen asleep in front of the fire.'

'Well, I'll need to talk to your daughter. Unless Colette turns up soon, of course. Which she probably will.' Howe produced a narrow smile, which Caroline Cassidy must have found as comforting as a shot of morphine. 'I don't suppose Jane's up and about yet.'

'I don't suppose she is,' Merrily said.

'Although *you* are.'

'In my job, you find it hard to sleep after six. Holy Communion and all that.'

DI Howe nodded.

'Ma'am.' A uniformed constable had come in. 'Got a minute?'

Howe and the PC moved over to the door. Merrily couldn't hear what they were saying, but the constable was pointing through the window to where another policeman was waiting, with a radio. Howe was looking interested, raising her eyebrows.

'Oh, my God,' Caroline said. 'Oh . . . my . . . God.'

Our Kind of Record

Nothing to worry about, DI Annie Howe had said, almost convincingly. And because Caroline Cassidy was clearly petrified by the possibility that the police had found a body, Howe revealed that it was simply a suspected burglary. At an isolated cottage in Blackberry Lane. Probably no connection at all.

To Merrily, this last statement sounded even less convincing.

Howe and Mumford had both left. Out on the square, a car was starting up. They were off to Lol Robinson's cottage.

It had to be. The police would have routinely knocked on the door to ask if anyone had seen or heard anything in the neighbouring orchard last night. They would perhaps have found the place empty, this Windling gone, but obvious signs of a break-in.

She stayed with the Cassidys, and when Caroline got up to fumble at the coffee machine, she said quietly to Terrence, 'If some of those kids were looking for somewhere to get drunk or smoke a little cannabis, and they found an empty house . . . you know?'

'Yes.' He looked, for a moment, more hopeful. 'She's easily led, you know, whatever anyone says. Just a child.'

Merrily said nothing. She needed to get back and tell Jane and Lol Robinson what had happened. Sooner or later, he was going to have to explain to the police what this was all about, and she hoped his story would sound more plausible than it had last night.

The phone rang on the wall behind the counter. Caroline stumbled across, snatched it down.

'Colette . . .? Oh.' She sagged. 'Hello, Margaret. No . . . No, I'm afraid not.'

'Mother of one of Colette's schoolfriends,' Terrence said to Merrily. 'We phoned as many as we could. Even though we'd seen some of them just an hour or two earlier when they came to collect their children.'

Merrily said, 'Did they *all* go with Colette into the orchard?'

'Some of them were too sensible,' Terrence said bitterly. 'Most of the others seem to have come back fairly quickly. Who wants to tramp around a place like that without torches or anything? Unless, as you say, they were looking for somewhere to experiment with drugs. I suppose you've seen some of that. You were in urban areas, weren't you?'

She nodded but didn't elaborate. The last thing he needed was to hear where some of these chemical experiments led.

Caroline said, 'Yes. All right. Thank you, Margaret.' Hung up the phone. 'Margaret says Cressida thinks we ought to talk to the DJ person, because Colette had gone off with his ghetto-blaster thing.'

'They found it,' Terrence said bleakly. 'The police found it in the orchard, batteries flat.'

Caroline's face crumpled like a wash leather.

'As for the DJ – Jeff Mooney – he stayed behind just about long enough to present me with his ridiculous bill.'

'Look.' Merrily stood up. 'I really think I ought to go back and talk to Jane. There's always the possibility she knows something that might help. I'd like to give her a thorough grilling before the police get round to it.'

'Would you?' Caroline dabbed at her face with a tissue and went back to the coffee machine. She pulled two cups from a shelf. 'Would you come back and tell us? If there was something. Anything at all?'

'Of course.'

Terrence suddenly moaned. 'The festival! I'd forgotten. We've got the ceremony this afternoon. To launch the festival. Crowds of people. We might even have the Press here.'

Oh yes, Merrily thought, you can certainly count on having the Press here this time.

'*Fuck* the festival!' Caroline slammed down both cups. 'How can you even think of that at a time like this?'

'I'm sorry.' Terrence's shoulders shook. His unshaven cheeks were wet.

*

At the entrance to the mews, Merrily almost bumped into a woman distractedly coming down from the market place.

'Oh.' Alison Kinnersley stepped impatiently to one side. She wore a genuine Barbour, one of the very long, expensive ones, like a highwayman's coat. Rural chic. 'Vicar. I'm so sorry. Excuse me.'

She hurried past Merrily into Church Street then stopped, called back.

'Lucy Devenish – the cottage with the red door?'

'I think so.' It was not yet seven-thirty, a little early for a social call. 'Brass knocker in the shape of an elf or something.'

'Thank you,' Alison said. It had begun to rain. It was clear she was in no mood for a conversation. She didn't seem to have heard about Colette's disappearance or noticed any police activity.

Alison strode off down the street in her highwayman's coat, and didn't look back. Merrily tried to imagine what she

357

could want with Lucy Devenish. Tried to imagine her with the less-than-flamboyant Lol Robinson – living with him, chatting with him over breakfast, sleeping with him. And couldn't, on either count.

She turned back towards the vicarage, almost running, because her legs felt too short and everything in her life seemed to be moving too fast for her and it was raining harder.

*

Jane had the door open before she could even get out her key. The kid's hair was uncombed, her eyes swollen. She looked very young and forlorn, like a battered child.

'Mum?'

'Could you make some tea, flower?' Merrily stepped inside, unzipped her coat. 'The sanctuary man still here?'

'You haven't had anything to eat again, have you?'

'What's eating? Remind me. Can you make some halfway-edible toast?'

She tossed her coat on to the hall table and went through to the kitchen.

'Mrs Watkins . . .' Lol Robinson was on his feet. 'It's OK, I'm going. I just wanted to say thanks for what you did.'

'Sit down, Lol,' Merrily said. 'You too, Jane.'

'I'm making the toast.' Jane walked across the stone flags, gathering up a half-wrapped loaf. She tossed three slices of bread into the toaster, plucked a butter knife from the drainer.

'Listen. Colette Cassidy didn't come home last night. The village is full of police.'

Jane dropped the butter knife.

'They've searched the village and the orchard. They're now starting to question her friends.'

Jane had gone pale.

'Which includes you, flower.'

'The stupid . . .' Jane picked up the knife and dug it into a slab of hard, cold butter.

'So if you know anything,' Merrily said, 'maybe you should tell me first.'

Lol said, 'This isn't any of my business. I should go.'

'You really don't have to go,' Merrily said. 'But you should know the police are at your house. They found it had been broken into. In the course of their inquiries.'

Lol didn't get up.

'They probably think it was a bunch of stoned tearaways,' she said, 'from the party. So perhaps you need to tell them about your unpleasant musician friend.'

But she found herself wondering if this evil musician really existed. And what else she didn't know about Lol Robinson, friend of Jane.

Lol was slowly interlacing his fingers. Jane pulled out the knife with a slab of yellow butter on the end, and looked at it. 'What do they think happened to her?'

'They don't know, flower. Do they? What do *you* think happened to her?'

The kid pulled a smoking slice from the toaster, oblivious to the heat, laid it carefully on a Willow-pattern plate and began buttering it.

Lol Robinson turned his head towards her. Merrily turned her back on the Aga but hung on to its rail.

The knife was scraping backwards and forwards across the same crisp slice. *Scritch, scratch*, over and over.

'Do they think she's dead?'

'Why do you say that?' Merrily's voice rose, like the voice of the single tone-deaf parishioner you regularly heard at the end of a hymn.

'Somebody will be.' Jane stopped buttering, picked up the plate and carried it across to her mother. Her hands shook.

'You're not making sense, Jane.'

'I thought it might be you. Came in last night and I . . . prayed for . . . for a long time. I was going to go to the church this morning, do it properly, but then I thought you'd be there, so it . . .'

'Prayed? You?'

'Only that you wouldn't die,' Jane said miserably. 'I always have. I've never prayed for anything else in my whole life except that you wouldn't bloody die on me.'

'Flower,' Merrily said gently, 'why did you think I was going to die?'

'When you see fruit and blossom on an apple tree at the same time, it means someone close to you—'

'We haven't got an apple tree.'

'It was in the orchard! That used to be the church's. The apple dropped off and rolled at my feet. *My* feet. Couldn't have been more obvious if it was that big finger in the sky from the national lottery.'

'That bloody Lucy Devenish!'

'No! You bloody Christians!' Jane said wildly. 'You'll believe any old shit if it's in the Bible. Anything else—' She sat down opposite Lol. 'I don't know. I don't know if she's dead or not. But somebody must be. These things don't just happen.'

Lol said, 'What happened with Colette?'

Merrily took a seat. All three of them around the table, like some screwed-up, dysfunctional family in a suitably dim and draughty kitchen. She told them everything that had happened this morning. Except for seeing Alison. And except for the poster about Merrily Watkins's black mass.

'Could she have gone off with some bloke?'

'Maybe,' Jane said moodily. 'I think she did want to get laid at her party. Although being sixteen and able to do it legally seems to have taken the magic out of it.'

'You think she wanted to go into the orchard to have sex with someone? Anyone in particular?'

'The mood she was in, anyone other than Dean Wall. And in the orchard, maybe because . . . because the orchard's a taboo place. Colette loves, you know, breaking taboos.'

'A taboo place? This is because of Edgar Powell's suicide?'

'Partly. And because things happen to you in the orchard, but they never happened to her. And—'

'Excuse me,' Merrily said. 'Stop. Just stop there a minute. *Things happen to you in the orchard*? What things? And to who?'

'Whom,' Jane said.

'Don't push it, flower. Because sooner or later I'm going to have to talk to you about your sitting room. Plus, I've had next to no sleep. Plus a lot of other . . . *What things?*'

Jane looked down at the table. There came a clipped, authoritative knocking on the front door.

*

'Oh.' Merrily found a narrow smile. 'I didn't expect you so soon.'

'Well, something was brought to my attention.' Annie Howe wore a loose, white raincoat over her dark business suit. 'Which rather puts Jane at the top of our list.'

'Oh?' Merrily held open the door, not daring to think what it might be. DC Mumford followed his boss into the hall.

Merrily shut the door. 'Er . . . before you talk to Jane . . .'

Howe tilted her head impatiently. Police officers always seemed to think only they were entitled to ask questions.

'How seriously are you, the police, taking all this? I mean, Colette's . . . how can I put it?'

'A bit of a trollop,' Mumford said. 'We know.'

'Or at least,' Annie Howe added, 'that seems to be what she'd like people to think. Times change, don't they, Ms Watkins?'

'No,' Merrily said. 'Not really.'

Howe smiled. It was glacial.

'You ask how seriously we're taking this matter. In view of the circumstances, more seriously than we would if she'd simply left home. You can appreciate that.'

'Yes. Right. Sure.'

She looked at Annie Howe and thought how clean-cut and purposefully single-minded she seemed. Merrily felt much older and yet younger. She felt vulnerable, somehow, for Jane and for herself too. Which was stupid. Wasn't it?

'We'll do everything we can to help,' she said lamely.

They followed her into the kitchen. Jane was at the sink, washing up. There was no sign of Lol. Merrily introduced the police, realizing that Jane was washing up to remove the cups – three of them – from the table, so Howe wouldn't suspect they had company. She'd even pushed the third chair under the table. Co-conspirators, Jane and Lol, in something else she didn't know about.

Merrily said, 'I'll stay. If you don't mind.'

'It's important that you do, Ms Watkins.'

'Merrily,' she said. 'I'm Merrily.'

Howe didn't say that she was Annie. What did I expect, Merrily thought sourly, instant bonding of two youngish professional women together in a man's world?

'Tea? Coffee?'

'Thank you, Ms Watkins, but we had more of both than we can handle at Cassidy's Country Kitchen.'

There was going to be no softening Annie Howe. She pulled out one of the chairs, like this was an interview room at police headquarters.

'Right, sit down, Jane, we won't keep you long. What time did you get home last night?'

'Not too sure.' Jane went around to the opposite side of the table and pulled out a chair of her own. 'After one.'

'After two,' Merrily said automatically. 'I heard you come in.'

Howe raised a hand. 'Let Jane answer, please, Ms Watkins.' She sat down. 'Colette Cassidy's a good friend of yours, isn't she?'

'Well, we've only known each other a few weeks. But . . . yeah. We get along OK.'

'Do you remember where you last saw her?'

'Yeah, it was . . . on the square. I mean, you know about what happened inside, with Barry?'

'Yes. Perhaps we can come back to that later. What happened on the square?'

Merrily went to lean against the stove, which put her behind Howe and facing Jane, while the kid, with – surely – transparent honesty, related what had happened when Colette Cassidy had decided to take the party outside after the row with Barry Bloom. How Colette had bullied Dr Samedi, the DJ, into setting up his boom-box outside and then, when people came out to protest and it looked like her parents were on the way, had run off with it towards the orchard.

Howe leaned towards Jane across the pine table.

'What exactly did Colette say when she invited everyone to go to the orchard?'

'Well, she just . . . I don't know. I don't remember.'

'Let me remind you then, Jane. We have several witnesses who say Colette shouted something like, "Follow me. Or Janey. Follow Janey. She knows." Would that be you she was talking about, Jane? Is that what she called you?'

'Yeah.' Jane blinked. The first sign of nerves. Merrily gripped the Aga rail. What was this about?

Annie Howe said, 'Yeah, that's what she called you, or yeah, it was you she meant?'

'Both, I suppose.'

'Good. All right.' Howe leaned back. 'Why would Colette have suggested they follow you? Why would she have said, "she knows"?'

Jane didn't hesitate. 'Because we got a bit pissed the other weekend and some boys were chasing us and that's where we wound up. In the orchard.'

'With the boys?'

'No, we'd shaken them off.'

'Did you and Colette often get pissed?'

'Just that once. It was only cider. I mean, I thought it was only cider. I'd never had it before. It was stupid.'

Annie Howe smiled. 'It's all right, we aren't going to charge you with under-age drinking.'

'Thanks.'

Howe frowned. 'But you didn't go with her into the orchard last night, did you?'

'No.'

'Why not?'

'Because . . .' Jane looked at Merrily. 'Because my mum wasn't very well, and I didn't want to stay out too late.'

'You didn't think two a.m. was already a little bit late?'

Jane shrugged, looked at Merrily again. Annie Howe, obviously suspecting eye signals, said, 'Ms Watkins, why don't you come and sit at the table with us?' And Merrily, not wanting to give the icy bitch any reason to suspect anything, reluctantly left the meagre comfort of the stove and went to sit down next to Jane.

'So,' Howe said, 'you watched her go off into the orchard, and then what did you do?'

'Just sort of wandered around.'

'You didn't talk to anyone?'

'No.'

'You're sure about that, Jane?'

'Yeah. Oh . . . Well, I did talk to Lloyd Powell.' Jane sighed. 'I asked him to go and get them out of the orchard. He owns it. His family.'

'Mr Powell seems to think you were worried about Colette.'

'I suppose so.'

'Because you thought she might be attacked?'

'No. I mean—'

'Then why?'

'Because . . . Colette's kind of headstrong. She gets like carried away.'

'You're saying you were more worried about what she might do than what might happen to her?'

'Yeah. I suppose I was.'

'What did you think she might do?'

'I don't know.'

'All right, let's go back to the party. Did you know there were drugs about?'

'I think so.'

'You knew the people who were supplying them?'

Jane didn't reply. Oh no, Merrily thought. Oh, surely not. I'd have known. Wouldn't I?

'Do you know Mark Putley?'

'Not really. We go to the same school, that's all. I don't think I've ever spoken to him.'

'What about Colette?'

'I don't think she knew him at all. She'd have no reason to. She goes to a different school.'

'Then why was he at her party?'

'Gatecrashed, I suppose. Him and a couple of others.'

'As far as you know, Colette hadn't invited them.'

'No. I mean . . . No.'

'Were you going to say something else there, Jane?'

Jane trailed her finger through some spilled tea on the tabletop. 'I suppose I was going to say not officially.'

'What do you mean by that?'

'I . . .' Jane hesitated. 'Oh hell . . . She thought the kids her parents approved of – because they knew the kids' parents and everything – she thought they were all going to be a bit like safe. She wanted to kind of spice things up a bit. So like, yeah, she might have made it easier for the local guys to get in. Like that's the sort of thing she does. I mean, you never really know what she's going to do.'

'Or who with?' Annie Howe stood up. 'Thank you, Jane. You won't be going out, will you? We may want to talk to you again. Thank you, Ms Watkins.'

Merrily saw Jane blow out her cheeks in some kind of relief, and in the middle of it, Howe suddenly turned back to her.

'Oh . . . one last thing, Jane . . . Did you see anyone else around after the party? Anyone you didn't know. Or perhaps someone you knew hadn't been invited?'

'No. I don't think so.'

Annie Howe said, 'How well do you know Laurence Robinson?'

Jane was caught out. She looked startled. Even Merrily thought she looked startled.

'I . . . I've met him a couple of times,' Jane said. 'He sometimes helps out at Ledwardine Lore. I've seen him there.'

'Have you ever been to his house?'

'No. Not really. I've been . . . sort of *past* his house.'

'And Colette. Does she know Mr Robinson?'

'I suppose so. I mean, yes. We all kind of know him, because he used to be a kind of rock star. Sort of.'

'When you say we *all* know him, who do you mean? Other girls?'

'No, just Colette and me. And Lucy Devenish.'

'When did you last see Mr Robinson, Jane?'

'I can't remember.'

'You can't remember all the way back to last night? When you were seen talking to Mr Robinson in Church Street?'

'Was I? Oh. Yes. I think I met him on my way to the party. Yes, I did.'

'But he didn't go to the party. Or did he?'

'No, he didn't.'

Howe smiled her ice-maiden's smile. 'Well, thank you again. As I say, we may come back. Or if there's anything you or your mother want to tell us, there'll always be someone at the Country Kitchen. Until we find Colette.'

*

Merrily followed them numbly to the door, where Annie Howe said, 'Do *you* know Laurence Robinson, Ms Watkins?'

Merrily said, 'I may have met him. I don't really know him.'

'He lives alone, doesn't he?'

'So I believe. He had a girlfriend. She left, I'm told.'

'And you felt . . . all right . . . about Jane seeing him. A man twenty years older, living on his own.'

Merrily said softly, 'Is there a problem?'

'He's just someone we need to eliminate from our inquiries. I suppose I can tell you. As a clergyperson. I know it'll go no further.'

'You have my word,' Merrily said.

'Mr Robinson isn't at home, but his cottage is in rather a mess. It may be a break-in, it may be a burglary – because there certainly isn't much furniture in there. But there are signs of what might have been a struggle. The stereo left on.

367

A damaged record on the turntable. There's no sign of the owner or anybody else. And Mr Robinson – this is the confidential part, at this stage – has a history. A record.'

'He made records,' Merrily heard herself saying, ridiculously.

'*Our* type of record, Ms Watkins. We believe he likes young girls.'

'What?'

'Laurence Robinson was convicted of having sex with a minor. Girl. Under-age.' Howe's smile was steely and barbed, like a safety pin opening up.

TWENTY-NINE

Cogs

By nine o'clock, they were putting up the last of the bunting and the fancy lights, Gomer Parry lifting Lloyd Powell in the bucket of his pet digger, Gwynneth, and not happy about this – a bit dangerous, it was, see, with no insurance to cover it and all these coppers around.

For once, though, the police never even noticed Gomer. Too busy trying to find the Cassidys' promiscuous daughter. Or was it precocious? No, this time Gomer reckoned he had it about right.

Got to feel sorry for them, though, the Cassidys. Moved out here to get away from, the big bad city. Wound up somewhere *little* and bad.

Gomer watched Lloyd Powell up in the bucket, attaching a string of wooden lanterns to a wrought-iron hook on the right-hand gable of the Black Swan. No coloured lights, this wasn't Christmas; these were Middle Ages-style lamps, handmade by this blacksmith bloke, from Croydon, had a workshop bottom of Old Barn Lane. Feller provided the lanterns free in the hope of picking up a few orders.

Take more than a few wooden lanterns to light up this place, though.

Little and bad.

Now why did he think that? It was a decent village, in many ways. Friendly, on the whole, nobody complaining about the newcomers. Not as it would make much difference if they did, mind, seeing as how the newcomers were now well in the majority, or maybe it just felt like that, on account of they ran everything, with their superior knowledge of marketing and public relations, fancy stuff like that.

Course, Gomer, he was a newcomer too. Not so much of one, like, on account of he only moved about twenty miles and he talked near enough the same, and he'd done a lot of work in these parts, over the years, so knew quite a few people before he moved in. Like Bull-Davies, whose fields he'd drained. Like Rod Powell, whose new cesspit he'd dug in '76, when Lloyd was no more than a babby and ole Mrs Powell, Edgar's missus, had been alive to terrorize Rod's wife. Drove her away in the end. Fearsome woman, Meggie Powell.

Aye, it was a hard place all round, was Ledwardine, when Gomer first come here. Lucy Devenish'd been right about that. Them days, some poor bloke with a Mr Cassidy accent ventured into the Black Swan, there'd be a red-cheeked, stone-eyed young farm-labourer, pissed-up on cheap scrumpy and just itching to punch his lights out for the fun of it. And for resentment's sake. Nobody hereabouts was rich, see, save for the Bulls, and they always punched back. Except when they punched first.

Sawdust on the floor of the Black Swan, them days, to make it easier cleaning up the blood and the puke.

There was an exhibition of posh watercolours opening in the Swan this evening, with a recital by a string quartet.

At the new tourist information office (once a butcher's shop, with slaughterhouse behind, blood and offal running down Church Street on Fridays) there was a display of local crafts, crafted by folk from London and Birmingham. On Monday evening, a poetry reading.

Gomer looked up at a movement. Out of Church Street

strode the Bull-Davies floozy, a little smile on her mouth. Now that was a funny business, the big Bull penned up by a woman came out of nowhere. Who was she, what had she got in mind for James, and where had she been this not-so-fine morning?

'OK, Gomer?'

The chubby face of Child, the organist, up at the window.

'Aye,' Gomer said. 'Have him all dressed up by eleven, the ole square, sure t'be. Some o' the little flags got pulled down last night, see, but we put 'em back, no problem.'

'Good man,' said Child. 'By the way, for my sins, I've been co-opted as festival co-ordinator for the duration of the present crisis. Poor old Terrence being hardly in the mood for public conviviality, as you can imagine.'

'Aye,' Gomer said. 'Wondered if they might call it off, under the circumstances.'

'We did think about it, but we've all put a lot of work in, and as it's going to go on for the whole season, postponing the opening ceremony would hardly seem like a good precedent. Besides, people coming from miles away, no way of letting them know. Anyway, it's not as if she's dead. She'll be on somebody's settee in Hereford, sleeping it off with her mouth open and her knickers round her ankles, what d'you say, Gomer?'

'Mabbe,' Gomer said, noting the relish in Child's voice. 'And mabbe not. 'Scuse me a sec.'

Lloyd Powell having given him the thumbs-down sign from the bucket, Gomer set about bringing him to the ground. Got to do it smoothly; one jerk and he'd be pitching the boy through the window of the public bar, and it was a good few years since anybody done that. Harry Morgan, the feed supplier, had probably been the last, slammed through the glass by John Bull-Davies, James's ole feller, for putting it around as the Bulls never paid their bills.

Hard men, the Bulls, always had been, and now here was James being led around the square and back again by the blonde floozie like there was a ring through his nose. Power of sex, eh?

'Leave you to it, Gomer.' Dermot Child busied off towards the Tourist Info. Lloyd clambered out of the bucket. Gomer leaned out.

'All finished then, is it? Good boy.'

'What did Child want?'

'Oh, he's in charge now, boy, is Mr Dermot Child. Gotter do what he says, see.'

'All we need,' said Lloyd. 'Got me in his choral thing, he has. *Auld cider*. Plus, we gotter do this barbershop kind of thing at the opening. Followed by a Cider Tasting.'

'That'd be for folk as dunno what cider tastes like, would it?'

'Kind of thing,' Lloyd said. 'Good stuff, mind.'

'The Wine of Angels?'

'Sharp, though. Dry. Take the hairs outer your nose.'

'Your dad done it all by isself then?'

'Old recipe, Gomer.' Lloyd tapped his nose. 'Cassidy, he wanted to make a thing out of it, let the visitors in, get a carthorse workin' the ole mill. Bugger that, Dad says, that's for the museums. So we done it all ourselves, the millin' and the pressin'. Served up the casks to Barry Bloom – least you can get some sense out of 'im – and he organized the bottles. It goes all right, we'll do it next year. Be a good crop. Plus we won't have to buy no apples in next time, looks of things.'

'Aye,' Gomer said and left it at that. Boy was right; never seen that much blossom in the Powell orchard, not in his lifetime anyway. Caused a fair bit of comment, too, grizzly farmers in the Ox mumbling about how it was Edgar's brains must've fertilized them twisted ole trees.

'Looks like that's it, then, Gomer.' Lloyd looking up at the bunting and lanterns. 'May's well take 'im home.' He grinned. 'If Minnie'll let you bring 'im through the gate.'

Gomer growled. Boy was more right than he knew. Minnie, she'd got this plan for a proper garden now, with rocks and a bloody fountain – cherub having a pee, no doubt. Which would require space, see. And what was taking up more space than a certain collection of near-vintage plant-hire equipment? Things was getting tense.

He pulled in the bucket, nice and tidy, and gently trundled Gwynneth to the edge of the square. By God, he loved this ole thing. The way she answered to every little flick of the levers. You could do anything with Gwynneth, with both eyes shut. Responsive, see, like a good sheepdog.

Waiting to get her into Church Street, Gomer saw two people. First was Lucy Devenish in her woolly cape-thing, striding out determined behind her moped. The ole warrior out for somebody's scalp this morning, sure t'be.

Second was that little Jane, the vicar's daughter. Not so bright and smiley today as she come out the vicarage gateway. A friend of that Colette Cassidy's. Lucky she hadn't gone with her last night to wherever it was. And Gomer was frankly a bit dubious about Dermot Child's theory that Colette'd been whisked off by some young stud with pleasure in mind. He did not like the feel of this, the way she'd disappeared into the orchard, no more than he liked the feel of the orchard itself, for all its explosion of blossom.

Too much blossom. They used to say that orchard'd been no good since it was cursed, back in the seventeenth century, by this Wil Williams, the vicar who done his bit of wizarding on the side and hung hisself when he was rumbled. Well, Gomer had no fixed opinions on cursing, and there was some as said the orchard was just let go on account of the crippling new tax on cider imposed by King Charles II – fifteen pence on a hogshead. But there was nobody could deny that if he'd hung hisself where they said he'd done it, the last thing this Wil Williams would've seen as he was swinging there . . . was that orchard.

He'd have stopped Lucy, got her opinion on a few things, except she looked so purposeful you'd have to block the way with ole Gwynneth to get her to pull up.

Unless you was young Jane, just as determined it looked like.

'Lucy!' The youngster running after the ole woman down Church Street.

Gomer saw Lucy stop in the middle of climbing on to her moped, and then they was talking something furious, arms waving and such. What he wouldn't've given to know what they was jabbering on about this gloomy ole morning.

*

'No, listen, Jane,' Lucy said. 'Please listen.'

Under her hat, her face was very red and her eyes were burning. She looked like an old-fashioned stove, this like huge, massive heat building up inside her.

'You know, don't you?' Jane said. 'You know where she is.'

'No.' Lucy took hold of both Jane's shoulders, propelled her backwards into the alley by the side of the Ox, where she and Colette had escaped from Dean Wall and Danny Gittoes. 'I *don't* know. But Jane, you must stay well away from it. Listen to me. What you must do is stay with your mother. Talk to her. Make her understand something.'

'Till the apple appeared on the ground, I thought, you know, I thought the worst that could happen was she'd get like . . . taken away. Like me. And maybe she wouldn't be able to handle that because of the kind of person she is, and—'

THE WINE OF ANGELS

Lucy's grip tightened on her shoulders. Her hands were terrifically strong, and there was so much heat there that Jane was scared into silence. She'd never seen Lucy like this before.

'Jane. Are you listening now?'

'Yes.' Jane felt very small. It was quite dim in the alley on a dull day like this. She could detect the thin, acid odour of urine from the Gents' toilet. It reminded her, in some awful way, of cider.

'Something happened to your mother last night,' Lucy said. 'In the church.'

'She was ill. Dean Wall and those creeps were making a big joke about it at the party and saying she was like possessed by a demon or something.'

'And they won't be the only ones,' Lucy said. 'Others may be subtler. There'll be pressure on her. Much of it from inside. Self-doubt. Do you know what I mean?'

Jane wasn't sure she did. 'She gets a bit overtired sometimes. She's not as certain about things as she used to be, but, like, she doesn't talk much about it. She just asks me questions I can't answer.'

'Yes, I know you can't. But what I mean, Jane, is that it will have occurred to her, consciously or not, that she became ill at the moment of taking her vows because she was not *meant* to take those vows. Not meant to commit herself to this parish. At some point, if it hasn't happened already, she'll be telling herself it was all wrong and that she really knew this all the time. That she made a mistake.'

'What, becoming a vicar? Going into the Church?'

'Possibly that. Or coming here. I know that must have been a shock for you, too, having a mother who suddenly decides to commit herself to God.'

'I'm not really jealous of the Old Guy.'

'I know.' Lucy's grip softened. 'But perhaps you haven't been as supportive as you might have been.'

375

'I've tried, really. I mean, we always talked the same language basically, if we stayed off religion. And like, after what's been happening I thought maybe there's some chance we could connect there as well, but we're coming at it from different directions, aren't we? I mean, sometimes I feel really . . . alight with it. But I can't tell her, she's like so blocked . . . yeah? With all the dogma and stuff. I mean, I left the Traherne book lying around, but she's always so busy.'

'Jane.' Lucy looked very serious. 'This is not the time to sit up on your superior teenager's perch . . . And don't look at me like that, you little snot. Your mother may have a restricted viewpoint professionally, but there's a thinking, feeling, responsive person under that cassock.'

'She doesn't wear that thing any more, thank goodness. Except, like, on the shop floor.'

'Yes. A sign, perhaps, that the person's re-emerging. She'll come to it in her own way, perhaps, and while you might have had a crash course, her knowledge is still a hundred times greater than yours. But you have to help her. If she won't come to me, and I can understand why she won't, then she needs you to tell her that coming here was not the mistake she's fearing it may have been. That she's very much needed here. She needs assurance from *you*, not from the bishop, not from the Cassidys, not from that pompous old fool, Ted Clowes.'

'She just asks me questions!'

'Then answer them as best you can, and pray for help.'

'Pray?' Jane turned away from the toilet smell, avoiding Lucy's hawk-like eyes. 'Who to?'

'You'll know,' Lucy said. 'And there's another thing. Last night, your mother indicated to me that she was going to refuse to allow Richard Coffey to put on his dreadful play in the church.'

'Yeah. We had a bit of a row about it. She talked to Stefan

Alder and she thought he'd got this unhealthy obsession. This kind of gay thing, you know? But that's not why she's against it. It's because he's in love with someone who's dead and it's like, you know, spiritual necrophilia and all that yuk stuff she doesn't think I know about. Like she doesn't want him to satisfy his weird lusts or whatever in church. I said I thought it was cool and kind of beautiful and she was being stupid.'

'You were right,' Lucy said. 'But for the wrong reasons. Jane, she must change her mind. She has to let Wil's spirit speak. She must be convinced. You'll have to be subtle.'

Jane was confused. 'But you said it was a *dreadful* play . . .'

'It's not the play, it's the machinery of it. The cogs it turns. The play may not be the play Coffey envisages. Not if Merrily stays. I thought she'd be a catalyst, but I thought it might take years, but it isn't, it's happening very, very quickly.'

'You've lost me.'

'It doesn't matter.' Lucy was looking feverish again, burning up inside. 'Jane, I have to go.'

'Where?'

'Perhaps I shall come and see you and your mother. It's too much for one person to carry, especially someone old and creaky like myself.'

'What is?'

Lucy lowered her arms, stepped away from Jane, looking about as old and creaky as a jumbo jet on the verge of take-off. Jane didn't think she'd ever seen anyone as powered-up. She thought she ought to tell Lucy about Lol and his problems, why he'd spent the night at the vicarage, how he'd inadvertently let Mum in to see the painted walls, leading to one of those questions Lucy said she'd have to try and answer.

'Go home, Jane. Remember what I said.'

'OK.' They walked out of the alley into Church Street, where Lucy climbed on to her moped.

A police car went past. 'I didn't tell *them* anything,' Jane said.

'The police? The police questioned you?'

'Inspector Howe. She was horrible. She looks like a sadistic dentist. She's coming back if they don't find Colette. She seems to think I know something.'

Lucy smiled briefly. 'Jane, if you told her what you know I think it would be safe to say she would never bother you again.'

'She'd think I was bonkers? She told Mum something I couldn't hear, when they were leaving, and Mum was a bit funny afterwards.'

Lucy stopped. 'Funny in what way?'

'Kind of shocked. And when I felt I had to come out of there and think about things on my own and I said maybe I'd go for a walk and kind of cool off, she seemed glad and she almost pushed me out, you know? I think that woman told her they thought Colette had been attacked or raped or something so bad she couldn't face talking to me about it. I mean, *you* don't think . . .?'

'I shall be honest with you, Jane,' Lucy said. 'I fear your inspector may be right.'

'No!' Jane stared at her, filled with a horrid, stark dismay. 'I wanted you to tell me I was wrong! Tell me that old apple was just . . . just like some stupid coincidence.'

Realizing as she said it that this was a stupid, make-it-all-right-mummy, little-girl reaction.

'Help your mother,' Lucy said. 'Be there, as they say, for her. I shall come and talk to you both.'

'You're not going to the orchard, are you, Lucy?'

Lucy's smile was somehow less . . . brave.

'Not exactly. Go to your mother.'

*

The vicarage looked at its biggest and drabbest when approached uphill from Church Street. Its timbers needed a few coats of paint or preservative, or whatever they used, its white bits were grey, its windows black, except . . .

Jane froze on the pavement, looking up. There was a light in the third storey. In the Apartment. A single, white light.

It was the sun, surely, the sun must have come out. She turned, looked all over the sky for the sun, catching a sliver of light between two bunches of cloud, but it wasn't enough. Something in that room was alive.

Wrong word, Jane thought, in terror. *Wrong word.*

Affliction

It was the way she looked at him.

Lol came in from the scullery.

She was waiting for him in the kitchen. Merrily. Little and dark and not girlish. This quietness around her.

The way she looked at him made him feel sick. The black-eyed dog was with her, like a shadow.

He'd listened to the detective dealing out the questions in a clipped and unsympathetic way that was surely all wrong for getting information out of a kid like Jane. Maybe, wherever the detective had come from, the teenagers she was used to questioning were hard and sullen, you had to be heavy with them. Lol thought Jane had been incredible, the way she'd handled it. So young, so much together.

And then the heavy one.

How well do you know Laurence Robinson? The question coming over like a missile, making him cringe into the corner of the doorway, a greasy, steel hinge biting into his forehead.

'OK,' Merrily said coldly, 'Sit down, Mr Robinson.'

He went and sat in the chair vacated by Jane and then wished he hadn't; she was looking at him like he was caressing some item of the girl's underwear.

'She told you, right?' Asking the question, but he couldn't look at her. 'The policewoman.'

'Told me what?'

'About Tracy Cooke.'

Merrily sat down opposite him, in a self-conscious way which showed she was forcing herself to do this, as an ordained church-person, a licensed member of the soul-police. He remembered the way his parents' minister had spoken to him, youngish guy called Gregory Wallace, meeting him at the door of the family home, informing him, on their behalf, that he was no longer welcome here. Suggesting he might care to join a church. Some other church, in some other town. Ask for God's help with his *affliction*.

'See, the way you're looking at me, Mrs Watkins, it's like you really ought to be handing me over to the police. Only, because you're a priest, you're going to give me a chance to unburden myself to you first. And then you'll persuade me to do the right thing and give myself up. That about it?'

'Whatever you think is appropriate. For a priest.'

'I don't think any of it's appropriate. But you don't ever get away from it.' He met her eyes again. 'Now you're thinking, would he have had time to sneak out of his sleeping bag, go and do whatever he did to Colette Cassidy and slink back before it got light?'

'I thought that about twenty minutes ago. It seemed unlikely.'

'But possible.'

'Yes.'

He blinked it away. Weeping would be like confirmation. The sex-offender breaks down.

'OK, then.' He stood up. 'I'll leave and you call the police. Or I'll just go back to the cottage and wait for them, and I've never been here. I won't tell them I've been here. If I could ask you one last favour . . . Is it possible you could look after Ethel? Not for ever, obviously. If you could tell Lucy, she'll take her. Or sort something out. That's if they . . . you know . . . if they take me away.'

'Oh, for fuck's sake.' Merrily closed her eyes in utter weariness. 'Can't you say anything without going round in circles? Tell me about this . . . Tracy.'

'Cooke,' Lol said. 'Tracy Cooke.'

*

The rain had stopped, but left a wind behind. Jane turned away from the vicarage, all of a dither. The bright light in the top window had gone out. The window was quite black now. It had not been a real light, had it?

No more real than the little lights in the orchard.

She had to think about all this, decide what was real.

The market square was full of strange vehicles, including two police cars and a red car with an aerial on top – local radio, and they weren't here for the opening of the Ledwardine Festival. Was Colette news? A girl who disappears during her sixteenth birthday party. Yes, it was, wasn't it?

And the festival was happening all around it. People rushing about: Dermot Child and Lloyd Powell and Uncle Ted – serious-faced people who should be smiling, making jokes, under the bunting and the fancy new lanterns. In front of the market hall, a little stage was going up, with a van like Dr Samedi's, only with permanent loud speakers on top.

Welcome to de carn-i-val.

The whole atmosphere was so weird. Like Ledwardine was inside one of those round glass ornaments and somebody was shaking it hard and everything was swirling around and when the village was eventually put down, when it all came to rest, nothing was going to be the same.

In the little globes, it was always snow that was swirled. Here it was apple blossom: specks of it everywhere, carried in on the wind, very white under the summerless, grey sky.

The orb had been shaken and the orchard was back in the village.

The thought made Jane quiver. She felt she had to cling to one of the pillars of the market hall or she'd be blown away in the blossom. Again.

Above her a new poster had gone up for Dermot Child's choral work.

𝕺𝖑𝖉 𝕮𝖎𝖉𝖊𝖗 . . . 𝖋𝖊𝖊𝖑 𝖙𝖍𝖊 𝖗𝖊𝖉 𝖊𝖆𝖗𝖙𝖍 𝖒𝖔𝖛𝖊.

*

Lol talked. It seemed very hard for him, but if it was an act, he was bloody good. If it was an act then everything else about him was false. He talked like he himself was hearing all this aloud for the first time.

And Merrily, willing Jane not to come back until this was over, found herself constructing a story around the faltering fragments, filling in what was unsaid.

This Tracy Cooke was nearly fifteen at the time. She had a friend called Kath Hurley, who was sixteen, though you wouldn't have known. You'd have guessed Kath was about twenty-five, and Tracy would have worn a lot of make-up trying to keep up. Merrily tried not to cast Jane and Colette in the roles; it was not appropriate.

Tracy and Kath were rock fans from Banbury in Oxfordshire. They went to a lot of gigs. Afterwards, they – Kath particularly – liked to talk to the musicians, if they were accessible. One night they went into Oxford, to one of the colleges, to see a band called Hazey Jane play this quite gentle, mostly acoustic music that wasn't all that fashionable at the time, and the audience wasn't very big, so it was easy for Kath and Tracy to get talking to the guys in the band.

Karl, who played bass and piano, was very extrovert and generous, and he said, would the girls like to come back to their hotel, have dinner? Dinner was what he said. Very sophisticated. That would have been the clincher for Tracy and Kath.

Turned out that only two of them were staying at the hotel – Karl himself and the singer, Lol – who was the one Kath really fancied, though he looked very young.

But Karl, who was in charge of this situation, he fancied Kath, who was the best looking, and so he made sure that Lol was sitting next to Tracy in the hotel, which was really just a pub with spare rooms. And when Karl and Kath went to the bar, Karl nudged her and laughed a lot as he got the barman to put vodka, lots of it, in Lol and Tracy's drinks. Karl, at some stage, said they would have dinner 'sent up', and Kath thought, yeah, fair enough, and so they went into their separate rooms and fucked, natch.

Which would have been OK. Which would have been fine . . . if Karl hadn't said after a while to Kath that maybe they should invite Tracy and Lol to join them, bring a little variation into the proceedings. And Kath, who – as Karl told him later, by way of consolation – had fancied Lol in the first place, said, yeah, why not?

And so Karl pulls on his briefs and strolls along to Lol's room. Not locked, of course, hotel rooms often weren't in those days, particularly a place this economical. Karl finds Lol and Tracy sleeping like the babies they were, and, being the considerate guy he is, he doesn't like to wake them up, he just squeezes himself in on Tracy's side.

'You were asleep all this time?' Merrily said. 'He didn't wake you up?'

'I was . . . drunk,' Lol admitted. 'Not used to it. You know what that's like.'

'Yeah,' Merrily said. 'So does Jane.' He worried her again then, the way he winced. But she said, 'Go on.'

Karl, of course, is not sleepy, and one thing leads to

another, and about five minutes later little Tracy wakes up almost suffocating, with her nose in this big, hairy chest and these big, sweaty hands easing her thighs apart.

Tracy goes berserk. Tracy has, presumably, just made love with gentle, hesitant Lol. Tracy is hysterical with shock and terror.

Guests in neighbouring rooms are awakened. One marches down to reception and demands that the licensee calls the police, and when they arrive they find a tearful Tracy over by the window, wrapped in one of the curtains, and the defendant-to-be, Laurence Robinson, 20, drunkenly fumbling some clothes on.

There is no one else in the room.

Questioned by police, Kathleen Hurley, 16, of Riverdale Drive, Banbury, insists that Karl Windling spent the entire night with her, and no, they didn't get much sleep which is how she knows he didn't slip away.

In the face of blanket denials, further investigation simply isn't worth the manpower. The police go with what they've got, which is Laurence Iain Robinson. The parents of Tracy Cooke insisting the prosecution should go ahead, as their daughter's reputation as a decent, modest person is on the line and these bloody pop people think they can get away with anything. Tracy tries to speak up for Lol; nobody listens.

*

Jane wandered into the mews. Cassidy's Country Kitchen was open as usual, and doing good business, although, not surprisingly, there was no sign of the proprietors.

Ledwardine Lore, however, was shut. Jane watched three obvious tourists walk up to the door and push and shake the handle and then walk away, shrugging. Business-wise, this could have been Lucy's best day for ages. Wherever she'd gone on her moped, it was obviously terribly important. Even the lights were out behind the Closed sign. Only a pale glimmering of fairy wings in the window.

Fairies. Yes, Lucy had said, people saw fairies with gossamer wings, fairies very much like these. It was how they were traditionally perceived, and how people liked to think of them. Like very tiny angels. Which was what they were. Tiny angels. But neither fairies nor angels were, in reality, like these images. And yet they were. It was complicated, Lucy said, and yet very, very simple. Simple as blossom, as lights in an apple tree.

'Excuse me.' At the mouth of the mews, a plump, twenty-something woman stepped out in front of Jane. 'I'm with BBC Radio Hereford and Worcester. I don't suppose you *know* Colette Cassidy, do you?'

She looked a bit harassed. She wore a black velvet hat and had a heavy-looking tape recorder clutched to her side; it looked as if the strap had broken.

'Sure,' Jane said.

'Thank God. Could I ask you a few things about her?'

'OK.'

'Terrific.' A microphone was unwound, with a blobby thing on the end. 'Be with you in a couple of seconds. Sorry, your name is?'

'Jane W— Wilkins.' It was OK talking about Colette, but she didn't fancy any vicar's daughter stuff.

'OK, Jane . . . So, were you at the party?'

'Yeah.' The microphone about six inches from her nose.

'I gather it was fairly lively.'

'No,' Jane said. 'Not really.'

'*No?*'

'It was quite dull, actually. People were just dancing and stuff. And drinking Coke.'

'Why did they all come outside?'

'Fresh air, I suppose.'

'Oh. I understood there was some dancing going on out here.'

'No, not really. People were just kind of wandering off. It was no big deal.'

'Wasn't Colette trying to . . . you know . . . get them going?'

'No, she's not like that. She's very quiet. I don't think she really wanted a party. It was just kind of expected. Normally, she liked, er, reading. And going for walks. Very interested in wildlife and, er, flowers. That sort of thing.'

'So what do you think's happened to her?'

'Well, knowing Colette, she probably went off somewhere with a friend to get away from it all. For cocoa or something. Stayed the night.'

'Oh.' The reporter switched off her machine. 'Well. Thanks, Jane.' Turned and walked off towards the radio car on the square. 'Thanks a fucking bunch,' Jane heard.

*

Merrily tried to remember if she'd read about it at the time, but as Hazey Jane were hardly famous, it probably hadn't been widely reported.

'They said I was very lucky,' Lol said. 'It could easily have been rape.'

'It *was* rape, surely?' Merrily said. 'And how on earth did he persuade that girl not to give evidence, if this was her friend?'

Lol was silent for a moment. 'I don't know. I imagine he threw her around a bit and gave her some money. Karl thinks on his feet, even when he's stoned.'

'So you were alone in the dock. What did you get?'

'Probation.' He was looking down at the table.

She could see him fighting the tears. Eighteen years ago,

and the wound was still wide open and oozing. Did she believe this? If it was true, it was hardly shocking when you considered it had happened nearly twenty years ago, when the alleged victim was not so much younger than the alleged criminal and probably emotionally more mature.

'I mean, I *did it*,' Lol said. 'I pleaded guilty. I had sex with an under-age girl. It was enough. In the eyes of God . . . as they say.'

'Who say?'

'My parents. Well, they're dead now. It was what they said at the time. Well, they didn't actually say it because neither of them ever spoke to me again. Only their minister. He spoke for them. And for God. As you priests do.'

'What denomination was this?'

'I can't remember. Big pink building, with posters outside.'

Merrily smiled.

'They'd caught religion in middle age. It just pushed everything else out. I was like a lodger by then. The old pictures of me as a kid all gone. Replaced by pictures of Jesus.'

'Only child?'

He nodded. 'But I'd stopped being their son in any real sense when I wouldn't go to their church. After they threw me out, they had my room . . . cleansed.'

Merrily said, 'Lucy Devenish know about this?'

'Some. After that, I went a bit . . .'

*

Gigging doesn't come easy when your last public appearance was in court. When your parents have thrown you out – spawn of Satan – and you're living in one room over a fish and chip shop in Swindon. And your music is stuck in a time warp and you keep dwelling on Nick Drake who was afraid of playing live and so never built up a following, so his records didn't sell and the black depression set in – the 'Black-Eyed Dog' at the door, like the 'Hellhound on my Trail' of the 1930s blues singer Robert Johnson who was so shy they had to record him facing the wall and died at twenty-six, just like Nick Drake. And you're getting more and more confused and taking pills and you get it into your head that there's some dark virus in the music, passed from Johnson to Drake and maybe other people in between, and now it's in you.

The band fizzles out, as bands do. You're living alone in one room and a toilet. One day, Dennis Clarke, the drummer, comes to see you.

Suburban Dennis is appalled at the way you're living, the stuff you're taking, your hair unwashed, your eyes way back in your head where it's always night. And your current girlfriend, who picked you up in a pub, is nearly old enough to be your mother, almost certainly on the game, and she takes your money and brings you drugs. You're ill and she's making you worse.

The truth of it was blindingly obvious to Merrily.

'You were afraid of young girls, weren't you? You were probably even afraid of girls your own age in case they turned out to be younger than they said they were, right? You felt safe with this woman.'

Lol shrugged.

'Are you still afraid of them, Lol? Were you afraid of Jane? Even though you came into the house with her last night? Went up to her room?'

Lol's fist tightened.

It was this Dennis who realized Lol had had a breakdown. Dennis who got him into the hospital. Dennis and a mate of his who was a doctor. Voluntary, of course. Lol was a voluntary patient. No kicking and screaming, no straitjackets.

On the other hand, no analysis. No therapy that you couldn't swallow with a glass of water. But he was glad of the rest.

And time passed.

'*How* long?'

'Yeah, I know, I know. It's very easy for people on the outside to say you should have got yourself out. But you get very . . . grateful. It's to do with people helping you. Stopping people helping you, that's the hard bit. Saying, no, I don't want help, I don't need your help. I'm all right, piss off. It was like Karl – he helped me get through the court thing.'

'How did he do that, Lol?'

Lol sighed. 'He gave me stuff to make it so that it didn't matter.'

'Or so you didn't have second thoughts about implicating him. Was that how you got started? Was it heroin?'

'No. I don't know what it was. Well, I do. But that doesn't matter. It wasn't addiction, just reliance. That's different. I think. But the more you took, the less it mattered, sure. In hospital, they call it your *medication*.'

'God.'

'Can we skip the hospital? I think they were doing their best. I did get out eventually. People helped. Dennis again. Then this sound-engineer we once worked with, Prof Levin, who was an alcoholic, nice guy, he put me in touch with Gary Kennedy, who was looking for a lyricist. So things looked up, money came in, quite a lot. Things were better.'

And then there was Alison. Alison was a friend of one of the nurses at the hospital, who'd become a friend of Lol's and kept in touch. Alison was the first girlfriend he'd had in a long, long time who was younger than him. So Alison was progress. She also made Lol realize *he* wasn't such a young person any more, and where had it gone, his youth?

Missing years. You never make up for missing years. But

he'd made it through to the other side of something. Unlike Nick Drake and Robert Johnson, he had not died, although there'd been a period when the thought of it hadn't frightened him too much.

Listen, Alison had said – this beautiful creature, too beautiful to entirely believe in – listen, why don't we get out of here?

They'd found the cottage the very next day. Like it was meant, Lol said, and something about the way he said it made Merrily wonder. She found herself thinking of Alison. On the square at night with an upper-class drunk calling her a whore, a slinky, slinky, whore. And that morning in the church. *James is full of shit, I thought I should tell you that.*

What are you full of, Alison?

She stood up. 'Let's have some more tea, Lol.'

He looked at her. He nodded. He didn't ask her if she believed him, and because of that she found she did.

*

On the square, a TV cameraman was unpacking his video gear. The local radio woman snorted. 'Bollocks.'

'Bella . . .'

The radio woman turned towards a man leaning out of the window of a chunky, blue four-wheel-drive thing. He beckoned her over. Jane followed, not sure why.

'You know where King's Oak Corner is, Bella?' the man in the four-wheel-drive asked.

'Maybe. What for?'

'Developments,' the man in the four-wheel-drive said.

'Oh yeah?' The radio woman hugged her tape recorder, looked unconvinced.

The man held up a mobile phone. 'I know a man with a police scanner. He reckons there's some interest in King's Oak Corner. Just if you're going that way, Bella, my darling, we could follow you, and don't say I never do you any favours.'

'Yeah, all right.' Bella nodded towards the cameraman, who'd met up with this sassy-looking girl in a long, black mac. 'Be casual. Don't want the circus, do we?'

He nodded, and the four-wheel-drive crawled to the edge of the cobbles. Bella made a play of standing around and looking at her watch before making her way to the radio car.

Where Jane was waiting for her.

'OK, if I come with you?'

'Certainly not,' Bella said.

'She's my best friend. Colette.'

'Sounded like it. I bet you don't even know what she looks like.'

Jane stepped out of the way of a troupe of jingling morris dancers alighting from a minibus. Several of them were laughing at something, evidently unaware of anything going on apart from the launch of the Ledwardine Festival.

'Please,' Jane said.

'We're not supposed to take members of the public in this.' Bella unlocked the radio car with a bleeper. 'BBC regulations. Sorry.'

'Oh, well, that's OK.' Jane sighed. 'I suppose I could ask those TV people.'

The morris dancers headed up the steps to the Black Swan. There was a muted cheer from inside.

'All right, you evil little bitch,' said Bella. 'Get in. But if they've found a body, you keep well out of the way or we'll both be stuffed.'

THIRTY-ONE

Accessory

Of the three roads close to Ledwardine, the B road to Madley, in the west, was the quietest. It was an old road which had been re-routed, straightened and widened, taking a strip off the great orchard and dividing two farmhouses, including the Powells', from the village. A mile out of Ledwardine, spectacular views opened up, across the lush, quilted Wye Valley to the Black Mountains on the Welsh border.

'It's beautiful, sure,' Bella said, 'but not so terrific as a news area. Well, not usually anyway.'

It was clear that Bella was secretly hoping Colette was dead. Jane thought you must really hate yourself for that, if you were a reporter or an ambitious detective – wishing for something really awful to happen to somebody while you just happened to be on the spot.

'I don't really work here,' Bella said. 'I'm on what they call an attachment. I was in Manchester for two years, then London for a bit, but I was a naughty girl and it was either this or back into researching or out. Six months, then they'll review my position, as we say. So how far's this King's Oak Corner?'

'Hang on,' said Jane, 'I thought you knew.'

'Do I hell. I did bloody well to make it here from Hereford. If I'd said I didn't know where it was, Chris might've clammed up.'

'So how would you have found it if *I* hadn't been with you?'

'Stopped and asked somebody, I expect. But you do know, don't you, chuck?'

'There's a pub called the King's Oak about two miles on, where you turn left. We go past it on the school bus.'

'Sounds good to me.' Bella speeded up.

King's Oak Corner. It was a long way from the orchard, wasn't it? Perhaps the message the guy had picked up on his police scanner related to something else entirely. Because it was a long way from the orchard.

In Jane's mind, an old, withered apple rolled along the snowy-petalled orchard floor to her feet.

She gave her head a brisk shake. 'What do you think they might have found . . . if not . . . you know?'

'Search me. Chris's mate could've got it wrong, but at least it gets me out of bloody Ledwardine for the big opening ceremony. If there are no developments on the missing girl or she gets found alive, I'm supposed to put together a package on the festival as well, yawn yawn. What I want is just to tie it into the main story . . . festival goes ahead despite missing girl drama. Rather than have to interview the little fat guy about his choral work, et cetera. What's she *really* like, bit of a sod?'

'Colette? She's OK.'

'Oh, so you do know her?'

'Yeah.'

'She got a boyfriend?'

'Nobody regular.'

'What about you, Jane? Gonna stick around and shack up with a farmer or get out soon as you can?'

'I don't know.' Bella was pretty direct; Jane could relate to that. 'I don't really know what I want to do. What's your job like?'

'Job's fine. It's some of the people you have to work for. What's your old man do?'

'He was a lawyer. He's dead.'

'Oh. Sorry, chuck.'

'And my mother's a priest.'

'Really?' Bella glanced sideways at Jane. 'Hey, hold on . . . bloody hell, Merrily—'

'Watkins.'

'Well, well. How d'you feel about that?'

'Mixed.'

'I've only seen her picture in the paper, but she looked like an otherwise normal person. Attractive. Why'd she do a thing like that?'

'Become a priest? God knows.'

'Grief? Like medieval widows used to go into a nunnery?'

'Definitely not. It started before he died, anyway. Like, I know she got pretty friendly with our local vicar and his wife – this was when my dad . . . when they were going through a difficult patch over a few things. And she started helping this guy with his parish stuff, advising people with problems. She's pretty smart. And then it just seemed she was reading the lessons in church and stuff like that, and it just sort of crept up, and one day it was like, Jane, we need to have a little chat, Mummy's going to train for a special new job. I was about nine.'

'Your dad was alive then?'

'Yeah. He got killed in a car crash. But he was alive when she decided to go for it. Hey . . . you're not planning to use any of this, are you?'

'Me? No way. How did your dad feel about it?'

'He was seriously pissed off about it. But things weren't good between them by then, anyway.'

She watched the countryside go past, views she'd seen a

hundred times, fields of sheep and cows. But it all looked different today. Like it had a pulse.

It was really weird, Bella asking about Mum, why she'd done it. Because there had to be *something*, didn't there? Or there would be with her. It wouldn't be like, Oh, I like helping people but I couldn't cut it as a nurse, so I'll be a vicar, *that's* cool. Like there was the problem with Dad, things he was doing that she thought maybe *she* ought to like atone for. But that's not enough, is it?

Realizing she wouldn't have thought, even a few weeks ago, that there would need to be anything else because the word *spiritual* didn't mean much until she was having long talks with Lucy. Until after she got pissed on cider and fell asleep in Powell's orchard and looked up.

'This the turning?' Bella said.

'What? Oh . . . Oh, yeah.' The black and white pub was up ahead. Vehicles including a police car on its parking area. Not far around the corner, Bella had to pull up for a hurriedly erected sign saying, POLICE. ROAD CLOSED.

'Oh my God,' Jane said. 'There really is something.'

Suddenly, she didn't want to get out of the car.

*

'All right,' Merrily said, taking control. 'You can't go back to Blackberry Lane. They'll nick you. Annie Howe will not believe you. She'll make your life unbearable. Until they find Colette or some . . . some other direction, you should stay here. The church does this sort of thing. It's called sanctuary.'

'It's called being an accessory,' Lol said.

Merrily laughed. She didn't know why.

'Listen, you have enough problems,' Lol said. 'The longer I'm missing, the more the finger's going to point my way. If they find out the vicar's hiding me, what's that going to look like?'

'Priest-in-charge,' Merrily said.

In charge? Five minutes ago, she'd taken a phone call from Uncle Ted who'd informed her that, in view of her illness, they'd organized a locum for Sunday, a retired rector from Pembridge, Canon Norman Gemmell. Only too glad to step into the breech, old Norman. Merrily, who had not been consulted, had suggested Ted telephone Norman immediately to say that it wouldn't, after all, be necessary to iron his surplice. Like the fallen jockey needs to get back into the saddle, the crashed pilot back behind the joystick, she had to get up in that pulpit, show to the congregation of doubters a face washed clean of vomit.

'If I quit, I quit,' she told Lol. 'But I'm not slinking out the back way. And nobody tells me who I accommodate in my vicarage.'

She saw he was looking at her with something verging on awe. She sat down, reached for cigarettes.

'Lol, do you never feel you've been pushed around once too often?'

'The problem is sorting out who's pushing you around because it serves their purposes or it's fun and who's genuinely trying to help you.'

And he's been pushed around by the best, she thought. Alison, this Windling guy, Lucy Devenish.

'That's too complicated for me,' she said. 'But if you ever think I'm pushing, you tell me, OK?'

The phone rang again in the hall. News travelled fast in Ledwardine. It was Dermot Child. He was delighted to hear she was so much better. He thought he just ought to mention – but, of course, everyone would understand if she still felt a little too *frail* – that she was to have said a few words at this afternoon's opening ceremony. Poor old Terrence had had her down for two-thirty.

'I'll be there,' Merrily said, not letting herself think.

It was that word *frail* that did it.

She put the phone down, went back into the kitchen, found Lol looking no less worried.

'What if it was Karl?' he said. 'He was drunk, he was angry, and he's not there any more.'

'Oh.' She sat down opposite him. 'If Colette came to his door – your door – at two in the morning, how would he react?'

'Like it was his birthday,' Lol said.

*

Bella pulled the Uher tape recorder from the well by Jane's feet. 'If you come, you keep quiet, OK?'

'I think I'll stay here.'

Bella flashed her a look of concern. 'She really *is* a good friend of yours, isn't she?'

'We go back,' Jane said. They went back less than a month; it felt like half a lifetime.

'Stay cool,' Bella said. 'It may not be.'

Jane sat and watched her stride boldly towards the police barrier, clutching the recording machine with the broken strap. The four-wheel-drive had pulled up behind them, and Bella was joined by the other reporter, Chris, and a photographer. A uniformed constable appeared, making these negative wiping gestures with his arms, but the photographer started taking pictures and Bella and Chris marched right up to the barrier.

Jane couldn't see, from where the car was parked, what was happening the other side. She was thinking about that faraway night in the orchard. Colette saying, *I often come here.*

And Jane had said, *Aren't you scared?*

And Colette had turned sly. *You mean of the ghost of Edgar Powell? Hey, listen, he's been seen. Old Edgar Powell, the headless farmer. All aglow and hovering about nine inches off the ground.*

Colette hadn't been scared of the ghost of Edgar Powell or anybody else. She thought it was all a joke. And yet – and this had occurred to Jane when she was giving Bella that spoof interview on tape – despite being a cool, city chick with a professed disdain for the countryside and wildlife and all that, Colette was secretly fascinated by the orchard. Compelled, kind of seduced. *I often come here*, she'd admitted, pissed. Before forcing Jane to look up into the branches. And then, when Jane's reaction had been . . . well, not what she'd expected, it must have hardened into a desire to really *know* about this. Giving Jane the third degree outside the chip shop, giving her the Hazey Jane album.

Colette must have gone again and again to that orchard, drawn by something she couldn't explain, that the cool chick in her sneered at but something deeper in her perceived as being sexy as hell.

And when something happened, it happened to Jane.

Bella was coming back, with Chris and the photographer, Chris smacking a fist into a palm. There was something. Jane tensed as Bella got into the car, handed her the tape machine.

'What?' Jane said. '*What?*'

Bella started the engine. 'They won't give us anything. They're holding a Press conference at four, at Hereford Police Station. They've found something, but I'm pretty sure it isn't a body. No sign of a meat wagon or anything. People in plastic suits, though. Chris is going to hang on here for half an hour, see if there's anything. I'll have to shoot back, grab some actuality of the opening of the festival in case the parents come out for it.'

'What do you *think* it is?'

'I don't know. Bastards. I'll have to put over a "mystery surrounds" piece, and then the telly'll be on to it. Bastards.'

Bella reversed the car into the entrance to the King's Oak car park and pointed it back towards Hereford and Ledwardine.

Jane said, 'What have you got against the TV?'

Bella laughed. Her side window was wound down and her elbow rested casually on the ledge. 'What could I possibly have against people who get paid about twice as much as me for working less than half as hard? I love those guys.'

There was no other traffic in sight in either direction, and when they rounded a bend and came upon the carnage in the road, Bella was doing over seventy.

*

'But where *is* he?' Merrily said. 'Where's he gone? What evidence have you got that he was even here, that he even exists, that you didn't make him up?'

'Jane saw him,' Lol said.

'When?' It was nearly lunchtime. Time Jane was making a reappearance. It no longer seemed an entirely good thing for Jane to be out there, despite the police on the streets.

'She came into the shop this particular afternoon . . . to ask about Wil Williams. I . . . asked her to mind the shop while I . . . went and hid.'

'Hid.'

'Upstairs.'

Nobody, Merrily thought, would make that up.

'She could see I was scared and she was having fun with that. Like building him up as a drug dealer or something. She seems to have . . . quite an active imagination.'

'You're not wrong.'

'So I told her to forget all about him. I said he was just a guy it was hard to get out of your hair. And to tell Colette to keep out of his way too.'

'Oh, Jesus,' Merrily said. 'You're not big on child psychology, are you?'

'Sorry.'

'So here she is – hypothetically – on the cottage doorstep at two in the morning. This is a girl who'd really quite like to get laid tonight – Jane said that. What happens? He invites her in?'

'Or he says, why don't I give you a lift home? You shouldn't be out on your own on a dark night like this. And – I know this guy – once he had her in the car, he'd just keep on driving.'

Merrily thought about this. 'All right. We'll wait till Jane comes back and we'll talk it over with her. She's had time to think about things. Several things, I hope. And then perhaps we'll both go and see Howe.'

'She'd only split us up, question us separately. That's what they do.'

'She couldn't,' Merrily said. 'I'm not a suspect.'

'You're an accessory.'

Merrily lit a cigarette. She said, 'It's at times like these when I usually suggest we kneel down together and pray for guidance.'

'You're not serious,' Lol said.

'It's what I do,' Merrily said.

'I'd forgotten.'

Outside, across on the square, a brass band began to play.

THIRTY-TWO

Bastard God

Bella spun the wheel, hand over hand over hand, and the brakes and the tyres screamed and the hedge burst out at them from the wrong side of the road.

'*Shiiiiiiit!*'

Bella shrieking as they were torn across a tangle of branches and thorns with a grating noise rising to a high, thin whine like a scythe on a sharpening wheel.

And '*Shiiiiiit!*' again, and a wing mirror snipped away as Jane lurched against Bella, all the breath kicked out of her, and the windscreen was full of slapping branches before the radio car seemed to wrench itself out of the hedge, hit the tarmac again with a clanging jolt.

The engine coughed once and stalled.

Jane wasn't aware of losing consciousness, but she seemed to awake into a deep, uncanny stillness, during which she could only think about that newspaper picture of her dad's car, balled like paper, with him and his secretary and lover, Karen, all mashed up together inside.

She became aware of a distant voice: Bella saying, almost calmly, 'Got to get out. We've got to get out of here.'

The voice repeating itself over and over again, but that was probably only in Jane's head because Bella was saying now, 'Are you all right? Are you all right, Jane?'

Jane's mind was searching back through thirty seconds of

snapshot memories for the horrific reason Bella had braked and swerved and they'd come off the road.

She sat up. The car was full of twigs and leaves. The heavy Uher tape recorder had fallen on to her trainers and she pulled one foot from underneath it, feeling for the door-pull. It still worked, but the door wouldn't open.

'Can't get out my side,' Bella said. Her velvet hat had come off and there were twigs in her hair and her face was raked with blood.

'Hang on.' Jane turned herself round, wedged both shoulders against the passenger door, her feet up against the handbrake. Heaved backwards, and the door sprang open and she slid out, clawing wildly at the air. Bella grabbed her hands before she could hit the tarmac. Let her sink down gently to the road.

Bella was easing herself out of the car as Jane struggled to her feet. She saw the car was side-on to the road, blocking one narrow carriageway and half of the other. The steeple of Ledwardine Church prodded out of some trees about half a mile away. Bella leaned back against the car, put a tentative hand to her face.

'Oh, shit,' Bella said. Jane remembered the window had been wound all the way down on the driver's side, Bella leaning an elbow out, offering a bare face to the slashing twigs.

'Jesus, my whole face is on fire. I'm gonna be disfigured for life. Still . . .' She smiled wanly at Jane through the streaks of blood. 'You're OK. And we're not dead, are we?' She pushed her hands through her hair, as though feeling for fractures. 'And it's not as if . . . Oh no.'

She sagged against the car, and they looked at each other, remembering. There was a white, almost wintry sun now, in a sky like tinfoil. Jane didn't seem to be hurt at all, no cuts, no scratches, no aches, except for an ankle where the recorder had fallen. But she felt sick with dread, remembering what had been in the road. What was now concealed by the radio car, side-on against the traffic, except there was none, no vehicles in sight, no sounds of traffic, the road clear in both directions. This was the straight stretch into Ledwardine from Madley and few people came this way on a Saturday.

Jane said softly, 'I'll look.'

'No.' Bella stood up stiffly. 'You stay there.'

But they knew they were both going. They went slowly around the car, taking different routes to show they weren't scared, Jane round by the boot, Bella by the bonnet.

Somewhere in the car, a phone bleeped. Neither Bella nor Jane looked back.

Jane saw the dead eyes of the ewe first. The ewe lay in a lump at her feet, like you sometimes came upon them dead in fields, bloodlessly dead for no apparent reason. Sheep seemed able to leave life behind in an instant, without suffering, without a thought. Poor sheep. They should die in grass, not on tarmac because of stupid farmers too mean to put in proper stock-proof fences. 'Poor sheep,' Jane said aloud, as though, by focusing all her sorrow on the ewe, there would be nothing more.

'Oh Christ,' Bella said.

There was some blood where she stood. Though not much of it. The blood was over a yard from the sheep, where there was another hump, a black and white checked blanket thrown over something. The blood was seeping from underneath the blanket.

Jane stared at it, rejecting it. It was a blanket. There was nothing underneath it. It was a familiar pattern. It was just a blanket.

'Please,' she said, feeling her eyes bulge, her lips already stretching in pain and shock. '*Please* . . .'

'Don't look,' Bella said. 'Let me.'

But Jane was already bending down and lifting the hem. Out of the corner of an eye, she could see a wheel in the hedge.

Jane looked down. Kept on looking.

Under the summer-fine wool, the old warrior's head lay in profile on the road. The lips closed under the hooked nose, one eye wide open, as blank as the ewe's. The face weathered and reddened by the many years of wind, and now by sticky blood.

When she'd come off her moped, the light, summer poncho had been thrown over her head.

Bella was back in the car. Jane could hear the tight little bleeps as her fingers stabbed at the mobile phone.

'No,' Jane said. 'No.'

She pulled the poncho away, sank down to the tarmac. She didn't know what to do. She was sure Lucy was breathing. She had to be breathing. She put her cheek against Lucy's breast. That was a heartbeat, wasn't it? She didn't know what do.

She looked up.

The sky wore a remote, uncaring sheen.

Through the blurred screen of her tears, Jane screamed into the mindless, heartless, self-satisfied face of her mother's bastard God.

THIRTY-THREE

Superstitious Crap

From the hall window, Lol watched her walking out of the gates, head down, shoulders squeezed in. He'd seen the shadows on her face and one of them was him.

Should have kicked me out when you had the chance, Vicar.

He looked around for Ethel, but she'd pattered off somewhere in the big, bare house in which they were both effectively trapped. Leaving him to walk round and round the kitchen in despair at what a really fucking *small* person he was, in every conceivable sense.

He thought of his suicide. All the care and logic he'd put into the scheme to bring Alison to his door. Which was, face it, an *insane* thing to do. As insane as going to Alison last night and asking her why she'd left him, like this was going to make her think, yeah, why *did* I leave the poor little guy, what kind of a bitch did I become? And then return. Which he didn't want. He didn't *want* Alison back. He didn't want his cottage back. He didn't want to pick up his car.

He was mad. Still very sick. He needed a small room and all his meals prepared. He needed his medication.

Lol walked round and round the kitchen like a mouse looking for a gap in the skirting.

*

Ascending the three steps to the wooden platform under the mirror sky, Merrily had this absurd vision of a scaffold, a beheading block. Or, even worse right now, the pulpit.

'Oyez! Oyez!' wailed the hired town crier, in his long red coat and three-cornered hat. 'Villagers of Ledwardine! Be it known that ye festival will be commenced at three of the clock!'

Merrily waited for Lucy Devenish to come striding out condemning it as a ludicrous travesty because, in over a thousand years of recorded history, Ledwardine had never had a town crier.

'Merrily.' Dermot Child clasped her right hand in both of his. 'Are you sure you're all right?' In a light-green polo shirt with an apple motif, he looked bright-eyed and excited. In the unfortunate absence of Terrence Cassidy, he appeared to have acquired a festival.

'Just one of those twenty-four-hour satanic viruses,' Merrily said tightly. 'I'm told it's going around.'

'Oh, *that* . . .' Dermot laughed. 'Some semi-literate youngster. Don't let it worry you.'

'What?'

'The posters, Merrily. Ignore it. It's a joke, albeit a poor one.'

'Posters *plural?*'

'Well, I did remove a couple. One from the market hall, one from the bus shelter in Old Barn Lane. *Hey.*' He squeezed her shoulders. 'Kids. It's kids.'

'I don't think so.' Someone was broadcasting a sick, specious rumour. Somebody out to do damage. The hi-tech version of the anonymous letter. With a printer, they could turn out dozens, hundreds.

'Anyway,' Dermot said, 'poor joke. How many would even understand it?'

And so she took her seat on the platform, at the opposite

end to Bull-Davies, festival president, who nodded. Council-lor Garrod Powell followed her up. 'Sorry I'm late. Car accident out on the Madley Road.'

Dermot glanced at him. 'Serious?'

'Didn't look much. Some young lunatic. Hadn't no time to find out.'

Well over a hundred people had drifted on to the square, which wasn't bad for a mere opening ceremony; opening ceremonies were for the organizers. There were quite a few strangers among the villagers, most of them either drinking outside the Black Swan, where tables and umbrellas had been set up, or gathered around the craft and refreshment stalls in the market hall. Or watching the police. The Ledwardine Festival providing the perfect cover for the curious.

'Oh, shit,' said Dermot Child. Wearing a dark suit and a pale face, Terrence Cassidy was crossing the cobbles. 'What we don't need is a spectre at the feast. Brave of him and everything, but bloody hell . . .'

'Give the man some credit, Child.' Bull-Davies stood up. 'Terrence . . . any news?'

Cassidy mounted the platform, smiled stiffly at Dermot and sat down between Bull-Davies and Powell. He shook his head.

'Never say die,' Bull-Davies said thoughtlessly.

'I had to come out,' Terrence said sombrely. 'Atmosphere's so utterly oppressive in there. Merrily, I don't suppose Jane . . .'

Merrily said cautiously, 'Jane has every confidence that Colette can take care of herself. But . . . no. She doesn't seem to have seen her after anyone else. I'm sorry.'

'Terrence,' Dermot said, 'I was simply going to pay tribute, in my opening speech, to the tremendous amount of work you've put in. But is there . . . I mean, the police presence is pretty obvious . . . What do you want me to say about . . .?'

'Nothing, Dermot. It has absolutely nothing to do with the festival.'

Terrence stared straight ahead as a photographer took a picture of him on the platform. Dermot Child scowled – not at the intrusion of the Press for the wrong reason, Merrily thought, but because the silent, tragic, dignified Cassidy was going to upstage him.

'All right, let's get on with it.' Dermot approached the microphone, tapped it. 'Ladies and gentlemen, could we have your attention now, please?'

He handled it well. He'd become Mr Ledwardine, round and rosy and polished. He thanked the tourist board, English Heritage, the Marches Development Board. Then he talked, as a native, about his village.

'A few centuries ago, we were a flourishing market town, as you can see from the beautiful little market hall behind me. In those days, like most country towns, we had half a dozen shops. We still have half a dozen shops. We remain as we were. But, like Pembridge and Eardisley and Weobley, we're no longer a town. We are no longer famous for our orchards and our cider. Indeed, we were in danger of becoming famous only . . . for what we were.'

Dermot paused. Merrily saw a police car, followed by another car, turning into Church Street from Old Barn Lane.

'It would have been too easy', Dermot said, 'to live in the past. To be a village of ghosts. To preserve our exquisite black and white buildings as no more than an open-air museum. But that would be to deny the power of the present.'

The police car pulled up a respectable distance from the square, the plain car behind it. Nobody got out. A policeman in the front was leaning over his seat, talking to people in the back. Merrily glanced at Terrence Cassidy. He was on the edge of his seat. Above his jaw, a muscle twitched.

'. . . the wealth of creative talent in our midst which makes Ledwardine a unique centre of excellence, an excellence which, between now and September, we plan – throwing off our traditional Herefordshire modesty – quite shamelessly to show off!'

Mild laughter. The passenger door of the police car opened and a policewoman got out, moved to a rear door. '*Please, God,*' Terrence whispered. '*Please.*'

'Later, there'll be concerts, exhibitions, morris dancing here on the square. But first,' Dermot said, 'we'd like to show off our very newest asset – our minister, our priest-in-charge, the, er . . .'

God almighty, Merrily thought, He's going to say, *The lovely* . . .

'. . . the Reverend Merrily Watkins.'

Behind the muted applause, as she stood up, Merrily distinctly heard a wolf whistle and at least two young male voices combining in a low, throaty, ritual '*phwoaw* . . .' As she moved towards the microphone, her calves felt weak. She saw the policewoman holding open the rear door of the police car.

'Thank you, Dermot,' Merrily said into the mike, the words slamming back from the twin speakers on the roof of a van parked in front of the Black Swan. 'Bit early to call me an asset. My predecessor was here for over thirty years, so I . . .'

A woman Merrily didn't recognize climbed out of the police car with a heavy-looking black case under her arm. At the same time, DI Annie Howe was emerging from the plain car. Followed by Jane.

'. . . I . . .'

Jane was shouting at Howe, who was holding up both hands. A policeman moved in behind Jane. Merrily couldn't hear the shouting, but she saw, in a moment of rigid disbelief, that Jane's face was pulsing with rage and tears.

'. . . have to go. I'm sorry.'

Sorry . . . orry, the speakers snapped back, as she stumbled away from the mike, down the wooden steps.

As she pushed through the crowd, she heard a man remark that if he'd known the vicar was coming he'd have worn a plastic mac.

*

Annie Howe said, 'I should take your daughter inside, Ms Watkins, she's had a shock.'

Jane glared at her, muttered, 'Cow.'

'Right!' Merrily pointed at the vicarage gates. 'In! Now!'

Jane scowled and walked about ten yards, to just inside the gates. Stood there, defiant, streaks down her face.

Merrily said to Howe, 'You'd better tell me.'

'There was an accident. One of the traffic people will be along in due course to take a statement from Jane.'

'Accident?'

Howe said impatiently, 'Jane appears to have bummed a lift from a radio reporter who'd discovered an aspect of our investigation we were not prepared to discuss. On the way back, they swerved to avoid a road accident which had already happened. Jane claimed to know the victim and became very distressed. She was reluctant to leave the scene, and we had to bring her back.'

'Who was it?'

'Not formally identified yet. Look, I have to go. I suggest that unless she has something specific to tell us, you keep the child out of our hair.'

'Look,' Merrily said, 'if one of my parishioners has been hurt in a car accident, I want to know about it.'

Annie Howe, walking away, told her who they understood it was and that she was dead.

*

Merrily thought Lol was going to collapse. She made him sit down. He sat at the kitchen table and stared at a white wall. He didn't move. Around him, the kitchen was black and white and grey. Jane's eyes were smudges. She was standing in the middle of the room, pulling at her hair.

'Stop it, flower. Please.'

'*That apple!*' Jane sobbed. 'The apple was Lucy. Why didn't I realize that?'

'Sit down, Jane. This is—'

'*She* didn't want to know.' Jane's eyes were hot and flashing. 'It was, Get traffic out here, Mumford, we don't want the damned road blocked all afternoon. I said, Do you know who this is? For Christ's sake, do you *know* who this is?'

'It was just another accident to her, Jane. And she's CID. Not her problem.'

'They wouldn't let me stay. I wanted to stay with her. I wanted somebody she knew to be there when she woke up.'

'But she wasn't going to wake up,' Merrily said gently. 'Was she? Look . . . it was one of those freak accidents. A sheep seems to have run out into the road and she hit it and came off her bike and hit her head on the road. It must have been instantaneous. She wouldn't have known a thing about it.'

'She was the apple,' Jane said bleakly. 'It was an old and withered apple. I even told her about the apple. I *told* her. I told her about her own death!'

She started to pull her hair again.

Merrily walked over and pulled her hands down. They stood there facing each other, Merrily clutching both Jane's hands.

'This is no time', Merrily said, 'for that superstitious crap.' And knew as soon as it was out, Jane's expression curdling, that this was about the worst thing she could have said.

Demarcation

Merrily was on her knees with a plastic dustpan over the rubble of mugs Jane had swept from the drainer.

She was very, very sorry about Lucy. She'd really liked Lucy for her independence, her forthright attitude, her wonderful eccentricity. But – she could hear Jane's feet on the stairs, big, childish clomps – the fact remained that the old woman had caused the kid to reinvent her life as a fairy tale.

The phone started ringing. Lol took over the dustpan. Ted Clowes's lawyer-voice on the line. The it's-my-job-to-protect-your-interests-but-you-aren't-making-it-easy-for-me voice. The sound of another gulf fast widening.

'You say you're well, but you clearly aren't. Far from it. Have to say, Merrily, that what I'd very strongly advise, as your churchwarden, is that you permit me to revert to my original plan. Bring in Norman Gemmell to conduct tomorrow's services.'

'Ted. No. Wait.' Everything spinning away from her, like the fragments of the mugs. 'If you're talking about the opening ceremony just now – the police brought Jane back. She'd just seen the accident . . . Miss Devenish? She was distressed. You see your daughter brought back in a police car, in tears—'

'Very tragic,' Ted said – his measured, will-reading voice. 'But everyone said it was going to happen one day, the way she'd ride that thing in the middle of the road, too old for it, refused to wear a crash helmet, and the local police too tolerant – or scared of her, more like – to enforce the law. Ridiculous situation. An accident—'

'—waiting to happen. Sure.'

Didn't some people just love it when an accident-in-waiting finally came through? She remembered Ted, in his quick guide to village characters, telling her how you'd find the famous moped on its side on some grassy verge and you'd slam on your brakes, only to discover Miss Devenish lying in a field on her back, smiling contentedly at the sky, a straw in her mouth.

'And the way Jane's been hanging around her . . . I did warn you about that. Don't get too close, I think were my words.'

'Yes. Thank you, Ted.' She felt like clubbing him with the phone. 'I need to ask you, are there any relatives in the parish?'

'None left alive I know of. McCready's her solicitor, he'll deal with all that.'

'No, I meant— Oh, forget it.'

'I'm trying to be down to earth, Merrily. Trying to rescue a runaway situation. Somebody has to.'

'*Situation . . .?*'

'You should never have gone out on that platform this afternoon. Here was I, telling people you'd contracted a stomach bug, and now it starts to look like, shall we say a nervous complaint?'

'Oh, a *nervous* complaint. I see.'

'Merrily, I don't know what your personal problems are, as you haven't seen fit to come and talk to me about them, but I do know that people are beginning to see you as a little too . . . too . . .'

He broke off. The line throbbed with the unspoken: he'd

seen the posters and God knew what else. And one did have to think of one's own position in the community.

*

'Lucy Devenish', Lol said, 'can't die like this.'

'Lucy Devenish just did,' Merrily said gently. 'And there's nothing you or Jane, with due regard to superstitions and omens, can do to alter that.'

He stopped pacing. From the market square came the merry wail and thump of an accordion band, for the morris dancing.

'Not Christian, I suppose. Omens.'

Merrily shook out a cigarette. 'You smoke, Lol? I can't remember.'

'Used to.' He took one, his fingers twitching. 'Thanks. There've been shocks, but this . . . She could make you believe you weren't abnormal, you know? Everything has a rational explanation, she'd say. Just that most people's idea of what's rational is severely limited.'

'Especially the Church's?'

'Maybe. She's dead, I'm alive. Where's the divine logic there?'

'I'm supposed to know that? Being a priest?'

'I can't see you as a priest,' Lol said. 'I don't know why someone like you would want to *be* a priest.'

'Lol.' She put her lighter to his cigarette. 'Is there something happening that it's not been considered suitable for me to know about? Because of me being a priest?'

'I don't . . .' He looked apprehensive. 'Maybe.'

'There have certainly been things I don't understand.' She took a lungful of smoke, breathed it out hard. 'And that the Church doesn't want to.'

'Like?'

'Like, the house haunts me. I hate it. Nothing's been

right since we moved in. I have bad dreams. The kind that make you wonder if they really are dreams. What would poor Lucy have said about that, do you think, if I hadn't been a priest?'

He took a small, self-conscious puff on the cigarette. 'She once said to me that I was living too near the orchard.'

'Meaning what?'

'Well, this was the Village in the Orchard. The orchard was its life-force. Now that's all gone, maybe the orchard isn't such a good place.'

'Resentful. *They grows resentful.*' Merrily put the cigarette in the ashtray, pushed it a couple of inches away. 'I'm having too many of these.'

'If an apple had rolled right up to my feet from a tree full of blossom,' Lol said, 'I'd probably feel much like Jane.' He looked at his cigarette as though it represented some aspect of his past he didn't really want to remember. He put it out in the ashtray. 'Sorry. Wasteful.'

'You always been superstitious?'

'Or paranoid? Is that the same thing? Like I was always influenced by this guy, Nick Drake. Called the band after one of his songs.'

'Hazey Jane.' Merrily started to sing it, went wrong and gave up. 'Never quite figured what that song was about, but she was obviously maladjusted. Cursing where she came from, swearing at the night. My step-brother had his albums. He was very appealing, was Nick Drake. But probably ill.'

'Probably was,' Lol said. 'For a long time, I was convinced I was going to die when I was twenty-six, like him. And then I was twenty-eight and I hadn't died, and so I felt guilty. And let down, somehow. That was when I went in for the second time.'

'The hospital?'

'Sounds' – he smiled – 'insane. But these things get inside

you and they get mixed up with everything else that's wrong, and it's like . . . *Is* it illness, or is there something else? Alison thought it'd be good for me, moving out here, fresh air, simple life. Only Lucy saw the problems. Everywhere has its own bag of superstition. Wherever I go, it all seems to connect. I remembered Nick's song "Fruit Tree", which more or less says you don't make it till you die. Sometimes, I had the feeling that Nick and Robert Johnson and these guys were out there, among the apple trees. That make sense? Does it hell.'

'Yes, it does. I'll tell you what happened to make me do it, if you like. I mean join the clergy.'

She undid her dog collar, placed it on the table so that it surrounded the ashtray and the smoking cigarette.

The past unclouding. The days when it all fell into place. Sean away in London for a week of meetings, and on the second day, there was this tentative visit from his anxious clerk, with a briefcase full of grief, and it was all laid out before her, all the corrupting entrails.

The third day, trying to lose the bad smell, she took her shrieking headache on a long drive into the country in the ill-gotten Volvo. Ending up at the unknown church of some saint with an obscure Celtic name – you could see the tower from a couple of miles away, but it turned out to be a tiny little place reachable only by a track. How could you put into words what happened in that bare, little church? What happened inside *you* that chose to happen *there*.

'See, for some time before this, I'd been helping our local vicar. Decent guy, but what a waste, this man being a vicar, collecting ten grand a year, whatever it was then – if you lived with Sean, everybody was rated according to their income: *he's a forty a year man*, whatever. So ten grand a year and a regular congregation of nineteen. What a loser.'

Merrily watched the smoke rising out of the white circle.

'It was funny – one of the things that occurred to me in that little church was . . . nineteen, that's a hell of a lot of lives. And that was when I saw the blue and the gold.'

Ah. The blue and the gold. An inner vision? *Hey, watch it – warning finger raised by Dr David Campbell – you're in danger of crossing the demarcation line.*

Aw, come on, David, aren't I allowed one mystical experience, if I don't talk about it too much? The sense of a huge benevolence, the awesome moment of cosmic awareness, the dwindling of self in an exhilarating vastness of blue and gold?

'Anyway, whatever it was,' she wound up, with a half-desperate cynicism, 'it got rid of the headache.'

'You ever experience it again?'

'A trace. An essence. Whenever I knelt to pray, it would be there, like a backcloth. This velvet security blanket of deep blue and gold. It kept me going.'

'And it isn't there now?'

'No,' Merrily said. 'It isn't, now. I don't quite remember when it stopped. These past couple of weeks have seemed like about ten years.'

'You ever go back to that little church?'

'I'd be scared to,' she said frankly. 'In case it was just a little, grey, empty building. Wow, you're really getting everything here, Lol. The full crisis-of-faith bit.'

She pulled the cigarette out of the ashtray, out of the dog collar.

'It's ironic, because I thought, the way you do, that I was being guided here. Like you maybe? Did you feel that?'

'No. Just Alison. Alison wanted to come here, and I was the guy who could afford to take on a mortgage. Nice place, no special sense of destiny.'

'I thought there was. Then, in a matter of weeks, the whole edifice is developing cracks. I don't know why that is.

Something I did, something I didn't do? Maybe women really *aren't* strong enough for this job. Shit, wash my mouth out.'

'Was that why you were ill in church?'

'Because I was feeling like a fraud? That doesn't matter any more, didn't you know? There's now a whole bunch of ministers within the Anglican Church ready to tell you the Virgin birth and the Christmas story and the resurrection are all myths and God as we know Him is just Father Christmas. No, I don't know why I was sick.'

A lie. Because she couldn't talk about the worst of it: that while her prayers had become flat and dead, while she was getting no comfort, no response, no sense of resonance, she was also becoming prey to cold visions from the other side of the demarcation line. Visions which began in dreams and finally made it. Finally got into the church.

Superstition. Mental illness.

'You know what occurred to me . . .' Lol hesitated, playing with the sleeve of his alien sweatshirt, winding it like a tourniquet around his forefinger. '. . . when you were on about the blue and gold?'

'Go on.'

'I thought of Jane's room. The ceiling. See, the night we brought Jane out of the orchard she was rambling about little golden lanterns.'

'She was drunk.'

'I don't think she was. I think she was . . . heavy word coming up, Merrily. Can you handle this?'

'Hit me.'

'Enchanted. She was enchanted. Everything that word says to you. All the different meanings . . . like, elated. Like, under a spell.'

'You're right,' Merrily said. 'That's a big word.'

'And what about you, when you were in the little church?'

'That', she said mock-primly, 'was what we like to call a religious experience.'

'There you go. Something's happened to Jane and you're in denial about it because she's just a kid and you're an ordained minister. Lucy would say that was a fairly primitive attitude – everything not connected with God must be . . .'

'Yeah,' Merrily said. 'I get the message.'

'I'm sorry. You've been really good to me and I'm insulting you.'

'Listen, I'm . . . OK, maybe what happened to Jane – and to you – was just . . . Lucy.'

'No,' Lol said.

'She was a very persuasive woman.'

'It wasn't just Lucy.'

'There's something else, isn't there? Something you talked about to Lucy Devenish.'

'Tried to,' he said cautiously.

'You and Lucy talked about my daughter and something that happened to her?'

'Kind of.'

'All right.' She put up both hands. 'I'm not accusing you of anything. But it relates to what you told me before? About the girls?'

'Everything relates to that,' Lol said. 'But this was scary.'

'It was scary, but nobody thought to tell me.'

'Like you said, I suppose it was because of what you are. Lucy said that when you were ready to hear this stuff, you'd go to her.'

'And now it's too late for that.' Merrily stood up. 'So let's go and ask Jane.'

'Both of us?'

'Oh yes. I think so.'

*

Together, in silence, they walked up to the Apartment. They were nearing the top of the second staircase when the radio came on in the sitting room/study. Newstime on Radio Hereford and Worcester.

'*The search for a Herefordshire schoolgirl has been stepped up following the discovery of clothing in a ditch two miles from her home. Police say they're now very concerned for the safety of Colette Cassidy, who disappeared from her sixteenth birthday party in the village of Ledwardine. This report from Bella Ford.*'

Bella Ford said over a telephone line, '*The items of clothing were found by a farmer about midday at King's Oak Corner between Ledwardine and Madley. Police have declined to say what exactly they were but confirm that they've been identified by Colette's parents as belonging to their daughter and probably worn by her when she disappeared.*'

'Oh God, that means underwear,' Merrily whispered, 'or they'd be sure she was wearing them.'

'*Detective Inspector Annie Howe, who's leading the search for Colette, says they now have to be worried for her safety and are appealing to the public for any information. It was around two o'clock this morning when Colette, a student at the Hereford Cathedral School—*'

'It's him,' Lol said. 'It has to be.'

'*—elderly woman has died in a road accident—*'

'You don't know that. Hang on. Lucy.'

'*—country lane near Ledwardine. The dead woman, who was riding a moped, has not yet been officially identified. No other vehicles were involved.*'

They heard Jane moan. 'You don't know. You don't know anything!'

'*—Meanwhile, a man who died when his car left the Hereford to Abergavenny road and smashed into a stone wall at Wormbridge late last night has been identified as Anthony*

*Karl Windling, from Abingdon, near Oxford. There's been a
mixed reaction to the news that fifty thousand pounds of
National Lottery money is to go to—'*

The radio went off. Merrily turned to find Lol sitting on
the stairs. She looked up to see Jane in the doorway of the
sitting room/study. Nobody spoke.

The Little Golden Lights

Lol looked up at her from his stair, like one of those small dogs that quivered. He was still institutionalized, Merrily thought. Looking, with Lucy gone, for someone else to administer the drug of reassurance. Mutely asking what he was supposed to feel.

'Where's Wormbridge?' he said at last.

'It's a place you pass through when you're heading for Abergavenny and the M4.'

'So he was leaving.'

'He must have been very drunk,' she said. 'That's the usual reason cars go out of control when no other vehicles are involved.'

'Yes.'

He shook his head slowly, like a boxer coming up after being knocked to his knees, only to be told that he might still win on points. Some part of him trying to equate the random, meaningless deaths of his mentor and his tormentor within the same twenty-four hours, both in road accidents with nobody else involved. Punch-drunk. Not sure what any of it meant.

'So Colette . . .'

'Ruled out, Lol. According to that report, he died last night. When she was still at the party. They never met. It's all a bitterly ironic coincidence.'

I've been there, she wanted to say, sensing Sean moving

towards her across bare, bedroom floorboards, smiling through his fatal injuries. *I've been exactly there.*

Feeling, in one of those spinning, crystal moments, that they must both be part of the same bizarre pattern.

And then, turning, she saw Jane looking down at them in manifest bewilderment from the doorway of the sitting room/study. Her face was white and blotched, her usually sleek dark hair like knotted string.

She said, 'Mum, will you come in? Please?'

*

They clung together for a long time, Jane's hot, wet, sticky face against Merrily's under the blue and gold ceiling, Jane's body shuddering as the accordion was wheezing up from the market square, and Merrily found she was crying too, for Miss Devenish and Sean and even the wretched Windling, united in road-death. Crying for Colette and the suffering Cassidys and other sufferings, known and unknown, and Lol and all his wasted years and all those senseless wasted days for Jane and her, hiding from each other behind screens of divisive superstition.

From the square came a chattering of polite, muted applause. Jane broke away and stood in the centre of the room as if unsure where she was. She swallowed. Merrily looked around.

The cheap stereo and its white-cased speakers sat on bare boards. There was also the old couch the kid had insisted on having in her bedroom in Liverpool, even though you had to climb over one of its arms to get to the bed. There were paperbacks in piles. There was Edwin, the teddy, one-eared and balding. Familiar items. But the blue of the timber-framed walls and ceiling made the room dark and mystical, like a grotto in a wood. The yellow-white lights were out of an over-the-top starry night by Van Gogh.

'Lucy said . . .' Jane sniffed and straightened up. 'She told me to like paint it out of my head. To externalize it.'

'She told you to paint all this?'

'She gave me this book of hers to read, *The Little Green Orchard*, and this kid in the book did that. She was afraid of the orchard until she brought it home in her head and did drawings and that gave her . . . not control, exactly, but like a stake in the orchard, a connection. I'd already told Lucy about the Mondrian walls idea, so . . .'

'This is what you saw in the orchard? The night you . . .'

'The night Colette dragged me into the orchard and she was trying to scare me, saying the ghost of Edgar Powell had been seen by the tree where he shot himself. But when I looked up, instead of seeing something horrible and grisly, it was—'

Jane looked up to the ceiling.

'It was beautiful?' Merrily said.

'Yeah. I was floating. It was awesome. And warm. Dreamy. It was like outside time. And all these little lights moving about among the branches, and they were like . . . like they had existence. Life. You felt they were responding to your moods. Needs. Lucy said it was kind of reaching out to me. The spirit of the orchard.'

'Why couldn't you tell me about it?'

'You need to ask that?'

Merrily remembered her anger at the absence of headache, queasy tummy, morning-after contrition. Lucy Devenish's explanation about the cider and the orchard, Like curing Like. Natural holistic medicine.

Crawl into the centre of the orb and curl up. Let nature do the rest. Wouldn't work for everyone. The orchard's a risky place, an entity in itself, a sphere. And this is a very old orchard. So it tells you – or rather it tells me – something about your daughter.

'All that evening,' Jane said, 'I'd had this kind of a sense of coming home. First it was Colette. She just like appeared in the Black Swan and we clicked, and that was great. But when I looked up in the orchard I was on my own again and it was like a different kind of bonding with . . . I don't know. I still don't know.'

'Something beyond everything,' Merrily said clumsily.

'She must have felt excluded,' Jane said. 'That was the problem.'

'Colette?'

'Yeah. She felt . . . That was why she tried to lead them all into the orchard at the party. She wanted to . . . I don't know.'

'Re-establish control. Inspector Howe said she was shouting . . .'

'*Jane knows*. Like it was a secret we had between us. But there wasn't. It's not something you can share. She didn't know anything about it. She was going in mob-handed, trampling on everything. She was going to cause offence.'

'What?' Merrily stiffened.

Going to cause offence. Miss Devenish on the night of the wassailing, nose twitching in disdain. *Can't anyone see that? Deep offence.*

Merrily said, 'Offence to whom?'

'The watchers,' Jane said. 'The watchers in . . . in the little green orchard.'

Merrily tensed. 'Who are the watchers, Jane?'

Jane's mouth opened, but the words wouldn't come. She saw Lol, standing shyly in the doorway.

'Poor Karl Windling,' she said. 'But you must be awfully glad.'

*

It was all very strange and cathartic. Merrily and Jane sat on the old sofa, Lol walked around, and they talked about levels of existence and the life-force in nature. The Lucy Devenish Memorial Discussion.

'So how does the Apple Tree Man come into this?' Merrily said. 'I thought he represented the spirit of the orchard.'

'Oh no,' said Jane. 'You haven't been listening. Lucy said that was wrong. That wasn't *local* folklore. She said different places grew their own customs and beliefs according to what was needed. She said Wil Williams knew the reality of it because he was so psychic. And all that about him being seen dancing with sprites, that probably had a basis in fact, because when he was in the orchard the spirits would show themselves to him.'

She and Lol explained about the Pharisees Reds. How, when the old farmers found out they had an exceptional cider apple that was different to the ones growing anywhere else, they thought it was a gift from the spirits of the orchard.

'Or the angels,' Jane said. 'Lucy said that in the seventeenth century if you said too much about fairies, you'd wind up . . . well, like Wil Williams.'

'Oh.' Merrily sank into the old sofa. 'I see. The Wine of Angels. Barry Bloom said that was Lucy's idea.'

'She wasn't happy about it though, Mum. She wasn't happy about the way the orchard had been let go and now it's all started coming back after the wassailing and old Edgar shooting himself.'

'Lucy thought things were coming to a head,' Lol said. 'And when Jane . . . Oh shit, this is really difficult.'

Down in the house, the phone was ringing. Jane exchanged a glance with Lol. 'I'll get it,' she said.

*

Lol said, 'She was just there. One second there was blossom on the ground, lots of it, and the next Jane was there, kind of . . . enshrouded in it. I don't know where she came from. I don't know how long she'd been there.'

'And what had you taken?' Merrily said coldly.

Lol sighed.

'I'm sorry.' She spread her hands on her lap and looked down at them. 'That was the scary thing, right? The thing you discussed with Miss Devenish. If there was anything calculated to scare you it would be the appearance of a fifteen-year-old girl lying on her back, wearing a school uniform and apple blossom. Could she have been there all the time and you just didn't see her until you were close up?'

'I don't know. It's possible. She had on this white school blouse. When she sat up, it was covered with petals. She sat up just like she'd been asleep, sunbathing. Except there was no sun. I took her right back to the cottage and phoned Lucy.'

'She could have been there all day, that's what you're saying. Since she failed to get on the school bus.'

'I don't know. Lucy said it . . . sometimes happened. Though not as often as you might imagine from all the folk tales. She said a day was nothing. Sometimes it could be a year before people came back, although it only felt like a few moments. And sometimes it felt like years but it was only a few moments. She showed me stuff in books.' He looked sick. 'You see why I was reluctant to tell you this. You imagine me telling the cops?'

'Don't even contemplate it.' Merrily placed a cigarette on the arm of the sofa, searched around for her Zippo. 'It's like these alien abductions. Was it a dream, was it hallucination? You want me to believe that, in some way, the orchard took her. That Jane has – or *thinks* she has – in some way been possessed by the orchard, which is itself an entity, a sentient thing. And that it's now taken Colette, maybe?'

Lol shook his head in defeat.

'Which,' Merrily said, 'I suppose could hardly be dismissed as entirely incredible by someone whose profession implies she believes a dead man appeared to his mates, displaying his crucifixion scars. Right?'

Lol shrugged.

'Except – ' Merrily located her lighter in a cuff of her sweater ' – that this is paganism.'

'I suppose it must be.'

'It really is, Lol. It makes me want to reach for my big cross.'

'Mum,' Jane said from the doorway, 'it's some solicitor in Hereford called McGreedy.'

*

'So you told her. You told her her daughter had been spirited away.'

'Something like that.'

'She scoff?'

'No. But that doesn't mean she believed it, though. You're going to have to be patient with her. Supportive, as they say.'

'That's what Lucy said.' Jane pulled the teddy bear on to her knees. 'She said Mum was the catalyst. I'm not sure what that means.'

'Means she's the one who's going to make things happen.'

'She's the one? We could wait for ever.'

'What for? What do you expect to happen? What happened to you? Where *did* you go? Did you just fall asleep or what?'

'It's a blank. I mean, maybe there's some part of my subconscious that remembers being prodded about by little green men or whatever, but it must be well buried. Suppose that's what happened to Colette. What can we do about that? Suppose, because she wasn't respectful, she's been received . . . less kindly.'

Lol was allowing himself to wonder whether they were really having this conversation or whether he himself had been abducted, slipped back into the hospital, back on to the medication, when Merrily returned, a little out of breath from all the stairs, her forehead furrowed.

'This your doing, flower?'

Lol, relaxed for the first time in nearly two decades in the company of a teenage girl, let himself think how very pretty her mother was.

'That was a lawyer called Harold McCready. He is Lucy Devenish's lawyer. He says she went to his office a couple of days ago to add a codicil to her will, appointing an extra executor. As though she knew she hadn't long to live, McCready said. A folksy, country lawyer. Seen it before, he said. People often know, even when they're not ill.'

Jane sat up. 'What's an executor?'

'Someone responsible for seeing that the wishes of the deceased are carried out to the letter. Normally, just a formality. Somehow, I suspect this is going to be more complicated.'

'Why?'

'Because it's me, flower. Things get stranger. Why would she do that? Someone who's had so little to do with her. It's weird. I'm supposed to look over her possessions for any indications of her last wishes . . . As vague as that. There's a clerk from McCready's office driving over with a key to her house. Have either of you ever been in there?'

'Just the shop,' Jane said. 'Mum, you have to take this very, very seriously. She said you might get cold feet and want to leave. Because of what happened in the church and stuff. She said you mustn't. She also said you should change your mind about not letting that play go on in the church. She said—'

'Flower—'

'I'm just a kid,' Jane said. 'Does executor mean the same as catalyst?'

Dancing Gates

'Disastrous,' Dermot Child said into the early evening still-ness. 'Totally disastrous. By the end of the afternoon it was fairly conclusive. About three dozen genuine ones, the rest were rubberneckers hoping for a body bag. When the police cars dwindled to one, they took themselves off home.'

He stood on the corner of Church Street looking out to the square, where the last stallholder was packing up, spread-ing stains of armpit sweat on his polo shirt uncomfortably reminiscent, for Merrily, of the menacing dream-Dermot.

'The bloody Press, too. Not an arts journalist among them. Ten people went into the exhibition, none of them bought a thing. Thirty tickets sold for the string quartet. Is it even worth it? Come and have a drink, Merrily. Do your understanding-vicar bit. Tell me you'll offer a prayer for the festival.'

'Priest-in-charge,' Merrily said dully. Lack of sleep was already corroding her resolve. The last thing she needed was a cosy drink with Dermot Child. 'Understanding-priest-in-charge. I'm sorry, I can't, Dermot. I have an appointment. I'll try and make it to the concert.'

'Perhaps it's telling us something. Controversy certainly attracts attention, but this was the wrong kind of controversy. Pulls in the wrong element.'

'The gossiping classes, as distinct from the chattering classes.'

He smiled. 'Clearly, the morris dancers were a mistake. Terrence's idea. Falls between two stools. The cultured consider it quaint but a little simplistic, the working class find it more than a bit of a yawn. Terrence is all for harmless tradition. I think we need to be a touch more avant-garde.'

'Like your Old Cider thing?'

'Ah.' His eyes went to sly slits and he tapped his nose. 'You haven't seen that yet, Merrily. And neither has Terrence, thank God. It might seem tame, but what you have is this *very male* celebration of fecundity.'

'Fascinating,' Merrily said. 'I'm sorry, I do have to go.'

'Approached it the wrong way at first, you see. I was looking for singers when I should've been seeking out untamed virility. Chaps who, with a little training, can learn to sing not from the throat, not from the stomach but from the, ah, loins.'

'Yes,' Merrily said. Dermot talking dirty only made her feel more exhausted. 'Well, good luck with tonight – I'm sure you'll get lots of people turning up on spec.'

She walked across the street, but carried on down past Miss Devenish's house, not wanting him to know where she was going. At the junction with Old Barn Lane, she turned, and he was gone. She walked back to Lucy's terraced black and white, taking out the key. As she pushed it into the lock beside the goblin knocker, a gruff and loaded male chorus sang in her head. *Auld ciderrrrrrrrr.*

Dermot's choral work was going to be a kind of aural hard-on.

She shuddered.

*

She was several feet into Lucy's living room when the door twitched shut behind her.

She started and turned her head, but no one was there. The silence, in fact, was almost companionable, and she understood that she was more afraid of Dermot Child having crept in behind her than she was of Lucy's ghost. Would almost have welcomed the jolly, ponchoed apparition.

To advise her, for a start, on what the hell she was supposed to be doing in here.

The muted evening light was a soft presence in the single, small window, leaded and lace-curtained. But not in the room, which was well into its own dusk. Merrily went back to the door and found a light switch, an old metal one like a pewter pip.

It activated two Victorian bracket lamps over an ornate, ebony desk which sat under the window and dominated the room like an altar. The beams above it were stained as black as the exterior timbers. There was a rigid-looking armchair and a Victorian chaise longue. All four walls were half-panelled, to waist level, white-painted above, between glass-fronted bookcases. There was a single etching – two Victorian fairies, elegantly pool-peering – in a thin black frame. And some framed photographs.

Merrily stood, for a moment, hands by her sides. Trying for quietness inside, receptivity.

The solicitor's clerk from McCready's office had arrived on a red Honda motorbike just before six, handing her a brown envelope containing only the front-door key and a smaller one. No instructions, no advice.

Jane had wanted to come across with her, but she'd felt that would be wrong. This apparently was between Miss Devenish and her. Although it would have been useful having Lol in here, the person who'd known her best of late, but who dare not be seen on the streets.

She was still reluctant to touch anything without at least a sensation of having permission. It was all so tidy. As though Lucy Devenish had actually walked out of here this morning under a premonition that she might not be returning.

Merrily folded her arms. 'What do you want me to do, Lucy?'

It didn't seem foolish to ask aloud. She'd always had the slightly unorthodox idea that the dead were not fully gone until after the funeral service. Sometimes she'd look at the coffin in the church and sense a relief, a gratefulness, emanating from it. Occasionally, a sense of indignation.

'What do you want me to know?'

Nothing happened. The lights did not go out. No bat-winged, hook-nosed spectre peeled itself from the panelling. Neither did she feel anything, nor hear any inner voice.

She went to look at the photographs on the walls. One, in blurry black and white, showed a much younger, bushy-haired Lucy in a summer dress sitting on a bench. A young, smiling man in cricketing clothes was leaning over the back of the bench, hands on her shoulders. Lucy wore a sad half-smile, as though she knew it wouldn't come to anything. In another picture, a shorter haired, middle-aged Lucy, trousers rolled into riding boots, held out a feed bucket for a piebald pony, while a younger woman looked on. She looked curiously familiar. Sister? Close friend?

Merrily peered into the bookcases without opening the doors. There was a surprising number of volumes on English and Welsh history, from the old, popular favourites, like Arthur Mee, to modern classics, like John Davies's *History of Wales* and, more specialist, Keith Thomas's *Religion and the Decline of Magic*. With the slump in congregations and the growth of New Age cults, somebody should have written one called *Magic and the Decline of Religion*. Someone like Lucy, perhaps.

She turned back to the desk.

There was a box on it. A Victorian writing box which should open out into a small, sloping desk-surface. Merrily saw that both bracket lamps had been angled to focus on it, pooling it in light.

'Spooky,' she said aloud, to show to herself that she wasn't spooked by this. Not at all. Good heavens no.

From the pocket of her denim skirt, she brought out the second key. A little brass key. The box had a brass escutcheon over its keyhole.

The key fitted, of course. The lock glided open with a discreet *pock*.

Eerie.

She made no immediate move to lift the lid, remembering the story of Joanna Southcott's box which could only be opened in the presence of about a dozen bishops and never had been because most bishops were too lofty or politically sensitive even to consider it.

She wondered if she should say a small prayer.

*

'This was it?' Lol picked up the hefty Lapridge Press paperback of Ella Mary Leather's *The Folklore of Herefordshire*. 'This was all there was inside?'

'Lucy's Bible. Careful, there are markers.'

Folded bits of paper had been placed between pages at intervals. Some had scrawled notes on them. When Lol put the book on the kitchen table it fell open at once to the section on wassailing the old girl had quoted on Twelfth Night.

'I'm at a loss.' Merrily sat down with a bump. 'I liked her. I want to honour her last wishes. I'm trying to feel flattered that she chose me as the instrument. But . . . you know . . . what are we looking for? And in what context?'

Jane perched on a corner of the table. 'It's obvious that we have to work it out for ourselves. Because if she just wrote it down in black and white we – or you, especially – would be able to say like, Yeah, yeah, very interesting, but the old boot was completely out of it. But if you have to spend some time working it out, you'll see the reasoning behind it.'

Merrily yawned. 'Can we look at this tomorrow?'

'Mum, it's important. It's vital!'

'Sure, but vital how? Vital to what?'

'Vital to *Lucy*!' Jane dropped her feet to the flagstones. 'Isn't that enough for you? It's enough for me. And Lol.'

Merrily smiled wearily. 'OK. You're right. We have a duty. *I* have a duty. No idea where to start, of course.' She plucked out one of the paper bookmarks, keeping her thumb in the place. 'Hannah Snell, 1745,' she read from the paper. 'That's all it says. What's that mean?'

'Mum, we can find out. You can find out anything if you put your mind to it.'

'Sure.' She pushed both hands through her hair. 'There're a few more obvious references to cider and apples. And this looks like a photocopy of a page from some other book, stuffed in here, something about Oxford University. Can't think what that connects to. There's a page marked here, lots of heavy underlining. Fairies again.'

It seemed to be a story told to Mrs Leather by an un-named woman who got it from her mother who said it had happened to her first cousin and she remembered it well.

> The cousin, a girl about eighteen, was very fond of dancing; she insisted on going to all the balls for miles around; wherever there was dancing going on, there was she. Her people told her something would happen to her some day, and one night when she was coming home

> just by the 'Dancing Gates' near Kington, she
> heard beautiful music. It was the music of
> the fairies and she was caught into the ring.
> Search was made for her and she appeared to
> her friends from time to time, but when they
> spoke to her she immediately disappeared.
> Her mother was told (probably by the wise
> man or woman) that if seen again she must be
> very quickly seized, without speaking, or she
> would never come back. So one day, a year
> after her disappearance, her mother saw her
> and took hold of her dress before she could
> escape. 'Why, Mother,' she said, 'where have
> you been since yesterday?'

Merrily looked up at Jane, now leaning over her other shoulder. 'I know what you're going to say. This girl's a nineteenth-century Colette. But I see no mention, in this curious precedent, of clothing found several miles away, do you?'

'What's this written inside the back cover? *Young Alison. 1965.* With a question mark.'

'It's not an uncommon name,' Merrily said. 'But Alison Kinnersley did go to see Lucy this morning.'

'Alison did?' Lol came over.

'This morning. Early. Just after I'd left the Country Kitchen. She asked me which was Lucy's house, and I directed her. I wondered at the time why she wanted to see her that early. Did they know each other?'

'Not that I know of. *Young Alison?*'

'It's just a pencil scrawl.'

'But, Mum, what if this was the last thing she wrote before she went out on her moped? The last thing she ever wrote?'

'Well, we aren't ever going to know that, are we, flower?'

The phone rang. Jane walked over to answer it. 'You in, or what?'

'Depends who it is. I'll leave it to your judgement. I might be having a bath.'

'Right.'

'I'm very confused,' Merrily said to Lol. 'I'm not happy.'

'And who's *that*?' Jane said into the phone. 'Oh. Right. Well, no, actually I'm her daughter, but if you tell me what it's about I might be able to find her.'

Jane listened, expressionless, for over a minute.

'Really,' she said flatly. 'And who told you that?' She smiled. 'No, I didn't think you would. Hang on, give me a couple of minutes, I'll wander over the vicarage, see if she's around.'

She inspected the receiver and then put it down on the window ledge and signalled to Merrily to follow her into the passage. 'Guy from *The Sunday Times* in London. Apparently, somebody's rung to tell them there's a row developed over you refusing to let Coffey do his play in the church. Looks like your chance to back off before they crucify you as a Philistine.'

'Damn.'

'You want to buy some time? How about if I tell them you're out at a string quartet recital and then you're going on to a fashionable village cocktail party?'

'And then they print it anyway and say I was unavailable for comment. Sod it.' Merrily went back into the kitchen, snatched up the phone. 'Hello. Merrily Watkins.'

'Mrs Watkins, hi. So sorry to bother you in the evening. Craig Jamieson at *The Sunday Times* newspaper. I'm just checking . . .'

'Sure. To be honest, I can't imagine why anyone should

want to cause mischief by telling you complete lies about an issue on which no decision's yet been announced one way or the other.'

'Really? That *is* puzzling, isn't it, Mrs Watkins?' Craig Jamieson sounded about seventeen, but Merrily supposed he must be at least a PhD to be a hack on *The Sunday Times*. 'You see, I've spoken to Richard Coffey and he told me he wouldn't be in the least surprised to find that you'd turned against the play. Because of all the pressure you'd been under.'

'Pressure?'

Craig Jamieson chuckled. 'I gather certain . . . well-established families are feeling threatened.'

'Look, I don't want to be cagey, but whoever told you this is going way over the top. There's been no row. Have you spoken to the member of the well-established family?'

'I was going to see what you had to say first.'

'Well, I'm sure that if you spoke to him he'd tell you he was right behind the play. Good heavens, when someone as distinguished as Richard Coffey wants to put your obscure little community on the literary map, you don't throw it back in his face, do you?'

God forgive me.

There was a pause. Then Craig Jamieson said, 'So you're going to let them do the play in your church?'

'I . . . Look, I can't just tell *you* that, can I? When nothing's been officially decided yet. I mean, there's . . . you know what the Church is like . . . there's protocol. I haven't even talked it over with the bishop yet.'

'He has to give his permission, does he? That's the Bishop of Hereford, right?'

'It's just . . . it's protocol. You know. I'm sorry, but there's really no story. You know?'

'I'm sure you're right,' said Craig Jamieson blandly.

Coffey, Merrily thought. This is Coffey. He wants to force the issue.

Perhaps it was time to call his bluff.

Replacing the phone, she saw Lol's fist connecting with the table. He was staring down at the scrawl in Mrs Leather's book.

'Young Alison,' he said. '*Young Alison*.'

Wil's Play

In a corner of the bar at the Swan, Gomer Parry sniffed suspiciously into his poncy glass. Not that he was any kind of connoisseur, see, but there was something . . .

'Stop that,' Minnie hissed down his ear. 'It's not French wine, you know. You'll be showing us up.'

'En't right, somehow.' Gomer shuffled uncomfortably inside what he'd always thought of as his laying-out suit. 'Nothing *wrong* with it, like, but it en't right.'

'The rubbish you talk, Gomer. Can't you just drink it?'

There was a free glass of the so-called Wine of Angels for everybody attending the string quartet concert – recital, Minnie kept stressing, I think it's a *recital*, Gomer – served in thin champagne glasses. Bottles of the stuff, with the picture of the church on the label, were set out on a special table, Emrys, the wine waiter, doing the honours to make everybody think this was a real privilege, like. 'Fermented in the bottle,' he kept telling the arty buggers from Off, whose Land Rover Discoveries were clogging up the market place – not that there was many of them, but a few of that sort went a long way, in Gomer's view.

On account of the tickets not going as well as they'd figured, Dermot Child's festival flunkeys had been doing the rounds, offering half-price seats to locals and finally fetching up at Gomer and Minnie's bungalow, the bastards. 'Oughter be called off, I reckon, in respect of poor Lucy,' Gomer had mumbled, but Minnie had shelled out for the tickets straight off, though neither of them'd know a string quartet from a dustcart crew.

There were other people you wouldn't expect to see at this kind of do. Effie Prosser, from the Spar shop, and Bernard and Norma Putley, from the garage, putting a brave face on it 'spite of their boy being grilled by the Law over drugs. Oh, and Bull-Davies with his blonde floozie.

No sign of the vicar, mind. Gomer was worried about that little lady. Needed friends, she did, and all that was happening was folk getting turned against her. Too many mischief-makers. Life was boring in the country now, for folk born and raised locally. No jobs worth getting up for, less they moved away, the telly always showing them what they were missing, the *Sun* telling them they ought to be having dynamite sex twice a night and different partners at weekends, drug dealers showing enterprising youngsters like Mark Putley how they could earn enough for a smart motorbike.

And no *characters* any more. Gomer fiddled in a pocket of his stiff, blue jacket for a cigarette he daren't bring out. No characters, now poor Lucy was gone. All gloss and no soul. The string quartet was made up of professional musicians from London with weekend cottages hereabouts.

And the so-called Wine of Angels, even that had no character. All this talk about the Pharisees Red and it tasted like supermarket cider. Whatever the old recipe was, the Powells had lost it.

'En't right,' Gomer mumbled, following Minnie into the big dining room, done out as a concert hall. 'Artificial.' That was the word. Whole village was artificial nowadays, but the cider, that needed checking out.

*

'Here for the concert, Reverend?' asked the fifty-something man at the hand dryer. Bank-manager type.

'Yes, I er . . . I'm staying with friends in Hereford.' *Try and project your voice more. Always sound confident.* 'I gather the Queen's Arms Quartet are building up quite a reputation.'

'Yes, indeed,' the bank manager said. 'I believe they are. Well . . . enjoy it.'

As the toilet door wheezed into place, the face of Sandy Locke came up in the mirror. The *Reverend* Sandy Locke. Whose parish was in Hampshire, who was spending a couple of weeks with some old college friends in the cathedral city and who, this evening, was indulging his fondness for chamber music.

In the mirror, the Rev. Sandy Locke produced a surprisingly encouraging smile. It scared him how plausible he looked. How confident, how relaxed. He actually wouldn't have recognized himself. A natural vicar's face, Merrily had told him. Kind of fresh and innocent.

God forbid.

The ponytail had had to go. It was quite reasonable for a vicar to have long hair these days, Merrily said, but in Ledwardine it would make some people look again. Jane had cut his hair, finishing off with nail scissors so that it looked neat and groomed. Merrily had produced the black jacket and black cord jeans, the black T-shirt thing and the dog collar, all out of her own wardrobe. Everything was very tight. The jacket buttoned the wrong way, but it wouldn't button anyway.

He froze momentarily when, on leaving the Gents, he brushed against a woman who turned out to be Detective Inspector Annie Howe, severely youthful in her business suit. Howe glanced at him and they both smiled and he was terrified, but Howe moved on, and that was the clincher: the

Rev. Sandy Locke bore no resemblance to the police picture of the young Lol Robinson, sex offender.

He went to the bar. He ordered a Perrier, carried it over to the window and stood there and watched the beautiful Alison Kinnersley, in a low-cut, wine-coloured velvet dress he didn't recognize, flashing smiles across a table at her lover, and he felt no longing.

Where he'd thought he'd be feeling ridiculous, in fact he felt controlled. It was a strange and powerful sensation, everything now tightly wrapped around this deep and focused curiosity. Wild. Exhilarating. And, in the garb of a church minister, entirely and ironically unexpected.

He stood there, by the long, floral curtains, the opulent scene before him glimmering with artificial candlelight from the oak-pillared walls, and he looked at Alison Kinnersley, as though he was seeing her for the first time and saw that she was focused, too. Every smile she flung at Bull-Davies had a weight of history behind it. Or was he imagining that because of what he now knew?

He went on looking at Alison Kinnersley, whose name just happened to be the name of a straggling village in North Herefordshire which you might pick off a map and think how solid and convincing it would sound as a surname.

He went on looking at Alison Kinnersley but he thought about the Reverend Merrily Watkins.

Look. She'd held the dog collar to his throat. *It'll work. This is the only way. It'll work.*

She'd seemed exhilarated by it, fussing around, attending to details.

She was very lovely. He only wished she hadn't seen Lol Robinson at his most pathetic.

Alison and Bull-Davies finished their drinks together and stood up together and walked together through a double doorway under a sign saying *dining room.*

In his strange, controlled way, the Rev. Sandy Locke followed them.

Where Lol Robinson would have hung around outside in the bar, hoping she'd need to go to the toilet, the Rev. Sandy Locke would take the seat right next to Alison.

Controlled?

Jesus, could it possibly last?

*

'You are happy to discuss this in front of your little daughter?' Richard Coffey said.

He wore a black leather waistcoat over a grandad vest. A rather good plaster facsimile of Michelangelo's David flaunted itself on a plinth beside his chair. On the flock-papered walls were some artfully lit but fairly blatant black and white photos of naked men.

'If there's anything I don't understand,' Merrily said, 'I'm sure she can explain it to me on the way home.'

Coffey didn't smile. The truth was, she hadn't been prepared to leave the kid alone in the vicarage. You might be able to lock Ethel the cat in the kitchen, but Jane disappeared too easily these days.

Jane sat on a cushion on a stone arm of the fireplace and gazed at Stefan Alder who shared the sofa with Coffey. Still young enough to think it just needed the right woman to come along to straighten him out. Merrily's view, looking at Coffey's bare, steely hawsered arms and his patchwork face, inclined more towards the right younger man. But to business.

'Reason I wanted to see you, Mr Coffey, was the telephone call I had from *The Sunday Times*.'

'Ah.' Coffey leaned an arm along the back of the sofa, behind Stefan. 'Dear Craig.'

'I presumed he got his initial information from you.'

Coffey scowled. 'He did not.'

The light in the lodge's cubical sitting room was fading and dusty. The room was furnished with reproduction statuary and thousands of books. No TV, only a small, portable stereo. Nothing valuable because the house was left empty for long periods, Coffey had explained, and who wanted to steal books? Not that their despicable neighbour, Bull-Davies, would do anything to stop them.

'If you're looking for Craig's informant,' Coffey said, 'I suggest you look no further than the festival committee. And I suspect that under the present circumstances one can rule out the unfortunate Cassidy.'

Merrily sat up even straighter than her pine Shaker-style chair demanded. 'You mean Child?'

Controversy certainly attracts attention, Dermot had said, bemoaning the poor attendance, in real terms, on Day One. *But this was the wrong kind of controversy.*

Coffey pursed his thin lips and raised his tightly plucked eyebrows and said nothing.

'For a quick blast of publicity for the festival?' It made sense; if the festival flopped now that Dermot was in charge, after his frequent disparaging of Terrence Cassidy, there'd be enough egg on his face to whip up mayonnaise.

Coffey leaned his head on his arm. 'Merrily, as I think I told you, I'm a thorough sort of chap, and I don't do business with unknowns. I had them all checked out, with particular reference to precisely what they were doing before they came to Ledwardine . . . or came back, in Child's case. Cassidy? Small beer, a polytechnic poseur who inherited his father's house and decided on a new start. Child. Hmm. Well. Stefan calls him the Goblin, don't you Steffie?'

'Goblins being the entities that enter your house at night and mess up your possessions,' Stefan said. He'd looked quite pleased to see them when he first opened the door. As though there was tension between Coffey and him.

'He's a failure, basically,' Coffey said. 'Started out as a music teacher at some comprehensive school, then decided his talents were worth more. Worked with an early-music ensemble and composed, in the loosest sense, the music for a television costume drama which was so awful they screened it around midnight. Been trading on it ever since, with diminishing returns. Child's a loser.'

'But a rather poor loser, I'm afraid,' Stefan said.

'A poisonous loser. Man's so embittered he doesn't care who goes down. So, if you're looking for the designer, if not the actual distributor, of, for example, certain posters branding you a person of satanic bent, you might begin by checking out the equipment at the festival office.'

Merrily was shocked. 'I can't believe that.'

'Of course you can't, he's a *charming* little man.'

Jane said, 'Posters?'

'Juvenile trivia, flower.'

'Only, Dean Wall and Gittoes and those hairballs were coming out with all that Satanism stuff at Colette's party.'

'Who?' said Coffey.

'Just some yobs from Jane's school.'

'Ah, well, schoolboys can be *terribly* useful,' Coffey said, with a certain insouciance. 'They always need money. And it doesn't have to be a great deal.'

Stefan glared at him.

'But why *would* he?' Merrily said. 'What have *I* ever done to him?'

'I really wouldn't know. Perhaps not enough. Who can say?'

'Christ,' Merrily said.

She couldn't look at any of them and stared out of the window, across a few semi-wooded fields to the village.

Between the lodge's Victorian Gothic mullions, smudges of evening cloud had blunted the church steeple.

*

After no more than about seventy-five minutes, the Queen's Arms Quartet were showing signs of strain, and the tubby, beaming guy – Dermot Child? – arose to lead a standing ovation. Seriously undeserved, Lol thought, having detected more than a few bum notes. Still, it was at this moment – when they all stood up, with an assortment of creaks from an assortment of chairs – that Alison glanced, for the first time, directly to her left and met the eyes of the Rev. Sandy Locke.

It was worth it. For a second, her face was frozen tight, before it imploded into a gasp. Another first. Maybe the gasp was even a tiny scream, but it was lost among the spurious applause, like a leaf in a gale.

Lol clapped harder so that he swayed against Alison. He put his cheek next to hers and in his jolly vicar voice he said, 'Alison Young, as I live and breathe.'

*

Stefan Alder began to look excited, leaned eagerly towards Merrily. 'So what are you proposing?'

It was quite dark now, but Coffey had not put on a lamp.

'I don't quite know,' Merrily said. 'It all seems to go deeper than I can say. Or you, I suspect.'

'It couldn't go any deeper with me,' Stefan said, and Coffey frowned.

'In the village, I meant.' Merrily thought of her afternoon with Lucy, who'd said she wanted the play to go on in the church so that the truth would come out. *When the ditch-waters are stirred, the turds often surface.* 'I think I want whatever's bubbling under there to come to the surface. Is that what you want?'

'It's all I want,' Stefan said humbly, without even a glance at Coffey.

'What I *don't* want, though,' Merrily said, 'and what I don't think the village deserves, is for it to happen in the middle of a media circus. I don't want – ' a sideways glance at Coffey ' – to play Dermot's game.'

Coffey said from the shadows, 'Don't try to be clever, Mrs Watkins. Spell it out.'

'All right.' She looked down to the village, where lights were coming on. 'I heard Stefan and your friends Martin and Mira discussing the idea of involving the community in the drama by having a few local people virtually take on the roles of their ancestors. So you'd have Wil Williams defending himself from the pulpit, explaining his . . . situation. And perhaps some reaction, whether it's surprise or dismay or sympathy. Who'd play Thomas Bull?'

'We'd have an actor,' Coffey said guardedly. 'I even considered doing it myself.'

Merrily said, before she could stop herself, 'You do like to live dangerously, don't you?'

A cold silence from Coffey's corner.

'We would hardly expect Bull-Davies to be there,' Stefan said.

'Don't underestimate him.'

'And don't underestimate *me*, Mrs Watkins.' Richard Coffey inclined his head to her. 'Don't push me too hard. There are other churches. There's even a cathedral.'

'No!' Stefan cried. Merrily raised a palm.

'I'm not pushing anybody. I'm just suggesting that if you want the local people on your side and no embarrassing interruptions, then you might like to try a private run-through with a private, local audience. Unpublicized. Word of mouth. I can guarantee an audience.'

'And Child would guarantee a television crew or two.'

'I think not,' Merrily said icily.

'And when were you thinking we might do this?'

'Tomorrow night?'

She heard Jane gasp. Two or three seconds of incredulous silence followed, before Coffey's forced laughter and Merrily interrupting it.

'Why not? It's all written, isn't it? Stefan's well into the role.'

'Mrs Watkins, your ignorance of the demands of a theatrical production I find—'

'But we're not talking about a theatrical production! We're talking about . . . I don't know *what* we're talking about . . . A confrontation. A dialogue. A dialogue with the past. The village facing up to its most shameful episode, seeking redemption. Looking into its own soul and groping for the truth after three centuries of ignorance. Trying to find the light.'

'The beginnings of a pretty soliloquy,' said Coffey. 'Who would you play, Mrs Watkins?'

'I understand what you're worried about. You're afraid of a shambles. Of word getting out that it was a disaster. Maybe Dermot Child shafting you. Well, all right, I can buy that. But this would be a village thing – the sort of thing churches were *intended* for.'

'She might be right.' Stefan Alder was on his feet, his back to the window, looking out over the lights of Ledwardine. 'We know everything about the village,' he said to Merrily. 'We've a great, thick file of information. Richard paid a chap who used to work for the local paper to collect stories and memories from local people.'

'Shut up, Steffie.'

'This chap was marvellous. He hung out in the Ox and places, he talked to a meeting of the WI. They all thought he was collecting information for one of those local history books. Nobody knew it was for us. We can use all that. We'll surprise everybody with how much we know, how much a part of this village we've become in such a short time. She's right, Richard, we can bond with these people, we can win them over, prove beyond all doubt that we're the right people to do this, to tell the truth.'

'She might very well be right, Steffie, but what she's suggesting is utterly impossible. Why tomorrow night anyway? Why not in a couple of months' time, when we know where we're going with this?'

'Because I don't know where *I'm* going with it, Mr Coffey. It keeps coming up in front of me. I keep telling myself it's only a bloody play, but . . .'

'It isn't,' Stefan said. 'It's a public redemption.'

'Yes. Whatever. Anyway, those are my terms. You want to do it somewhere else, you go ahead. You know my number.' Merrily stood up. 'Come on, Jane.'

'All right.' Stefan Alder turned towards them, a shadow, even his ash-blond hair black against the blue-grey window. 'We'll do it. We'll do it tomorrow night. Bring who you want. Fill the church.'

'Stefan, don't be a bloody fool.' Coffey sprang up, his face pulsing. 'Leave us, Mrs Watkins.'

'Sure. Flower?'

Jane crept quietly away from the empty hearth. They let themselves out. In the dark room behind them, they heard Richard Coffey snarl, 'You stupid little shit. It's *my* play.'

'I'll see he's there,' Stefan called after them, his voice high and tremulously theatrical. 'I'll have him there.'

'It's *my play*!'

'Not *you*,' Stefan sang out, with stinging contempt. 'Wil. It's *Wil's* play.'

Winding Sheet

Mum drove them slowly home in the Volvo with the *Hazey Jane* album playing quite loudly on the CD, a signal she didn't want to talk. Maybe this was just as well, Jane was thinking. She'd only have said something really crass about Mum coming on, at last, like an actual catalyst.

It was like Lucy was in the back seat.

And what was so crazy about that? Jane looked out of the side window as they came into the village as if she might spot the lamp of the moped bobbing into the market place, a little golden light. What had they done with Lucy's moped? Probably being examined by some police mechanical expert, who'd say the brakes were crap or something and the little bike was a death trap and why wasn't she wearing a helmet?

Because it wouldn't fit over her big hat, you cretins! You want Lucy Devenish to go out without her hat?

There *was* life after death. There had to be. Or there was no justice; no justice for good people like Lucy. Who nobody could replace; something had died with Lucy, a spirit. It was mega-depressing.

She glanced at Mum's profile, the dark curls in need of a cut. *Run with this, Vicar, don't let her down.* And then thought about Colette. Where was she tonight?

It's like somebody cuts out a section of time and joins the ends together, second to second. Like with the dancing girl in

Mrs Leather, maybe Colette will be visible occasionally in the little, green orchard.

The thought wasn't scary; it was hopeful. It had been there on the back burner since she first read that story. If Colette was *there*, somebody should try and reach her.

The market place was still full of cars, but, at barely ten, people were already dribbling out of the Black Swan under the hanging lanterns. Not much of a gig, then. She wondered how Lol was getting on. It had just been so much fun making him look like a vicar, like traditional country vicars were supposed to look, kind of weedy and innocent. In the end he looked much more like one than Mum, but then Mum never really had.

Before they left for Coffey's place, Mum had told her the whole story about Lol and Karl Windling and the young girls in the hotel – which she'd found so awful and so barely credible that she wanted to go and find these girls and their smug parents and tell them just what they'd done. As for that bastard Windling . . .

On the CD, Lol was singing, the low, breathy voice solo with acoustic guitar, about being alone in the city in a cold January rain but not wanting to go home.

It made such horrifying sense. It made her want to cry. It made her wish she was old enough to marry him or something.

A police car rolled out of Church Street. The awful Howe would be hoping now, like Bella, that Colette was dead, turning it into a big case for an area like this. Dreaming of picking up Lol and shoving him into a little grey-walled room, like on *The Bill*, her and that Mumford asking him kind of nonchalantly what he'd done with the body. Telling him they just wanted to help him. That was what the police always did, they told you they just wanted to help you. But they were just in it for themselves. Like everybody was.

Except Mum.

'Suppose they've got him?' she said as they pulled into the vicarage drive.

'If they'd got him,' Mum said calmly, switching off the engine and the stereo, 'I think they'd be waiting for us, too. I don't see anybody, do you?'

'Lol wouldn't finger us.'

'No,' Mum said. 'I don't think he would.'

Inside the vicarage, she seemed to collapse. No sleep, not much food for over a day. Running on empty for too long. She was trying to open a can of sardines for Ethel, but the metal key thing snapped, and she just stood there in the kitchen and started to weep.

Somehow, the vicarage did this to her. The vastness of it, the emptiness, was far worse for Mum than it was for Jane, who still thought a big house was cool. Not as if it was haunted or anything. It just seemed to do Mum's brain in. She'd been dynamite at the Upper Hall Lodge, pushing even the scary Coffey into a corner, getting what she wanted. And now, here she was, sobbing her heart out in her own kitchen, and Jane just knew she was thinking about Dad and what a balls they'd made of their marriage and everything and how stupid she'd been to think she could manage a parish and all the other stuff that came down on you when were exhausted in a place you hated.

'Go to bed, Mum. Please go to bed. I'll look after everything.'

'I can't. What about Lol?'

'I'll wait up for him. Please go to bed.'

Mum wiped her eyes with the sleeve of her jumper. 'Sorry.'

'You're overtired.' Jane eased the sardine can out of her hands.

'I gave him a key,' Mum said. 'Didn't I?'

'I think you did. Don't worry. Sleep.'

Mum looked at her, just about finding the energy for suspicion.

'I'll go up too,' Jane assured her. 'I won't go out again, I promise.'

Not tonight, anyway. Got to prepare. Got to get it right.

*

There was a lounge, for residents only, with a TV set tuned to a film about surfing, with the sound down. A waitress served cocoa to two elderly couples at a window table.

Lol took a seat by the door. One of the elderly ladies smiled at him, and Lol said, 'Good evening,' in his soft but resonant vicar's voice and sat, composed, his fingers loosely entwined.

She would come. She'd directed him here. Smiling and nodding pleasantly for the thirty seconds she'd been speaking to the Rev. Locke, smiling for the benefit of James Bull-Davies, who'd been getting drinks at the time. An actress. Every move she made powered by this low-burning, high-octane fury.

He saw that now. The Rev. Sandy Locke, one step removed from it all, seemed able to see so many things concealed from screwed-up, introverted Lol Robinson.

'Two eggs,' one of the elderly men said. 'Bacon, sausage, liver, onions, black pudding, chips. Nine ninety-five.' He sat back, triumphant. 'Inclusive of sweet.'

'The toilets weren't clean, though,' his wife said. 'At least the toilets are clean here. And what's more, what I always think is important in a hotel—'

She broke off as Alison glided in, both elderly ladies looking rather shocked when this blonde in the revealing dress went to sit next to the clergyman, the old men looking pleased.

'Hi.' Lol smiled. 'Where did you tell him you were going?'

'Powder my nose. Evidently, I bumped into someone I knew in the Ladies', you know what women are like.'

'I'm kind of learning,' Lol said. 'At last.'

'He'll find someone's ear to bend. Won't notice I'm missing for a while. As to that – ' Alison gestured at his dog collar ' – I'm not going to ask.'

'A drink?'

'No time.'

'So you talk,' Lol said. 'And I'll listen. I won't interrupt.' He felt like he was hovering, very steadily. Everything delicately balanced but, for the first time in his adult life, he was keeping the balance.

Alison shook her hair back. 'I suppose Devenish told you, God rest her heathen soul.'

'No, it was insight.'

'From *you*?'

He grinned. She couldn't touch him tonight. He lowered his voice. He took this great leap in the dark.

'I can't help wondering what James would say, if he knew he'd been fucking his . . . what? Half-sister?'

She remained entirely calm. 'You going to tell him?'

Jesus. It's right.

'Probably not,' he said.

*

In the darkness of her too-big bedroom, Merrily knelt to pray by her too-big bed.

'I, er . . . I don't know what I'm asking for. Strength, certainly. Yeah. I'm not strong. But You know that.'

She went quiet. Receptive. Opening up a space in her heart. Wanting very much to receive something, if it was only an upsurge of blessed scepticism. She didn't *want* to believe in bloody ghosts and fairies.

In the silence, there was no sense of blue or gold. Was that itself a sign? Was the lack of response, the sense of praying into a black void, an indication that she should harden herself against phoney mysticism, spurious super-stition? She felt distantly angry at God for never giving it to you straight.

*

Of course, it was Lol himself who'd pointed her at Lucy.

Mentioning, when Alison had talked about the Bull-Davies tradition of keeping horses, that James's old man seemed to have carried on the equine tradition purely for a steady supply of stable girls.

The first chance she had this morning, Alison had been off to pursue this angle with Lucy Devenish, good friend of Patricia Young who'd slaved in the Bull stables in the early 'sixties.

'And came home pregnant to Swindon,' Alison said. 'Steadfastly refusing to name the father. My gran was very supportive, although God knows she had enough on her plate at the time, with Grandfather failing fast. He died, in fact, the night after I was born, so we came back to a house of mourning, Mother and I.'

The waitress returned and, evidently thinking the minister was a hotel guest, asked if they would like anything. Lol ordered coffee, figuring this was going to take longer than Alison imagined.

'I don't think', he said, 'that Lucy mentioned anything to me about her friend being pregnant. I don't think she knew. She said she'd warned her to get out of Upper Hall and she'd taken the advice.'

'You're right, Devenish didn't know about the pregnancy. She said this morning that that was what she was afraid of. My mother would come to her in tears, asking what could she do when she needed the job and the money. In the end, Devenish gave her some to get away. Which was kind. But too late. No, she didn't know about a baby. How did you?'

Lol explained, without mentioning Merrily, about the book in the box. The word Young and then Alison. How he'd kept looking at it and puzzling and then remembered the name, Patricia Young. All those weeks of agonizing over why she left him, and then this moment of blinding certainty. Intuition.

'I had no choice, Lol.'

'No,' he said neutrally.

'You don't believe that. Hell, you don't owe me any generosity, I don't expect any. I needed to live in a certain posh village, couldn't afford a mortgage.' She shrugged. 'You were there. You needed help too. I'm sorry. But I'd do it again.'

Lol didn't react. He understood now. He didn't care.

'So when did your mother eventually admit the old Bull was your father?'

'Never. Never did. My gran said she'd sometimes imply it was one of the village boys. Unconvincingly.'

'You must have asked her who your father was, as you got older.'

'No, no you don't understand.' Shaking her head impatiently. 'I don't *remember* Patricia. I don't remember my mother at all. That's the whole point. One day, when I was about eighteen months old, she left me with my gran, said she was going back to Hereford to see some people. Get some money out of the father, that was always Gran's theory, because they had money problems at the time, after the old man died. Bills. Debts. He was a farmer, too, of sorts, my grandad. So Gran didn't try to stop my mother going. Died regretting that.'

'Why?

'Because she never came back, Lol. She returned to Ledwardine to face the father and she never bloody well came back. Gran reported it to the police and they made cursory, routine inquiries in Ledwardine and said nobody had seen her, and that was that.'

'That was *it*?' He thought of the way the police were turning over the village for Colette Cassidy.

'Grown women, Lol, sometimes choose to disappear. The police were suggesting she'd only come back to Swindon to dump the baby, make sure I had a good home. Then off to join some man, with no inconvenient little kid in tow.'

'They check with old Bull-Davies?'

'Oh, sure. Squire John, county councillor and magistrate. Local constable deferential on the doorstep. Sorry to disturb you, sir, tug-tug on the forelock, but this silly girl you once kindly employed . . . Just a formality, sir, if you'd be so good as to confirm you never saw her again, thank you very much, sir, sorry to have bothered you.'

Alison tossed back her hair.

'People like you, Lol, into all this progressive 'sixties music, forget that it was still quite primitive then, in country areas. You didn't ruffle the hawk's feathers.'

'What do you think happened to her?'

'I used to think she was given money to go abroad. But now I know they hadn't got that kind of money. No way. And this is the country. What do you do with nuisances in the country? What do you do with the dog that's worrying your sheep? What do you do with the badgers you're convinced are spreading tuberculosis to your cows, even though badgers are officially protected? What do you do with the woman who's threatening to expose you to the county?'

'Was she?'

'No way. She probably just asked for a few thousand quid. Perhaps *he* was worried she'd be into him for money for the rest of his life, but I can't imagine she'd have even thought of that. She just went to ask for a bit of help.'

'Lucy said she was naive. Kind of innocent.'

'Which would've made it even easier for him.'

'Easier?'

'To get rid of her. The way people always did in the countryside. With pests.'

'That's . . .'

'More difficult than it used to be. But not that much more difficult. I knew it as soon as I came here.'

'With me?'

'No . . . years earlier. Ten years ago. With a couple of girl friends. Camping holiday. It had been gnawing at me more and more. The number of times I found this place on the maps, circled it and circled it until the biro went through the paper. Then, when Gran died . . . I mean, she died hard. She was working well into her seventies, cleaning people's houses so I could stay on at school, go to university. She died hard and she died full of regrets and remorse – with no reason, whatever, she was a saint, my gran. She died when I was in my final year and I dropped out at once and I got a job and I thought, those fucking rich, smug bastards, they killed my mother and they killed my grandmother, and I . . . *I just wanted* . . .'

She was hunched up now, gripping the sides of her chair with both hands. A side of her she'd never before let him see. She tossed back her hair again, getting herself together.

'So we were on this camping holiday, Julie, Donna – mates from college. I made sure we came here, never told them why. Yeah, it would be twelve years ago, the year after I dropped out. It was a good summer, we hired mountain bikes. I had the route all marked out on the OS map, and when we came to Upper Hall, there he was, the good and great John Bull-Davies, overseeing the haymaking. Sitting on the edge of the bottom meadow in his linen jacket, with his fat bum on a shooting stick. John Bull-fucking-Davies.'

'How did you know it was him?'

'I didn't. At first. I walked over on my own and asked for directions to Canon Pyon. It was very hot, and I was wearing shorts and a skimpy top and sweating profusely, and he said I looked awfully hot and I could probably do with something long and cool. Always remember that. Something long and cool. He leered. Must've been in his sixties. Then he saw the other two waiting for me down by the field gate. Too many. Too awkward. So he gave me the directions to Canon Pyon.'

'You think he'd really have made a play for you, with all the blokes at work in the field?'

'Absolutely. Probably wanted them to see. The old squire as potent as ever he was. They've always fucked who they liked. It was the way. Their right. Droit de seigneur. Before I went back to the bikes, I stood there and looked at him. Full in the face. Memorizing every little, poxy detail. Been a good-looking guy in his time. I stood and I kept on looking at him, until even he became uncomfortable and turned away. Then, that night, in a pub – in this pub, actually – I stared at myself in the mirror and I was nearly sick with disgust.'

The coffee came, and Lol paid for it. It was a different waitress, who clearly recognized Alison, so Lol said, 'Oh, and Auntie Doris sends her love, by the way.'

Alison poured the coffee with a steady hand.

*

Cramp in her left leg awoke her.

She'd fallen asleep in the middle of her attempted prayer, head in a curled arm on the duvet. The arm was numb. She was cold. She needed to pee.

She struggled upright, rubbing at the cramped calf. There

was no sound from above or from below. What time was it? She groped for the alarm clock, peered at its luminous hands.

Nearly half-twelve. Sunday. The Sabbath. The Working Day. Holy Communion. Morning service. An unusually full church. What would the vicar look like? How would she behave? Would she be pale and penitent? Would she have crimson eyes and drool? However the vicar looked, there'd be enough material for a whole week's gossip.

The efficient Ted would have rung back while she and Jane were at the lodge, and, on getting no reply, gone ahead and summoned the trusty, retired minister from Pembridge. Making long-term plans, no doubt, to distance himself: a discreet word here, an expression of concern there. *Did my best for her, but the traumas of the past, you know. My fault, should have realized her nerves were simply not up to it, parish this size . . . all the pressure . . .*

Pressure on her bladder. Merrily slid her feet into her sandals, found the sweater at the bottom of the bed and pulled it on over her nightdress. Shuffled to the door, aching with weariness, feeling old and beaten, worn out, done in.

For several minutes after she'd finished, she sat there on the lavatory, bowed over, her face in her hands. Her nerves were shot. It made her ashamed. Dozens of people in the village had real, solid, frightening problems – serious illness, recent bereavement, job loss, the prospect of a house being repossessed because they couldn't meet the mortgage, and, of course, the extreme and constant anxiety and fear when a daughter has disappeared. Compared with all of this, her own problems were meaningless, ephemeral, fatuous.

Merrily washed her hands and face in cold water.

Go back to bed, forget it. Don't think about tomorrow night either, or how you're going to organize it; if it's meant to happen, it will; if it isn't, let it go, let the original decision stand, no Wil Williams in the church, thank you. Thank you and, if necessary, goodbye. She pulled the bathroom door closed behind her.

Something rushed at her from the blackness. In a vivid instant, she had the clear impression of a hard nucleus of bitter cold, rolling along the lightless passage like a soiled, grey snowball, rapidly gathering momentum, frigidity.

She shrank away, flattened herself against the bathroom door, turned her head into the wall.

The cold hit her. It stank of misery. It wrapped itself around her, a frigid winding sheet. She couldn't breathe.

She squirmed. *Wake up.* Lips pulled tight around a prayer: *O God, yea, though I walk through the darkness of the soul, though my heart is weak . . .*

At the end of the passage, a light hung over the stairs.

Wake up, wake up, wake up, wake . . .

The light was a lean, vertical smear. It wasn't much, promised no warmth, but she reached out for it, her hands groping for the stair-rail on the landing.

Should she try to run downstairs? She looked down. She tried to call down to Lol, who might not even be there. There was no easier name to say, but she couldn't say it. 'L . . . L . . .' Her tongue stuck to the roof of her mouth and all that emerged was a sound like an owl-hoot, weak and lonely, and looking down the stairs was like looking down an endless, cold, black well.

The only way was up.

She looked up, just as the light flared over the stairs, like a small, contained area of sheet lightning behind cloud and she was briefly caught in its periphery, which sent a jagged shock into her still-tightened chest, and she stumbled in panic, fell forward on to the stairs into a clinging, damp vapour, dense with particles of fleeing light, and the wooden stairs under her were very rough and the air around her cold. Cold for January, desperately cold for May. She pulled herself up and was nearly pulled down again because her heart was so packed with pain.

Despair. A worm of liquid despair wriggling inside her. The light flared again for a moment, and she felt a penetrating agony in her chest as she toppled into the attic.

There was no sound but the whine of the night wind in the exposed roof timbers and her own breathing.

As she pulled herself up, the tightness fell away and she breathed odourless air. Stood, panting on the top floor of the vicarage, a place of dreams, where there were no doors. No bedroom, no sitting room/study.

No Jane.

Only a long empty space, with a sloping roof, where something cold and naked, wretchedly embracing an unending misery, metamorphosed for a wild, defiant instant into a spinning, swirling, silken vortex of silver-grey and then was gone.

Levels

Downstairs in the drawing room of the vicarage, the lights were on. There were brown, smoking embers in the grate. She was wearing a shapeless, green polo-neck jumper over a white nightdress. It was still night. She'd lost a sandal. She felt cold and drained and heartbroken.

And didn't know why.

'She's sleeping,' Lol said. 'I went back and stuck my head around the door. She's fine. Everything's normal.'

'Except me.' Merrily threw coal on the fire. She would never be warm again.

Lol contemplated her seriously through his glasses, round and brass-rimmed like some old, nautical telescope.

She said, 'Where was I?'

'At the top of the stairs. Swaying about. I thought you were going to fall.'

'What did you see? What was it like? Was it a kind of big, open space? Rough joists. Damp . . .' Her voice faded. She knew what he was going to say.

'It was normal. Just like now.'

'You didn't go to the right place,' she said.

'Maybe not.' He sat her down on the sofa and positioned himself at the other end, his back against the arm. Ethel jumped into his lap. 'Maybe not, no.'

Seconds passed. He was thinking.

She said, 'You're still wearing your vicar's gear.'

Absurd reversal of roles.

'Mm.' He was calmer than she'd seen him, or maybe that was merely relative to her own condition.

'Time is it, Lol?'

'About twenty past one.'

'You been back long?' His sleeping bag was on the rug in front of the fire, still rolled up.

'Hour or so. I was wandering around the garden for a while. Thinking things out.' He looked down at his black chest. 'Scared to take these off, I suppose. This guy looks at things objectively.'

'Let's put some more coal on the fire,' Merrily said.

*

She told him about all the times it had happened before, from that first night when she thought she'd followed Jane and she'd kept opening doors and wound up at the foot of the stairs, looking up to the third floor.

She shut her eyes and rolled her head slowly around, small bones creaking at the back of her neck.

'And then Sean.'

'Your husband?'

'My dead husband. I know it wasn't a dream, because . . .'

She told him about the door handle which fell out again, proving she'd been in the empty bedroom when she saw him and not in her own bed, dreaming.

In the fireplace, cool yellow flames were swarming over the new coal. Lol pushed in the poker.

'What happened?'

'I don't know. I did wake up in bed, and it was morning, and I thought it had been a dream. It was a hallucination, I suppose. I went into that room and I hallucinated Sean. A source of guilt, because I didn't help him when he needed help. But he didn't want me to. He had another woman.'

'You're the kind of person always feels responsible.'

'Jane tell you that?'

'No. I've actually started figuring things out for myself.' He prodded at a cob of coal until it developed fissures and opened up and let more flames through.

'If it's not the house,' Merrily said, 'it has to be me.'

'Could it be a combination of both? You and the house setting something off in each other? Or you and the house . . . and Jane?'

'Yeah, I know. Like adolescents cause poltergeist phenomena. I've heard all that. But this doesn't happen to Jane. Nothing happens to Jane here.'

'Only in the orchard.'

He looked into the fire for a while and then he said, 'This question of different floors. When you've read lots of books on psychology like me . . . That's what I used to read in hospital. They had a library, for the doctors and the staff, with a resident librarian, and I got to know her, and that's where I used to spend . . . days. Whole days, I suppose. Reading books on psychology and psychiatric syndromes. Some of it made more sense than the patronizing crap I was getting from most of the staff.'

'How did you stand it?'

'Time passes,' Lol said. 'You don't notice. But, anyway . . . levels. The floor where you're sleeping, that's where you're at. That's your situation. Your husband's there, your past, all your problems, your insecurities, your fears, your guilt. That's where you keep opening doors and they lead nowhere, except into the past. That's where you saw Sean. And when it gets too stifling, just when you feel there's no escape, you wind up at the stairs leading to the third floor.'

Psychological claptrap. She needed a cigarette.

'But, up there, Merrily, is the Unknown. It could be Enlightenment. But it could also be madness. You're afraid of what you might learn.'

'I didn't learn anything. I'd fallen asleep in the praying position and woke up feeling really low and beaten and hopeless. But until I went up into that attic, I didn't know what sorrow was. Or felt like, because I still don't know what it was. Why I felt so bad.'

'And it was different.'

'I wasn't frightened. I had this freedom up there. The freedom to cry for ever. And I knew I couldn't. I couldn't make a sound. Mustn't be heard.'

'By Jane?'

'Jane wasn't there. Nobody else was there. It was different time, Lol. It was a time of indescribable unhappiness.'

Merrily wept.

The sorrow she was giving off was so profound, he had to blink back his own tears.

He wanted to hold her.

He didn't touch her.

He went to make tea.

*

Later, he lay on the sofa and watched her sleep in front of the fire, curled up in the sleeping bag there like a child, the orange coals and the wire fireguard making glowing, crisscross patterns on her face. The cigarettes and Zippo lighter on the rug, a few inches from her nose, Ethel by her feet.

Never had got around to telling her about Alison. He'd wanted to ask her, How will this end? What can we do about it? He'd asked Alison. She said she had no idea.

But it'll be on my terms. When I tell him.

You still hate him?

How can I hate him? My own flesh and blood.

Alison had laughed.

Yesterday morning, she'd told most of this to Lucy and then Lucy had died, bequeathing the responsibility to Merrily Watkins.

Lol was back in the alien sweatshirt, the vicar's clothes neatly on hangers behind the door. Merrily had not told him what had happened when she and Jane had gone to Richard Coffey's place.

Lol looked at Merrily, sleeping. He thought of Lucy on her back on a mortuary table in Hereford, cold and hatless and awaiting her post-mortem. This made him anxious, too anxious to sleep.

Ethel, the cat, wasn't sleeping either. She lay at the bottom of the sleeping bag, where Merrily's ankles were, and she watched Lol, golden-eyed and purring gently.

Merrily's face was flushed by the firelight. He couldn't stop looking at it.

Twice in the night, he got up to put more coal on the fire to keep her warm.

FORTY

Bad Year for Apples

'Oh, wow,' Jane said.

She was standing in the drawing-room doorway, fully dressed. Lol came up behind her from the kitchen, with tea things on a tray. Over Jane's shoulder he could see Merrily, hurriedly propping herself up in the sleeping bag.

'Flower, before you say a word—'

'Well, well,' Jane said. 'So you got it together.'

It was nearly eight a.m. Substantial sunshine had collected in the bay window, coloured pale green by the trees.

'You slept together,' Jane said.

'No!' Merrily sat up in the sleeping bag. 'I mean yes, but no.'

'This' – Jane ambled into the room, hands on hips – 'is really quite seriously cool.' She turned, beamed at Lol. 'And she looks so much better. Don't you think she looks fantastic?'

'Yes,' Lol said honestly. 'However—'

Merrily stood up. The sun shone through her white nightdress. Lol thought maybe he should close his eyes. Couldn't quite manage that.

'That's it. That is just about enough.' Merrily looked around for her sweater, failed to find it, covered herself with the sleeping bag. 'Make some toast, child.'

'Right,' Jane said. 'Anything you say.'

The phone rang. '*I'll* get that.' Merrily gathered the sleeping bag around her. Jane giggled. Lol moved out of the doorway. Merrily passed him without a glance.

Lol shut the drawing-room door behind her, faced up to Jane.

'Vicars don't lie. Nothing happened.'

'In which case – ' Jane frowned ' – you ought to be bloody well ashamed. She doesn't attract you?'

'Well . . . ye-es . . . yes, she does.'

'God.' Jane breathed hard through her teeth. 'She's not quite a *nun*. She needs somebody.'

'But preferably somebody stable.'

'Oh yeah, somebody really, really stable.' She glared at him. 'Come *on*. My *dad* was stable. My dad was this like utterly focused individual who knew exactly where he was going the whole time.'

'I thought he was bent.'

'And getting away with it! Because he knew he could. Because he was stable inside. Focused. Balanced. Never worried about anything, not really. My dad thought a neurosis was . . . was . . .'

'Something you can grow in a window box, with care.'

'Yeah. Exactly. So, you know, screw *stable*. Life's too short. Look, I know you've had your problems. I listen at doors sometimes, I'm not afraid to admit that.'

'You do, huh?'

'Those back stairs are very useful. You could go through life really ignorant if you didn't listen at doors. Like, Colette always saying you were scared of her, like it was really cool having somebody who's scared of you, but it wasn't her at all you were scared of, I know that now, and I'm glad. And I'm glad Karl Windling's dead. I mean not glad he's *dead*, like if there was some other way he could be completely out of your face . . .'

'Well, I haven't figured out how I should feel about that either.'

'You should feel free. Hey, I forgot . . . Did you get to see Alison last night?'

'I have a problem with free,' Lol said.

'Just that I keep seeing people, twice, three times, Jesus, *four* times as old as me, and they *still* haven't done anything. And then they die.' Jane slumped into the sofa. 'I don't know what I'm trying to say. Everything's peculiar. I've decided if I don't want to believe things, then I won't. So I don't believe you and Mum didn't sleep together and I don't believe Lucy's dead, OK?'

'OK.'

'And they haven't found Colette. I had the radio on at seven. It was the same stuff, more or less, as last night.'

'That's starting to not make sense.'

'Depends on how you look at it, doesn't it? Suppose I don't want to believe Colette's dead either? Or gone off with anybody. Anybody human.'

'That's even more dangerous ground.'

'Everything's *dangerous* to you, isn't it, Lol? Even Mum. What's the matter with you? All I cut *off* was your pony-tail.'

*

Stefan Alder on the line.

'It's sorted.' He sounded very calm, very purposeful. 'It's on. I'm going to make it happen, Merrily.'

'Well, good. That's wonderful. I'll put the word around.'

But what if nobody came? What if the church was empty save for Stefan and Coffey and the sick priest?

'Come and see you, shall I, Merrily, after your morning service?'

'No, that would be— I'm not actually doing the services

today. But if you want to . . . rehearse or anything, the church should be empty by twelve.'

She was calmer this morning. At least the villagers, old and new, would be given the chance. If nobody came, then it suggested nobody, except James Bull-Davies, was bothered, so the play could go ahead, in the church, whenever Coffey and his team were ready. It all seemed so simple now.

'I hope this hasn't caused problems between Richard and you.'

'No . . .' Stefan hesitated. 'Perhaps it's resolved them. You see, Richard . . . he won't be having anything to do with this. It's going to be entirely down to me.'

Oh God, Merrily thought. Sulks.

'This is how it should have been in the first place. It was my idea. I discovered him.'

'Wil?'

'It's a one-man show, Merrily. It comes from the heart, not the page. Some of it was going to be improvised anyway. I'm a performer. A stage, an audience, you know? Give me one and a half hours. Or more.'

'Shall we say seven p.m.? We don't have an evening service any more, so that's not a problem.'

'Could you make it half-eight? Nine? I'd prefer it to get gradually darker.'

'All right.'

They agreed to meet in the church at one.

'I'm bringing him home, Merrily,' Stefan said.

Merrily put down the phone and stood for a moment, thinking about last night. She'd slept easily between the fire and Lol Robinson. Daylight had cancelled the fear.

Although there wasn't any at the end; only sorrow.

She wouldn't forget that.

*

When she came back to the drawing room, Lol and Jane had one of the Sunday tabloids spread out on the coffee table. 'Oh well,' Lol was saying, 'it had to happen at some stage.'

The page two headline was,

Fears Grow for Party Girl Colette

There was a picture of a rather younger, more innocent Colette, with no nose-stud and an unfamiliar smile. The fact that it was quite small was a strong indication this was not the picture the paper had wanted, given the comments gathered from 'neighbours'.

> 'Colette was a bit of a handful,' one said. 'A real wild child.'

Most of the story was an innuendo-laden account of

> the steamy sixteenth birthday party which brought midnight chaos to a sleepy village.
>
> Music was provided by notorious Voodoo DJ Dr Samedi, who has been banned from several clubs following claims of blood sacrifices.
>
> The 29-year-old DJ, real name Jeff Mooney, said last night, 'Compared with some of the gigs I do, this seemed like a really tame venue. But as soon as I met this chick, I knew she was trouble.'

'He's actually OK,' Jane said. 'The blood sacrifice stuff's probably a bit exaggerated.'

'Like, only small amounts of blood.' Lol pointed to the end of the piece.

Police also want to talk to the owner of a cottage close to the orchard, songwriter Laurence Robinson.

'We think he may have information that could help us with our inquiries,' DI Howe said.

Mr Robinson, who has been working on new songs with 'seventies rock-hero Gary Kennedy, was still not at home last night.

'Speaks for itself, doesn't it? I'll go and see her. I'll explain about Karl. I'll spell it all out.'

'Are you completely crazy?' Jane snatched up the paper, waved it in his face. 'She'll nail you to the wall. How are you going to explain where you've been?'

'She could be right, Lol,' Merrily said. 'With hindsight, it would've been better if you'd been sitting there when she came to talk to Jane yesterday. You're still the best they've got. There's at least enough circumstantial evidence to hang on to you for a few days. Which would be . . . a strain.'

Thinking that if Howe's team found a body Lol would be signing a confession before the week was out, just to get them off his back.

'Give it another day,' she said. 'None of us needs to have seen a paper. Perhaps they'll find her.'

'Every day drops me further in it.'

'Why? They carefully haven't named you as a suspect.'

'She cares, Lol.' Jane smiled mischievously. 'Don't knock it.'

'Don't push it, flower.'

'It was that good, huh?'

'Make the breakfast.' Merrily picked up the paper. 'Where did this come from, anyway?'

'It was on the mat,' Lol said. 'Is this the only Sunday paper you take?'

'I don't take it.'

'I *told* you she didn't,' Jane said.

'I normally collect the papers from the newsagent on the way back from Communion. This isn't one of them.'

'Well, it was on the mat,' Lol said. 'It must be a mistake.'

'Laurence, in a village this size, you don't mistakenly deliver papers to the vicarage. Somebody wanted us to see it.'

'*Us?*' Lol said.

'Alison know you're here?'

'Yes.'

'That wise?'

'She'll keep quiet; she's on her own knife-edge. I'll tell you about that.'

Jane blinked. 'Young Alison? You cracked it?'

Merrily said, 'Make the breakfast, Jane. All right?'

*

Jane found some eggs. Put the toaster on. It was infuriating, but maybe, after what she'd said to Lol, this was not the best time to listen at the door.

And also, Mrs Leather's *The Folklore of Herefordshire* was still open on the kitchen table. It had fallen open at *that* page. Portentous, right?

> Search was made for her and she appeared
> to her friends from time to time, but when
> they spoke to her she immediately disap-
> peared.

But suppose the friends had known the score? Suppose the friends had it totally sussed?

> Her mother was told (probably by the
> wise man or woman)

. . . for whom read Lucy Devenish . . .

> that if seen again she must be very quickly
> seized, without speaking, or she would never
> come back. So one day, a year after her
> disappearance, her mother saw her and took
> hold of her dress before she could escape.
> 'Why, Mother,' she said, 'where have you
> been since yesterday?'

Jane had this sudden, crazy image of grabbing hold of the shoulder of the freshly materialized Colette's sexy black dress, and Colette rounding on her, shrieking, 'What the fuck are you playing at Janey? This is *my* poxy party!'

Jane laughed.

But why not? Why the hell not? OK, if it was all airy-fairy nonsense, total cobblers, if Colette had actually gone off with some smooth crack dealer from Hereford, then what was lost? Who was hurt?

The plain fact is, nobody, but nobody, apart from me, is ever going to try it.

OK. Practicalities. She couldn't simply keep taking walks through the orchard on the off chance Colette would show. There had to be method in this. She thought back to the night it all began. The apple tree, the little golden lights.

Another element, though, if you followed Lucy's logic, was crucial.

Cider.

*

'Does she know what she's playing with here?'

Merrily had a clear picture of Alison in the church that morning. Black shirt, gold pendant, knowing smile. *James is full of shit.*

Oh yes, Alison knew precisely what she was playing with.

And Lol, who'd been used and discarded, seemed to be able to live with that, now that he knew the circumstances, now that he understood. He was either a natural-born Christian or a natural-born sucker.

'It's good, at least, to have explanations,' he said. 'Looking back, my life's been pretty short on explanations.'

'It's horrifying. What's she want out of it? Half the hall? The farm? Half the debts?'

'Goes deeper than money.'

'Obviously. But this is a very old-fashioned guy. I really hate to imagine how he's going to react when he finds out he's been f—'

Merrily glanced at the door. They'd been whispering, but the kid had good ears and no scruples.

'. . . and that his father may have killed someone. There's certainly enough ground there to bury a body in.'

'I don't think', Lol said, 'that Bull-Davies is under any illusions about his family. Last year, he apparently spent a lot of money on the only copy of some unpublished, handwritten addendum Mrs Leather had written to her folklore book. It was going to be auctioned; he got in first. It was all about apple orchards. With special reference to Wil Williams.'

'Lucy know about it?'

'Found out too late, presumably. Maybe she doesn't have friends in auction houses. Alison came across it a few weeks ago. Not on the bookshelves. Rotting in the attic.'

'It shows the Bull family in a bad light?'

'All it shows is how flimsy the evidence against Williams

was. The farmer who accused him of bewitching his orchard
. . . according to Mrs Leather, all that amounted to was that
it had been a very bad year for apples, except in the Ledwardine orchard, where the crop was very acceptable. The
orchard, at that time, belonging entirely to the Church.'

'So? God looks after his own. That was it? He bought the
thing purely because it suggested his ancestor accepted iffy
evidence of witchcraft in the year sixteen sixty-whatever?'

Lol shrugged. 'Just, you know, an illustration of the level
of James's paranoia about his family. According to Alison.'

'She's got to be hard as nails.'

'Hardened by circumstance.'

'You are too generous, Lol. This is her brother.'

'Half-brother.'

The sun had gone in. Another capricious spring day.

'Lol, did she mention anything about another document?
The Journal of Thomas Bull?'

'There're some volumes of it in a bank in Hereford.'

'Which is where, I suppose, they're destined to stay,'
Merrily said.

*

Breakfast was a muted meal.

Jane produced boiled eggs and toast. Nobody mentioned
Alison or Bull-Davies or the deaths of Lucy and Karl Windling or little golden lights or the Nighthouse. They talked
like ordinary people with ordinary lives and only ordinary
undercurrents. Like a family, thought Lol, who'd forgotten
what a family was like.

They discussed how Merrily was going to spread the word
about the personal appearance in Ledwardine Parish Church
that night of its former incumbent, the Reverend Wil Williams, without attracting unwelcome publicity.

'It's a village thing,' Merrily said. 'And it has to stay that way. That's why I want it done quickly. Done, finished with, everybody gets their say. The issue decides itself. That's the theory, anyway. It would be good to get the Women's Institute out in force. They'll all fall for Stefan in a big way, lots of tear-filled hankies.'

'What about the Press?' Lol said. 'You can't keep them out.'

'The way I see it, the search for Colette will overshadow everything. I really don't think the Press would be interested. Unless someone told them.'

'Dermot Child,' Jane said. 'The Goblin.'

'I'm going to deal with that.' Merrily bit decisively into a slice of crisp toast.

*

From mid-morning, she hung around the churchyard, under apple trees, listening to the leaden, Victorian hymns, feeling redundant and rejected. She should be in there, today of all days, offering prayers for Colette Cassidy and her family, holding the community together, siphoning God's comfort from the chancel to the nave.

Stupid. *Stupid, stupid, stupid.* Hadn't thought of the implications of not being there today. But Ted presumably had, the machiavellian bastard. It had taken her rather too long to see Ted, not as an uncle, but as the worst kind of country solicitor, a man who'd spent his adult life smoothing over, glossing over, planing off rough edges. Female priest? A nice idea that failed. Too soon, my friends, too soon.

And there he was, as the main doors opened, fawningly attendant upon the imposing figure of the Rev. Norman Gemmell – tall, stooping, pointed beard, gravely patriarchal. Presiding in the porch, dispensing cordial clerical aftercare.

Bowing over hands, tilting his head with concern, as though he'd known these rusticized city folk for many, many years, followed their family heartaches and triumphs through the generations. A true professional.

The worst moment came when the Cassidys emerged – the Cassidys, who rarely attended morning worship because of the Sunday lunch stampede. Norman Gemmell held Caroline's fingers tenderly, led her a few yards away from the porch, bent his head to her pale, tight face. Spoke with earnest sincerity, and then patted Terrence on the shoulder as Caroline began to cry and two press photographers recorded the moment in a discreet chatter of motordrives.

Seemed like a good time, before the saintly Gemmell returned to the vestry to change into his civvies. Merrily crept from under her apple tree and made for the small rear door which led to the Bull chapel and the organ.

Pushed open the small, Gothic door and stopped.

There he stood, in his friar-like organist's robe, pensive by the effigy of the Bull. Looking up – an initial shock at seeing her, plumped up in a second into the charming, old Dermot.

'Why, Merrily, I thought . . .'

'We need to talk.'

'Ah, if only I'd known, I should have re-arranged my lunch appointment.'

'You know now,' Merrily said coldly.

'Perhaps this evening? A table at the Swan?'

'Dermot,' Merrily said, 'get your chubby little arse through that door before I rip my sweater and make allegations.'

'Merrily!'

'Calling as a witness, Mr Watts, the organ repair man . . . among others.'

'Merrily, what are you saying?'

She looked him steadily in the eyes and slowly lifted her sweater, exposing her midriff and the base of her bra.

Then she screamed.

'All right!' Dermot scowled and scurried after her out of the church, hitching up his robe.

FORTY-ONE

Home Cooking

At the bottom of the churchyard, where apple trees in bloom overhung the graves, Dermot Child sat, legs crossed, on a nineteenth-century tombstone, looking very affronted and – disturbingly – very much like a goblin. *A poisonous loser. Man's so embittered he doesn't care who goes down.*

And Merrily, gripping a gravestone, had cold feet. Supposing they were wrong about him? Suppose he was just a funny but basically harmless little man with a perfectly harmless, perfectly natural, perfectly healthy . . .

. . . *about a hundred buttons down the front, and you imagine yourself undoing them all, very slowly, one by one. Oh God. White collar, pink body, brown nipples . . .*

. . . lust for female clergy.

'Let's be frank with each other, shall we, Dermot?'

His button eyes arose to level on her. No smile, possibly the beginning of a sneer. 'Let's do that, Ms Priest-in-Charge. Oh yes, I'm all for that.'

Merrily thought she could see, behind the blossom on the apple trees, the first small swellings of the embryo Pharisees Reds.

'What do you know about the posters scattered around the village? The ones we discussed yesterday.'

The eyes were still. 'A poor joke, as I said. Not terribly funny.'

'Except there wasn't really time for subtlety?'

'Wasn't there?'

She took a chance. 'I gather they were done on the festival office printer.'

The eyes flickered. 'Really?'

'You supervise that?'

'The printer or the production of the posters? Yes to the printer. And the posters . . . well, indirectly, who knows? Do *you* know, Merrily?'

'And *The Sunday Times*. Did you, perhaps, speak to them?'

There was nothing prominent in today's *Sunday Times*, as it happened. At least, not the edition she'd picked up on the way to the church. The story had evidently been judged insufficiently strong at this stage, which was fine.

'Oh yes,' Dermot said. 'Of course. I've spoken to all the quality papers. I have to try to interest them in our lovely festival. Part of my function, in the absence of poor, dear, tragic Terrence.'

'And told them about the storm-in-a-teacup over Coffey's play?'

'More than that, surely, Merrily. A storm, at least, in a hogshead of cider. Old cider. A dark storm fermenting for many years. Centuries. Let's not make light of these things.'

'And you told *The Sunday Times* about it.'

He shifted on the tomb, uncrossed his legs under the thin robe. 'Did I?'

'Did you?'

He giggled. 'Did I?'

She gritted her teeth.

'Did I?' Dermot said gaily. 'Did I? Did I? Did I? Oh, Merrily, my dear, you don't know a thing, do you? You're fishing in the dark with a twig and a bent safety-pin, and you don't know a thing about our ways, any more than poor old

Hayden did, but he, at least, was content with that and went his bumbling way, the very model of a genial, faintly tedious country cleric. Ghastly, though not everyone agreed. Oh Lord, how I wanted you as his replacement, a jolly little dolly of a clergyperson with nice legs and dinky titties, oh what fun.'

Merrily cut off a shocked breath. *Don't react.* She stayed very still, tried not to look away from his eyes, although Dermot had certainly looked away from hers, blatantly lowering his sardonic gaze to her breasts.

'What fun,' he said coldly. 'But don't dare imagine that you, any more than Cassidy, any more than the obnoxious Coffey, could ever know the essence of our quaint little village ways.'

She bit her lip. He wasn't supposed to behave like this. Back in the church, she was convinced she had the little bugger. She was going to threaten him, quite calmly, in an absolutely straightforward way – tell him about the projected Wil Williams event, a village affair, and warn him that if the merest whisper of it got out to the media, she'd know precisely who to blame.

She rallied. 'And what do *you* know about the village ways, Dermot? About Ledwardine life as it's been lived in the past two decades? Having spent over half *your* life away, trying to make it in the big cities.'

A plump cheek twitched.

'With no conspicuous success,' Merrily said.

He scowled. 'And so feisty, aren't we? The new woman, oh *my*. Well, as a matter of fact, Ms Watkins, being born and raised here and then separated from it for a while gives one a highly individual perspective. The incomers don't see at all, the locals see but don't *notice*. But someone like myself, with a foot in both camps, observes all. Knows all the pressure points. Knows where a tiny *tweak* may have maximum effect.'

'And you do like to tweak, don't you, Dermot?'

Dermot grinned. He leaned back on the tombstone, legs apart, hands behind his head. 'I like to think', he said, 'that I *orchestrate*. The parish organist. One takes great pleasure in that. The first, dramatic chords which stir the blood and energize the sleeping church. Like *auld ciderrrrrr* . . . does to a man. Wonderful.'

He stretched and spread his legs, assisting the slippage of the dark, cotton robe from his fat, red, naked thighs.

'Cassidy hates all that, as you know. To him, it's an academic exercise, for purely commercial purposes. Like his phoney wassailing. I didn't go to that. It was always going to be a silly charade, with his pompous speeches and Caroline fussing and tinkling. Mind, wasn't a charade in the end, was it? Old reality burst on to the scene with a vengeance. Thank God for the Powells.'

Merrily realized she'd lost it. He couldn't care less whether she knew about him or not. He felt completely secure in revealing the side of him that, when you thought about it, he'd never entirely hidden behind the civilized glaze of educated frivolity.

She said, 'I suppose you'll say old Edgar topped himself at the wassailing specifically to show up the superficiality of it all.'

'Shouldn't think so.' He smiled. 'Can't see Edgar throwing away a good old country death on the Cassidys. Salt of the earth, the Powells. A bloody good phrase, *salt of the earth*. Overused, devalued. But it's a good one for the Powells. A good, dark, old family.'

'Older than the Bull-Davieses?' This was ridiculous, she was merely making conversation now. He'd insulted her to her face and she was just sidling away from it.

'The Bulls?' Dermot snorted. 'Norman blood, there. Acquired the Davies adjunct a few generations ago to highlight a little Welsh strand amounting to nothing. The Bulls of Ledwardine. Sounds good, doesn't amount to a lot. Always liked to think they had control, but they were still newcomers compared with the Powells. Something strong and tight and sturdy about the unassuming Powells. That's where the real tradition lies.'

She was picturing Garrod Powell in his well-pressed slacks and his blazer.

'Rod?' He startled her, seeming to snatch the thought from her head.

'Can't see it in Rod, is it? Well, you can't see anything, can you? You're an outsider. Even if your grandfather did farm at Mansell Lacy, you're way out of it now and you'll never get back in. Let me tell you about Rod. Raised the old way. Ever hear talk of Edgar's wife? Scabby old harpy, she was, but eyes like diamonds. I remember her on Pig Friday, marvellous great toothless grin and blood up to her elbows. And then home to teach young Rod a thing or two. If you know what I mean.'

'What?' Merrily's legs felt suddenly weak.

'Ha! Shocked you at last, have I, Reverend? What d'you think traditional country life's about if not fecundity and potency? And making sure your eldest boy knows what a woman likes best on a dark night in front of the fire. Country life, Merrily: home cooking, home sex and plenty of *auld cider*, home milled with a dead rat or two thrown in, for flavour. The farmer's wife hoisting up her skirts and pissing into the mix.'

'I'm going.' Merrily turned away. 'Thank you for the anthropological lecture.'

'Go on, give us a *real* blush, girlie. How's this?' He leaned right back on the tombstone, grinning into the sun, sliding the robe to the tops of his flabby thighs where the thin fabric rose up triumphantly. 'Whoops,' Dermot said.

'Well, that's that, isn't it?' Her voice distressingly shrill. 'You've finally made sure we aren't going to be able to work together again.'

'Sad, isn't it? We could have got on so well.'

He pulled down his robe, the smile vanishing.

'Where will you go, Merrily? Leave the clergy, perhaps? We all make mistakes, don't we?'

'I could have you arrested. Enough police about the place.'

Dermot sat up. 'Ah, yes,' he said soberly. 'I'm glad you reminded me. I *do* have to see the police. Did you notice the prowler in your garden? In the vicarage garden? Last night? Latish?'

'No.' She began to walk away along the blossom-strewn path, the big sandstone church in front of her, the old country church with its erect steeple. She wanted to scream. The bloody goblin had been creeping about her garden?

'Not a very big chap,' he called after her. 'Spectacles.'

She froze.

'Just had a haircut, one couldn't help noticing that. And dressed, bizarrely, as a clergyman. What happened, you see, I'd returned to the church to collect some music and couldn't help noticing him going through your gates. I think the lady inspector would want to know about that, don't you? What d'you think, Merrily? Or should one tell Ted Clowes first? Good old Uncle Ted. No, the police, I think. It might be important.'

His forced but merry laughter followed her all the way to the lych-gate. She slowed, evened up her pace, would not show him her panic.

He delivered Sunday papers, too, then.

*

'Oh,' Jane said, like this was an afterthought. 'And a couple of bottles of that – what's it called? – Wine of Angels.'

Jim Prosser, who always looked too big for the counter at the little Spar shop, reached up instinctively to the shelf and then paused.

'How old are you again, Jane? Fourteen, is it?'

'Fifteen!'

'Old enough to know the rules, then.'

'Oh, come on, Jim, it's only cider.'

'No such thing as only cider. Cider's stronger than beer, and this stuff's stronger than your average cider.'

'It's not for *me*. It's a present.'

'That's what they all say, my dear.'

'Bloody hell,' said Jane, exasperated. 'You're always selling cans of Woodpecker and stuff to Dean Wall and his mates. This is sexism.'

'Oh, come on now,' said Jim. 'Don't give me a hard time. The place is crawling with coppers, and you *are* the vicar's daughter.'

'For my sins.'

Jane paid for the two bags of Doritos. This was going to be a problem. There was whisky in the house, a few bottles of wine. No cider.

'You wouldn't like it, anyway,' Jim Prosser said. 'It might be in a fancy bottle, but you can get better at half the price, I reckon.'

The North Side

Merrily stood in the Sunday morning square and prayed silently for guidance. Two parishioners discreetly crossed into Church Street, pretending they hadn't seen her.

Or perhaps she'd become invisible now. A nine-day wonder and the nine days were over. Nobody special any more, just another single mother to be ignored, gossiped about, sniggered at, flashed at.

Stop it!

All right. So Dermot Child had recognized Lol Robinson, knew where he was hiding. Had gone to the trouble of delivering a late-edition Sunday tabloid to make sure Merrily knew the police had named Lol as someone they wanted to question. The devious Goblin planning ahead. Setting something up.

Blackmail? Would he have held on to the information and tried to blackmail her? Demanding what, in return for his continued silence? Precisely *what*? The mind boggled. The loins shrivelled. Her hand went to her mouth, stifling reaction.

'Vicar . . .'

Gomer Parry stood a few yards away, breathing heavily, cigarette waggling whitely in his teeth. He'd run after her.

'A word, Vicar?'

'Sure.' She followed him between the oak pillars into the market hall.

'Apologies for the state, Vicar. Cleanin' out your boundary ditch, I was, see.' Gomer held up both mud-red hands. 'I know, I know . . . the sabbath, it is, but there en't gonner be a fine day for near-enough a week, 'cordin' to the farmin' forecast, so I reckoned I'd get to grips with the bugger, do the manual 'fore I brings in ole Gwynneth, see?'

'I see. Well, just – you know – keep the lid on it. We have our zealots. You didn't actually have to inform me.'

'And wouldn't 'ave, Vicar, no way. If, that is, I hadn't been down in this yere stinkin' ditch, keepin' a low profile, as it were, when our friend Mr Dermot Child happens to take up occupancy of the ole Probert family tomb just this side the hedge, followed by your good self.'

'Oh.'

'You want my personal stance on the issue, I reckon that feller oughter be strung up by the nuts, but that's only my personal opinion, like.'

'Gomer,' Merrily said fervently. 'It's a very valid one.'

'Tried to rope me in for this *ole cider* rubbish. I sez, Mr Child, I can't sing worth a bag o' cowshit. Don't matter, he sez. Long's you got it *down there*. I sez, whatever you got down there, I sez, is between you and your ole woman and you don't bring it out in no church.' Gomer coughed, embarrassed. 'Or churchyard.'

'No.'

'If it'd gone any further, see, I'd've been up outer that ole ditch. But you was off. An' Child, he just stays there, lyin' on the stone, chucklin' and schemin'. Anyhow, all I'm tryin' to say . . .' Gomer looked down at his mud-caked boots '. . . is that's a dangerous feller. An' he en't on 'is own. So for what it's worth, Vicar, you got my full support, whatever goes down. Like if you wants a witness . . .'

'No, I don't think I'll be taking it any further.'

'What's happenin' yereabouts, see, it smells *off*. I were you, I wouldn't trust nobody. I know that en't in the spirit of your profession, like, but that's my advice, see. It smells *off*. An' that's comin' from a man who was once up to 'is Adam's apple in Billy Tudge's cesspit.'

It was time, Merrily decided, to take Gomer Parry seriously.

'I suppose', she said delicately, 'that you heard the bit about the intruder.'

'Sure t' be,' Gomer confirmed, producing a soggy match, bending down to strike it on a cobble. 'That would be Mr Robinson, mabbe?'

'Oh dear,' Merrily said.

Gomer stood up, his cigarette burning. 'Vicar, there's no problem, yere. Friend of poor ole Lucy's, right? So *no problem*. See?' He rubbed mud from his glasses and winked. 'All right?'

'Thank you,' Merrily said.

'En't done nothin', yet. Jus' lettin' you know I'm yere. Anythin' I can do, say the word. 'Cause, I never told Lucy Devenish, see. I never quite said that to Lucy, and now she en't yere no more, which was a funny sort of accident, my way o' thinkin', and so the only other person I can say it to's you, an' I'm sayin' it.'

'You knew I was her executor?'

'Nope. That matter?'

Funny sort of accident?

'Gomer, can we talk?'

'We're talking, innit?'

'Not here. Back at the vicarage?'

'Hell, I wouldn't go in the vicarage in this state. Minnie'd never speak a civil word to me again. I'll mabbe get a bath and catch you later, if that's all right with you.'

'No. Please. Gomer, listen, there is something you can do. You come into contact with quite a few people, and Minnie's secretary of the WI.'

'On account of nobody else'll take it on. Aye.'

'OK.' She told him briefly about Stefan Alder's private preview of the Wil Williams play. To be performed in about ten hours' time. It didn't sound remotely possible.

Gomer whistled. '*Tonight*? So this – let me get this right – this is like a play, but it's . . .'

'It's a partly improvised drama. Stefan Alder, as Wil Williams, presents a kind of sermon, telling his life story, how he came to be in the mess he's in. His congregation, as I understand it, will be able to question him. And anyone else.'

'But they'll all know it's just an act.'

'Gomer, when half the nation's watching a soap opera, everybody knows it's an act, but does that stop them getting involved? Does that stop the tabloid papers printing stories about *Coronation Street* characters as though they're real people? This guy's an experienced actor, and this is a role he cares deeply about. They're the congregation, this is their church. Within half an hour, they'll have forgotten who Stefan Alder *is*.'

'By golly,' Gomer said. 'You really *are* gonner throw the shit in the mincer.'

'You can get the word around the village? You and Minnie?'

'Bugger me, the ole phone'll be burnin' up. Anybody in partic'lar you *don't* want?'

'At the moment, I can only think of Dermot Child. Bull-Davies is an optional.'

'Right then.' Gomer nodded, stamped out his cigarette. 'Consider it spread.'

*

'Well, I suppose there comes a point in your life,' Lol said, 'when you start to accept that some people are just not good people and you can't do anything about that. I know it's your job to try and put them on the path of righteousness and all that, but that's not always the wisest strategy. Sometimes.'

'I suppose, tackling Coffey last night, I thought I was on a roll again. It was a mistake. I shouldn't have gone to see him.'

'Perhaps Child wanted you to. I think people like him quite like to be discovered. I'm really sorry. This means you can't accuse him of indecent exposure. But then he'd know that.'

'Friday I throw up at my installation service. Saturday, I go to pieces at the opening of the festival. Sunday, while admitting to sheltering a man the police want to question, I claim my organist flashed at me. I think we're looking at a resignation situation here, at the very least.'

'Don't even think of it,' Jane said. 'Lucy said—'

'Sure. The catalyst. Where do you go, Lol? Don't say the cops, that's not an option. Not with Child working against us.'

'Why is he, Mum? Why's he doing this?'

'Because . . . because he obviously has the most incredible ego. And no remorse.'

'He's a psychopath,' Lol said. 'Very few of them actually kill people, they just do damage.'

Merrily smiled in spite of it all. 'Lol has read widely on psychology. Come on, we may not have much time. Where shall we put him, flower?'

'Lucy's house? Or Lucy's shop?'

'With the cops hanging round the Country Kitchen?'

'The Reverend Locke again?'

'Won't work. Child's sussed that. And we don't know what else he knows. We don't know if or when he'll go to the police. It's very unsettling. Look, I have to go and meet Stefan. I'm going to leave Lucy's house key on the mantelpiece. If you can think of any way of getting across there without being seen, do it. Otherwise, sit tight.'

'And pray, right?' Jane said.

*

'Tell me about these people,' Stefan Alder called down from the pulpit. 'These villagers. Who'll be here? The older residents, particularly. The ones from the older families.'

'I've no actual idea.' Merrily sat alone, in a pew halfway down the nave. 'We're hardly issuing specific invitations. But, in my experience, anything mysterious, anything faintly bizarre happening in the church'll still pack them in. They won't come the following week, but in this case that doesn't matter, does it?'

'No. But who specifically?' Strange, stained-glass colours blurred in Stefan's thick, pale hair. 'Who comes to all your services? I've been twice, if we include your ill-fated induction ceremony. I made a few mental notes on both occasions. For example, the old lady who arrives in a wheelchair but insists on leaving it in the doorway and have people help her into a pew? Looks terribly fragile. Who is she?'

'That's Mrs Goddard. Priscilla. Lives in the Stables House at the end of Old Barn Lane.'

'What's wrong with her?'

'Osteoporosis, quite advanced.'

'Brittle bones, yes? I wonder what they called it in the seventeenth century. Is she in much pain?'

'Much of it emotional. She used to be an enthusiastic horsewoman. Ran a riding school from her home. Now the

497

stables are empty, she's looking out on an empty field and she feels her life's effectively over. Needs to be handled with great care.'

'I understand.' Stefan made a note in the stiff-backed book he'd brought with him. He asked about any other people who were chronically ill, or who'd been recently bereaved, or had sick and disabled children or grandchildren . . . or conspicuous money worries, marital problems, difficulty conceiving a child.

All a little disturbing. Audience participation was one thing, meddling with a congregation something else. And what good would it do him if he made a mistake and insulted someone?

'Stefan, you can't hope to absorb all that information. Even I still have problems remembering everybody's name.'

'Not a problem for me, Merrily. Indeed, my notes are a formality. I don't forget faces. I have a photographic memory. I'm not boasting, it's a simple fact, I can learn a fifty-minute television script in a night. And today – ' he leaned over the pulpit ' – today, I am concentrating.'

He was certainly a presence in the church. Although he wore tight black trousers and a billowy white shirt out of one of those old Douglas Fairbanks Jr movies, there was nothing effete about his movements or his speech today. He had, Merrily thought, stepped out of Richard Coffey's shadow oozing intensity of purpose. No more toyboy.

'You're taking this very seriously, aren't you?' she said, without thinking, the echo emphasizing the stupidity of the question.

'It will be the performance of my life.' He said it simply, quite quietly, no histrionics, no camp melodrama. 'Perhaps', he said, 'there won't be another.'

'Oh, I think there will. I think, somehow, you're going to

win a lot of support. It's already quite a talking point. I suspect everyone's going to rather enjoy it.'

'*Enjoy?*'

'Wrong word?'

He came down the pulpit's wooden steps, stood behind the carved-oak eagle lectern. Oh my God, Merrily thought, he's going for the full Messianic bit.

'I should like one spotlight, if I may. Just . . . here.' He stood at the foot of the pulpit. 'One of the high, rear ones, so that it's quite wide. Is there someone who could operate that? Merely a question of switching it on shortly before dusk, say half an hour into the performance, so that everyone will have become accustomed to it by the time it takes effect.'

'Jane could do that. As you can see, we've actually got several spots up there, which we could vary without too much difficulty. I mean, I don't know much about theatrical lighting, but—'

'Just the one will be sufficient. In the pulpit and elsewhere, I shall be using candles. Do you have candles?'

'Few dozen.'

'I'll bring more. I want these people to believe totally that they are in the seventeenth century and that Wil Williams is their minister. If that doesn't offend you.'

'No, that's . . . that's fine. In fact that may be easier than you think. You know the pageant thing the Women's Institute are organizing for the festival – the working life of Ledwardine through the ages?'

'I'm afraid I've paid scant attention to the other aspects of the festival.' Even his speech pattern had altered, become more formal, a touch archaic.

'They've been making costumes,' Merrily told him. 'Authentic stuff. It's not all seventeenth century, obviously, there'll be Victorian and medieval . . .'

Stefan said warily, 'There won't be Roman soldiers or anything, will there?'

'No Roman soldiers. No Tudor doublets and ruffs. No Second World War fighter pilots. I'm not saying there won't be anachronisms, but they're unlikely to be glaring. Besides, working country clothes have always been very muted and they haven't changed much – look at the Barbour.'

'Yes.' He considered. 'Yes. That would be wonderful. It would add to that sense of otherness. Do you understand what I mean?'

'Take them out of themselves.'

'Absolutely.'

'I also thought . . . Well, the seating pattern. It was different then. I mean, the arrangement of the pews, facing the chancel, facing the pulpit . . . that was roughly the same. But in those days pews were allocated according to your social standing. Areas were set aside for the gentry and other areas, well away, for the servants, and the servants were packed in like sardines, while the nobs had room to lounge about. Now, obviously we can't attempt to segregate people in that way. But . . . well, men and women were also separated.'

'Were they really?'

'Women were generally relegated to the north side.'

'Why is that?'

'Because women were naturally considered less important, and the north side of the church – any church – was supposed to be more exposed to the influence of the devil, I don't quite know why. Certainly people didn't want to be buried at the north end of the churchyard. Look at any church around here and you'll find the more recent graves to the north, and not many of them.'

'And would they do that? Will the men sit separately?'

'They will if their wives tell them to. Times seem to have changed in that respect, at least.'

'And the women will go to the north?'

'I'll organize it. What about the Bull-Davies pew? If he doesn't come, which he probably won't, it's going to stand out as conspicuously vacant. Do you want—'

'No. It must remain empty. I can use that.'

'It's your show,' Merrily said.

'Thank you. You're a good person, Merrily. I . . . Yes. I've studied the parish records and various histories. There are certain old families who I know have descendants in the village: the Monks, the Prossers, the Woods, the Cadwalladers . . . Will you stand with me this evening, somewhere discreet – the Bull chapel, perhaps – and point out the various people as they come in?'

'All right. And then disappear, huh?'

He smiled. 'Once they enter the church, I want it to be my church again.'

'You going to spend the afternoon here, rehearsing?'

'I don't need to rehearse. I shall walk among the apple trees. I want to meditate. Open myself to him.'

'Right. I'll leave you then.' Merrily stood up, not entirely comfortable with this. 'Good luck . . . Wil.'

'Merrily!' She stopped. 'Don't . . . don't joke about this,' Stefan said. 'I beg you. The performance of my life, re-member?'

'Yes.'

Meant

Gomer's lunch was on the table, Minnie's potato pie, when the phone rang. 'Tell them to call back,' Minnie shouted through from the kitchen. 'And if it's that man about the septic tank, don't forget – you're retired.'

'Ar,' said Gomer non-committally.

'If you can't bring yourself to tell him, you put him on to me,' Minnie went on. 'I'll give him septic tank!'

Gomer groped for the phone.

'Jeff Harris, Gomer. You were right, boy. Wouldn't use this stuff to unblock my sink.'

Gomer sat up.

'Shirley was coming through Ledwardine this morning, so I asked her to call for a bottle. You had me worried, see. Got to protect the image of the product or we're all done for. Uncorked it – not so much a pop as a fizzle. Poured half a glass, took it to the window, held it up to the light . . .'

'And?' Gomer was on the edge of his seat now. If you couldn't trust the word of a man who'd worked for Bulmer's, Weston's, Dunkerton's and God knew who else during a forty-year career, you couldn't trust nobody when it came to cider, but he did like to make a performance of it, did Jeff Harris.

'Well, that about the sink . . . exaggerated a bit there, I confess. It's not abso*lute* piss, but if that's the original old

Pharisees Red, I'll drink six pints of Australian lager out of my old farm boots.'

'Gomer!' Minnie came in from the kitchen, all pink and homely and steaming angry. 'If you don't get back to that pie in thirty seconds, it's going back in the oven. D'you realize how much I've got to do before tonight?'

Gomer raised a finger, pleading for one minute.

'It's bottle-fermented, all right,' Jeff said, 'but there's a difference between fine champagne and two-quid fizz. All right, if the Powells want to take these daft Londoners for a ride, they might think that's all right, and at six pound fifty a bottle they can be pretty sure none of us is ever going to taste it, but in my book you don't misrepresent cider. The Wine of Angels, indeed. What you gonner do about it, Gomer?'

'Well . . . not my place, is it? Just wanted to know, like. Talkin' to young Lloyd, I was, see, yesterday, and he reckoned they had to buy some apples in, not havin' enough of the ole Pharisees to produce the kind o' quantity Cassidy was after. That account for it?'

'Bought the damn lot in, if you ask me. *And* got somebody to produce it for them.'

'But why'd they wanner *do* that?' Gomer asked, watching Minnie ceremoniously carrying his pie-dish through to the kitchen.

'Didn't want to lose face, I suppose,' said Jeff Harris. 'Hadn't made cider in more than a generation, except perhaps a drop or two for themselves; now here's Cassidy saying they must have the traditional stuff and talking about grants from the tourist board and all this. They came to an arrangement with Jeremy Selby or one of those boys, that's my guess. Save a lot of work, make a few hundred quid each and that idiot Cassidy and his cronies, never having tasted cider in their lives, are none the wiser.'

'Wouldn't've thought it of Rod. His ole man, mabbe.'

'Like father like son, my boy. Man's a councillor, isn't he? Most councillors are in it for what they can shovel into their back pockets. Fact of rural life. Let me know of any further developments.'

'Sure to,' Gomer said and hung up, puzzling hard.

Of course, Minnie brought his lunch back, and while he was eating it, she paraded before him in a long, dull-brown woollen dress with a wheaty-coloured shawl round her shoulders. Gomer didn't think much to it.

'We en't short of a bob or two, Min. You don't have to go as a peasant woman.'

'This isn't peasant's clothes. Sunday best, this is, for an eighteenth-century farmer's wife. Still pass for seventeenth century, though wouldn't it?'

'Give up trying to look nice once they got married, did they?'

Minnie snorted. 'I only wish I had a veil, too, to hide my blushes. We all know what kind of play that Coffey's likely to've written.'

'Aye, well, that's why we're all gettin' a chance to see it first, innit? You don't like it, you think it treads on too many ole corns, you get your chance to say so out loud. Not that you will, you women, you'll all just sit there all po-faced and then pull it to bits outside, and 'ave another go at the vicar for good measure.'

'I never said a word against that young woman.'

'Aye, but you done your share of noddin' and frownin' and glancin' sideways.'

'You would say that – you're a man. If she was fat and fifty, you'd be having second thoughts just like the rest of us. Especially when she's letting something like this go on in the church.'

'That don't stop you goin', though, do it?'

'I like to make up my own mind.'

'Oh aye. And you'll all be gatherin' round like them women round the ole guillotine, hopin' she's put both feet in the slurry again.'

'That's not fair. Anyway, when you've finished your pie, we'll sort something out for you, my duck.'

'Gerroff, woman. I en't goin'. I done my bit. Me bein' there en't gonner help the vicar. Anyway, they didn't 'ave no plant hire in the seventeenth century.'

'Never mind plant hire, you're a retired businessman!'

Gomer closed his eyes in anguish.

*

It was simple really. Or so Jane said. Lucy's house, like most of those on the vicarage side of Church Street, backed on to the old bowling green, which in turn was accessible from the orchard, which you could access from the bottom of the vicarage garden.

So if Jane were to let herself into Lucy's by the front door and go round and leave the back door open for Lol . . . geddit?

'And while you're in there, maybe you find out whatever Lucy was trying to tell us.'

'If she was trying to tell us anything.'

'I know she was,' Jane said.

*

Soon after she'd gone, with Merrily still organizing Stefan Alder, the phone rang, the answering machine kicking in.

'Merrily, it's Ted. What the hell d'you think you're doing? Don't you think there should have been a meeting of the church council before you let these people take over the place at short notice, especially for something so politically and morally sensitive? I cannot believe you went over all our heads in this

deplorable fashion, and I have to say that if this is an example of the kind of behaviour we can expect from you in the future, then I'm afraid you can no longer count on my support and I wish, herewith, to dissociate myself entirely from tonight's outrage.'

That was the first.

The second one, just under ten minutes later, said sternly, *'Councillor Powell, Mrs Watkins. I should be glad if you would telephone me immediately upon your return.'*

Within two minutes, the third.

'Ah, Merrily, my love. No wonder you don't need a man. You're obviously quite capable of fucking yourself. My condolences.'

*

Firmly and decisively, Jane shut the door of the house in Church Street and then was stopped, very scared, by the sight of the winter poncho draped over the post at the bottom of the stairs.

The poncho hung there, dark and sombre like a kid's idea of a ghost. It was both frightening and awfully moving. It made her wish she hadn't come because it brought home to her – more even than the sight of the body in the road – the cruel reality of Lucy's death.

To banish the fright, she threw her arms around the poncho, buried her face in its folds. Burst at once into sobs, hugging the woollen thing tight, but the hardness, the deadness of the oaken post beneath only made it worse, its rigid, knurled point imprinting on her forehead the message that the wonderful Lucy Devenish really was never coming back.

When she pulled away, the poncho fell in a heap to the floor, as if the spirit had drifted away from under it. She gathered it up quickly and carried it up the narrow stairs, finding Lucy's bedroom, putting the poncho on the bed and walking out without looking at anything because a bedroom was private.

She went into the bathroom and looked at her face in the mirror. She looked like a child, and the tear stains didn't help. She washed her face, dried it on an Aztec-patterned bathtowel that reminded her of the summer poncho and was just so Lucy she nearly wept again.

Wipe your eyes, you little snot! Pull yourself together!

She tried to hear Lucy's voice saying it, but it wasn't there, was it?

She wasn't here, and there was nobody else who knew the real truth about Ledwardine. The place was all tarted up and polished like the archaic tools and farm implements on the walls in the Swan that nobody quite knew the original purpose of any more.

Downstairs, in the low-ceilinged living room, she felt a bit better. There were photos on the walls to look at, which was different to photos in some dusty album at the bottom of a wardrobe. And, of course, the bookshelves beckoned.

But first, Jane went into the little kitchen, which faced north – always the bleakest light – and overlooked the old bowling green, a few morose sheep nibbling out there now. Under the window was a Belfast sink beside a sturdy-looking cast-iron cooker, and there was a small fridge and a kind of sawn-off Welsh dresser with a cardboard box on it. A note was tucked into one of the box's flaps.

> Compliments of the Ledwardine Festival.
> Thanks for your help,
>
> Barry Bloom

The box contained six champagne bottles. She lifted one out. Its ornate label featured the familiar black line-drawing of the parish church, and, in archaic lettering,

The Wine of Angels.

Oh, Lucy. Oh, wow.

Jane went quickly to the back door, unbolted it, turned the key and then removed two bottles from the box.

It was like they'd been waiting for her.

She looked out of the window, giving Lucy's hook-nosed ghost a chance to manifest among the sheep, its arms rising angrily from the dark poncho's folds. *Put those back at once, you tripehound!*

But nothing appeared. The Wine of Angels lay heavy in her arms. Jane carried the bottles out of the back door and over the fence on to the path bordering the bowling green.

It was meant.

*

'*You duplicitous woman. Your hypocrisy defies belief. You lied to my face.*'

The machine, as Merrily came in, recording a message. Distorting badly.

'*To my face, Mrs Watkins.*'

'And good afternoon to you too, James.' Merrily dumped her bag on the hallstand. When the shit hit the fan, an answering machine was mercifully absorbent. She saw Lol in the kitchen doorway and smiled weakly. 'I get more popular all the time.'

'*It is clear to me now that you were, from the beginning, conspiring with certain subversive elements to undermine the stability of my village. I am a soldier. I cannot tolerate that.*'

Lol said, 'Is he real?'

'*My information is that tonight you propose to allow this man to lay out his foul smears in public. I am giving you this opportunity to call it off. You may consider this an ultimatum.*'

'My God,' Merrily said. 'This is a prepared statement.'

The red light on the answering machine blinked and swelled like some warning vein in Bull-Davies's forehead.

'If I do not hear from you before four o'clock, I shall personally take action to put a stop to this homosexual farce. And to ensure that you never again have an opportunity to use Church of England property to defame and to destroy. If you are representative of women priests then, by God, I shall make it my business to ensure this village will never have another when you are gone. Good-day to you.'

*

Lol said, 'And you thought Alison was playing with fire.'

'Sometimes,' Merrily said, 'you do things without quite understanding why.'

'You don't know why you're doing this?'

'Well, I know how it started.' She leaned against the hallstand with her back to the flashing red light. 'It started with me feeling pressured by anonymous letters and veiled threats and people trying to use the media to get what they want and . . .'

She sighed and dug in her bag for cigarettes.

'And then we were sitting there in Coffey's house, and this idea was suddenly taking shape and it all came pouring out almost like I was speaking someone else's thoughts. I hadn't reasoned it out, it just . . . I don't know, maybe my self-destruct mechanism came into play.'

'Maybe, when it's over,' he said, 'they'll all wonder why they made such a fuss.'

She looked at him over her lighter, shaking her head. 'You don't think that.'

He didn't know what to say.

'I suppose I was kind of hoping Coffey would put the arm on Stefan and it would all fall through, and then I'd have done my bit, given them a chance. But of course Stefan got

his way. And then this morning I mentioned it to Gomer
Parry and now we have a whole bunch of people due to turn
up in fancy dress. So it's been generating its own momentum.
Like it was meant. Pre-ordained. Destiny. Fate. Something
working me like a puppet. Out of control. Except of course
it isn't. I could stop it now.'

Lol turned to her and put out a hand and she took it.

'What should I do?' she said. 'Looking at it objectively.'

He had no idea what to say. How could he be objective
when he was falling in love with her?

'Is it the *right* thing?' Merrily said. 'That's the only
question, isn't it, when you think about it.'

Part Four

A mist involves the eye
While in the middle it doth lie
And till the ends of things are seen
The way's uncertain that doth stand between.

Thomas Traherne,
The Demonstration

Pink Moon

Stefan Alder was waiting for her under the lych-gate just before eight. She'd expected some smart, stately late-Stuart gentleman, but he was no more in period costume than he had been this morning. The neutral black trousers and white shirt, a little crumpled now, a smudge of green mould on the arm where it reached a muddied open cuff. A deep, red scratch dividing the back of one hand.

'I don't want . . .' Stefan stepped away from her scrutiny as though it were a court summons. 'I don't want a twee little costume drama. I don't want a pantomime. They understand this, don't they?'

'It's all right.' Merrily backed off, putting up her hands. 'Nobody wants that, Stefan.'

'Sorry.' He smiled palely. 'First-night nerves.' He laughed, as if this was a private joke.

'You eaten?'

'An apple.'

Symbolic, but insufficient calories. He looked lonely and he looked frail. Merrily suspected he'd been given a bad time at the lodge. She imagined the patchwork face sneering, but inwardly Richard Coffey would be eaten up with unquenchable jealousy because his beautiful Steffie was in love with a ghost.

The sun was going down behind the church, which had faded from red to brown and would soon be black.

Merrily wasn't in costume either. Not period, nor clerical. She wore a long black skirt and a black, high-necked cashmere sweater – another relic, like the Volvo, of Sean's boomtime. There would only be room in there for one minister tonight.

'Stefan,' she said. 'What's in this for you?'

He looked frightened of the question. The moon was rising over his shoulder. An unusually distinct moon, already yellow.

'Redemption,' Stefan said bleakly. 'Isn't that what we all want?'

'I suppose. But for whom?'

He didn't answer that. He looked out across the empty market place, where the first lights were coming on. 'Which way will they come? Where shall we stand?'

She led him to a tree. An apple tree, as it happened, which in the evening was absorbed into the big shadow of the church. He stood rigidly, a bag of nerves. Bloody Coffey. He might have helped; he could have been here for moral and artistic support, he could have enlisted the aid of his technical friends. Or did Coffey, perhaps, want this to fail, so that the whole project – not his idea, anyway – might be discreetly dumped? Had she actually been playing into Coffey's hands?

Stefan was watching her now. The evening was quite warm, and ashen hair hung damply over his ears. He pushed some back. 'And what's in it for you, Merrily?'

'I don't know,' she said truthfully. 'I really don't know. Answers, perhaps, to the things I don't know.'

'Anyone can ask questions. That's the point, isn't it? There's nothing I won't be able to answer. I've read all Richard's research, but I've thrown away the script.'

*

Merrily walked into the empty church and sensed at once a disturbance.

There'd been a temporary estrangement between her and the church, but when you preached and prayed in a building, it began to send messages to you in the atmosphere and the echo.

Tonight, the church was agitated, and it wasn't with anticipation. Something had happened. She walked out past the font and into the nave. In the north-west corner, the door to the tower and steeple was closed and padlocked. The vibration was not like the shiver of bells, but it did seem to be on this side of the church.

She stood by the tower door and looked along the northern aisle towards the organ pipes. The curtain screening the organ was drawn. She thought of malevolent goblins, strode up the aisle and swept it aside.

The organ loft was curiously like the cockpit of a very old-fashioned aircraft. Merrily switched on the curling brass lamps which lit the keyboards and the panels of knobs. Nothing seemed disturbed, but she lingered, allowing herself to consider what, until today, had been unthinkable: that Dermot Child might be connected with the disappearance of Colette Cassidy.

He might have been giggling when he exposed himself on the tombstone this morning, but it was in fact an act of rage, of violence. She'd made Dermot lose his temper, and he'd brandished his cock like a knife. A peevish child grown into a bitter, screwed-up, middle-aged man who thought he was entitled to more. Arrogant enough to believe younger women could fancy him. Remorselessly devious enough to lie in wait for a sixteen-year-old girl who everyone said was asking for it?

She backed out, snapped off the lights, drew back the curtain. Perhaps she should play Dermot's own game and send an anonymous note to Annie Howe. Perhaps she should swallow her pride and go to see Annie Howe.

Still unsettled, she moved up the steps and under the rood screen into the chancel. The altar shone down at her in white and gold. Nothing wrong there.

She entered the side chapel which began a few yards behind the organ and ran parallel to the chancel. The Bull chapel. Its high east window was dulled now, but the bigger, north-facing, leaded panes cast a hard and coarsening light on the face of Thomas Bull, on its trim beard, its bulbous lips, its scarily wide-open eyes.

In the bleak, northern light, this was a dour and creepy place. But there was nothing here but the unsleeping Bull in his frugal sandstone clothing, the dull blade of his naked stone sword quiescent at his side. It irked her that this chapel should be next to the chancel, so that you couldn't approach the altar without getting a glimpse of him.

Her shoe crunched something. She bent down. Cement or sandstone dust on the flags near the foot of the tomb and directly below the place where it seemed to have been repaired at some stage, where, she remembered thinking, it looked as though Tom Bull had stretched out his legs and kicked out a couple of bricks.

She sprang back in horror. It looked as though he had.

Merrily took a long breath, gritty with still-floating cement dust. The eyes of Tom Bull sneered at her as she pulled up her skirt and then, lowering herself beyond his field of vision, knelt on the flags by his stone-booted feet on their stone cushion.

She saw that all the cement had been chipped out around two bricks.

She put hands either side of one and lifted it. It was old and parched and not very heavy, and it came out easily and she laid it on the floor.

Removed the second brick, revealing a hole like a large letterbox.

It was black in there, and she had no torch. With a rising dread, she slipped a hand in. *He's bones. Unless you touch him, and then he's dust.*

She didn't touch him. A small draught caressed her fingers. She snatched her hand back, shaking.

*

'You'll be OK, Lol?'

Jane seemed quite anxious to get away.

'Sure,' he said.

'She's not here, you know. In case you were worried.'

'I wasn't.'

He was sitting at Lucy's desk, with the two lamps on and the velvet curtains drawn. The windows faced the street, but Jane had been outside and said no chinks of lights were visible. Unless they wandered round the back and into the garden, no one would have reason to think the house was occupied.

'I thought she would be here,' Jane said gloomily. 'I really didn't think she'd left us for ever.'

'Well, maybe she's . . . gone on, as they say. To something better.'

'But her work here isn't finished!'

'No,' he admitted. 'Perhaps it isn't. What are you going to do now?'

'Just muddle on, I suppose.'

'No, I meant now as in . . . now.'

'Oh. I'm going to the church. I'm supposed to be in charge of lights. Wow. It means I get to switch on one spotlight just before it goes dark.'

'That's it?'

'She just wants me there to keep an eye on me.'

'So suspicious,' he said, 'mothers.'

Jane turned in the doorway. 'She does like you. I can tell. I think, on reflection, the way things turned out, you probably did the best thing not actually sleeping with her.'

'That's what you think.'

'It will stand you in good stead,' Jane said solemnly.

When she'd gone, he thought about Lucy and he thought about Merrily.

He looked around the tidy little room. Jane was right. Lucy's spirit was not here. Perhaps it never had been. You could look around this room and you would not know her. You'd know what she'd looked like from the photos on the walls, what she'd eaten from the food in the kitchen, what she'd worn from the clothes in the wardrobe, but you would not know Lucy. If there was a shrine, it would be the shop with its fruit and its fairies.

It seemed to Lol, though, that the spirit was too small to be confined in one small space. It would have to hover over Ledwardine, its guardian hills and its apple trees. The spirit would want to light up the orb.

But it was too late to help Lucy in any practical way. Lol opened the annotated copy of Ella Leather's *Folklore*.

The living light tonight was in Merrily Watkins, and he was scared because it was flickering.

*

'Let me help you. Please.' Outside the porch, Stefan was bending over Mrs Goddard in her wheelchair, a rug over her knees. The stress lines had vanished from his handsome face, concern glowed out, the setting sun colouring his hair.

Stefan was acting. Or something.

'Thank you,' Mrs Goddard said, 'Mr . . .?'

'Williams,' he said simply.

The daughter pushing the wheelchair frowned, Merrily noticed, but Mrs Goddard smiled. 'They didn't want me to come, but I insisted.' She patted his hand resting on the arm of the chair. 'I believe in you.'

'I am glad,' Stefan said.

'And, you know, I believe what poor Miss Devenish often used to say, that until we face up to our history and uncover the truth, we shall never be a real village again, merely a tourist museum. A sort of black and white theme park.'

Stefan listened and nodded. Merrily marvelled at the old girl, although she'd noticed this before, the way disabled people often became clearer sighted, more focused and certainly more outspoken.

Most of the others had been less forthcoming. A couple of men had uncomfortably declined to shake the hand Stefan offered them, as though they might contract the HIV virus or something. A retired headmaster called Carrington had pushed past him into the church, grunting, 'Don't take us for fools, Mr Alder.' But most of the women had seemed charmed, if, in some cases, reluctantly. They'd all seen him on television, many had been scandalized and titillated by the news that he was living in Ledwardine with an older man who was also a controversial playwright. But he was young and good-looking, magnetic, charismatic . . . and he was performing exclusively for them, and they were part of that performance.

'Boy knows what he's doing.' Big Jim Prosser, from the shop, had come to stand with Merrily, on the grass to the left of the porch. 'Look at 'em all. Nearest they'll ever get to being extras in *Pride and Prejudice*. I know that's a century or so out, but what do they care?'

'Yes.' There was an unfortunate number of rather showy

dresses drifting along the path from the lych-gate. Jim himself, in a striped apron over a collarless shirt, was rather more than a century out, but he didn't seem to care either.

'What's the feeling in the village about this, Jim?'

'Caused a bit of a flurry, Vicar. Nothing else got talked about in the shop this afternoon, that's for sure.'

'You know what I mean.'

'Aye. Mabbe I do.'

Ted Clowes walked in on his own. He was wearing his dark churchwarden's suit. He did not look at Merrily.

'And?'

Jim grinned. 'You know as well as I do that most folk yere tonight don't give a toss about Wil Williams. Never even heard of the feller until all this fuss started. But the old timers and the WI ladies and the ones who've been around a while are all of a flutter 'cause they seen the effect it's having on some folk. They wanner be able to say, I was there, all dressed up, the night of the fireworks.'

'Fireworks,' said Merrily.

'Some folk gonner be real disappointed if there en't, Vicar.'

'You haven't seen James Bull-Davies around by any chance?'

'Not yet.' Big Jim twinkling with anticipation.

'Good evening, Ms Watkins.'

Merrily turned to find Detective Inspector Annie Howe stepping on to the grass. She was not in costume.

'Hello,' Merrily said, 'Annie.'

Howe stood quietly, watching the villagers gather in the churchyard. She wore jeans. She carried her white mac over her arm.

'Night off?' Merrily said.

'What do you think?'

'Depends how close you are to finding Colette Cassidy, I suppose.'

'You think we might be close?'

Tell her about Dermot. Tell her about the desecration of the tomb.

'I pray that you are,' she said.

Thinking this was precisely what Alf Hayden would have said, a platitude.

*

All right. Be practical, Lol told himself. Be objective for the first time in your life. She's out there. She's presiding over something she doesn't understand. There are people there who want to stop her. There are people who want to destroy her. And people who want to watch.

At the centre of all this is a secret involving the death of a man more than three centuries ago.

Merrily doesn't know the secret. Ignorance is dangerous.

If you want to help her you have just a short time to discover the secret.

'Help me, Lucy,' Lol said.

He didn't know where to start. He switched off the lamps and drew back the curtains. Church Street, draped in dusk, was deserted. Above the house across the street, the moon rose. It was almost full.

It was pink.

No other way to decribe it. This was a pink moon.

Nick Drake's bleak last album was called *Pink Moon*.

The title track was this short song with very few words. One verse, repeated. It didn't have to explain all the folklore about a pink moon, that a pink moon meant death, violence, was tinted by blood.

The song just said, in Nick's flattest, coldest, most aridly refined upper-middle-class tone, that the pink moon was going to *get ye all.*

'I'm over that,' Lol howled, wrenching at the curtains, his legs feeling heavy, his arms numb, his heart like the leaden pendulum of some old clock. 'I'm over it . . .'

The Eternal Bull

'And let us pray', Stefan said, 'for Tom Bull.'

It was as though the red stone of the church had trapped the sunset, as it had on the night of Merrily's non-installation as priest-in-charge. The remains of the evening travelled through all the apples in the windows – the Pharisees Red in the hand of Eve, the cluster of green and orange fruit around the nucleus of the big circular window above the pulpit, where Stefan stood, collecting the last light in his hair and face and shirt.

'The man,' Stefan said, more loudly. 'And the Bull.'

The pulpit steps creaked as he came down, the nave echoed back the rapid crackling of his shoes on the stone flags.

'Bull of Ages!' Stefan cried, mock-heroically.

He stopped in front of the organ, half-turned towards the screen which hid the chapel.

'The Eternal Bull.' An edge of desperation. 'Will you be joining us, Thomas? Will you pray with us before you take me? I'm your priest, Thomas. Still your priest, when all is said. Tom? Tom Bull? Will you come and pray?'

There was an almost audible apprehension in the church, faces lifting to the organ pipes and the wooden panel which sheltered them from the eyes which were open for eternity.

Merrily watched from the rearmost pew of the northern

aisle, where the women sat. Stefan, it seemed, had had no difficulty at all in persuading the women away from their husbands, and they all clustered in the Satan sector in their variety of costumes, Minnie Parry at the front in dark brown wool, the velvet wives, mostly incomers, conspicuously in the middle, like visitors from Restoration London.

Silence apart from some shuffling, a few coughs. Stefan wiped his brow with an arm. He sniffed. He looked beyond the burnished walls and pillars into the blackness of the rafters.

'It goes dark,' he said sadly. 'We have so little time.'

He was at the front of the northern aisle now, close to Minnie. Merrily could see Gomer Parry, sitting just across from her in the central nave, squeezed into his inquest suit. He looked in need of a cigarette; she could sympathize. In the otherwise empty pew behind Gomer sat the only woman who, unsurprisingly, had resisted attempts to put her in the northern aisle, but Annie Howe looked curiously uncomfortable.

'Bessie!' Stefan called out suddenly. 'Where are you, Bessie Cross?' Advancing down the aisle, looking this way and that over the heads; wherever he went he seemed to take the light with him. 'Bessie Cross! Nay, don't deny me now, woman!'

He stopped three pews from the bottom of the aisle. He waited.

'Bessie?'

Two rows in front of Merrily, a woman moved: Teresa Roberts, a farmer's widow in her late sixties, a friendly, decent soul and a regular churchgoer. Earlier, she'd been one of several people Stefan had asked Merrily to point out to him.

Teresa said hesitantly, 'Bessie Cross . . . she was my

grandmoth—' But Stefan was leaning over the pew end, reaching for her hands to pull her to her feet.

'Bessie! How is the girl now? How is Janet? For I myself have prayed for her many times. Bessie, don't be affeared, he's not here. The Bull's not here yet, we have time for this. How does she lie now, Bessie, is Janet Cross at peace?'

The woman next to Teresa looked up quickly and Merrily saw, with widening eyes, that it was Caroline Cassidy in a dark brown cape. She must have come in alone, after the others.

Still holding Teresa's hand, Stefan turned to the wider congregation, raised his voice.

'You all know about this. All of you know what happened to Bessie Cross's girl, who went into the Bull's meadow to look for her cockerel at close of day, fearing the attentions of the fox, and was caught and branded for a poacher.'

A murmuring. Merrily remembered what Stefan had said, before Coffey could shut him up, about hiring a researcher to gather memories and old stories from the village. But, if this was about Teresa Roberts's grandmother, it was Victorian – for Wil Williams, a couple of hundred years in the future.

It didn't seem to matter. Stefan was clearly invoking memories of a figure which bestrode the centuries: the Eternal Bull.

'And the Bull said to the child, did he not, "Now, Janet, would you appear in court and bring shame down upon your family or have me deal with you now?"'

Stefan paused.

'*Deal with you now*,' he repeated quietly, with low menace. 'Bessie, my poor, dear woman, is what I say true in every detail?'

Teresa Roberts, entirely in shadow, said, 'Well, my mother, she used to tell me—'

'How old was she, Bessie? How old was Janet when she was brought before the Bull?'

The church had gone very quiet. Some had turned to look at the dim tableau of Stefan and Teresa. Others gazed stoically in front of them as if they were afraid to respond, afraid of repercussions. Merrily marvelled at the willingness of a group of disparate people in an enclosed space to relinquish their world for another . . . indeed, their inability *not* to. The power of theatre. Power. She'd never had, nor wanted, power, but this was what being a successful minister was still all about.

Twenty minutes, and he's got them in his hands. They've never given me half this much attention.

Teresa said, 'Twelve. Twelve year old.'

'Has she stopped crying now?' Stefan asked gently. 'Has the poor child stopped crying in the night?'

'She . . . she never stopped. Hardly a week went by they wouldn't hear her crying in her bed. Hardly a week, my mother used to say.'

'*Deal . . . with . . . her . . . now.* A whipping? Was that not what you were told by the gamekeeper, when he brought the child home?'

'It was.'

'A whipping? Does a whipping do that to a girl? A farm girl, a big, hardy, raw-boned girl, a scamp? Does a whipping do that?'

Teresa Roberts said, pain coming through, 'Please . . .'

'Don't worry,' Stefan whispered, just loud enough for Merrily to hear. 'This should be heard.'

The air inside the church was thicker and darker now, the walls like dull earth, but a heart of pure red fire in the circular window. All that was visible of Stefan was the white of his shirt. He moved around the pew like a restless ghost.

'Does a whipping do that, Bessie? I'll bet she'd been whipped a time or two at home.'

'Aye.' Teresa Roberts was a talking shadow. 'We all were, back then.'

'How long did she cry at night?'

'They say she was never at peace and she couldn't look no man in the face from that day till—'

'Where did the Bull take her, Bessie? Don't be afraid. Let it be told, in this holy place, for this haunts your family still.'

'The cider house! He took her in the ole cider house, where they say he took all his women. Because the air itself in there, they used to say, the smell of it could make you drunk. So's you wouldn't notice. The cider house. It was always the ole cider house. It made you drunk, to be in there. And . . . wanton.'

Merrily froze up in the darkness. Images came alive in her head, the dream she'd had in the afternoon in the Black Swan, the dream of Dermot Child in the foetid, sweating cell.

'The cider house,' Stefan said with satisfaction. 'The old Bull cider house. God bless you, Bessie, for your courage! God have mercy on the Bull! And God bless the child who cries in the night!'

'No!' The voice of Teresa Roberts was ragged. 'She don't cry n'more, Reverend. Don't cry n'more . . .'

'How old was she?' Stefan's voice gentle but full and round and relishing his punchline. 'How old was she the day she hanged herself in the barn?'

'Sixteen,' Teresa whispered. 'Sixteen that day, sir.'

In the long, hollow silence that followed, Merrily was aware of Gomer Parry edging out of his pew and then Stefan Alder was leaning over her, his lips against her ear. She could smell his sweat.

'The light, please, Merrily. The spot. Five minutes?'

*

He was so screwed up he couldn't think. He kept walking around the room, pulling books from the shelves. He didn't know where to start. He had so little time and no idea where the hell to start.

He made himself sit down.

Traherne. Start with Traherne. How did Traherne come to know Wil Williams? Help me, Lucy. Just remind me.

Thinking back to when Lucy had first introduced him to Traherne, who had a link with Ledwardine through Wil Williams and . . .

Hopton.

Susannah Hopton. The patroness.

It took Lol nearly twenty minutes to discover, from the various histories of Herefordshire, that Susannah Hopton had been the wife of a judge on the Welsh circuit who lived right on the border at Kington and was a devout high Anglican with some kind of circle of disciples. During the puritan Cromwellian years, Mrs Hopton had moved towards Roman Catholicism but returned after the Restoration of the monarchy. She had a strict and punishing regime of daily worship, which began before dawn. She was very fond of clergymen and her best-known protégé was Thomas Traherne.

But Wil Williams, Lucy said, had become virtually a part of her household.

His background had equipped him to meet her schedules without difficulty.

*

'I was born,' Stefan said, 'on a grey and wind-soured hill farm at Glascwm in Radnorshire.'

He looked down at his fingernails, as if remembering a time when they were black and ragged.

'My father held seventy acres of rocky, boggy, clay-heavy,

God-deserted earth. My father had little faith. No hope. And no conception of charity . . .'

Stefan moved around the church; you could hear the crackling of his footsteps, the only sound, and wherever he would stop light would flare.

Candles.

All around the church, faces were lit by little, oval spears, and in this timeless light, the centuries dissolved, and you saw that essentially nothing had changed, farming faces no less rough and reddened than ever they were, than the stones themselves. And no face more severely stony than Garrod Powell's. *An axe to grind* . . . Merrily recalled the councillor's fist striking the table in the village hall . . . *Let him grind it somewhere else, sir. Not in our church.* And would he say a word tonight? Probably not. No muscle would twitch in Rod's puritan face, no eyebrow rise.

There were no stray breezes in the church tonight, and the flames were vertical, sending up wispy tapers of smoke and that faintly bitter, singeing aroma.

Faces. She saw the moon-bland countenance of Dermot Child. He had not looked at her. She saw the pert, urban features of Caroline Cassidy made gaunt and austere by the wan and waxy light and the anxiety that many a mother knew in the seventeenth century when so many children would expire in infancy. Caroline had not noticed her.

Then she saw Alison Kinnersley. Who had slipped into the back central pew occupied, at the other end, by Annie Howe.

Behind them, Jane hovered. Merrily walked over, made a little signal with a forefinger to tell her to put on the left-hand spot. She could easily have done the lights herself, but it was an excuse to have the kid safely in the building. Jane nodded.

By the time the spot came on, a dusty yellow tunnel from

the rafters to the area below the pulpit, Stefan was there, sitting on the second step, half in the beam, half in shadow. He began to speak conversationally, as though to friends, about his adoption by a rich and pious woman who recognized in him an intelligence, a longing and a purity of spirit so rare it required special nurturing.

He had everyone's attention. The world of Wil Williams. But he spoke boastfully, and that wouldn't go down well. Herefordshire people were generally laid-back and self-effacing.

All around her, Merrily felt a cloudy, ancient atmosphere, but when she looked at Stefan she saw . . . an actor.

Why? She rubbed her eyes. Was it jealousy, because they were never so silent, so attentive to her? She went and stood against the back wall of the nave, next to the heavy curtain covering the entrance to the vestry, and listened to Stefan telling of his introduction to Traherne. How Traherne, with, perhaps, financial assistance from Hopton, had secured Wil's acceptance to his old Oxford College, Brasenose.

Merrily felt very strange. She felt a tightness in her chest. She leaned against the wall, took deep breaths until it subsided.

Stefan was saying something about him and Traherne being two halves of the same apple. Traherne was a poet and a mystic, Wil was deeply sensitive, a natural psychic, a visionary in the most direct sense. When Wil walked out on the hills or into the oak woods, the spirits came to him like the birds and animals to St Francis. He was a wild child, possessed of a raw, exciting beauty.

Where was this leading? Traherne's rough trade, or what?

Merrily felt that alarming tightening in the chest and this time she couldn't make it go away. She held on to the curtain to the vestry to prevent herself falling to her knees. When she began to wheeze, heads turned.

Oh no, not again. Not again, no way.

Merrily walked out.

*

'Mum?'

Jane stood in the porch, watching her anxiously.

Merrily took gulps of air. All around her, the graves were washed amber-pink by the moon.

'You're not ill again, are you?'

'Sorry, flower, I think it's the fumes from all those candles. You go back. Stefan'll think we don't like it.'

'I don't. Do you?'

'I'll tell you when it's finished. Just go back, Jane, OK? There's nothing to worry about. I'm just going to have a cigarette, OK?'

'God,' said Jane. 'You can't go an hour without one, can you?'

She gave her mother one final disapproving glance before disappearing into the porch.

Merrily turned away and leaned her arms over a tall gravestone as a red speck came up from behind another stone.

'Sorry, Vicar, went and hid, I did. Thought it was gonner be my Minnie.'

His cigarette end made a glowing triangle with the twin moons in his glasses.

'Hello, Gomer.'

'Lost track of time in there. En't allowed to wear my watch tonight. Digital, see, gives a bit of a bleep on the hour. Minnie says, What's that gonner sound like in the seventeenth century, eh? Had to sit at the back, too, on account of not havin' a proper fancy-dress costume.'

'Still. You came. I'm glad.' Out here, the pain in her chest had dulled to a throb.

Gomer took a pull on his cigarette. 'En't workin', is it?'

'What en't? Sorry.'

'Thought 'e was gonner hit the spot, that young feller, when he got on to cider, but it went by, see.'

'How do you mean?'

'The cider house. Got me thinkin', that did, so I come out to think sumore. Does a lot o' thinkin' these days. Too much time.'

'The cider house?'

'Where the Bulls took their women. Not their wives, like, you know. Their women. Them as was old enough to qualify as women.'

'Their mistresses?'

'Not even their mistresses, Vicar. The ones they used for their sport, you might say. The ones as didn't count for shit, 'scuse my language.'

'There were more like this . . . Janet?'

'I should say. God bless you, Vicar, it were cheaper than fox 'untin', and no hounds to feed.' Gomer shook his head sadly. 'You looks in need of a ciggy. I got a few yere, ready rolled.'

'Thanks, but . . . Oh, sod it . . . if you can spare one.'

Gomer produced a skinny roll-up and lit it for her.

'When you're retired, see, God damn it, you gets to hangin' around and dwellin' on things and all the folk you ever worked for or had a pint or two with, and they all gets jumbled up in your memory, and then a coupler things rolls out when you en't expectin' it, and you thinks, well bugger me. Why'd ole Edgar Powell shoot 'isself . . . *accidently*, like? Why en't the cider the real stuff?'

'I don't understand.'

'I'll tell you, you got time. I'm sick of keepin' it all up yere. 'Cause I don't understand, neither, and I reckons it's time we did.'

'Go on.'

'Well, you start with the ole cider house. That's the Powell cider house now, see. The Bulls originally, but the Powells, they had it off 'em, way back when the Bulls got rid of all that ground. Interestin', when you works out just how much Bull ground's now Powell ground. I reckon it's gotter be . . .'

Gomer stopped talking. Merrily followed his gaze towards the lych-gate, through which they could see car lights.

'You notice when you come in, Vicar, them cars parked on the edge of the square just across from the church.'

'So many these days. Why?'

'Miserable Andy Mumford in one, coupler young fellers in the other usually wears uniforms, but plain clothes tonight. Mind if we just . . .?'

Gomer set off towards the lych-gate, Merrily following.

'They're on to somethin', I reckon. Don't waste man-power on that scale, less they got somethin' in mind. And that lady copper in the church? They're lookin' for some-body. Or they got somebody in mind. Where's your friend Mr Robinson tonight?'

As they approached, one of the parked cars had put on its lights and pulled out to make way for another vehicle which took over its space just left of the lych-gate. The new vehicle was a battered blue Land Rover with a torn canvas. The driver's door opened as the wheels gritted to a halt.

Gomer put a hand under Merrily's arm and pulled her into the trees beside the gate, as James Bull-Davies stepped down and ducked quickly under the lych-gate, slamming the Land Rover door behind him.

Both front doors of the parked police car opened. Mumford and another man followed Bull-Davies at a distance.

Gomer looked at Merrily.

'Not my place to ask, mabbe, but they clear this with you, the police? Stakin' out your church and whatnot?'

She could hear Bull-Davies's voice crackling into the answering machine. *I shall personally take action to put a stop to this homosexual farce. You may consider this an ultimatum.*

'No,' she said. 'They bloody didn't.'

'You better get back in there. Wouldn't be anythin' I could do, would there?'

'I think there would.'

*

From the apple trees next to the porch, Jane watched James Bull-Davies go in, followed by the two detectives.

The Eternal Bull. It could start to get interesting at last. Sadly, she couldn't stay for it. She waited for Mum to come back – on her own and looking pretty fired up – before she slipped away.

Pretty Foul

'The orchard was mine,' Stefan Alder said.

The spotlight hugging him like a sunbeam from a high window as he knelt at the pulpit steps, looking up towards the rood-screen, where a hundred apples were carved.

'Oh, yes, it belonged to the church, the whole forty acres, but it also belonged to me. It was where I found my peace. And my God. God was always in the orchard.'

He turned full into the light, his hands held out in supplication, half an apple in each. His face was creamed with sweat. Even from the back, Merrily could see the film of desperation over his eyes.

He was losing it. He'd gone on too long. Without Coffey's cohesion, his performance had become shapeless and over-emotional. The dramatic edge was blunt. The audience shuffled and coughed, older Ledwardine folk beginning to see the holes.

And there *were* holes, despite the research. Richard Coffey had not wanted this because he was not ready, but Stefan had been lured here by Merrily and when the evening was discredited as a piece of faintly tedious, overdramatized, gay propaganda the remaining fragments of her own credibility would go with it.

By the light of a cluster of candles, she could see a satisfied smile on the face of Dermot Child. Occasionally he would glance towards one or other of the police.

He would have told them Lol could well be here. Knowing that the vicarage was now unsafe, where else would she hide him? One of the few pieces of information to escape Dermot's intelligence net, perhaps, would be Merrily's appointment as Lucy's executor, her receipt of the keys to Lucy's house. Although you could rely on nothing in a village this size.

But where – much as he would enjoy the sight of Lol being taken away with Merrily as an accessory – did Bull-Davies come into this?

She'd followed them into the church prepared to battle this out; now she felt drained again. Get it over. *Whatever it is, just get it over.*

'For God was inside every apple.' Stefan held up the halves. 'And here had left his mark, the five-pointed star of wisdom.'

'That's not God,' a woman called out scornfully from the middle of the Northern aisle. 'I've seen that. We all know that. That's a pentacle. It's satanic. It's the mark of the serpent! That's why you're supposed to cut the apple the other way.'

Stefan reeled for a moment, as if struck in the face and then, in a graceful piece of theatre-craft, came back.

'There!' Dropping the apple halves, he arose, pointing, straight-armed, at the woman. 'This is how it starts. What upon a tree is more beautiful, more wholesome, more sacred than an apple? The whole world is in an apple. The apple was God's most precious gift to Hereford. The apple heals! And yet . . .'

His arm and voice dropped together. He backed against the pulpit, glanced from side to side, hunted.

'. . . in the wrong hands, even an apple can be poisonous. And this is how it began. This is where the hounding began.'

In front of Merrily, Annie Howe leaned forward, revealing the fine, light hair cut close to the nape of the neck, the ears exposed, no earrings. Raised a forefinger to someone.

Towards the front, a hand went up. Merrily saw that it belonged to James Bull-Davies, sprawled now in the Bull family pew, an arm stretched along its back. Although every eye was focused on him, he seemed entirely relaxed.

Stefan had left the spotlight, was walking from candle to candle in a circle round the church, showing how the net had gathered around Wil Williams. Who was alone now in Ledwardine, the much-respected Thomas Traherne, although still nominally the vicar of Credenhill, having gone to London as chaplain to Sir Orlando Bridgeman. Now Wil had no champion, no defender. No lover was the implication.

'And one enemy,' Stefan said, arriving back at the pulpit.

A buzz. With those words he had his audience back. They didn't want to hear about his sensitivity, his affinity with nature, his perception of the whole world in an apple. They wanted the full, unexpurgated chronicle of hate.

'We were friends, Tom Bull and I,' Stefan Alder mused. 'He was not a well-schooled man, but he had some small understanding of Latin and of the Welsh language and was always eager for news of advances in the physical sciences. He would dine at the vicarage and sometimes I would spend an evening at the Hall and talk of letters we had received from Oxford and London. So what went amiss?'

It was clear that Stefan had not yet noticed James.

'I will tell you,' he said. 'The Bull discovered – or redis-covered – an aspect of himself that he could not bear to confront.'

Stefan rose up several inches in the pulpit, as though

jagged lightning was working through his body. Abruptly, he turned away and vanished into the darkness, reappearing at the foot of the pulpit, sitting on a step, full in the spotlight.

'What do you think?' he said. And laughed. 'Tom Bull had fallen in love.'

*

A tapping on the window this time.

Lol stood in the dark, with his back to the kitchen door. The front doorbell had rung twice, the back door had been knocked on.

'Mr Robinson? Lol Robinson? Gomer Parry, it is, see.'

Well, everybody knew Gomer Parry, even Lol. Genial, harmless Gomer.

It was the name you'd announce yourself by if you didn't want to scare someone away, if you wanted them to open the door, nice and quiet . . .

'You listenin', Lol?' the voice said. ''Cause this is what the vicar told me t'say, see? 'Er says – you ready for this? – 'er says, have you noticed . . . the Dick Drake Moon? Hope I got that right.'

Lol let him in anyway.

*

Now that the blossom had dropped from neighbouring trees, and because it was lighter tonight than the last time, you could see that the Apple Tree Man was actually very sad. Half-dead. Covered with scabs and sores and his branches stuck up like an umbrella with its fabric torn away, some of the prongs bent.

The more Jane drank, the more bent they would seem against the brown sky and the brick-coloured moon.

She lay with her back to the tree, roughly where she'd lain the night Colette had brought her here. It had been easy to find the Man, in his small clearing, but now she was here nothing was quite as she remembered it. It was a different kind of night.

And a different kind of cider.

She'd come in over the wall from the vicarage, tossing the strong, heavy, dark green bottles before her. The idea she'd had from Lucy, of this traditional Ledwardine drink, made from the legendary Pharisees Red, was that this was the booze endorsed by the fairies, who were the little angels of the orchard, and so it would be like nectar, right? The cider itself would have mystical properties.

She'd eased out the champagne-style cork, expecting an emphatic pop, like a magical starting pistol. *This is where it begins.* But the cork had merely fallen out and rolled away and, although the bottles must have been shaken up getting here, there was no exciting frothy rush either, just this joyless dribble.

Oh well. Jane had leaned back against the trunk, trying not to think of Edgar Powell with his grizzled old head blown off – that episode was a complete irrelevance – and had gripped the lips of the bottle with her own and thrown her head back.

And then came the real shock.

The Wine of Angels was actually pretty foul.

To begin with, it was dry. Horribly dry. The cider she and Colette had drunk that night in the Ox was cheap and sweet and went down very easily and made you happy and bubbly. But the Wine had this cloying taste that was more like soil than apples. She recalled the first time she'd had real champagne, at a wedding Mum had conducted up in Liverpool, and what a bitter disappointment that had been, especially out of such a brilliant bottle. This was worse.

And this was The Wine of Angels, named by Lucy Devenish.

She sat in the toffee-coloured night and felt like crying. What it was – she was bloody useless on her own. She was just a kid and a townie kid as well. She'd tried to imagine Lucy walking alongside her into the orchard, but Lucy was cold in the mortuary, Lucy was never coming back to the orchard.

Upset and furious and frustrated, Jane had another drink. It couldn't really be so *yuk*. Must be another sign of how immature she was that she couldn't appreciate the quality of a fine cider made to an ancient recipe, fermented in the bottle.

But she wasn't bloody well going back now. She had to go all the way with this, so that nobody could say she hadn't tried. She'd even put on the same old blue Pulp T-shirt she'd been wearing when Colette had first brought her in here. All for Colette.

Do it. Be there for her. Use your *contact*.

What she needed was to get into the same mood, to find the same state of mind. She went over all the events leading up to the golden lights moment, getting the sequence of it, starting with the outstanding time they'd had in the pub, laughing at people like James Bull-Davies, realizing they had this repartee going between them, that they could be good mates, if not exactly soulmates. Then that sweating boil, Dean Wall, and his cronies eyeing them up and coming after them, the smell of urine from the Gents toilets, the flight past the old bowling green to the church porch, the after-hours social club, Colette's delight at Jane throwing up all over . . .

Her stomach lurched at the thought of that and she pressed her hands down on it and belched. This cider was so much gassier. And it wasn't working. She'd drunk masses of the stuff, or it felt like it, and yet she didn't seem to be particularly drunk. Certainly didn't feel at all happy. All the optimism was long gone, the feeling that Ledwardine was her real, pre-ordained home, that she could really *function* here, help Mum make a go of it, have some laughs with Colette – maybe find some cool guys together – help Lol get himself straightened out and organized and recording again, work with Lucy on re-establishing the natural way of things, become more aware of the *orb*.

The orchard smelled damp and mouldy. She was sure it hadn't been like this before. She tried to remember the moment they'd both flopped down under the Apple Tree Man, but she couldn't. Her only memory was of saying she was dying and then Colette's voice, so cool, so smokey, so sassy, coiling out of the ground beside her.

You ain't felt nothin' yet, honeychile.

Those really prophetic words. Like she really knew the score. But it was just some scam to scare Jane. Colette hadn't known a thing. Not then. And afterwards was far too cool to think she had anything to learn from a weird old bat like Lucy Devenish. But she'd hated to feel she'd been left behind by anybody. She had to be the leader, and on the night of her party she'd impulsively led some kind of raiding party on the orchard, determined to break through to whatever it was Jane had accessed. Bust into what Lucy called the orb, find the contact.

And had vanished.

Search was made for her and she appeared to her friends from time to time, but when they spoke to her she immediately disappeared.

Jane took another swig of the awful Wine of Angels and slumped back with her hair against the knobbly bark of the Apple Tree Man, still clutching the big bottle by its neck. She closed her eyes, lay very still and tried again. She imagined Colette in a land of lights, separated from the orchard by a billowing night mist. The point being that

Colette was nobody special in this place; she was learning that there were higher forces and inner structures and that most of the things she thought were really cool were actually quite trivial and insignificant.

It was time for her to return, chastened.

'Colette,' Jane whispered. 'You hear me, you dumb slag? It's me. I've come back. I've come to fetch you.'

There was an answering rustle of leaves from somewhere beyond the edge of the clearing. It was probably a fox or a badger, but in her mind Jane turned it into Colette.

She had a clear picture of Colette strolling through the orchard. She could see the nose stud and the red plastic windcheater open over the daring black dress.

The rustling came closer. If she opened her eyes now, she would *see* . . . She was getting shivery vibrations at the back of her neck, remembered Dr Samedi: '. . . *and de drummin' begin, feel de drummin' inside, fingers dancin', dancin', dancin' up an' down yo spine . . .*'

Colette. Colette was coming. She was coming back. The urge to open her eyes was overpowering.

But she didn't. She mustn't. The moment must be absolutely right.

She must be very quickly seized, without speaking, or she would never come back.

She heard breathing. It wasn't a fox or a badger, it was her old friend Colette Cassidy, and she'd stop in the clearing, the cynical cow, and she'd go, Aw, Janey, you're not still here? This is just so sad. And then they'd both crease up laughing.

Come on, lady.

She concentrated on keeping her eyes squeezed tight, tight shut and holding her breath, and putting everything she had into the image of Colette, summoning this incredible detail: a light sheen of sweat on the forehead overhung by a wing of hair, a blob of mascara on the end of an eyelash, the weird red moon glinting in the nose-stud, a slick of crimson lipstick on her avaricious little teeth when she smiled.

She heard Colette's voice calling to her across the nights. *Look up. For me. Just look up, once. And then we'll go.*

Jane looked up.

FORTY-SEVEN

False Lover

Gomer said, 'Don't suppose Lucy kept the odd bottle about the place? Helps you think better, it do, my experience. Well, not better, mabbe, but a bit *wilder*, like. You gotter think wild to get your brain round this kinder business.'

He certainly looked wild tonight. Lol recalled them watching the little guy troop past the shop one afternoon and Lucy saying Gomer Parry was an object lesson on the dangers of retirement. Not the man he used to be. Not the man he was a year ago.

Tonight though, Gomer's springy white hair was on end like a lavatory brush and his eyes looked hot enough to melt the wire frames of his glasses.

'No accident?' Lol said, going through to the kitchen. 'You sure of that?'

'Course I en't,' Gomer snapped. 'All I'm sayin', see, is I've used bloody *hedge trimmers* with more power than that little bike. And it never got much stick from Lucy Devenish. You know Lucy, it makes no sense.'

'They're calling it a freak accident.'

'Freak accident my arse,' said Gomer. 'Lucy seen a ewe amblin' out the hedge, she'd just pull over and wait for the ole thing to get across. This is a country woman, born, bred and what you like, through and through. That woman could *sense* a sheep from fifty yards. But you try tellin' that to one

544

o' these bloody inquests. It'll be Edgar Powell all over again. Accidental bloody death!'

'If it wasn't an accident, what was it?'

'Suspicious is what it was.'

'You think somebody *killed* Lucy?'

'That's a wild question,' Gomer said. 'But it's gotter be asked, see. Gotter be asked. En't nobody else gonner ask it, are they? All right then, it's n'more than a feelin'. En't never gonner be no evidence now, coppers've made up their minds. Open and shut. Shut for ever, like a lot o' stuff in this village. But when the wind's in the right direction . . .'

Pulling his tobacco tin from his jacket pocket, Gomer got going furiously on a roll-up.

'Put it this way, boy. You don't dig out two thousand cesspits in thirty years without learnin' what shit smells like. I know the vicar's taken a few shovel-loads she en't deservin' of, and we had a bit of a chat about tonight and 'er says, do me a favour, you go round and talk to Mister Lol Robinson about this and anythin' else that's on your mind, give him summat to think about 'stead o' worryin' about the colour of the moon, like.'

'She said that?'

'Give or take. So yere I am.'

'Well.' Lol brought the presentation case of The Wine of Angels into the living room. 'I'm glad to see you, Gomer. I've been sitting here getting nowhere fast.'

'We can pool what we got, mabbe. I told you that about Lucy, see, 'cause I know you and 'er was friends . . .'

Lol nodded. Point taken. Resolve strengthened. He put down The Wine of Angels box, the only bottles he could find in the house. Gomer sniffed.

'No thank *you*, boy. Once was enough.'

'Looks like a present to Lucy from the festival committee.'

''Er was mabbe keepin' it to donate to the Christmas raffle.'

Lol observed that two bottles appeared to have been drunk already.

'Impossible,' Gomer said. 'Nobody'd ever drink a second. Wine of Angels? Balls. Must be fifteen year back, Rod Powell, he calls me in to dig out a couple hundred yards o' drainage ditch. Well, Edgar'd made a few barrels of Pharisees Red cider, strictly for their own consumption, like, and it was a hot day, see, and they gives me a jugful and, by God, that weren't the kind o' cider you forgets. And this – ' Gomer brandished a bottle with some contempt ' – en't it.'

'What is it?'

'Supermarket cider, boy. Pop. Not quite cheap muck, not far off. This never come out o' the ole Powell cider house, the Bull cider house as was, I'd stake my JCB on it. They bought this in, knowing poor bloody Cassidy and his flash friends wouldn't know the difference if it come out of a fancy bottle. Now why they done that?'

'That's a mystery,' Lol said dubiously.

'Aye.' Gomer's glasses gleamed. 'Another bloody mystery, boy. You might reckon that en't got nothin' to do with nothin'. But cider, as Lucy used to say, was the lifeblood of Ledwardine. This is central, boy. Central.'

'I know I'm not thinking too well tonight,' Lol said, 'but I don't see where this is going.'

'Nor me,' said Gomer. 'Not yet. But it all smells *off*. We looks at things and we draws conclusions and sometimes they're wrong – like the vicar sees all these coppers movin' in on the church and she reckons they're after *you*. I think there's summat else afoot, but we'll have to wait and see, isn't it?'

'Except we don't have time to wait,' Lol said. 'Merrily's playing it by ear in there, Bull-Davies is planning to get it stopped and drive her out of the village for good, and a lot of things are . . . closing in, you know?'

'Ar,' Gomer said.

They stood there in Lucy's living room, two little guys in glasses who wanted to help and didn't know how. Eventually Lol said, 'You know anything about Wil Williams, Gomer?'

'Not a lot.'

'Thomas Traherne?'

'Know Lucy was keen on the feller. That's about it.'

Lol looked across at the framed photograph of Lucy and a young, blonde woman feeding a pony from a bucket.

'Patricia Young?'

Gomer thought for a moment. 'No.'

'Susannah Hopton?'

Gomer shook his head.

Lol picked up Mrs Leather, opened it to the handwritten notes on the inside back cover. 'Hannah Snell?'

'Ar.'

'Sorry?'

'Hannah Snell,' Gomer said. 'I know who she is, all right.' He cleared his throat and began to sing in a tuneless tenor.

> '*All ye noble British spirits*
> *That midst dangers glory sought*
> *Let it lessen not your merit*
> *That a woman bravely fought . . .*'

Gomer beamed. 'Thought you was some sort o' folk singer, Lol. You en't never yeard that? My ole gran used to sing me that as a nipper. Hannah Snell. Bugger me, that takes me back.'

'Tell me,' Lol said. '*Tell* me.'

When Gomer had finished, he said, 'Tell Merrily.' And 'Christ.'

*

James Bull-Davies came almost languidly to his feet.

'So.' He leaned forward, both hands on the rim of the prayer-book rack. 'You're suggesting my ancestor was, ah . . . gay.'

Stefan Alder stood defiantly in front of the pulpit.

'He was in love with me.'

'Gord's sake, man, do we have to have this bloody play-acting?' His voice filled the church. 'You make accusations about my family, you don't hide behind bloody Wil Williams. You, Stefan Alder, are saying Thomas Bull was a poofter. Correct?'

'That's not a word I would use.'

'I'm sorry. A homosexual. This man with four children.'

'It doesn't make any difference. You must know that.'

'But that's what you're alleging. Come on, man, you can't libel the dead, spit it out.'

'All right. I believe that Tom Bull had a physical relation-ship with the Priest of Ledwardine and when there was a danger that it would become a matter of general knowledge in the village, in his family, in the courts where he presided, he sought to have Wil condemned as a witch. He had a neigh-bouring farmer accuse Wil of diminishing the productivity of his orchard. He had a local artisan who was dependent on his patronage invent a story about him dancing with sprites, or even . . .'

Stefan glanced around his silent congregation.

'Don't stop, Alder,' Bull-Davies said. 'We're all agog.'

'. . . or even paid some of the local youths to disport themselves naked in the orchard to torment poor Wil beyond his powers of endurance.'

Murmurs of disbelief and disapproval, mostly from the northern aisle.

Bull-Davies sighed. 'Went to an awful lot of trouble, didn't he?'

Stefan had been too long in the light. His hair was damp and darkened, his shirt hung limp and grey with sweat.

'What I find most objectionable, is your slur on the *integrity* of the man.'

'You don't understand.' Stefan's face streamed. He refused to move out of the light. 'I do think Tom believed in what he was doing. He convinced himself that Wil Williams had occult powers. How else could he, a Bull, possibly fall in love with a man? Unless that man had bewitched him.'

A hush. Merrily saw James's hands tighten on the prayer-book shelf of the Bull family pew. Very slowly, James straightened up and walked out of the pew and into the well below the pulpit, stopping two yards from Stefan Alder.

'And on what', he said, with a clear menace, 'do you base your evidence?'

Stefan didn't move. 'He kept a journal, did he not?'

'And you, of course, have seen this journal?'

'You know I cannot possibly have seen it, as your family keeps it in a bank vault in Hereford.'

Murmurs in the pews.

'And unless and until you are prepared to produce this journal, you're in no position even to pretend to refute any of what I've said. Are you?'

James said confidently, 'There is no journal relating to your spurious allegations in any bank vault, to my knowledge, in Hereford or anywhere else.'

They faced one another at the end of the tunnel of light, James heavy in tweeds making Stefan look even more pale and fragile. Somebody should stop the fight, Merrily thought absurdly.

'So you've taken it out of the bank, have you?'

Stefan stared into James's eyes, his body arching towards the big soldier, his hands weaving in the light in an almost womanly distress. When he spoke again it was in a soft, imploring voice.

'Please tell us the truth, James . . . Please don't hold back any more . . . You know that Tom, before he died, made a confession to the then priest, together with an enormous donation to the church in order that his body might lie where it lies now – behind me – in the area between the altar and the orchard where his beloved Wil lay, in unhallowed ground; a man who took his own life rather than face conviction for the crime of being gay. Conviction – and betrayal – at the hands of a dishonest man and a false lover, who—'

'You . . . little . . . shit . . .' With a roar James was on him and the church exploded into light. Some women on the left screamed, men in the centre were on their feet.

Blinded by the glare, Merrily threw both hands up to her eyes and through the fingers saw figures converging on the threshing bodies below the rood screen. She stumbled down the aisle towards them, aware of Annie Howe striding in front of her. Scrambling up the steps under the chancel arch she saw policemen holding back Bull-Davies and Stefan Alder, and she filled her lungs and screamed out, 'In the name of God, stop this!'

And for a moment, there was quiet.

Annie Howe looked up at Merrily and smiled pleasantly. 'Thank you, Ms Watkins.'

The two detectives holding James Bull-Davies let him go and James stepped away from them, brushed down his jacket and straightened up and stood quite stiffly, looking directly across the nave at nobody.

The detective holding Stefan did not let him go. It was

Mumford. Stefan sullenly tossed his head back against Mumford's shoulder. Mumford went rigid. Annie Howe said, 'Bernard Stephen Alderson, I'm arresting you for the murder of Richard Coffey. You don't have to say anything, but if you fail to mention something you later rely on in court . . .'

The rest was lost in the tumult.

Merrily closed her eyes.

Thank You, Lord

Full of breathless excitement and bad, gassy cider, Jane looked up.

Looked up in hope and then began to scream. The figure rearing up in the clearing, the shape hiding the moon was not Colette. Was far too big to be Colette.

She shrank back against the Apple Tree Man, let go of the neck of The Wine of Angels, the bottle rolling away, sloshing cider over her jeans. Her lips went soggy and a whimper began in her throat. *Please*, she was trying to say. *Please, I'm drunk.*

The figure didn't move. If it was the police, there'd have been a powerful torchbeam in her face. She was pushing herself back so hard that a spiky piece of bark was stabbing into the top of her head, the pain brutally assuring her that this was not a dream.

'Jane Watkins.' The voice was sorrowful. And male. And local.

'Oh God,' Jane said. Her head was all fogged up. She knew the voice, couldn't identify it.

'What you doing yere, Jane Watkins?'

Whoever it was, he knew the orchard too well to need a torch.

'This is not in the best of taste, I'd say.'

'Oh God!' Jane sat up. 'It's you.' The last time they'd

met, she'd rushed up to him in a panic in the market place, and he'd put his big hands on her shoulders and said yes, all right, he'd go into the orchard after Colette and see what he could do, and his eyes had looked sort of rangy and fearless under his Paul Weller fringe, but even then she hadn't held out any great hopes of everything being all right.

'Two things,' Lloyd Powell said. 'One, you're too young to be drinking that ole pop. Two, this is where my grandfather died and if he's looking down now he's gonner be disgusted, he is.'

'Sorry, Lloyd. I really didn't mean to be disrespectful.'

'I thought better of you, I really did, young lady. But you en't such a lady, after all, are you? Look at you . . . You stink of it. Disgraceful.'

'I let the bottle go and it all came out.'

She struggled to her feet, stumbling about a bit, which she hadn't expected; The Wine of Angels had been so foul she hadn't really thought it would have any effect.

'I dunno at all,' Lloyd said. 'Just look at the state of you.'

Jane gritted her teeth. He might look cool and hunky, but he was just like his dad, all strait-laced and backbone of the community and no sense of humour at all.

'Well,' he said. 'I don't hear an explanation.'

Oh sure. Well, actually, Lloyd I was conducting a mystical experiment, on the lines indicated by Mrs Leather, to try and bring Colette back from the Land of Faerie, which isn't as stupid as it sounds, if people like you had ever taken the trouble to listen to Miss Devenish, we're simply talking about a parallel dimension, and I know it exists because I think I've been there, although I don't remember a thing, it was a kind of trance state, and all right, it was a long shot, but . . .

Oh, *sure*.

'Come on, Jane. We better get you back to your mother before something happens to you.'

Jane stood up straight. Well, almost. She pushed her hair back behind her ears, bits of bark and stuff dropping out.

'I can get myself back, thank you.'

'Oh aye? And how am I gonner feel, something happens to you or you goes off like your friend? Though heaven only knows why a decent girl would want a friend like that. Looking at you now, mind, I'm not sure you're a decent girl after all.'

Jane dragged an angry breath between her closed teeth. You could only stand so much of this. 'Look. I'm sorry for trespassing in your precious orchard. I'm sorry for resting under your grandad's tree. And, most of all, I'm sorry for drinking your disgusting cider. I shall go.'

'And I said . . .' Lloyd stood up right in front of her, about a foot taller and nearly twice as heavy '. . . that *I* will take you home, miss. Come on. Pick up that bottle – litter, that is.'

'I wasn't going to *leave* it. I care for the countryside.'

'Oh aye,' Lloyd said. 'All you incomers care for the country.'

'And all you farmers are just so smug. You always think that whatever you do's got to be right because you've been doing it for centuries or whatever.'

Jane bent and picked up the bottle. There was another one somewhere, but what would he think if he saw she'd brought two of the things? Probably that she was expecting a bloke. She stuck the empty bottle under her arm and turned back towards the church. But Lloyd was in front of her again, spreading out his long arms like an official police barrier.

'No, you don't. Not that way, Miss Watkins. Got my truck over the other side, isn't it?'

'Oh, for God's sake, that's stupid! It's only a few minutes' walk back to the churchyard.'

'You're going back in the truck and that's final. I wanner keep my eye on you, make sure you goes in the right door.'

She was furious. But she was also a bit drunk. Damn Lloyd Powell. Damn Lloyd and damn Rod and damn bloody old Edgar who was too gaga to point his gun in the right direction.

Feeling really sullen, sickeningly bloody *teenage*, she let Lloyd steer her out of the clearing in the opposite direction to the way she'd come in, towards the farm entrance to the orchard which was out near the 'new' road. She noticed he never touched her, just put out his arms like barriers. The Powells were such puritans. Or could it even be that it was like with Lol, and Lloyd was afraid of teenage girls? Guys could be so strange.

'I didn't think there'd be anybody around tonight,' she said when they picked up the rough path through the apple trees, still floury with yellowing blossom against the treacly sky. 'I thought you'd be in church with everybody else.'

Lloyd snorted. With an unexpected venom, he said, 'Why'd I wanner to listen to the ramblings of some poncy, posing little queer who thinks he can rewrite other people's history?'

It wasn't clear whether he was talking about Stefan or Richard Coffey. Nothing was too clear, actually. She'd deliberately drunk too much, hoping to disconnect her mind, and she'd succeeded. Hazey Jane again.

'We supposed to sit around and allow that?'

'It's only a play, Lloyd. Nobody's saying it's true.'

'En't they?'

'No.'

'All you know, miss. All you know.'

As they emerged, quite suddenly, at the roadside, Jane said, resentfully, 'You'd be surprised what I know.'

Lloyd stopped. His famous white truck was parked by the

kerb without lights. Lloyd got out his keys, unlocked the passenger door. 'All right.' There was a kind of resignation in his voice. He held open the door. 'You better get in.'

Standing on the footplate, hauling herself up, she got dizzy, stumbled again and clutched at the side-panel to stop herself falling off.

In the back of the truck, the pink moon shone out of dead eyes.

*

Mumford and his colleague took Stefan away. Nobody in the church attempted to follow them except for Annie Howe. Merrily caught her arm as she walked down from the chancel.

'Excuse me, Inspector. Do I have to disturb the bishop and ask him to disturb the Chief Constable or do I get to hear an explanation?'

Annie Howe half-turned in irritation. And then – the woman of the hour who could afford to be magnanimous – she relaxed, comfortably resigned.

'Ms Watkins . . . I really am very, very sorry. But it did seem inappropriate at the time to tell you what we were doing. Besides which, we didn't, at that stage, have what I would have considered sufficient evidence, so I actually hadn't yet decided precisely how I wanted to handle it. It was what you might call an ongoing situation. Sor-ry.'

'Just go on talking,' Merrily said. 'I'll tell you when I've heard enough.'

Oh God, but it made terrible sense. *It's sorted*, Stefan had said. *Richard won't be having anything to do with this.*

Because Richard had died a bloody but not protracted death in the living room of Upper Hall lodge, under repeated blows from a blunt instrument. Merrily pictured some statuette of a nude biblical male spattered with blood and brain.

It will be the performance of my life. Perhaps there won't be another.

James Bull-Davies had discovered the body when he went to confront Coffey after learning about the proposed evening of drama cooked up by Stefan Alder and the vicar. The living-room curtains had been drawn, but on the front-door frame was a blatant and unavoidable handprint in blood. Bull-Davies had kicked the door in.

Stefan, it seemed, had made very little attempt to conceal the killing – a crime, very definitely, of passion, but the passion was for a man over three centuries dead. Perhaps, after tonight's performance, he would have given himself up.

'So why didn't you just arrest the poor sod before the performance? Did the idea of an audience appeal to your—?'

'Ms Watkins. I'm really not obliged to justify my choice of procedure to you, nor even to—'

'It was James, wasn't it? He wanted the entire village to know that the man attempting to defame his ancestry was not only a liar but a murderer. Or to conclude that, because he's now revealed as a murderer, he must also be a liar.'

'Inspector,' Bull-Davies boomed from behind her, 'as you so rightly say, you are under absolutely no obligation to defend your methods to this woman, who, in my view, is simply wasting police time. As she has wasted everyone else's. She might also care to consider that had it not been for her irresponsible promotion of this impromptu fiasco, Richard Coffey would in all probability not have died.'

'It's not my place to say he's right,' Annie Howe said. 'But I do have to go now. Nobody's been permitted to leave yet, by the way, because we shall need the name and address of everyone here tonight. DC Thomas will stay and take them down.'

'Why?'

'Possible witnesses.'

'To what? James's assault on Stefan Alder?'

'May I have a word in private, Ms Watkins?'

Merrily followed her down the central aisle, through a parted sea of appallingly excited faces, to the south porch.

'Look,' Howe said, 'I'm still looking for Colette Cassidy. It's possible that the death of Richard Coffey has absolutely no connection with that, but in a village this size it would be amazing if there wasn't some kind of overlap, however peripheral. So that's one reason I want to know precisely who is in this building.'

'It's a church.'

'It's just another public building to me.'

'I thought you were looking for this ... Laurence Robinson.'

'He's one of the people we want to eliminate from our inquiries. Why, is he here?'

'I wouldn't know,' Merrily said.

'No? Well, I'm going back to Hereford now to talk to Mr Alder, but there will be other officers around should you wish to give them any information.'

'A celebrity murder,' Merrily said tonelessly. 'Aren't you lucky?' It would sound grudging, mean-spirited. Distinctly unsaintly. 'I need some air,' she said.

*

Outside, she lit a cigarette and walked among the graves.

So that was it. All over.

Richard Coffey dead and his play stillborn. Stefan Alder destroyed. Wil Williams reburied in a deeper grave. The troublesome and ineffectual woman priest publicly discredited, last seen plucking feebly at the sleeve of the younger woman who took all the honours.

God and the Fates had conspired to make the world secure again for the Bulls of Ledwardine. Thank you, Lord.

And the pink moon shone down.

After a while, Merrily squeezed out the cigarette and went back into the church to find Jane and go home.

Wherever that was.

Badger Baiting

Lloyd laughed. 'Just an ole ewe, Jane. Picked her up from the north field this afternoon, forgot she was still in the back. Second one just dropped dead in two days, you get weeks like that. No reason for it.'

A spent eye gazed past Jane, who shuddered, thinking of the ewe Lucy had run into, the one that killed her and itself. That was one of the Powells', too, presumably.

The truck's engine rattled into life. Lloyd threw it into gear, switched on his lights and pulled out.

The last time Jane had been on this road it was with Bella, the radio reporter, bound for King's Oak Corner, where the police had found some of Colette's clothing. She didn't want to be on it again, heading for the spot where Lucy had died.

'Why are we going up here?' She looked over her shoulder. 'The village is that way.'

'Because the truck, he was pointing *this* way,' Lloyd said, exasperated. 'And it en't a good road for doing a three-point turn in the dark. We got to carry on up yere a mile or so then reverse into Morgan's yard, all right?'

'Oh.'

Which meant they were going to pass the section where Lucy had hit the sheep. And then they'd have to pass it *again*, when Lloyd had turned round. He had no right to do this. Who was he anyway? Who did the Powells think they were? Generation after generation of boring councillors and self-righteous farmers who slagged off townies for never having shagged a sheep or whatever.

Sheep. She thought of the poor, lifeless ewe slung in the back of the truck and then, with a flush of anger, realized that if the Powells had been such brilliant farmers, Lucy would still be alive.

'That was one of your sheep, wasn't it, that Lucy Devenish hit?'

'Like I said, two ewes gone in two days,' Lloyd said.

It hadn't been quite what he'd said, but Jane pressed on, not wanting to lose the impetus.

'So where did it come from?'

'I dunno. The field across from the orchard, presumably.' He was driving with one hand on the wheel. His right elbow was resting on the ledge of his wound-down window. He looked pretty cool actually. One of the girls at school had said she'd tried to snog him once at a Young Farmers' dance, but Lloyd had just kissed her limply and walked off like he had better fish to fry.

'How did it get out?'

'What you on about?'

'The sheep.'

'I got no idea, Jane.'

'You would if you bothered to check your fences,' Jane said tartly.

Lloyd eased off the accelerator. 'What you mean by that?'

'Next to a road like this, you should have decent fences and check them regularly. That way, sheep wouldn't get out and run in front of people and cause accidents. It wasn't the sheep's fault, it was yours.'

She thought he'd be angry, and she didn't care, but he seemed relieved, making a small sound that was almost a laugh.

'You're a cheeky little devil, Jane.'

'And you're just . . . irresponsible,' she said ineffectually.

The truck jolted to a standstill.

Jane looked out of the window for lights and saw none. 'Why've you stopped?'

'Morgan's Yard. Morgan's bloody *yard*, Jane.'

'I can't see anything.'

Lloyd sighed. 'Morgan's farm's been derelict these past twenty years.'

He reversed quickly and carelessly, as though he'd done it a thousand times at night and then, with the car pointing at ninety degrees to the road, took his hands off the wheel.

'Well, go on, then.' Jane felt suddenly quite nervous of him. 'Take me home.'

'No,' Lloyd said. 'You got a bee in your bonnet about this Devenish business, I want it sorted.'

'She was good to me. And if you'd seen her lying dead in the road—'

'Well, I didn't. But if I had, I'd still've thought she was a cranky, meddling old troublemaker, and this village better off with her gone.'

'You rotten bastard,' Jane blurted. 'What did she ever do to you?'

'Plus,' Lloyd said pedantically, 'she was a danger to herself and every other road-user. Two reasons – one, she never wore protective headgear.'

'She liked her cowboy hat, and everybody knew it was her coming along, it was part of her im—'

'Two, that ridiculous Mexican poncho thing. Get the wind under that, it blows up over your handlebars. Up over your head, if you're unlucky. Which was exactly what happened, wannit?'

'Yes,' Jane whispered, shutting her eyes as if that would

drive away the picture of Lucy's face under the happy, summer poncho.

Lloyd revved hard and she was flung back into the passenger seat. 'Silly bugger,' Lloyd said and put both hands on the wheel, sending the truck bolting back in the direction of Ledwardine.

Thank God for that, Jane thought. Suddenly, the idea of being dumped back at the vicarage or outside the church with some snide little comment to Mum about keeping her daughter off the booze seemed almost cosy. She only hoped, the speed Lloyd was going, that no more sheep had strayed on to the road.

There was a cold explosion in her head.

Oh God.

Second one just dropped dead in two days, you get weeks like that. No reason for it, he'd said.

Not, *And that makes it two with the one Lucy Devenish ran into.* He was saying it had already dropped dead. How could he possibly know that?

Plus *that poncho thing. Up over your head, if you're unlucky. Which was exactly what happened, wannit?*

How did he know that? How did he know Lucy had been lying dead with the poncho over her face, when he said he hadn't seen her? Nobody had, except Jane and Bella and the police who'd immediately concealed the area.

Lloyd put his headlights on, as the truck began jolting like all the tyres had gone flat or something.

'What's happening? Why's it gone all bumpy?'

'Short cut,' Lloyd said tersely. In the green glow from the dashboard, he looked angry.

'No, it's not, where are we going?'

He rounded on her. '*Shut up!*'

'What's the matter? What have I done?'

'This is all your bloody fault, you stupid little cow. I never bloody wanted this. I tried to be fair with you and you just kept pushin' it and pushin' it and pushin' it. You couldn't leave well alone.'

'I don't know what you mean. What have I said?'

'It's not what *you* said, it's what you made *me* say. Leadin' me on all the time, laying traps. You come yere, you all think you're so smart. You and your university-educated parents and all I ever went to was the local agricultural college, all laughing behind your hands, bloody ole yokels, we'll show 'em how to organize 'emselves, oh you think you're so—'

'We're not . . . My mother dropped *out* of university,' Jane said. Desperately grabbing at a change of topic, anything not to do with sheep and road accidents. 'She got pregnant. She's worked really hard all her life. We're not posh townies, Mum's family came from—'

'Shut your bloody clever little gob.' The truck slithered to a greasy stop. 'Let me think!'

'Take me home.' Jane discovered she was crying. She didn't feel disgusted with herself, anybody would cry in this situation. 'Please, Lloyd.'

'You've had that, miss. You won't get home now.'

'Where are we?' She made a grab for the door handle; he reared over her. She screamed. The scream floated away out of the window, into nowhere.

'Don't make me touch you,' Lloyd said.

Jane got both hands to the door-pull, but it just kept clicking and the door didn't open.

'Don't work from the inside n' more,' Lloyd said. 'I was gonner get him fixed, then I saw he had his uses.'

*

Gomer caught up with Merrily under the porch lantern.

'Vicar. Hold on.' He was out of breath.

She stepped outside again, although she didn't think she could bring herself to explain what had happened.

'Gomer—'

'Seen 'em fetchin' 'im out, Vicar. At least four people told me the story 'tween Church Street and the market. Should be more'n halfway round the county by now. Forget that. That don't matter, see. You gotter get back in there, 'fore they all leaves.'

'Sorry?'

'You gotter tell 'em the truth.'

'Dear Gomer.' She sighed. 'I don't know any truth any more. And if I did, nobody would want to hear it from me.'

'*I* know the truth. Me and Lol, we figured it. If you'd just give me chance—'

'Gomer, whatever it is, it's too late.'

'En't,' Gomer said obstinately.

She shook her head. 'I've got to find Jane.'

He followed her back into the porch. 'Vicar, you gotter listen. Lol, see, he's been puttin' me in the picture 'bout a lot o' things you been keepin' to yourself too long.'

'Then he shouldn't have. It's all been a waste of time and I should've known better.'

Inside the porch, sitting on the stone bench like a smug gnome, Dermot Child smirked at her. 'Quite an interesting night, Reverend. In spite of everything. I'm sure the repercussions will be many and varied.'

'Who's that?' Gomer peered sourly at him, 'Ah, it's you, Mr Child. Didn't recognize you with your dick in your pants.' He held open the church door for Merrily.

'Gomer—'

'Hear me out, Vicar.'

At the prayer-book table, just inside the door, Detective Constable Ken Thomas was sitting taking names. Ken was local, well known to most of the villagers and Merrily too.

He was a nice man, overweight and approaching retirement age, therefore consigned by Howe to such menial, clerical tasks as this. He didn't seem to mind.

'You en't gonner write my full name down, are you, Ken?' Jim Prosser was saying. 'Just put Jim, Shop, you'll remember.'

'But she won't, and she's the one matters.'

'That girl?'

'That *girl* could be divisional commander next year, way things are going. It's called accelerated promotion. Tonight's likely shoved her up two more rungs.'

'Bugger me,' Jim Prosser said. Behind him, Effie, his wife, fussed with her inappropriate crinoline. Behind her Dr Kent Asprey looked impatient, Rod Powell dignified and unconcerned. James Bull-Davies, heritage vindicated, hung out by the pulpit, aloof, chin thrust out, gazing up at the opaque apple window, on the opposite side of the church to the Bull chapel where, Merrily was convinced, he'd earlier hacked his way into a seventeenth-century tomb. But who would ever learn about that now?

Nobody seemed to notice Merrily. There was no sign of Jane.

'Prob'ly gone home lookin' for you,' Gomer said. 'We'll find her, don't you worry 'bout that. Now, where's quiet? Vestry?'

He held back the curtain and almost pushed her inside.

*

Jane wrapped her arms around herself, shrinking into the corner where the sunken passenger seat ended and the metal partition separated her and the dead sheep in the back of the truck.

This was the Powell farm, on the wrong side of the new

road, the village a sparse and distant glimmering through the orchard.

'I'm not getting out. I want to go home. You've got to take me home.'

'Stop whining, bitch,' Lloyd said. 'I gotter think.'

He was clutching the steering wheel tightly with both hands as though he wanted to bang his head on it. The film of sweat on his forehead was lime-green in the dashlight. The engine was chunnering. A smell of petrol inside the cab, mixed with cattle feed and manure.

'Then let me get out. I'll walk home. I can see you've got a lot on your mind.'

'I've told you to stop that.'

Lloyd looked up from the wheel, his face severe but kind of bland, like his dad's. Like being moved by anything was a weakness genetically eradicated in the Powells centuries ago.

'You think we're stupid. You think you can soft-talk me and I'll let you go and you'll toddle off back to your mother and tell her all about what the bad Powells done to poor Miss Devenish.'

'I don't know what you're talking about,' Jane lied desperately. 'I know you wouldn't do anything to Lucy. Just let me go home, Lloyd. I'm a bit pissed and everything, and I probably won't remember a thing in the morning. Just let me go back to the orchard and I'll find my own way home, all right?'

'Why'd you do that?' He leaned back, curious now. 'Why'd you take that bottle of cider into the orchard?'

'Couldn't very well drink it at home, could I? And that was where Colette and I came on—'

'Why there? Why under that tree?'

'I don't know. Colette—'

'Colette, Colette, Colette!' He slammed a fist into the

wheel. 'That little slapper! *You want me, don't you? Don't you, Lloydie?* Piece of rubbish. Piercing her body, advertising herself. And they paid for *that* to go to the Cathedral School.'

Jane said, 'I think I'm going to be sick.'

'Right.' Lloyd leaned on his door. A second later he was opening hers from the outside. 'Out.'

She didn't want to get out. She wondered if she could slide across and somehow start the truck and . . .

Lloyd gripped her arm above the elbow and squeezed on the muscle until she screamed in pain.

'*Out.*'

Outside, there were hulking buildings without lights. Barns and sheds. The air smelled of working farm.

'Go on then, Jane.'

She struggled out on legs that felt like foam rubber and stood shivering in a stiffened rut made by tractor wheels. The raspberry moon shone out of a bitter chocolate sky. She did want to heave now, but she wouldn't, not in front of *him*. Not to order, like a prisoner.

I'm a prisoner.

'You wanner be sick, be sick.'

'It's gone off.' She looked around for somewhere to run, but they were in a kind of stockade, fencing topped by barbed wire.

'You en't leaving now, Jane. Don't get ideas. And don't try and fool me with any ole crap about you don't understand. I'm gonner tell you, so you *will* understand. Only fair, that is. Lucy Devenish, see, she come up to talk to Father about Colonel Bull-Davies and his ole man, thinking as Father could help her clarify a few points.'

'It's nothing to do with me.' Jane said hopelessly. 'Honestly. Can't you—'

'No I bloody can't! Too soft-hearted, that's my trouble. I can feel sorry, see, but it don't get you nowhere. The little fluffy lamb's still gotter be killed, the ole sow's still gonner wind up hanging by her back legs, it's the way of the world. And some you en't sorry for, like the fox. When the ole fox starts rootin' around, he's gotter go. Fast. *Bang.*'

Lloyd clapped his big hands.

'And that was the way Lucy Devenish went. Clean and neat and efficient.'

'No!' Jane threw her hands over her ears. 'I don't want to know!'

'Father driving the truck, he pulls in front of the little bike, I tumbles out the ole dead ewe . . . *smack*. Happens in a twinkling. She don't know a thing. Takes off like an owl from a branch. Dead before she hit the ground, wouldn't surprise me. Their hearts en't too strong, that age. Efficient, that was.'

'Efficient? You're completely insane!'

'She wouldn't've suffered anyway,' Lloyd said reassuringly. 'We'd just've banged her ole head one more time on the tarmac. We can be humane, see, when we need to be. Ole Lucy, she was a nuisance, no question, got these funny ideas and she couldn't leave well alone and she got Father in a right state the stuff she was comin' out with, but' – he shrugged – 'she was still one of us. So when she's in the way, when she's gotter go, then it's done humanely.'

He nodded and smacked the side of the truck. His clean-cut face shining in the moonlight with pride at a job well done. He straightened up, stood with his hands on his hips and contemplated Jane.

'And then there's you,' he said.

'I suppose I'm in the way, too.'

Momentarily astonished at how calm her voice sounded now there was no need to pretend any more, now that there was nowhere to run and nobody to hear her screams. She looked up at the pink moon, and it occurred to her that this could be the last moon she would ever see. She felt full of hate and terror, but hazy too. Hazey Jane cursing the night. But remote from it all, somehow because people like Lloyd just couldn't *be*, not in the modern world.

'I can't make up my mind, see,' Lloyd said, 'what you are. A fox or a lamb. Or even a badger. You ever been on a badger-dig?'

'No! That's disgusting—'

'Illegal now, mind. But it goes on. It has to go on, see, else how we gonner keep 'em down? Had him near enough wiped out in these parts once, ole brock, pesky ole bugger, but the conservationists, who know best, see, from their offices in London and them places, they lets the badger back to spread tuberculosis through our herds. Badgers coming back as fast as townies in their holiday cottages, and they said we couldn't touch 'em.'

'That was never proved,' Jane said, clutching at another conversational straw. 'Tuberculosis.'

'Never *proved*. Arseholes, it wasn't. All I'm saying, badger on my land, he goes down, and if I can have a bit of fun with him before he goes, where's the harm there? He's dead anyway at the end. What difference is half an hour gonner make?'

'Not badger *baiting*?' Jane said faintly.

'Aye, if you wanner call it that. Feller from up north, he brings his terriers once in a while. Ole brock, he gets dug out, we throws him to the dogs. It's a bit of fun. It's cheap. Nobody gets harmed, 'cept the badger and that's his fault for being a badger. And the dogs sometimes, but we stitch 'em up, no problem.'

'That's *despicable*.'

'Why?' His face puckered slightly in genuine puzzlement. 'You don't look at things the right way round. A savage bastard, he is, the badger when he gets going. Or if it's a female with young. Or any kind of female. Asking for it. Daring you to do it.' Lloyd leaned against his white truck, arms folded. 'Asking for it,' he repeated. He looked up at the moon. In a parody of a wheedling, posh, female voice, he said, *'You want me, don't you, Lloydie?'*

Turned to Jane. 'They all want you, see, women. Bit of a catch, a farmer, always was. You get stuck with the wrong one, mind, she's hard to dislodge, so you gotter get it right. Drummed into me from early on, this was. *You gotter get it right.'*

She didn't know what he was saying.

'Gotter get it . . . *right.'* He hacked a heel into one of the truck's back tyres. 'Meantimes,' he said, 'you does a bit of badger-baiting, kind of thing. Come along, Jane, I'll show you the ole cider house.'

Deep Offence

As each name was written down by DC Thomas, the person was allowed to go. Few had. There was, perhaps, a sense that this electric night was not yet over.

The laborious procedure at least had given Merrily time to assemble her thoughts. After Gomer had told her about Hannah Snell and the rest, they had gone back outside, Gomer to report back to Lol and find Jane.

While Merrily had made three slow circuits of the church, trembling with a fearful excitement. All the time, the thoughts assembling in her head like blocks falling together, compacting, until she found she was looking at a solid, stone staircase. Leading all the way to the top of the vicarage.

Now she was walking back into the church, where Ken Thomas was coming to the end of his list. She stopped by his table.

'Merrily Watkins,' she said. 'The Vicarage, Ledwardine.'

I, Merrily Rose Watkins . . .

The image, from the Installation service, of an empty church. Something crawling up the stone-flagged aisle, naked and pale and wracked and twisted.

Poor Wil. You came in the evening.

When the weight was too much to bear, you came in and you locked the door behind you and shed your hated clothing and went down on the cold stones and crawled, sobbing, on

hands and knees, along the aisle and up the chancel steps until
the altar was above you.

And there you showed yourself to God and you called out, 'Is
this right . . . IS THIS RIGHT?

'You all right, Vicar?' Ken Thomas said.

'Sorry. Miles away.'

'Been a long night,' Ken said. He lowered his voice.
'Bloody disgrace, her not saying a word to you. Humiliating
you like that. Should've told you. No excuse for it. Complain, I would.'

Merrily shook her head. 'Thanks, anyway.' She started to
walk away then went back. 'Ken, I don't suppose you'll be
hanging around for a while?'

'Well, I'm supposed to call in, but most times they've got
a job remembering who I am these days. You rather I stayed
until you locked up?'

'I think I would. We had a bit of . . . vandalism, earlier.'

'What was that, then?'

'Well, it's kind of complicated. If you stick around, all will
be clear. Possibly.'

She moved slowly towards the chancel, past James Bull-
Davies, who was still standing on his own, while Alison
watched him thoughtfully, leaning over the back pew of the
northern aisle. Merrily didn't look at James. She walked
halfway along the chancel, past the choir stalls, to the spot
where she'd imagined the twisted, naked thing that was Wil
Williams asking, *Is this right?*

Is it the right *thing?* she'd said to Lol. That's the only
question, isn't it, when you think about it.

And it had seemed right, to find the truth and lay it out.
She could have become a lawyer, working the criminal and
civil courts towards a similar end. The first courtrooms had
surely been constructed in imitation of churches, down to
the presence of the Bible. But in church there was only one

judge; the preacher in the pulpit was merely an advocate, at worst a hell-and-damnation prosecutor . . .

But is it the *right* thing to do?

Merrily walked up to the altar and knelt and prayed for guidance.

'If this is wrong,' she said aloud, 'maybe you could just strike me down.'

Everyone else seemed to have.

*

Lol looked into the box of The Wine of Angels to confirm that two bottles were indeed missing. He showed Gomer the Dancing Gates story in Mrs Leather's book.

'It's obvious. She thinks she can reach Colette. She thinks Lucy wants that.'

Gomer was dubious. 'She'd go down there on her own? To the place where ole Edgar done isself in?'

Merrily had given him a key to the vicarage and he'd been in there to make sure there was no Jane. All the way to the top floor. Nothing, except for a little black cat watching him from the hallstand.

'It's where they both went once. Whether she fully believes it or she'll think she has to try it.'

'Right then,' Gomer said. 'Let's not waste no more time.'

With a long, rubber torch they'd found in the kitchen, they went the back way, over Lucy's fence, across the old bowling green towards the orchard.

'I don't know what to say about this kind o' thing,' Gomer said. 'When I was a boy, people laughed. When my granny was a girl, nobody laughed. What's that? Barely a century. For hundreds of years, folk never questions there's more in an orchard, more in a cornfield. Few decades of computers and air-conditioned tractors, even the farmers thinks it's all balls. Sad, en't it? Computers and air-conditioned bloody tractors.'

'Watch yourself,' Lol said, 'there's brambles all over the place.'

'Aye.' Gomer chuckled wryly through his ciggy. 'Some orchard, this is. Never could figure it. They gets bugger-all off it, but they keeps it tickin' over. Plants a couple o' new trees every year, chops down a dead 'un for firewood. But they won't plough him up, start again, do it proper – Superstition, I used to reckon, disguised as concern for the village heritage. But you look at Rod Powell, do he *look* like a superstitious man.'

'What's a superstitious man look like?'

'Superstitious man looks more like you, Lol, you want the truth.'

'Thank you, Gomer.'

'More like you than Powell is all.'

'Why'd he go along with the wassailing, then?'

'No way he could refuse. Cassidy says it's in the interests of the village, Powell's a councillor . . . *Bugger me!*'

Gomer stopped in the clearing where the Apple Tree Man stood. Twin pink moons in his glasses gave him a nightmare quality.

'I've fuckin' got it, boy! Why The Wine of Angels tastes like it's been through a horse! Listen. Cassidy, he wants to revive the ole cider industry, right? Well, that's a tall order, given all the established firms. But if they does manage to get it off the ground, the first thing happens, see, is they get the experts in, and they looks at this lot and cracks up laughin'. Grub the bloody lot up, they'd say, not cost effective. Plough up the whole flamin' orchard, plant some nice neat rows of dwarf trees—'

'Could you have a dwarf Pharisees Red?'

'Pharisees Red, Red Streak, where's the difference? Orchardin's moved on, it en't what it was.'

'So why don't the Powells want it dug—' Lol stared down at the base of the Apple Tree Man. 'Oh, Jesus.'

Gomer's grin was savage. 'You're thinkin' wild at last, boy.'

*

When Merrily came down from the altar, Caroline Cassidy was waiting for her.

'I don't know why I'm still here. I don't really know why I came. Terrence refused. He said he would prefer to wait by the phone. I almost walked out when poor Stefan made that woman tell the story about the girl who was raped and then hanged herself.'

With that story, Merrily realized now, poor Stefan was making more of a point than he imagined.

'Knowing that these things have always happened to young girls doesn't make it any better,' Caroline said.

'People got away with it then,' Merrily said. 'Now they seldom do.' Perhaps, she thought, we're here to bring peace to the spirits of old victims. Perhaps that's the secret of restoring balance to a community.

'They've been stopping motorists and showing them her photograph,' Caroline said. 'Now they're even talking about some sort of reconstruction, though what use that would be in a village this size, I can't imagine.'

'Get it on television again.'

'What's the use of that? Colette's dead. No . . . No . . .' Caroline warded off Merrily's protests with an impatient wave. 'Don't give me the obligatory platitudes. I only wish . . . I only wish she'd been going through a *nicer phase* when she . . . I mean, some people had a chance to grow up, to change for the better. And didn't. Won't be many mourners for Richard Coffey, will there, horrible man? It's poor Stefan one feels sorry for. I would hate . . . I'm sorry, don't think I know what I'm saying.'

'Stefan could be a free man in a few years and getting more acting jobs than ever,' Merrily said. 'It is, actually, Coffey I feel sorry for. Caroline, look, I'm going to start something in a minute, and if the other bit disturbed you, it could be fairly painful. So, if you want to leave, this might be a good time.'

'It won't be,' Caroline said absently. 'There won't be any more good times for us here.'

Merrily stepped up to the pulpit and, for the first time ever, took out the microphone from the shelf underneath. She pushed in the jack-plug, switched on, tapped the mike, heard a thump from both sides of the rood screen. She needed this tonight; there were a lot of people, a lot of tension and she didn't want to have to shout, to sound like a preacher.

Right.

'Erm . . . could I . . . could I have your attention?'

The sound was far louder than she'd expected. Everyone stopped speaking, even Bull-Davies turned round. Merrily moved back from the mike.

'Perhaps, when Ken's finished taking the names, those of you who are interested in, er, the truth about Wil Williams and, er . . . and other things . . . might like to return to your pews. Thank you.'

*

Lol held up The Wine of Angels bottle in the beam of Gomer's long, black torch.

'Unopened.'

The Apple Tree Man was still heavily blossomed, despite the dead branches. Lol thought of Dickens's Miss Havisham in her wedding dress. Grotesque. Wrong.

Gomer bent down to sniff the grass. 'The other bottle got opened, my guess, and some got spilled. But where's he gone, that bottle?'

Was it likely she'd wandered off, drinking out of the bottle? But that wasn't what happened last time. She'd be trying to replicate that, to summon the little golden lights. And then Colette.

'Maybe she cleared off when she heard us coming. She wouldn't know who it was. Jane? *Jane!*'

No answer.

'What do we do now, Gomer?'

Gomer was looking at the Apple Tree Man.

'I was yere when ole Edgar blowed his head off. Accident? Balls if that were an accident, any more'n Lucy.'

'What, somebody killed—'

'No, you pillock, he killed hisself, all right. But it weren't no accident. Bull-Davies fixed that inquest verdict, I reckon, just like the Bulls always fixed things for the Powells on account the Powells fixed other things for the Bulls.'

'How do you know it was deliberate?'

'Comin' to it, en't I? See, Edgar Powell, he was ninety year old, near enough, and quite a few bales short of a full barn by then. So Edgar's standin' yere with both barrels ready to go, and anybody can see the poor ole bugger can't remember why the hell he's come. Wassailin'? What the hell do Edgar know about wassailin'? 'Specially not the foreign kind them Cassidys organized. All he's pickin' up is aggravation, Mrs Cassidy yellin' at Lucy, Lucy yellin' back, and it all boils up into a mush until it's time to do the business and Rod gives the ole feller a nudge, and mabbe up until then he's been asleep on his feet like an ole shire horse. And he comes round with a jerk . . . I seen this. He's standin' . . .'

Gomer walked about five yards back from the tree and dug a Doc Marten heel into the grass.

'. . . yere. Just about. And he looks down, and I swear to God, the look come on his face, I thought the ole boy was gonner mess his britches. Not scared exactly, more . . . hunted, like . . . Hunted. Aye. Days later it come to me what Lucy Devenish said mabbe a split second 'fore that. Can never remember the exact words, see, but it was about causin' *offence*. To the tree and all that . . . lives yere, lies yere . . . *Deep offence*. Summat like that. And that was what put the shits up ole Edgar, I reckon. And then he done hisself.'

Gomer spat out the remains of his roll-up before it could burn the skin off his lips.

'She meant the spirits,' Lol said.

'Ar. But what did *Edgar* think she meant? You know what I'd like, Lol? I'd like to bring ole Gwynneth out yere and 'ave a bit of a dig around this yere tree.'

'But if there's something buried here and the Powells know about it, why would they let them hold the wassailing here?'

'Where else in this orchard you gonner 'ave it? Nice clearin', see, for the folk to gather in and so Mrs Cassidy don't ladder her tights on no brambles. 'Sides, it wouldn't worry Rod. Rod wouldn't turn a hair. It was just Edgar comin' out of his stupor, realizin' where he is and hearin' the voice of doom.'

'Lucy.'

'Lucy. God rest her soul.'

'Meanwhile, there's Jane.'

'Ar. Let's be realistic yere, Lol. Some bastard mighter took 'er.'

Lol said, 'You don't like the Powells, do you?'

*

Important to get the voice right. Firm, but not preachy, not hectoring, not *clever*. After Stefan and James, they wouldn't be sure who they could believe. And on the last occasion the Reverend Watkins stood before them in this church, she'd had to be helped out of it.

She looked around the congregation. There were about sixty people in church, though the men and women were not separated any more, except for Alison Kinnersley and the eternal Bull, sprawling in the Bull pew. Ted Clowes had gone. Dermot Child had gone. Possibly a good sign, who could tell?

'OK.' Pushing up the sleeves of her ill-gotten, black cashmere sweater. 'Earlier tonight, someone went into the Bull Chapel and broke into the tomb of Thomas Bull.'

Fewer gasps than might have been expected, but understandably so, given the preceding drama. Ken Thomas appeared interested.

'Anyone want to confess?' she asked Jim Prosser, who couldn't have appeared less guilty.

Not a murmur.

'Anyone like to finger anyone else? Too public?'

Merrily looked directly at Alison Kinnersley. She was wearing a dark tweed suit with a cameo brooch. She didn't look like a mistress.

'I mean, it wasn't *desecration*. It wasn't *black magic* . . . In that, as far as I could see, the body remained undisturbed. But something, I think, was removed. Whatever it was, there was a little space for it, just under the feet of the effigy of

Tom Bull. My guess is a journal. Or part of one. Just the relevant pages.'

She paused. 'Say, for instance, the record of a certain incident.'

She waited. She shifted her gaze from Alison, now a shadow, to the roof timbers. Clasped her hands loosely in front of her.

'I know this sort of thing is often best kept . . . in the family, in the loosest sense . . .'

'O . . . K.' Alison Kinnersley's long sigh was audible the length of the nave. 'What do you want me to say? You've been very astute, Vicar. He brought it into the Hall when he came back to phone the police about Coffey. Under the circumstances, he was less careful than he usually is. He slipped it into a drawer in his desk.'

Merrily risked a glance at Bull-Davies. He remained motionless, his arm along the back of the pew. There was enough light to show that his face had hardened, his mouth tightened; his eyes seemed to have retreated under the heavy brow.

'I read it, of course,' Alison said. 'And you're quite correct. It relates to Wil Williams and it looks pretty genuine. I suppose you want to know what it says.'

Bull-Davies stood at once and spun like a soldier on parade. He pointed, as he'd done earlier at Stefan, throwing out an arm as though it held a sword.

'You,' he said. 'Have no damned *right*.'

'I have *every* right.' A voice that wanted to shed some old burden. 'As you implied, Vicar, I'm fam—'

'Miss Kinnersley . . .' Merrily tapped on the microphone. Not the time, not yet. 'I don't want to cause any undue distress. Perhaps it would be better if you didn't actually reveal the contents of those papers at this stage.'

There was a low but perceptible moan of disappointment from disabled Miss Goddard, sitting next to Minnie Parry, who still kept looking around for Gomer.

Merrily said into the microphone, 'Perhaps I can save you the trouble, anyway. Does it, perhaps, offer an entirely new perspective on Wil himself?'

A hush.

'I don't actually know what you mean,' Alison said.

'Like that I am not actually the first woman priest of Ledwardine?'

Vision

The cider house! He took her in the ole cider house, where they say he took all his women. Because the air itself in there, they used to say, the smell of it could make you· drunk. So's you wouldn't notice. The cider house. It was always the ole cider house. It made you drunk, to be in there. And . . . wanton.

The description, with its overtones of the erotic and the forbidden, had lodged in Jane's mind.

But surely the woman whom Stefan had called Bessie couldn't have been referring to this hellhole.

Jane was no longer in the least bit drunk. She was far from wanton.

She was frightened of what would happen. She was cold.

The cider house was damp, had no windows, was lit by a fluorescent strip set into the low roof of blackened timber which sent a wobbly, purplish, hospital sort of light up the thick walls of old, discoloured bricks. There was a putrid smell, like rotten potatoes.

The cider house was a nasty place. No one would ever buy a bottle of The Wine of Angels if they thought it had been produced in here. It couldn't have been. Surely.

Yet all the equipment was here. There was a mill: a big stone-sided tub that you put the apples in so that they could be crushed to pulp by the great stone wheel. It was pulled round by a horse or, in this case, pushed by men leaning on a projecting pole of wood or metal – this one was so dirty it was difficult to tell which.

And there was a press, like a giant printing press: a wooden scaffold with an enormous wooden screw down the middle, to tighten a sandwich of slabs and squeeze the juice from the pulped apples.

Over the mill was a kind of hayloft full of black bin sacks. There was no sign of apples, even rotten ones, but why should there be? The harvest was five months away.

Still, it was all wrong. So filthy that the old, rustic machinery looked like engines of pain from some medieval torture chamber.

Jane sat huddled against a wall, describing the cider-making process, as if to a party of visitors, going into all kinds of detail, most of which was probably wrong. You had to give your mind something to do, try and think of something normal and interesting. It was useless, in this atmosphere, closing your eyes and trying to put yourself on a beach in Tunisia or a fishing harbour in Greece or an exhibition of nice, clean paintings by Mondrian.

'Of course, hygiene was never considered terribly important in cider-making in the old days,' Jane said. 'Indeed, it was frequently asserted that in some areas a dead rat would always be added to give it a certain piquancy.'

Which was one ingredient they wouldn't go short of in this dump.

In trying to make herself laugh, Jane only succeeded in crying again and asking herself, between sobs, why a respectable councillor and his son should want to kill a lovable old lady on a moped.

. . . come up to talk to Father about Colonel Bull-Davies and his ole man, thinking as Father could help her clarify a few points. Got Father in a right state the stuff she was comin' out with.

It was the way he was so matter of fact about it. Lucy must have gone to see Councillor Powell directly after talking to Jane in the street. What could she possibly have said to get Garrod Powell in 'a state'? And how could you tell?

Jane started to laugh again. Was this what they called hysteria?

The lock scraped and the great, thick oak door cranked open and Lloyd was standing there, the big key dangling and night behind him.

'He en't back, Jane,' Lloyd said grumpily. 'Said he'd be back before ten.' He stared at Jane, suspicious. 'What you laughing at? What you done?'

Normally, she would have said, *Wouldn't you like to know?* – something sarky. Not with Lloyd. Lloyd wouldn't recognize even sarcasm. It wasn't that he wasn't intelligent. He probably was. That was what was so awful. You learned that you had to play everything dead straight. Like when she'd said – in sudden disgust at his sniffy, narrow-minded attitude towards Colette – that she was going to be sick, he'd taken it literally.

She was scared to mention Colette. Didn't dare ask herself why.

'Nothing,' she said. 'I haven't got anything to laugh at, have I? I don't understand why you're doing this. You don't think people aren't looking for me by now, do you?'

Lloyd looked appalled, insulted. 'Nobody ever looks *yere*! Father's a *magistrate*. He used to be on the police committee. Grandfather was Chairman of Planning for many years. Great-grandfather was to have been Mayor of Hereford, but he died.'

Like a litany.

'I expect you'll be standing for the council, too, then,' Jane said.

'When I'm thirty-five.'

'Jesus,' said Jane.

'Nice language from a vicar's daughter.'

'Oh, yeah!' Jane lost it. 'And how nice is it' – she sprang to her feet – 'to keep a vicar's daughter in this disgusting pit?'

Lloyd's expression didn't change.

'Two things,' he said. 'One, my father was not in favour of the appointment of your mother but he was prepared to support her in the interests of local democracy. Two, you wouldn't be yere if you hadn't behaved like a little slut, would you?'

Jane pushed her knuckles into her eyes. He couldn't be like this, really. Not cool, slim-but-muscular Lloyd Powell in his denims and his white truck, not hunky Lloyd, the *Young Farmers' News* centrefold. How could genetics be so horribly linear? How could this not be a stupid nightmare?

Not going to cry this time.

She wrenched her fists away from her face and blinked. He was still there.

'And to think we thought you looked like a young Paul Weller.'

'Who's Paul Weller?' said Lloyd.

'God.'

'Anyway,' Lloyd said. 'I just come to say Father en't back yet and when he is I'll be bringing him in to you and let him decide.'

'Decide what?'

'You know,' he said uncomfortably.

Don't ask. She bit her lip hard.

'I don't know what you're going on like that for,' Lloyd said. 'It's all your fault. We got that much on now, see, with the festival and all.'

'What did . . . what did Lucy tell your father to make him so upset?'

'Business is that of yours?' he said sternly.

'I'm sure she didn't mean to.'

'Oh, you are, are you?'

'It was probably all a mistake. It's very easy to get things all wrong. If you let me go . . .'

She let the sentence trail off because Lloyd had put his hands on his hips and his head to one side.

'You really do think we're stupid, don't you?'

'No, I . . . I don't.'

'Trying to soft-talk me now, is it, like I'm some mad psycho? Lord above, Jane, *it en't like that*. We are ordinary people who serve the local community as best we can and have done for many generations.'

God, he was as much of a museum piece as the cider press.

'And you always serve the Bull-Davieses, don't you?' she said. 'The Bulls.'

'Our families have had a close relationship for a number of years, yes. We don't *serve* them. That time's gone. We *respect* them and they respect us. It's mutual respect that holds a rural community together in a way you don't get in the cities, that's why you got all this crime and drugs and street violence.'

'What . . .?' She couldn't hold it back. 'You just confessed to a murder!'

'*Confessed?*'

Lloyd stormed into the cider house, kicked the door shut with his heel.

'You calling me a common criminal, miss? Like it was *wrong* to stop that woman spreadin' her filth and lies and undermining a stable community built on respect? That's what's criminal, Jane.'

He towered over her, one foot half over both of hers. She cowered instinctively, which seemed to excite him.

'Father en't back soon,' he said. 'I en't gonner wait.'

'Why don't you go and look for him?'

'Shut your mouth, Jane, before I . . .'

He stepped back and pulled something out of his jeans. Jane screamed.

'Only my mobile, Jane.' Lloyd opened the phone and moved closer to the fluorescent tube. 'I phoned him twice, but he won't take his phone into church, see. Not respectful.'

He stabbed out the number and waited, with the phone at his ear. 'Come on, Father, come *on*. Funny thing . . .' She saw his mouth twist in amusement over the lip of the mobile. 'I thought you were a bit different at first. Even thought you might make a wife in a year or two. Funny how first impressions can be deceiving.'

*

'It was Lucy Devenish who put us on to it,' Merrily said. 'Though I suspect it was me coming here that put Lucy on to the idea. I don't think she could prove it, but she was expecting it to *be* proved. The arrival in Ledwardine of a female minister . . . Well, she seems to have thought that would set something off, and perhaps it did. Certainly in the vicarage. But that's . . . I'll come back to that, if I can.'

The amazing thing was not that everybody she'd looked at – including James Bull-Davies and Alison Kinnersley – had shown genuine surprise, but that nobody out there now looked sceptical. Most were clearly intrigued. Bull-Davies seemed confused and unhappy. Only Garrod Powell, as usual, was expressionless.

Merrily felt strangely and completely relaxed. All the pressure had lifted from her chest. She was not nervous. Her breathing was even.

'There's no reason to doubt that the person who became

Wil Williams was indeed a protégée of Susannah Hopton, of Kington, having been introduced to her in the 1660s. It seems more likely to me that Mrs Hopton would have taken a girl into her house than a man. And a hard-up Radnorshire hill farmer would be rather more likely to spare his daughter than his son. Certainly Mrs Hopton would have been fascinated by someone so utterly committed to the Christian life that she was prepared to abandon her womanhood for it.'

'Let me get this right, Mrs Watkins,' Bull-Davies said. 'You are suggesting that Williams managed to con his – or her – way through university and bamboozle the Church of England into accepting her as a man, and then went on to practise as a clergyman for several years without once—'

'Yes.'

'It's ridiculous. No one would get away with it.'

'Have you heard of Hannah Snell, James?'

'Should I have?'

'Hannah Snell was born in Worcester about a century after Wil Williams. She made a name for herself on the London stage, singing songs and telling tales of her bizarre life which began – the bizarre part – when her husband, a Dutch sailor, disappeared. Hannah went off to try and find him. Joined the army, later the Marines. Travelled as far as India. Was obliged, on occasion, to share a bed with servicemen and was also, allegedly, stripped to the waist for a flogging. During all that time, nobody seems ever to have spotted she was a woman.'

'That's true,' Jim Prosser shouted. 'A fact, that is. And she wasn't butch, neither, apparently.'

Merrily said, 'And there was nothing about this in the Bull journal? They must have discovered the truth about Wil after death, at least.'

'Nothing that I could see,' Alison said. She'd left her seat

589

at the back and moved to the choir stalls, possibly to observe James's reaction. 'It concerns the death itself more than anything.'

James looked sullen again.

'We'll come to that,' Merrily said. 'I'm just trying to show that if Hannah Snell could pass herself off as a front-line fighting man for over five years, then it would certainly be possible for a young woman to get through college and become ordained and serve as a priest. Especially if she had the support of people of the order of Susannah Hopton and Thomas Traherne.'

Merrily switched off the microphone, leaned over the pulpit.

'Look, we know hardly anything about the real Wil Williams and I doubt we're ever going to. We presume she went to Oxford as a man – perhaps there are records, I don't know. We can only speculate. About many things. Like why the estimable Thomas Traherne, who so loved Hereford and delighted in the countryside, should have gone so readily to London. Perhaps he too was in love and knew better than anyone why it was doomed.'

'That's an enchanting thought,' said Mrs Goddard, the crippled horsewoman. 'He never married, you know. He died at thirty-seven.'

Bull-Davies snorted. Merrily wondered whether Lol Robinson, who was also thirty-seven, knew that Traherne had died at precisely that age. She was suddenly worried about Lol. And Jane. She would have to end this soon.

'What must it've been like for her, though?' Effie Prosser said. 'A woman alone in that big vicarage, pretending to be a man.'

Merrily thought for a moment before responding.

'I know exactly what it was like.'

'You're really a man, are you, Mrs Watkins?'

'Mr Davies,' said Mrs Goddard, 'I'm getting rather tired of the sound of your voice. Please go on, Mrs Watkins.'

'Well, she wouldn't have *been* alone,' Merrily said. 'That's the first point. Ministers in those days, I gather, were rather more up-market than they are today. So there would have been servants. Certainly other people in that house from whom she would have had to hide the truth. Can you imagine the problems that would cause? She'd have no privacy in her own house. Except . . .'

Merrily no longer wanted to be in the pulpit. She wanted to be a woman, not just a minister. She came down and sat on the chancel steps, as Stefan, as Wil, had done.

'. . . except in the attic. I . . . feel . . . that the attic was the only place where she felt free to be a woman. Even her bedchamber on the first floor would have been cleaned and tidied by a maid. So it would have to be a masculine room. When I'm on that floor, particularly, I sometimes sense a . . . constriction. Perhaps I imagine that. Perhaps it's psychological.'

'Or perhaps you are psychic,' said Mrs Goddard brightly.

Merrily tried to look dubious.

'I feel she went through quite a lot of pain, both emotional and physical, flattening her chest, deepening her voice, never daring to show herself in public without the bindings or corsets or whatever she wore. Unlike Traherne, she couldn't go out in the countryside with any sense of freedom. She couldn't even go into her beloved orchard and just be herself, without the risk of being seen.'

The images were coming to her as she spoke. She felt she was quivering with vision.

'So she made a place for herself. A dark, secret place, where she could perhaps keep women's clothes. Parade at night in the flimsiest, most frivolous of dresses. And weep. Silently, of course. Always silently. In the attic of the vicarage.'

I saw her. Oh my God, I saw her.

'I . . . It's funny . . .' She looked up. 'My daughter, Jane, was drawn to the attic from the moment she entered the house. I was thinking what a miserable, draughty-looking house it was, and Jane was dashing upstairs and claiming the attic for herself.'

She thought of the Mondrian walls which had become orchard walls. Had whoever became Wil Williams lain up there and closed her eyes and dreamed of walking out as a woman, smelling apple scents. Seeing those little golden lights among the branches and floating, like Jane on cheap cider? Had the presence – the spirit – of the orchard manifested there?

*

It was getting on for midnight. Gomer sat down at the base of the tree, where the moon couldn't find his glasses.

'All right,' he said, 'I'll tell you why I don't like the Powells.'

Lol was getting restive. He didn't know what to do but he wanted to be doing it. Could Gomer make it brief?

'En't a long story.'

Went back mainly to that day fifteen or so years ago, when Rod hired Gomer Parry Plant Hire to dig some drainage ditches. The hot day, when he'd had some of Edgar's excellent cider, made from the Pharisees Reds. Except the cider wasn't served up by Edgar or Rod, who were both at a cattle sale that day.

'Jennifer, it was. Jennifer Powell. Jennifer Adair, who used to work in the kitchen at the Black Swan.'

'Lloyd's mother?'

'And Rod's missus, and a hell of a nice girl. 'Er'd've been about thirty at the time and Lloyd was ten and Rod was forty and a bit more. They likes 'em younger, the Powells and they don't marry till late.'

Cut a long story short, it was clear Jennifer Powell had been crying and if you knew her mother-in-law, Meggie Powell, it didn't take long to work out she was the reason.

Tough wasn't the word for Meggie Powell.

'Built like a Hereford bull, face to match,' said Gomer. 'Bit less feminine, mabbe. When the 1959 flu epidemic took off half the fellers worked at the slaughterhouse there used to be, bottom of Ole Barn Lane, Meggie filled in for a fortnight. That kind o' woman, you know? Good wife to Edgar, mind, all senses of the word. Good mother to Garrod, likewise. By which I means . . . likewise.'

'Aw, shit,' said Lol.

'Ar, sixty-seventh woman Edgar slept with, sure t' be. First one for Rod.'

'You're kidding.'

'It was normal enough then, boy, some families. Normal sex education, like. Well, not normal, but not uncommon. Teach 'em young. Teach 'em how it all works. Self-sufficiency, see. Look after your own, don't make a mess, but if you do, make sure you clears up after yourself. And, above all, *keep it quiet.*'

What rural life was all about in the old days. Feller beat up his wife in the city all the neighbours knew about it. Same thing happened in the country . . . well, all the neighbours knew about it too, but they kept *quiet.* Anybody got really out of hand, they got dealt with. One way or another.

The Powell women were chosen with care, Gomer said. There were traditions they had to observe. Had to be a special sort of woman, which was not always the prettiest . . . Well, look at Meggie. By the time a Powell married, usually at thirty-five-plus, he'd sown his wild oats over a wide area and was ready to settle down and pass on his knowledge to the next generation. By Powell standards, however, Rod chose unwisely. Jennifer Adair was too prissy, too genteel and on the day, fifteen years ago, when Rod and his old man were at the cattle sale and Jennifer Powell learned, in a heart to heart with Meggie, what was going to be expected of her in relation to Lloyd in a couple of years' time, Jennifer fled the premises and wound up weeping into the upholstery of Gomer's Jeep.

'What it come down to, 'er knowed Rod must've put it about, though he never said much and she never asked, like. But one thing she couldn't cope with was the thought of spendin' the rest of her life sleeping next a feller slept with Meggie.'

'What happened?'

'I seen her point and give her a lift to Hereford Station and a hundred quid and she en't been back to this day, and not a word, Lol, boy, 'cause if Rod ever finds out I'm a dead man, and that en't a figure of speech, like. Behind that wooden mask, Garrod Powell's the bitterest bastard you'll ever meet. Never married again after Jennifer walked out, never a girlfriend – not seemly, like, not *proper*. Plus, he's doubly suspicious of all women, he don't *like* women. But you puts that together with a sex drive could light up half the county, you got a few big question marks, innit?'

'This common knowledge, Gomer?'

'Were never exactly *common* knowledge, except to the few of us working over a wide area of farms and such. And nowadays, when half the folk in Ledwardine was living other side of the country three year ago, ole Rod's a councillor and a gentleman and Lloyd's the decentest, politest boy you'd want your daughter to fetch back for Sunday tea.'

'I'm confused.' Lol massaged the back of his neck where

the ponytail used to lie. He was thinking about Patricia Young. 'I don't know whether we're looking at the Bulls or the Powells.'

'There you hit it, boy. People's always looked at the Bulls in the big house. Looks at the Bulls, don't see the Powells. But them two families been linked up for years, centuries. Lives are entirely separate, o' course. Bulls is walkin' out with nice ladies, doin' the hunt-ball circuit and what have you. The Powells is huntin' on another level. When mammy done her bit, see, the old man'd take over their education. Take the boy into town – bit further away, Ledbury, Abergavenny mabbe, show him how to hunt and not get hunted. Powells liked to marry late, like I said, so there'd be plenty of huntin' for a good few years. But there's huntin' . . . and there's baitin'.'

'What the difference?'

'Baitin's where you brings 'em back,' Gomer said grimly.

FIFTY-TWO

The Loft

It was the part she'd been worrying about. Merrily walked up the two steps to the chancel to whisper to Alison in the choir stalls.

'I know,' Alison said. 'I know what you're asking, and now I'm not so sure. I mean, for Christ's sake, look at him.'

James sat with his head bent, as if in prayer, revealing a bald patch like a tonsure.

'Sooner or later, somebody's going to have to explain what's in the Journal,' Merrily said, 'and it isn't going to be James, is it?'

'And if I don't do it, you'll tell him who I am, what I'm doing here, right?'

'No,' Merrily said. 'I'm never going to tell him. It's not my place.'

Emotions crowded Alison's starkly beautiful face. Merrily tried to see a resemblance there to James and couldn't.

'You see, it's changed some things,' Alison said. 'Fundamental things. I haven't taken in half this stuff tonight, I've just sat there going over and over it.'

'Look,' Merrily said. 'Whatever's in there, both you and James know exactly what it is, while everybody else is going to speculate for generations. It needs to come out. We're exorcizing this village tonight; you must have sensed that.'

'I don't trust what I sense,' Alison said. 'Not any more.'

*

As Alison walked from the choir stalls to the chancel steps, James Bull-Davies came out into the aisle.

'Alison. No. *No.*'

Alison walked down the steps. Merrily moved back against the pulpit.

'It's getting bloody late and I'm tired,' James said. 'I'm tired of defending my family against a load of pure fantasy. And I'm tired of you, Mrs Watkins. I'm tired of your smugness, your high-handedness, and I'm tired of your bloody voice.'

'Mr Davies, sit down *this instant*!' Mrs Goddard shook off her daughter's hand and rose painfully from her pew. 'I want to hear what Mrs Watkins and this young woman have to say and I want you to hear it too. You're emerging as even more of an obnoxious man than we thought and a liar to boot. Don't show yourself to be a coward as well. *Sit down!*'

He didn't sit down, but he didn't leave. He went to stand at the back, near the vestry curtain. DC Ken Thomas was watching him.

Alison stood just forward from the rood screen with its wooden apples. Her voice was muted but distinct.

'What we learn from the Journal is that Wil Williams was buried on the wrong side of the ditch. He . . . she . . . did not commit suicide.'

'Yes,' said Mrs Goddard, as if she'd known all along.

'Thomas Bull says nothing about having a physical infatuation with the minister, but he does say he came to believe he was bewitched. The implication is by Wil.'

'He doesn't *say* that!' Bull-Davies shouted in pain from the back of the church.

'Of course not,' Merrily said. 'But he wouldn't, would he? I think we can assume he was tortured in all kinds of ways. He was frightened of his own feelings, which were foreign to everything he'd always understood about himself. And perhaps he was worried about it coming out. I'm not qualified to comment on the level of anti-gay prejudice in the seventeenth century or whether Tom Bull was particularly homophobic. But he must have been pretty scared.'

Alison said, 'What seems likely – and this is very *strongly* implied, Jamie, whatever you say – is that Tom, having built up this spurious witchcraft case against Wil, then became extremely paranoid about what might come out in court.'

Merrily came to stand next to Alison, to give her some support. 'She wasn't even hanged, was she?'

'Oh, she was hanged, Merrily. She was hanged after death. They took the body out to the orchard and put a rope around its neck and hung it from the tallest apple tree.'

'No!' James howled.

'She was probably strangled,' Alison said.

Merrily said, 'Tom Bull admits that she was murdered?'

'Tom Bull agrees that Wil Williams was murdered. The extreme remorse he shows only really makes sense when you start to think of Wil as a woman.'

'He was not a *bad* man,' James said. 'Not the brutal arch-villain you're making out. He overreacted.'

'Ha,' said Mrs Goddard.

'James,' Merrily said, 'for God's sake . . . there's a lot of things you could clear up. You took those papers out of the tomb, so obviously the family knew they were there. I don't understand why, if the Bulls and Bull-Davieses were so embarrassed by all this, that journal wasn't simply destroyed years ago.'

'Because you're not damn well *supposed* to understand. It's no one's business but ours.'

'Oh, you pompous prick!' Alison threw up her arms. 'Can't you ever see the virtues of opening out, hanging out the dirty washing? You're so curled up and tight inside it's a wonder you can breathe. Come on, James. For Christ's sake, come out here.'

'You don't understand, you can't understand . . .'

'But we need to,' Merrily said. 'Because we know that poor Wil Williams was only the start.'

Alison put out an elegant hand. 'James . . .'

For close to half a minute, James Bull-Davies remained motionless.

Then, slowly, he pushed himself from the back wall and moved into the central aisle.

Alison didn't move.

Jim Prosser started to clap.

As James walked towards the chancel, other villagers joined in the applause, and Mrs Goddard banged her stick on the stones. When James Bull-Davies was halfway to the front, someone squeezed out of a pew, and he and James glanced at each other once. James carried on walking. The other figure moved silently towards the south porch, where Ken Thomas blocked his way.

'I think it's better nobody leaves just yet, if you don't mind, sir . . . Oh, sorry, Rod.'

'Bit late this, Ken, for a farmer.'

'Sorry, Rod,' said Ken, moving aside at once.

*

Lloyd had gone out again to wait for his father. Periodically she would hear him tramp past the door or the beep-beep of his fingers on the phone as he tried to reach his father's mobile.

Jane seethed. The idea of this brutal, humourless tosser sizing her up as a future bride blew through her fear. She would refuse to think what he might do to her. She'd think instead of what she might do to *him*.

She got to her feet, her jeans feeling disgustingly damp from the straw, and crept silently around the cider house. Perhaps there was a wooden paddle or something they used to push the apples around in the mill. She imagined herself waiting behind the door with it raised and smashing it down on him when he next came in. It always worked in films.

But then, in films, there was always something handy. The only stave in the cider house was the one used to turn the screw mechanism on the press and this proved to be metal and bolted firmly into place, and the bolts were so rusty even a wrench wouldn't dislodge them.

She kicked about in the hay, in case there was something underneath. Only flagstones.

Nothing. Nothing, nothing, *nothing*.

She flung herself at a wall, scratching at the bricks on the off chance one was loose and could be prised out and she could throw it at him.

Hopeless. Was she even strong enough to hurl a brick with any force? She still tried, going from wall to wall, even looking up at the roof to see if there was a loose slate (which she could send skimming at his throat, oh, sure . . .) arriving finally at the hayloft over the mill. She'd forgotten all about that.

Worth a try. She might be able to hide up there and drop something on his head. Height was always an advantage, wasn't it?

There was no ladder (which, anyway, she would have broken up for a hefty stick) but only a couple of feet separated the loft from the top of the stone millwheel.

No problem, probably. Jane tested the thick wooden axle stuck through a hole in the middle of the stone. It was all so crude, in a Flintstones kind of way, but the wood wasn't rotten and she was able to get a foot on it to hoist herself to the top of the wheel.

She had an awful vision of the wheel suddenly rolling away, leaving her dangling from the rafters, but it was as solid as a rock, which she supposed it actually was, and she hauled herself up, quite easily in the end, into the loft, where she rolled over and flopped on her stomach between a couple of black bin liners. (She could wait behind the door with one and throw it over his head, then duck behind him to freedom; oh Jesus, this was getting ridiculous.) It seemed much brighter up here; the fluorescent tube was only about three feet away; and she felt exposed and pushed herself back from the edge until she felt her feet slot into the narrow area where the rafters met the sloping slates.

Now she was up here, the total seriousness of the situation clouded around her. Her bowels felt suddenly weak and she threw her arms over one of the bin sacks to stifle a sob. *Oh, Mum, please be looking for me. Please, please, plea—*

The evil little smell from the bin sack had entered her nose like a thin needle.

Not a smell she knew, but one she had a horrid feeling she ought to.

Before she realized what she was doing, she'd drawn the plastic back.

Over the damp hair and the soft, white skin, purpled by the light. The open, bulging eyes and the big, squashy lips, and the tongue out like a dog's.

The diamond nose-stud winking in the clinical light.

Watching

'I'm a bloody madman, en't I?' Gomer said. 'Even look like a bloody madman, so people tell me. I got a wife en't gonner speak to me for a month as a result of what I already done tonight this far. So what do we do, boy? What we gonner do about this?'

'The cider house?'

'The cider house where the Bulls took their women until they give it to the Powells. Soon as Tess Roberts told that story tonight, it bothered me. Had to go out, have a ciggy. Whatever they're doin' in that cider house it en't makin' cider.'

'Whereabouts is it?'

'Top of a field, other side o' the new road, as I recall. A barn, an ole sheep shed and the cider house. Used to be a tiny little shepherd's cottage there at one time, but that got pulled down years back.'

'You want to take a look?' Lol said. 'Put your mind at rest?' Meaning put *my* mind at rest. If they'd found Jane he'd have said, Let's call it a night, let's go and find Merrily and talk about all of this, see how it looks in daylight.

But they hadn't found Jane.

'Unpredictable kid, though, Gomer. She comes and goes. Has her own ideas, her own apartment in the vicarage. She could be back there now, for all we know.'

'All right, boy, I'll tell you what we does.'

Gomer said he'd go back via the old bowling green, through into the churchyard, check on the situation there and whether the kiddie had been found, grab his Jeep off the square – always felt better on wheels, never much of a foot soldier, see. Lol, meanwhile, would torch-sweep as much of the orchard as he could before making his way to the gate opening on to the new road, where Gomer would pick him up in about half an hour.

'That way, we covers both exits. If her's in the orchard, one or other of us'll mabbe stumble—' Gomer coughed, shuffled. 'Sorry, didn't mean . . .'

'She'll be OK,' Lol said. 'She'll be OK.' Like repeating it was going to make it so. 'She's always OK.'

But when Gomer had gone, the Garrod Powell in his head faded into Lloyd Powell and both of them merged into Karl Windling and the white-robed apple trees stood around like bent old druids at some woodland ceremony, and he didn't think Jane was OK.

He was very fond of Jane. He could say that to himself now. It was OK to be fond of a fifteen-year-old girl. It was OK to fall in love with her mother. He walked away. The salmon moon was entangled in a cluster of spiky dead branches projecting from the blossom below. Gomer was right; the only way to make any kind of productive orchard here was to start again.

He walked quickly, pointing the torch at what remained of the path, sometimes apprehensively sweeping it from side to side, and finding patches of fungus pale as flesh and exposed roots like withered limbs.

*

She went as far away as she could get, squeezing herself into different corners, squatting in the straw. But wherever she

603

was, she could still see the loft and the bin sack. Wherever she went, she thought she could see Colette's eyes, popping out at her like marbles.

Even though she'd dragged the bin sack back over the face, she seemed to see the eyes making little round bulges in the plastic.

What a bummer, eh, Janey? Ain't this just the pits?

But the cool, sassy voice she remembered no longer matched the face. Colette, dead, had a child's face again, this was what was so awful. She looked so pitifully young. *Younger than me.*

And the smell. Colette's sickly new perfume. Putrefying. A putrefying child. A little, swollen doll with a livid throat.

'*Pleeeeeease.*'

The folds of the bin sack settled around Colette's face with a crinkling sound.

'*Naaaaaw!*'

In a frenzy, Jane scrambled back on to the Flintstones mill wheel and balanced there, piling more and more empty bin sacks over the corpse, to lose the shape, lose the smell, a stink which would have so disgusted Colette. Her thoughts flitting fearfully into the forbidden unknown. How long had Colette been kept here before they killed her like a turkey? What had they done to her before they throttled her and took her clothes and dumped them in a ditch at King's Oak Corner and dressed her in a crinkly black shroud? Hunky Lloyd Powell and his dignified father. *What had they done to her?*

She remembered what Lloyd had said about pests and badger-baiting. *It's a bit of fun. It's cheap. Nobody gets harmed, 'cept the badger and that's his fault for being a badger.*

Behind her, the door swung open. She didn't even try to get down. What was the point?

'Ah, you found her then, is it?'

Lloyd standing in the doorway with his legs apart. Lloyd sounding quite pleased, like Colette's body was a birthday present they'd hidden.

'Amazing what you find when you snoop around, girl. Still. It's not very nice. Shouldn't leave 'em unburied. Health risk, it is. I apologize.'

He sighed.

'We got too much on, see, at present. And too many strangers about. We never *wanted* the slag, mind. We never done anything like that before. You don't, not on your own doorstep, not on your own *land*. Stupid, that is. And then we couldn't even bury her with all these police tramping around. Untidy. Hate that, I do.'

'*Stop it!*' she screeched, jumping down, putting the mill wheel between them. 'I don't want to know. You disgust me.'

Lloyd folded his arms, affronted. 'Now, don't you bloody come on like that with me, Jane. It was your fault. It was you sent me after the bitch. *Oh, you gotter stop them, you gotter get them out, Lloyd, please, Lloyd, please, please, please* . . . You think I wanted that? Last thing we bloody wanted after that one Father brought back from Kingsland, did nothin' but bloody cry, day and night . . . But no, you had to keep on at me. *Please, Lloyd, oh please, please—*'

'*Stop it!*' Jane shrieked and bent her head into her arms between her knees.

'So I find the slag, and she's looking at me like I'm God's gift. Throwing herself all over me in the middle of our own orchard. Got rid of her mates fast enough, she had, and here she is, wandering around half naked all by herself. What was I supposed to do? You tell me that, Jane. Fetch her back to the restaurant, with her slobbering all over me, making up her lies? What would that do to my reputation. What would it do to Father?'

'You didn't have to bring her back *here*. Why couldn't you just . . . just make love to her . . . whatever she wanted. *You didn't have to bring her back here!*'

'But we always fetches 'em back yere.'

Lloyd looked momentarily puzzled, like even he wasn't quite sure why they always fetched them here. Just what he'd been brought up to do. A few stupid city people might think it was cruel, but it was a different way of life out here, wasn't it?

Nobody gets harmed, 'cept the badger and that's his fault for being a badger.

Colette's fault for being a slag.

Jane didn't know how to talk to him any more. He wasn't mad in the normal sense. He didn't have the imagination to be mad. You couldn't humour him; he had no humour.

Jane said, in a very low, faint voice, 'I didn't throw myself at anybody. I'm not going to spread any lies. Why can't you just let me go?'

Lloyd shook his head in his brisk and businesslike way. 'Not an option, Jane. You gotter see that. 'Specially now.'

'I'm sure your father'll say to let me go. He's a councillor, for God's sake. My mother's the—'

Lloyd sort of smiled. 'You don't really know Father, do you, Jane?'

And there, suddenly, was Mr Powell in her head, his council-chairman's chain wound around his hands and tightened.

She braced herself to attack Lloyd. She would go for his balls.

Lloyd leaned back slightly on his heels and regarded her sorrowfully. 'You try anything, Jane, on me, I got to tell you I'll punch your face flat. Won't offend Father. Won't put Father off. Don't look at the ole mantelpiece when you're—'

She saw that Mr Powell wore no trousers and his shirt flap was sticking out. In Lloyd's hip pocket, the mobile phone had begun to bleep.

'And about time, too, Father,' Lloyd said. 'Excuse me.'

When he'd shut the door efficiently behind him and locked it again, Jane gave up, threw herself into the filthy straw. She was thirsty. She had no more tears left. Her chest hurt from sobbing. It was over. All she had left to hope for was that they would see her as a fox – *fast, bang*.

Please God, not a badger.

She thought back in horrified amazement to the side of herself which had persuaded her to go into the orchard with two full bottles of gassy cider. When you knew you were going to die quite soon, your body put into a clammy bin liner, the idea of being suspended in some parallel, ethereal, faerie universe was just the most awful, self-deluding crap imaginable. Lucy Devenish believed all this shit and they'd killed her too, and she hadn't come back because all that afterlife stuff Mum preached was utter crap as well. What she'd had in the orchard that day had been some kind of black-out; she probably had a brain tumour and would have died anyway.

Jane lay there and sniffed the stinking straw because it was better than the piercing perfume of Colette. She, too, would start to smell like that, quite soon, when she was lying in her own bin sack, she and Colette decaying side by side, good mates turning bad. Jane sobbed and snuffled over this until, weak and exhausted – *please God, not a badger* – her body slackened into a thin sleep and Mr Powell was there, with his chain tight and his thing out, not smiling.

*

James lifted his chin, his eyes focused on the rafters. His tone was clipped.

'Many times, I gather, the destruction of that document was mooted. But there was a sound reason for it being preserved. Eventually, about a hundred years ago, my great-grandfather suggested it should be entombed with its author. That's all there is to it.'

'James,' said Merrily. 'You can't just tell us there was a sound reason without saying what it was.'

'It's a private—'

'James, listen to me. About thirty years ago, a girl called Patricia Young went to work for your father in the stables. She got pregnant – never mind how I know, I *know*. She returned after the child was born, to try and persuade the father to face up to his responsibilities. He obviously did. He faced up to the responsibility he obviously felt to his family, and she was never seen again.'

Someone shouted out, 'Patricia came *back*?'

'This is disgraceful,' James snarled.

'Bloody well come clean, Bull-Davies,' a man yelled. Several people were on their feet. Ken Thomas had put on all the lights. Bull-Davies's face was white, a vein throbbing in his forehead. He flung out his pointing arm at Merrily.

'If there's a bloody witch here, it's you.'

'Shame!' Minnie Parry cried out and was echoed by at least a dozen people, some of them out in the aisle.

'All right!' James threw up his hands. 'Reason we didn't destroy that document is because it also vindicates Tom Bull. Didn't kill Williams. Didn't even order it done. Truth of it . . . like Thomas à Becket all over again. *Will no one rid me of this troublesome priest?* One of his . . . servants did it. And that's all I'm saying. That's it. Show's over. I'm leaving. Goodnight.'

To a chorus of groans and protests from the pews, he strode away to the south porch, didn't look at Ken Thomas, went out. Alison glanced at Merrily then followed him.

Merrily shrugged and followed Alison. Behind her, a score of conversations were detonated.

*

Garrod Powell had a Sunday car, a silver-grey Ford Escort. Whenever he came to church, he parked it in the same place on the square adjacent to the market hall where it reached out towards the mews where Cassidy's Country Kitchen was and Ledwardine Lore. Rod's space. Only tourists parked there when Rod wasn't in town.

When Gomer spotted the car, Rod was in it, talking on the phone.

Gomer pulled his Jeep into the kerbside at the mouth of Church Street and waited.

Bull-Davies strode past towards his blue Land Rover, almost dragging the floozie behind him. He was unlocking the driver's door when the little vicar caught them up.

*

Alison suddenly snatched her hand away and turned on James like a cornered cat.

'Tell her, you bloody fool. Why don't you just tell her everything you know? This has nothing to do with honour or tradition.'

'If that were true . . .' He leaned back against his Land Rover and breathed in through his teeth. 'If that were true, my darling mistress, this would not be a problem.'

'The problem is', Merrily said, 'that I think we're talking about a tradition that's far from honourable.'

'You're very clever, Mrs Watkins.'

'No I'm not. I've not been very clever at all. I've got people killed.'

'If you're talking about Coffey—'

'You didn't kill Coffey, did you, James?' It just came out.

'What?' James's jaw fell open like a padlock. He blinked. 'Good Lord. You saw Alder in there. Fellow as good as confessed. Didn't say a word in denial, took it' – he grunted – 'took it like a man.'

'He's an actor,' Merrily said. 'His great performance was dying on its feet. I wondered if he was just grabbing the chance of getting out on a moment of high drama.'

'Look. Mrs Watkins . . . Mrs Watkins, *no*. I did not kill Coffey. Found the man and went to the police, co-operated fully. Even let them take my fingerprints. No. Did not kill Coffey. May have wanted to, but that's not my way. Couldn't. All right?'

'Tell her, then,' Alison said. 'Tell her that the Bulls don't kill. Tell her who—'

'Stop. Please. All right. According to his own account, Thomas Bull got very drunk one night. Opened his heart to the only man he felt he could still trust. His bailiff, game-keeper, head groom, land steward, his . . .'

Merrily, shuddering, had a vision of big brown hands around a small, white throat.

'His Powell,' she said.

'Now do you see?' James bellowed. '*Now* do you bloody well see?'

'The . . . this Powell . . . killed her.' Merrily felt breath-less, felt the sudden closeness of the woman who was Wil. 'Strangled her.'

'Robert Powell, his name. He was trying to help Tom Bull, and he did a terrible thing.'

'Even more terrible,' Alison said, 'because he'd have soon realized he was killing a woman. It's not so easy to strangle a man.'

'He didn't just strangle her,' Merrily said. 'He raped her first. He raped the minister. He went to kill a priest, and—'

'Don't make it *worse*, woman!'

'But it *is* worse, James. It got worse. Because it didn't stop. From then on, the Powells had a hold on the Bulls, and maybe it strengthened over the centuries because of the things the Powells would do without compunction. Things it wouldn't have been proper or seemly or honourable . . . Who killed Patricia Young?'

Bull-Davies reeled. 'I don't know that! Gord's sake, don't know anything. Don't know if the damned woman *was* killed. I was a boy then, probably still away at school, nobody would have told *me*. I don't *know* anything. Just inherited all this shit, been trying to keep the damned toilet lid down ever since.'

Merrily looked at Alison.

Alison gave a tiny nod, her face flushed with anticipation.

'Who do you think killed her?' Merrily said.

'Do you never give up? Presumably the father of her child, whoever . . .' James swallowed. 'Whoever that was. Certainly not *my* poor bloody father who for the last twenty years of his life was impotent through illness and drink and got his only pleasure from . . .'

James clenched his teeth.

'. . . watching.'

Alison gasped.

'Watching who, James?' Merrily's voice was very faint.

He wouldn't answer. He hardly needed to. An engine roared suddenly and the side of the Land Rover was blasted by headlights.

'Vicar!'

'Gomer?'

Merrily saw, with a spasm of panic, that he was alone behind the wheel of his jeep.

'Where's Jane?'

'You en't seen her?'

'Oh *Christ*!'

Gomer reached over and threw open the passenger door.

'Get in, Vicar.'

Way to Blue

Lol stumbled out into the road before he knew it, the tarmac unrolling to either side, a fence opposite with a ploughed field rising steeply behind it, pink moon on pink soil, to a bristle of trees.

No vehicles, no lights, no sign of Gomer.

He felt confused and upset, didn't know how much time had passed, swinging the torch from tree to tree, tensely shining it under bushes and briars. Once, he'd lit up a rag and nearly thrown up with dread.

There was no pavement; he'd have to stand in the hedge if a vehicle came past. He stared down at his feet on the tarmac and found himself praying that Jane was alive and back at the vicarage, then stopped, scared it might do more harm than good, as if he was tapping into Merrily's line to a God he wasn't sure of and Jane often mocked. Omens and portents seemed to have soaked up all his spirituality. Pink moons and black-eyed dogs. *Please, Jane.*

He looked up then and saw her.

She was standing in the middle of the pink, ploughed field. She didn't smile at him or come running towards him. She didn't seem to notice him at all. She was standing very still, although a wind he couldn't feel lifted her dark hair.

And then there was only the field and the distant trees with buildings behind, under the hardening moon, and Lol knew the curse, by way of Robert Johnson and Nick Drake, was reaching for him.

*

Merrily was struggling not to give way. She asked Gomer if he'd tried the vicarage. Had he been upstairs? Had he called out? Had he called out to the third storey?

Gomer told her no way was Jane in the vicarage, but Lol had spotted two cider bottles missing from a case in Lucy's kitchen.

Merrily let out a long, serrated breath. 'I know Lucy's dead, I know she was your friend. But I wish to God Jane had never known her.'

'Lol's in the orchard now, searchin'. She's there, he'll find her.'

'How is he?'

'How d'you mean like?' Gomer was watching a car on the other side of the square.

'Lol is – ' she bit off the word unstable ' – unsure of himself sometimes.'

'He's all right. Good boy, I reckon.' Gomer pointed across the cobbles. 'That's Rod Powell's car, see. Keepin' an eye on him, I am. He's on the phone. Now who'd Rod be callin' this time o' night, you reckon?'

Merrily was silent.

A second later, Rod was getting out of his car and walking, in his stately and confident way, across to the Black Swan, where a lemony light still burned in windows either side of the front door. Rod went up the steps and rapped on a window. Presently the door opened and he was admitted. A couple of minutes later, he came out with a bottle of whisky.

'Councillor Powell keeps his own licensin' hours,' Gomer said. 'How about that? Man's gonner have himself a drink in his car, I shouldn't wonder. Coppers in and out, every hour on the hour lately, that's how arrogant the feller is.'

'Perhaps he needs some courage. Perhaps he could see a few things starting to . . . ooze out of the woodwork.'

She told Gomer, very briefly, what she'd learned in the last hour and what she'd surmised. Everything, except for the very mixed implications for Alison.

'Bugger me,' said Gomer. 'Wouldn't it just suit the bastard to get his end away with the Bulls' women? Where'd that happen, I wonder. No prizes.'

'The cider house?'

'Likely why John Bull-Davies give Rod that bit o' land with the ole place *on* it.'

'With a convenient hole in the wall?'

'Hole in the loft prob'ly. That bloody ole John Bull-Davies. He weren't never any good. You look at that whole situation, Vicar, you can see why James is the screwed-up bugger he is. Obvious, he's backin' off from the Powells. Tryin' to.'

'I think he perhaps wanted to do that on his own terms, but circumstances aren't letting him.'

'They comes over so loud and haughty-like, the Bulls, but they're weak underneath, most of 'em. They'll always come back to the Powells. It's like some ole magnetism. They might think they got away, but they en't.'

As the tail lights of Rod Powell's car came on and the strings of medieval, electric lanterns across the square were extinguished by some timer mechanism, Merrily thought of James and Alison, free to resume their odd relationship.

James Bull-Davies and Alison Kinnersley. Or Powell, as she might have been. The Bulls and the Powells. She hoped there would never be a child.

*

Lol ran across the road. There was an iron gate on the other side, leading to the pink-washed field. For a moment, as he climbed over, he thought he saw her again, a flitting thing, a wisp, a trick of the light.

He turned and looked back across the road towards the orchard. He should wait here. He should wait for Gomer.

There was a flash, like magnesium, on the very periphery of his vision and he spun round and once more saw her, in total, absolute clarity, standing in the centre of the field with her arms by her sides. She was dressed in black.

This time, he saw, in a heart-freezing moment, that her feet were not quite touching the soil. A girl dressed in black, hovering under a pink moon.

He stood with his back to the gate, snatched off his glasses and rubbed his hands over his face, replaced the glasses, looked back at the road and then spun around again. But there was nothing now.

He wasn't sure if it had been Jane.

Or Colette.

Both of them? Both of them out here?

His hands were trembling as he pushed himself away from the iron gate and began to walk across the churned-up field, soil the colour of raw meat, the pink moon above him, the black-eyed dog, he was sure, at his heels.

He knew where he was going. Among the farm buildings behind the trees was the cider house, where The Wine of Angels had not been made. The place where the Bulls had once taken their women.

Lol stopped and looked once over his shoulder before walking steadily towards the buildings.

*

The Escort had turned down Church Street for Old Barn Lane before Gomer started to follow. He'd pulled back into the shadows to avoid Minnie spotting the Jeep when she came out of the lych-gate, accompanied by Tess Roberts and the Prossers. 'Never get to keep my ole Gwynneth after this,' Gomer muttered.

Rod was turning into Old Barn Lane.

'Never even signalled,' Gomer observed. He sucked on his ciggy. 'What you reckon a man like Powell does, he sees the blinds come down after three hundred years?'

'Wondering that myself.' Merrily thought about the unmissable password she'd given Gomer to identify himself to Lol. Nick Drake's 'Pink Moon' was the song of his that seemed to get played more often than any other when she was a kid. She used to ask her step-brother, Jonathan, to put it on again because the idea sounded so pretty. It was years later before she found out the message was far from comforting, spoke of no escape. For anyone.

'Magistrate like Rod,' Gomer said soberly, 'he feels it's all over, last thing he wants is to sit the other side o' the ole courtroom.'

Merrily fastened the webbing seat-belt. 'I don't know where this is going to end. I think we lost control a long time ago.'

'Will of God.' Gomer turned into Old Barn Lane. 'En't that the bottom line of it for you, Vicar?'

'I'm a bit unsure about the strength of my faith, Gomer. If something happened to Jane I'd be swearing at the heavens and cursing in the night like nobody ever did.'

The sights and smells of the dream cider house swelled in her head. In the vaporous humidity, no longer the pulpy, sweating cheeks of the pumping Child but the emotionless, rhythmical rise and thrust of a piece of well-preserved, well-oiled farm machinery.

Gomer glanced at her and then turned back to the lane.

*

Lol had spoken to him only once before, when he and Alison had bought the apple wood for fragrant fires. But on another occasion, the week after Alison had left, he'd seen Lol buying cat food in the Spar shop and had laughed quietly.

'What you doin' yere?' Lloyd Powell said now. Not a man who smiled, but he laughed sometimes.

Lol stood uncertainly on the edge of the field, where it gave way to a weed-spattered gravel forecourt.

'I'm speaking to you, sunshine,' Lloyd said. 'Come over yere in the light.'

The only light was a dome-shaded bulb in a holder like a question mark over the door of what Lol took to be the cider house. He moved shyly to within six feet of it.

'Hello,' he said.

Lloyd was Marlboro County Man in denims but with no cigarette. Lol saw Karl Windling with no beard.

'Ah.' Lloyd put his hands on his hips. 'I know who *you* are. You're that bloke Alison Kinnersley left for James.'

Lol nodded. The pint-sized cuckold.

Lloyd's expression was blank.

Pint-sized cuckold. With no bottle. Just phrases he'd overheard in the shop when they were laughing quietly, Lloyd and another bloke.

Lloyd examined him for a moment then seemed to lose interest. 'Go away, little man,' he said. 'I'm busy.'

He turned his back on Lol, taking some keys out of his pocket.

'No,' Lol said. 'I won't, if you don't mind.'

'What was that?' Lloyd didn't turn round. Lol saw that his dashing white truck was parked a few yards away with its tailgate open. In the back was a dead sheep and something not much bigger wrapped in bin sacks.

'Got it all loaded then, Lloyd?'

Lloyd still didn't turn.

'Give you a hand, maybe?'

'I don't think so,' Lloyd said. 'Don't reckon you'd have the strength. Bugger off. Go'n look at your owls, your badgers, whatever you little fellers do at night.'

The pink moon shone surrealistically down on a pastoral dreamscape. Lol wasn't quite sure if he was actually here. He glimpsed the past few days in a series of frozen incidents fanned out like playing cards – the vicarage days, his own mirror image bizarrely in a dog collar, Alison unmasked, the glow of firelight on Merrily's eyelids – and then the fan was closed and he was standing back where it all began, in Blackberry Lane, in front of the invaded cottage, the torn-up pages of Traherne like petals on the lawn, Karl Windling in the window.

'I thought as I was passing,' Lol heard himself saying, as though from some distance, 'that I would take Jane home.'

Lloyd turned slowly back from the door.

'Come yere a minute.'

Lol heard Karl Windling say, *Now you fucking stay there. You understand? You go anywhere, I'll find you. You don't move the rest of the night. I'm coming over.*

He walked up to the door and stood there.

'Right, then,' Lloyd said.

The pink moon bulged as Lloyd half turned and hit him in the mouth. As he fell back, Lloyd hit him in the stomach. As he doubled up and his face came down, Lloyd's fist was waiting to meet it, crunching his glasses into his eyes.

As he rolled over on the gravel, Lloyd kicked him in the head.

*

'Tell me the truth,' the vicar said as they came up to the junction of Old Barn Lane and the new road. Terrible stupid junction, this was, Gomer reckoned, right on a bad bend.

'You don't actually think Lol's going to find her lying drunk in the orchard. Do you?'

'Oh, Vicar . . .' Gomer slowed down, not wanting to come up to the junction right behind Rod, pretending that concentrating on his driving was the reason he hadn't finished the sentence.

'You think she's in the cider house, don't you?'

'En't my place to think nonsense like that,' Gomer said gruffly.

'What happens in the cider house?'

'They makes cider. Used to.'

They passed into a tunnel of trees, blocking the moonlight.

'I dreamt about it once.' Her voice was very low. 'I've never been in one, but I dreamt about it. It was Dermot Child in there.'

Gomer thought that Dermot Child, nasty little bugger though he was, wasn't in the same evil league as the Powells, so inbred, deep-down evil they didn't even know they *was* evil. He turned out on to the new road and had to brake sharply on account of Rod Powell's Escort was dead in front of him, having slowed for a big lorry rumbling round the bend.

'Strewth, you don't expect heavy goods traffic this time o' night.'

It was a low loader with a big stack of crates on the back. The driver cranked the gears and the lorry built up to a steady speed as they approached the spot where poor ole Lucy bought it, just before you hit the straight, Powells' farm turning about half a mile off.

Too late. Before Rod, too, changed gear and speeded up, Gomer saw him look in his mirror to see who'd come up behind him. Not many folk in this village drove a US Army Jeep with a cigarette glowing in their gobs.

'Bugger.'

He'd have seen the vicar, too. He'd know they were following him. He wouldn't like that.

Gomer eased up, left some space between him and Rod. His view of it was that Rod was heading home fast to check everything was in order, mabbe throw some disinfectant around then figure out how he was going to play it. He wouldn't want no company tonight.

But whatever he did to clean up the cider house, there wasn't a thing he could do about the orchard. About this Patricia Young, who Gomer was convinced lay under the Apple Tree Man. He weren't that old. Thirty years was a good age for an untended apple tree.

Bugger. Rod giving it some clog now, getting up behind the lorry so he could get past when they hit the straight. Gomer put his foot down.

What happened next happened so quick that he'd hardly registered it before the Jeep was up the bank and not-so-clean through the hedge.

*

'Where are you? Where are you? Where you gone?' Moving about in the bilious fluorescence, throwing hay around, old bin sacks. 'Don't mess me about, you bitch, you little scrubber. You come out now and mabbe I won't give you to Father for his pleasure, mabbe I'll just finish it quick, quick as a chicken, see, humane . . . You want humane, you come out now. Father, he en't humane, n'more. You come out now, you hear. I know you can't've got out, had my eye on you the whole time I'm removin' your friend, efficient, we are, you don't get round the back of *us* . . . Don't mess me about, Jane, you listen to me, I en't got time . . . When I find you I'm gonner hurt you, gonner hurt you very bad, you hear me, Jane, you hear me, you little slut? You can't've gone, you can't've gone, you cannot've *gone*, Jane. Jane. *Jane. JANE!'*

He comes out, boiling with bewilderment.

'Where is she?'

Advancing on Lol, tottering away from the truck, half blind, body burning.

'Think I'm daft enough to leave the keys in, is it? Think you can drive off? Think I'm *daft*?'

Big, tough hands, farmer's hands, bass player's hands, picking him up and slamming him back against some wall.

And he can feel the freshly washed hair of a girl called Tracy Cooke in his eyes and mouth in a dingy hotel bedroom and he can see Karl Windling's yellow grin as he pushes Tracy over onto Lol's arm and goes down on her.

I'm gonner hurt you, gonner hurt you real bad, you hear me, Jane . . .

Jane?

'Where is she?' Lloyd's screaming, his hard face up close. 'What you done with her? I'm gonner tear your other eye out, mister!'

Lol's hand comes up with the bottle in it. The empty bottle he found rolling around in the back of the truck. The bottle coming up and striking Lloyd on the point of the chin with a small click.

Lloyd stumbling and spitting a little blood.

'Right then.' Rubbing his jaw once. 'You done it now, boy.'

Lol swaying, hearing the words of Thomas Traherne.

. . . to love all persons in all ages, all angels, all worlds, is divine and heavenly . . . To love all . . .

Lloyd comes for Lol.

Karl Windling says, *And you . . . you're just . . . I mean, who'd notice? Who'd give a shit? Who'd put flowers on your grave?*

Lol, with both hands smashing the bottle into the side of Lloyd's head, whispers, 'Jane?'

There is no reply. Lloyd is on his knees. The bottle falling to the gravel and rolling over, its label lit by the moon.

The Wine of Angels.

Tears are the wine of angels. Traherne sighs. *The best to quench the devil's fires.*

*

You'd've thought it would be all over the road, but it was very neat. From the bank, Gomer was looking down on it, the moon so warm and bright you could see everything. Very neat indeed, the car looking like it had taken a bite out of the bed of the lorry, like the car roof was its upper lip, clamped down.

'No, you don't,' Gomer said, putting out an arm to bar the vicar's path. 'Call me sexist, Vicar, but this is gonner be no sight for you. You stay in this yere field. I'll go down and check this out first, see.'

He slithered down to the mangled wire fence, stepped over it and through the gap the Jeep had torn out of the hedge. Lit himself a ciggy then went to look under the deck of the lorry, where the bonnet of the Escort was barely visible. The end of the deck had gone through the windscreen like a wide-bladed stone chisel.

Gomer bent his head, sniffed, then straightened up and wiped his hands on his trousers.

The lorry driver was down from his cab. He'd thrown up in the road. He wore a baseball cap and a big earring.

'Well, well,' Gomer said. 'Jeremy Selby.'

'Gomer?'

'Bit late for a consignment o' cider.'

'Going down Southampton way. Bit of a rock festival.'

'Ar,' Gomer said. 'Best place for it. All be too stoned to taste the ole muck.'

'It was so *bloody* quick, Gomer. Couldn't believe it. He was right on my arse, then it just come running out the hedge, I didn't know what it was at first, just slammed on, you know, instinctively, it was a really big one, all white.'

'Hang on, get a hold, boy.' Gomer extracted the ciggy. 'What did? What exactly come runnin' out the hedge?'

'Bloody great sheep. White as a bloody polar bear.'

'Ar.' Gomer walked round to the front of the lorry. No sign of a sheep. Naturally. Gomer nodded, ambled back. 'Where'd it go, then, Jeremy?'

'Fuck knows. It was here one second, gone the next. I swear to God, Gomer, it—'

'All right, boy.' Gomer patted him on the shoulder. 'If the coppers asks, I'll say I seen it too. You rung 'em?'

'On my mobile.'

They both stepped into the road. It was dead quiet.

'Poor bugger,' Jeremy said. 'I suppose there really is no . . .'

'What, with half of him in the front, half in the back and his head—'

'All *right*! Christ, I'm still shaking. Don't suppose you recognize the car?'

'Oh aye. Rod Powell, that is. Was.'

'You what?' Jeremy Selby snatched off his baseball cap in horror. 'I just killed *Councillor Powell*?'

'Ar.' Gomer's beam was a bright gash in the night as he stuck out his hand. 'Put it there, pal.'

*

It was a cawing sound, like a nightbird, sporadic but coming closer.

'. . . *ane* . . .? *ane* . . .'

Merrily stood in the pink ploughed field exactly where

Gomer had left her, not looking where he'd told her not to look. It was as though all her muscles had seized up. She felt raw and frozen and unable to think clearly. She saw a large hole in her cashmere sweater, just below the elbow. She could throw it away now.

Something was standing about fifteen yards up the field. It cawed again.

'J . . . ane?'

Merrily looked up. 'Lol? Is it *Lol*?'

'. . . 'errily? Sorry, I can't . . . glasses gone.'

He stumbled down a furrow. Before he fell into her arms she saw his face was full of blood and his mouth was up on one side. One eye was closed.

They crushed each other and Merrily began to cry. 'Oh, Lol, what have they done to you?' She felt his blood on her face. He looked like his cat had. She remembered waking up by the fire, seeing him looking down at her, closing her eyes again, content. She closed her eyes now and the night swirled around her, not pink but deep blue. She couldn't understand that when everything told her it should be black, streaked with red.

*

'Lol, boy!'

Merrily blinked. Gomer stood a few feet away.

'Take it easy,' Gomer said. 'Everybody take it easy.'

The night became real and hard-edged. Memories battered Merrily. A flame of fear enveloped her. She stared into Gomer's terrifying face, with the white spikes of hair and the core of fire in his teeth.

'Bloody useless, you are, Lol, boy,' Gomer said. 'Wouldn't find an elephant in your own backyard. 'Er just comes walkin' out the orchard, cool as you like, through the ole gate.'

Merrily swam upwards through the blue.

'Flower?'

*

Next to tough, wiry old Gomer, she was looking very small and young and fragile. Her face was as white as bread. Her eyes were on the move, still travelling back.

'Oh, Christ,' Lol said.

Breaking away from Merrily to let Jane in, he looked up.

Through a single, watering, blood-blurred, short-sighted eye, he saw a curious cloud formation above the moon, a dark cloud hanging there making a curving V-shape. So that the moon, for a long, undying moment, was like a big, red apple.

*

He heard Jane saying,

'Mum . . . where have you been since yesterday?'

H.L. McCready and Partners,
Solicitors,
Apex House,
King Street,
Hereford.

3 June

The Revd. M. Watkins,
The Vicarage,
Ledwardine,
Herefordshire

Dear Mrs Watkins,

I shall be writing to you more formally about this matter in
due course but felt I should give you informal advance
warning of something which, until now, has been subject to
a degree of secrecy. I am sure that, were she alive, the police
would be more than interested to talk to Miss Devenish in
the light of recent events! In the circumstances, one can
only mutter about there being more things in heaven and
earth . . .

First, may I say how pleased I have been to learn that
you and your daughter are fully recovered from what
must have been a most disturbing night. I doubt if
Ledwardine has weathered a more eventful period in its
lengthy history.

But to business. Many people, no doubt, will be wondering
who is to receive the bulk of Miss Devenish's legacy, which

will amount principally to the proceeds of the sale of her house and shop, both highly desirable properties in a much sought-after village. In January this year, Miss Devenish placed before me a proposal which I confess I greeted with some dismay. It was her intention that all the money should be left in trust to the Diocese of Hereford for the purchase of the orchard immediately adjacent to the Parish Church whenever it might come on the market, the land to remain as an orchard in perpetuity.

As the aforementioned orchard had, for several centuries, been in the ownership of the Powell family and there seemed little prospect of its being relinquished, I was at pains to discourage Miss Devenish from this course of action, but, as you know, she was a most determined person and was insistent that her wishes be adhered to.

Following the death, in the early hours of Monday morning, of Mr Garrod Powell, the property passed into the ownership of his son, Mr Lloyd Powell. However, with the death in hospital yesterday of Mr Lloyd Powell (which I am informed is unlikely, under the circumstances, to give rise to any criminal proceedings against his assailant) it seems not improbable that the orchard will indeed shortly become available for purchase.

Attempts are being made to contact Mrs Jennifer Powell, from whom, it may surprise you to learn, Mr Garrod Powell has never been legally separated and to whom it appears the Powell Orchard may now belong. In view of her long estrangement from Mr Powell, it seems likely that Mrs Powell will wish to dispense with the property, especially in view of the gruesome discoveries there over the past few days.

Be assured that I shall keep you fully informed of any future developments; meanwhile, please accept my very best wishes for your Installation Service next Friday.

Yours sincerely,

Harold L. McCready

CLOSING CREDITS

The research for this novel meant bothering various vicars and historians, principally The Revs. Richard Birt (the great Traherne expert), Philip Clarke (Priest-in-Charge) and John Guy, Bob Jenkins and Ron Shoesmith. None of whom should be blamed for any errors, distortions or complete lies.

Many thanks also to Penny Arnold, Wendy and Paul Gibbons, Lara Latcham, June and Doug Mason, Jeanine McMullen and the late, great Graham Nown.

The book was dissected and probed in depth over two gruelling weeks by my wife Carol, the finest plot doctor in the business, overviewed by the uniquely patient, perceptive Peter Lavery and dispatched on time, against all the odds, by the fastest postmistress in the mid-West, Gwen Lewis.

*

Ella Leather's classic *The Folklore of Herefordshire* is now available from Lapridge Publications, the full story of the amazing Hannah Snell is told in *The Folklore of Hereford and Worcester* by Roy Palmer, from Logaston Press, who also publish, with its author Elizabeth Taylor, *King's Caple in Archenfield*, the outstanding, elegantly written and massively detailed history of a Herefordshire village which provided many little details about churches and cider. The tragic facts about Nick Drake (whose albums are seriously recommended) are revealed in Patrick Humphries' evocative biography, *Nick Drake*, published by Bloomsbury, and Penguin Classics do the *Selected Poems and Prose of Thomas Traherne* of whom I was reminded, just in time, by Sue Gee's moving and atmospheric novel *The Hours of the Night*.

Candlelight

CONTENTS

THANKS

To Carol, my wife, who found all the flaws and inspired me to start again. To Anna Haycraft and Peter James for being encouraging about the revised opening chapters.

To Hedd Bleddyn Williams, Don Leach and the Revd Geraint Hughes, for information about bodies and tombs and how to get one out of the other.

To Dr Viv Davies, for medical background; Richard Livsey, by-elections; John Higgs, Volvos; a coroner. And finally, the *Gwrach y Rhibyn* and its Press agent, Alun Lenny.

These were the people I actually approached for information. Scores of others, all over Wales, have unwittingly contributed. The late T. Gwynn Jones's *Welsh Folklore and Folk Custom* was invaluable – as were the people who told us about their own uncanny encounters.

If any of the research material has been misused or distorted, I'm sorry – but nothing's sacred in this business, thank God.

PRONOUNCING WELSH

This is not as difficult as many tourists imagine, but there are some names in this novel which are not pronounced as their spelling might suggest.

For instance, Buddug is pronounced *Bithig*. This is because, in Welsh, the vowel 'u' is pronounced 'i' as in 'big'. And 'dd' is '*th*' as in 'this'.

In Welsh, virtually every letter in every word is sounded. Thus the place name Y Groes (the cross) comes out something like *Uh Groyce*. Croeso (welcome) is *croyso*. And Pontmeurig (Meurig Bridge) is *Pontmayrig*.

The letter 'w' is usually pronounced '*u*' as in 'rule'. So Owain Glyndwr is a bit like *Owine Glyndoor*.

The letter 'c' is always hard as in 'cat'. So the name Ap Siencyn is pronounced *Ap Shenkin*.

The letter 'f' is pronounced '*v*' as in 'van', so Y Groesfan (the crossing place) is *Uh Groycevan* – unless there are two 'f's, that is, as in the name Gruffydd, which is pronounced *Griffith*.

Here are a few more names:

Dai, pronounced *Die*

Guto, pronounced *Gitto*

Alun, pronounced *Allin*

Sali, pronounced *Sally*

PART ONE

PORTENTS

CHAPTER I

LAUGHTER trickled after him out of the inn.
Ingley's mouth tightened and he would have turned
back, but this was no time to lose his temper. In a hurry
now. Knew what it was he was looking for. Could almost hear
it summoning him, as if the bells were clanging in the tower.

Besides, he doubted the laughter was intended to be offensive. They were not hostile in the village – yes, all right, they
insisted on speaking Welsh in public all the time, as if none
of them understood anything else. But he could handle that.
As long as they didn't get in his way.

'Torch,' he'd demanded. 'Flashlight. Do you have one I
could borrow?'

'Well . . .' Aled Gruffydd, the landlord, had pondered the
question as he pulled a pint of beer, slow and precise as a
doctor drawing a blood sample.

The big man, Morgan somebody, or somebody Morgan,
had said, very deadpan, 'No flashlights here, Professor. Blindfold we could find our way around this place.'

'. . . and pissed,' a man called out by the dartboard. 'Blindfold and pissed.'

Aled Gruffydd laid the pint reverently on a slop-mat and
then produced from behind the bar a big black flashlight.
'But we keep this,' he said, 'for the tourists. Rubber. Bounces,
see.'

Morgan laughed into his beer, a hollow sound.

'Thanks,' Ingley said, ignoring him. 'I . . . my notes. And
a couple of books. Left them in the church. Probably there in
the morning, but I need to know.' He smiled faintly. 'If they
aren't, I'm in trouble.'

The landlord passed the rubber torch across the bar to him.
'One thing, Doctor Ingley. Batteries might be running down
a bit, so don't go using it until you need to. There's a good
bit of moon for you, see.'

13

'Quite. You'll have it back. Half an hour or so, yes?'

'Mind the steps now,' Morgan said.

There was a short alleyway formed by the side of the inn and the ivy-covered concrete wall of an electricity sub-station. From where it ended at some stone steps Thomas Ingley could hear the river hissing gently, could smell a heady blend of beer and honeysuckle.

This pathway had not been built with Ingley in mind. The alley had been almost too narrow for his portly body, now the steps seemed too steep for his short legs. On all his previous visits to the church he'd gone by car to the main entrance. Hadn't known about the steps until somebody had pointed them out to him that morning. The steps clambered crookedly from the village to the church on its hillock, an ancient man-made mound rising suddenly behind the inn.

As the landlord had said, there was a moon – three parts full, but it was trapped behind the rearing church tower (medieval perpendicular, twice repaired in the nineteenth century) and there were no lights in the back of the inn to guide him up the steps. So he switched on the torch and found the beam quite steady.

Ingley had lied about leaving notes in the church. Kept everything – because you couldn't trust anybody these days – under the loose floorboard beneath his bed. He wondered what the hell he would have done if one of the regulars had offered to help him. Can't go up there on your own in the dark, Professor – break your neck, isn't it? He'd have been forced to stroll around the place, pretending to search for his documents, the tomb tantalisingly visible all the while, then have to wait for the morning to examine it. Too long to wait.

He never put anything off any more. If one had a line to pursue, strand to unravel, one should go on regardless of ritual mealtimes, social restraints, the clock by which man artificially regulated – and therefore reduced – his life.

And depressingly, with Ingley's condition, one never knew quite how much time one had left anyway.

He set off up the jagged steps.

14

A bat flittered across the torchbeam like an insect. Bats, like rats, were always so much smaller than one imagined.

Ingley paused halfway up the steps. Had to get his breath. Ought to rest periodically – doctor's warning. He scowled. Stood a moment in the scented silence. Did the sense of smell compensate for restricted vision in the dark? Or were the perfumes themselves simply more potent after sunset?

A sudden burst of clinking and distant chatter, then a strong voice in the night. A voice nurtured, no doubt, by the male choir and the directing of sheepdogs on windy hills.

'Professor! Dr Ingley! Where are you, man?'

Morgan. Dammit. Dammit. Dammit. Snapping off the torch, he held himself very still on the steps. Or as still as one could manage when one was underexercised, overweight and panting.

'Prof, are you all right?'

Of course I am. Go away. Go away. Go away. Thomas Ingley stayed silent and clenched his little teeth.

Another voice, speaking rapidly in Welsh, and then Morgan said '*O'r gorau*' OK, then – must mean that, surely. And the heavy front door of the inn closed with a thunk that sounded final.

Ingley waited a while, just to be sure, and then made his way slowly to the top of the steps. Emerging onto the plateau of the churchyard, he stopped to steady his breathing. The sky was a curious moonwashed indigo behind the rearing black tower and the squat pyramid of its spire. All around him was warmth and softness and musty fragrance; wild flowers grew in profusion among the graves, stones leaning this way and that, centuries deep.

Not afraid of graves. Graves he liked.

'*Dyma fedd Ebenezer Watkins,*' the torch lit up, letters etched into eternity. '*1858–1909.*'

Fairly recent interee. Ingley put out the light again, saving it for someone laid to rest here well over four centuries before Ebenezer Watkins. Excited by the thought, he made straight for the door at the base of the tower, straying from the narrow path by mistake and stumbling over a crooked, sunken headstone on the edge of the grass. Could fall here, smash one's skull on the edge of some outlying grave and all for nothing, all one's research. 'Don't be stupid,' he said aloud, but quietly. He often gave himself instructions. 'Put the bloody light back on.'

Followed the torchbeam to the door, which he knew would be unlocked. 'A hospice, sanctuary I suppose you would say, in medieval times,' Elias ap Siencyn had told him. 'And today, is there not an even greater need for sanctuary?' Impressive man, ap Siencyn, strong character and strong face, contoured like the bark of an old tree. Too often these days one went to consult a minister about the history of his church to be met by a person in a soft dog collar and jeans who knew nothing of the place, claiming Today's Church was about people, not architecture.

At the merest touch the ancient door swung inwards (arched moulded doorway, eighteenth century) and the churchy atmosphere came out to him in a great hollow yawn. He was at once in the nave, eight or nine centuries or more enfolding him, cloak of ages, wonderful.

All the same, was it not taking tradition too far to have no electricity in the church, no lights, no heating?

Inside, all he could see were steep Gothic windows, translucent panes, no stained glass, only shades of mauve stained by the night sky. He knew the way now and, putting out the torch, moved briskly down the central aisle, footsteps on stone, *tock, tock, tock.*

Stopped at the altar as if about to offer a prayer or to cross himself.

Hardly. Ingley didn't sneer this time, but it was close.

Table laid for God. A millennium or more of devotion, hopes and dreads heaped up here and left to go cold. Confirmed atheist, Thomas Ingley. Found the altar just about the least interesting part of the church.

He'd stopped because this was where one turned sharply left, three paces, to get to the secret core of the place, the heart of it all. Simply hadn't realised it until tonight. Been up here five times over the weekend. Missing, each time, the obvious.

Decidedly cool in the church, but Ingley was sweating in anticipation and the torch was sticky in his hand. A sweeping sound, a skittering far above him in the rafters: bats again. Then a silence in which even the flashlight switch sounded like the breach of a rifle.

Clack!

And the beam was thrown full in the face of the knight.

Like a gauntlet, Thomas Ingley thought, in challenge. Slap on one cheek, slap on the other. This is it. Lain there for centuries and nobody's given a sod who you were or what you were doing here. But you've slept long enough. Taking you on now, sir, taking you on.

The stone eyelids of the knight stayed shut. His petrified lips wore a furtive smile. His stone hands, three knuckles badly chipped, were on his breast, together in prayer. The beam of light tracked downwards, over the codpiece to the pointed feet.

'All right, friend,' Thomas Ingley said, speaking aloud again, laying the torch on the effigy, taking out a notebook, felt-tip pen, his reading glasses. Nuts and bolts time. 'Let's get on with it.'

He made detailed notes, with small drawings and diagrams, balancing the notebook on the edge of the tomb beneath the light. He drew outlines of the patterns in the stone. He copied the inscriptions in Latin and in Welsh, at least some of which he suspected had been added later, maybe centuries after the installation of the tomb. Tomorrow, perhaps, buy a camera with a flash, do the thing properly. Tonight, just had to know.

Finally he took from his jacket pocket a retractable metal rule and very carefully measured the tomb. It was about two feet longer than the effigy. The inscription in stone identified its occupant as Sir Robert Meredydd. An obscure figure. If indeed, thought Ingley, he had ever existed.

The main inscription, he was now convinced, had been done later, the slab cemented to the side of the tomb; he could see an ancient crack where something had gone amiss, been repaired. He put away rule, notebook, pen, spectacles. Picked up his torch from the knight's armoured belly.

Got you now, friend. Yes.

17

For a moment, in the heat of certainty, all his principles deserted him and he wanted to tear the tomb open, take up a slegehammer or something and smash his way in.

Involuntarily, he shouted out, 'Got you!' And now he really did slap the effigy, full in its smug, smiling face.

A certain coldness spread up his arm as the slap resounded from the rafters.

Ingley stepped back, panting, shocked at himself. He felt silence swelling in the church.

The knight's cold face flickered. The torch went out.

Batteries.

Couldn't say he hadn't been warned. Too absorbed in his work to notice it growing dim. He shook the torch; a mean amber glimmer, then it died.

Mission accomplished, anyway. Retreating into the aisle, he glanced over his shoulder at the stone husk on the tomb, its dead lips luminously purpled by the colour of the night through the long windows. He would go now. He hurried down the aisle, *tock, tock, tock*.

As if to guide him on his way, five yards distant, at the entrance to the nave, close to the font (heptagonal, nineteenth-century replacement) a meagre flame appeared, like a taper. When he moved forward to try and see it more clearly, the small light moved with him, as if whoever held it was backing away.

'I'm sorry,' Ingley said, raising his head and his voice, authoritative, irascible, producing an echo. 'Who is there?'

there . . . there . . . ere . . .

He registered, disturbed, that the little flame cast no ambience. It was like the light through a keyhole, something on the other side of the dark.

Then it went out.

Was somebody with him now in the church? Somebody who'd seen him by the tomb, who would tell them what he'd been doing? Who'd now doused his light to . . . .

Blindfold we could find our way around this place . . .

18

More likely he was simply overexcited and overtired. He stood very still, disgusted at his heart for suddenly pulsing in his chest like some squirming animal. Pills, where were his pills?

'Finished now. Leaving,' he said to nobody.

ving . . . ing . . .

Back in the inn, that was where they were, the pills. On the dresser in his room.

'. . . Leaving, all right . . .?'

. . . ight.

There was nobody. Nobody at all. He walked down the aisle to the great door, which was open a crack – had he left it like that? Thought perhaps he had, certainly didn't remember closing it. He glanced back into the church, towards the altar and the tomb, neither visible now. Saw only the tall Gothic windows tinctured in amethyst. He grasped the iron ring handle and hauled the door closed behind him, hearing the muffled echo of the latch from within.

Out then, gratefully, into the remembered warmth of a summer night, into the churchyard's terraced circle, from where one could look down on the yellow glowing of the village. Relieved, he took a great gulp of the soft night air.

The air was hard and slammed into his throat and locked there.

Ingley spun round, blinking.

No lights.

No village.

No moon.

He clutched at the stone porch and the breath came out of him like razorblades.

The circular cemetery was an island in a dark, polluted sea. The sky was black, and something was swirling about him, plucking playfully at his jacket.

He hauled in another breath; it didn't want to come. He slapped at his jacket where the dark wind was fingering it like a pickpocket.

The breath came up like an anchor through mud. His chest seemed to creak. Cold too out here now, and damp. No sweet smells any more.

Then the true essence of the place came to him, faint at first, and shocking because . . .

'Oh, Christ!' The little fat man, clamping a cupped hand over his mouth and nose, was thrown back by the stench.

Stench?

Yes, yes, vile, decaying, putrid . . . as if the season had betrayed them and the scented flowers had choked and bloated on their stems. He knew that stink, had always known it. He knew it from hospital wards and his stricken mother's bedroom, from dustbins in summer and the yard behind his father's butcher's shop. And he knew, sad and angry now, that it was not as it seemed. It was within him – had to be – the blackness, the smell, the withering.

His own lights going out.

Poor old Ingley, historian, antiquary, awkward customer, abrupt sometimes, knew it – but so little time to do things, always so little time. Hang on to things. Hang on to reality – single-chamber church with tower to the West, perpendicular, wooden bell-stage, pyramidal two-tiered roof . . .

Then, at first vaporous and indistinct, above a middle-distant grave, possibly the grave of Ebenezer Watkins, rose the little flame. Rose up and hovered, steamy and flickering as if in the hand of a still, dark figure, waiting. And blue this time, a cold and gaseous blue.

Ingley began to sob, and it was bitterly painful in his chest.

CHAPTER II

THE corpse wore a shroud and a silly smile, and its hair was sticking out like wires. The five people standing around its coffin were gloomily dressed in black or dark brown – but they too were smiling.

Bethan was not smiling. It ought to have been comical, but

it seemed all the more sinister and graphically real without the benefit of perspective. With the figures ludicrously out of proportion, big heads like grinning toffee apples on black sticks, it resembled some crude medieval engraving.

She turned over the exercise book to look at the name on the cover, and she was right. Sali Dafis, it said unevenly in capitals. She turned back to the drawing. Underneath it the childish script said in Welsh,

> *Old Mrs Jones, Ty Canol, died on Friday. We all went in to see her. She was in her coffin. It was on the table. Nain said she knew Mrs Jones would die soon because she saw the cannwyll gorff in the churchyard and it went all the way to Mrs Jones's door.*

On the facing page, another drawing showed a white gravestone against a sky crosshatched with dark-blue crayon. In the sky were a half-moon and several stars and something that looked like a bigger star hanging over the grave. Underneath this one was written,

> *Here is the cannwyll gorff over the grave of Mr Tegwyn Jones. He is sending it to fetch his wife.*

'God,' Bethan said and slapped the exercise book face-down on the sofa.

She'd told the children to pretend they were working for the *papur bro*, the community newspaper in Pontmeurig, and to write about something that had happened in their own village which they thought people ought to know about. Of the results she'd seen so far, most had been predictably innocuous. Carys Huws had written about the haymaking and how the farmers were hoping to have it finished in time to go to the Royal Welsh agricultural show. Bobi Fon had described the chairman's chair his father, the carpenter, had made for Glanmeurig District Council.

But both Cefyn Lewis and Glyn Jones had described the *Gorsedd Ddu* meeting in the oakwoods at dead of night to

21

judge the traitors and the cowards – writing as if it had really happened, although both were old enough to know the difference between history and legend.

And now Sali had written again of some sinister, imaginary aspect of death.

Slowly, to calm herself, Bethan poured out a mug of tea. Yesterday she'd overheard Glyn and Cefyn telling little Nerys Roberts about the *toili*, as if it were a regular feature of village life. Nerys was big-eyed and pale. Bethan, furious, had sent the two boys out into the yard, from where they'd grinned slyly at her through the window.

Buddug, she thought. Buddug is behind this.

She sipped the tea; it was horribly strong and bitter. Bethan grimaced. Corpse candles, phantom funerals. The knocking, the moaning, the bird of death. It was insidious.

The tea in the pot was as dense as peat. She went into the kitchen to make some more, pulling the rubber band from her black hair, shaking her head and letting the hair fall softly, comfortingly around her shoulders. She felt very alone.

Waiting for the kettle to boil, Bethan stood by the window, wondering whether to take up smoking again, and she thought, I hate weekends.

Outside the window it was Saturday night in Pontmeurig. Only eight miles – and yet a whole world – away from the village of Y Groes. Barely four thousand people lived in this town now, but it still had seventeen pubs. Considering how much of the population was either too young, too sick or too ostensibly clean-living to go out for a drink, that left . . . well, it made Bethan wonder how they'd all survived, the seventeen pubs.

She took off her glasses and rubbed at her eyes, smudging the remains of her make-up and not caring; she would not be going anywhere tonight.

Just before ten o'clock, Guto Evans phoned.

'What are you doing then, Bethan, at this moment?'

'Nothing illegal,' Bethan said cautiously.

'That's a shame,' Guto said. He paused, hesitated. 'Look,

22

the night, as they say, is young. Why don't we go out and paint the town? Any colour you like, except for grey, which nobody would notice.'

Bethan pictured him with the phone tucked into his shaggy beard, like a big terrier with a bone, his stocky frame wedged into a corner of his mother's front parlour amid hundreds of plates and china ornaments.

'I don't think so,' Bethan said solemnly into the phone. Her glasses slipped and with one finger she pushed them back along her nose. 'I have my reputation to protect. You would lead me into bad ways.'

'One drink, then? A chat?'

'I'm sorry, Guto, I do appreciate it. It's just . . . well, I've such a lot of work to catch up on.'

And she drew him away from the subject by asking if he'd heard about the unfortunate incident at that afternoon's protest demo by some of their mutual friends in the sometimes-militant Welsh Language Society. The society had targeted a particular estate agent in Aberystwyth who specialised in selling country cottages in Welsh-speaking areas to affluent English people looking for holiday homes.

'It got seriously out of hand, of course,' Bethan said. 'Some of the boys had collected For Sale signs out of people's gardens and heaped them up outside Hughes's door. And what should someone do but pour paraffin over the pile and set them alight. If the fire brigade had not arrived in time, who knows, the whole building might have gone up.'

'Would have been no great loss. Bloody Emyr Hughes. Him and his new Mercedes. And a helicopter now, did you hear?' Guto snorted. 'Traitorous fat bastard. Grown fat on English gold.'

Bethan smiled. Guto sharpening up his rhetoric, now, because it was rumoured Burnham-Lloyd was a very sick man and there might soon be a by-election. 'So Dewi and Alun Phillips were arrested,' she said. 'They will probably be charged tomorrow. Wilful damage, I hope. Not arson.'

'Of course, I would have been there myself,' Guto said. 'But I am keeping a low political profile until such time as I am called.'

'Well, there's sensible,' said Bethan, in mock-surprise. She paused. 'Um, it was nice of you to ask me out.'

'Yes,' said Guto. 'I am a nice man, this is true.'

'But I must get back to my marking.'

'Should I call again some time?'

'Yes. When I'm not so busy.'

'And when will that be? No, no, it's all right. I might be nice but I'm not daft. Goodnight, Bethan. *Nos da*.'

'Guto, have you ever found . . .?'

'What?'

She had been going to ask about the *cannwyll gorff*. She stopped herself. What could she say? Guto, I'm scared. There is something badly wrong in the village and I don't think I can handle it.

'Hello . . . Bethan . . .?'

But if she said any more then Guto would say it was quite clear that in her state of mind Bethan should not be spending the night alone, and so . . .

'Are you still there, Bethan?'

'Yes . . . I . . . It doesn't matter,' she said. '*Nos da*, Guto.'

'You take care of yourself,' he said.

It would have been nice to go out for a drink. And a chat. Just a chat. She wondered: did I say no because it would not be seemly for a widow of less than a year to be seen out with Guto Evans on a Saturday night in Pontmeurig?

No, she decided. If I'd thought that, I would have gone.

Saturday night was probably the reason the seventeen pubs survived.

They had come into Pontmeurig now, from all the outlying villages and the hill farms, sometimes six or seven of them in a single Land-Rover. Farmers, farmers' sons, farmers' grandsons. Even a few women, these days. Some of the men would get quietly and expertly drunk. A handful would make a macho celebration out of it, and there would perhaps be a fight, a smashed window, a beer glass flung into the street, splintering against the kerb or somebody's head.

24

A yellow haze of smoke and steam, beer fumes and chip fat settled on the street below the lighted window of the apartment over Hampton's bookshop. In the window, Bethan was a still silhouette.

She drew the thin curtains, turned back to the sadly over-crowded sitting room, drank tea and glared at the dark green cover of the book lying on the sofa. Sali Dafis. Aged seven.

A bright child. Confident too – winner of the recitation prize for her age-group at this year's Urdd Eisteddfod, where three other children from the school had also won prizes. Which was incredible for a little village school with just twenty-four pupils. One of the judges had commented that this was clearly a school where children were encouraged to be imaginative. He could say that again, Bethan thought. She remembered Buddug, huge and beaming, in the audience. Buddug, quite rightly, taking all the credit because Bethan had been away looking after a sick husband,

Then mourning for a dead husband.

She was back now. She didn't have to return, she'd terminated her lease on the cottage. She could have gone anywhere, stayed in the city, where there was no silence and no sense of a gathering darkness.

Parting the curtains, Bethan looked down into the street, watched four youths standing outside the Drovers' Arms nursing beer glasses, admiring a motor bike. She thought, I should have gone. Maybe it was my last chance. I've been too long with death.

Irritated and restless now, she snatched the green exercise book from the sofa. Sali Dafis was the daughter of the man who ran the garage. Her mother had died when Sali was a baby; the child had been raised by her grandmother, Mrs Bronwen Dafis, a withered crone who dispensed herbal remedies and told fortunes.

And who, Bethan thought, frowning, was also a friend of Buddug's.

She got out her red pen, intending not to mark Sali's exercise but to write, 'See me after school' at the bottom of it, because the child needed help. She had a vague memory of

Sali's mother, a little blonde-haired secretary from Essex whom Dilwyn had met on holiday.

As she started to write *'gwel . . .'* at the bottom of the second drawing, Bethan's red ballpoint pen ran out. Without thinking, she bustled into the bedroom to pinch a pen from the inside pocket of Robin's jacket in the wardrobe. Stood there with the wardrobe door half-open, a hand inside feeling from coat to coat. *Her* coats. Realising then that Robin's jacket had never been in this bedroom, had gone long ago to the Oxfam shop, probably with the pens still in the pocket.

I'm not going to cry, she told herself. I'm going to laugh. But she couldn't make her lips go through the motions.

She heard a scornful, trailing cheer from the street outside, as she went back into the living room, edging around cumbersome furniture she didn't need any more. A male voice hooted and a girl screamed in excitement as Bethan sat down at the table to continue her note to Sali in pencil.

'Geraint, don't . . .!' the girl squealed in the street, and Bethan knew that whatever it was Geraint was doing, the girl really didn't mind. It was about romance.

Bethan looked up from the table. By the wan light of the Victorian brass standard lamp, their first Christmas present from Robin's mother in Durham, she saw a little attic flat over somebody else's failed bookshop in a town which had been falling apart for five centuries.

Single person's accommodation, Bethan thought.

She broke down then, a hot rush of despair, over the horror-comic drawings of Sali Dafis, aged seven.

For three nights before Robin died, the village women said, the *cannwyll gorff* had been seen. First in the churchyard. Then over the river.

Finally, hanging solemnly in the still air outside their cottage.

When Bethan raised her head from the table she saw that the pages of the exercise book were crumpled and tear-stained.

I spilled tea on your book, she would tell Sali on Monday. I shall have to give you a new one. I'm sorry. All your nice drawings.

Feeling suddenly light-headed, she almost rang Guto back to say yes, she would go out with him and they would get very, very drunk.

She didn't, though. It was not the time.

CHAPTER III

ABOVE him the whitewashed ceiling gleamed faintly between beams as thick as railway sleepers. The heavy bed of Victorian mahogany was creaking below like the timbers of a sailing ship.

Sinking.

Head rolling back on the pillow, he closed his eyes.

. . . And his mind was alive with images, burgling his brain like fragments of a dream getting through from the other side of sleep, as if they couldn't wait. Black tower in a purple sky, perpendicular tower, wooden bell-stage, in tiers . . .

Always ends in tiers, he thought ludicrously. Opening his eyes again, he tried to calm his thoughts, remembering pushing at the door of the inn to escape from the cloying dark. Then the yellow light, beer haze, oak beams, the ceaseless banter – the overwhelming relief of it, of being back amongst these tiresome people with their impenetrable language. Still not closing time when he'd returned. How had he made it back so quickly?

Pounding pain in his chest now. He reached to the bedside cabinet for a Trinitrin. Slipped it under his tongue. How had he got back? He remembered the stink of decay all around him in the churchyard. Remembered trying to find the steps in the mist. Then nothing until the door and the yellow light. Inside, they had seemed almost pleased to see him.

'All right then, Professor?'

'Well hell, man, you look cold . . .'

'Course he's cold, Morgan. Bloody church – sorry Reverend

27

– always cold, that church. No heating, see. Get him a drink, for God's sake, Aled.'

'Oh, I'm so sorry, Doctor Ingley. Should have replaced these batteries weeks ago, but you know how it is. Look, my fault, have a drink. What is it to be now, nice drop of brandy? Best Welsh brandy, mind . . .'

'Thank you, no. I think I'll go directly to bed.'

'Big mistake, Professor. First time this year Aled's offered anybody a free tot of his precious bloody brandy. Never see it again.'

'Leave him be, Morgan. Poor man's knackered.'

'Oh aye, leave him be, now, is it Aled? Any excuse, you bugger.'

'I'm sorry, I . . . good night.'

'Night, Professor.'

'*Nos da i chi!*'

Still the pain.

Another Trinitrin. Worked in seconds, they always worked in seconds. He lay there in the bed, not moving, the pill under his tongue. It was a small room; just beyond the bed was a lumbering Victorian wardrobe, to its right the uncurtained window hanging open for air, bringing in the sounds of glasses jingling as they were collected in the bar below, laughter, oaths, a *nos da* or two.

He was uncomfortable and tried to roll over. But when he moved the pain ripped through his chest like the roots of a tree being torn out of the ground.

Christ.

Breathe. Come on, breathe steadily.

His eyes closed by themselves.

Creaking of the bed. Wooden bed. Wooden bellstage, moulded doorway eighteenth century, heptagonal font, perpendicular tower . . . black on purple . . . falling . . . Oh God in heaven, I don't know where I am . . .

Blindfold we could find our way . . .

Calm down. It wasn't a candle.

candle, andle, ndle . . .

Sharp, probing pain now, deep in his chest, like a slender knife going in . . .

. . . and his eyes came open, to show him there *was* a candle. At the bottom of the bed. Just above his feet. The flame did not waver.

He shut out the image in frozen panic. It was only a symbol, a motif summoned by his subconscious, an hallucination, a manifestation of the corruption in his system – a sick body's attempt to bring down the mind to its own level of decay.

Dying people, he thought in silent hysteria, conjured up choirs of angels, all that nonsense. Chemicals. And his own chemicals now, flooding about uncontrollably, mixing their toxic cocktails, how ironic that they should throw off such an image. The corpse candle. Harbinger of death. Flickering from the periphery of his scholarly probings into a society still obsessed with its own mythology.

He could make this candle go away. He could send it back to his subconscious. He was furious now. He would not submit to this invasion. And he would not die. Damned if he would. Damned if he . . .

Ingley squeezed his eyes shut, trying to squeeze rationality into his thoughts.

and found himself walking up the aisle of the church, footsteps on stone, *tock*, *tock*, *tock* . . .

Turn back, turn back, turn back . . .!

tock, *tock*, *tock* . . .

Can't . . . Can't go on . . . Must go back . . .

Drawn steadily down the aisle towards the steep windows leaking livid light into the nave.

He struggled frantically to open his eyes, didn't care now what arcane symbol they would show him, so long as it could pull him out of this place of old, forgotten, stinking evil. He felt himself rolling about in the bed, sweating cold fluid, screaming inside. But his eyelids, fastened down like heavy blinds, would not move. He remembered as a boy being shut by older boys inside a wall cupboard where there was barely room to breathe and heaving at the door in helpless panic, his first experience of claustrophobia, the stifling terror.

tock . . . *tock* . . .

Please. Let me go. I'm sorry, oh God, I'm sorry.

It was cold in the church. The altar cloth was white, with a mulberry splash, like an old bloodstain, where it caught the light through the long windows. The altar was where you turned left, three paces to . . .

No . . .!

Three paces.

tock . . .

The air thickened and vibrated with a frigid energy.

tock . . .

No. Please . . . Can't . . . Jesus Christ, let me out!

tock

A long black shadow arose in his path. He screamed. Screamed to get out of the church. Screamed for his eyes to open. But it was as if, while his mind was elsewhere, both eyelids had been very precisely stitched up.

. . . but the stone eyelids of the knight sprang open, and his eyes were of cold amethyst light. His hands unclasped from prayer, chipped knuckles, white bone beneath the stone, seeking one's throat. His stone mouth splintered into a grin.

Thomas Ingley threw all that remained of his strength into the fight to re-enter his bedroom at the inn, like pushing and pushing at a seized-up manhole cover to escape from some fetid cellar, the strain tearing at his poor exhausted heart, stretching and popping like rotted rubber.

Don't want to know who you are. Don't care any more who you are! But please . . . don't let it happen here, not here, to be held for ever among the deep shadows and the misty mauveness . . .

The stone hands locked around his windpipe. His eyeballs bulged.

And his eyes opened.

Lids flicking up with a butterfly motion. Effortless.

The room was quiet and the air was still. He could see the wardrobe in the corner by the door. The moon through the uncurtained window. The luminous green hands of the travel alarm clock, although he couldn't make out how they were arranged. Inside his chest he felt nothing at all. The bed was silent now, no creaks. He expected to find the bedclothes in knots, but the sheets were still stiffly tucked in around him. Hospital corners. He lay calmly motionless and listened to his breathing, steady now. Nor could he feel his heart pounding any more.

So peaceful.

The relief was so great that he didn't try to move, just let his head sink into the pillow and his gaze drift up to the ceiling, where the little light hung in a frosty miasma about six inches above his temple. He went on watching the light, fully resigned now, as it turned from blue to pink . . . to blood red.

He tried to scream then, his face twisting, but it came out as a parched rattle.

CHAPTER IV

THIS was the thing about Wales. Some places seemed cursed – filthy weather, soil you could hardly grow dandelions in – and some places, like this village, had it all. The change, when you came out of the forestry, the other side of the Nearly Mountains, was dramatic and yet subtle too . . . the landscape greener, the weather milder, the whole atmosphere all-round mellower.

It embraced you, he thought, like a good woman.

The better to appreciate it, Dai Death, the undertaker from Pontmeurig, stopped his hearse in the middle of the road, where it left the forestry, and looked down on the village in its little cwm. Sunday afternoon. No hurry. It had looked like rain in Pontmeurig, but the sky over Y Groes was as deep a blue as you could ever expect to see in Wales. The cottages were a clutch of eggs in a nest; the church a benevolent old bird.

A clutch of eggs, yes. Nice metaphor. Dai liked to write a bit of poetry and aspired to the crown of the Glanmeurig

31

Eisteddfod. Sitting at the wheel of his hearse, window wound down and the sunlight warm on his bald head, he lit a cigarette, feeling happy because he liked doing business in Y Groes and it wasn't often he got the chance – not because nobody died here, but because they had little use for undertakers. He wondered, not for the first time, how anyone could look out at such a place from his deathbed and hold on to any hopes of going to a greater paradise.

By all accounts, though, today's customer had been in no position to dwell upon the relative merits of a hypothetical heaven and the village of Y Groes. He'd gone in the night, when, Dai supposed, Y Groes looked much the same as any other village.

An engine grumbled at him from behind. In his wing mirror he saw a tractor that couldn't get past, it being a narrow road and the farmer not wanting to sound his horn because he could see a coffin in the back of Dai's hearse and how was he to know it was empty?

'All right, man, I'm off.'

Dai tossed his cigarette out of the window, raised an apologetic hand and put the hearse in gear. Normally he might have let out the clutch sharpish like, and shot off with a spurt – bouncing the pale utility coffin into the air and giving the bugger on the tractor one hell of a shock. But he didn't like to do that now.

Not here.

For Dai's greatest aspiration, even closer to his heart than the thought of wearing the plastic crown at the Glanmeurig Eisteddfod, was to get himself a cottage in this village, to retire one day to paradise.

He was on his own today, his brother Harri still in Bronglais Hospital with his back. So he had to ask the landlord to give him a hand with the customer.

'Police sent you, is it?'

Dai nodded. 'Said could they have him stored until they find his relatives down in England.' He lifted up the tailgate of the hearse and pulled out the lightweight fibre-glass coffin with one hand. 'Well, see, I don't mind jobs like this, even on a Sunday. Sooner or later some bugger pays the bill.' He smiled slyly. 'English prices, isn't it?'

The bedroom was almost directly over the bar. It had a very low ceiling and wasn't really big enough for three men, even if one would be forever still.

'Above and beyond, this is, Dai.' Aled grunted as they laid the body on a plastic sheet next to the coffin. It was going to be a tight fit. 'Not what I'd call a small man, the Professor. Also, seemed to smell a good deal better, if I remember, when he was alive.'

'Obviously went off in a bit of a sweat,' Dai observed.

The customer was somewhere between late middle-aged and elderly. There was a touch of froth, which nobody had bothered to wipe away, at the side of his mouth.

'Professor, you say?' Dai said conversationally, trying not to react to the expression on the face of the customer. He was reminded of the time he'd removed a body from a dentist's chair, a man, who – mortally afraid of dentists all his life – had expired at the very moment of extraction.

'Well, of sorts.' Aled was small, but wiry and strong enough to take the corpse's weight at the shoulders. 'Big Morgan, it was, first started calling him that. Retired teacher, I suppose, or a college lecturer. Some sort of historian. Always walking around making notes, looking at things, never at people, you know the kind. Oh, Christ, I forgot they did that. Pass me that cloth, will you, Dai.'

'Sorry, Aled. Should have thought.' In this part of the world most people still knew the basics of it. They had not grown up with funeral parlours; laying out their relatives was something most of them had had to learn, like changing a wheel. Not only was it uneconomical to pay somebody like Dai to prepare a corpse, it was also still considered in many homes – and particularly, he'd found, in Y Groes – to be less than polite to the deceased.

'Can you do anything about that?' Aled asked, nodding at the face. 'Or does he have to go to his maker looking as though somebody was amputating his leg without the anaesthetic?'

Dai made a professional appraisal of the customer's blue and twisted features, working out how they might be rearranged. 'Easy,' he said loftily. 'Piece of piss. What was it, anyway?'

'Well, heart. Angina, something of that order. Dr Wyn said he was not surprised at all. Been coming here for months, see. Had his pills through Dr Wyn regular.'

'Why was that?'

'Well, convenient, I suppose.'

'No, no, I mean why did he come here? The fishing?'

'No, I was telling you. Historian or something. Into old churches.'

'Not old houses?' In Dai's experience, most of the English people who persistently returned to this area were looking to buy a piece of it, some little stone cottage with an inglenook and a view of the mountains. 'Buggers go crazy over places like this.'

'Do they now?' Aled said. 'Well, well.'

'Name your price, man, place like this. Name your bloody price.'

Aled made no reply. Dai looked for an expression in the landlord's compact face, but none was apparent. All the same, he decided this was as good an opening as any, and so he said carefully, 'You know . . . I was only thinking to myself, well, I wouldn't mind retiring to Y Groes, me and the wife. Nowhere quite like it, see, for the peace and quiet.' Casual like. In passing. Not sounding as serious as he really was. 'But hell, man, I don't suppose I could afford it any more, even with selling the business, the way things are going, the prices.'

'Where do you want him?' Aled asked, as if he hadn't heard any of this. 'In that thing, is it?'

'In the shell.'

'The what?'

'Shell. What we call it. Utility job, see. Just to get him to the warehouse, and then the relatives choose something more tasteful.' Dai tapped the side of the light-coloured coffin to show how cheap and flimsy it was, then returned, hopefully, to his theme. 'What's the answer, though? What is the answer?

34

Local boy wants a home of his own, priced out of the market before he starts. Got to go, isn't it? No option. Winds up in bloody Birmingham or somewhere and all the rich buggers who couldn't tell a Welsh mountain ewe from a Beulah speckle-faced if you drew 'em a diagram are moving in and building bloody squash courts. Well, of course, I have nothing against the English, as a race . . . Right, now, you get the other side and we'll . . . Ah, lovely job.'

Both men stood back. Dai Death mopped his bald head with a handkerchief. 'So, tell me, purely out of interest, like . . . How much are they fetching?'

'Beulah speckle-faced?'

'Houses, man! What would it cost for me to get a place here? How much did the last one go for?'

'I can't remember. It was a long time ago.'

'Oh, come on now!' Dai was getting a bit exasperated. What Aled was supposed to say was, well, Dai, funny you should bring that up because there's this very interesting little place I know of, not on the market yet, but if they thought you were keen – you being a local boy, a Welsh-speaker and a respected professional man – I'm sure a nice quick deal could be arranged, no fuss, no estate agents.

'That it?' Aled demanded. 'Finished, have we?'

'I can't credit that at all,' Dai said. 'Bloody hell, in Pont, I'm not kidding, the estate agents' signs have been going up faster than the TV aerials when we got the first transmitter.'

'So they tell me,' said Aled.

'But not here.'

'No.' A note of finality. 'Not here.'

Dai was baffled and felt slighted. What, he wondered, had happened to Tegwyn Jones's place now his wife was also dead? Every village always had a couple of houses ready for the market, especially now, when the English would pay a small fortune for something you wouldn't keep chickens in. And what about – now here was a point – what about the judge's house?

'Having the lid on, are we, Dai?'

'I'll deal with that. Tricky, this sort. Professional use only.'

35

Dai straightened up, gathering what was left of his dignity. They only ever called him out here for the foreigners, like that chap Martin, the curate. And poor Bethan's man.

He sniffed. For Judge Rhys there'd been a coffin custom-made by Dewi Fon, the carpenter, gravestone by Myrddin Jones, the sculptor. He went out to the landing and returned with a rectangular strip of fibreglass, which he slotted into place, concealing the dreadful face of the Professor. Wondering gloomily who would be doing this job in ten years' time when he and Harri had retired, Harri being a bachelor and Dai's son away at university to study engineering. No doubt the business would get taken over by one of these national chains with colour brochures of coffins and off-the-peg shrouds. Well, bollocks to that.

'So what happened,' he asked bluntly, 'to the judge's house?'

'Well done, Dai,' said Aled, ignoring the question. 'Look, come and have a drink before we take him down.' He towed the coffin away from the bedroom door so they could get out. 'There, see . . . getting soft, I am, helping you with your bloody corpse then offering you a drink.' He smiled. 'Stiff one, is it?'

'Very funny,' said Dai Death. 'I'll have a pint and I'll pay you for it.'

'Good God. Epidemic of something fatal, is there, in Pontmeurig, that you're so wealthy?'

'The judge's house,' Dai reminded him, annoyed now and showing it. 'Just tell me what happened to the fucking judge's house?'

Driving away, customer in the back, Dai took careful note. And, yes, it was true enough. Not a For Sale sign anywhere in the village. He shook his head in disbelief, afflicted by the usual aching longing as he took in the mellow stone and timber-framed dwellings, the crooked stone steps and walled gardens, the soft fields and the stately oaks, the wooded amphitheatre of hills sloping to the Nearly Mountains. Even the bloody

Nearly Mountains, wind-blasted and conifer-choked . . . even they looked impressive when viewed from Y Groes.

He looked back towards the lane which led to the judge's house. It would have been perfect. Not too big, not too small, nicely screened. But a lost cause. Christ, he'd never even heard of the old chap having a grand-daughter. Recluse who never left the village, never even went into Pontmeurig. Maybe – he brightened momentarily – maybe she'd want to sell. But then – his spirits sagging again – what would she do but advertise it in the London papers?

It was, he thought, only a matter of time. They were bound to discover this place, the English. Some young stockbroker-type would cruise out here in his Porsche and spot a derelict barn, ripe for conversion, and make the farmer an offer he'd be a fool to refuse. And another farmer would hear about it and he'd sell *two* of his buildings. Then some poor widow would be staggered at how much she could get for her cottage. And, in no time at all, there'd be a little colony of English, enough to hold a bridge party with After Eight mints.

Dai gave Y Groes a final rueful glance before turning into the forestry.

And in time, he thought, the little clutch of eggs will turn rotten in the nest.

PART TWO

NOT MEANT TO
BE THERE

CHAPTER V

ENGLAND

LYING back, red hair all over the pillow and the cane headboard too, Miranda applied the Zippo to the end of her cigarette and said, 'So, how was it for *you*, Miranda?'

Berry Morelli said, 'Huh?' The sweat on his back was merely damp now, and chilly. It was an hour before dawn, the bedroom half-lit from the street.

In a dreamy voice, Miranda replied, 'Well, since you ask, Miranda, not too wonderful. I can say, with some degree of confidence, that I have definitely had better. I suppose, as rapes go, it was not *without* consideration . . .'

'Rape?' Berry Morelli sat up. 'You said *rape?*'

'Well, if it was meant to be love-making,' Miranda said, 'it was distressingly short on the customary endearments. In fact, now I think about it, it was entirely silent, bar the odd sharp intake of breath.'

'Hey, listen, I . . .' Berry leaned over her and helped himself to one of her cigarettes from the bedside table.

'. . . And then I began to detect in this rapist a . . . sort of underlying absence of joy, would that describe it? One's first experience of *pre*-coital tristesse. Or perhaps it was simply lack of interest, which would be *considerably* less tolerable.' Miranda turned onto her side to face him, looking pale and fragile – which she wasn't – in the hazy streetlight from the uncurtained window.

'OK,' she said. 'What's eating you, Morelli?'

Berry hauled black hair out of his eyes. The hair was still wet. From the rain not the sweat. 'Listen, I'm sorry, kid.'

'Oh, please . . . not the apology. I expect I enjoyed it more than you anyway.' She covered up a breast and stared into space, smoking. 'And don't call me "kid", all right?'

This Miranda. You could never figure out if she was deeply

41

wounded or what. Berry rolled out of bed and into his bathrobe. 'You want some tea?' He was fully into tea now, no coffee these days. Very British.

'No sugar,' Miranda said. 'No, wait . . . make that two sugars. I suspect, God help me, that the night is yet young.'

'I'll fetch a tray. Black?'

'Morelli, we haven't all got the zeal of the converted.'

'OK.' While Berry's hands moved things around in the tiny kitchen, his head was still walking the streets. There'd been cabs around the hospital but he'd needed to walk. Death did that to you, he thought. You had to keep moving, proving to yourself you still could.

A bad night, in the end.

And he'd lost a friend.

He couldn't afford to lose a friend in this country. It only left one, if you didn't include Miranda. Which he didn't, yet.

'Biscuits, too, Morelli,' she called imperiously from the bedroom. Miranda, whom he'd often find in his bed but whom he hesitated to call his regular girlfriend. Who'd gone home with him the first time because, she explained, she liked the sound of his name, the way you liked the sound of Al Pacino and Robert de Niro. There were dukes in Miranda's family and her aunt had once been a temporary lady-in-waiting to Princess Anne. Berry liked the sound of Miranda's name too, the way you liked the sound of cucumber sandwiches and Glyndebourne.

'Morelli!'

'What?'

'Biscuits.'

'Yeah, I heard.'

'The chocolate ginger things from Sainsbury's, OK?'

'Right.'

Earlier tonight Miranda's good mood had blown like a light bulb after she'd produced tickets for Peter Gabriel and he'd told her he wouldn't be able to make the gig on account of it was Old Winstone's farewell binge. Old Winstone, his friend.

She hadn't believed him. 'What's he doing having it on a Sunday night?'

'All about Monday morning. If he gets smashed, he doesn't wake up till way past the time he normally goes to work. Thus avoiding the initial trauma of his first day of retirement.'

'You think I'm awfully stupid don't you, Morelli?' Miranda had said.

'Listen, I'm . . .'

'Sorry. Yes.'

Berry put on the light as he carried the tea tray into the bedroom. 'I didn't figure on you being here when I got in.'

'I suppose that explains it,' Miranda said. 'You thought you were shagging someone else.'

'You never came back before. Not the same night. Not after a fight. How'd you get in anyway?'

'I'm frightfully unpredictable,' she said, sitting up, breasts wobbling at him and somehow making the trayful of cups jiggle in his hands. 'It's part of my appeal.' She giggled, a sound like Chinese bells, signifying things were OK again, for the time being. 'And I'm not going to tell you how I got in, because I'm also terribly clever and rather mysterious.'

Mysterious, she wasn't. In spite of everything, he grinned, wishing he could say she was his girlfriend. Why was he so goddamn insecure? He set the tea tray down on the bed and Miranda reached across to pour. 'Too strong as usual, Morelli. You're an awfully selfish bastard.'

He flinched a little. It was what his old man had said, leading to Berry's decision to leave the States. *You're a goddamn selfish bastard. You don't have to agree with a fucking thing I stand for, but when you screw things up for me to further your own pissant career, that's indefensible, boy.*

'Listen, I guess what happened was I used you,' he confessed to Miranda, 'to reinforce my hold on life. How's that sound?'

'Pretentious.'

'It was kind of a heavy night.'

'You're not pissed, though, are you?'

'No, I . . . Jesus, this guy – a friend – he just died on me.'

'To be quite honest I thought somebody was dying on *me*,' Miranda said. 'Don't do it again. Wake me up first, I might've missed it.'

'Yeah, I'm . . .' Shit, he seemed to spend half his time apologising to people. Maybe he should apologise for apologising too much. He felt he could still hear the ambulance siren, the efficient clunk of the rear doors after they'd loaded the stretcher. The finality of it. He'd known then that it was final.

'Oh for God's sake, Morelli . . .' Miranda drowned her cigarette end in the dregs of her tea, a small rebellion against her refined upbringing. 'Tell mummy all about it. Who died on you? You don't mean mean really died? As in, you know . . . turning up one's toes?'

Berry drank his tea, not quite knowing where to start. He detected mild amusement in Miranda's green eyes. How could it be really serious if he'd strolled in afterwards and screwed her, however perfunctory that had been?

'I ever tell you about this guy I know, Giles Freeman?'

'The political reporter? I met him, if you remember, that time at Verity's. Very dashing and sporty, but terribly earnest. Quiet little wife, a bit hamsterish.'

Berry admired the way Miranda took in the essence of people she'd met only in passing. Ought to have been a much better actress than she was – maybe she just found it hard to let her own outrageous personality be submerged by lesser ones.

'You're saying Giles Freeman is dead?'

'Huh? No, shit, Giles is fine. That is . . .' He put the empty cup on the tea-tray and set it down on the carpet. And then he asked her, because this really was the bottom line, 'You ever get to Wales?'

'Wales?' Miranda patted around the duvet for her cigarettes. 'What's Wales got to do with it?'

'You ever go there?'

'Morelli,' she said, 'do I look like the kind of person who has Welsh connections? Like someone who reads the Bible all the time, plays rugby and eats seaweed?'

Berry thought about this. 'Maybe not,' he conceded. He found her cigarettes in a fold of the duvet, lit two and passed her one. 'Folks do that in Wales? They eat seaweed?'

'So it is said. They make some kind of bread from it. I went there once, but it was depressing. It rained.'

Miranda. If she visited the Taj Mahal during a monsoon it would forever be depressing.

'But this is Britain, right?' Berry said. 'This is Wales, England? Same island. What I mean . . . Welsh folks live in England, English folks live in Wales.'

'If they're desperate enough. Or they've been offered some terribly lucrative job out there, and there can't be many of those. Why do you ask?'

'OK,' Berry said. 'Hypothetical, right? If you had friends aiming to move to Wales, what would you say to them?'

Miranda's mouth twitched impatiently. 'I'd probably say au revoir rather than goodbye because most of my friends wouldn't even survive in Dorking. Morelli, what is all this about?'

Berry sighed. 'Listen, forget the hypothetical shit. What it's about is there's this guy moving to Wales and I find myself in the position of having to try and prevent that. I mean, Christ, I never went there, I don't plan to go there, but I got to talk this guy out of it. Guy who wants to make his home there more than anywhere else in the world, however bizarre that sounds to you. That's it. That's the situation.'

Under the duvet Miranda ran a hand across his thigh and back again. 'Nothing doing, then?' she said, affecting a squeaky East End accent.

'Gimme a break.'

'Morelli, I'm sure there's an awfully interesting story behind all this but I don't somehow think I want to go into it after all. It sounds frightfully complicated, and' – she reached over to her teacup on the bedside cabinet and tipped her cigarette into it half-smoked – 'quite honestly, I find the whole subject of Wales the most awful turn-off.'

Miranda snuggled down, poking her bottom into Berry's right thigh and within a minute was asleep, leaving him to switch off the light and stare uncertainly into the blotchy dark, trying to figure out how this situation came about.

CHAPTER VI

THAT evening, seeing Winstone Thorpe flick open his ancient hooded eyes, Berry had thought of an old tomcat on a back-porch alerted by the flutter of wings.

'Where's that then?' Winstone had asked in that tired, diffident way he had.

'It's a smallish country sort of welded onto the side of England, Winstone,' Giles Freeman explained, and he giggled drunkenly. 'It's where the M4 peters out. They've got mountains there. Play rugby. Sing a lot.'

'Oh . . .' old Winstone Thorpe chuckled and his chins wobbled. 'You mean Wales. Sorry old boy, must've misheard.'

Sure you did, you old bastard, Berry thought affectionately. He looked at Winstone across the pub table. Then he looked at Giles, who was clearly too drunk to realise he was being set up. Several of the other journalists, who knew Winstone of old, glanced up from their drinks and grinned.

'Wales, eh?' Winstone said. 'Oh dear.'

There he goes, Berry thought.

'All right,' Giles Freeman said testily. 'What's that supposed to mean?' Giles had drunk maybe five pints of beer, and he wasn't used to it. His fair hair was in disarray and his long face was hot and shiny, freckles aglow. He was too drunk to realise how bored they all were with hearing about his incredible piece of luck – well, Claire's actually, her inheritance. But an utterly amazing old place, splendid countryside, absolutely terrific atmosphere. Just being there made you realise how totally cardboard and artificial your urban environment was.

So Giles had fallen heavily for some backwoods shack. And now old Winstone Thorpe, who had retired that day after more than half a lifetime on the *Daily Telegraph*, was blinking lazily beneath eyebrows like thatched eaves and saying 'Oh dear.'

'Well, come on, Winstone,' Giles was leaning aggressively across the table now. Berry had never seen him like this before;

somebody had hit a nerve. 'If you've got something to say, just bloody say it.'

'But, dear chap . . .' Winstone put down his empty whisky glass and looked around vaguely until Ray Wheeler of the *Mirror* slipped him a replacement. 'Ah, a fellow Christian. Thank you. No, you see – am I stating the obvious here? You're an Englishman, old boy.'

Somewhere a clock chimed. It was eleven o'clock, and there was a momentary silence in the battered Edwardian bar of what old Winstone Thorpe maintained was the last halfway decent pub in what used to be Fleet Street.

Berry found himself nodding. Aside, perhaps, from old Winstone himself, Giles Freeman was just about the most English guy he'd ever met, even here in England.

'Now look, Winstone,' Giles took an angry gulp of his beer. 'That is just incredibly simplistic. I mean, have you ever even been to Wales? Come on now, tell the truth?'

Wrong question, Giles, thought Berry. You just walked into it. He leaned back and waited for Winstone Thorpe's story, knowing there had to be one.

'Well, since you ask . . .' The venerable reporter unbuttoned his weighty tweed jacket and lifted his whisky glass onto his knee. 'Matter of fact, I *was* in Wales once.'

'No kidding,' Berry said and then shut up because there were guys here who still had him down as a no-talent asshole on the run. Things had changed since his last time here, as a student in the seventies. People had gotten tighter, more suspicious – even journalists. They were coming across like Americans imagined the English to be – stiff, superior. And they were suspicious of him because he wasn't like Americans were supposed to be – didn't drink a lot, never ate burgers. They weren't programmed for a vegetarian American hack who'd come up from the Underground press and dumped on his distinguished dad. Berry looked around the three tables pushed together and saw complacent smiles on prematurely-florid faces. These were mainly Parliamentary reporters like Giles. In this job, after a while, after long hours in the Westminster bars, journalists began to look like MPs.

'Early sixties, must've been,' Winstone said. His face had

long gone beyond merely florid to the colour and texture of an overripe plum. 'Sixty-two? Sixty-three? Anyway, we were dragged out to Wales on a Sunday on the sort of story that sounds as if it's going to be better than it actually turns out. Somebody'd shot this old farmer and his son, twelve-bore job, brains all over the wall. Lived miles from anywhere, up this God-forsaken mountain. Turned out the housekeeper did it, sordid domestic stuff, only worth a couple of pars. But that's beside the point.'

Berry glanced over at Giles who was trying to look bored. Giles caught the glance and rolled his eyes towards the ceiling. Berry got along OK with Giles, who was less clannish than the others.

'Point is,' Winstone said, 'Locals treated us as if we were lepers. Here we are, sitting in this grim, freezing so-called guest house like the lost bloody patrol – Sunday, so all the pubs are closed, can you imagine that – and all we can hear is the rain and the natives jabbering away at each other in Welsh, which is just about the world's most incomprehensible bloody language. We try to quiz the landlady: "Are you sure you didn't know them, Mrs Davies, they only lived two hundred yards away, surely you heard the shots, didn't you?" Everybody in Wales is called Jones or Davies, terrible interbreeding. "Will you take your tea now?" she says, "It's nearly time for chapel." Then she waddles out on us. And she'd been to chapel twice that day already!

'And we're there for hours and bloody hours, Freddie Payne of the *Express*, Jack Beddall of the *Sketch*, and me, knocking on the doors of these broken-down farmhouses, trying to drag a statement out of Chief-Inspector-bloody-Davies-no-relation. Trying to cultivate the local reporter who didn't even drink, even when it wasn't Sunday. Getting absolutely nowhere. Dreadful times, old boy.'

Giles Freeman sighed. 'Look, that's . . .'

A restraining hand went up. Nobody deflected old Winstone Thorpe from his punchline.

'So, what I did in the end, I went over to the local chapel and picked a name off a bloody gravestone. Emrys Lloyd –

never forget it. And I wandered back to the pub and button-holed one of these local shepherd-types. "Look here, I suspect this is a long-shot, old boy, but I don't suppose you knew this great-uncle of mine. Emrys Lloyd, his name. Told he used to live in this neck of the woods . . ." '

He paused while everybody laughed, except Giles.

'Told 'em my name was Ivor Lloyd and I'd been born in Wales but moved out at an early age, always regretted I'd never learned the good old language, all this bullshit . . . Well, dammit, you couldn't stop the sods talking after that. Gave me everything I wanted. No longer one of the enemy, you see. I could be trusted. They even felt sorry for me because I was a bloody exile in England, can you believe that?'

'No,' said Giles Freeman loudly, something catching fire behind his freckles. 'It's utter bollocks. You made it up. You've always made things up, you old bastard.'

Winstone Thorpe looked hurt. 'Not a bit of it, old boy, that was precisely what happened. And the thing is—'

'Utter balls,' Giles said contemptuously. He glared across the table at Winstone. 'You're just a boring old con-man.'

And that, Berry perceived, was the point at which the other guys decided that Giles, irrespective of the amount of booze he'd put away, had overstepped the mark and should be dealt with for pissing on a national monument.

Giles didn't notice the guys exchanging glances. 'You know why the Welsh are suspicious of the English?' he demanded, slapping the table, making waves in all the glasses.

'Actually,' said Shirley Gillies, one of the BBC's political reporters, 'I once—'

'Just hang on a minute, Shirley. Listen, I'll tell you why. Because we're so . . . bloody . . . smug. We think we're the greatest bloody race on earth. We think we're great by tra-dition. And the idea of people here in Britain, in our island who don't want to speak English . . . we think that's a joke. Because ours is the language of Shakespeare and Keats and Barbara bloody Cartland . . .'

'Actually,' Shirley Gillies repeated, as if Giles was some stray drunk who didn't really belong in their corner. 'I had rather a similar experience of being frozen out in Wales. Only I wasn't as clever as you, Winstone. I rather left with egg on my face.'

And this mention of egg reminded Charlie Firth, of the *Mail*, of the time he and he his wife had gone into this Welsh snack bar for a meal just as it was about to close. The waitresses had muttered to each other – in Welsh, of course – and eventually served Charlie and Mrs Firth a couple of scrambled eggs which had left them both with seriously upset stomachs. 'Had to stop off at about seven public lavs on the way back,' Charlie said. 'Like, you expect it in Spain, but . . .'

'Poisoned,' said Max Canavan, of the *Sun*. 'They poisoned you on account of you was English, yeh?'

Voices had risen, everybody grinning, suddenly having fun thinking up horror stories about Wales. Or more likely, Berry figured, *making them up* as a communal putdown for Giles. Other hacks in the bar, not part of Winstone's farewell piss-up, were gathering around, sensing that electric change in the atmosphere, noses almost visibly twitching. The pack instinct was always strong among British national journalists. Guys from papers which were bitter rivals hung out together like a street gang.

'Oh dear me, look,' Old Winstone said. 'I didn't want to start—'

'Always been like that,' said Brian McAllister of the Press Association. 'I remember once I was in Colwyn flamin' Bay . . . Anybody ever been to Colwyn Bay?'

'Called in once, but it was closed,' Charlie Firth said.

'Bloody Welsh,' one of the newcomers said. 'Frogs, Krauts, Eyeties – I can get along with all of 'em, but the bloody Welsh . . .'

'Right.' Giles was on his feet, swaying, freckles ablaze. 'I've fucking had enough of this.' He was very angry and began to extricate himself from the table. 'Bigoted, racist bastards . . .'

'No, mate, they're the racists,' Ray Wheeler of the *Mirror* said gleefully. 'The Welsh. Ever since we beat the brown stuff out of 'em back in, when was it, I dunno, Edward the First and all that.'

'Piss off,' Giles snarled, and slammed his glass down so hard that it cracked in two places. Giles being Giles, he paid for it on his way out.

Berry hesitated a moment, then followed him.

CHAPTER VII

GILES had been pacing the pavement under a mild summer drizzle. As Berry came up behind him he swung round murderously. Berry swiftly put a lamppost between them.

'Who the hell's that?' Giles said.

Berry stepped out from behind the post.

'Oh,' Giles said. 'You.'

'Yeah.'

'If it was that fucking Firth I was going to—'

'Sure.'

Giles grinned, white teeth flashing in the headlights of a Bentley whispering somebody home. 'Bit pissed. Sorry. Those bastards.' He pushed fingers through his heavy fair hair. 'Feel a bit of a prat now, actually. Shouldn't have let them wind me up. Shouldn't have gone for old Winstone like that. Not like me. Am I very pissed?'

Berry looked him up and down. 'Smashed outa your skull,' he said.

Giles laughed. 'You're probably quite a decent guy, Berry, for an American. You didn't say anything bad about Wales.'

'That's because I never went there, Giles. It most likely is the armpit of Britain.'

'Bastard.'

'Sure.'

The pub door opened and Giles swung round again in case it was somebody he felt he ought to hit. Ted Wareham, of the *Independent*, came out grasping a bottle of Scotch. He didn't notice them.

'So you're leaving us, Giles,' Berry said.

51

Giles said, rather wearily, 'I don't know. Don't know what to do. For a while I've been looking around and thinking it's time I moved on. Where do you go? It's a trap.'

'Trap?'

'The money for one thing,' Giles said. 'We moan sometimes, but, bloody hell, where else can you collect on this scale in our job? Plus, it's an addictive sort of life. Policing the Great and Good, or whatever it is we do. But the thought of spending another thirty years around this bit of London, drinking with the same blokes, getting older and shabbier and ending up, at best, as some lovable father figure with a face full of broken veins and a knackered liver . . .'

'That wouldn't happen to you, Giles,' Berry said, meaning it. 'You're not in that mould.'

'What's that mean?'

Berry shrugged.

'Anyway I reckon we've been thrown a lifeline, Claire and me. To pull us out of our complacency. Just came out of the blue. Something we'd just never thought of. We drove out there – couple of weeks ago – first thing in the morning. Quite a grey morning, everything really drab. But by the time we got there it was a gorgeous day, and it got better and better. And we found the cottage almost straight away, just as if we were being guided. Up the street, over the bridge, past the church, along this shady country lane and there it was. I felt—'

Giles hugged the lamp-post in a burst of passion, then pulled away. 'Bloody beer. This is not like me, not like me at all. You'll go back in there and tell them what I said and all have a fucking good laugh.'

'Aw, Giles, come on . . .'

'Sorry, sorry . . . an injustice.'

'Those guys didn't even notice me leave, 'cept for Winstone. So what did you feel?'

'What?'

'When you saw the place. What did you feel?'

'Look, here's a cab. I'll have to grab it, OK? Excitement, Berry. Only more than that, much more. I didn't want to come back. Course it was all locked up, we couldn't get in that day, just peering through the windows like Hansel and bloody Gretel. It was enchanting. I'd have stayed there all day and slept on the grass when it got dark.' Giles got into the taxi. 'Tell the buggers that, why don't you. I don't care.'

Berry watched the cab's tail-lights vanish into the traffic along what used to be Fleet Street.

Then he went back into the bar.

'Those stories,' Berry said. 'All shit, right? Kind of, let's put the frighteners on ole Giles.'

'Yes and no, old boy.' Winstone Thorpe said. 'Yes and no.'

'Meaning?'

'Meaning, probably, that nobody poisoned Charlie Firth. Can you really see that man dining on unlicensed premises?'

At close to midnight, old Winstone and Berry Morelli were the only two left, Berry because he thought he had nobody to go home to tonight and Winstone because – as he'd told them all earlier – he suspected that when he walked out of the bar this time he'd never come back. People had been shaking his hand and promising to look in on him sometime. Berry didn't think any of them ever would.

'And no?'

'No what?'

'You said "yes and no".'

'Ah.' Winstone finished off his last Glenfiddich. At this hour even he wouldn't get served again. 'I suppose . . . Well, I was drinking with our property chap the other day. Do you know how many English people have bought homes in Wales over the past few years? Tens of thousands, apparently. Mind boggles. Got them cheap, you see – well, cheap compared with the south-east. Plenty of spare cash about down here these days. So it's holiday homes, retirement homes, views of the mountains, views of the sea.'

Winstone put his glass down, sat back. 'Backs to the wall, now, the Joneses and the Davieses. Getting driven out, along with what's left of their language, by all these foreigners searching for the old rural idyll bit.'

Like Giles.

'Very pretty and all that, apparently, this cottage of Claire's. They're so enchanted with the place, they're talking about leaving London altogether and trying to make a living out there . . . or even commute, for God's sake.'

Winstone shook his head sadly. 'Pretended I was asleep, but really I was the only one listening to him. Oh dear . . . Bad news, old boy. Going to get ugly. Seen it before. Nothing drives people to loony extremes more than religion and national pride.'

'We never learned much about Wales at school, back home.'

'A hard and bitter land, old boy. Don't have our sensibilities, never been able to afford them. We go there in our innocence, the English, and we're degraded and often destroyed. I'm talking about North Wales and the West, where they've always danced on the edge of the abyss. Look, this is most unlike me, but is there some club we could go on to?'

Berry smiled. 'It isn't the end, Winstone. They said you could freelance for them, right?'

'Not the same, old boy. Wife gone, kids abroad. Paper's been my family.' Winstone put a hand on Berry's arm and the ancient eyes flickered. 'Look, you put the arm on young Giles. Persuade him to get the bloody place sold. Soon as he can. We're really not meant to be there, you know, the English. Stop him. I mean it. You have to do this for the boy. He won't survive. *Listen* to me, this is not the drink.'

Berry met Winstone's urgent, bloodshot gaze and saw some long-buried sorrow there. 'C'mon,' he said. 'I know somewhere.' He thought Winstone was suddenly looking too old and too sober. 'Anyway, you try and talk Giles out of something, he just gets more determined.'

'He's a decent chap, compared to most of us,' Winstone said. 'But naïve. Innocent. Throw everything away if somebody doesn't stop him. You see – as an American you may not understand this, but the thing is, Giles made the big time too soon. What's he now, thirty-three, thirty-four? My day, you were lucky if you'd made it to the Nationals at all by that age. So now Giles is looking around and he's thinking, where on earth do I go from here? What's there left to do? Sort of premature mid-life crisis, everything comes younger these days. And of course he can see all the editors getting alarmingly younger too. One day his copy's being handled by some chap who only shaves twice a week. Or worse still,' Winstone got unsteadily to his feet and reached for his raincoat, 'not shaving at all, if you see what I mean.'

'Women,' Berry said.

Winstone scowled. 'So he's looking for a new adventure. But he thinks – fatal this – he *thinks* he's looking for his soul.'

'In Wales?'

'Insanity.' Winstone paused in the doorway, took a last look around the almost deserted bar. His face was pale, his jowls like tallow dripping down a candle. 'The boy was right. I talk too much nonsense. So now nobody believes my stories any more.'

'Winstone, Giles was smashed.'

The old journalist smiled wistfully and walked out into the street, where the night was warm but rain was falling.

'You know, old boy,' he said after a moment, turning and looking around him in apparent confusion. 'I must say I feel rather odd.'

'It's gonna pass, Winstone, believe me, it's gonna pass. You just got to find a new . . . Hey—'

Winstone gripped the lamp-post which Giles had hugged in his drunken excitement. 'Do you know what, old boy?' he said conversationally. 'I'm think I'm having another stroke.'

'Huh . . .?'

Winstone Thorpe quietly slid down to his knees on the wet pavement, as if offering a final prayer to the old gods of what used to be Fleet Street.

'Shit,' Berry breathed. He stared down at Winstone in horror. The old man smiled.

Berry dashed back and stuck his head round the pub door. 'Somebody call an ambulance! Listen, I'm not kidding. It's ole Winstone!'

He rushed back to the old man. 'Hey, come on, let's get you back inside, OK?'

But as he bent down, Winstone toppled – almost non-

55

chalantly, it seemed – on to his face. As if his prayer had been answered.

CHAPTER VIII

'DEAD?' Giles said. 'But that's wonderful.'

Claire passed him his coffee. 'Oh, Giles, let's not get—'

'I know, I know, I'm sorry, it's the beer. Bit pissed. But it is rather wonderful, isn't it? Not for the old boy, of course, but we've all got to go sometime and, bloody hell, he couldn't have chosen a better time for us, could he?'

'You can't say that yet,' Claire said. 'They might not even let you do it.'

She'd been waiting up for him with the news, that mischievous little tilt to her small mouth; she knew something he didn't. It was as near as Claire ever came to expressing excitement.

Giles had both hands around his coffee cup, squeezing it. 'Let them try and stop me,' he said. 'Just let the bastards try. Did it say on the news what his majority was?'

'I don't think so. They may have. It was still dawning on me, the significance of it, you know.'

'Right then.' Giles sprang to his feet. 'Let's find out.'

'Will you get anybody? It's nearly one o'clock.'

'No problem.' He was already stabbing out the night desk number on the cordless phone. Standing, for luck, under the framed blow-up of Claire's first photograph of the cottage, the one taken from between the two sycamores at the entrance to the lane. They'd taken down a Michael Renwick screenprint to make space for it on the crowded buttermilk wall above the rebuilt fireplace.

'Peter, that you? Oh, sorry, look is Peter there? It's Giles Freeman. Yes, I'll wait.'

There were blow-ups of five of Claire's photographs on the walls. Not of the award-winning Belfast stuff, nothing heavy.

Just the atmosphere pics: the old woman collecting driftwood on the shore, the shadowed stillness of a cathedral close at dusk, that kind of thing. The picture of the cottage was the only one that hadn't appeared in a paper or a magazine. Giles loved it. He was still amazed by Claire's ability to move at once to the right angle, to link into a scene.

'Peter. Listen, sorry to bother you, but I've just heard about Burnham-Lloyd, the MP for Glanmeurig. Was there time for you to run it in the final?' Giles sniffed. 'Well I think you should have, Peter, I really do, even if it *is* only Wales.' He and Claire exchanged meaningful glances. 'Anyway, listen Peter, what was his majority?'

Giles waited. Claire perched on the edge of the sofa and cupped her small face in her slender hands, short, fair hair tufting through the fingers. She wore a cream silk dressing gown and wooden sandals. Giles, re-energized by the news, eyed her lustfully.

'Bloody hell,' he said. 'That's not bad. That's not at all bad. Thank you, Peter, thank you very much indeed.'

He cleared the line and made a whooshing sound.

'Narrow?' Claire asked.

Giles said, very slowly and precisely, 'Eight hundred and seventy-one.' His freckles were aglow again. He tossed the phone almost to the ceiling and caught it. 'Eight hundred and seventy fucking one! It's marginal, Claire! Plaid's been slowly gaining on him for years! Oh God, I really do feel something's working for us.'

'I suppose,' Claire said thoughtfully, 'I feel a bit scared now. It's all coming at once. Propelling us into something. Out of our control.' She was still feeling upset, actually, by her mother's reaction. She'd phoned her while Giles was out, to explain about the inheritance, tonight being the first opportunity since her parents had returned from their cruise.

Giles was hungrily pacing the carpet. 'What I'll suggest is a bit of a recce. Zoom up there this weekend. Take the air. Talk to people.'

'I can't. I've got that thing for the *Observer* in Norwich.'

Claire was glad to put it off. She'd been frightened by her own emotional response when they'd first gone to look at the cottage. The feeling that somehow she was *meant* to live there. Now she wanted to slow things down, give them time to think. Giles, however, had to be firing on all cylinders or none at all.

'Well, all right, *next* weekend,' he said impatiently. 'You see, what we have to do is build this up as a really significant mid-term by-election, knock off a couple of prelim pieces, hype it up a bit. We can have the cottage as our base, save them hotel bills and stuff. And while we're there . . . I mean, with the run-up and everything, we're talking well over three weeks for a by-election campaign. So we can do all the groundwork, either for persuading them they really need a full-time staffer in Wales or setting up some decent freelance outlets. I would have sounded people out tonight, but they were all being so bloody snide and superior.'

Slow down, slow down, Claire yelled inside her head. But Giles in overdrive was not open to reasonable argument. She wanted to tell him about her mother, but in his present state of drink-enhanced euphoria he wouldn't take it in. And even when stone cold sober, hearing what she'd had to say – the bitch – would only harden his determination.

As expected, her mother had been stiff and resentful, so Claire herself had gone on the attack.

'Mother, why didn't you tell me he was dead? Why did I have to find out from the solicitor?'

Elinor made an impatient noise. 'Because . . . Oh, look, we only found out the day we left. I mean, really, what was I supposed to do, put it in a postcard from Greece? Weather fine, old Rhys dead?'

Old Rhys. Claire's grandfather.

'But – I can't believe this – he was your *father*.'

A distant snort.

'I know, I know,' Claire snapped. 'But that doesn't alter anything, does it?'

'It clearly altered things for him, if he's left his awful hovel to *you*. He only ever saw you once. I wonder what he did with his money.'

'It seems,' Claire said icily, 'that he left most of it to the Church.'

There'd been a silence, then Elinor gave her a short, false cackle. 'Oh dear, do excuse me. It's simply that the idea of God and my father discovering each other in that ghastly Welsh backwater is rather too much to take at this hour of the night.'

Claire had expected bitterness, had been ready for *some* of this. But nothing as unpleasant as . . .

'What happened to his whores, I wonder. Perhaps he was predeceased. Do you think he died alone and unloved? I do hope so.'

This is awful, Claire thought. She knew her mother did not need the money. But she must, all the same, have hoped for some token in the will, a sign that Thomas Rhys even remembered once having a wife and a daughter . . . as well as a grandchild.

'Did you – tell me the truth now, Claire – did you ever go to visit him, you and Giles?'

'Of course not! I mean . . .' There had, it was true, often been times when Claire had felt powerfully drawn to seek out the mysterious Judge Rhys. That tug of curiosity edged with an undefined sense of guilt and longing, whenever she'd come across a picture of Welsh mountains on some holiday brochure. And then there'd been that electric moment when she'd first seen the village – a mere three months ago, but it felt to Claire as if she'd known it all her life in some unexplored part of her soul.

'Then why?' Elinor's voice was flat and hard. 'Apart from a desire to spit on your grandmother and me. Why? Can you explain it?'

'No,' Claire said in a small voice. 'Mother, look, I – I know you must be terribly hurt—'

'Don't patronise me, Claire. I'm extremely glad the old swine's gone, I didn't want a penny of his money and I shall be thankful when you've sold that damned house for as much as you can get.'

'Sell it?'

'Well you're hardly going to live in it are you?' her mother had said.

'I've been thinking,' Giles was saying. 'Perhaps we should make contact with a few of the local tradesmen – plumbers, carpenters. Book them in advance. Sometimes guys like that can be jolly hard to find in rural areas, and they need lots of notice. Then we're going to need an automatic washing machine and all that. We shall have to work pretty fast.'

'Yes, but Giles . . . what if the by-election goes ahead before probate's complete. There's no way round that, you know. We can't let workmen into a house that isn't ours yet.'

Claire somehow felt she had to create as many obstacles as she could to counteract the awesome pull of the village. To make sure that it was the right thing to do, that it really was *meant*.

'Won't happen,' Giles said confidently. 'No way there'll be a by-election until all the party conferences are safely over. We're talking November at least.'

Claire realised then that this by-election could be quite a good thing after all. It would give them a trial period to see if life in Wales really suited them. Trying to get the cottage into some kind of shape and cover an election campaign at the same time would be quite a testing experience. And if they realised they were making a big mistake they could always come back here and either sell the place or keep it as a holiday home – and feel grateful they hadn't burned their boats.

'I'll tell you one thing, though,' Giles said, leaning against the remoulded plaster of the fireplace. 'Those bastards tonight, my so-called colleagues. It's made me realise how badly I want to get out of all this. It's a phoney life, a façade, just a garish backcloth we think we can perform against. Not real at all. I mean, I can't get on with those guys any more. Even Winstone – Christ, I thought he was a friend.' He shook his head, mouth tight.

Then he loosened up and flashed Claire a grin. 'What have you got on under there?' He tossed the phone into an armchair, threw off his jacket and plunged at the sofa.

Claire let him pull the dressing gown off her shoulders and suddenly quivered.

Nothing to do with Giles. Something her mother had said was replaying itself. She hadn't realised at the time, hadn't seen the significance.

. . . left his awful hovel to you. He only ever saw you once . . .

When? Claire didn't remember ever seeing her grandfather. She'd always understood there'd been no contact whatsoever since the day, two years before she was born, when Judge Thomas Rhys had gravely announced that he would be returning to the place of his birth, but his family would not be accompanying him.

So when?

Excitement and dread combined to make Claire shiver.

Giles moaned, lips tracking down her bare shoulder. 'Darling . . .' he breathed.

CHAPTER IX

'LOOK,' Miranda said. 'I just don't see it. Why don't you come back to bed?'

The sun had emerged, and Miranda looked rosy and warm and inviting.

'I didn't expect you would,' Berry said, standing by the window, turning to look into the street three storeys down. 'What counts is how I see it.' He gazed out towards the Thames. This building did not itself overlook the Thames but you could see some other buildings which did.

'Well it certainly isn't *my* idea of a dying wish or a last request or whatever,' Miranda said. 'To make a last request you have to know you're dying. And from what you say, he didn't.'

At the hospital, the tired-eyed young doctor on night-duty,

jeans under the white coat, had said it looked like a small stroke followed by a second, massive stroke. Happened like an earthquake, or maybe an earthquake in reverse, a mild fore-shock and then the big one. Bip, bam! Good a way to go as any, better than most. And he'd had a minor one before, had he? Say no more. Later, the cops had gone through the motions, because of the way it happened.

'I'm gonna call Giles,' Berry said. 'Maybe we can organise lunch.'

. . . *Look, you put the arm on young Giles. Persuade him to get the bloody place sold. Soon as he can.*

'You were going to have lunch with *me*, remember, if you were in town.' Miranda pulled the duvet over her breasts and went into a pout.

Shit, how was he supposed to get this across?

'See, it's just . . . when I first came over here I didn't know England from a hole in the ocean and ole Winstone, he kind of initiated me.'

'Is England so complicated?'

'Minefield,' Berry said. He'd taken the job with the agency, American Newsnet, without thinking, in his haste to get out. Mario Morelli's son guilty of unAmerican behaviour.

'The English National Press, they were a club I didn't know how to join,' he said. 'I walked in this bar one night and sat down and all these guys stared at me like I'd thrown up on the table. After a while one leaned over and said out of the corner of his mouth, "You do know you're sitting in Win-stone's chair." '

'I think I've seen that film,' Miranda said.

'So I apologised to Winstone.'

'As you would.'

'And he became the first one of them I really talked to, you know? I asked him a whole bunch of those questions I didn't dare ask anyone else. By closing time he'd explained how Parliament worked and all those British niceties. Why it isn't done to talk to the Queen without she talks to you first, or label a guy a killer after he's charged and like that. No big deal, but he saved my ass a few times, while certain people stood around waiting for me to fall on it. He was always there, anything I needed to know. He drank like prohibition was starting tomorrow, but it didn't matter to him that I didn't join him.'

'So long as you paid for his I shouldn't imagine it would bother him in the slightest,' said Miranda. 'You're endearingly naïve sometimes, Morelli.'

'The only other guy ever spared the time to help me along was Giles,' said Berry.

Stop him. I mean it.

'Morelli,' Miranda said. 'You're overreacting. If Freeman is loopy enough to want to throw up his career to go and live in wildest Wales it's his decision. None of your business. And if you think old-what's-his-name is going to come back and haunt you, you must be even simpler than most of your race. Now come back to bed. I warn you – last chance.'

We're really not meant to be there, you know, the English.

'How much of a generalisation is it, that stuff about rugby and the Bible?'

'Wales? Who cares? It's still an awfully long way from Harrods.'

'You're a big help, Miranda.'

'Oh, you are a pain, Morelli. Look, I haven't been very often. It's got lovely mountains and nice beaches here and there. And in the south there used to be a lot of coal mines, and Cardiff's fairly civilised these days but terribly bland . . . But, from what you say, your friend is off to one of the primitive bits, about which I'm really not qualified to comment. You know me and the primitive. Admittedly, there are *times* for being primitive . . .'

Miranda put on her most lascivious smile which, Berry had to admit, was pretty damn lascivious.

'Yeah, OK,' he said. 'Maybe I'll call Giles later.'

CHAPTER X

WALES

IT WAS the third headline on the BBC Radio Wales news at 8 a.m.

'. . . and Sir Maurice Burnham-Lloyd, Conservative MP for Glanmeurig for more than thirty years, is dead.'

Guto Evans felt unexpectedly nervous. He lay in bed and waited for the full report. By the time it came on, he'd convinced himself that he definitely wasn't going to get the Plaid nomination. Dai Death had been right: no chance.

The whole report lasted just over one minute. After a summary of the high points of Burnham-Lloyd's career (Guto wondered how they'd managed to pad it out to twenty seconds) there was a short clip of the Secretary of State for Wales speaking over the telephone to the studio.

'. . . but most of all,' crackled the Secretary of State, 'Maurice was a constituency man, a farmer among farmers. He was always *deeply* concerned that people in London and in Brussels should be *aware* of exactly how their policies would affect a sheep farmer in the heart of Glanmeurig.'

Guto groaned, snapped off the radio and pushed back the covers. 'Mam!' he shouted, hearing the clatter of a pan from downstairs. 'Mam, no breakfast for me, I've got to go out right away, OK?'

Bethan. He had to see her before she left for school or he'd spend the day in a state of advanced paranoia. Being a widow seemed to have endowed Bethan with a certain aura of wisdom.

He found her making her way across the car park below the castle ruins. She was carrying her briefcase and a pile of exercise books to the little green Peugeot.

'What should I do then, Bethan?' Guto demanded without preamble.

'Now,' said Bethan thoughtfully, leaning into the car. 'Do

you think I should put all these books into the boot or will they stay on the back seat without falling over?'

'Do I phone anybody or do I wait for them to contact me?' said Guto in agony. 'Don't want them to think I'm pushing, see.'

'I think what I shall do,' said Bethan, 'is put them on the back seat and prop them up behind the briefcase.'

'I've got to be well placed for it. I mean, I'm pretty well known locally.'

Bethan straightened up. She was wearing a black cardigan over a white cotton dress, and big gold earrings. Guto felt a pang of something not connected with politics.

'Well Guto,' she said. 'There you have identified the problem. You are *exceedingly* well known locally.'

They stared at each other across the roof of the little car.

'What are you getting at?'

'Well, who in this town has not heard you ranting on at length about the English and what we should do to keep them out? Ah, they say to strangers, you know who that is don't you? That is Guto Evans the famous extremist.'

'Well, good God, woman, they all *agree* with me.'

'Of course they don't, and neither does the party. Guto, the one thing you must never suggest these days is that Welsh Nationalist means anti-English.'

'I know that, but . . .'

'And a by-election! In-depth scrutiny by the media of all the candidates, especially ours. Muck-raking. Well, think about it – can Plaid credibly be represented by a man who once had a homing device attached to the underside of his van so the police could keep track of his movements?'

'Oh, now, that was a mistake. They thought I was—'

'But it will come out. So will the pub brawl—'

'I was never charged, for God's sake—'

'Only because all your friends lied through their teeth. Now Guto, I'm not saying that, in one respect, a man of your talents would not be the best hope in a by-election. But you have a lot of work to do. Have to change your image, Guto. People must get used to seeing you around in a smart suit and a tie.

And er – ' Bethan smothered a giggle ' – kissing babies.'

'Aaaargh,' growled Guto in disgust.

'English babies too.' Bethan slid into her car.

Guto watched her drive away, dragging a cloud of early-morning exhaust across the Pontmeurig bypass and on to the mountain road to Y Groes. Though still warm, it was the first grey morning in three weeks. There was rain in the air and mist on the hills.

'Damn it, Bethan,' Guto mumbled wistfully, shambling back into the town, past the castle destroyed by his hero, Owain Glyndwr. 'If I could have you, they could stuff the bloody nomination.'

Impossibly, as Bethan drove out of the forestry, the mist appeared to evaporate and the church tower of Y Groes shimmered in a shaft of gold.

It's a blue hole, this place, Bethan thought, but she took no great pleasure in the thought these days.

The school was on the other side of the river in a little lane of its own, screened from the village by a row of elms which had somehow survived successive epidemics of Dutch Elm Disease when nearly all the others for miles around had succumbed.

Bethan liked to get to school at least ten minutes before the first of the children, but Guto had delayed her and there was a small group of them around the wooden gate, chattering in Welsh. They stopped when they saw Bethan and chorused dutifully, '*Bore da*, Mrs McQueen.'

'*Bore da, blant*,' said Bethan, shouldering the gate open, arms full of briefcase and books. The children followed her in, all good Welsh-speaking children from Welsh-speaking families, not a single English cuckoo. Which disappointed Bethan in a way, because she used to enjoy the challenge of taking a handful of children from London or Birmingham at the age of five and then sending them on to the secondary school completely fluent in Welsh, even starting to think in Welsh.

The school had been lucky to survive so long with only

twenty-four pupils. Twice the education authority had attempted to close it down and transfer the children to Pont-meurig. But that would have meant an eight-mile journey for them along a mountain road that was often impassable in winter, and the local councillors had won the day.

Bethan waded into the school through a puddle of children, the smallest ones pulling at her skirt to attract her attention. She never discouraged them. The school had a warm family atmosphere.

'*Bore da*, Mrs Morgan,' the children sang, as Buddug entered, the deputy head teacher or Bethan's entire staff, depending on how you saw it. Buddug, a big woman in her middle fifties, a farmer's wife with red cheeks full of broken veins, like a map of the London Underground, had taught at Y Groes for over thirty years and was regarded as the head of the school by everyone except the county education officials who'd appointed Bethan.

'*Eisteddwch!*' Buddug commanded, and the children squeezed into their seats and snatched a final few seconds of chatter as Buddug strode across to the piano for the morning hymn which was only changed once a week and was limited to the three tunes Buddug could play, except at Christmas when carols were sung unaccompanied.

'Buddug,' said Bethan in her ear, 'can you spare me a couple of minutes during playtime? Something is bothering me.'

Buddug beamed and nodded and crashed her stiffened fingers down on the keyboard like a butcher cleaving a side of beef.

'It's this,' said Bethan determinedly, and opened the child's exercise book to reveal the drawing of the corpse and the corpse candle over the grave.

'Yes, isn't it good?' said Buddug. She turned over the exercise book to read the name on the front. 'Sali Dafis. Her writing has improved enormously over the past few weeks, and look at the detail in those drawings!'

'I'm not objecting to the quality of it,' said Bethan. 'It's more the content. I asked them to pretend they were working for the *papur bro* and to write about something which had happened in the village.'

'Excellent,' said Buddug. 'And were any of the others as good as this one?' She stared insolently at Bethan out of dark brown eyes.

'Oh, Buddug, what are you trying to do to me?'

'I don't understand. What are you objecting to? What sort of ideas have you brought back from the city? Would you rather the children wrote about one-parent families and lesbians?' Buddug laughed shrilly.

Bethan snatched back the book and turned away, blinking back angry tears. Seeing, out of the window, the children in the playground, seeing a certain corruption in their eyes and their milk-teeth smiles.

'I accept,' she said carefully, still looking out of the window, her back to Buddug, 'that a child has to learn about death. I don't believe that being taken to view a neighbour in her coffin and being informed that her dying was foretold by the corpse candle is a particularly healthy way of going about it.'

She gathered her resolve and whirled back at Buddug, who was wearing a expression of mild incomprehension now, like a cow over a gate.

'I don't believe,' Bethan said furiously, 'that little children should see the woods not as the home of squirrels and somewhere to collect acorns but as the place where the *Gorsedd Ddu* hold their rituals. I don't believe that when they hear the thunder they should think it's the sound of Owain Glyndwr rolling about in his grave. I don't want them looking at storm clouds and not seeing formations of cumulonimbus but the Hounds of Annwn gathering for the hunt. I just don't believe—'

'You don't believe in anything!' Buddug said, smiling, eyes suddenly alight. 'And this is not a place for people who do not believe in anything. Playtime is over. Time to bring them in.'

She rang the brass handbell with powerful twists of an old milkmaid's wrist.

CHAPTER XI

ENGLAND

THE rolling countryside of the Cotswolds was turning out to be good therapy for Berry's car, which had been a mite bronchitic of late.

He drove an old Austin Healey Sprite of a colour which, when the Sprite was born, was known as British Racing Green. He loved this car. It coughed and rattled sometimes and was as uncomfortable as hell, but it was the fulfilment of a dream he'd had since seeing an old detective show back in the States called Harry O, whose hero drove a British MG sports car and was, even by Californian standards, very laid back.

The Cotswolds, also, were laid back, often in a surprisingly Californian way: rich homes sprawled languidly behind lush foliage which was not so lush that you couldn't admire the beautiful bodies of the houses and their gorgeous Cotswold tans. Was this what remained of olde England: a burglar alarm and a Volvo estate car outside some cottage originally built for farmworkers who couldn't afford their own cart?

Touch of therapy for Berry too, to be out here. Distances were negligible in Britain. Couple of hours ago he'd been in the office, the combination of events and Miranda ensuring that by the time he arrived at work he was already feeling overtired. This had cut no ice at all with American Newsnet's London bureau chief, Addison Walls, who'd ordered him to go at once to Gloucestershire, where the Government's Energy Secretary had his country home. The Minister was to give an unofficial Press conference explaining why he'd chosen to resign over the Oil Crisis.

'Anybody in the States give a shit about this?' Berry had asked, and Addison Walls looked at him like he was crazy.

'Morelli, watch my lips. The Oil Crisis. O – I – L.'

'Yeah, yeah, OK. Just tired, is all.'

'Get outa here,' muttered Addison Walls. 'Fuckin' radical.'

When he finally arrived at what turned out to be quite a modest Cotswold farmhouse – barely an acre of land around it – Berry learned he'd missed the Press conference by a good twenty minutes. He found two reporters chatting by their cars in the lane. One was Shirley Gillies of the BBC with a black Uher tape recorder over her shoulder. The other was Giles Freeman, his wheat-coloured hair uncombed and grey circles under his eyes.

'Don't worry about it, mate,' he told Berry, waving a weary, dismissive hand. 'Wasn't worth coming. Terse statement, nothing new in it. Wouldn't answer questions. Posed for few simpering pictures with his wife. Didn't offer us coffee.'

'Giles rebuked him for wasting our time,' Shirley Gillies said. I'm afraid if I spoke like that to a Government minister, the next farewell piss-up would be mine, but he as good as apologised to Giles. Who can be quite impressive when he's sober.'

Giles, who was wearing a crumpled cream suit, shrugged in a what-the-hell kind of way. The attitude of a guy who wasn't planning to be around much longer, Berry thought. He hesitated then said, 'Ah, talking of farewell piss-ups. I suppose you . . .'

Giles sighed. 'It was all round the office. What can I say? I feel awful. Easy to say, "if only I'd known." I mean, God—'

Berry wondered if this might be the time to fulfil his obligation to put the arm on Giles. He couldn't, however, say anything with Shirley around. Couldn't think, anyway, how to start. Suppose Old Winstone was simply paranoid?

'Still, I suppose if he'd had a choice of where to snuff it,' Giles said, 'he'd probably have opted for the pub.'

'I gather you were still there, Berry,' Shirley Gillies said brightly, 'when it happened.'

'Yeah,' Berry said. 'Tell you about it sometime.'

'Yes,' Shirley said, clearly meaning no. 'Look, I must go. See you around, Giles.'

Giles and Berry stood in silence in the Cotswold lane as

Shirley loaded her gear into her car. It was a soft, dull summer morning, still moist from last night's rain.

'Bloody awful smug place, this,' Giles said. 'Not exactly nature in the raw, is it? Not like—' He broke off.

'You gonna give me the Minister's statement?'

'Sure. Let's find a pub. You don't have to rush back?'

Berry shook his head. Giles said abruptly, 'We're nowhere near bloody Painswick, are we?'

'Now how would I know that?'

'Claire's mother lives near Painswick. Wouldn't like to run into the old bat. Not just now. I wouldn't be responsible.'

Berry followed Giles's silver BMW in his beat-up Sprite. They motored through shimmering ochre villages before pulling up at Hollywood's idea of an olde English pub, outside which Giles had detected an obscure Real Ale sign. They sat on upholstered wooden stools at the bar, the first customers of the day. On Giles's recommendation, Berry ordered two halves of something even thicker and murkier than Hollywood's idea of English beer.

'Hair of the dog,' Giles said. 'Bloody animal.'

'He'd hate you to feel bad about this, Giles. He was very fond of you and Claire. Winstone, I mean.'

Giles found a lop-sided smile. He told Berry a couple of funny Old Winstone anecdotes from way back. Berry had heard both before, but he chuckled over them anyway, for Giles's sake, assuring him again that Winstone had in no way been offended by the way he'd stormed out of the bar and no, there was no way it had caused any stress which might have hastened the stroke.

'That story he told,' Berry said, fishing for a reaction. 'About the domestic murder and the Welsh landlady and all. I guess it was kind of a Winstone parable. He'd been hearing about how bad things were over in Wales. Folks feeling their heritage was being ripped off. Dumb foreigners on a back-to-nature trip stampeding the sacred cows.'

'Yes,' Giles said. 'But, don't you go thinking we're going to be like that, Claire and me. We aren't going to march in like bloody yuppies on the make. We'll learn the language,

71

the whole bit. Go, er, go native. Well . . . I . . . You're not really interested in hearing this, are you Berry?'

'I am, Giles.'

'You sure? I think people were bored last night.'

'No way, Giles. Jealous, is all.'

'You think that?'

'Sure. Tell me about Wales, Giles.'

Giles shrugged and had a slurp of Real Ale.

'Well, for a start, even though she'd never even been there before this, Claire has very strong family links with this village, Y Groes. So we feel we're . . . reviving something. And reviving ourselves in the process. Do you know what I mean?'

'When I was a kid,' Berry said, 'they used to tell me my great grandpa made the best pasta in Venice. That doesn't mean that to find eternal fulfilment I have to be a fucking gondolier.'

Giles gave him a warning look and started rocking on his bar stool. 'Look, poor old Winstone struck a nerve when I was pissed. I'm sorry about that, but it doesn't change anything. You hear about Burnham-Lloyd?'

'Who?'

Giles told Berry about the impending by-election. It seemed to restore his mood. 'Brilliant timing, don't you think? Not just another mid-term by-election, old son.' He was holding his beer to the light and nodding appreciatively at tiny specks in the umber fluid. Berry pushed his own glass away in disgust.

'Burnham-Lloyd,' Giles said. 'Tory, OK? Held that seat for over thirty years on the strength of being a local chap, well in with the farmers, all that. But Plaid Cymru – that's the Welsh nationalist party – have been slowly gaining on him for years. The other parties haven't much support, so it's a two-horse race. Going to be a cracker. Gives me a chance to go in there as a reporter, meet the local people, discover all the key local issues. So when we move we won't be going in cold.'

Berry nodded. Maybe Giles wouldn't get along with the local people, would discover he was out of sympathy with the local issues. Well, maybe . . .

'What about you, Berry? Has it got Newsnet potential? I'll

tell you – mass-immigration by English people is sure to be a major issue. And the one that could give the seat to Plaid. Absolutely fascinating.'

'What are we looking at here Giles? Beginnings of an Ulster situation?'

'Oh, good God no. They're just after devolution to begin with, power to run their own affairs. Then to become a free state within Europe. Not a huge step for Wales – or Scotland, for that matter. And in spite of the odd bits of terrorism, it's not a nation inflamed by anti-English passions, whatever Old – whatever people say.'

'Yeah,' Berry said non-commitally. Most Americans didn't even realise Wales was a separate country. If they mentioned it at all they talked about 'Wales, England,' like it was some district.

'We were going to drive out there this weekend,' Giles was saying. 'Make a few political contacts and have a little drool over our cottage at the same time. Won't be ours for a couple of months yet – legal red-tape – but it's a wonderful feeling, just standing in the lane gazing at it through the trees, making plans.'

Berry noticed the grey circles under Giles's eyes had shrunk and his freckles were aglow.

Look, you put the arm on young Giles.

'Only we can't go because Claire's saddled with this job for the *Observer* in East Anglia—'

'Too bad,' Berry said.

'Unless . . . Hey look, Berry, what are you doing next weekend?'

Playing with Miranda. 'Nothing fixed,' Berry said.

'Feel like taking a drive out there?'

'To Wales?' She'll kill me, he thought.

'You could get it on exes, surely? Bit of research?'

'Well, I—'

'And you could come and see our cottage, see Y Groes – and then you'd realise why we're so excited about it.'

Persuade him to get the bloody place sold.

'Come on, Berry, it'll be fun.'

Not meant to be there, the English.
'What do you say?'
Stop him. I mean it.
'Yeah, OK,' Berry said. 'Why not?'

CHAPTER XII

WALES

'M ISS SION!'
Bethan turned at the school door, the key in her hand. 'You decided you'd better come back then, did you Sali?'

She was small for her age, Sali Dafis, and looked more fragile than other members of her family. Her father, Dilwyn, and her *nain* had coal-black hair, but Sali's was wispy brown. A legacy from her mother, the secretary from Essex whom Dilwyn had met on holiday at Butlins, Pwllheli.

'It's a bit late now, though, isn't it?' Bethan said. 'And I'm not Miss Sion any more, remember?'

They were alone in the yard. It was a gloomy afternoon now. Overcast. A reminder of how rapidly the days were shortening. Locking the school door, Bethan had heard a child's shoes tripping across the yard towards her and wondered if it would be Sali.

'See me after school, please,' she'd finally written in the exercise book, but Sali had gone off with the others half an hour ago. Now she was back, alone. An indication that she didn't want her friends to know she was seeing the teacher.

'But Miss Sion, your husband is dead.'

Bethan breathed in sharply, as if stabbed. Children could be vicious.

'Mrs McQueen, if you don't mind. I won't tell you again. We don't go back to our old names just because—' Bethan had a thought. 'Who told you to start calling me Miss Sion again?'

74

Sali Dafis looked at her feet and said nothing.

'Never mind,' Bethan said. 'I think I can guess. Look, why don't we talk to each other tomorrow. We don't want your *nain* wondering where you are.' Or the old hag will put a curse on me, she thought, then decided that wasn't funny.

Sali looked up at Bethan very solemnly and seemed about to say something.

'Well?'

'Mrs McQueen,' said Sali innocently. 'Would you like to see a dead body?'

Bethan put the key in her bag and snapped it shut. 'All right, we'd better have our talk right now. You wait there while I put my things in the car, then we'll go for a walk.'

She was definitely not in the mood for this.

They followed the river from the rear of the school towards the oak woods, most of which were coppiced by Meirion, the forester whose father had done it before him. It was like entering a huge, entimbered medieval cathedral. Awesome in the right light, but dim and heavy now, the trees immense and gnarled, prickly bushes in the shade of some of them. The river entered the woods and and then went off on its own, away from the path.

'So whose was the dead body – the one you thought I might like to see?'

Bethan knew very well that nobody had died in the village recently, except for the antiquarian at the *Tafarn* and Mrs Tegwyn Jones, Ty Canol, over a week before that.

'Don't know,' Sali said.

'Why would you think I might even want to see this . . . this dead body?'

'Don't know,' Sali said.

They were approaching the thick wooden gate draped with creepers that said on it one word.

Rheithordy.

The rectory. It was the only house in the wood. Well, not quite in the wood: the house itself was in a green clearing, but the encroaching oaks had claimed most of its garden, heavyweight sentinels around it. The rectory was itself hugely timber-framed, and Bethan found it all a bit ominous, as if the beams in the house's skeleton had only been borrowed from the wood.

Hurrying the child past the gate, because the rector also tended to give her the creeps, Bethan said, 'You know what a dead body is, don't you Sali?'

She saw the child nod without looking up. This was not going to be easy. Why did she feel, uncomfortably, that the big trees were listening to her with more attention than Sali?

'Do you really know what a dead body is? It's nothing to do with the person who used to be in the body. That is why we bury them – because they are no use to anyone any more. What people are is nothing to do with their bodies. The really important part is something that just uses the body to get around in. And when it's too old or badly damaged, we discard it, throw it away.'

Bethan felt inadequate to the task of explaining to an eight-year-old the things that few adults claimed to understand. This was no time to be trite or patronising.

'When someone brings an old car or a Land Rover into your dad's garage, he . . . he mends it. If he can. And if it's just too old and tired out, then he has to send the car to the scrapyard. And the driver gets a new one. That's what happens to our bodies when we've used them up – we get rid of them and then we get a new body – a heavenly body.' This is pathetic, Bethan thought.

'I know *that*,' Sali said scornfully, kicking at the dirt. 'My *nain* can see people in their heavenly bodies.'

Bethan stopped walking.

'Sometimes,' Sali said, walking on then turning round on the path, 'she asks me if I can see people in their heavenly bodies.'

Dear God.

'But I can't,' Sali said. 'Well, I don't think I can. *Nain* says that is because my mam was English. She says the English haven't got the gift.'

Lucky them, thought Bethan. They were following the path deep into the wood. It would soon be strewn with acorns. Season of mists and mellow fruitfulness and nature rambles and autumn leaves to press. Once, autumn had excited Bethan – the scent of burning leaves, logs gathered for the fire, newly made toast. Someone to eat it with. She thought, that's right, burst into tears in front of the child.

Instead she sat down on a big tree stump and pulled Sali towards her, gripping the girl's arms. 'Sali, look at me.'

Sali gazed into Bethan's face. Disturbingly, she was reminded of the way Buddug had looked at her that morning. Condescending.

'Sali, some . . . some people don't want to let the dead go. Do you remember last year . . . my husband died.'

The child stood stiffly between Bethan's hands. She did not seem interested.

'I was very sad,' Bethan said. 'I didn't want him to be dead. I used to think about him all the time. I still—'

'He was only English,' Sali said.

'I – what did you say?'

Sali pulled quickly away and ran off.

'Sali! Come here!'

The child had vanished, as if the woods had absorbed her. Alone now in this sombre place Bethan thought, I've blown it. We're on different sides of some invisible barrier. She's gone to Buddug and Mrs Bronwen Dafis.

'Sali, come back now, we have to go home.'

The child had disappeared.

'Sali, where are you?'

The wood was heavy with age and stillness. No birds fluttered in the undergrowth. Overhead the branches formed a great canopy of darkest green, no breath of Autumn yet among the foliage.

'Sali! This instant!'

Bethan had risen to her feet, feeling cold now in her white cotton dress. She stepped off the path and a bramble ensnared her shoe, pulling it off.

'Damn you, Sali—'

She tore her shoe away from the spiny tendril, scratching her hand, drawing blood. What was she bothering about? The kid probably knew every inch of these woods, and there were no marauding paedophiles in Y Groes.

'I'm going home now, Sali. If you want to stay here all night, that's up to you.'

What if she'd fallen somewhere? Pushing on through the bushes, Bethan suddenly became aware of the sound of rushing water.

What if she'd fallen in the river?

'Sali! Shout if you can hear me!'

She saw where some of the undergrowth had recently been flattened, and she moved towards it. Overhead, the sky had darkened and mingled with the interwoven leaves. There was a harsh spattering of rain. She could hear it but couldn't feel it yet.

'Shout, Sali!'

She prised her way through the bushes towards the sound of water and felt her dress tear at the hem.

'Damn you, Sali, if you're—'

A blackberry had been squashed against her hip and she looked down and saw bubbles of juice like dark blood. Then she slipped and fell down the river bank, rolling over and over.

The crows had taken his eyes.

That was the first thing she saw.

She was winded by the fall and lay on her back, a few yards from the water. Pain rippled up her left leg: ankle twisted.

A muddy boot swung gently about a yard above her head. She must have caught it as she rolled past. The boot made a sort of click as it swung against the other boot.

Bethan retched.

'I said, didn't I, Miss Sion?'

Sali Dafis was standing at the edge of the river looking proudly up at where he hung, nylon climber's rope under his chin, knotted around the branch, his tongue out, black now, and a dried-out pulp where the crows had taken his eyes.

CHAPTER XIII

PONTMEURIG was eight miles from Y Groes, on the other side of the Nearly Mountains. A slow, messy drive, especially for a hearse.

It was an untidy town, mottled grey and brown, something that had rolled down from the hills in the Middle Ages and was still rolling, new housing estates and factories spilling over the old boundaries on either side of the river.

Still puzzled by the attitude of Aled Gruffydd, Dai Death drove the corpse into town past the cattle mart and the new car park and past what was left of the medieval castle, looming grey in the dusk. Sometime in the early fifteenth century the castle had been burned down by Owain Glyndwr, it was said, in retribution for something, and had never been rebuilt because nobody could remember why the hell they'd ever needed a castle in Pontmeurig anyway.

In a street squashed behind the ruins, almost opposite one of the town's three chapels, was an offensive new fast-food take-away, The Welsh Pizza House, owned, of course, by English people. Next to it was a small yard with a sign that said: V. W. Williams and Sons, Funeral Directors. Dai was parking the hearse under the sign when the police car drew up alongside and a constable wound down his window.

'You've done it again, Dai. He's not yours yet, he's ours.'

'Oh, bloody hell,' said Dai. 'I'm sorry, Paul. Automatic pilot I'm on today. You back into the entry and I'll turn around.'

'Daft bugger, Williams,' he told himself, switching his lights on then putting the hearse into reverse. Understandable, though; it had been a year since the Dyfed-Powys police had last used him as a meat wagon.

He pulled out into the main street and drove past the police station to the cottage hospital at the bottom of the town. The forecourt wasn't very big and was packed with cars, because it was visiting time, so he had to park on the pavement outside.

He got out, hoping the police would find him a space. He didn't like having a fibre-glass shell seen in public; people would think he specialised in cheap coffins.

A thirtyish couple walked past in identical outsize lumberjack shirts and baggy corduroy trousers with turn-ups. The man had a baby strapped into a sort of sling around his chest. 'Pity, really,' he was saying. 'Super view, I thought.' The voice carried across the quiet street.

'Look at that,' Guto Evans said, walking up behind them on his way to the Drovers. 'The Ethnic Look. Designer working clothes. And of course they have to pretend they can't afford a bloody pram. Evening, Dai.'

'What do they call those things?' Dai asked him. 'Something Red Indian.'

'Papoose,' said Guto in disgust. 'The day you show me a Welshman with a papoose around his neck is the day I emigrate to Patagonia.' He peered into the back of the hearse. 'Who have you got in there?' His black beard split into a wide, carnivorous grin. 'Burnham-Lloyd himself is it?'

Dai did not find this funny. He'd had a vague hope that he, the local man, would have been chosen to handle the Burnham-Lloyd funeral, but the more he thought about it the less likely it seemed.

'Let me tell you something, Guto,' he said. 'Even if, through some insane aberration, they were to make you the candidate, I don't even think your mother would vote for you. It's a hiker.'

'What is?'

'Him. In the back. They found him in the woods by Y Groes.'

'English?'

'Probably.'

'Second one in just a few days. Bloody hell, Dai, might as well be working for the council, the times they send for you to cart away the rubbish.'

'Anybody can tell, Guto, that you are a natural politician. That sense of fair play, of diplomacy, the way you choose your words so as not to cause offence.' Dai opened up the tailgate of the hearse so fast that Guto jumped back. 'How would you like to help me carry him in?'

'Me? Carry a coffin? An Englishman's coffin?'

'Don't like the thought of death, do you, Guto?'

'Get lost,' said Guto.

Dai nodded knowingly. Most people were made instantly uncomfortable by the arrival of himself and his hearse. Except for those in professions touching on the death business – doctors, nurses, solicitors, monumental masons. And the police.

By the time Dai had arrived the body had been cut down and lay on the river bank in the manner of a determined sunbather, vainly stretching out his head to catch what remained of the light.

Then Dai saw the rope still dangling from the branch and realised what this was all about.

'Oh dear,' he had said to Chief Inspector Gwyn Arthur Jones, and the policeman nodded.

'I've never understood why they come out here to do it,' Gwyn Arthur said, taking out his pipe. 'Three or four a year, I reckon. If it's not here it's the Elan Valley. If it's not a rope over a tree it's a rubber pipe from the exhaust.'

Dai did not mention that it was his personal ambition to die here too in case the Chief Inspector got the wrong idea. 'Well, they come here for holidays. Happy memories, isn't it. Want to go out where they were happiest.'

'Bottle of pills and a photo album would save us all a lot of mess,' said Gwyn Arthur.

The corpse looked to be in his mid-forties and quite a seasoned hiker, judging by his clothing and well-worn boots.

'Who found him?'

'What's her name – the teacher. Pretty girl.'

'Bethan? Oh God.'

'Well, one of the kids it was originally. Anyway, Dai, we want to have a little poke around the woods, just to make sure he was alone. Then you can cart him up to the hospital mortuary. Why don't you go and bang on the Tafarn door and get

Aled to give you a pint. If you leave your casket on the bank, by there, my boys will have filled it up for you by the time you get back.'

Dai made his way back to the hearse. He'd managed to squeeze it into a bit of a clearing by the roadside so it wasn't very far to carry the coffin down to the river – not as far, anyway, as it would seem to the coppers carrying it back.

It was less than a quarter of a mile to the village, so he walked, feeling the air – so much lighter, somehow, than the air in Pontmeurig.

He strolled across the bridge to Tafarn y Groes. It was just gone six. Aled rarely opened before seven-fifteen. Dai rapped briskly on the pub door. Forgetting, until the pain stung his knuckles, what a solid oak door this was.

For a long time there was no response.

Dai was about to knock again when the door opened slowly and unwillingly, and in the gap he saw Aled's worried face. His white hair was uncombed; he had a hunted look about him.

'Coffee, Aled?'

'What?'

'Coffee. I won't ask you for a pint, but I wouldn't mind a coffee.'

'What are you doing here?'

Dai was thrown by this. All right, he was early and some landlords could be expected to be inhospitable. But not Aled. Aled was flexible.

'Something wrong, is there?'

'No . . . Well, Gwenllian's not so good. Bad throat. Awake half last night. Got a bit behind, we have.'

'Oh, I'm sorry. In that case I won't bother you.'

'No, no,' Aled said, opening the door wider. 'Come in. I want to talk to you.'

Aled made him coffee in the bar. There was no sign of Gwenllian. But then, in Dai's experience, there rarely was; she kept herself to the kitchen and served infrequently in the bar.

'Another body then,' Dai said.

'What?' Aled dropped a saucer.

'A body. Up by the woods. Hiker. Strung himself up, poor bugger.'

'Oh.' Aled was staring at the broken saucer as if someone else had dropped it. He began to pick up the pieces.

Dai drank his coffee in silence, burning his mouth in his haste to be away. There was clearly something wrong here, more than a bad throat.

Aled said, a bit hoarsely, 'How did you get on with Dr Ingley?'

'The Prof? Shipped back to – where was it now? Basingstoke.'

'Gone?'

'Gone,' said Dai.

'Where did you keep him?'

There was an odd question.

'How do you mean?'

'Where did you put the body?'

'Well, chapel of rest.'

'No . . . no problems?'

What the hell did that mean?

'I was asked to embalm him. Usual thing. Why do you ask?'

'No reason,' Aled said. Though it was not quite dark yet, he moved to the switches on the wall and put all the lights on.

Blinking in the sudden glare, Dai thought at first he must be seeing things when he noticed how badly the landlord's hand was shaking.

PART THREE

SICE

CHAPTER XIV

'I KNOW what you're thinking,' Giles said.

They were driving inland on roads that became narrower, through countryside that got bleaker. Camouflage country, Berry thought. Weathered farmhouses were hunched into the hillsides; tough, cynical-looking sheep grazed mean fields the colour of worn khaki. And then the forestry began, rank upon regimented rank of uniform conifers, a drab army of occupation.

'But you're wrong.' Giles was trying vainly to stretch his legs. Claire had taken the BMW to Norwich while her own car was being serviced, so they'd come in Berry's little old Sprite, lanky Giles wedged awkwardly with his knees around his chin because of the bags and stuff behind his seat.

They were passing a derelict lead mine in a valley, broken grey walls and tin-roofed shacks. A thin river seeped along the valley bottom, tired as a drain.

'Just you wait,' Giles promised.

Berry's first time in Wales. They'd driven in from the South-East, which he found pretty much like England, except more of it was rural. Wherever they stopped for a meal or cigarettes everybody seemed to speak English too, in quite intelligible accents.

Then they'd hit the west coast, checking into a hotel in Aberystwyth where quite a lot of the people around them were speaking a language Berry didn't understand. It sounded European, but it had a lilting quality, and the speech of people in the street was flecked with English phrases. They were only a couple hundred miles from London. Weird.

'So this cottage,' Berry said. 'All comes down to Claire, right?' He was quite enjoying himself. A whole new scene.

They came to a T-junction. A sign pointing right said: Pontmeurig, 5 miles.

'Go left,' said Giles. 'Yes. What basically happened is that sometime back in the fifties Claire's grandparents split up, and the old man – well, he couldn't have been that old then – he came back to his native Wales. Back to the actual village where he'd been born.'

'How Welsh does that make Claire?'

'Not very. Second generation, or is it third generation? Point is, Claire's mother was furious at Granddad, just buggering off like that, so they never had anything to do with him again. But then he dies – and he leaves his house to the granddaughter he never knew. Rather romantic, isn't it?'

'How far now?'

'No more than four. Of course, Claire's kicking herself now, that she never came to see the old chap while he was alive.'

'He, ah, had a lot of dough?'

'He was a judge,' said Giles. 'Qualified as a barrister in England, worked in London and the South East for years then became a circuit judge or a recorder or something – one of those chaps who used to take the old Quarter Sessions in provincial towns, it's all changed now. But yes, he did all right. She's English, of course, his wife, Claire's granny. She did all right too, out of the settlement. Nobody in the family talks much about why they split up. He'd just retired. Maybe he wanted to come back to Wales and she didn't.'

'Kind of a drastic solution.'

'Ha. When you see the village, you can imagine people doing pretty drastic things to get back.'

'Not if it's like this,' said Berry.

There was forestry now on both sides of the road. Berry liked country roads, as did the Sprite. But this route was no less claustrophobic than some concrete canyon in Brooklyn.

'Here?'

The sign said Y Groes, 2. Giles gave a confirmatory grunt.

They turned left. At the entrance to the road another sign had a broad red line across it: dead end. After Y Groes – nothing. For over a mile the forestry stayed close to the road on both sides.

'What's it mean, this place? The name.'

'Y Groes?'

'Yeah.'

'It means The Cross,' said Giles.

'Like in religion?'

'Must be. It has a very impressive church. Look, there it is – see?'

'Oh, yeah. Hey—' Berry's head swivelled. 'Where'd the forest go?'

Something lit up underneath Giles's freckles.

'Great, isn't it, the way you come out of the forestry so fast and everything changes. Notice how the trees are all broadleaf now? Look at the variety of wild flowers on the verges, don't see that in many places nowadays. And, look – what about the *sun*, for Christ's sake!'

'What *about* the sun?'

'It's come out!'

'Big deal,' said Berry.

All the same, he was getting an idea why Giles was so excited. Something in the light, was that it? Maybe it was because the journey across the hills had been through such harsh and hostile country that Y Groes seemed subtly translucent and shimmering like a mirage. Maybe the sun looked suddenly brighter and warmer here because, along the road, its rays had been absorbed by the close-packed conifers. Something like that.

They drove on down, and it got better.

Most of the other villages Berry had seen on the way from Aberystwyth had consisted of a single street, with cold-looking houses, a shop and a big grey chapel all strung out like damp clothing on a frayed washing line. Here, chunky, timber-frame cottages were clustered below the old church in a way that seemed somehow organic, like wild mushrooms in a circle. An image came to Berry of the cottages pushing themselves up out of the ground, chimneys first, each one in its naturally-ordained space.

Weird thought, but kind of charming. And natural – none of that manicured Cotswold gloss. You went behind that ochre Cotswold stone and you were in Hampstead. Here . . . he didn't know.

For the first time this weekend, he wished Miranda were

here. She'd approve, although she hadn't approved when he'd said he would not be seeing her that weekend and explained why. 'Morelli,' she'd snarled, 'as far as I'm concerned you don't ever need to come back. You can bloody well stay out there with the leeks and the seaweed bread and the Bibles.' Then things had got heavy.

'Looks like a nice old pub too,' Berry said, slowing down, wondering where they'd got the stone from because it seemed to have a more softly-luminous quality than the rocks they'd passed. Although the soil here seemed lighter too, so maybe . . .

'I've never been in the pub,' said Giles. 'I was sort of saving it.' Giles was hunched forward in his bucket seat, excited in a proprietorial kind of way, pointing out this feature and that, the natural amphitheatre of hills, the steps leading up behind the inn to the churchyard, the path to the river.

Berry eased the Sprite over the narrow river bridge, the inn directly ahead. Its sign, swinging from a wooden bracket – or it would have been swinging if there'd been a wind – had a fading picture of the same church tower they could see jutting out of the hilltop behind. The inn sign said, *Tafarn Y Groesfan*.

'Just carry straight on up the hill, as if you're heading for the church.'

Two old men with flat caps and sticks leaned against the side of the bridge. Berry gave them a wave and, to his vague surprise, one returned a cheery, gap-toothed smile and the other raised his stick in greeting.

Giles raised a friendly hand to the two old men and grinned delightedly. 'You see . . . absolutely nothing like old Winstone's picture of Wales, God rest his soul. Super people here; everybody you meet has a smile.'

Backs to the wall now, the Joneses and the Davieses . . .

Yesterday Berry had been to Winstone's funeral. The old reporter had gone down into the flames just like he always said he would and all the hacks had gone back to the last halfway decent pub in what used to be Fleet Street and drunk, between them, what Berry figured must have been several gallons of Glenfiddich in memory of one of the Scottish distillery's most faithful supporters. Giles had been unable to attend, having been sent to cover a much-heralded speech by Labour's shadow chancellor at some local government conference in Scarborough. Berry suspected he was glad to have avoided the occasion. Somebody – Firth or Canavan – would have been sure to make some discreet reference to Giles's behaviour on the night of Winstone's death.

Berry could still feel Winstone's hand on his arm. *Stop him.* But this village wasn't helping.

He'd been hoping for somewhere grey and grim. Instead, he was charmed. There was a surprising air of contentment about the place.

The Thorpe funeral had been conducted by a retired Fleet Street chaplain, the Revd Peters who'd known Winstone from way back. In the bar afterwards Berry had bought the old guy a drink, and it had emerged he was Welsh, from the industrial south east of the country. He'd laughed when Berry had told him of Winstone's gloomy warnings. His part of Wales, he'd said, had the warmest, friendliest folk you could wish to meet.

Up the short street Berry could see just two shops. Three women stood chatting outside one, shopping baskets on their arms. One woman had a cloud of fluffy white hair and wore a white summer dress with big red spots. Berry just knew they were speaking in Welsh. Something about the way they used their hands.

'Hey Giles—' He'd been trying to work out what it was made Y Groes different from anywhere else, even allowing for the absence of tacky modern storefronts among the old buildings.

He realised. 'Giles, we're the only car here!'

'That's right. What do the villagers need cars for? Going to drive fifty yards to pick up the groceries?'

'What I'm saying is, village this attractive – how come there're no tourists, 'cept us?'

'Well, it's not on a tourist *route*,' said Giles. 'Lots of attractive villages don't get hordes of visitors simply for that reason. I mean, we're in the middle of some pretty rough countryside, the sort that tourists just want to get through quick to get to somewhere else. I suppose they get a few walking enthusiasts and people of that sort, but obviously not enough to be worth catering for – as you can see, no souvenir shops, no cafés, no snack bars. Don't even think the pub does overnight accommodation.'

'Shame.'

'Not for me,' said Giles. 'I hate bloody tourists. Pull in here. We'll walk the rest of the way.'

A track led between two outsize sycamore trees. It was blocked after about twenty yards by a rusted metal farm gate.

'OK to park here?'

'Private road,' said Giles. '*Our* private road. Or it will be.'

They got out and stood looking down on the village in the vivid light of early evening. To the left of them stood the church tower, like a monolith. The church was built on a big hump, around which cottages fitted – or grew, as Berry liked to fantasise – in a semi-circle. The church tower had a short pyramid for a spire with timbers around the belfry. It seemed very old, older than the village. Older than the goddamn sky, Berry thought, for some reason.

A palpable silence lay over the scene, like a spell. No dogs barked, no radios played. It was calm and mature and the air was scented. The sycamores framed the view as if they'd been arranged by some eighteenth-century landscape painter.

'Nice,' said Berry 'Hey, pal, I apologise, OK? You were right.'

'Yes,' said Giles.

'This is some place.'

'Isn't it.'

They stood in silence for almost two whole minutes.

Birds sang. Butterflies danced up and down invisible staircases of warm air.

That church. It was bigger and taller and more quietly dignified than any of the others around here, where it was mostly chapels anyway. It was like some country cathedral, Berry thought. Except villages didn't have cathedrals.

'You really gonna commute?' he asked. 'Can you *do* that?'

'The way I see it,' said Giles, 'I'm working this four-day

week, OK? So, let's say I'm working Monday to Thursday. I get up really early and drive down Monday morning. On Thursday night I drive back. That means I only have to spend three nights in London.'

'Lot of travelling, ole buddy.'

'I don't care. I just want to spend as much time in this bloody glorious place as I can wangle.'

'Sounds good to me,' said Berry, wondering if it really did.

He thought, could I go for this, all this rural idyll stuff, four nights out of the rat race? Well, maybe. Maybe, with the right lady. Maybe for a few months. Maybe in the summer.

You put the arm on young Giles. Persuade him to sell the bloody place, soon as he can . . .

But what would Winstone Thorpe have said if he'd seen this place?

'Tell you what,' Giles was saying. 'Why don't you come down for a weekend, or even a holiday, when we're settled in? Bring whoever it is you're with these days.'

'Miranda,' said Berry doubtfully.

'Oh yes, the one who—'

'Thinks I look like Al Pacino. When he was younger, of course.'

Giles, face bright with pride, opened the iron gate and carefully closed it when Berry was through. Then he led the way along a track no more than eight feet wide, lined with hawthorn and holly.

They came at last to the house. And that was where, for Berry Morelli, the idyll died.

CHAPTER XV

THE dead, lower branches of the close-packed conifers, pale brown by day, were whitened by the headlights – the only kind of direct light they'd ever known, Berry thought. He was aware of just how narrow a channel the road made between the bristly ranks. Like driving down the middle of a toothbrush. He wondered what it would be like in the frozen days of January.

Berry shivered.

'You thought of that?' he asked, needing to talk.

'Thought of what?' said Giles.

'How it'd be in winter. Like when you have to get up at 5.30 on some freezing dark morning and drive to London on icebound roads and wonder how you're ever gonna make it back if there's snow. You ever think about that?'

'Nothing's without its problems,' Giles said. 'If you start to dwell on things like that, you never try anything new.'

The forestry was thinning out now. Berry braked as a rabbit scooted across the road. How about that, something alive in this place. He shivered again.

Pull yourself together, asshole.

It wasn't so dark yet, not when you got through the forestry. When they cleared the next ridge they'd get the benefit of the light coming off the sea. A sign said Pontmeurig 5, Aberystwyth 16. One-horse resort or not, he'd be glad to see Aberystwyth again. Least it had a few bars and a pier with coloured lights and gaming machines. Familiar, tacky things.

'Berry?' Giles said.

'Uh huh?' He turned briefly to look at Giles, saw only a hunched-up shape in a space too small for it and the glow at the end of a cigarette.

Giles said, 'Are you trying to put me off?'

'Put you off?'

They came into the valley of the disused lead mine, stone towers black against the western sky. It looked powerfully stark, quite impressive now it was too dark to see all the drab detail. Wales's answer to Monument Valley.

Yeah, he thought, damn right I'm trying to put you off.

Berry snapped the headlights on again. This was going to need careful handling.

It had seemed, in all the obvious ways, a good house. Barely fifty yards off the road, but nicely private, screened by laurels and holly and hawthorn, hunched into the hillside, protected from the wind. It had a view of the church hill some 250 yards away. Below that was the village; on winter evenings they'd be able to see the smoke spiralling from the village chimneys, warming the grey sky.

Nice. Cosy.

So the cottage looked, too, from the outside. Its walls were that warm, rusty grey that softened the outlines of the whole village. Its windows, six of them on the front, were small and quartered like in the picture books.

And clean. Somebody had been and cleaned the goddamn windows.

Not only that, they'd taken care of the garden too. It should have been overgrown, yet the small front lawn had been mown, the flowerbeds tended, even the roses deadheaded.

This did not look like the empty house of a man deceased.

Berry had said, 'You're sure we got the right place here?'

'No, I just thought we'd poke around somebody else's garden first, to pass the time. Of course it's the right bloody place!'

'Only somebody's taking good care of it for you. Why would they do that?'

'It was the judge's house, Berry. People respected the man.' As if to make his own mark on the garden, Giles bent down to a clump of pansies, and pinched off a couple of dead flowers. 'Perhaps the gardener and the cleaner wanted to maintain the place as he'd have wanted. Maybe they got a little something in the will.'

'I get it,' said Berry. 'So the lawyer wouldn't give you a key but he gave one to the cleaner so he or she could keep the place like the judge was still around.'

Giles clearly hadn't thought of this. Visibly miffed, he turned and walked off round the side of the cottage.

Berry caught him up.

'Hey, don't worry about it, fella. What d'you expect? You're English.'

'Now look!' Giles snarled. He spun round and shoved under Berry's nose an elegant English forefinger. 'Just stop trying to wind me up, all right? Me being English doesn't come into it.' And then he strode off across the back lawn that would be *his* lawn, olive-green waxed jacket swinging open to reveal his olive-green army-officer's pullover. An urban man who thought his life would be made suddenly healthier by driving an extra five hundred miles a week.

Berry looked at the cottage, soft-focus through the bushes. It was like most of the others in Y Groes, seemed as if it had grown out of the soil, its timbers forming together, like a developing bone structure.

Inevitably, the thought came to him: Giles might need this house, but the house doesn't need him.

Giles strode back across the lawn. He wore a wry half-smile. 'Sorry, mate. I'm touchy, OK? It means a lot to me. To be accepted. To be, you know, part of all this.'

'I can buy that,' said Berry. 'It's a good place to have.'

Maybe good wasn't quite the word. It was its own place.

They peered through a few windows, but even though the glass was clean and sparkling it was too dark inside to see much. One downstairs room they couldn't see into at all.

'That's the study,' Giles said. 'Somebody must have drawn the curtains to protect the books from too much light.'

'Thoughtful of them,' said Berry.

And that should have been it. He should have told Giles how nice the cottage looked and what a lucky man he was and they'd have walked around a while then maybe gone down to the pub, had one drink, then off back to the coast. They would have done just that if, while strolling by the rear of the cottage, he, Berry dumb-ass Morelli, had not spotted a dark line along the edge of a window. Now the late Winstone Thorpe had himself a firm ally.

'Hey Giles – you want to get in here?'

'What d'you mean?'

'See, if I go fetch a screwdriver from the car, I can slide it into this crack, push up the lever and maybe – well, just a thought, ole buddy . . .'

'Ha,' said Giles. 'One in the eye for Mr Goronwy Davies, I think. Well spotted, Berry.'

'Who's Mr Goronwy Davies?'

'The lawyer in Pontmeurig. The chap who won't give us a key until probate's complete.'

'Ah, right.'

And from then on they'd been like two schoolkids on an adventure. The goddamn Hardy Boys strike again.

'You did like it, though?'

'Oh, yeah. Sure. It looked in pretty good condition. All things considered.'

'That's not what I meant.'

'We still on the right road, Giles? It looks different.'

'Just getting dark. Bound to look different. You seem a bit nervy tonight, Berry.'

'Me? Naw, tired is all. Been a long day.'

'I'm not tired. I'm exhilarated. It always seems to renew me, going back there. I feel it's my place. Becoming more like my place all the time. And Claire's of course, I mean—'

'Sure,' Berry said.

No, he thought. It's not your place at all. It's somebody else's place. Always be somebody else's place.

CHAPTER XVI

H E'D dropped to the floor and found himself standing next to a sink. An old-fashioned sink of white porcelain sticking out of the wall. No cupboards underneath, just a metal bucket. It was gloomy in here, but there was no smell of damp. Two spiders raced each other along the rim of the sink. Spiders didn't like damp either – where had he read that?

It had been quite a squeeze getting through the window, which was only a quarter pane. It seemed unlikely that Giles would be able to manage it.

'Listen,' he'd shouted through the open window, 'why don't I come round, open the back door?'

'Good thinking,' said Giles. 'Only, don't shout, all right? We don't want to advertise ourselves.'

Berry threw the screwdriver out to Giles and carefully closed the window.

'Always knew I could've made it in the CIA,' he said aloud, and was surprised at how firm his voice sounded in here. You expected an echo in an empty house, but this was acoustically very tight, like a recording studio. He looked up, saw heavy oak beams and more beams sunk into the walls. That was it: timber-framing, low ceilings. A vacuum for sound.

Also, it wasn't an empty house. Much of the furniture, it appeared, was still here.

He looked around. The kitchen, right? It was quite small. Probably all cottage kitchens were small when this place was built back in the – when, 1800s, 1700s . . . earlier? Whenever, no dinner parties in those days. Was there going to be room here for the dishwasher, the freezer, the microwave oven and all the other sophisticated stuff he was pretty sure Giles and Claire must possess?

Berry chuckled, which was a very intimate sound in here. He stifled it.

In one corner he could see a big Aga-type stove, the only substantial piece of the twentieth century, if you didn't count the taps and the electric light, which was just a bulb with a white porcelain shade shaped like a plant pot.

There were two doors. He opened one and found some kind of storeroom or scullery. He hit his knee against a stack of shelves, still loaded with provisions. A packet fell off and he caught it. Paxo sage and onion stuffing. Judge Rhys's concession to haute cuisine?

The other door led him into a dim hallway, low ceiling, beams black and sagging. He could have used some light in here, but the power wouldn't be connected. The passage led straight through to the front of the house and ended at the front door and some narrow stairs. So which way was the back entrance? There were more doors on either side of him, so he tried one and found himself in a room where the light was rationed by drawn curtains. The judge's study.

'Christ,' Berry said.

It could have been a homely room: fireplace, book-lined walls, low ceiling with beams. Place where you could come and put your feet up, have a TV dinner, glass or two of beer. Warm your ass by the fire.

Except the fireplace was Victorian, an ugly iron thing, cold and dead, and the black beams seemed to press down like the fingers of a gloved hand.

And the books. Well, as Berry saw it, there were basically two kinds of books. There were warm, friendly books with bright dust-jackets that gave you the come-on, brought a room alive.

And there were books like these.

Thousands of them. The shelves ran floor-to-ceiling, taking up most of two walls, dark oak shelves of dark old books, heavy, black-spined books. The kind of books you felt it would be a breach of protocol to take down without you were wearing a tie.

It was a coldly austere room, this study, like . . . what? Some old-fashioned classroom? Air of discipline. Severity.

The window, quite small, was set uncommonly high in the wall, faded grey curtains pulled across as if for a passing funeral. Opposite the window was a huge old desk, like a monument; behind it a chair, thronelike, with a tall back and carved spindles. Heavy, dour, forbidding.

No, not a classroom, Berry thought suddenly. A courtroom. It's like a very small courtroom. Is this what happens when old judges retire and have no lowlife scum to send to jail any more? They have to bring with them that ambience of old-fashioned judicial disdain?

Above the fireplace was a single picture, a framed photograph of what he took, at first, to be a gathering of the Ku Klux Klan, everybody in long white robes. Then underneath he saw the words *Eisteddfod Genedlaethol 1963*. Ah, the annual Welsh festival of poetry and song and stuff where all the head guys dressed up like Druids. Was Judge Rhys one of the men in white?

Berry stood in the middle of the floor, which was stone-flagged, a single rug beneath his feet, on it a threadbare red dragon spitting faded fire.

He hesitated, then crossed to the shelves and pulled down one obese volume, expecting a small dust storm. It didn't happen. Even the damn books were still being cared for. In case the judge came back from the grave and had nothing to read?

When that thought – a typically trivial, facetious thought – occurred to Berry Morelli, he felt a chill that came and went, like the door of a freezer opening and closing with a hiss. A cold hiss, like the hiss in ice . . . *iiiiice*. Did he hear that, or did he imagine it?

He opened the book, and that hissed too, tissue-thin pages whispering secrets denied to him . . . because every word was Welsh. He quickly pulled down three more fat, black books at random – and they were all in Welsh too. Hard to imagine so many books being published in a language spoken by so few. But then it *was*, according to Giles, supposed to be the oldest language in Europe. And these were real old books.

As he returned the book to the shelf, he felt suddenly guilty. And furtive, like a kid who'd left sticky fingermarks on the school Bible. He thought, somebody's watching, and he spun round and there was nobody. But in his mind the freezer door opened and closed again. With a hiss . . . *iiiiice* . . .

It was darker, too, he was sure the air itself had got darker. And yet there was a sunset out there (so why are the damn curtains washed with grey?)

Berry's gaze travelled across the patchy gloom, from the ranked books, to the drab lumps of furniture, to the picture of the procession of men in white. He felt the weight of something old and hallowed.

He didn't care for it.

In the room, and yet beyond the room, he felt kind of a coiled malice. And the air was too thick. How could the air be thick in a room with no dust?

The air came in shifting shades of black and grey and a poisonous off-white, like dirty milk. And it hissed, short gasps, like bellows. He felt, with an astonishing wrench of panic, that if he stayed in here much longer, Judge Thomas Rhys would materialise, fully robed, in the tall gothic chair, his eyes giving off dull heat, a bony finger pointing, trembling with a focused fury.

'*Sice!*' he'd breathe, the word coming out in a short, hideous rasp, like a cobra rearing to strike.

And the air hissed, the bellows, the freezer door opening and closing. The air said,

'*SICE!*'

'Fuck this,' Berry said, suddenly very scared. He stepped back into the hallway and closed the door of the study firmly behind him, then backed off, afraid to look away in case it should open by itself, releasing the air, the wafting hate.

CHAPTER XVII

THE door hung ajar.

Aled Gruffydd stepped back quickly, as if afraid something would reach out and snatch him inside.

'I will not go in there with you,' he said. 'You do understand?'

The tall man with white hair only smiled.

'Did not happen immediately, see,' Aled said. 'Quiet it was, for more than three days.'

It was gloomy on the landing, the day closing down.

'We cleaned out the room and stripped the bed,' Aled said. Gwenllian said to burn the sheets, but I said no, isn't as if he had anything contagious.'

The tall man looked at the opening and did not move. He was very thin and his greasy suit hung like leaves blackened by a sudden overnight frost.

'So she took off the sheets for washing and brought clean ones and put them on the bed. And as she is tucking in the sheets, it flew off the bedside table. The vase. She had sweet peas in it, to sweeten the air, see.'

The white-haired man silently put out a forefinger to the door but did not quite touch it.

'Flew off the table, flew within an inch of Gwenllian's head. Smashed into the wall. Gwen came tearing down the stairs, almost falling over herself.'

Aled looked over his shoulder, down the stairs. His companion said, 'And then?'

'I came back with her and we picked up the pieces of the vase and the flowers. All quiet. No disturbance. I would not doubt her, though. I shut the door and locked it, and we came downstairs and did not go in again until this morning.'

With a small coughing sound, the bedroom door moved inwards, revealing a slice of white wall. Aled recoiled. 'There – can you smell it?'

The Reverend Elias ap Siencyn remained motionless. His pale eyes did not blink. His long nose did not twitch at the stench, which included, among other odours, the smell of hot decay.

'We have not been in since,' Aled said. 'We've left it the way we found it this morning.'

'Only this room? He has not come to you in the night? Or to Gwenllian?'

Aled gripped the banister. 'Oh, good God.' He was shaking at the thought. 'No. Nothing like that.'

'I doubt if he knows, you see,' the rector said. He had a surprisingly high voice, though with a penetrating pitch, like organ pipes. 'Sometimes it takes quite some while before they can fully accept their condition.'

'I don't want him, Reverend. I don't want him here.' Aled tried to make a joke of it. 'Not as if he's paying me now, is it?'

The rector had not taken his eyes from the door. 'Tell me again. What you found.'

'Oh Christ – sorry Reverend. But can't you smell it?'

'Bodily fluids?'

'Shit, Reverend. And the other stuff. Slime. Mucus. All over the sheets. Soaked-in, dried stiff. And splattered on the walls. Like those prisoners in Ireland did to their cells.'

'All right, Aled. About a week ago, yes? Since he died?'

'A week ago tonight. Exactly.'

'Very well. I may need assistance. Perhaps you could fetch Mrs Dafis. Or Buddug Morgan from the farm.'

'Yes indeed,' Aled said, clearly glad to have an excuse to go outside. He went downstairs very rapidly, but at the bottom he turned and shouted back, 'I swear to God, I locked the door! I put the key in the glass with the others. In the bar, see. I swear to God, nobody could get in.'

'Aled, I *believe* you.'

'So how can it be? He's *dead*, Rector. Dead and gone. I know there are things the dead can do, but this . . . How can it be?'

'Because,' said the Reverend Elias ap Siencyn, 'he cannot adjust. And he cannot contain his fear and his – I don't know, there is something else.'

With a single finger he pushed open the door.

'Also,' he said quietly, when Aled had gone, 'like others of his race, he is vermin. Vermin make a mess.'

The rector walked into the bedroom and looked around.

The sheets and the walls were spotless. Whatever Aled had seen was gone. But the stink remained. The stink was obnoxious, and carried a sense of fear and pain and suffering. As well as deep frustration, a helpless rage and a terrible confusion.

'Alien contaminant,' he muttered to himself, a fragment of an old verse, 'a foul disease now chokes the oakwood.'

He stood at the foot of the bed and spoke, with the clarity and resonance of the first words in a sermon.

'You expect my pity?'

He smiled coldly, putting down a scuffed attaché case. Then he straightened up and looked at the bed, at a spot just above the pillow.

'You can't stay here,' he said. 'You are over. The air's too strong for you, the light's too bright.'

CHAPTER XVIII

WHEN they drove at last into Aberystwyth, the coloured lights were on at the entrance to the pier. Green and yellow lights, rippling up and down in a sequence. It wasn't Coney Island, but it made Berry feel a little happier.

'Giles, I— You ever talk to anybody about the house? Anybody local?'

'How d'you mean?'

'—'bout its history. Anything.'

'No, not really. We didn't like to go round asking questions. Nosey newcomers. Why?'

Berry took the first left after the pier and found a parking space in a sidestreet, a block or two away from the hotel. He could see its sign and an illuminated advert for Welsh Bitter. He switched off the engine and lay back in his seat and let out a sharp breath.

'Look, what's up, Berry? You're behaving pretty bloody strangely tonight.'

'Giles, you're gonna think I'm crazy—'

'I always have.'

'Listen,' Berry said. 'You remember ole Winstone Thorpe—'

'Oh no!' Giles snapped. 'We're not going into that again.'

Berry had come out the way he'd got in, landing this time less easily, on a gravel path, ripping a hole in his jeans and grazing a knee.

Giles had found him on the lawn. He must have looked like hell, but Giles didn't seem to notice.

'Berry, you cretin,' he'd said when Berry told him he hadn't been able to open either the front door or the back door. 'Why didn't you shout? There's a back door key in the bottom of an old vase in the scullery. I remember seeing the solicitor put it there when he was showing us round. You'll just have to get back in through the window.'

Berry was already shaking his head. Uh huh. No way. No time now. Gonna be dark soon. Anyway, had plenty time to look around. Let's go, OK . . .?

'Well, go on,' Giles snapped, 'Say it. Say what you've got to say.'

His lean, freckled face, lit up by the headlights of a passing car, looked aggressive, affronted and defiant, all at once.

A girl with luminous green hair and a man in a tight silver jacket, as worn on the Starship Enterprise, walked past the car, laughing at each other, but probably not because of the jacket and the hair. They went into the hotel.

'C'mon, let's go in,' said Berry. 'Get a drink.'

The hotel bar was quite crowded, but they managed to find a table, one people had avoided because it was next to the men's room. Giles went to get the drinks and Berry leaned back in his chair and closed his eyes, letting the voices wash over him, soporific, like surf. He could hear people speaking in English and in Welsh and even, he was sure, in Japanese. University town. Kind of a cosmopolitan town. He liked that. Made him feel secure. Like New York, except if you closed your eyes in a New York bar you'd open them half a minute later to find you'd lost your wallet or your watch or, where applicable, your virginity.

There was a crush of people around the bar; it took Giles a while to get served. Berry sat quietly, half-listening to the multilingual voices and half-hearing his own voice talking to him, saying all the real obvious things.

. . . you dreamt it, it was your imagination, you're making it up . . .

No way.

Something had been in there, something heavier than the desk, harder than the oak beams, blacker than the books.

'Here we are,' said Giles. He put down two beers. 'I know how you like to try local brews, so this is . . . dammit, I've forgotten the name, but it was in a bottle with a yellow label with a red dragon on it.'

'Thanks, pal.' He hated local brews. 'I was just thinking, I could quite get to like this town. Good mix of people here, you know?'

'Yes,' said Giles. 'But what about Y Groes? What about my cottage?'

'Hell of a place,' said Berry. '*Hell* of a place.'

So, OK, he thought, let's work this out rationally, bearing in mind that at the end of the day, this is not your problem. Tomorrow you drive out of here and you don't come back. Let Giles find out for himself. It is *his* problem.

So you didn't like the cottage. No, get it right, there was nothing so wrong with the cottage, it was the room you didn't like. You didn't like the furniture. You couldn't understand the books. You were inexplicably disturbed by a photograph which, in other circumstances, might have seemed faintly comic, bunch of old men in christening robes.

So how come you were squeezing out that window like some guy breaking jail. Grown man, smooth-talking wise-ass reporter, scampering away like a puppy, oh, Jesus, this can't be happening, too bewildered to crank up the mental machinery to attempt to analyse it.

'Berry, are you going to come on like the rest of them. Like Winstone Thorpe – "But you're an Englishman, old boy, you don't belong there." '

'No,' Berry said uncertainly. 'That's not how I—'

'Fuck 'em all, that's what I say.' Giles stared into his beer. 'I've had it with all these smug London bastards. They're the ones who're out of touch, you know. Had it with Westminster too. And newspapers that try to tell the public what's important in life, what they should be concerned about. This is a place where you can't bargain on London terms. Listen to this – I wasn't going to say anything about this, I thought you'd snigger—'

Giles leaned back, drew in a breath and said,

'*R'wyn dysgu Cymraeg.*'

Berry stared him, expressionless.

'Means "I am learning Welsh." Been working at it for several weeks now with cassette tapes. When we move in here I'm going to take proper lessons. What d'you think about that?'

'Let me get you another drink,' said Berry

He pushed his way through to the bar and said to the barman, 'Gimme a couple those beers with the dragon on the label.'

It was worse than he'd thought.

So Berry said casually, 'Listen, Giles, that . . . study. You didn't feel it was a mite depressing in there, all that heavy furniture, those old books?'

Giles put down his glass and laughed in amazement. 'Depressing? That study has to be absolutely the best part of the house. Super atmosphere. Real old Welsh. Stark, strong—'

'Yeah but, Giles, what if . . . what if it was, you know . . .?'

He couldn't say it. He just couldn't bring himself to say it. 'So you're learning Welsh, huh?' he finished lamely.

'We have these cassettes,' Giles said. 'We play them in the car, Claire and I. Try and talk to each other in Welsh, over breakfast. *R'wyf i eisiau un siwgwr.* I should like one sugar.'

'Could be real useful that, Giles, you have to use a teashop making so much money they can refuse to serve people who don't place their order in Welsh. What else can you say? How about, "Don't spit in my beer, I can't help being English." '

'You're not into this at all, are you, Berry?'

Berry smiled sadly.

'*Cwrw*, that's beer. *Peint o gwrw.* Pint of beer. The C in *cwrw* mutates to G after a vowel. More or less everything mutates in Welsh; once you grasp that you can start making progress.'

Berry lost patience with him.

'OK, then, Giles, ole buddy. You go over to the bar and order us up a couple half pints of whatever it was, guru, right?'

'I *could* do it, I expect,' Giles said. 'If I really had something to prove.'

'Ten pounds says you won't go through with it.'

Giles, eyes flashing, pushed back his chair and rose decisively to his feet.

'Right,' he said. 'Put your money on the table.'

Berry pulled his wallet out of the hip pocket of his newly torn jeans and placed a ten pound note under the ashtray.

Giles put on his stiff-upper-lip expression. 'Right, you listen carefully.'

Aw, hell, Berry thought. Can't you ever keep a hold on your mouth, Morelli?

Through his fingers, he watched Giles march to the bar. Two men in front of Giles who'd been conversing in Welsh ordered a pint of lager and a whisky and soda in English.

Berry saw Giles stare down his nose at them. When it was his turn he said loudly.

'*Hanner peint o gwrw, os gwelwch yn dda.*'

Lowering his voice and pointing at the bottle with the dragon on it, he added, 'Er, make that two.'

Berry thought he'd never seen so many wry smiles turned on at once. It was like a *chorus* of wry smiles. You had to feel sorry for Giles; he was a brave man and a born fall-guy.

He was still cringing on Giles's behalf, when, at the adjacent table, the young man in the Starship Enterprise jacket nodded towards Giles and said laconically to the girl with the luminous green hair,

'Sice.'

Berry spilled a lot of beer. He felt himself go pale.

Within a minute Giles was back, red-faced, slamming two glasses on the table and snatching the tenner from beneath the ashtray.

'Bastard,' he said.

'I'm sorry, ole buddy. I didn't plan to set you up.'

'You're a bastard,' said Giles. 'I think I'll go to bed.'

'What about your beer?'

'You drink it,' said Giles. 'I'll see you at breakfast.'

'Giles, what's "sice" mean?'

'Piss off,' said Giles.

'Come on Giles, I'm serious, what's it mean?'

'Piss off, you know what it means.'

'Aw, for Chrissakes, Giles, if I knew what it meant would I be asking you?'

'*Sais*,' Giles hissed. '*Sais*.'

'Yeah, right, sice.'

'English,' said Giles. 'It means English. Often used in a derogatory way, like the Scots say Sassenach. Satisfied now?'

'I don't know,' said Berry. 'Maybe, I . . . I don't know.'

'I'm going to bed,' said Giles. 'OK?'

PART FOUR

CROESO

CHAPTER XIX

ENGLAND

FOUR or five times Berry had picked up the phone, intending to call Giles, each time pulling back. In his head, he'd almost had it figured out. 'See Giles, I've always been sensitive to atmospheres and I just had the feeling there was something badly wrong in there. Humour me, OK? Have a priest take a look.' Every time he heard himself saying that, he chickened out. A priest! Had he really been about to say that?

From the Newsnet office, the day after they'd got back from Wales, Berry had called Giles's paper and asked if he was around. 'It's Gary Willis here,' a guy said. 'Giles has taken some leave. Gone to move some of his stuff out to this place he's got in Wales.'

'When's he gonna be back?'

'I don't know, mate, and Roger's not here at the moment. But it can't be more than a week or two.'

Berry stood at his apartment window, looking out at the block from which you could see the Thames. He clenched his fists.

All the way home from Aberystwyth, he and Giles had discussed their respective careers in journalism, the differences between the British and American media and even the rift between Berry and his dad and what had caused it, the ethics of the job, all this stuff.

Everything, it seemed, except the cottage in Y Groes, Giles's future there, Berry's feelings about the place. It was clear that Giles, having brought Berry to see the house without getting the expected result – 'Gee, Giles, this is just amazing, you're a lucky guy, I can't tell you how jealous I am' – had been studiously avoiding the issue.

While Berry . . . Well, what was *his* excuse?

You asshole, Morelli, he told himself. You blew it again. All ways, you blew it.

111

This was three days ago. It was now Wednesday night. It was well into October. It was dark. He had nobody to talk to.

Miranda had landed a part in a TV commercial for perfume. Although the perfume was made in Wolverhampton, they were making the commercial in Paris. She'd left a message on his answering machine to say she might be back by the end of the week if she didn't run into any vaguely interesting Frenchmen looking for a little fun.

Berry sat down and tried to watch a re-run of an episode of *Cheers*. Even that didn't lift him out of his private gloom. When it was over, he switched off and lay down on his bed, missing Miranda, haunted by the same crazy question.

Am I psychic or just neurotic?

'*The kid's neurotic*,' Mario Morelli had said. It was the first time he was conscious of hearing the word. He'd been – what? Nine, ten? The year he went to summer camp and was so unhappy they sent him home, scared – he heard his dad telling his mom – that he was going to walk off on his own and drown himself. After that, Mario took no chances; he wasn't having a son of his bringing down scandal on the family.

His career. Really, he was afraid of what it would do to his career.

In subsequent years they reluctantly took him with them on vacation, which was how he first saw London. He'd been happy then, although he knew things between his parents were not good. He'd pretended he was there alone, pretended it was his town. Felt the history of the place; imagined he was part of it, not part of his dad's vacation, which seemed to be full of inefficient service and lousy Limey food.

How long after that was The Gypsy?

Whenever, that was the year the vacation coincided with his mom being in hospital having this Ladies' Surgery – he never did find out whether it was a hysterectomy or new tits – and his dad had to take custody of the kid. Berry had spent this dismal fortnight down in Florida, where Mario – already a high-profile newsman with NBC – had borrowed a beach house from a friend. Come to think of it, this friend had been a senator, the bastard already getting too close to politicians for a guy who was supposed to be ruthlessly impartial.

Anyhow, that had been the summer of The Gypsy. He didn't know if she *was* a gypsy, but that was how he always thought of her. He didn't know, either, if she was a phoney. Just always hoped she was. Better to be a basic neurotic than what she said.

He remembered the nights spent holding the pillow around his head to muffle the sound of Mario humping Carmine, his mistress, in the next room. One night he didn't go back to the beach house, just walked until dawn, a night of spinning pinballs and hard coloured lights and cheap music. And The Gypsy.

She was this mid-European lady, with a sign over her door covered with coloured moons and stars. He couldn't imagine now how the hell he'd found the courage to walk in there with his five dollars. She'd said, 'You not a happy boy, you mixed up.' He thought she was about to use the word neurotic, like his old man. But she went on, 'It affect you more on account of you sensitive, right? Have eyes inside, yes?' Berry staring at her blankly. 'One day something happen to you. Wow! Crash! Boom! And then you know what you got.'

Crazy. The lights, the hot music, and The Gypsy. Sometimes – occasionally in the years before The Gypsy and increasingly afterwards – he'd got feelings about things or places. Small things, stupid things. Feelings that said: don't get closer to this, back off. And The Gypsy's words would come back to him, and he'd laugh. Try to laugh, anyhow. She'd been called Rose-something, weren't they all? She'd taken his money, but afterwards given it back to him. 'You and me, we in same shit. You find out. Good luck, huh.'

Most likely, she was neurotic too.

The thing that really got to him was old Winstone. Put the arm on young Giles, stop him, not meant to be there, all that crap. The sequence of events leading up to him standing in a dark, cold room permeated by hatred.

Or maybe simply a perfectly ordinary room with a certifiable neurotic standing in it.

On Friday night Miranda called Berry from her mother's house in Chelsea to say she was home.

113

'Did you get my message?' she asked him.

'Did you get a Frenchman?'

'They all tried too hard,' Miranda said. 'I wanted one who really didn't want to know, but they all tried too hard. I'm afraid Paris has become rather tedious.'

'As tedious as Wales?'

'Do me a favour. How did you get on, anyway?'

She seemed to have forgotten about telling him not to bother coming back.

'Oh, you know, OK,' Berry said. 'Interesting place, good scenery. Crazy language.'

'And you spelled it out for him? As stipulated in the dying wish of old what's-his-name?'

'Kid, it was complicated.'

'Complicated. I see. What you're saying is you didn't sort it out. You didn't, did you? You really didn't tell him. You spent the whole weekend poncing around with a lot of Celtic sheep-shaggers and you didn't say a word.'

'That isn't quite fair, Miranda. What happened . . . Listen, can I see you?'

She hung up on him.

Angrily, Berry broke the line and tried to call her back. Then he changed his mind and called Giles at home. This was it. The end. He'd lay the whole thing on him, the whole Winstone bit, the bad vibes in the judge's study, everything.

Giles's phone rang five times and then there was a beep.

'This is the London home of Claire and Giles Freeman. We're not here, so you can either leave a message after the tone or ring us on Y Groes 239.'

Beep.

Berry put the phone down.

Y Groes 239.

'Shit,' he said, dismayed.

Giles had complained it would be months before all the legal stuff was complete, what did they call it, probate.

'They're living in that goddamn house,' Berry said aloud. 'They moved in.'

He'd blown it. He'd let everybody down again. Giles, Winstone. Even Miranda.

You're a waste of time, boy. You know that?
Mario Morelli's words, of course.
You got no guts is the problem.

CHAPTER XX

WALES

ONE of the first things they did was to go into Pontmeurig and choose a bed.

Nothing else. Not yet, anyway. Any changes, they had agreed, should be dictated by the cottage itself. They felt that after they'd spent a few weeks there they would know instinctively which items of new furniture the judge's house might consider permissible.

But a new bed was essential. There was only one in the place, an obvious antique with an impressive headboard of dark oak which was possibly Claire's grandfather's deathbed. Hardly be seemly for the pair of them to spend their first night in Y Groes squashed into that.

So they ordered the new bed from Garfield and Pugh's furniture store in Stryd y Castell, Pontmeurig. It wasn't the kind of bed they would have bought under normal circumstances – it had a headboard of shiny pink vinyl – but there were only three to choose from and Giles was adamant that they should support local traders.

'We can soon pick up a new headboard somewhere,' he whispered to Claire. 'I mean, it'd look pretty bad if we walked out now without buying one.'

Young Mr Pugh, son of one of the partners, was standing no more than four feet away with an contemptuous smile on his pale, plump face. He had obviously heard every word and was not bothering to conceal the fact.

'I cannot see us having anything that would suit *you*,' Mr Pugh had told them bluntly. 'No brass bedsteads here. No pine. Nothing – how can I put it – nothing *cottagey*. Have you tried Aberystwyth or Lampeter?'

'We'd rather shop locally,' Giles had replied stiffly. 'Now we're living here.' He was furious. This youth was treating him like one of the mindless incomers who wanted to turn Wales into an English colony. He imagined a headline in the local paper.

SNOOTY LONDONERS SNUB LOCAL BEDS

'We'll have this one,' Giles said. 'Nice cheerful headboard.'

Mr Pugh shrugged. 'We can't deliver until Monday.'

'That'll be fine,' Giles said, wondering where the hell they were going to sleep over the weekend.

'*Blaen-y-cwm*, is it?' Mr Pugh asked.

'What?'

'Mrs Harris's old place. Where you're living?'

'No,' Giles said. 'We've taken over my wife's grandfather's house at Y Groes. Judge Rhys.'

'Oh, I see,' said Mr Pugh, with a little more interest. '*Siarad Cymraeg*?'

'I'm afraid not,' Giles said. 'But we hope to learn.'

'They don't speak much English in Y Groes,' Mr Pugh said with a smirk.

'Good,' said Giles.

When they left the shop, Claire said, 'Not very friendly, are they? He didn't particularly want to sell us that bed.'

'He's probably sick to death of posh English people buying things and then seeing something better and cancelling their order.'

'They weren't very friendly in the Drovers' Arms either.'

'They were OK. They didn't all start speaking Welsh or anything when we walked in.'

'Oh yes, most of them were speaking English,' said Claire. 'But not to us.'

'For God's sake—' Giles snapped. 'Give them a chance, can't you?'

Claire's small face was solemn, and Giles's mood softened.

He knew she was looking for reasons not to stay here. Not because she didn't want to, but because she did want to, very badly.

'Look,' Giles said. 'We can't expect them to rush out and welcome us with open arms. We're just another English couple in love with a dream. They've seen us before. That's what they think.'

Claire smiled. 'I doubt if anyone has seen you before, Giles,' she said.

Giles ignored this. 'We've got to persuade them we're not the usual kind of pompous self-satisfied shits who come in and throw money about until they get bored and move to Provence or somewhere the weather's better.' He put an arm around Claire. 'Come on, let's go home.'

He loved the sound of that. Home.

Y Groes was home now.

Giles had taken a fortnight's leave to coincide with the move, which had become possible far sooner than they'd imagined. It turned out that the usual six months' probate period did not apply in the case of property bequeathed to a close relative.

Suddenly the judge's house was theirs. The weather was still warm, the travelling was easy. There'd never be a better time, Giles had maintained, freckles aglow, hustling Claire.

So they'd done it.

As they were retaining their London flat – for the time being, at least – and the cottage was already furnished, there wasn't a great deal to bring, and the removal firm had used its smallest van.

Now, as they drove back from Pontmeurig with groceries and things in the boot of the BMW, Giles was once again aware of the difference in atmosphere as they came out of the Nearly Mountains.

It wasn't simply the transition from the bleak forestry to the broadleaved haven of the village. It was the striking difference between Y Groes and Pontmeurig – a town Giles had never actually visited before today.

He tried to explain it to Claire. 'A definite air of depression. I don't mean the people. The shops weren't exactly over-stocked. And there was quite a lot of, you know, not exactly dereliction, but peeling paintwork, that sort of thing.'

'Not a prosperous town,' Claire conceded.

'Dying on its feet, if you ask me. All right, there were a couple of shiny new shopfronts – the bookshop and that awful pizza joint. But you get the feeling they won't be there this time next year – or they'll be replaced by other experiments in the art of retailing.'

'Not enough money,' Claire said. 'Because there aren't enough people. I bet . . . I bet all the incomers get their provisions from the supermarkets in Aberystwyth. They're used to travelling a fair distance on shopping trips back in England – big discount furniture places and hypermarkets.'

'Well *we* won't be doing that,' Giles said firmly, turning into the track between the two sycamores. 'I don't care what it costs or how many different shops we have to go to. These people deserve our trade.'

They found the gate already open and two women by the front step. Oh God, Giles thought. What have we done wrong? If there were neighbours outside the flat in Islington, they'd usually come to complain.

He remembered what young Mr Pugh had said about Y Groes. '*Bore da*,' he said uncertainly, then realised it was no use wishing them good morning at three-thirty in the afternoon. He tried again.

'Er . . . *Prynhawn da*.'

The first of the ladies came forward, smiling, hand out-stretched. 'Oh, Mr Freeman, good afternoon,' she said. 'We are terribly sorry to trouble you, but the telephone people arrived to reconnect your line and could not get in. I am Mrs Huws, from the Post Office, this is Mrs Hywels.'

Mrs Huws and Mrs Hywels both shook hands with Giles and with Claire. 'Pleased to meet you, Miss Rhys.'

'Oh gosh,' Giles said. 'I mean, there was no need for you to come all the way up here just to—'

'Well, they could hardly ring to tell you they had been to connect your telephone.' said Mrs Hywels.

'We are delighted to help in any way we can,' said Mrs Huws. 'Moving house is such a trial. You must be exhausted.'

'What you must do,' said Mrs Hywels, 'is to tell Mair when it is convenient for the telephone people to come to you, and she will ring them.'

'Good God, no.' Giles was glowing with pleasure at their kindness. 'There's a phone box in the village. I'll ring them. We can't put you to that kind of trouble.'

'Now, Mr Freeman,' said Mrs Huws severely. 'We are a very close village. When you come to live amongst us, you are part of our community whether you like it or not, isn't it. Now is there anything you need for tonight. Tea? Sugar? Bread?'

'Thank you,' Giles said. 'But we're fine. We've got everything. Everything we could wish for.'

The small dark eyes of the women were darting about like bluebottles, over Giles and Claire and the BMW beyond the gate.

'Would you like a cup of tea?' Claire asked. 'Before you go?'

The ladies said they would not put her to such trouble but when Mr and Mrs Freeman had settled in they would be pleased to accept their hospitality.

'Super,' said Claire.

Walking the ladies to the gate, holding it open for them, Giles asked how well they'd known Claire's grandfather. They told him the judge was a very quiet and dignified man, who never came out, even in the height of summer, without a jacket and a tie and a watch and chain. Claire, they said, would have been proud to know him. And he, they were sure, would have been very proud of his granddaughter.

'Er, we . . . We don't know an awful lot about the judge,' Giles admitted. 'That is, his death . . . The solicitor, Mr Davies, implied it had been fairly sudden. Quick, I mean.'

'And without pain, wasn't it, Eirlys.' Mrs Huws said. 'Very weak, he was though, at the end. Weak in body, mind, not in spirit. And he was over ninety. Dr Wyn wanted to send him to the hospital in Pont, but he refused. He knew he was going, see, and would not leave Y Groesfan.'

'In case his spirit could not find its way back,' Mrs Hywels said. Giles smiled, acknowledging that no spirit in its right mind would want to leave Y Groes.

'Don't forget now,' Mair Huws said. 'If you find you have run out of anything, come to the shop and knock on the door if we are closed.'

'Great,' said Giles. 'Er, *diolch yn fawr*.'

'Goodbye then Mr Freeman. 'And welcome to Y Groesfan.'

Giles went back to the house, his gratitude brimming over. Life in Y Groes was already turning out exactly as he'd hoped it would.

That night they built a big log fire in the inglenook (Giles, with a howl of delight, had uncovered what looked like a year's supply of cut, dry logs in a shed) and spread two sleeping bags on the living room floor. Claire, ever efficient, had brought them just in case. The house really was remarkably clean, and Giles was surprised how generally trauma-free the move had been. They hadn't had a single row – although Claire was the sort of quietly-efficient professional person it was hard to pick fights with anyway.

Giles did get rather angry with himself as he discovered he had no natural ability when it came to making log fires and had to keep getting up in the night to feed the thing. At this rate what looked like a year's supply of logs would probably last about six weeks. Altogether Giles reckoned he got about three hours' sleep, and he awoke next morning with a slight headache.

Of course, the ache began to fade as soon as he looked out of the window and saw the hills freshly speckled with early sun. He pulled on his trousers and went barefoot through the primitive kitchen to fill the kettle with spring water which came, apparently, from their own private supply and in as much quantity as if it were from the mains. He cupped his hands under the tap and tasted it – probably better than the stuff they bought in bottles from Sainsbury's – and rubbed the rest into his eyes, rinsing away the remains of his headache.

He went back into the living room and stared down at

Claire, still sleeping, curled foetally in her yellow sleeping bag. He didn't think he'd ever seen her looking so relaxed, so untroubled. Even her hair – short, blonde, businesslike – mustn't have it flying over the lens, ruining a shot – seemed to have loosened up and was fanned out over the edge of the sleeping bag and onto the hearthrug below. She really did, he thought, look reborn.

Giles felt his lungs expand with something he identified as joy. It felt quite strange and moving.

'This, my darling,' he said softly, a little chokily, 'is where it really begins.'

Claire slept on.

CHAPTER XXI

O N Sunday evening, Giles decided to make his first visit to his new local, *Tafarn y Groesfan*. Claire watched him walk out of sight down the hill before setting off alone to chase the spirit of the place in the only way she knew how: by taking pictures of things.

She walked out of the front garden gate and did not look back. She wanted to photograph the cottage last of all. That was the natural sequence. She didn't want to take its picture until she'd made other connections . . . out there.

Feeling as if she were descending into a dream, Claire walked into the last burst of brilliance from the setting sun. It forced her to look downwards, denying her a view of the church, denying her a picture too, because from this side the tower would be hard against the light and it was too bright yet to make any dramatic use of that.

There was nobody on the main street. Dark blinds were down in the windows of the post office – *Swyddfa'r Post*, it said above the door, without a translation. Claire took a picture of the post office, with herself reflected in the dark window, a slender, crop-haired woman, face semi-concealed behind the battered Nikon. This was a picture to prove that she really was here, an image in the window along with two terraced cottages and a black cat. Part of the scene.

She photographed interlocking beams in the end wall of the general store, pushing out like bones under a taut white skin.

Then she became aware of a very distinguished old oak tree, standing at the bottom of the street, above the river bridge. She filled the frame with the stern expressions on its trunk, and then took another shot on wide angle, to get in a heavy tractor looking flimsy and transient in its shade. Claire could almost feel the ancient male arrogance of the tree, its roots flexing in the earth.

That made her wonder about her own roots, how deep *they* were here.

She'd phoned her mother to explain that they would be spending a few days at the cottage. Not yet telling her, however, that they actually intended to make it their permanent home – although Giles had thought they should. Indeed, he seemed to be looking forward to it. 'Christ, I'd love to see the old bag's face, when she finds out.' he kept saying. Giles, who had never got on with his mother-in-law, was taking full advantage of her being out of favour with Claire as well.

'You're doing what?' Elinor had said.

'It seems only right, mother. He *did* leave it to me. Do you really think I could sell it without a second thought?'

'You can't sleep there. It'll be damp.'

'Why should it be? It hasn't been empty long. I gather he hadn't been in hospital for more than a few days when he died.'

'And dirty.'

'We'll clean it.'

Elinor was breathing very hard.

'Mother . . .'

'What?' Elinor snapped.

'You said my grandfather had only seen me once.'

'When did I say that?'

'When I rang you two weeks ago.'

'Well, I – I've told you about that, surely.'

'No.'

'I must have.'

'You haven't.'

'Well, I don't want to talk about it now.'

'Oh mother, please – this is ridiculous.'

'You don't know what that man was like, Claire.'

'I expect I'll find out this weekend then. I shall ask people in the village about him. I'll find out from them when I saw him. Somebody must know—'

'No!'

'What?'

'Listen . . . We went to see him just once, your father and I,' her mother said, 'when you were a very small child, three or four. I've told you before, I'm sure, but I don't suppose you were very interested at the time. Anyway, we thought he ought to see his granddaughter. Just once, for the sake of—'

Appearances, Claire thought.

'—the family. Old times. I don't know why we went really.'

Because you wanted a good snoop, Claire thought.

'But – My God, we soon wished we hadn't. It was *the* most embarrassing day I can ever remember. He seemed to have nothing to say to us. A *stranger*, a strange man to me – my own father. Just some old, some old . . . Welshman. Who didn't even look the same, somehow. His . . . housekeeper prepared this very basic lunch of ham salad, I remember. She also did most of the talking. And then after lunch he said, let's go for a walk, something like that. And your father got to his feet and the old devil waved at him to sit down. Not you, he said. The child and I will go. I was speechless.'

'And what happened?' asked Claire.

A silence.

'You went,' her mother said coldly.

'Really?' Claire had been expecting to hear how she'd burst into tears and clung to her mother's skirt, demanding to go home. She was thrilled. 'I really went with him?'

Elinor didn't reply this time. She obviously regarded it as an act of almost unbelievable treachery.

Claire said, 'You never told me that before. I know you never told me.'

'Why should I? It's hardly been a fond memory.'

'Mother—' Claire thought, *that feeling . . . the feeling that it was meant . . .* I was simply *remembering . . .* 'What happened,' she said, 'when I went for this walk with my grandfather? I mean, where did we go?'

'Claire, it's thirty years ago, and it's not something—'

'Oh, come on, mother, you must remember. You remember everything else that happened.'

She heard Elinor drawing in a long, thin breath. 'All I remember is that you were both gone for what seemed an awfully long time and I ran out of things to say to this frightful woman, the so-called housekeeper, and your father got increasingly embarrassed, so we went outside to look for you. George was getting rather worried because it was hardly a big place and yet we couldn't see you anywhere. And then the old swine came up the lane from the church. He was holding your hand and we could hear him – well, I was disgusted. I snatched you away at once.'

'Good God, Mother, what on earth—?'

'I put you in the car and I made your father drive us away from there. We didn't bother to say goodbye. We'd been insulted enough.'

'But what was he doing? Did he say something to you? To me?'

'And we swore never to go back there again, ever. And we never did.'

'But what—?'

'I don't *know*!' her mother had almost screamed. 'He was talking to you in *Welsh*, for God's sake!'

The old oak tree stood there, as if it were absorbing her thoughts and her emotions and considering what to do about her.

Claire looked up the lane towards the church and pictured a distinguished gentleman in a black suit walking slowly down it, a little girl clinging to his hand.

But, of course, this was all imagination because Claire had

no idea what her grandfather had looked like. She'd never seen a single photograph of him. Her mother wouldn't have one in the house.

CHAPTER XXII

WALKING towards *Tafarn y Groesfan* Giles felt undeniably nervous. For some reason, he started to think about Charlie Firth, of the *Mail*, and the allegedly poisoned eggs. All that absolute nonsense.

But, bloody hell – if, in parts of Wales, there *was* a lingering suspicion of the English, was it not amply justified by people like Charlie Firth and the others? If the locals were suspicious of *him*, better to find out now. Show his face, let them get used to it.

It was the last week of British Summertime. The evening sun was losing strength, although it was still remarkably warm, as Giles approached the huge oaken door which hung ajar, giving direct access to the bar. As it swung open, the heads of three men inside slowly pivoted, as if they were part of the same mechanism, and three gazes came to rest on Giles.

He blinked timidly.

The bar was so small and – well, *woody*, that it was almost like being inside an ancient, hollow tree. Beams everywhere, far thicker than the ones in the cottage. It was lit only by the dying sun, so it was dark. But dark in a rich and burnished way, rather than dim like, say, the judge's study.

It was palpably old. The phrase 'as old as the hills' – a cliché too hackneyed for Giles ever to use in an article – suddenly resounded in his head, making dramatic sense.

All the richness came from the age of the building, for it was very plain inside. No brasswork, no awful reproduction warming pans.

In a most un-publike silence Giles approached the bar. From beneath a beam the shape and colour of a giant Mars bar, a face peered out.

The landlord, if indeed it was he, was a small man with white hair and a Lloyd George moustache. Aled Gruffydd, it had said over the door. What Giles had presumed was the familiar line about Aled Gruffydd being allowed to sell liquor pursuant to sub-section whatever of the Licensing Act had been given only in Welsh.

Either side of the bar a man stood sentinel-like. Giles tentatively flashed each of them a smile and recognised one immediately, having almost run out of petrol on the way here in his determination to fill up locally, at this wonderfully old-fashioned grey stone garage. It had tall, thin pumps, no self-service and a small, rickety sign outside which said Dilwyn Dafis and something in Welsh involving the word *modur*, which he'd taken to mean motor.

This was Dilwyn Dafis. He was in his thirties, wore an oily cap and had a spectacular beer belly. The second customer was a contrastingly cadaverous chap with large, white protruding teeth and thick glasses which were trained now on Giles, like powerful binoculars.

Giles had to bend his head because the great beam over the bar was bowed so low. Too low for an Englishman's comfort. All three of them stared at him.

Should he try greeting them in Welsh? *Nos da*? No, that was good night, said when you were leaving. *Nos . . . nos . . . noswaith da*? Was that it? Was that good evening? Bloody hell, he ought to know something as simple as that, he'd learned a whole collection of greetings weeks ago. *Noswaith da*. It was close but it wasn't quite there.

The three men went on staring at him in silence.

Giles began to sweat. Come on, come on, say *something*, for God's sake.

'Er . . . evening,' he said lamely. 'Pint of bitter, please.'

The landlord nodded and reached for a pint glass.

'And please,' Giles added earnestly, flattening his hair as if trying to make himself shorter and thus less English. 'Absolutely no need to speak English just because I'm here.'

Christ! What a bloody stupid, patronising thing to say. Especially as nobody, as yet, had spoken at all. He wanted to go out and never, ever come in again.

Still nobody spoke, but the white-haired barman gave him an amused and quizzical look, into which Giles read withering contempt.

'I mean—' he floundered, feeling his face reddening. All those years a journalist and he was going red! But this wasn't an assignment, this was the first faltering step into his future. 'If I want to know what's going on around here, I'll just, er, just have to learn *your* language, won't I?' Christ, worse and worse . . .

Dilwyn Dafis, the garage man, chuckled quietly.

Aled the landlord stepped back to pull the pint. The pump gurgled and spat.

It was the thin man with the sticking-out teeth who finally spoke. He said,

'Well . . . *there's* a thing.'

What the hell did that mean? For the first time, Giles came close to wishing he were back in London.

Aled Gruffydd topped up Giles's pint, leaned across the bar with it. 'Nobody expects that, man.'

'I'm sorry . . .?'

'I said nobody expects you to learn Welsh. Right Glyn?'

'Good God, no,' said the thin man.

'No indeed,' said Dilwyn Dafis, shaking his head and his oily cap.

Giles inspected the three faces, found no hint of sarcasm in any of them and was nonplussed. 'That's very generous of you,' he said. 'But I *want* to learn Welsh. I believe it's the least one can do when one comes to live in a Welsh-speaking community.' How pompous it sounded, how horribly, unforgivably, tight-arsed *English*.

Aled Gruffydd said, 'Why? What is it you think is going to happen if you don't?'

'Waste of time for you, man,' Dilwyn Dafis said. 'We speak it because we grew up speaking it, the Welsh. No great thing, here. Just the way it is, see.'

'Have a seat,' said Glyn. A faded tweed suit hung limply from his angular frame. 'Tell us about yourself. We won't bite you.'

Giles sat down rather shakily on a wooden bar stool. The

whole atmosphere had changed. He'd walked into silence and stares, and now they were making him welcome and telling him there was absolutely no need to learn Welsh – in a village where little else ever seemed to be spoken. He was confused.

'Where is your wife?' Aled Gruffydd said.

'Oh, she's . . . out. Taking a few pictures.'

'Photos, is it?'

'That's what she does. She's a photographer.'

'Well, well,' said Aled.

Giles had the feeling Gruffydd knew this already. A feeling there was very little he could tell them about himself that they didn't already know. But he explained about his wife's inheritance and they nodded and said 'well, well' and 'good God' a few times as if it was the first they'd heard about it. They were unbelievably affable. And this made it more important for them to know he and Claire were not just going to be holiday-home-owners, that this was now their principal residence and they were going to preserve its character; there'd be no phoney suburban bits and pieces, no patio doors, no plastic-framed double-glazing, no carriage lamps . . .

'Good house, that is, mind,' thin Glyn said. 'Been in that family for . . . what is the word in English? Generations.'

'You mean the Rhys family?'

'Generations,' said Glyn. 'Many generations, the Rhyses.'

Bloody hell, he'd never thought of that – that he and Claire were actually maintaining a family chain of ownership going back possibly centuries. They really didn't know anything, did they?

'Gosh,' Giles said. 'I suppose – I mean, is that why Judge Rhys came back? Because somebody left *him* the house?'

'Well,' said Glyn. 'I suppose that was one of the reasons. From England, he came, as you know, having spent most of his life there.'

This was actually marvellous. This gave them a solid, copper-bottomed basis for residency. This gave them a right to be here.

'What is that other word?' said Glyn. 'Continuity. We believe in that, see, in Y Groesfan. Continuity.'

Giles understood now. When he first came in they weren't quite sure who he was. Now they knew he was the husband of a Rhys. Knew he belonged. He settled back on his wooden stool and began to look around. What a superb old place it was. He remembered Berry Morelli telling him on their way back to London how the buildings in Y Groes had struck him as having grown out of the landscape as part of some natural process. This pub was like that, its oaken interior so crude and yet so perfect. He felt privileged to be here. And proud too, now.

He bought them all drinks.

They told him about the village.

They told him it had about two hundred and fifty people, if you included the outlying farms.

It had two shops, the general store and the post office. One garage, one school, one church.

They told him the original name of the village was Y Groes-fan – the crossing. But when non-conformism had taken Wales in the nineteenth century a chapel had been built and the name shortened to Y Groes – the cross – because it seemed more holy. When Giles said he hadn't noticed a chapel, Dilwyn Dafis smiled. Glyn, who apparently was something of an historian, said non-conformism had been a passing phase here, although nobody had bothered to change the name back.

'I suppose,' Giles said, journalistic antennae finally pushing through, now he was more sure of his ground, 'that you must be pretty sick about all the English people moving in.'

'What English is that?' Aled said. He took a cloth from a shelf below the bar and began to polish glasses.

'Well, you know . . . I mean, we were in Pontmeurig this morning and at least half the people we met, half the shop-keepers for instance, were incomers. I just hadn't realised it was that bad. I mean, it must irritate you, surely.'

'Ah, well, see, that is Pontmeurig,' said Dilwyn Dafis.

'Pont is different,' said Glyn. 'They are always moaning about the English in Pont. But we don't moan about them here, do we boys? No cause to.'

Aled Gruffydd shook his head. Glyn drained his beer glass

and Giles seized the opportunity to buy everyone another drink. He was dying to ask all kinds of questions but settled on just one more as the glasses were passed over and the three Welshmen said 'Cheers' rather than *Iechyd Da!* out of deference to their English companion. They really were remarkably accommodating. Indeed if everyone was as gently hospitable as these chaps and Mrs Huws and Mrs Hywels it was really no wonder the country was being overrun by the English.

But they hadn't been like this in Pontmeurig. Only in Y Groes. A special place.

'So, what,' Giles asked, 'is the actual percentage of incomers in Y Groes? I mean, you know, roughly.'

Dilwyn Dafis looked puzzled. 'How's that, like?'

'What he means,' Aled said, 'is how many English compared to Welsh.'

'In this village?'

'Right,' said Giles.

'What English?' said Dilwyn.

'You mean—?' The truth hit Giles like a brick. 'You mean that the entire immigrant population of Y Groes is—'

Glyn smiled, his large front teeth standing out like a marble cemetery in the moonlight.

'—*us*?' said Giles.

'Well, there we are,' said Dilwyn Dafis, raising his glass to Giles and smiling slowly. 'Makes you a bit of a novelty, like, isn't it?'

CHAPTER XXIII

CLAIRE climbed into the riverside field by a convenient stile to photograph a lone sheep, somebody's initials SE scrawled across its back in lurid crimson, like a splash of fresh blood. The sheep was lying apart from the rest of the flock, benign head lifted, gazing beyond the field to the village street. Through the lens, Claire followed the sheep's gaze but saw only a litter bin attached to a low wall with grass growing out of the top. She took a picture, the sheep dark in the foreground.

The river was beautiful. It splashed and fizzed amiably over the rocks, calling out so strongly to Claire that she just had to scramble down the bank, camera bouncing around on its leather strap, until her feet slipped into the soft, cool water. One shoe floated off and she had to rescue it. Then, on impulse, she put the blue shoe back in the river and took a photograph of the clear water swirling gently around it, in the background the river-washed stonework of a bridge support.

The river, the bridge, her shoe – part of the scene.

She should have come to see him. If she'd known about him wanting to take her, just her, for that walk, down the lane to the village, past the church; if she'd known that, she would have come. She imagined him talking to her softly, musically, in Welsh – how beautiful. If she'd been told about that, she would have come. No doubt her mother had thought of that. Bitch. Until that phone call Claire had assumed she'd never met her grandfather, never been to Y Groes in her life. No wonder the village called out to her to come back.

Bitch.

Y Groes – always 'some ghastly God-forsaken place in the middle of nowhere' or 'some damp, dreary hellhole.' If only she'd known . . .

It was her own fault. Such a placid child, people always said. Incurious about everything until her teens, when she began to take photographs and the world opened out like a huge flower. And then always too busy: leaving home, catching up on everything she'd missed, carving out a career in what then was still seen as a man's world. And forgetting for years at a time that she had a grandfather on her mother's side, an estranged counterpart to good old Reg with his garden and his golf.

And here, unknown to her – all this.

Bitch.

Sitting on the river bank, in the lengthening shadow of the bridge, strange, conflicting emotions crowded in on Claire and she wept silently. Not soul-wrenching, God-cursing tears, as often wept by Bethan, whom she did not as yet know, but quiet tears of regret.

Another shadow fell across her and she looked up, a tall figure blocking the dying sun.

It's *him*.

Claire's heart leapt in fear. Fear and—

—and longing.

The voice was soft and high and sibilant, like the wind in a cornfield.

'I'm afraid I don't know your name. So I shall just call you Miss Rhys. How are you, Miss Rhys?'

CHAPTER XXIV

THREE-FIFTEEN. Home time.

Bethan was bustling about the school hall attending to children's major crises: the four-year-old boy whose shoelace had come undone, the girl of six with a broken nail.

'Try not to get it wet or it will come off,' she said, adjusting the Band-aid round the child's finger then turning to help a small boy who'd buttoned his coat all wrong.

A handful of mothers were waiting for the smallest children. They watched her with indulgent smiles, none of them rushing to help her. Perhaps they thought this was the kind of therapy she needed to cure her of widowhood.

The mothers took their kids and left, leaving Bethan with just three small pupils waiting to be collected and a strange woman standing hesitantly in the doorway, clutching one of those slim, garish packages in which prints and negatives are returned from processing.

'Mrs Freeman,' Bethan remembered. 'You rang this morning. You wanted to see me.'

'Hello,' the woman said. She looked down at the photo envelope. 'I usually do my own or take them to someone I know in London,' she said half-apologetically. 'I've been to one of those fast-print places in Aberystwyth. Just, you know, wanted . . . to see how they'd turned out.'

She seemed embarrassed. Bethan couldn't think why. She smiled at the woman. 'Come in,' she said. 'Try not to fall over Angharad, she thinks she's a sheepdog.'

Buddug had left early, to Bethan's relief. In the emptying school hall, where an electric kettle was coming gently to the boil on the teachers' table, Bethan looked at the woman and the woman looked at Bethan. They were around the same age, one dark, one blonde, one Welsh, the other . . . well, very English, Bethan thought, but who could really say?

'I'm still rather feeling my way in the village,' the blonde one said. She was dressed like a very urban explorer, in fashionably-baggy green trousers and red hiking boots. 'I don't know quite how I should behave.'

Good heavens, Bethan thought, they aren't usually like that, the English, when they move into Pontmeurig, joining this and organising that and introducing themselves everywhere and even buying people drinks, sometimes.

'Don't be silly,' she said, pouring boiling water into a chunky earthenware pot. 'Sit down. Have a cup of tea.'

'Thank you,' the judge's granddaughter said, lowering herself, quite gracefully under the circumstances, into a tiny chair designed for a seven-year-old. 'That's kind of you, Miss Sion.'

'Mrs McQueen.'

'Oh, I'm terribly sorry, I was told—'

'Bethan. Call me Bethan.'

'Oh. Yes. Thank you. I'm Claire Freeman, but everyone seems to know that.' She laughed. 'Although they all seem to call me Miss Rhys – the women in the post office and Mr ap Siencyn, the rector. My grandfather, you see, he was—'

'I know,' Bethan said. 'I'm afraid I never really met him. A bit before my time. He was staying in his house most of the time, when I was here. He used to study a lot, people said. In the village, I believe, he was very much . . . well, revered.'

This had the desired effect of pleasing Claire Freeman, who told Bethan how wonderful it had been to discover in the cottage and in the village this whole new aspect of her ancestry, long hidden, like the family treasure.

'But you said you didn't really know him,' Claire said. 'So you can't have been here all that long yourself.'

Pouring tea into a yellow mug, Bethan told her she'd been here nearly a year, then left, then come back. No she hadn't been here all that long, when you added it up.

'But it's different for you,' Claire said, 'and that's what I've come about, I suppose.' She'd opened the envelope and was flicking through the photographs without looking at them, still rather ill at ease, the child, Angharad, scampering around her feet.

'Milk?' said Bethan.

'Just a little.'

'Sugar?'

Claire paused. '*Dim siwgwr*. Is that right?'

'Yes,' said Bethan, smiling a little, passing her the mug of tea. 'But only if you're trying to lose weight. Can I see?'

'I haven't really looked at them yet. They won't be very good. They're just snaps.'

Bethan pushed back her hair and adjusted her glasses. She opened the envelope and saw clear water swirling around a bright blue shoe. It was a startling picture. She drew it out and below it saw the judge's cottage, twilit. Then she saw the village street looking very still, with deep shadows; various close-ups of the timber-framed houses – including the tiny terraced cottage where she and Robin had lived, with the setting sun floating in its upstairs front window. Then a solitary sheep, a view of the darkening hills, of the rigidly-upright figure of the rector standing in the grass above the river, of Mair Huws outside her shop, of the church tower braced against the dying light and photographed from a steep angle that made it look as if it was falling towards you.

She felt something at once in the photographs. This woman had plucked ripened images of Y Groes out of the air like apples from a tree, and caught the glow.

'They're wonderful,' Bethan said. 'They're like something out of a magazine. No, that's inadequate, that cheapens them.'

'Oh dear,' said Claire, 'I was hoping they'd be like holiday snaps. I can't seem to take snaps any more.'

She looked so seriously disappointed that Bethan had to laugh, quite liking her now. Out of the window she saw two mothers appear at the gate, and excused herself and rounded up the remaining three children – '*Dewch yma, Angharad*, wuff wuff' – gently pushing them out of the door into the playground, waving to the mothers.

When she returned, Claire was thumbing rapidly through the photographs, looking puzzled.

'Anything wrong?'

'No, I – a couple seem to be missing, that's all. My own fault, I should have waited to have them done in London. That is—'

She looked embarrassed again, as if expecting Bethan to say, Oh, so our Welsh film processing isn't good enough for you, is it, Mrs Posh Londoner?

'Well,' said Bethan, 'they *are* a bit slapdash, some of these quick-processing outfits.'

Claire looked grateful. 'What I've come about – I – somebody in the pub told Giles, my husband, that you were rather brilliant at teaching English children to speak Welsh, and so we wondered—'

Bethan explained that it wasn't a question of being brilliant; English children, the younger the better, picked up Welsh surprisingly quickly. By the age of seven or eight, if they attended a Welsh-medium school, they were often quite fluent. Claire said they had no children yet, but when they did have a baby she would like it to be raised in a bilingual home, and so— 'It's funny really, some people in the pub told Giles there was no need to learn Welsh in Y Groes.'

Bethan raised an eyebrow. 'They told him that?'

'I think it was because we seem to be the only English people in the village. I think they were just being kind, probably.'

'Probably,' said Bethan, thinking how odd this was.

'We'd fit in, of course, with your arrangements,' Claire said.

Bethan thought about it.

'I've never done it before, taught adults.'

'Is it so different?'

'I don't know,' Bethan said.

'They say the brain starts to atrophy or something, when you pass thirty. Isn't that what they say?'

'Well,' said Bethan, pouring herself a mug of strong, black tea, coming to a decision, 'let's prove them wrong. I could come to your house after school for a short time, how would that be?'

'That would be super. I mean, Giles will have to go back to London during the week, but I'll be staying here, and I could bring him up to date at weekends on everything I've learned.'

Bethan said slowly, 'I'm . . . often free at the weekend too.' All too free, she thought. 'The thing to do is to work on it every day if you can, even if it's only for twenty minutes. I'm sure we could do that most days. And perhaps at weekends we could have a revision session, with your husband.'

Claire flung out a big smile, and Bethan thought she was going to hug her. 'That's absolutely marvellous, Bethan. I mean, we'll pay whatever you think is—'

'Don't worry about that. I'll enjoy it, I think.'

Bethan had caught a breath of something from this woman, something she realised she missed, a sense of the cosmopolitan, a sense of *away*.

Bethan closed the school door behind her and looked around her nervously, half expecting to find another child inviting her to inspect a dead body. She shivered, although it was a pleasant evening, still warmish, still no sign of the leaves fraying on the trees. In Pontmeurig many already were brown and shrivelled.

The arrival of Claire Freeman and her husband had, she thought, opened up the place, making a small but meaningful crack in its archaic structure. All villages needed new life, even one as self-contained as Y Groes. *Especially* one like Y Groes.

Learning the language was good – and something that few of the incomers to Pontmeurig bothered to attempt. But she

found herself hoping (Guto would be horrified) that the Free-
mans wouldn't try *too* hard to fit in.

As she drove the Peugeot out of the school lane towards
the bridge, she saw Claire Freeman standing in the middle of
the village street gazing out at the river. Nobody else was on
the street. Claire looked abstracted, a wisp of blonde hair fallen
forward between her eyes.

Bethan paused for a second before turning the wheel
towards the Pontmeurig road, and Claire saw her and began
to run towards the car, waving urgently.

She wound down her window.

Claire, flushed and panting, leaning against the car, said,
'Bethan, I think I must be going mad. I can't seem to find my
tree.'

'Your tree?'

'It's a huge oak tree. Very old. It's . . . I'm sure it was in
that field. You see, I took some pictures of it, but they weren't
there, with the others.'

'Perhaps they didn't come out.'

'My pictures,' said Claire, '*never* don't come out – I'm sorry,
I didn't mean – but they don't. I've been through the negatives
and the tree pictures aren't there either. And now the tree's
gone too. I'm sorry, this must sound ever so stupid.'

'Well, perhaps—' Bethan was going to say perhaps somebody chopped it down, but that made no sense either and she
wasn't aware of there ever having been a tree down there
anyway.

'The tractor!' Claire exclaimed. 'Look, see that yellow
tractor . . . *that* was there when I took the picture, standing
next to the tree. The tree was *there*!'

'Well, that explains it,' said Bethan. 'Somebody has moved
the tractor and confused you. Your tree is probably further
up the bank.'

'No—' Claire brow's was creased and her mouth tight. 'No,
I don't think so.'

There is more to this than photos, Bethan thought.

'I'm sorry,' Claire said, pulling herself away from the car.
'It's professional pride, I suppose. You always know exactly

what you've shot, and there are a few things on that film I don't— Look, I'm delaying you again, you're probably right, the tree's somewhere upstream and it doesn't matter anyway, does it?'

Claire tried a weak smile. 'Perhaps my brain really is starting to atrophy,' she said.

Bethan didn't think so.

CHAPTER XXV

GILES was setting up his word processor in his new office, plugging the printer into the monitor and standing back to admire.

It was all just too bloody perfect.

Well, all right, *almost* too perfect. His one disappointment had been not being able to organise his office in the old man's study. He'd pictured himself in the Gothic chair behind that monster of an oak desk, surrounded by all those heavy books in a language which he couldn't as yet understand – although that was only a matter of time.

Last night, after returning from the pub, Giles had unpacked his word processor and was struggling into the judge's study with the monitor in his arms, fumbling for the light switch, when he found there wasn't one.

There was no electric light in there!

Not only that, there were no bloody power points either.

'Bit of a primitive, your granddad, was he?' he'd said in some irritation.

Claire's reply had been, 'Oh, didn't you know about that?' Which could have meant anything. Giles had resolved to contact an electrician. He really wanted that room.

Meanwhile he'd decided to adopt the smallest of the three bedrooms for his office, and he had to admit there were compensations.

Not least the view, through a gap in the trees (an intentional gap, surely) and down over the rooftops of the village towards the Pontmeurig road. The church was just out of sight, seemingly behind the cottage at this point, but he could sense its presence, somehow.

There was another window to the side and it was against this one that Giles had pushed his desk, which was actually their old stripped-pine dining table from the flat in Islington, one of the comparatively few items of furniture they'd brought with them. Claire had insisted they should eat at her grandfather's dining table, which was a terrible fifties-style thing with fat legs. Giles himself would have chopped it up for kindling; he hated its lugubrious lack of style.

Through the side window he could look out from his desk on to an acre of their own land sloping down towards the river. The neighbouring farmer apparently had some sort of grazing right, and the field was full of fat sheep. Giles was thrilled. He could gaze on all this and the enclosing hills with one eye while keeping the other, so to speak, on the VDU. He was, he felt, in the vanguard of journalism: living in this superb rural location, yet in full and immediate contact with London. Or he would be once he'd installed a fax machine.

He didn't think he'd ever felt so happy or so secure. For the first time in years the job was not the most compelling thing in his life. And he knew that if he did have to quit the paper and go freelance like Claire – a freelance specialising, of course, in honest features about the *real* Wales – they'd be cushioned for the forseeable future by the no doubt astonishing amount of money they'd get for the flat in Islington.

Giles was feeling so buoyant he told the computer how happy he was, typing it out on the keyboard in Welsh: *R'wyn hapus.*

He examined the sentence on the screen. It wasn't right, was it? It didn't look right at all. He hadn't had much chance to work on his Welsh since moving to Y Groes. Awkward bastard of a language; back in London he'd been sure he was going to have it cracked in no time at all.

Still, no doubt it would start to improve again now Claire was arranging a teacher for them. 'Well, all right then, why don't you have a word with Bethan at the school,' Aled in the

139

pub had said finally, when he'd emphasised how determined they were to learn the language. 'She used to teach a lot of English kids in Pont. Must be good at it.' 'Right,' Giles had said. 'Tremendous. Thanks.' Getting somewhere now.

'I'll go and see her,' Claire had said that morning, when Giles got up with another headache. 'Then I'll drive over to Aberystwyth and get my film processed and get some food and things. You take an aspirin and sort out your office.'

The headache had completely vanished now, the office was in order, everything was fine. He rather wished he'd gone with Claire. He'd been wondering which of the teachers this Bethan was, what she looked like – just hoping she didn't turn out to be that female-wrestler type he'd seen stumping down the lane to the school. He understood she was called Mrs Morgan and was in fact their neighbour, wife of the farmer who raised sheep in their field. Mrs B. Morgan. Bethan Morgan? He did hope not.

Giles leapt up in alarm when, down in the living room, the phone rang for the first time since the Telecom blokes had reconnected it. He charged downstairs, thinking he'd get them back to scatter a few extensions around when he and Claire had worked out which rooms they were using. At present the only phone was on a deep window ledge in the living room.

'Hullo, yes. This is, er, hang on – Y Groes two three nine.'

'Giles? Is that you, Giles?'

'Certainly is.'

'Giles, this is Elinor. Could I speak to Claire?'

Oh hell. He should have known it was all too good to last.

'Sorry, Elinor, Claire's out with her camera. I'm not sure when she'll be back. Might be staying out late to photograph badgers or something.'

'Don't be ridiculous, Giles. Now tell me what on earth you're doing *there*. Why is there a message on your answering machine referring people to *this* number? What's going on?'

Giles smiled indulgently into the phone. 'Going on? Nothing's going on. That's the whole beauty of this place, nothing *ever* goes on.'

'Giles—' The voice of his mother-in-law had acquired a

warning weight. 'Am I to expect any sense at all out of you? Or should I call back when my daughter's in? Look—' Being reasonable again, the old Mrs Nice and Mrs Nasty routine, Giles thought. 'I'm aware that hovel may not be in a fit condition to sell, but surely you could afford to pay someone to *do* something with it. You didn't have to go there yourselves.'

'It's already in good enough condition for us, old darling,' said Giles. 'Well, virtually. I mean, it needs a few minor alterations, mainly of a cosmetic nature. Anyway, look, I may as well tell you. Expect Claire's been too busy to fill you in about our plans, but the current situation is that we're actually living here now.'

The silence lasted nearly half a minute, it seemed to Giles. Why did she always have to phone when Claire was out? He'd have to suffer it all twice now – the heavy threats over the phone from Elinor and then, when he'd told her about the conversation, half an hour or so of Claire pacing around saying what an old cow her mother was.

'Elinor, you still there?'

'In . . . in that house?' She was sounding very far away. '*His* house?'

'No, Elinor. *Our* house.'

'Oh, Giles.' Unexpectedly her voice had turned itself down low, with apparent anxiety rather than anger. 'What about your work, both of you?'

'No problem,' said Giles, enjoying talking about this bit, as he always did. He explained how fate had intervened in the form of the Glanmeurig by-election, how he was taking a fortnight's holiday by the end of which, with any luck, they'd be into the campaign. Could be weeks before he'd have to return to London, give or take the odd day, and then, afterwards—

'And *then* you'll sell it, that's what you're saying, when this election is over. Because—'

Giles mentally battered his forehead with an exasperated hand.

'Good God, no, you're not getting this at all, are you? We'll still have our base here. I'll travel to London during the week,

Claire will work directly from here – good as anywhere – and then we've got a few long-term plans to make sure that Wales remains our home. I mean for good. For ever. Got it now?'

There came a stage with Elinor when only brutality would work. He heard her breathe in sharply and then force herself to calm down and reason with him.

'Giles, listen – before this nonsense goes any further—'

Oh, bloody hell, it isn't . . .

'—I – I *can* talk to you, can't I? I've always thought I could – most of the time.' She drew a long breath. Christ, Giles thought, get me out of this. 'Now, I assume this is some insane idea of Claire's . . . You have to talk her out of it, do you understand? I can't do it, never could once she'd made up her mind about something – now that's an admission, isn't it, from a mother? Giles, please, I'm relying on you, and one day you'll thank me for this—'

'I'll do it now, in case we don't see you for a while. Thanks, Elinor. Now if you don't mind—'

'Giles, don't you dare hang up on me! Listen—' The old girl was racing along breathlessly now. 'You could probably get rid of it – the house – quite quickly, if you put your mind to it. I'm sure, if you really want to live in the country, you could get quite a nice property in . . . in Berkshire or somewhere, for the money. Isn't there some land to sell?'

'Strewth,' Giles said. 'We don't want to live in bloody Berkshire. I mean, don't worry, we'll still come to see you at Christmas, it's not exactly the other side of the world.'

Christ, how could somebody as balanced as Claire have a mother like this? She reflected all the worst aspects of Home Counties womanhood – smugness, snobbery, inability to conceive of civilised society anywhere north of—

'Giles, this is not funny. You must fetch Claire home at once.'

He felt a warning ripple behind his forehead.

'Home? Home? Listen, Elinor, if you want the truth' – the headache was coming back, bloody woman – 'If you really want the truth, I've never felt more at home in my entire bloody life. OK, sure, we all know you and the old man were not exactly close but – well, it's not as if he's still here, is it?'

'Isn't it?' his mother-in-law said, sounding suddenly strained and old and tired.

Then she hung up on him.

'All fixed,' Claire said. 'Starting tomorrow evening.'

'What's she like?'

'Very pleasant.'

'I mean, is she young or . . . not so young?'

'I suppose,' said Claire, 'that depends on what you mean by young.'

Getting a bit cryptic these days, Claire. Must be exposure to the Welsh.

'What's she called. I mean, what's her last name?'

'Something English. McQueen – or is that Scottish? Although, obviously, she isn't. Anyway, she's going to pop round after school as many nights as she can manage. We didn't get round to agreeing a fee, but I'm sure it'll be reasonable.'

'Doesn't matter,' Giles said. 'Where else would you get Welsh lessons in your own home? But, look, we've got lots to talk about, so why don't I light a fire? Brought some more logs in. Marvellous logs, you know, these, dry as bone.'

Going dark earlier these nights. Colder too, Giles thought, glad Claire was back; it was good to stride around the place during the day but he could never go too long without a spot of company. He was dismayed when Claire said, 'I have to go out again.'

'Go out? Where?'

'I've got some more pictures to take.' A wry little twitch of the mouth. 'I'm photographing my way into the community, aren't I?'

'Christ, haven't you got enough pictures yet?'

Claire didn't reply. She began to load a film into her newest Nikon as if leaving for a major assignment in the jungles of Nicaragua. It had been like this all day, as though he didn't really exist. She'd just announced what she was going to do and then done it.

Giles said plaintively, 'I was waiting to light the fire, have a discussion about, you know, the future. I mean we've hardly had much chance to talk, the past few days. Also, your m—'

No, he wasn't going to go into all that Elinor business. Not now.

'We can talk later,' Claire said. 'I have to catch what's left of the light, OK?'

'Bugger all left, if you ask me. Why not leave it till tomorrow?'

'Also,' Claire mumbled, snapping the camera shut. 'I have to find my tree.'

'I see. And which tree is that?'

'Just a tree I shot last night, and then it went missing.'

'I see,' said Giles, gritting his teeth. 'Now look, Claire, I really do think—'

But Claire had shouldered her camera and was off before he could even tell her about the call from her mother.

Fuck her, thought Giles, and then realised he hadn't done that for quite a while either.

CHAPTER XXVI

THROUGH the living-room window, Giles watched Claire approach the iron gate. The trees seemed to close around her, and it was as though she were passing quietly into some other dimension. Claire opened the gate without effort and went through, and the landscape appeared to absorb her on the other side. She fitted. She blended with the scene. It welcomed her.

Croeso.

As if she's lived here all her life, Giles thought.

The illusion frightened him. He thought, has she ever really blended with me like that? For the first time since they'd come to live in Y Groes he felt heartsick and alone. And vaguely jealous of the village, which was ridiculous.

He was becoming aware of how differently they regarded this move, this new life. It had been, for him, the big adventure, the great expedition into the unknown, a terrific challenge. It had filled him with energy just thinking about the future. Now he felt his wife was not tuned to quite the same wavelength.

With her it was not elation. It was less of a fun thing. Here they were, just of the two of them in a totally strange place and, far from getting closer, confiding more in each other, there was a hazy space between them. Well, not so much between them as around Claire, who had always been so practical and clear-sighted. Now she was altering in unpredictable ways. Like tonight, doing what she'd never done, in his experience, before: going out to take pictures, not in a professional way, but just snapping things, looking for some special sodding tree, for God's sake! This, especially, had got to Giles because only rarely could Claire be persuaded to get out her camera for holiday photos and family occasions. He remembered once suggesting she might knock off a few pics at the christening of his cousin's new baby and she'd gone very huffy indeed, asking him how he'd feel about being asked to write features for the local parish magazine.

Giles sat down at the bloody awful fat-legged dining table and looked into the fireplace which he'd laid with paper and kindling and three small logs and didn't feel like lighting any more.

He ought to try to understand her instead of feeling sorry for himself. She was obviously preoccupied, something here she was struggling to come to terms with. A responsibility to her surroundings that she'd never felt before? Because of her grandfather, yes? Filling in for a missing generation, her mother, who had spurned everything the old man wanted out of life? And what *had* he wanted out of life except for a bit of peace and quiet, back among his compatriots?

For the old man perhaps, this had represented peace and quiet, but for English people it was a lot more demanding, Giles thought, only now realising how clean-cut their life in London had been. *That* was the simple life, when you thought about it, for people with their background. He was a hack. Claire took pictures for money. Professionals. The flat in

Islington had been like a station waiting room where they'd passed the time until trains took them in different directions. Maybe he only knew Claire as a kind of intimate colleague.

Stuff this! Giles stood up angrily and reached on the deepset window sill for a box of kitchen matches. He struck two at once and flung them at the fireplace, watched the paper flare, listened to the kindling crackle. Life. Energy.

Early days. Give it time. Be positive. Be practical.

In the diminishing light, he moved purposefully around the house, thinking about the improvements they could make without spoiling its character. He took with him the slimline pocket cassette-recorder he used sometimes for interviews.

The living room – well, that was more or less OK. Beams, inglenook fireplace – great. A wood-burning stove might be useful in the inglenook, more energy-efficient. It would save a lot of work too; amazing how many logs you got through on an open fire, and most of the heat went up the chimney anyway.

Giles went out into the hall, trying to remember where he'd seen a shop specialising in woodstoves.

'Was it Aberystwyth?' he said into the slim, leather-covered cassette machine. 'Check in Yellow Pages.'

The hall, too, was basically all right. Bit dark, and you had to walk permanently stooped or risk collecting a pair of black eyes from the low-slung beams.

'Hall,' he said. 'Perhaps some diffused lighting under the beams.'

He came back through the living room to the kitchen. This, of course, would need the most attention. In Giles's view only the solid-fuel Aga-type stove was worth keeping. It hummed and belched a bit, but he liked that. Also, it took both coal and wood.

'OK,' Giles said into the recorder. 'New sink, for starters. Fitted units, maybe the wall between the kitchen and the pantry knocked out. Discuss with Claire . . . *if* she can spare the time.'

Right, OK . . .

The study.

'Now, we shall have to be a bit careful here,' Giles told the machine.

After all, one wrong decision and they could easily ruin what was undoubtedly the most interesting room in the house. Again, he found himself groping for the light switch before remembering.

'Unbelievable,' he said. 'How the hell did the old boy manage without any power in here?'

Wrong there, Giles, he thought. There's certainly power in here. Shelves full of it. But how did he read without a light?

He almost bumped his head on the answer, a big oil lamp of tarnished brass Claire had found in the pantry. It was now hanging from the central beam – she must have done that this morning. He tapped the lamp and gave it a swing, trying to find out if there was oil in it. It didn't sound as if there was. The lamp just rattled. It needed polishing up, too.

'OK, memo: buy paraffin. Also chase up that electrician.'

It was darker in here than anywhere else in the house, and yet the room was facing west. Must be all the books, no light reflected from the walls. He wondered if the books were valuable. He wondered how he was going to make space in here for his own books when he brought them up from London. OK, they'd look a bit odd, glossy paperbacks among the stark black spines of Judge Rhys's library. But if it eventually was going to be his office, the judge would just have to move over a bit.

It was chilly in here too. Giles wondered if they could run a radiator from the kitchen stove; it wouldn't be far to bring a pipe. First things first though: let there be some bloody light.

'Suggestion,' he said to the tape. 'What about removing some of the shelving in the middle of the two side walls and installing some wall-lights? Have to be tasteful ones of course. Convert a couple of antique oil lamps or something.'

He glanced up at the framed eisteddfod photograph, full of dignified, white-clad bards and shivered pleasurably, remembering how this room seemed to have spooked Berry Morelli. Great. That picture was definitely going to stay. He wondered which of the bards, if any, was his grandfather-in-law.

The picture seemed dusty and unclear in the dim light and he took a tissue from a hip pocket of his jeans and rubbed at the pale faces of the bards, thinking perhaps he might catch an image of Claire in one of them. Peering at the picture, he felt a dull throb behind his eyes. Bloody headache again. The strain of trying to make out details in semi-darkness.

He backed off, rubbing at his eyes. The room was all shadows now and the only light seemed to be coming out of the picture, out of the white robes of the bards, who appeared to be walking slowly towards him in solemn procession, as if they were about to drift out of the picture and into the room to stand around Giles like a chalk circle and then to melt into the blotchy air.

Back in the picture, meanwhile, the bards had turned black.

'Aspirin,' Giles mumbled. He left the study and closed the door behind him and gave it a push to make sure it really was shut.

Where was she?

Giles looked out of the window and it was utterly black, he couldn't even see the lights of the village. How could she take pictures in this? He was pretty sure she hadn't taken a flash unit with her. He looked at his watch and saw it was nearly eight o'clock – she'd been back by seven last night.

He felt a pang of anxiety, unable to shake the ludicrous image of Claire being absorbed by the trees or the village or the night or some numinous combination of all three. And then thought: of course, somebody must have asked her in for a cup of tea, that's what's happened. A bit bloody silly worrying about her being out after dark in Y Groes when she'd survived the streets of Belfast and photographed call-girls on the corners and junkies in the darkened doorways of the nastier crevices of London.

All the same he went out to the porch to wait for her and found the night wasn't as dark as it had seemed from inside. There was a moon, three parts full, and the tallest village roofs were silvered between the two big sycamores. Giles moved out onto the dampening lawn and the church tower slid into view, the tip of its spire appearing to spear the moon, so that it looked like a big black candle with a small white flame.

Giles's heart thumped as a shadow detached itself from the base of the tower and came towards him, as if a piece of the stonework had come alive. But it turned out to be Claire herself, camera hanging limply from the strap curled around a wrist.

'Bloody hell,' Giles said. 'I didn't know you were going to be so long. I mean, all right, muggings are decidedly uncommon in this area, but all the same—'

'Darling,' Claire said briskly. 'Go back inside, will you, and put all the lights on for me. *All* the lights.'

'People will think we're extravagant,' Giles protested – halfheartedly, though, because he was so pleased to have her back. 'I mean, not a good image to have around here.'

'Oh, Giles—'

'All right, all right—' Giles switched on everything, even the light on the little landing upstairs, thinking: we'll change some of these old parchment shades when we get time, they're more than a touch dreary. All the upstairs windows were open and he could hear Claire darting about, aperture wide open, shutter speed down. Thock . . . thock . . . thock. A great tenderness overcame him, and when she came in he kissed her under the oak beams of the living room, next to the inglenook where they'd have log fires all through the winter. His headache had receded and with his arms around Claire's slim, functional body he felt much better.

'Sweetheart, where precisely have you been? Your hair feels all tangled.'

Claire laughed and Giles heard a new boldness in that laugh, all the London tightness gone. Earthy too.

He joined in the laughter.

'You're really happy, aren't you?' he said.

Claire pulled away from him and went to stand by the window.

'Yes,' she said. 'I'm very happy.'

Giles said. 'Did you find your tree?'

'Yes,' said Claire. 'I found my tree.'

And then, without a word, switching lights off on the way, she led him up to bed . . .

. . . where they made love for the first time since their arrival, the first time in the new bed. And it was really not how Giles had imagined it would be in this pastoral setting. Nothing languid and dreamy about it at all; it was really pretty ferocious stuff, the old fingernails-down-the-back routine, quiet Claire on the initiative, hungry. Nothing distant now.

Giles told himself it had been very exciting.

CHAPTER XXVII

HE WAS exhausted and slept like the dead and woke late next morning. Woke with another headache and this one was a bastard. Eyes tightly shut, he ground his head into the pillow. It was as if somebody were slicing his skull down the middle with a chainsaw.

'Change of air,' Claire diagnosed. 'You're just not used to it yet.'

She swung both legs simultaneously out of bed and walked naked to the door.

'Yeah, sure, air like bloody wine,' Giles groaned into the pillow. 'Air that gives you a bastard hangover.'

A few minutes later, he was slowly pulling his trousers on, the sight of the pink vinyl headboard making him feel queasy, when Claire returned from her bath, still naked, tiny drops of water falling from her hair onto her narrow shoulders. She seemed oblivious of her nakedness which, for Claire, was unusual: to be nude, in daylight, when Giles was obviously feeling too lousy to be turned on.

'I may stop rinsing my hair,' said Claire, looking out of the window. 'What do you think?'

'I think I need a cup of strong tea,' Giles said.

'There's no point in being artificially anything around here,' Claire said.

Giles looked up, a pinball of agony whizzing from ear to ear with the movement.

'I like you blonde,' he said. 'I always have.'

Claire just went on gazing out of the window, across the village to the Nearly Mountains and the neutral sky.

In a bid to lose his headache, Giles took a couple of paracetamol tablets and went for a walk down to the village, where autumn, it seemed, had yet to begin – even though tonight would see the end of British Summertime.

'*Bore da*,' he said, as cheerily as he could manage, to Glyn, the angular historian chap, doing his Saturday shopping with a basket over his arm.

'Good morning, Mr Freeman,' said Glyn with a flash of his tombstone teeth.

'Wonderful weather,' Giles said, not failing to notice that Glyn, like everyone else he spoke to in the village, had addressed him in English. He'd never learn Welsh if people kept doing that.

'Well, yes,' said Glyn, as if warm weather in October was taken for granted here. Perhaps it was, thought Giles. He walked across the river bridge, past the entrance to the school lane and on towards a place he'd never been before: the great wood which began on the edge of the village.

Sooner than he expected he found himself in what seemed like an enormous wooden nave. He was reminded of the ruins of some old abbey. It was almost all oak trees, freely spaced as if in parkland. Oak trees bulging with health, with the space to spread out their muscular limbs, no decaying branches, no weaklings. Some of the oaks were clearly of immense age and had a massive, magisterial presence.

Giles wondered if this was what Claire had meant when she talked of 'my tree'. Had she come up here alone at dusk?

It occurred to him that he was standing inside a huge ancient monument. Most of these trees were centuries old, some perhaps older than the castles the English had built to subdue the people of Wales.

And this was what most of the Welsh forests used to be like, from pre-medieval days to the early part of the twentieth century, until the now-ubiquitous conifers had been introduced – quick to grow, quick to harvest, uniform sizes. Drab and characterless, but easy money for comparatively little work.

This wood was awesomely beautiful. This was how it should be. Giles felt a sense of sublime discovery and an aching pride. He felt he'd penetrated at last to the ancient heart of Y Groes. Surely this was where it had all begun – the source of the timber-framing of the cottages, all those gigantic beams, the woody spirit of the place.

Giles felt, obscurely, that this place could take away his headache.

He wandered deeper among the trees, which were still carrying the weighty riches of late summer. The wood seemed to go on and on, and he realised it must form a great semi-circle around the village.

He came upon two great stumps, where trees had been felled. Between them, a young tree surged out of the black soil. The wood, obviously, was still being managed, still being worked as woodland had been in the old days. Whereas, elsewhere in Wales, it sometimes seemed as if all that remained of the great oak woods were knotted arthritic copses used by farmers merely as shelter for their sheep, devoid of new growth because the sheep ate the tiny saplings as soon as they showed.

No sheep in here. No people either, except for Giles.

He'd heard talk of foresters in Y Groes and assumed they were blokes who worked for the Forestry Commission in the giant conifer plantation along the Aberystwyth road. Obviously they were in charge of maintaining this huge oak wood, selecting trees for unobtrusive felling, planting new ones so the appearance of the place would never change from century to century. He also knew there was a carpenter, a Mr Vaughan – or Fon, as it was spelled in Welsh – who made traditional oak furniture. And Aled in the *Tafarn* had mentioned that a new house was to be built near the river for Morgan's eldest son and had laughed when Giles expressed the hope that it

would not look out of place. 'When it is built,' Glyn had said,
'you will think it has always been there.'

God, Giles thought, the village is still growing out of this
woodland just as it always has. An organic process. Morelli
had been right when he said it was like the place had just
grown up out of the ground.

Giles raised up his arms as if to absorb the soaring energy
of the wood but felt only insignificant among the arboreal
giants and decided to turn back. It was too much to take in
all at once. Especially when he wasn't feeling awfully well,
nerves in his head still jerking, like wires pulled this way and
that by a powerful magnet.

He almost got lost on the way back, taking a path he was
convinced was the right one until it led him to a pair of
blackened gateposts where the oaks formed a sort of tunnel.
At the end was something big, like a huge crouching animal.

A house. Somebody lived in the middle of the wood.

Well, what was so odd about that? Lots of people lived in
woods.

Yes, but this wood was special. The village was down
below; this was where the *trees* lived.

There was no gate but on the left-hand post it said, carved
out of the wood,

Rheithordy.

Above the word, which Giles had never seen before, a rough
cross had been hewn.

'*Helo.*'

Giles stopped, startled, as a small dark figure darted out
from behind the gatepost.

'Hello,' Giles said. 'Who's that?'

It was a little girl – maybe eight or nine – and she was
dressed mainly in black – black skirt, black jumper, black
shoes. Even so, she seemed to fit into the backcloth, like some
woodland sprite. '*Pwy y chi* ?' she demanded.

'Sorry,' said Giles. ''Fraid I don't speak Welsh. Yet.'

The child had mousy hair and a pale, solemn face. 'Are
you English?'

Giles nodded, smiling ruefully. ''Fraid so.'

The child looked up at Giles out of large brown eyes. She said seriously, 'Have you come to hang yourself?'

'What?' Giles's eyes widened in amusement. 'Have I come to—?'

But she only turned away and ran back behind the gatepost.

Giles shook his head – which hurt – and strolled on. Soon the path widened and sloped down to the village. It was easy when you knew your way.

There was only one paracetamol left in the packet, but he took it anyway and sat down at the fat-legged dining table. They were going this morning to Pontmeurig, where Giles was to meet the chairman of the local Conservative Party to get a bit of background for a feature he was planning in the run-up to the Glanmeurig by-election. It wouldn't be long now before a date was set.

'And while we're in Pont,' he shouted to Claire, who was in the bedroom, changing out of her old, stained jeans into something more respectable, 'there're a few things we could be on the lookout for, if you're agreeable. I had a walk around the place last night, making a few notes on tape.'

'Super,' Claire said, appearing at the living room door, still wriggling into clean, white denims. '*Da iawn*. How's your head?'

'Could be worse. Don't you want to hear the list?'

'Oh, I hate it when you put ideas on tape and we have to unscramble all this distorted cackle. Why can't you write it out?'

'All right. I mean o'r . . . o'r . . .'

'*O'r gorau,*' Claire said, zipping up her trousers as she went through to the kitchen.

While still in London they'd taken to peppering their conversations with a few Welsh phrases. Giles now tried to think of a suitable comment to make in *Cymraeg* but nothing came to him and his head still hurt. How long had they had these bloody paracetamol? Maybe they were losing their potency.

He found his pocket cassette recorder and ran the tape back to transcribe the aural memoranda into a notebook. Concealed lighting for the hall, electrician, plumber . . .

'. . . and the pantry knocked out,' his voice crackled back at him from the tiny speaker. 'Discuss with Claire . . . *if* she can spare the time . . .'

Giles hurriedly lowered the volume, hoping she hadn't heard the last bit from the kitchen. He put his ear to the speaker in case he'd said anything else vaguely inflammatory, but there was nothing.

Nothing at all.

Hang on, where was the stuff he'd recorded in the study, something about wall-lights, right?

It had gone.

He must have wiped it by mistake.

Bugger.

And yet – turning up the volume as high as it would go – he could still hear the ambient sounds of the room, the hollow gasp of empty space, as if it was only his own voice which had been wiped off. Which was stupid; he must simply have left the thing running.

'Recorder batteries,' he wrote in his notebook, at the head of the list. Better make sure of that before he started doing any actual interviews. Over the past few years Giles had relied increasingly on pocket tape-recorders; his shorthand was all to cock these days.

Not that the batteries seemed low, but there was an awful lot of tape hiss.

sssssssss, it went. *ssssssssssssssssssssss*

CHAPTER XXVIII

BETHAN had never been to Judge Rhys's house before. She'd been past it enough times – shepherding the children on nature rambles up in the hills, trying to spot the Red Kite, Britain's rarest bird of prey, which nested there.

Occasionally, over the hedge, she'd seen the judge in his garden. Not actually gardening, of course. Other people did his gardening. Simply standing there, not moving but not really looking as if he was admiring the scenery either.

He used to be like that in church too, always in the same pew, two rows from the front, very still in the black suit, not visibly singing and not visibly praying.

Strange man.

Now there was only the house to stand there gazing towards the hills, its windows darkened. As she lifted up the metal gate and pushed it open, Bethan was trying to imagine what it would look like here when Claire had her children and there were toys all over the lawn and perhaps a swing.

She really could not see it.

A fine dusk was purpling into night as Bethan walked up the path. A light came on in a front window, and by the time she reached the front door, arms full of books and things as usual, it was open. A tall, fair-haired man was there in a sleeveless V-necked pullover over a checked shirt, looking, she thought, distinctly relieved when he saw her.

'Great. Hi. Giles Freeman. Bethan, right?' Standing back to usher her into the warm living room with the Welsh dresser and the inglenook and a muted glow from a reading lamp with a brown ceramic base. 'Super of you to do this for us, it really is.'

'Super of you to *want* to do it,' Bethan said. 'Not many of you –. your – people who move in from England—'

'Bastards,' Giles said vehemently, closing doors. 'No sense of where they are. We— Ah, here's Claire.'

She wore a grey skirt and a white blouse, looking like a schoolgirl, no make-up. She did not smile. 'Bethan, hello. Coffee now? Or later?'

'Whichever suits you.' Had there been a row, she wondered.

'How about during,' Giles said. 'I'll make it.'

'I'd like to start, I think,' Claire said. 'We don't want to delay you. You'll want to get home to your husband.'

'My husband is dead,' Bethan said casually, standing in the

middle of the floor looking for somewhere to put down the pile of books, pretending not to notice the familiar silence which always followed this disclosure.

'Oh,' said Claire mildly, as Giles was saying, 'I'm awfully sorry. We didn't know.' The unspoken question was hanging around, so Bethan answered it.

'He died about a year ago. Leukaemia.'

'That's really terrible,' said Giles. 'That really is a bastard of a thing.'

'It was very quick. By the time it was diagnosed he was dying. Three weeks later, he—' Bethan made a mouth-smile. 'Right. That is over with. I am at the stage where sympathy only depresses me. Look, I've brought you these little books. They're grown-up cartoons with all the bubbles in Welsh and a lot of the everyday kind of words you don't find in the more formal textbooks.'

Giles moved to take the other stuff from her (why did people always rush to help as soon as they learned she was a widow?) so she could open a little paperback called 'Welsh is Fun'. She showed him a drawing of a woman in her underwear. Little arrows pointed to things, giving the Welsh, with the English in brackets. Like *bronglwm* (bra) and *bol* (belly).

'I've also brought you some leaflets for *Pont* – have you heard of that?'

Giles shook his head.

'It's an organisation set up to form links between native Welsh people and the, um, incomers. *Pont* means—'

'Bridge, right?' said Giles. 'As in Pontmeurig. Rehabilitation, eh?'

'There we are,' said Bethan, glancing towards the fat-legged dining table at which only two chairs were set. 'That's a start. Now, where shall we sit?'

'Not in here,' Claire said quickly.

Giles looked at her. She said, 'I've set up a table in the study.'

'What's the use of going in there? There's no bloody electricity!'

'I filled the oil lamp. And lit the fire. Will you light the lamp, Giles? Please?' It was a command, Bethan thought.

'Oh, for Christ's sake . . . What's wrong with staying here?'

'It's more fitting,' Claire said quietly.

'Goodness,' Bethan said, looking at the rows of black books.

'Can you tell us what they are?' Giles was turning up the wick on the big oil lamp dangling from the middle beam. 'Claire, is this really going to be bright enough?'

'If we put the table not quite underneath, it'll be fine.'

She'd erected a green-topped card table and placed three stiff-backed chairs around it. A small coal fire burned rather meanly in the Victorian grate. Bethan also would rather have stayed in the living room. She would never have tolerated a classroom as stiff and cold as this. She crossed to the shelves.

'I don't recognise most of these.' Taking books down at random. 'They're obviously very old and must be very valuable indeed. See . . .' She held out a page of text. 'This is in medieval Welsh. These must be some of the oldest books ever printed in Welsh – although copies, I expect, in most cases. There seems to be a lot of old poetry – Taliesyn, is this? And these three are quite early versions of The Mabinogion. I've never seen them before, although I'm no expert. Oh—'

'What've you found?' Giles wandered over, craning his neck.

'Nothing really, just a modern one amongst all the old stuff. It hasn't got its dustjacket so it looked like all the rest. It's ap Siencyn, one of his early books of poetry.'

'What, you mean ap Siencyn, the vicar here?'

'The rector, yes. He used to be a poet.' Bethan smiled. 'What I mean is, he used to publish his poetry. Many years ago.'

'That's amazing,' Giles said.

'Not really, there are poets everywhere in Wales and quite a few are ministers.'

Giles nodded solemnly. 'Exactly. That's the whole point.' He folded his arms, rocking back on his heels in the middle of the room on the dragon rug. 'What I mean is – We've become so smug and cynical in England because our cultural heritage is so *safe*. We've got the world's number one language, we've got Shakespeare and Jane Austen and all these literary giants planted in state in Westminster Abbey. But Welsh culture's about ordinary people. I mean, your writers and poets don't spend all their time poncing about at fancy publishers' parties and doing lecture tours of the States. They're working farmers and schoolteachers and – clergymen. And they'll never be remotely famous outside Wales because virtually nobody out there can understand a word they write. It takes real commitment to carry on in a situation like that, wouldn't you say?'

Bethan watched Giles's lean English face shining with an honest fervour in the unsteady lamplight. How could the issue of Wales be seized on with such vigour by people like Giles and Claire, who had not been brought up in the warmth of a Welsh community, not had bedtime stories read to them in Welsh, sung Welsh nursery rhymes or made their first terrifying public appearance performing a little recitation before a critical audience of neighbours at the local eisteddfod? Did they equate Wales with whales? Were the Welsh suddenly interesting because they looked like a threatened species?

Then Bethan glanced at Claire and drew in a sharp breath. Claire, small face not mellow but stark in the lamplight, was looking up at Giles. And wearing a rigid expression of explicit contempt.

'You know,' Giles was telling Bethan enthusiastically. 'I wouldn't mind doing a feature sometime on old ap Siencyn. What's he like?'

'He's – *You've* met him, Claire, what did you think of him?'

Giles looked hurt. 'Claire, you never mentioned meeting the rector.'

'I—' Claire didn't look at him. 'Our paths crossed while I was out taking pictures.'

'She took *his* picture,' Bethan said.

'I didn't see that,' Giles said.

'It didn't come out,' Claire snapped. 'Can we make a start?'

Bethan thought, Her pictures *never* don't come out. Besides, I saw it.

'Well, I think I've seen his house,' Giles said. 'Up on the edge of the woods. Very impressive.'

Bethan said, 'Sometimes I take the kids up to the woods, but we go the other way. I don't like that part somehow.' Especially now, she thought, shuddering at the image, which came to her unbidden, of two leather hiking boots slowly swinging overhead.

'I thought it was magnificent,' Giles said, freckles aglow in the lamplight. 'You get the feeling that's where the whole village was born – you know, the timber for the cottages. I think it's fantastic the way they're managing it, renewing the trees and everything. I mean, who actually does that? Who are the foresters?'

Claire, face taut, severe in the oil-light, said, with quiet menace, '*Ydy chi'n barod*, Bethan?'

Giles fell silent, looked embarrassed.

'Yes,' Bethan said, feeling sorry for him. Why did his innocent ardour seemed to irritate his wife so? 'Yes, I'm ready.' When she'd agreed to teach them Welsh, she'd been looking forward to a chat over coffee with people who weren't a part of this stifling community. Not this formal, frigid atmosphere, this sense of . . . ritual, almost.

It's the house, she thought. It's the damned house.

She opened one of her books on the card table. Aware, on the periphery of her vision, of the old, heavy desk and the Victorian Gothic chair across the room, beyond the dome of the lamplight. As if they were awaiting the arrival of the real teacher.

It was nearly eight o'clock when Bethan left.

There was no moon. It was very dark.

'Where's your car?' Giles asked.

'I left it at the school, it's only three minutes' walk.'

'It's pitch black. I'll come with you, bring a torch.'

'Thank you, but I used to live in this village, there's no—'

'There is,' Giles said firmly, grabbing his green waxed jacket from behind the door, switching his heavyweight policeman's torch on and off to make sure it was working.

'Well, thank you,' Bethan said. Oh God, she thought. I don't really want to be alone with Giles now. I don't need this.

Following the torchbeam, they walked down the hill and over the bridge, the river hissing below them. There was an anguished silence between them until they reached the entrance to the school lane.

'Christ,' Giles said.

'Look—' Bethan put a reassuring hand on his arm. 'Don't worry, all right?'

'Huh—' Giles twisted away like a petulant schoolboy then immediately turned back, apologetic. He expelled a sigh, full of hopelessness, and rubbed his eyes.

'You will soon get the hang of it.'

It was too dark to see his face.

'But you don't understand,' Giles said desperately, 'I thought I *was* getting the hang of it. I've been working at it for weeks. Before we even came, I used to spend all my lunch hours swotting. I mean, you know – I really thought I was getting pretty good. It's just so bloody embarrassing.'

'Don't worry,' Bethan said. 'Everybody has days like that. When they're beginning. A few weeks really isn't very long, you know.'

'All right then, what about Claire? I mean, she hasn't spent anywhere near as much time on it as me.'

'Look,' Bethan said, as they reached the Peugeot. 'The very worst thing you can do is worry.'

'But I couldn't put together even the simplest sentences! I mean things I know!' Bethan heard Giles punching the palm of his hand in bitter frustration. The violent movement seemed to hurt him more than he'd intended because he gave a small moan of pain.

'Mr Freeman, are you sure you're all right?'

'Giles. Please. I hate being Freeman, so bloody English. Yes I'm fine. Well, I've got a headache, but that's nothing unusual. I'm sorry, I'm being ridiculous.'

'I know it means a lot to you,' Bethan said gently. She felt

161

terribly sorry for him. He wanted so badly to be a part of this culture. It had been awful watching him agonisingly entangled in the alien grammar, tongue frozen around words he just could not say, getting stuck on the same ones again and again, stammering in his confusion. Sometimes – his hands gripping the edge of the table until the knuckles were white as bone – it seemed almost as if his facial muscles had been driven into paralysis by the complexity of the language.

'Look,' Bethan said. 'Get a good night's sleep. Don't think about it. Don't look at any books. I'll see you again tomorrow. Maybe . . . Look, maybe it's something I am doing wrong. I'm so used to teaching children.'

'But what about *Claire*?' he cried. 'I mean, for God's sake, how do you explain that?'

CHAPTER XXIX

ENGLAND

BERRY MORELLI had not long been in the office when his boss threw a newspaper at him.

'For your private information,' Addison Walls said.

Newsnet's London bureau chief was a small, neat, precise man with steel-rimmed glasses, a thin bow tie that was always straight and an unassuming brown toupée. It was Berry's unvoiced theory that Addison possessed a normal head of hair but shaved it off periodically on account of a toupée was tidier.

'Your buddy, I think,' Addison said and went back to his examination of the *Yorkshire Post*. He was a very thorough man, arriving at work each day somewhere between 8.0 and 8.03 a.m. and completing a shrewd perusal of every British national newspaper and five major provincial morning papers by 9.15 when his staff got in.

The staff consisted of a secretary, a research assistant and three reporters including Berry Morelli. Although there would usually be orders for the major stories of the day, Newsnet specialised in features dealing with peripheral issues of American interest which the big agencies had no time to mess with. Occasionally, compiling his morning inventory of the British press, Addison Walls would suddenly zap an item with his thick black marker pen and announce, 'This is a Newsnet story.'

Berry noticed the item flung at him had not been zapped, although the paper had been neatly folded around an inside-page feature starkly headlined,

THE ANGRY HILLS

Above the text was a photograph of a ruined castle which resembled the lower plate of a set of dentures, two walls standing up like teeth. The view was framed by the walls of more recent buildings; a FOR SALE sign hung crookedly from one.

Underneath the picture, it said,

> Giles Freeman, of our political staff, reports on what's shaping up to be a dramatic by-election battle in wildest Wales.

Berry smiled and sat down and lit a cigarette. So Giles had pulled it off. They'd let him cover the Pontmeurig by-election. Filing his stuff, no doubt, from his own cottage, probably over the phone from the judge's study. Two weeks had passed since Berry had fled that place. Two weeks in which to consider the possibility that he'd been overreacting. Him and old Winstone both.

He started to read the feature, thinking Giles would be sure to hype up the issue to persuade his editor that this election was worthy of intensive on-the-spot coverage.

It was not the usual political backgrounder. Giles had gone folksy.

> Idwal Roberts smiled knowingly as he laid out his leather tobacco pouch on the bar of the Drovers' Arms.

'This,' he said, 'is going to be a bit of an eye-opener for a London boy. I imagine you've reported a fair few by-elections, but I can tell you – you won't have seen one like this.

'Oh, I know they've had them in South Wales and the Borders in recent years. But this time you're in the *real* Wales. A foreign country, see.'

Idwal Roberts, a retired headmaster, is the Mayor of Pontmeurig, a little market town at the southern end of the range of rugged hills called in Welsh something long and complicated which translates roughly as 'the Nearly Mountains'.

This is the principal town in the constituency of Glanmeurig, which recently lost its long-serving Conservative MP, Sir Maurice Burnham-Lloyd and is now preparing for its first ever by-election. Local people will tell you that the last time anything really exciting happened in Pontmeurig was in the fifteenth century when the Welsh nationalist leader Owain Glyndwr (or Owen Glendower, as they call him east of Offa's Dyke) set fire to the castle.

The gaunt remains of this castle still frown over the cattle market and the new car-park. The fortress was actually built by the Welsh but subsequently commandeered by the English king Edward I. One story tells how the wealthy baron in charge of the castle offered to support Glyndwr's rebellion, but Owain set light to the place anyway on the grounds that you could never trust the word of an Englishman.

The Mayor of Pontmeurig (an 'independent' like most councillors hereabouts) reckons opinions have not changed a great deal in the intervening years.

Giles went on to outline the problem of comparatively wealthy English people moving into the area, pricing many houses beyond the range of locals, often buying shops and pubs and post offices and conducting their business in English where once Welsh had been the language of the streets.

'What say we take at look at this?' Berry said casually, and Addison Walls gave him a wry smile that said no way.

'They may be a big deal over here, but you think back, son, and tell me how many British by-elections you saw reported in the *New York Times*.

'It's been known,' said Berry.

'It's been known if the Government's on the brink.'

'I just thought, maybe this language angle.'

'Forget it. You compare this situation with Ulster, it's chickenshit.'

'Yeah,' Berry said.

'Housing and immigration are going to be key issues in this election,' Roberts says. 'People are getting very angry, seeing their sons and daughters having to leave the area because they can't afford a house any more.'

One local estate agent admits that more than sixty per cent of the houses he's sold this year have gone to English people moving to rural Wales in search of what they see as a 'healthier' lifestyle.

'There is going to be acrimony,' says Idwal Roberts. 'Sparks will fly. You can count on that, my friend.'

'You can sure count on it with Giles around,' Berry muttered. The article went on to discuss the two leading contenders – the Conservative Party and the Welsh nationalist party, Plaid Cymru. The Conservatives had chosen their man, a local auctioneer called Simon Gallier. But Plaid, as Giles explained, had a crucial decision to make.

If Plaid want to play safe, they'll go for Wil James, a mild-mannered Baptist minister from Cardigan. He's well liked, but party strategists are wondering if he really has what it takes to slug it out with a man used to the cut-and-thrust of the livestock sales.

If Plaid want to live dangerously, however, they'll take a chance on Guto Evans, a 44-year-old part-time college lecturer, author and one-time bass-guitarist in a Welsh language rock and roll band.

Evans is a man not known for keeping his opinions to

himself – especially on the subject of mass-immigration by well-off English people.

'Ah, yes,' says the Mayor of Pontmeurig, relighting his pipe. 'Guto Evans. Now that really *would* be interesting.'

And he gives what could only be described as a sinister chuckle.

It's now felt the election is unlikely to take place before December because of . . .

'Addison, I can't help wondering if this isn't gonna get heavy,' Berry said.

'Anybody dies,' said Addison, 'you can go out there.'

'Thanks.'

'Meantime, listen up, I got something here the West Coast papers could be clamouring for by tonight so I figure we got no time to waste.'

'Right, I . . .' Something had caught Berry's eye. It was the picture byline.

It was placed unobtrusively in the top right hand corner of the photo of the castle and the 'FOR SALE' sign. Tiny lettering, as was normal in Giles's paper, especially when they used a freelance photographer.

It said

Picture by Claire Rhys.

'Now that's weird,' Berry said. 'That is real weird.'

'What?' said Addison Walls.

'Sorry,' Berry said. 'You go ahead, I'm listening.'

Maybe it wasn't that weird. People often changed their names for professional purposes. Women reverted to their premarital names. Claire, of course, had never been called Rhys, but maybe she thought a Welsh name like that would attract more work within Wales. Also, when people moved to a different country they altered their names so as not to sound unpronounceably foreign. A lot of Poles did that.

But English people called Freeman?

No, he was right first time.

It was weird.

PART FIVE

TOILI

CHAPTER XXX

BY mid-November the weather had turned nasty.

There had been much heavy rain, with three Red Two flood alerts for the River Meurig in as many weeks. And it was suddenly much colder. On the tops of the Nearly Mountains the rain fell as wintry showers, leaving premature patches of stiff snow behind the crags.

In its bowl of snow-encrusted hills, the village of Y Groes was, as usual, preserved from the worst of it. A blue hole, they called it. Bethan thought scientists might explain this in terms of changes in atmospheric pressure brought about by the geophysical features of the surrounding landscape. But the truth was she didn't know, so there was little she could say when Buddug told the children that Y Groes was especially favoured by the heavens because it had preserved the old traditions more faithfully than anywhere else in Wales.

'If you pay attention,' Buddug said, wagging a fat forefinger, 'you will see how clouds shrink away from the tower of our church. As if they are afraid.'

Crazy old bat, Bethan thought, leaning moodily on the piano, as Buddug lectured the assembly, two dozen scrubbed, rapt faces.

Later, as she drove home in the sepia dusk, she glanced towards the church tower and noted with some annoyance that the timbered belfry was hard against an almost perfect cloudless circle.

That day the Conservative Party had moved the writ for the Glanmeurig by-election, naming the day as December 15th – unusually late in the year. A week ago, the prospective Conservative candidate, Simon Gallier, a local auctioneer and valuer, protégé of Burnham-Lloyd and well in with the farmers, had officially been adopted by his constituency party in the suitably dignified setting of the Plas Meurig Hotel. The other parties were not far behind – except for Plaid Cymru which, as usual, took its time selecting a candidate, with predictable implications for Guto Evans's nervous system.

'Quite honestly,' he lied that night, 'I don't bloody care any more. If they go for the soft option and choose Wil James, they won't be the party I joined all those years ago, so it won't matter anyway.'

Guto was slumped in the shabby lounge of the Drovers' Arms with Bethan and two other friends, Dai Death, the funeral director, and Idwal Roberts – the 'independent' Mayor of Pontmeurig.

In Pont it was raining hard again.

Although the public bar was half full, the less-dedicated drinkers had been deterred by the weather and Guto's table was the only one occupied in the lounge. Because of the shortage of custom the lounge bar itself remained closed, its shutters down. This meant they had to fetch their own drinks from the public bar, but it also meant nobody could eavesdrop on what they were saying. Which was fortunate because the little gathering had turned into an impromptu training session for Guto's final interview by the Party's selection panel.

It was not going well.

Bethan thought this was not altogether surprising in view of the publication that morning in Wales's daily newspaper, the *Western Mail*, of the story Guto had been dreading.

It was brief but slotted significantly into the front page. It said police had confirmed having interviewed Guto Evans, a short-listed contender for the Plaid Cymru candidacy in the forthcoming Glanmeurig by-election, following an incident in a public bar a few weeks ago, during which a 26-year-old merchant banker had been slightly hurt. The injured man, who came from Surrey, had just bought a farmhouse on the outskirts of Pontmeurig at auction when the incident occurred at the Drovers' Arms in the town centre. He had been treated at Pontmeurig Cottage Hospital for minor facial injuries. However, police said they had no evidence of an offence being committed and charges were unlikely. Mr Evans had been unavailable for comment last night.

'It could have been worse,' Bethan said.

Her companions clearly disagreed. Plaid's riskier option for the Glanmeurig candidacy was miserably mopping beer froth from his beard with a frayed tartan handkerchief. The Mayor, a solid man with crinkly grey hair, sucked morosely on an empty pipe. Dai Death just stared sorrowfully into space in his best graveside manner.

They looked as dismal as the lounge, which was lit by naked bulbs in tarnished brass wall-brackets and smelled of beer and mothballs.

Bethan said, 'I accept that over-confidence is not to be recommended, but I can't help feeling . . .'

She sighed and gave up.

'Warning him weeks ago, I was,' said Dai Death. 'The day of the activist is over, see. Public displays of anger, all this oratory and rhetoric – forget it, man. Plausible on the telly is what it takes now.'

'Oratory and rhetoric have rather more to commend them,' Idwal Roberts said heavily, 'than physical violence. But I follow your reasoning. Give him another question, Bethan.'

Bethan looked at Guto, who shrugged and nodded gloomily.

'All right,' Bethan said, straightening her skirt and adjusting her glasses to consult the clipboard on her knee. 'So, Mr Evans, there's been a lot of debate about the upsurge of terrorism in Wales, with the burning of English-owned property and a wave of anti-English feeling. Where do *you* stand on this controversial issue?'

Guto cleared his throat. 'Well, er . . . I, of course, abhor all terrorism, while recognising that the present economic situation, the price of housing, the shortage of low-cost homes for local people, the mass immigration – all this, sadly, is an invitation to those for whom democracy seems such a painfully *slow* way of bringing about change. But nonetheless, we— Ah, I am tying myself up in knots trying to avoid saying that while I might deplore their methods I applaud their aims – ask me an easier one, I'll be all right on the night.'

'Hmmm,' Bethan looked doubtful. 'All right, then. So why, if you abhor all terrorism, did you—?'

She stopped when she saw Idwal Roberts pursing his lips and shaking his head.

'That reporter fellow,' Idwal whispered, 'has just walked past the door.'

Giles Freeman had only really called in at the Drovers' to use the lavatory. He'd spent four days at the paper and was on his way home, still wearing his dark suit, still looking and feeling very London. Far too London for the Drovers' Arms, but he really did need a slash.

Feeling better though, the nearer he got to Y Groes – in spite of the weather, the rain coming at the windscreen so hard it was like being permanently stuck in a high-powered car wash.

Feeling better the further he got from London. Feeling especially good because he would not now have to return until after the by-election. When his fortnight's holiday had ended and still no date had been fixed, he'd had no alternative but to spend four days a week in London. And, in these conditions, the journey had been more gruelling than he could have imagined.

On each of the three weekends, he'd started out happily for home. But each time the drive seemed to get longer – perhaps because he was getting used to the scenery, an element of the routine setting in. And when he arrived back in Y Groes the effects of the journey would hit him like an avalanche and he'd feel utterly exhausted, waking up the following morning with a ghastly headache. A couple of days at the cottage – most of them spent recovering in bed – and he'd had to make his way back to the Islington flat and another week on the paper.

'Giles, you look bloody awful,' his boss, the political editor had told him bluntly last week. 'Commuting's one thing – I mean we all commute, up to a point – but commuting a couple of hundred miles each way is bloody lunacy, if you ask me.'

'Don't worry about me,' Giles had said. 'It's just there's a lot of extra pressure, what with moving stuff out there and everything.'

'You're nuts,' said the political editor.

'It'll be OK,' Giles insisted. 'Soon get used to it.'

But he knew he wouldn't. He knew he was trying to marry two totally incompatible lifestyles.

The headaches, he realised now, had been the result of years of grinding tension: smoking, drinking, late nights, junk food, driving like a bat out of hell – his system had adjusted itself over the years to that kind of lifestyle. And now it had reacted perversely to intensive bursts of fresh air, relaxation and healthy eating.

Withdrawal symptoms. A sort of Cold Turkey.

This had become clear over the past few days, after Giles had been ordered to return to London and plunge back into the urban cesspit. His system had reverted to the old routine, the familiar self-destruct mechanism clicking back into place, the body throwing up the usual smokescreen telling him it didn't mind being abused, quite liked it really and look, here's the proof: no headaches while you're down in the Smoke, drinking, slugging it out with the traffic, pressurising politicians who've been barely on nodding terms with the truth for years.

One good thing, though – the Welsh. Every night in the Islington flat, with no distractions – for the first time he was glad to have the kind of London neighbours who wouldn't notice if you were dead until the smell began to offend them – Giles would sit down and spend at least ninety minutes with his Welsh textbook and his cassette tapes.

And, though he said it himself, it was coming on a treat.

'*Noswaith dda*,' he said affably to the young man next to him at the urinal in the Drovers' gents.

Feeling friendly, feeling good about the language again. Glad to be using it.

He'd been left badly shaken by several nights of humiliation in the judge's study, the last one ending with an almost unbearable headache. But now the grammar was making sense again. Bethan was a great girl, but perhaps he was more suited to working on his own than having lessons.

'*Mae hi'n bwrw glaw*,' he observed to the youth in the adjacent stall, nodding at the rain dripping down the crevices of the bubbled window above their heads.

'Yeah,' said the youth. He smirked, zipped up his fly and turned away.

Incomer, Giles thought disparagingly.

The youth went out, glancing over his shoulder at Giles.

Giles washed his hands and stared at his face in the mirror above the basin. He looked pale but determined.

Already his new life in Y Groes had shown him the things which were really important. Shown him, above all, that London and the paper were no longer for him – unless he could convince them that they needed a full-time staff reporter in Wales. After all, the *Telegraph* had one now. Failing that, he and Claire would flog the Islington flat for serious money and then set up some sort of news and features agency in Wales, supplying national papers, radio, television, the international media. He had the contacts. All he had to do now was make sure this election generated enough excitement to convince enough editors that Wales was a country they needed to keep a much closer eye on in the future.

Giles and Claire would be that eye. Claire Rhys. He liked the way she'd changed her name for professional purposes. Added a certain credibility. One in the eye for Elinor too. He only wished he could call himself Giles Rhys.

He decided to go into the public bar for one drink before tackling the Nearly Mountains. Unfair to use the place merely as a urinal.

Guto said sharply, 'Is it that bastard from Cardiff?' He was halfway out of his chair, face darkening.

'That's right,' said Dai Death sarcastically. 'That's just the way to handle it. You get up and clobber him in public. He's probably got a photographer with him, you could hit him too. Would you like me to hold your jacket?'

Idwal Roberts said, 'Sit down, you silly bugger. It's not him, anyway, it's the other fellow, the English one.'

Bethan said, 'Giles Freeman?'

She hadn't seen Giles for nearly a week. If he was back from London, she wanted to talk to him.

About Claire, of course.

Claire was still wandering around with her camera as the days shortened and the hills grew misty. Bethan thought she must have photographed everything worth photographing at least five times. Before she realised that Claire was just drifting about with the camera around her neck – but *not* taking pictures at all any more.

Then there was no camera, but Claire was still to be seen roaming the village, wandering in the fields, by the river, among the graves in the churchyard.

As if searching for something.

'Is there something you've lost?' Bethan had asked the other day, taking some of the children into the woods to gather autumn leaves for pressing, and finding Claire moving silently among the trees.

'Only my heritage.' Claire had just smiled, wryly but distantly, and moved on. Bethan noticed she wore no make-up; her hair was in disarray and its colour was streaked, dark roots showing. She seemed careless of her clothes too, wearing Giles's waxed jacket, conspicuously too big and gone brittle through need of rewaxing.

'Did you ever find that oak tree?' Bethan had asked her on another occasion.

'Oh that,' said Claire. 'I made a mistake. You were quite right.'

And explained no further.

Bethan asked her, 'Does Giles never go with you on your walks?'

'Giles?' As if she had to think for a moment who Giles was. 'Giles is in London.' Her eyes were somewhere else. 'He's having great fun,' she said vaguely.

'She is a very nice girl,' Buddug said surprisingly as they saw Claire one afternoon, flitting like a pale moth past the school gate.

'You've had much to do with her?'

'Oh, yes indeed. She's our nearest neighbour.'

'I suppose she must be.' Bethan had forgotten the judge's

175

cottage was on the edge of the seventy-or-so acres owned by Buddug and her husband, Morgan.

'She's had her eggs from us. And sometimes a chicken.'

Buddug killed her own chickens and occasionally pigs.

'I can't say much about *him*,' Buddug said.

'Giles? I like him.'

'Well, you would. Wouldn't you?' Buddug had turned away and scrubbed at the blackboard, smiling to herself.

Something had happened, Bethan thought. In a few short weeks Claire had changed from a smart, attractive, professional person to someone who was either moody or dreamy or pre-occupied with things that made no sense. There was no longer that aura of 'away' about her, that breath of urban sophist-ication which Bethan had so welcomed.

Bethan stared hard at Buddug's back, a great wedge between the desk and the blackboard. Buddug. Mrs Bronwen Dafis. The Revd Elias ap Siencyn.

And now Claire.

A chasm was opening between Claire and Giles, with his boyish enthusiasm for all things Welsh and his determination to be a part of The Culture. Bethan wondered if he could see it.

CHAPTER XXXI

'*H*ANNER *peint o gwrw*,' Giles told the barman, pointing at the appropriate beer-pump and climbing on to a barstool. '*Os gwelwch yn dda*.'

He was pleased with his accent, the casual way he'd ordered the drink. Grammar was all well and good but if you wanted to make yourself understood you had to get into the local idiom, had to sound relaxed.

The barman set down the glass of beer and Giles handed over a five pound note. '*Diolch yn fawr*,' Running the words together, as you would say thanks-very-much.

Convincing stuff.

The public bar was less than half full. Giles thought of

another bar, in Aberystwyth, where everybody had stared at him, amused by his stumbling debut in the Welsh language. Nobody smiled this time. With those few slick phrases nobody, he felt, could be quite sure he wasn't a native.

The barman gave him his change.

'*Diolch yn fawr iawn,*' Giles said in a louder voice, more confident now.

To his right, there was a sharp silence, somebody putting the brakes on a conversation. 'What was that?' a man's voice said in the centre of the hush.

'Beg your pardon—?' Giles turned, thinking, damn, should have said that in Welsh, blown my cover now.

On the next stool sat the youth he'd spoken to in the gents. Not looking quite as youthful now. Around twenty-three, twenty-four, thick-set, face pitted, lower lip sticking out like a shelf, eyes deep-sunk under short sandy hair. He nodded towards the bar. 'What you ordered.'

'Well,' Giles replied, holding up his glass to the light. 'It should be a half of bitter.'

The young man was not looking at Giles's glass, he was looking hard at Giles. He said, 'Oh, that's what it was.' Behind him was another young man on another bar stool. This one had prematurely-thinning black hair and a slit of a mouth, like a shaving cut.

'What I actually said to the barman here was *hanner peint o gwrw*.' Giles explained. 'I'm learning Welsh.' He smiled sheepishly. 'Got to practise.'

Two mouths went into simultaneous sneers. The eyes were still fixed on Giles, who realised he'd got it wrong; this chap wasn't an incomer at all.

The man turned to his companion. 'Learning Welsh, he is, this . . . *gentleman.*' Turned back to Giles, unsmiling. 'Go on then, say it again.'

'What d'you mean?'

'Go on – *hanner* . . .'

Giles said quickly, '*Hanner peint o gwrw.*' Not liking the way these two were looking at him, almost smelling the sour hostility.

A blast of rain splattered a window behind his head.

177

'Didn't catch that.' Slit-mouth. 'Say it again.'

'*Hanner* . . . oh, come on!'

'No, we want to learn, isn't it?' the other one said. He had a face like the cratered moon. 'We want to speak our own language as good as you, see.'

'I reckon that's all he can talk about, the beer.'

'Oh no, talking to me in the lav, he was. He's an expert. He can do the weather too.'

'Maybe he was takin' the piss, Gary.'

'Fuck, I never thought of that.' Heavily-feigned surprise. Still staring at Giles. 'Takin' the piss, is it?'

Giles said evenly, 'I can assure you I was not taking the piss. If I'm trying to learn the language, I've got to use it, haven't I? Is there any other way? I mean, what am I supposed to do?'

Definitely uncomfortable now – bloody yobs – he glanced around to see if there was anybody he knew even slightly, some group he could join. Didn't recognise a soul. Apart from a handful of men around the dartboard the customers were all sitting at tables. There were no more than fifteen people in the room. The barman was at the other end of the bar, watching the darts.

The silence set around Giles like cement. Clearly, Pontmeurig was just like any other town these days, full of night-time aggro. All very sad. Disappointing.

'Well now, there's an answer to that,' Crater-face said, all casual, elbow on the bar, hand propping his chin. 'I can tell you what you ought to do, English. Ought to fuck off back where you came from, isn't it.'

'Yes, all right, I will.' Giles made himself take a longish drink. He'd finish his beer and get out. This was not convivial. What a country – layer upon layer of resentment.

'We'll come with you,' Slit-mouth said.

'That won't be necessary,' Giles muttered.

'Least we can do.' Crater-face smiled with lurid menace. 'Show you the right road, see.'

'Hate you to get lost,' Slit-mouth said.

'Finish your drink, English,' Crater-face said.

He had lowered his voice so as not be overheard by a

stooping man with a bald head who was paying for a tray of drinks: three pints of bitter and a glass of dry white wine.

'. . . Ah, no, well, that Freeman does not seem a bad chap,' Idwal was saying as Dai laid the tray on the table. 'Compared with some of them.'

The training session had been abandoned.

'That's because he turned you into an overnight superstar,' said Guto. 'Idwal Roberts, political pundit, social commentator, media personality . . .'

'He *is* actually OK,' Bethan said, lifting her wine glass from the tray 'Quite fair minded. Thank you, Dai.'

She was sure Giles had learned about Guto and the pub incident. But he hadn't used it in his article – even though it would have underlined the point he was trying to make about Guto being the party hard-man.

'What I mean is,' she said, 'Giles is sympathetic. He can see what the incomers are doing to Wales and he doesn't want to be that kind of incomer. That is why he's so concerned about learning Welsh.'

Dai Death said, 'You're acquainted with this reporter from London then, Bethan?'

'Who do you think is *teaching* the bugger Welsh?' said Guto.

'He wants to learn Welsh for the election? There's enthusiasm.'

'No, Dai,' said Bethan. 'He is thinking longer term. He has acquired a house in Y Groes.'

A short but volcanic silence followed this disclosure.

'Y Groes!' Dai's voice rose to a squeak. He lurched in his seat, his bald head shining with hot indignation. 'How the hell did he find a house there?'

Of course, Bethan realised. A sore point.

Amid muted rumblings from Guto about wealthy bloody incomers being able to find anything they wanted anywhere at a price, she briefly explained how Claire and Giles Freeman had gained admittance to Paradise.

Dai scowled.

'I've never been one to attack the incomers,' he said. 'Nothing personal, like. But the first house since I don't know when to come available in Y Groes . . . and it goes, without a word, to a bloody Englishman. There is no justice.'

'English*woman*,' Bethan said.

Idwal Roberts sniffed.

'I will tell you one thing,' he said, tamping down the tobacco in his pipe. 'You would not catch me living there. Godless place, that village, always has been.'

Bethan, who had begun her teaching career as a member of Idwal's staff at Pontmeurig's Nantglas Primary School, had heard that since his retirement he had somewhat deepened his commitment to non-conformist religion.

'Godless,' he said.

'Only on your terms, man,' said Dai, still annoyed. 'Just because there is no chapel any more.'

'No.' Idwal waved his pipe in the air. 'That's not—'

'Still a *church* there,' Dai said. 'Bloody good church.'

Guto looked up innocently from his beer. 'Still a chapel, too. Had my car repaired there once.'

Dai nodded. 'Yes, well, plenty room for the ramp, with that high ceiling.'

'What I was meaning—' Idwal said.

'What is more,' said Guto deadpan, 'give Dilwyn Dafis a couple of quid on top, and you can have your bloody brake-linings blessed.'

'This is getting stupid,' Giles said.

Light conversation, in both English and Welsh, went on around them, the thump of darts on the board, nobody appearing to notice anything amiss or picking up on the tension. Giles knew how it must look – as if the three of them were having a nice quiet chat about beer-prices or the prospects of the Meurig bursting its banks.

Slit-mouth made a narrow smile. 'He thinks you're stupid, Gary.'

Getting into the comedy routine. But Giles had had enough. You really did find them everywhere, didn't you, always looking for somebody whose night they could spoil. A few casual remarks in the toilet and he'd set himself up as tonight's target. Well that was it, he wasn't taking any more.

'Look,' he said firmly. 'I just came in here for a drink. I've moved into the area, I'm trying to fit in. I didn't mean to cause any offence, all right? What else can I say?'

He felt his voice quiver. Bastards.

They were both studying him now with their stone-hard, hostile eyes.

'Got a house, have you? How much you pay for that?'

'Oh, for Christ's sake, this is getting awfully tedious.'

'Oh dear,' Slit-mouth said, mimicking Giles's accent. '*Awfully tedious.* Oh, my—'

Crater-face said to Giles, 'See, I've got this mate lookin' for a house. Gettin' married, he is. And you know what . . . you won't believe this, but this boy, my mate, he's been lookin' all over town for fuckin' weeks and he can't find one anywhere. Not as he can afford. You know why . . .?'

Leaning forward now, beer-breath sour in Giles's face. '*Know why, English?*'

Oh yes, Giles knew why all right. 'Now look, if you really want to talk about this—'

''Cause they've all been bought by your kind, is why, you bastard.'

Giles got an explicit close-up of the angry, pitted skin and the eyes, wells of malice.

'Kid on the way, see.'

Giles felt bits of beery spit spatter his face.

'Goin' to be really in the shit, he is, can't get a fuckin' house for his woman.'

Edging his stool closer to Giles, he whispered, 'I hate cunts like you, think you can buy in wherever you like. Come on, English, finish your drink.'

Giles put one foot on the floor. Get out. Get out fast.

'But you think you're all right, isn't it?' Lower lip out and curling. 'You think you're laughing, cause—' Eyes glittered and the hand shot forward as if reaching for cigarettes or something.

'—cause you're learnin—'

Then pulled casually back, toppling Giles's beer glass, still half full, off the bar and into his lap.

'—*Welsh*.'

'You bast—!'

Leaping up in outrage, beer soaking invisibly into his dark suit, Giles was drowned out by Crater-face crying,

'Aaaaw!'

And leaping from his stool too, knocking it over. Crash of the stool, splintering of glass on the linoleum.

'Aaaaaw, I'm sorry! My fault entirely, clumsy bugger I am. See, go in the lav, quick, sponge it off before it stains, I'll get you another – I'm sorry, pal, I really am!'

Everybody in the bar looking up now, vacant grins from around the dartboard. Obvious to Giles that nobody realised they were setting him up.

'Excuse me,' he said stiffly and made for the door that said bilingually TOILETS/TOILED.

'—accident,' he heard behind him. 'No sense of humour, the English . . .'

Stumbled into the passage, but instead of going to the gents he dashed in the opposite direction. A door before him, ajar, LOUNGE on frosted glass, group of people huddled over a table. Giles saw them look up as if disturbed in some conspiracy – more hostility, Christ. Turned quickly away and saw, to his overwhelming relief that the passage was empty all the way to the front door. Going to have to get out of here quick before those two went into the gents and found he wasn't there. Giles glanced apprehensively behind, but they hadn't emerged.

Years since he'd been in such a panic. Memory-flash: hiding from older kids in a cloakroom at school. The famous wheedling lie: *Come out Freeman, we're not going to hurt you . . .*

Giles charged along the corridor, not caring how much noise he made, knocking over an umbrella stand. He looked behind him one more time – thought he saw a pitted face – and then, with his right arm outstretched like a lance, he sent the swing door flying open and lurched into the street, into the hard, stinging rain, slanting golden needles in the streetlights.

He stood in the cold rain, cold beer in his crotch, telling himself, you're never – breathing hard – *never* going to get in that kind of situation again.

And thinking of the ancient wooden warmth of *Tafarn y Groes*, where he was known and welcomed, he turned and ran through the rain to his car, his shiny new Subaru four-wheel-drive, the thinking driver's answer to the Nearly Mountains on a cold, wet night.

They were waiting for him in the shiny wet car park, rainwater streaming down their ghastly, grinning faces.

'What I like . . . out this pub . . .' – words fractured by the wind – '. . . two doors.'

Lower lip jutting like a waterspout.

Gargoyle.

Giles mentally measured the distance to the car. Fifteen yards. Might as well have been a mile. Not a hope of making it.

Through the blinding downpour, he sized up the opposition. They were both shorter than he was, but the crater-faced one had a rugby player's physique, wide chest, arms like double-barrelled sawn-off shotguns.

'Look, lads . . .' he said weakly, accepting beyond doubt that he was in deep trouble here. What could one say to people like this?

Rain coming down like nails. Giles was suddenly terribly frightened. And heartsick to think this should happen to him in the land he'd chosen for his own, for his unborn children. He wanted to weep.

The dark one, Slit-mouth, hard water plastering down his sparse black hair, pouring like furious tears down his concrete face, said,

'You're dead, you are, fuckin' Saxon git.'

Giles folded in two as a big shoe went into his stomach and his hair was torn back and something that could only have been a fist but felt like a steel spike was driven into his left eye.

CHAPTER XXXII

IN Y Groes, around midnight, the air was still.

All that night there would be violent rain in Pontmeurig. Over the Nearly Mountains there was sleet. The River Meurig was savagely swollen.

Y Groes, around midnight, was another world.

True, it *had* been stormy and the barometers still registered minimal pressure. But now the rain had stopped and the wind had died. The clouds slid back theatrically and there was a full moon over the church. Wherever you stood in Y Groes, the moon always seemed to be over the church, like a white candle flame.

Just before midnight, Claire came down the ribbon of lane from the church among a group of people. They included the rector, the Revd Elias Ap Siencyn, Glyn Harri, the amateur historian, Mrs Bronwen Dafis, mother of Dilwyn and grandmother of Sali. And the Morgans – Buddug Morgan and big Morgan Morgan.

They walked down towards the river and Claire, seeing the moon on the thrashing water, became excited.

The river had been rising all day and something in Claire had been rising with it. She felt drawn to the water, but a gentle hand held her back.

'*Dim nawr.*'

Not now.

Mrs Bronwen Dafis explained that if she went down now she might not get back. It was too dangerous. Too dark.

But the moon . . .

Indeed, Mrs Dafis said cryptically. The moon.

'*Wel, pryd?*' Claire said. When?

'*Bore fori,*' the rector said quietly. Tomorrow morning.

He turned and walked away up the hill.

Tacitly dismissed, the group split up in silence. Glyn Harri followed a respectful distance behind the spindly figure of the rector. Then went Buddug and Morgan. Mrs Bronwen Dafis was the last, a tiny, upright figure, alone. None of them looked back at Claire, who stood staring into the dark water.

The river was still gathering rage, although there was no wind or rain here. As if driven by the moon, it hurled itself at the stone buttresses of the bridge.

No lights now in the village, except for a lone streetlamp with a small yellow bulb under a pan-lid shade. The rector's long shape vanished beyond the light.

She was alone on the bridge, but unafraid. Inside her dwelt a great calm which stilled her thoughts and her emotions. She was content. She was *here*. Home.

At last.

Time passed. True darkness came, as a dense cloud formed around the moon and then a final fold of cloud came down over it like an eyelid. The air was still, but the water rushed and roared, filling the atmosphere with rhythmic sounds. Claire could hear the night now and feel its essence inside her.

Eventually, she began to walk away from the bridge and up the hill towards the church.

Although she was moving further from the bridge, further from the water, the sounds were going with her, swirling around her and then separating, dying off then wafting in. And mingled with the water noise was the sound of singing, uneven and hesitant. A frail organ wail, like cat-cries, and the sonorous rhythm of measured footsteps.

An arm brushed against Claire and a hand touched her shoulder.

Misty people were drifting around her. She was carried among them up the hill.

And they sang. With uncertainty in their fractured, mournful voices, they sang, in Welsh and then in English,

Love is kind and suffers long
Love is meek and thinks no wrong

The amorphous crowd split in two and something long and narrow slid between the two lines and a darker mist closed around it.

As the singing fell away and the people dissolved into vapour, Claire felt a momentary heart-stab of pain. But a cushion of warm air settled around her and the pain became a soft and bearable memory. With no light to guide her, she turned into the track leading to her cottage.

Soon after, the rain returned. But there was no wind until daylight came.

CHAPTER XXXIII

IT WAS probably the cold water that deadened the pain. He was lying in a puddle. Or perhaps it had been raining so hard that the entire car park was a great lake.

A blow. He heard rather than felt it.

Bastards. He cringed. How long would they go on hitting him and kicking him before he lost consciousness? He lay very still; perhaps he should pretend he was already unconscious. Perhaps that would stop them.

no need for you to speak Welsh, man . . .

How friendly they were in Y Groes. How hospitable.

makes you a novelty, like, isn't it . . .

A Rhys. He was a Rhys. Sort of. In spirit.

He was *with* them.

His head imploding as they kicked it. Far away though, now. He closed his eyes, wished he could keep them closed for ever, feeling nothing but the icy balm.

But they wrenched him to his feet again, flung him back against the wall. His stomach clenched, waiting for the pain. He felt the vomit rising again.

White figure swimming towards him.

From the picture. Pale figure from the photograph in its frame in the judge's study. *Eisteddfod Genedlaethol*. White-robed, bardic, druidic.

It shimmered.

'No.' he said weakly. 'No . . .'

'Giles.'

'No.'

Bethan pushed back the hood of her white raincoat. 'Giles, can you *see* me?'

'No,' he said. 'No. Get away from me.'

'Got him, have you? Where's the other?'

'Don't . . . know. Keep still, you bugger. You bite me again, I'm going to break your nose. What should I do with this one?'

'What you should do is to get rid of him very discreetly before he sees your face. You have enough problems as it is.'

'Big bloody help that is. Where am I going to put him?'

'Well, hell, I don't know – drag him over to the castle and throw him in the moat. Take him a good while to extricate himself, by which time we'll all be away.'

Guto looked puzzled. 'There is no moat any more.'

Dai Death looked up into the plummeting night sky.

'There will be by now,' he said.

Giles stared at Bethan as if he didn't know whether to push her away or to hit her. As if he couldn't decide if it was really her. Or, if it *was* her, whose side she was on.

In the shelter of the eaves, he was propped into a corner like a broken scarecrow, fair hair spiked and bloody, his suit vomit-soaked, beer-soaked, puddle-soaked and torn in several places. But it was his eye Bethan was most worried about.

'Giles, can you see me now?'

'Yes. Yes, of course I can.'

'Can you see me through *both* eyes?'

'I think so. I don't know. Christ, what happened to me?'

'You – you were mugged,' Bethan said.

'Mugged?' Giles started to laugh and went into a coughing fit, vomit around his mouth, blood in his left eye. 'Is *that* what you call it?'

'We knew something must be wrong when we saw you racing past the door, knocking everything over.'

'Where are the bastards now?'

'One got away. Guto has the other.'

'Who?'

'A friend. Giles, you're going to get pneumonia. We have to get you to hospital.'

Giles said, 'Am I hurt?'

Bethan said, 'Your eye. How does it feel?'

'Cold. A bit cold. My whole head, really. Cold, you know—'

'Idwal, stay with him. My car's over there. We'll get him to the hospital.'

'No!' Giles straightened up and stumbled. 'I've got to get back to Y Groes. My car—'

'Oh, Giles, how could you drive? Where is Claire?'

'At home. I suppose. I mean, she's not expecting me tonight. It was . . . When we heard the weather was going to be bad we decided I'd travel back on Friday – tomorrow. I – I couldn't wait. Left early. Thing is – I always phone her, you know, every night.'

Bethan thought Giles looked as pathetic as seven-year-old Huw Morus had looked that morning after wetting himself in class.

'I'll ring her for you later,' Bethan said. 'We've got to get you to the hospital.'

'Bethan, I'm OK. Really, I am.'

'I'll bring the car. Idwal will stay with you. You remember Idwal Roberts whom you interviewed?'

'Hullo again, boy,' said Idwal. 'Talk about politics, is it?'

Pontmeurig Cottage Hospital accepted patients from within a fifteen-mile radius. As with most local hospitals in Wales it did not have a permanent medical staff of its own but was run by the local family doctors. Anybody in need of complicated treatment or surgery was referred at once to the general hospitals in Aberystwyth or Carmarthen.

They took Giles into a small treatment room with whitewashed walls. A local doctor was summoned to look into his left eye, which was cleaned up by a nurse and then re-examined. Serious bruising. Permanent damage unlikely.

The doctor, a youngish man of perhaps Middle-Eastern origins, said to Bethan, 'How did this happen?'

'Slipped in the car park,' Giles replied quickly. 'Running to the car through the rain. Fell into a puddle and hit my head on somebody's bumper.'

'What about the vomit?'

'Turned me sick,' Giles said. 'Hell of a blow.'

'I see. Were *you* there, Mrs McQueen?'

'I came along afterwards.'

'Did you. Look, Mr Freeman, I think I'd like to keep you in overnight, OK?'

'Oh, come on – is that really necessary?'

'I don't know,' said the doctor, who had an educated English accent. 'But let's not take any chances.'

'Well, can I get cleaned up?'

'I sincerely hope so. We're not going to admit you in that state, we have our standards, you know. Excuse me a minute.'

'Just look at my clothes,' Giles said in disgust when the doctor had gone out. 'What am I going to do? I can't put these back on.'

Bethan thought about this. 'What we'll do, Giles – how does this sound? I'll ring Claire and tell her what happened. She can get a change of clothes ready for you and I'll drive over early tomorrow and bring them back.'

Giles shook his head. 'I can't ask you to do that. You'd have to leave at the crack of dawn to go over there and bring the stuff back and then get back in time for school. You can't go to that trouble. No way.'

'How else are you going to get anything. Claire hasn't a car there yet, has she?'

'She hires one from Dilwyn when she needs to go somewhere.'

'And I doubt if anything of Guto's would fit you.'

'This Guto,' Giles said slowly. 'Guto Evans by any chance?'

'Shhhhh,' said Bethan. 'He was not involved, all right? You did not see him.'

Giles tried to smile. 'Thank him for me anyway. I'd have been half dead if he hadn't – hadn't not been involved. Who were those guys, anyway, d'you know?'

Bethan said, 'Dai – that's Dai Williams who was with us – he thinks they work in the kitchens at the Plas Meurig. They are not local boys, I am thankful to say.'

Sitting on the edge of the treatment table, looking down at his stockinged feet, Giles told Bethan how it had come about, how the whole thing had developed from one swift *hanner peint o gwrw*.

'I'm confused,' he said. 'I thought if one was making the effort to learn Welsh . . . That's what you want, isn't it?'

Bethan gave a frustrated half-laugh. 'Most likely those boys are not Welsh speakers anyway. Some Welsh people are very aggressively opposed to the language. It's not black and white, you must realise that by now.'

'I'm getting better again, Bethan. With the language. I've done a lot of studying.'

'Good. Listen, Giles—'

'I don't know what came over me before. Tired, I think. Headaches. But I'm much better now.'

'Giles, can I ask you a question?'

'Ask away. What have I got to lose?'

'Everything,' said Bethan. 'That is just it. You have everything to lose. You are a successful journalist with a—' She hesitated. '—a good marriage. A good career, plenty of money, I suppose.'

'Well, you know, enough to be going on with.'

'So why do you want to be part of this mess?' she asked bluntly.

'Mess?' Giles moved along the plastic sheet to detach his sodden trousers which were sticking to it. 'I don't think it's a mess. Politically, it's very stimulating. I mean, in England most people just vote for whichever party they think is going to benefit them financially. To be in a place where the main issues are cultural and linguistic – national identity at stake . . . Hey, listen, I'll tell you one thing—' Giles grinned like an idiot, through his pain. 'I bet I'm the first ever English guy to get his head kicked in for speaking Welsh in public.'

'Oh, Giles,' Bethan said. 'It isn't fair, is it?'

How could she tell him that tonight's fracas was probably the least of his problems?

Her face must have become overcast, because he said, 'Look, Bethan – we should have a proper talk sometime, you know.'

The doctor came back before she could fashion a reply.

'Mr Freeman, we've prepared a bathroom for you. The nurse will help you. How does your head feel?'

'OK. Just cold. Quite cold.'

Giles dropped to the floor and winced.

'Do you have pain anywhere else?'

'Nothing much.'

'I think,' the doctor said, 'that you should go to Bronglais tomorrow—'

'No! No bloody way!'

'—if not tonight. We should have X-rays.'

'For Christ's sake,' Giles snapped. 'It was only a fall. It doubtless looks much worse than it actually is.'

'All right,' the doctor said. 'We'll talk about it tomorrow. Now come and get cleaned up. Would you excuse us, Mrs McQueen?'

'Of course.' Bethan went to the door and looked back at Giles. 'I'll be back early in the morning.'

'You've been wonderful,' Giles said. 'I think I'm in love with you, Bethan.'

'Join the queue,' the doctor said.

When Bethan got back to her flat over the bookshop, the phone was ringing. Guto.

She told him how it had come about that Giles Freeman had been assaulted in the car park.

'Bastards,' Guto said. 'Ought to have handed that bugger

191

over to the cops, but Dai said I could wave goodbye to the candidacy if I was linked to another assault, even as a witness. A minefield, it is, politics.'

'You didn't harm that one, did you?'

'Well, the odd tweak, kind of thing. Nothing that will show. I quite enjoyed it, to be honest. Tell your English friend that when I am MP for Glanmeurig I shall recommend we erect a monument on the Drovers' car park to commemorate his historic stand on behalf of the language.'

It was an ill wind, Bethan thought. Guto seemed to have cheered up considerably.

She switched on lights, plugged in the kettle and sat down to telephone Claire, wondering what the reaction would be. Perhaps this would bring Claire down to earth again. Giles would need some looking after.

In Y Groes the phone rang five times. Then there was a bleep, a pause and Claire's recorded voice said,

'*Y Groes dau, tri, naw. Dyma Claire Rhys . . .* '

The message, in near-perfect Welsh, said Claire Rhys was not available to come to the telephone but the caller could leave a message after the tone.

Bethan's own answering machine had a message in Welsh, followed by a translation. Thousands of answering machines in Welsh-speaking areas of Wales now carried messages in Welsh, almost invariably with a translation; nobody wanted to lose an important caller because he or she, like the majority of Welsh people, spoke only English.

Claire's message was given only in Welsh. Bethan hung up, troubled.

Three times a week now, she went to the judge's house for the Welsh lesson – with Claire alone, of late, because Giles had been in London. One to one. The oil lamp hanging from the beam in the judge's study surrounded by the judge's black books. Sombre yellow light. Deep, deep shadows.

And Claire, face gaunt in the oil-light, hair drawn tightly back, showing the dark roots.

A student so brilliant it was unnerving.

She dialled the number one last time.

'*Y Groes dau, tri, naw. Dyma Claire Rhys . . .* '

Not the kind of problem you could explain to an answering machine. She would get up very early and go to the judge's house.

Bethan put the phone down.

The rain and wind attacked her window.

CHAPTER XXXIV

LIKE some spurned, embittered lover, the wind-driven rain beat on Bethan's bedroom window all night. She got little sleep; every half-dream seemed to feature Giles's wet and bloodied image. Its screams were frenzied but inaudible, as if it were separated from her by thick glass – a windscreen or a television screen.

Before six o'clock, Bethan was up, making strong, black tea, peering out of the window and half expecting to find Pontmeurig's main street under two feet of water. Ironically the rain, having deprived her of sleep, had now stopped. There were no signs of flooding in the street, although the river must surely be dangerously high.

It looked cold too. Bethan put on her white raincoat, with a long red scarf and a pink woolly hat which she pulled down over her ears as she stepped out into the street.

By six thirty she was collecting the Peugeot from the car park under the castle's broken tower. She looked down, with some trepidation, into the ditch below the outer ramparts, as if she might see a rigid, clawing hand emerging from the watery mud in which its owner had drowned. On the eve of the selection meeting, it would be just Guto's luck.

Before leaving she had telephoned the hospital, where the sister in charge reported that Giles had had quite a painful and restless night.

But yet, she thought, unlocking the car door, if Giles were writing a report of last night's incident he would deal seriously and sympathetically with the dilemma of the non-Welsh-speaking Welshman.

That English sense of fair play.

The town was quiet, cowed – as though people were deliberately lying low, apprehensive about getting up to find their gardens underwater or their chimney pots in pieces on the lawn. Driving over the Meurig Bridge in the steely-grey dawn, Bethan saw that it had indeed been a close thing. Trees sprouted from the water, where the river had claimed its first meadow.

Allowing for weather problems, storm debris on the road, it would take about twenty minutes to get to Y Groes. Bethan knew Claire rose early and guessed she might be waiting for the light to see what pictures she could obtain of storm damage. If she was still actually taking pictures. She'll probably want to come back with me to the hospital, Bethan thought. Another lost opportunity to talk to Giles.

Part of Bethan said it was not her problem, she should keep out. Another part said Giles was a decent man who needed saving from himself. Too many English people had given up their jobs and come to Wales with new-life dreams, many of them to start smallholdings on poor-quality land from which they imagined they could be self-sufficient. She saw a parallel here with Giles, who seemed about to abandon a highly paid post to spend his life ploughing this infertile place for news, in the naïve belief that the public over the border cared as much about Wales as he did.

In Bethan's experience, the only immigrants who really could be said to have fitted in were those who came to take up existing, steady jobs. Like Robin, her husband, who had worked with the British Geological Survey team near Aberystwyth.

Bethan's eyes filled up.

Stop it! Her hands tightened on the wheel. The Nearly Mountains rose up before her, tented by cloud.

Bethan had experimented with a number of different methods of tackling these sudden rushes of grief. Anger, the least satisfactory, had usually proved, all the same, to be the most effective.

So she thought about Buddug.

Yesterday Huw Morus, aged seven, had wet himself in class. Bethan had led him into the teachers' toilet and washroom to get cleaned up.

Huw had been very distressed. Bethan had taken him back into her office, sat him on a chair by the electric fire and asked him if he was feeling unwell. Huw had started crying and said he wanted to go. Again.

Bethan had sent him back to the teachers' toilet and then said, 'OK, we'll take you home.'

'I am sure he'll be happy now,' Buddug commented. 'Now he's got what he wanted.'

'It seems likely to me that he has some kind of bladder infection,' Bethan said.

Buddug had sniffed dismissively. 'Lazy. He is lazy.'

Huw lived in the village. where his father was a mechanic, the sole employee at Dilwyn Dafis's garage.

'Did you ask Mrs Morgan if you could go to the toilet?' Bethan asked, as the boy trotted beside her past the *Tafarn* and the post office to a timber-framed terrace of cottages at the end of the street.

It emerged that Huw had asked Mrs Morgan at about half past nine by the classroom clock and she had allowed him to go. Then he'd asked her again at about a quarter past ten and she'd told him he could wait until break. He'd barely made it in time.

At about twenty minutes past eleven Huw had again raised his hand and sought permission to go to the lavatory and Mrs Morgan had shaken her head and told him he must not try it on with her again.

Ten minutes later Huw, by now frozen to the chair with his legs tightly crossed, had appealed again to the teacher. This time Mrs Morgan had walked over and bent down and whispered in his ear.

Bethan questioned the seven-year-old boy in some detail, because she wanted to be sure about this.

It seemed Buddug had reminded Huw that the end of the yard, where the children's toilets were, was very close to the woods.

Which, as everyone knew, were guarded by the the the *Gorsedd Ddu*.

The dark bards.

And the *Gorsedd Ddu* would view Huw's repeated appearances as a mockery.

If they found him there again they might catch him and take him with them into the woods, and there would be no relief to be found there. Not for a stupid little boy who tried to deceive his teacher.

Bethan, coming down now out of the Nearly Mountains, swung the wheel of the Peugeot to avoid a grey squirrel in the road. The squirrel shot into the forestry.

In Bethan's experience, small children were often terrified by their first sight of a *gorsedd* of bards, those poets and writers who had been honoured at *eisteddfodau* and walked in solemn procession wearing their long ceremonial robes and druidic headdresses. These archetypal figures, in the garb of ancient pagan priests, could seem quite awesomely sinister to little kids until they found out that under those white robes you would usually find genial grandfatherly figures who would occasionally dispense sweets like Sion Corn, the Welsh Father Christmas.

The *Gorsedd Ddu*, the black bards – there was a difference here. They were meant to be terrifying.

The lower slopes of the Nearly Mountains were sparsely wooded and Bethan had to slow down to find a path between branches torn off the trees in the night. She would not have been surprised to find the road blocked by an entire Sitka spruce, its roots ripped out of the shallow soil.

This never happened to the oak trees in the old woods. The reason, Buddug would probably say, was not only that the soil was thick and deep and the area so sheltered. But that the oak woods were protected by the *Gorsedd Ddu*.

Most parents and infant-teachers, in fanciful mood, might tell children the woods were the home of, say, the *Tylwyth Teg*, the Welsh fairy folk. But that would not satisfy the streak of cruelty in Buddug. First she had refused to consider that the child, Huw Morus, might be ill, and then she had made wetting himself seem the safer option by invoking the insidiously horrifying image of the mythical assembly of black-robed bards who were said to convene to judge the traitors and the cowards.

Bethan decided there were certain aspects of the Welsh national heritage which she disliked intensely – and most of them were represented by Buddug, who would not be happy until children were sitting at their desks dressed stiffly in Welsh national costume, drawing pictures of corpse candles and sin-eaters consuming their lunches from the shrouded chests of dead people.

There was still a strong wind, but no trees had been blown down on the lower slopes of the Nearly Mountains, and Bethan arrived in Y Groes well before seven to find the last few lights glimmering in the cottages, the village enfolded in the dark hills like antique jewellery in velvet, under a delicate oyster sky.

But the wind was high, the sky unbalanced, a sense of something wild beyond the horizon.

Bethan parked in the entrance to the school lane and set off across the bridge. Below it the swollen Meurig frothed and spat. 'Big, tough river now, is it?' Bethan said. 'You never had much to say for yourself in the summer.'

She walked past the *Tafarn* and up the lane towards the church and then between the two sycamores to the judge's house.

The iron gate was open, but nobody was in sight. The wind perhaps? Bethan closed the gate behind her, walked up the path, knocked on the door.

She would tell Claire everything, including the probable reasons for the attack on Giles. Everything except the involvement of Guto who must, for the sake of his image, remain an anonymous hero.

Claire could pack a change of clothes and Bethan would take them – and Claire, if she wanted – to the hospital. There should be plenty time to get back to school before the first children arrived.

The door opened.

'Oh Claire, I tried to ring you—' Bethan said, then stopped and drew back.

It was Buddug.

CHAPTER XXXV

BUDDUG did not seem surprised to see her. But then Buddug never seemed surprised.

She wore a high-necked, starched white blouse and – Bethan would swear – a smudge of make-up. As if she had arrived for an Occasion. She filled the doorway. Bethan could not see if Claire was in the room behind her.

'Where is *Claire*?' she said flatly.

Buddug stared impassively at her.

'Where is Claire?'

'Not here,' Buddug said calmly.

'Out? So early?'

She'd been out last night too. The answering machine.

'And what are *you* doing here?' Bethan demanded. Her mind could not grasp this situation. Buddug in Claire's house. At little after seven in the morning.

And formally attired. Looking quite grotesque – there was no other word for it.

'Are you alone here?'

Buddug did not reply. There was a silence in the room behind her but it was the kind of silence which implied *presence*, as if a still company was sitting there. Bethan found herself thinking of the drawing in Sali Dafis's exercise book, dark brown stick-people around a coffin on a table.

'Are you not going to answer me?' Her voice shook. 'Where is Claire?'

Buddug did not move. The thought came to Bethan that this woman was big enough and strong enough to kill her, as simply as she killed chickens and turkeys, huge hands around her throat. A swift, dismissive jerk of the wrists.

'Look, I want to know. Where is Claire? *What have you done with her?*'

Buddug came alive then, bulging out of the doorway, the veins in her face suddenly lighting up like an electric circuit.

'What is it to you?' she shrieked. 'Who said you could come here? Get out! Get back to your school, you stupid, meddling little bitch!'

Bethan went pale. 'How d—!'

The front door leapt on its hinges, as if hit by a gale, and Bethan lurched back, clutching at the air, as the door crashed into its frame and shuddered there.

A sudden stiff breeze disturbed the giant sycamores and prodded her down the lane. There was a ball of cold in the pit of her stomach as she walked back towards the river.

What she felt for Buddug had gone beyond hatred to the place where nightmares are born.

'You are early, Bethan.'

He was sitting on a wooden bench under the *Tafarn* sign, which was beginning to swing now in the gathering wind.

'You also are early, Aled,' Bethan said, groping for composure. 'For a landlord.'

'Could not sleep, girl. The wind rising.'

'The wind's nothing here, compared with Pontmeurig. Well, last night . . .'

'Ah, well, see, so little of the wind we get here that the merest flurry we notice. I do, anyway. Because the river is so close, see. The river goes mad.'

Aled's hair was as white and stiff as the icy snow on the tops of the Nearly Mountains. Bethan had always found him a droll and placid man, easy to talk to, in Welsh or English. She wondered if she could trust him.

'Do you . . .?' She hesitated.

He looked quizzically at her.

'Do you find things are changing, Aled?'

'Changing?'

'Here. In the village.'

Aled looked away from Bethan, over the oak woods and back again. 'Things changing? In Y Groes?' He smiled.

'Perhaps it's me. Perhaps I should not have come back.'

'Why do you say that?'

'I don't know. Too many memories, perhaps.' Although, of course, that was not it really.

'He was a nice boy, your man. A terrible shame, it was, that he . . . well.'

Bethan asked him, 'What do you think of Giles Freeman?'

'Nice fellow,' Aled said. 'Well meaning, you know.'

'He was—' No, she could not tell him what had happened. Not even that Giles had fallen in the car park. Not until she'd told Claire.

'I think, Bethan,' Aled said. 'I think you have a decision to make.'

'What kind of decision?'

'Well, as you said . . . about your future. Whether you stay here, perhaps move into one of the cottages.'

'There are no cottages for sale.'

'No, but . . . well, Tegwyn Jones's old place. It might be available. If you—'

'If I wanted to settle down here?'

'—to settle down, as you say. To become part of our community. It is . . . well, as you know, it is a rare and beautiful place.'

'Yes.'

'But it makes . . . demands, see.'

'Does it make demands on you, Aled?'

There was rarely much colour in his face. He was not an outdoor man, like Morgan, or even Dilwyn Dafis. All the same, he did not look well. Bethan had not seen him face to face for several weeks, and she felt a tiredness coming from him.

'Oh yes,' he said. 'It has made demands on me. Bethan, would you excuse me. I have the bar to clean.' He stood up. 'Nice to see you, as always.'

Face it, Bethan told herself. No one here is going to help you.

Suddenly she wanted to dash back to the Peugeot, shut herself in, wind up all the windows, lock the door, put the radio on – loud, loud rock music – and race back over the Nearly Mountains to sanctuary and sanity.

I could do that, she thought hysterically. I could have a nervous breakdown. God knows, I'm halfway there. I could go to the doctor, get signed off. Nobody would be surprised. The Widow McQueen. Came back too soon.

Too soon.

Obviously she had come back too soon this morning. What was going on? What had she disturbed?

Did she really want to know?

Had to pull herself together. Her main task was to get clean clothing for Giles. If she couldn't get into the house, it would have to be Guto – he must have *something* that would not look entirely ludicrous on a man six inches taller and at least two stones lighter. Or she could even go to Probert's and buy some things.

She set off purposefully across the bridge to her car.

But made the mistake of looking over the stone parapet.

To where, fifty yards downstream, a woman had her head in the water.

Bethan looked around for help but there was nobody on the main street at this hour. She ran across the bridge, crying out 'Aled! Aled!' at the closed door of the *Tafarn*, but the wind ripped the words away and there was no response as she scrambled down the bank to the where the woman's head was being tossed this way and that by the thrashing river.

Halfway down, Bethan lost her footing. Her left shoe skated on a grass-slick, the wind seemed to flick her into the air and she was thrown, screaming, full length down the slimy, freezing river bank.

For a moment Bethan just lay there and sobbed with anguish and incomprehension. And that amply-justified sense of *déjà vu* which told her she would look up to find two large, muddy hiking boots swinging one against the other.

But the only thing in focus was the hard grey stone of the bridge support. All around her was just a wash of glacial green and white, the abstract colours spinning past her eyes, because this time her glasses had gone.

'Oh no. Oh no, please God . . .'

Trembling with cold and shock, Bethan put both hands in the sodden, slippery grass and pushed herself to her knees. Then she began to crawl awkwardly up the bank, groping at the grass on either side.

Stricken with the fear that if she slipped again her hands would find somebody's dead skin, the scaly contours of a drow ed face. Or chewed-out eye sockets where the crows had .

Her hand touched something smooth and wet and she snatched it back in dread, before realising she'd found the glasses. Half retching with relief, she fumbled them on, rubbing the grass and mud from the lenses which were still, oh thank God, apparently intact.

On her knees now, pink woolly hat missing, hair ravaged by the wind, skirt torn almost up to the waist, Bethan looked around her and then down to the river no more than four feet below her.

The woman was naked from the waist up, bent into the river. Either her body was being thrown about by the wind or . . . Bethan, crouching, half sliding, edged her way to the water.

She reached the spitting river just as the woman's head came up, black and dripping, and her eyes were like chips of ice and she was Claire, and Bethan arched back in horror and bewilderment.

Above the frenzy of wind and water, Claire was making a noise as harsh and chill as the river itself. It seemed at first as if she was crying, with great jagged wails. Then Bethan realised, with shock, that Claire was laughing, which somehow was far, far worse.

'Claire . . .?'

Bethan felt a piercing of fear. Claire just went on laughing, rising up on the bank, breasts ice-blue, marbled with the cold.

'What's wrong? What's happening? What are you doing? For God's sake! Claire!'

Bethan pulled off her raincoat and went to wrap it around Claire, although she was really afraid to go near her. But Claire stood up and backed off. She was wearing only jeans and her red hiking boots.

'You are crazy,' Bethan breathed.

Claire's small mouth was stretched wide with grotesque mirth. She ran her hands through her hair, wet and dark as a seal.

Bethan saw that almost all the blonde had gone, just a few jaundiced patches.

'*Dychi ddim yn gweld?*' Claire hissed. '*Dychi ddim yn gweld?*' Can't you see?

The river writhed among the rocks.

Bethan, face damp with cold sweat and spray, didn't move. She was very scared now, wanting to clamber up the bank and get away, but afraid of somebody or the crazy wind pushing her back to the river, and the river was slurping at the rocks and the bridge support as if licking its lips for her.

She thought of Giles lying restlessly in his unwanted hospital bed, while his wife cavorted like some insane water-nymph.

Claire started to move back along the bank towards the stile that led into one of Morgan's fields. Black cloth, a shawl, hung from one of the posts of the stile and she pulled it off and wrapped it around her. A sheep track curved up through the field and ended near the judge's cottage.

When she reached the stile, Claire turned one last time towards Bethan, tearing at her once-blonde hair, screaming gleefully through the wind. '*Dydwy ddim yn Sais!*' I am not English!

And burst out laughing again, in raucous peels like church bells rung by madmen.

CHAPTER XXXVI

'FORGET it,' Giles said. 'Just forget it, OK?'

'You're being very foolish, Mr Freeman.'

'Look, mate,' Giles said, 'it's my bloody head and if I don't want it bloody scanned, or whatever they do these days, I don't have to comply. So bring me the sodding papers or whatever I'm supposed to sign.'

'All right, just supposing you have a brain haemorrhage.'

Giles shrugged.

'I can't stop you,' the doctor said. 'I can only warn you. And all I can say is, if somebody had given *me* a kicking . . .'

'I *fell*.'

'. . . If somebody had given me that kind of kicking, I'd want all the medical evidence I could get.' Dr Tahan, unshaven, was clearly suppressing rage. He'd been awoken by a nurse on the phone telling him Mr Freeman was threatening to walk out in his underpants if they didn't bring his clothes immediately.

'Look . . .' Giles passed a hand over his eyes. 'I'm very grateful for all you've done, but there's nothing wrong with me that sleep won't cure, and I'm not going to get any here. Bring me whatever I have to sign and my clothes. I want to go home.'

'Come and see me tomorrow,' the doctor said curtly. 'If you want to.' And walked out of the room.

Not you, Giles said to himself. I'll go and see Dr Wyn in the village, if I have to. *If* I have to.

A nurse brought his clothes, put them down on the bed, did not speak to him. If you didn't want to play by their rules, Giles thought, they didn't want to know you. The clothes had been dried and straightened out, as far as was possible with all the torn bits, and the lining hanging out of his jacket. Giles held up the jacket and grinned savagely. He felt removed from all this. He felt he was standing a foot or so behind the action, watching himself hold up the jacket, controlling his own responses at arm's length, pulling strings to bring on the savage grin.

In truth he felt awful – physically and emotionally in a similar condition to his clothes.

But he was going home.

Guto was wearing a tie.

An unheard-of phenomenon.

'I borrowed it,' he said. 'From Dai.'

'But it's one of his *working* ties,' Bethan said.

'Looks all right though, doesn't it?'

'It's black.'

'Reflects my new image. Sober. Caring.'

'Take it off, Guto. I shall go and buy you another. Meanwhile, there is something you could do for me.'

'No time – to get a new tie, I mean. I'm meeting Dafydd and Gwynfor in Lampeter at ten. Then we are all going over to Rhayader for the selection meeting.'

'It's not until tonight, is it?'

'A lot to discuss before then. Hell of a lot.'

They were alone in the house, Guto's mam having gone for the early bus to Aber, as she did every Friday. Bethan had driven over from Y Groes in a kind of trance, going deliberately far too fast so that she would have to concentrate hard on her driving to avoid disaster and would not be able to think about anything else.

'There are big green stains on your mac,' Guto observed.

'So there are,' said Bethan.

It was not yet eight o'clock. No more than half an hour since she'd scrambled up the river bank away from the madwoman who had almost been her friend.

'Guto, Giles might be coming out of hospital this morning. You know the state of his clothes. I was wondering if you had anything that might fit him.'

'What about his own clothes? He's got more than that suit at home, hasn't he?'

'Yes, but . . . there are problems in bringing them across.'

The central problem, she now realised, was that Giles would actually be going home – she had no illusions that the doctor might persuade him to be examined at Bronglais – and walking into a situation which he might have difficulty coping with even if he were fully fit.

She simply did not know what to do for the best.

'I'll make some tea,' Guto said. 'You look as if you need it.'

'No, you go,' Bethan said. 'You get off to Lampeter. It's your big day.'

'Are you all right, Bethan?'

205

'Of course I am.'

'Listen, go upstairs now. Second door on the left. Just inside the door there's a wardrobe. Some of my dad's old clothes you'll find in there. A big, tall man, he was, my dad. Well, compared with me he was. Take what you like. Bit old-fashioned, mind, but if it's only to get him home . . .'

Guto straightened his undertaker's tie in the gilt-framed mirror over a mantelpiece heavy with cumbersome Victorian pottery. From a chair he took his briefcase.

His *briefcase*! A tie *and* a briefcase. On any other day but this Bethan would have found the spectacle richly amusing.

'I'm off,' said Guto. 'Just slam the door behind you when you've finished.'

'Thank you. Guto . . .'

He looked back, mute appeal in his doggy eyes.

What the hell, Bethan thought, and went over and kissed him. On the cheek, of course.

'Good luck, Guto.'

Guto snatched her by the arm and kissed her on the lips. He'd trimmed his beard too.

'There,' he said. '*Now* I feel lucky.'

When he'd gone, Bethan went upstairs and found his late father's wardrobe. Guto's dad had been a miner in the Rhondda who had suffered badly with his chest. When Guto was twelve or thirteen the family had moved west for his father's health, taking over a small tobacconist's shop in Pontmeurig. Bethan remembered Bryn Evans as a man who coughed a lot and laughed a lot, spent each night in the Drovers' Arms until closing time but was never conspicuously drunk.

Inevitably, as she pulled open the mahogany doors, Bethan remembered going through Robin's wardrobe, packing up all his clothes, taking them to the Oxfam shop in Stryd-y-Castell. Easily the most heartbreaking task she'd ever performed. She remembered folding his beloved sheepskin-lined flying jacket, then changing her mind and taking it out of the cardboard box and stowing in the bottom of her own wardrobe, where it still lay, and she—

Stop it, stop it, stop it!

On a shelf above the stiff, dark suits, she found a pair of light slacks and a thick, grey rollneck pullover. Could be worse.

With the clothes under her arm, she ran down the stairs and out of the front door, shutting it firmly behind her. Five minutes past eight. Not much time. She wondered how Buddug would react if she didn't turn up for school by nine o'clock. And would Buddug herself be on time, or would she be otherwise engaged?

Bethan shuddered at the memory of Buddug, enormous in the doorway, made-up like a fat corpse.

She put the clothes on the back seat of the Peugeot and drove to the cottage hospital. On impulse she went into the phone box in the hospital foyer and dialled Y Groes 239.

Last chance to speak sensibly to Claire, otherwise she would have to tell Giles everything.

Tell him everything?

But what was she doing in the river, Bethan?

She was washing her hair, Giles.

I see.

In Y Groes the telephone rang out. Six times, seven times, eight.

Bethan hung up and left the box and walked across to the reception desk.

'Giles Freeman,' she said to a woman who had been a couple of years ahead of her at secondary school in Aber.

'You'll be lucky,' the receptionist said. 'Do you want to speak to Dr Tahan?'

'What do you mean?'

'I'll bleep him,' said the receptionist. 'He'll want to talk to *you*, I imagine.'

Bethan went cold. 'Is Giles all right?'

'No, he's not all right,' the woman said smugly. Bethan could tell that, as she spoke, she was busy fabricating an interesting relationship between the schoolteacher and the Englishman. 'Not for me to say, though, is it?'

The doctor was more forthcoming. He led Bethan to his office in the new wing and closed the door.

'Delayed concussion, fractured skull, brain haemorrhage,

you name it,' he said. 'It could be any, it could be none. But how are we to know? I don't particularly want to know precisely how he came by his injuries, but I do want him to be fully examined. Call it selfishness. Call it protecting my own back, I don't care.'

'Hold on,' Bethan said. 'You are saying he's gone?'

'Your friend discharged himself half an hour ago. There was nothing I could say to stop him. We don't, unfortunately, have powers of arrest.'

'Oh God,' Bethan said.

'I don't know how much you are in a position to influence him, but if he blacks out and runs his car off the road . . .'

'All right,' Bethan said, looking at her watch. Twenty past eight.

She ran down the hospital corridor and did not look at the receptionist on her way to the door.

CHAPTER XXXVII

TIRED. Desperately, desperately tired.

He had thought the fresh air would revive him, but walking to the car park was like he imagined it would be for a deep sea diver staggering across the ocean bed, the air heavy on his shoulders, powerful currents pulling him this way and that. In reality the wind was not so strong any more and the sky all rained-out.

Stepping from the kerb, Giles lost his balance and fell sideways across the bonnet of a parked car. People stared at him, as though he were some rare species of breakfast-time drunk.

When he got into his own car, the new Subaru, it felt strange, as if he hadn't driven it in years. When he pulled out of the car park below the ruined castle, his hands on the wheel seemed a long way away, as if he were driving from the back seat.

He steered stiffly across the Meurig bridge and on to the

bypass. The Nearly Mountains were above him now, wispy grey clouds around the tops like smoke-rings.

Just hadn't realised what complete fatigue could be like. Except this was more than fatigue: his whole body aching, bloated, lumbering. His head feeling as though it were encased in some huge metal helmet, like the Man in the Iron Mask.

A truck blasted its horn behind him as he swung the car off the bypass and on to the mountain road, and he realised he'd forgotten to signal.

After three miles, Giles began to see double. Twin roads snaked into the hills, two wooden fences sealed off the forestry. He pulled into a lay-by. Switched off the engine, sat back, and the seat pulled him in and his eyelids crashed down.

He remembered Bethan then. How she was going to fetch him some clothes. He'd forgotten all about that. He must stop her, tell her he was going home. He sat up, hands scrabbling at the carphone. He would call home, tell Claire, get her to ring Bethan or something. Or something.

His fingers kept pushing all the wrong numbers. The carphone squeaked impatiently. He saw the message NO SERVICE printed out across the illuminated panel on the receiver. Giles groaned. He must have passed the point at which the Vodaphone signal faded out. Perhaps it would return. He must remember to try again. Must remember . . .

Really he felt like stumbling off into the forestry and curling up on the brown carpet of dead needles, knowing he would fall asleep there instantly. But he heaved his body into position on the seat, switched on the engine again and drove very, very slowly over the crest of the Nearly Mountains, where the snow snuggled into the crags and hollows. He could have stopped and walked out and gone to sleep in the snow, like Captain Oates. Just going out. May be some time.

He didn't have to analyse why it was so vital for him to get away from Pontmeurig and back to Y Groes. Couldn't have managed any heavy thinking in his state anyway. But he knew why it was. It came down to this: the first seriously unpleasant thing had happened to him in Pont, the thing that backed up everything they'd said, the hacks, at Winstone Thorpe's farewell session. While in Y Groes, everything disproved it. The warmth, the open friendliness, the generosity, the feeling that here were people who were confident enough of their heritage, their place in the world, not to suspect everyone with an English accent of trying to rip them off.

Something like that.

He glanced back at the phone. NO SERVICE it said still, NO SERVICE. Why should it just say NO SERVICE in English? Why not in Welsh, too? DIM . . . DIM whatever the hell service was in Welsh.

Down now, into the forestry's gloom. Sitka spruce stamping in dispiriting symmetry down the hillside, stealing the land and the light. Giles clung to the wheel of the Subaru, wipers scraping at the spray thrown up as the car slogged through a roadside river left by the storm. The rhythm of the wipers wafted waves of sleep into his head.

soon-be-home, soon-be-home, soon-be-home.

Only when his chin hit his chest did Giles awake to his peril, violently jerking himself upright, a bumper scraping the forestry fence as he swerved back into the middle of the road.

Breathing hard, he wiped the palm of his hand across the windscreen and smeared cool condensation into his hot, hurting eyes.

Presently, the sky brightened. He pulled down the sun-visor then flung it up again, tears in his eyes, realising this was the brightness heralding home. He saw the church's two-tiered belfry, and he stopped the car, his heart tugging weakly but triumphantly.

The church was a symbol for Giles of what this village was about. Not some grey chapel behind back-street railings, but a great, soaring tower stabbing the sky, announcing Y GROES. The cross. Y GROESFAN. The crossing place.

He had never been to a service at this church, never been to any kind of service since his wedding, but he told himself he must go this Sunday. Renew his faith, give thanks to the village and to its people and to the Almighty for bringing him here.

Battered, beaten-up, bedraggled, Giles wrapped both arms

around the steering wheel and wept. And looked up and saw, through his tears, two towers, two bridges, two roads. But he would make it now. Back home to sleep. Sleep until church on Sunday. Sunday. When was that? What day was it? Was it Sunday tomorrow?

The car rolled out of the forestry as if someone else were driving it, Giles's senses somewhere around the rear parcel shelf.

Across the bridge, up the hill, past the lych gate of the church, a couple of hundred yards then right, between the two great sycamores in full autumnal glory.

Oh God, thank you, thank you.

Giles almost fell out of the car, heedless of the pain, and breathed deeply of the soft air. The metal gate was open for him. They must have told Claire he was on his way. What he wanted most in the world was to fall into bed, holding her to him, and sleep. Sleep for ever.

'Claire . . . darling Claire . . .'

He realised he'd said that aloud as he staggered up the path. The judge's house – no *his* house surely, his house now – sat before him, grey stone under a milky sky.

The front door also was open for him. He stumbled gratefully over the step. 'Hello, darling, I tried to phone . . .'

There was no Claire waiting for him in the little stonewalled hallway.

Giles went into the living room. It was silent. No fire in the hearth, no cups on the table.

'Claire?'

He shouted out, 'Claire!' His voice almost breaking into a wail of disappointment. She wasn't here.

But the gate open, the front door. Couldn't have gone far, surely.

Giles went back outside, looked around the garden, called out, 'Claire!'

The wind brought only a sheep's bleat back to him from Morgan's field.

He returned to the house, upset and angry now, feeling deserted. And terribly, terribly tired. Too tired to think sensibly.

'I'm going to bed,' Giles said thickly. 'Sod you, Claire, I'm going to bed.'

He staggered through the passage to the bottom of the stairs, still clinging to the hope that he would meet Claire coming down, smiling with welcome and sympathy and a hot cup of coffee.

Three doors in the passage, the one to the judge's study hanging open. But no light leaked out of the gap into the already dim passage. Irritably he pulled the door closed, but it swung open again as he turned away.

Angrily he spun round and snapped it shut.

In the passage he stumbled over something that should not be there, could not take in at first that this was the pink vinyl headboard, cheap and brash, from Garfield and Pugh in hostile Pontmeurig. What was the bloody headboard doing at the foot of the stairs?

'Claire? Claire!!' He began to climb the stairs. It was too bad. Just too bloody bad of her. Not even a fire lit.

Halfway up the stairs he looked back and saw that the door of the judge's study was hanging open again. He turned away from it and carried on to the upstairs landing.

He went into his office and looked around. Aghast.

His office had gone.

It was a bedroom.

His office was a bloody bedroom again!

Giles squeezed his aching eyes with trembling fingers. Illusion, fatigue, hallucination?

Let it be that. Please let it be that, God.

But when he opened his eyes, it was still a bedroom, and now he recognised the bed. Two green mattresses and a frame of light pine. It was the bed which had come into the house with the ghastly pink vinyl head-board.

'Claire!!' he screamed, his throat choking on the word. He began to cough.

He backed out of the room and threw open the door of their own bedroom, his and Claire's, knowing in an icy part of his stomach what he would find there. Whose bed, with its frowning headboard of carved oak.

'Thank God,' Bethan said, seeing Giles's car parked in the track between the two sycamores.

She'd driven straight out of the forestry and into the village at close to sixty miles per hour, knowing that at this time there'd be no children in the road – they'd all be in school by now, wondering where their head teacher was.

At seven minutes to nine, the head teacher had been shattering a wing mirror on the parapet of the bridge as the little Peugeot whizzed across like a frightened squirrel.

All the way across the hills she'd been peering nervously over walls and hedges and fences, expecting to see a car on its side somewhere, or bits of wreckage.

Well thank God he'd made it. Thank God for that, at least. For what it was worth.

Bethan thought, on reflection, that perhaps the best thing that could have happened would have been a minor crash, something to get Giles towed back to Pont, deposited safely in the hospital with a broken leg, something minor but incapacitating.

For a few seconds she debated going up to the house to ask if Giles was OK. But really it was none of her business. All right, a bruised and beaten man and an increasingly loopy woman. What could she do about that? She was a primary school teacher, not a psychotherapist or a marriage-guidance counsellor.

Besides it was almost nine o'clock.

Christ. She felt as if she'd put in two full days' work, and it was not yet nine o'clock.

Five minutes or so later, Buddug's hands froze above the piano keyboard as Bethan slid into the school hall.

She stood in the doorway in her white mac with the streaks of mud and the huge grass stains. The children, sitting in five

213

short rows, all turned towards her, and Buddug's head swivelled round slowly, her lips drawn back into a smile of incandescent malevolence.

'*Bore da*,' the children chorused. '*Bore da*, Miss Sion.'

She sat down at her desk in the hall, still wearing her mac, too weary to say anything as Buddug's hands smashed into the opening chords of the hymn.

Buddug sang with shrill, ferocious zest, hammering the keys like a pub pianist. Energy rippled through the room as the children yelled out the words, gleefully discordant.

Bethan sat in her soiled raincoat and stared at the wall, utterly defeated.

Giles came out of the bedroom and stood at the top of the stairs, swaying.

He could not believe the agony.

Like a flower it had opened out. Bursting free inside his skull like some huge multi-petalled chrysanthemum. And at the end of every petal, a poisoned barb prodding into each tiny fold of his brain, awakening every nerve to the dazzling white light of purest pain.

He could not even bear to scream.

Mercifully, perhaps, the pain had deadened his emotions. Except for one. Which was rage.

Rage gathered in his throat, choking him. Rage against *her*.

And against him.

Her dead grandfather.

He began to walk down the stairs, each soft step detonating a new explosion in his brain.

He walked across the hall, past the pink vinyl headboard, to where the door of the judge's study still hung ajar.

Giles went in.

PART SIX

BLACK TEA

CHAPTER XXXVIII

WALES

NO RACISM HERE – WE'RE BRITISH

by Gary Willis, political staff.

Candidates in the Glanmeurig by-election have denied it's
going to turn into a bitter Welsh-versus-English clash.

Launching his campaign yesterday, Conservative
Simon Gallier said, 'I might have been born in England,
but I've spent all my working life in Wales. I believe I
stand for the quality of independence which has won
worldwide respect for the Welsh nation.'

And his Labour opponent, Wayne Davies said, 'The
main issue here is the threat to the rural economy and
the urgent need for new jobs.'

It was a quiet start to a campaign expected to produce
electoral fireworks. Everyone here is now waiting for the
Welsh Nationalist candidate to show his hand . . .

'You really write that, Gary?' asked Ray Wheeler, of the
Mirror, grinning through Guinness froth.

'Do me a favour,' Gary Willis said. Twenty-six years old,
the only reporter in the pack with a degree in economics and
political science. 'Do I strike you as being that inane?'

'You'll get used to it, son,' Charlie Firth said, lighting a
thin cigar.

'But what's the point in sending us out here if they've made
up their minds what the issues are? Or in this case, what the
issues are not.'

'Don't be so naïve, mate,' Ray Wheeler said. 'You really
think your rag's going to give any credence to people who
figure Great Britain needs fragmenting? Take my advice, send
'em the stuff and try to avoid reading what the buggers do
with it.'

'And console yourself with one thought.' Charlie Firth produced an acrid cough. 'However hard it is for you to take, it would have been a bloody sight harder for poor old Giles.'

'That,' said Ray, 'is very true. Does this dump do sandwiches?'

'If it's *egg* sandwiches,' Charlie said, 'count me out. The Welsh aren't poisoning me a second time.'

English was the dominant language tonight in the public bar of the Drovers' Arms, where all five rooms had been taken by representatives of the British national Press. Accommodation, reporters were learning, was not plentiful in this area. Max Canavan, of the *Sun*, had been left with an attic, while Peter Warren, of the *Independent*, couldn't find anywhere in town and would be forced to commute each day from a hotel on the seafront at Aberystwyth.

'Bloody BBC,' said Ray Wheeler.

'What have we done now?' Shirley Gillies demanded.

'Only block-booked the best hotel in town.'

'Advance-planning.' Shirley smiled sweetly. 'I shall think of you guys when I'm sitting down to dinner at the Plas Meurig in approximately an hour's time. Still, it's awfully, you know, *homey* here, isn't it.'

'Piss off, Shirley,' said Charlie Firth.

'The Plas Meurig,' Gary Willis said, 'is where the Tories'll be having their daily Press conferences, yeh?'

'And the Liberals,' Shirley said. 'It's a big place. They're at opposite ends. I'm not sure where Labour are, but at least you won't have to get up too early to cover the Plaid pressers, will you?'

'They've got bloody great green signs all over the door of the other bar,' Ray Wheeler said. 'Listen, are we going to tackle the bugger about this assault stuff tomorrow?'

'Assault stuff?' Shirley leaned forward. 'Do tell.'

'Come on, Shirley,' Ray said. 'Everybody knows about that.'

'The merchant banker he filled in.' Charlie bunched a fist. 'Think you can buy up all our farms and get away with it, do you, you English swine? Take that.'

Charlie pretended to hit Gary Willis.

'Oh, that,' Shirley said. 'Is it actually true?'

'What's that matter to these buggers?' Gary said.

'Watch it, Willis.' Ray held Charlie's beer glass over Gary's head and tilted it threateningly.

Just then a customer put down his glass of lager, detached himself from a small group of companions and leaned across the reporters' table in a conspiratorial fashion, like a trader in dirty postcards.

'Not met him yet then, this nationalist maniac?'

Charlie and Ray favoured this native with their open, friendly, reporters' smiles. They couldn't see him very well because the public bar had bad lighting, as distinct from soft lighting.

'Do you know him, then?' Shirley Gillies asked.

'Surprisingly distinguished-looking, he is. Not, you know, tremendously *tall*. But powerfully-built. What the Welsh consider a fine figure of a man.'

'Like, short and fat?' said Charlie.

'Stocky,' corrected the customer. 'A good beard on him, too, but tidy. Dresses casual, like, but not . . . not a *slovenly* man.'

'Looks a bit like you, then?' Ray Wheeler said.

'Indeed.' The man put out a hand. 'Guto Evans, my name.'

He took a deep breath and, with visible effort, added, 'At your service.'

A dark-haired man came in through the bottom door and quietly took a seat at the adjacent table, behind Shirley Gillies.

'Hullo, Berry,' Shirley said.

'Hi,' he said quietly.

'Where are you staying?'

'Dunno yet. I just got here. Where are *you* staying?'

'Plas Meurig,' Shirley said smugly. 'Beeb's taken about ten rooms, what with all the telly boys and the technicians. Charlie and Ray are awfully miffed.' She lowered her voice. 'That's Guto Evans, by the way, the Plaid Cymru candidate. Isn't he perfect?'

'You here on your own, then?' Ray Wheeler said to Guto. 'No aides, agent, entourage?'

'My local, this is,' Guto told him. 'I tend not to require any political advice on which brand of lager to select. Can I get you boys a drink, or is the English Press immune to bribery?'

'Son,' said Ray Wheeler, 'you've obviously got a big future in politics. Mine's a brandy.'

'Come and talk to us,' Charlie said. 'Tell us what this election is *really* about.'

'Off the record, is it?' Guto said dubiously. 'I've been warned about you boys.'

'Oh, sure,' Charlie said. 'Don't you worry about a thing, Guto. We're all old hands at this game, except for Gary, and his paper ignores everything he writes anyway.' Gary Willis looked very annoyed, and Charlie chuckled and offered Guto a cigar.

'Look, I have to walk back to the Plas Meurig,' said Shirley Gillies, 'Or I won't get my dinner. I'll talk to you again, Guto, OK?'

'I'll walk with you,' Berry Morelli said. 'Dark out there.'

'Amazing, isn't it,' Shirley said, plump body even plumper in an enormous pink padded ski-jacket. 'I mean, it's just a village, really. A big, untidy village.'

Seven p.m. The lights of Pontmeurig seemed vague and sparse, suffocating in a cold night mist. There was no moon, no stars.

'You were expecting neon?' said Berry.

Shirley shivered and wobbled. 'I suppose not. Still . . .'

'Yeah, I know what you mean. That frontier-town feel.'

They walked across the Meurig bridge. No lights were reflected in the river heaving sluggishly below.

'Berry, look, I was awfully sorry about Giles,' Shirley mumbled. 'We weren't very kind to him, were we?'

'Kind?'

'It's horribly ironic, though, isn't it, that we're all out here and he's . . . I mean, I was picturing him in that pub. He'd have been centre stage, holding forth, correcting our pronunciation of Welsh names. Absolutely in his element.'

'Yeah.'

'I mean, isn't it just so *cruel*?'

They walked down from the bridge and after a few yards there was a right turning, a sweeping drive and pillars supporting illuminated AA and RAC signs. In the middle distance, a floodlit façade, a colonial-style verandah. The Plas Meurig Hotel. Two-star.

'Thanks Berry. I don't think I would've enjoyed walking down here alone. Are you here for the duration?'

He shook his head. 'Two days.'

'So where are you going to sleep tonight?'

'This an invitation, Shirley?' He was being polite.

'Gosh . . .' Shirley simpered. 'I suppose it is rather a cold night to spend in one's car. But I think not, really. Not at the *start* of a campaign. I generally prefer to let the excitement build a little before I start to let myself go.'

Shit, Berry thought sourly, heading back over the bridge. This was what they meant by election fever?

The thought of even attempting to spend a night in an Austin Healy Sprite made Berry quicken his pace. It hadn't occurred to him that accommodation might turn out a problem.

What he didn't want was to stay in the same establishment as Firth and Wheeler and those guys. He was here on a mission, and it didn't have anything to do with politics.

He speeded up, seeking to stride through his own sadness and guilt, but they were frozen around him in the mist. It had made big, deep razor-slits in his life, this thing. Might have cost him the only person who could still make him laugh.

'Well, really, it's no good, is it?' Miranda had said as he brought down the lid of his suitcase. For once, being low-voiced, low-key, absolutely and uncharacteristically serious. Sitting on a hard wooden chair well away from the bed.

'Honestly,' she'd said. 'I'm terribly, terribly sorry about your friend.'

'But?'

'But I'm not sure I want to be associated with a really crazy person any more.'

So, there it was. The bottom line. The boy's neurotic.

'Listen, maybe you're right.' Spreading his hands, appealing for some understanding. 'Like, I can't say if I'm crazy. How can I know that? I just have to go find out. I got no choice. Not now.'

Miranda had looked about as sad as she was capable of looking. Berry had made her take his key in case she needed a nice central place to sleep, throw wild parties.

'Oh God,' Maybe a spark of her old self. 'I've got the awful feeling I once played this scene in a World War One spoof at the Edinburgh fringe. Go away. Go and play with your ghosts, Morelli. Your *Welsh* ghosts.'

Walking back now into this one-horse town in search of some place to sleep. Solitary like Clint Eastwood in a spaghetti Western. Except Clint was tough, needed no friends and no reassurance. Also Clint knew he was not neurotic.

Berry Morelli stared savagely down the underlit street. It was just about the last place anybody could imagine being part of Britain. Sunk so far into its own private gloom that when people moaned about the place, they moaned in a language nobody outside even wanted to understand. Some deep irony there. He wondered what it would be like for whoever won this election, sitting up there in the Mother of Parliaments, representing *this*. Honourable Member for Shitheap, Wales.

Berry chuckled cynically to himself. As the evening advanced, the town could almost be said to be filling up with people. A Land-Rover disgorged four men and a woman into the main street. Two kids on motor bikes cruised down the street, circled the castle car park and then cruised back. Night life in Pontmeurig. A black-haired woman in a white mac glanced at Berry as she walked past. She had an oval face and heavy eyelids and she looked no more happy than he might have expected, given the surroundings. He wondered if she was a hooker, but decided not.

CHAPTER XXXIX

S HE poured another cup of tea, having a sour, perverse kind of competition with herself to see how strong she could make it, and how strong she could drink it.

Outside the window it was not Saturday night in Pontmeurig, but it *looked* like Saturday night. That is, there were more than half a dozen people on the streets, the town having come alive in the hour after nine o'clock.

They weren't all here for the by-election. The sudden excitement had brought out local people, hoping perhaps to catch sight of some half-famous politician, here to campaign for Simon Gallier or Wayne Davies. Tomorrow night, two of Plaid Cymru's MPs would be here to support Guto. Big deal, she thought.

Knowing that really she ought to be throwing herself into this campaign, knocking on doors, scattering leaflets. Support your local boy and your local party, you know it makes sense.

Her hands tightened on the window ledge. Street light was washing in the pits and craters of a face beneath the lamp.

Bethan drank some dark tea, which was horrible and burned her mouth. It seemed as if every time she looked out of her window she saw one or both of the boys who'd attacked Giles. Shambling out of the Drovers' or into the tobacconist's that Guto's parents used to own. Grinning at each other. Arrogant, like crows.

Or perhaps it wasn't them at all. She didn't trust her own perceptions any more.

This morning she had been to County Hall in Carmarthen to see an assistant in the office of the Director of Education. She had asked for Roy Phillips, who was nice and had helped her in the past and who could be relied upon at least to give her a sympathetic hearing. But Roy had taken early retirement,

223

she'd been told. They'd sent her to a chisel-faced young man with rimless glasses, like a junior officer in the Gestapo, and she hadn't known where to begin.

Eventually, Bethan had made herself say it, and the junior officer had leaned back in his leather swivel chair and blinked.

'Mrs McQueen . . . I hardly know how to react. Have you discussed this with the parents?'

'No. They would, naturally, object strongly. Parents always do.'

He was looking urbane and half-amused. They were speaking Welsh.

'I confess, this is the first time such a proposition has ever been put to me by a head teacher. I find it rather extraordinary.'

'The circumstances are fairly unique. The village is very enclosed. Too self . . . self-absorbed. I've been convinced for some time that the children need exposure to a wider culture. All I am asking is that it should go on the next list. That the possibility should be debated at county level.'

'You are aware that this was mooted some years ago, when we were particularly short of money.' He had probably still been at university at the time, Bethan thought. 'And there was an enormous row. If you remember, the committee decided that this was a good school with a terrific record . . . And, of course, there was the question of transportation in winter.'

'I remember, but . . .'

'And now, with the roll approaching a reasonably healthy level for a rural area, the prospect of fifty pupils in a year or two, you come here – one of our, ah, brightest head teachers – to say you think your school should be closed down.'

'Yes.' Bethan had stuck out her jaw, determined. 'I don't think it's educationally viable. I used to believe in small schools. I no longer consider them valid. Not this one anyway.'

'Extraordinary,' he said. 'You would be putting yourself out of a job.'

'Yes.'

'I think you should put all this writing, Mrs McQueen.'

Oh God, Bethan thought. What am I doing here? He thinks I'm off my head.

The education official was peering at her over his glasses in the manner of a far older and more experienced man. Bethan hated him already.

'I'm wondering,' he said, 'if there isn't something more to all this. How do you get on with the other teacher? Mrs Morgan, isn't it?'

'I am sorry to have troubled you,' Bethan said tightly, in English. 'You are right. Perhaps I'll put this in writing to the Director.'

'It would be best.'

She'd left then, her dignity in shreds. She hadn't gone back to the school. Could not face Buddug – who, she felt, would know exactly where she had been and why.

Bethan had gone straight home – just over an hour's drive – where she'd thrown her coat on the settee, put the kettle on and was plugging in the electric fire when the phone rang. It was a welfare adviser in the education department, a woman she knew slightly. They had wasted no time.

'We think you should take two or three weeks off.'

'Oh?'

'You've obviously had a very stressful time lately. Finding that body. And the man who . . . Why don't you go and see your doctor? Get him to give you something to help you relax. Some of us thought you went back to work rather too soon after your husband died.'

'What about the school?'

'Don't worry about that. We've spoken to Mrs Morgan, and offered her a relief teacher. But she says she can manage very well on her own.'

The phone shook in Bethan's hand.

They had rung Buddug. Well, of course they had. They must have rung her within minutes of Bethan leaving Carmarthen. She could almost hear the shrill babble over the phone . . . 'Oh, the poor girl . . . yes, very, very sad, I have tried to help her, but it has all been getting on top of her . . . No, indeed, I don't think she is good for the children in this state, not at all . . . Perhaps a different post somewhere would be the answer . . .'

Bethan had flung her coat back on and walked around and

around the town in the dark, feeling like a ghost condemned to an endless circuit. Well, she had to do it. She had to try.

Now there was nothing left to try. She'd returned to the flat over the bookshop and made strong tea, her final bitter refuge.

Standing in the window now, watching the town filling up with strangers. New life out there.

Finding that body. And the man who . . .

. . . had been lying face-down among a scattering of books. Black books. Hands frozen like claws. Hands which had torn the books from the shelves in a frenzy, nail marks scored down black spines.

Morgan had turned him over with one hand, effortless. His bloodless lips pulled back in a snarl. Eyes glazed-over but still screaming. How could eyes scream? Bethan had turned her head away and run from the house. Run down the path, between the sycamores, leaving the iron gate swinging behind her.

Oh, Giles.

Oh, God.

'Where'd the guys go?'

He was addressing the Nationalist candidate, Evans. Nobody else in the bar he recognised, apart from a couple of MPs drinking Scotch and examining a map. 'Buggered if I know, Keith,' one of the MPs was saying. 'By tomorrow night, I'll have done my stint, so I couldn't care less.'

'Charlie and Ray,' said Guto, 'and young Gary . . . have gone for a meal. I recommended the Welsh Pizza House.' He grinned malevolently. 'Serve them right.'

Berry Morelli noticed how Guto's beard split in half when he grinned. The guy looked like some kind of caveman.

'American, eh?' Guto said.

'Sure am.' Berry said, like an American. 'Just great to be in your wunnerful country,' he added wearily.

'Yes, I bet,' said Guto. 'You want to ask me any questions before I get too pissed?'

'No,' said Berry, who wasn't expected to file a story the following day, unless something happened – and Addison Walls's definition of 'something' usually meant several people dead.

'Good,' said Guto. 'Bloody shattered, I am. I think I shot my mouth off again.'

'I thought that was what politics was about.'

Clearly less inhibited in the presence of someone who was neither English nor Welsh, Guto affected a drawling English accent. ' "Seeaw! Tell us about yourself, Guto! Why does it say in your Press handout that you're only a part-time lecturer?" ' His voice sank bitterly. 'Because this is Wales, pal. I could only get a *full*-time lecturer's job in England.'

'You wanna drink?' said Berry.

'Aye, why the devil not. Pint of Carlsberg? What can you say, eh? One day in politics and I've had it up to the bloody eyeballs.'

'One day in politics is a long time, buddy.'

'You know what else they asked me? What was the name of the rock and roll band I played bass guitar with? *What was the name of the flaming band?* Why the hell would they want to know that?'

'You really are new to this game, aren't you?' said Berry.

'Is it that bloody obvious?'

'They had to know the name of the band so they could have it checked out in the morgue.'

Guto looked mystified.

'Most members of most rock bands,' Berry said patiently, 'have stuff in their past that doesn't lie down too easy with a career in politics. Like getting busted for dope, smashing up hotel rooms. Yeah?'

'Ah . . . right,' said Guto. 'But no. Not me. Once got busted for Woodbines in the school lavatories, I did. But drugs, no.'

'Hotel rooms?'

'The hotels in these parts, nobody would notice.'

'Mr Clean, huh?'

'Mr Bloody Spotless,' said Guto. 'Well, you know . . .'

'Yeah.'

Guto grabbed his pint with both hands. At which point, a thought seemed to strike him and he put the glass tankard down on the bartop and said seriously, 'I never asked – are you a reporter?'

Berry started to laugh. He laughed so hard he thought he was going to lose control of his bladder. He laughed so hard people began to stare at him.

'What did I say?' said Guto.

Berry shook his head, tears in his eyes. He was thinking of the po-faced front-bench bastards in the House of Commons. He was thinking of the Energy Secretary making a careful statement at the bottom of his manicured lawn in the Cotswolds. He was thinking of his dad and a particular senator.

In the normal way of things, none of this would have seemed funny enough to make him lose control in a public bar.

He wondered, after a few seconds, if what he was really doing wasn't crying.

'I'm sorry,' Berry said, getting his act back together. 'Yeah, I'm a reporter, but I don't think I came here to report. I think I came to go to a funeral.'

Guto said nothing.

'My pal died,' Berry said. 'Tomorrow he gets cremated.'

'Oh Christ,' said Guto. 'Giles Freeman, is it?'

Berry looked hard at the Nationalist guy. What did he know about Giles Freeman? 'I'm looking for someplace to stay,' he said. 'One night, maybe two.'

'Every hotel in this town is booked solid,' said Guto.

'That's what I heard.'

'Giles Freeman, eh?'

'Yep. You knew him? I guess he knew you.'

'We met,' said Guto. 'Just the one time. But memorably. Looking for a posh place, are you?'

'Huh?'

'To stay.'

'I'm looking for a bed.'

'My Mam is feeling aggrieved,' Guto said. 'She does bed and breakfast all through the summer. Now, when everybody wants to stay in Pontmeurig, I have to tell her: forget it, Mam. What is it going to look like, you taking in party workers or reporters? *English* reporters, for God's sake! Me out there on the hustings and you cashing in. So, very aggrieved she is feeling.'

'What's she charge?' Berry noticed Guto was suddenly looking at him the way business people the world over looked at Americans.

Guto's eyes gleamed. 'Thirty-five quid a night?'

'Th . . .?'

'Big breakfast, mind,' said Guto.

Guto's mother was a small, scurrying, squeaky creature with an agonisingly tight perm. In a living room so crammed with little jugs and vases and thousands of polished plates that Berry didn't like to move his arms, she told him seriously that Guto would be the death of her.

'She is delighted, really,' Guto said. 'She's never had an American to stay. What's your name anyway?'

'Morelli.'

'That's an American name?'

'Don't be so rude, Guto,' Mrs Evans snapped. She smiled at Berry and her teeth moved. 'We had some Morellis, we did, at the back of us in Merthyr. Do you know Merthyr . . .?'

'Of course he bloody doesn't, Mam. Listen, Morelli, we can't do hash browns or steak and eggs for breakfast. Well, eggs are OK, but . . .'

Berry told them he was vegetarian.

'Oh dear, oh dear, we haven't any of that,' wailed Mrs Evans, squeezing the corners of her apron in anguish. 'What will you think of us?'

'Toast?' said Berry. 'Marmalade?'

'An American vegetarian?' said Guto, aghast.

'He'll be the death of me, this boy,' said Mrs Evans.

CHAPTER XL

BERRY spent the night under a mountain of blankets in a bed like a swamp. He slept surprisingly well, and, at eight-fifteen on a grey Pontmeurig morning, came down to a table set for one, with a spare napkin. There was thick toast, thin toast and toasted rolls. There were three kinds of marmalade.

'These jars are new,' Berry said.

'I sent Guto for to wake them up at the shop,' Mrs Evans explained. 'I still don't feel right about it. I can't have you paying for a proper breakfast.'

It occurred to Berry that Mrs Evans did not know she was charging thirty-five pounds a night.

'Guto had to leave early to prepare for his Press conference,' she said. 'He'll make a terrible mess of it, I know he will. He'll say all the wrong things.'

He already did, Berry thought. 'He'll be fine,' he said.

'Do you think so?'

'Guy's a natural politician.'

'He won't win, I'm afraid,' Mrs Evans said. 'And then he'll come on with all this bravado. And then he'll drink himself silly.'

'They say he has a good chance.'

Mrs Evans shook her head. 'Any chances he has he'll ruin. That kind of boy. They offered him a job once, down in Exeter. Head of the History Department. He wouldn't have it. That kind of boy, see.'

'This is great,' Berry said, munching a slice of toast with ginger marmalade.

'It's not a proper breakfast.'

'It's my kind of breakfast,' Berry said, 'Can you tell me where I find the police department in this town?'

There were two public buildings in Pontmeurig built in the past five years. This morning Berry would visit both. One was the crematorium, the other was the police station.

The police station was so modern it had automatic glass doors.

'Who's in charge here?' Berry said.

'I am,' said an elderly police constable behind the latest kind of bulletproof security screen. 'So they tell me.' His voice came out of a circular metal grille.

'You don't have detectives?'

'Detectives, is it?' The constable looked resentful. 'What is it about?'

'It's about what I guess you'd call a suspicious death,' said Berry.

The policeman's expression remained static. He picked up a telephone and pointed to some grey leather and chrome chairs. 'Take a seat, my friend,' he said. 'I'll see if Gwyn Arthur's arrived.'

Above the security screen, the digital station clock was printing out 8.57 a.m.

The huge oak hatstand was a determined personal touch in Detective Chief Inspector Gwyn Arthur Jones's new office, where everything else was plastic or metal or glass and coloured grey or white. Berry decided the Chief Inspector must be the only guy in the CID who still wore a hat.

'I can appreciate your concern,' Gwyn Arthur said. 'I can even understand your suspicions.' He spread his long fingers on the plastic of his desktop. 'But none of us can argue with a post mortem report.'

He took an envelope from a drawer of the desk. 'You realise I don't have to show you this.'

'Good of you,' Berry said.

'Trying to be cooperative I am. As I say, I can understand your suspicions.'

Before consenting to discuss Giles Freeman, the Chief Inspector had spent a good ten minutes lighting his pipe and asking Berry a lot of questions about himself. Casual and leisurely, but penetrating. He'd examined Berry's ID and expressed considerable curiosity about American Newsnet before appearing to accept that Berry's interest in this case was personal, as distinct from journalistic.

'This is the autopsy report, yeah?'

'You can skip the first three-quarters if you aren't interested in things like what your friend had for breakfast on the day he died. Go to the conclusion.'

'I already did,' said Berry. 'Some of these medical terms elude me, but what it seems to be saying is that Giles died of a brain tumour. Which is what we were told.'

'Indeed,' said Gwyn Arthur. For a Welshman, he was surprisingly tall and narrow. He had a half-moon kind of face and flat grey hair.

'I don't get it.'

'What don't you get?'

'This stuff. These . . .' Berry held up the report. 'This mean bruising, or what?'

'More or less. Abrasions. Consistent with a fall on a hard surface. Consistent also, I may say, with a blow. Which occurred to the doctor who examined him in the hospital and who passed on his suspicions to us.'

'He died in hospital?'

'No, he died at his home. Let me explain from the beginning.'

'Yeah,' said Berry. 'You do that.'

Gwyn Arthur Jones talked for twenty minutes, puffing his pipe and staring down at his fingers on the plastic desk. He talked of the doctor's suspicions that Giles had been in a fight and Giles's insistence that he'd fallen in the Castle car-park.

'Which, considering the state of his clothes, was plausible enough. And was not something we could contest as, if there was another protagonist, we have not found him. Or her – who can tell these days? And I would add that the doctor did suspect at the time, from the way Mr Freeman was behaving, that there might have been brain damage. He wanted to make an appointment at Bronglais Hospital in Aberystwyth, but your friend flatly refused and discharged himself.'

Berry smiled. 'Sounds like Giles.'

'They parted with some acrimony. Personally I think the doctor ought to have exercised his prerogative to prevent your friend from driving. Still, he appears to have made it home, without mishap, to Y Groes. Where, it seems, his luck ran out.'

Claire Freeman, who told the police she knew nothing of Giles's fall, had been out when he arrived home. She was not expecting him back from London until that evening.

Gwyn Arthur said, 'Why did he come home early, do you know?'

Berry shrugged. 'Any chance he had to get out of London, he took it. He was kind of obsessed with Y Groes – with having this bolthole, you know?'

Gwyn Arthur sighed. 'It is a common aberration. Among the English.'

'So what happened?'

'There is a schoolteacher in Y Groes. It seems she had become quite friendly with Mr and Mrs Freeman and was giving them lessons in the Welsh language. She was among a group of people who saw him lying in the car park on the Thursday night and went to help him. The following day, Mrs McQueen – that's the teacher – learned that your friend had discharged himself from the hospital and gone home. So, in her lunch break, she went up to his house to see if he was all right. She knocked and got no reply, so she looked through the downstairs windows and saw a man's body, in a collapsed state, on the floor of one of the rooms. She went to the pub for help and two of the customers went back with her and broke down the rear door.'

Berry was picturing the judge's house, the back porch near the window he'd prised open with a screwdriver on a late summer's afternoon.

'Mr Freeman had probably been dead for over an hour by the time they got to him.'

Gwyn Arthur took another envelope from a drawer. 'Do you want to look at these?'

'What are they?'

From the brown envelope Gwyn Arthur pulled a dark-grey folder, about six inches by eight, on which was printed, in black, the words DYFED-POWYS POLICE.

'As I say, it did look somewhat suspicious at first. Mrs

McQueen telephoned the police. I drove across, with the scenes-of-crime officer. These photographs were taken before the body was moved.'

Berry felt a little sick, tasted ginger marmalade. He opened the dark grey folder.

'They would have been produced at the inquest, had there been one,' said Gwyn Arthur.

The pictures were in colour. They'd been taken with flash. Berry flinched.

Giles's lips were drawn back into a twisted parody of a grin. Both eyes were open, the left one purple and black. The bruising spread down one side of Giles's face and mingled with the freckles.

Another picture was taken from further back and higher up, like the photographer had been standing on a chair.

'Shit,' Berry breathed.

It showed Giles sprawled crookedly, arms extended. All around him were scattered black books. One had its binding partially torn away, and curling pages lay around.

Tissue-thin. Berry could hear the pages whispering.

Next to Giles's head was a red dragon's head, spitting faded, threadbare fire into the dead man's right ear.

'The study,' Berry said, going cold. 'He died in the study.'

'You have been in this house?'

'Once,' Berry said. 'Just once. What happened to the books?'

'He appears to have had some kind of, er, final fit, should I say? Obviously grabbed at the shelves to try and prevent himself falling. Dragged out the books. Quite a frenzy.'

'So you ordered an autopsy.'

'Naturally. The state of the room suggested a possible struggle. Oh yes, we had the portable incident room on standby, I can tell you. But by teatime it was clear we had all overreacted. These things happen.'

'Brain tumour.'

'It had been forming for – well, who knows how long. Weeks, months, years? His wife tells us he had been suffering from very severe headaches. Mrs McQueen confirms this. Perhaps, you yourself . . .'

'No. He never mentioned headaches.'

'You see, with a condition like this, his apparent black-out on the car-park . . . Hit his head on a car bumper, he said. All consistent. It is a great tragedy, but that's all it is. Natural causes. No inquest. Unless there's something you feel you can add?'

'No,' Berry said. 'Nothing I have to add. Thanks, Inspector.'

Gwyn Arthur Jones put the slim photo-album back in its envelope. 'I'm very sorry.'

'One thing,' Berry said. 'His wife. Claire.'

'Quiet little girl,' said Gwyn Arthur.

'Where was she when they found Giles?'

'My, you are a suspicious chap,' said Gwyn Arthur with a half-smile. 'Mrs Freeman was quite a short distance away, at a friend's house, as it turns out. Mrs Dafis, is it? I don't know without looking up the statement. Obviously she feels very bad about not being there when her husband arrived home and him dying like that, on his own. I hear the funeral is today.'

'You going?'

'Well, see, I don't mean any disrespect, but not appropriate, is it, now?'

'Guess not.'

'See, even if he'd gone to Bronglais, as the doctor wanted, the chances are it would have been too late, the size of that bloody thing. Any time he could have gone.'

'Malignant? I was kind of shaky on the big words.'

Gwyn Arthur's pipe had gone out. He laid it on the grey plastic desktop and looked at it.

'As the devil,' he said. 'As the bloody devil.'

CHAPTER XLI

THEY came in from the Lampeter end, George twice stopping to consult the map, slowing at every signpost. Terribly galling, because he was normally such a fast driver, often recklessly so in his wife's opinion.

'Pretty obscure place,' George grunted. 'Don't want to get it wrong.'

'You don't want to get there at all,' Elinor said icily.

'Elinor, I still say . . .'

'And *why* do you think we weren't told?' Elinor demanded. 'Because I didn't tell her about *his* death. As simple as that.'

'I can't believe,' George said, slowing the Volvo for another signpost, 'that she would be quite so petty.'

'You mean, not so petty as me?'

'That is *not* what I said. Elinor, for Christ's sake will you stop this.'

'We can't be far off,' Elinor said and affected a shudder. 'I can feel it somehow.'

George sighed and kept quiet. He was a rumpled man with hair of nicotine and white. He'd never really taken to his son-in-law, she thought. George avoided people in high-profile jobs. He wasn't a high-profile person. He'd never minded his daughter being a photographer, though, because the photographer was the one person guaranteed always to be *behind* the camera.

She was like him in a way. Claire. George's daughter. Wife of Elinor's dead son-in-law.

The shock, for Elinor, had been quite stunning. And to chance upon it, without warning, in Giles's own newspaper, spread on the ceramic worktop after breakfast, four brief paragraphs of obituary, a quote from the editor: immense flair . . . terrible tragedy . . . so young . . . will be hard to replace.

Elinor had *liked* Giles. He'd been strong in his opinions, forthright. Whereas George had always been so *grey*. She'd been sure that Giles would, after a few weeks, realise the impossibility of living in Wales and lead Claire back. Lead. That was it. He'd always been a leader. That was what she'd liked about Giles, that staunchly English quality of leadership.

'I don't know where we're going to stay,' George was saying. 'You do realise there's a by-election on.'

'We'll find somewhere,' Elinor said, more briskly than she felt. 'Just get us there.'

'It's four miles,' George said. 'That's what the signpost said. But you know what they say about Welsh miles.'

The aftershock had been the discovery that Giles's funeral was not to be in London. Elinor had learned this by telephoning his paper. She'd phoned the number in Y Groes about twenty times, of course, and got an answering machine, Claire's voice . . . in Welsh! She'd refused to leave a message after the tone. 'Claire, I'm sorry, I refuse to leave a message,' she'd said once, voice faltering, and hung up, regretful and feeling rather stupid.

At the paper, the political editor said he too was surprised that the funeral was being held in Wales, although with both Giles's parents being dead he supposed there was no special reason for it to be done in London. And with the by-election on, there'd at least be enough reporters out there to make a respectable showing.

Elinor had been glad, at least, to learn that Giles was not to be buried in the churchyard at Y Groes. Even the ceremony would not be held there.

And yet she did wonder why.

And still she had not spoken to Claire. Her daughter's reaction on their appearance at the funeral was something she could not even attempt to predict. She accepted that they had not parted on the best of terms, but for the girl to avoid her own mother at a time when a mother was needed the most . . .

George had taken a hopelessly circuitous route and they had turned into the road linking Aberystwyth and Pontmeurig, entering the grim valley of the disused lead mine.

Feeling at once sorrowful, offended and inadequate, Elinor experienced the pinprick of a small tear. Her daughter was a widow. A widow and childless.

'I suppose she'll marry again,' George said suddenly, as if he'd picked up her thoughts. Which was something he never did, being far too insensitive.

'What do you mean?'

'She's young. I suppose if she stays out here, there'll be lots of chaps . . . that is, I mean . . .'

'Stays?' Elinor's body went as rigid as the stark towers of the lead mine. 'Stays *here*? Are you *quite* mad?'

Guto was in deep shit.

Berry had seen it coming, a whole dump-truck load. Guto underneath, apparently oblivious of the danger.

The man steering the dump truck, one sure finger on the wheel, was F. C. W. 'Bill' Sykes, Political Editor of the *Daily Telegraph*, one of fourteen reporters and two TV crews, ranged in a three-quarter circle around the candidate. Television lights were belching hot glare into the makeshift gladiatorial arena in the shabby lounge of the Drovers' Arms.

They were mob-handed now, no longer the inoffensive affable guys in the public bar last night. Notebooks and pocket cassette machines next to the cups at their elbows. No alcohol, just hard caffeine. They meant business.

Berry Morelli had covered one British by-election before and knew they were basically all the same: every morning, for about a fortnight, each of the political parties would hold a Press conference with the candidate and some heavy back-up from Westminster – a minister or a shadow-minister or, on perhaps one occasion, the party leader. In Plaid Cymru's case, Berry guessed, the leader would show up pretty often, on account of the party had only three MPs to pull out.

They must be saving the big guns for later. Guto was doing his first conference solo, accompanied by only one minder – Plaid's General Secretary, a diffident guy in tinted glasses. This afternoon they'd be out on the streets, canvassing, pressing the flesh, as they put it. And then, each night there'd be public meetings to address.

Hard grind.

And this morning, the baptism of fire.

It started with a question about an act of vandalism perpetrated by the Welsh Language Society against a leading high-street building society which had been unwise enough to refuse a mortgage application in Welsh.

'Ah, well,' Guto explained, 'they are youngsters with a mission and sometimes they get carried away.'

'Usually by the police,' Ray Wheeler said from the table nearest Guto's. There was laughter.

'All right then, old boy,' rumbled Bill Sykes, 'While we're on the subject of brushes with the law . . .'

He was unfolding a cutting from Wales's national newspaper, the *Western Mail*.

'Let's get this one out of the way, eh?' Sykes said kindly. 'Clear the air. This business of you being questioned by the constabulary about minor injuries inflicted on some poor chap from London who'd had the temerity to buy himself a farmhouse near here. Small incident in a pub, I believe.'

'*This* pub, Bill,' Charlie Firth said. 'May even have been this very room. This is where they hold the auctions, isn't it?'

'Was it *really*?' said Sykes, as if he didn't know. 'Anyway, let's polish it off now, shall we? Then we can all have a nice peaceful campaign. What exactly happened, Mr Evans?'

The room fell into a hush.

What the hell was this? Mr Clean? Mr Bloody Spotless? Berry caught Guto's eye and raised an eyebrow.

Guto appeared unconcerned.

'Well, you know,' he said to the silent, expectant Press, 'I feel a bit offended. I cannot understand why you boys are concentrating on this one little incident. Here I am, the party hard-man, scarcely a night goes by without I don't beat up an Englishman . . .'

The head of the General Secretary of Plaid Cymru swivelled through ninety degrees. Berry couldn't see his eyes behind the tinted glasses but he was pretty sure that here was one worried man.

'. . . and you pick on the one occasion when I am standing by that very bar across the hall, minding my pint of Carlsberg, and suddenly I am at the centre of a most regrettable kerfuffle for the sole reason that I happen to be in the path of a gentleman who falls off his stool.'

There was a hoot of derision from the floor.

He's on a tightrope here, Berry thought. These guys catch him out in a lie, he's finished. He was surprised to find himself caring, just slightly, that Guto's campaign should not come to an ignominiously premature conclusion. Even if the guy *was* staging the bed-and-breakfast scam of the century.

'Then why did the police find it necessary to question you?' demanded Gary Willis. Berry could see one of the TV cameramen going in tight on Guto's face. He could see Shirley Gillies urgently adjusting the level on her tape-recorder.

'I think perhaps,' said Guto, glancing across the room, maybe not so sure of himself now, 'that you should direct that question at my good friend, Chief Inspector Gwyn Arthur Jones. Not for me to answer on his behalf, is it?'

Playing for time, Berry thought. But these guys have all the time in the world.

'Come now,' said a rat-faced reporter Berry didn't recognise. 'Let's not evade the issue. The inference is that you feel so strongly about English people buying up all the best property in these parts that you're liable to lose your temper when faced with a blatant example of . . .'

'I think . . .' Guto's voice was raised.

'I think perhaps you should give the question rather more serious consideration before you answer, Mr Evans,' said Bill Sykes with magisterial menace.

'Come on, Guto,' Charlie Firth said. 'Let's have the truth.'

He's had it, Berry thought sadly. They're gonna rip him apart.

Guto raised a hand to quell the murmurs. 'I think we can resolve this very minor issue . . .'

'Not minor for you,' somebody said.

'. . . if I introduce you to a friend of mine.'

At the back of the room, a metal-framed chair fell with a clang as a man got to his feet. 'Terribly sorry,' they heard, a kind of Chelsea purr. 'I do seem to have a knack of knocking furniture over in this place.'

Everybody turned, including the TV cameramen. Everybody except for Berry, who was standing at the back of the room next to the guy who'd deliberately knocked his chair over.

And was therefore the only one to see Guto expelling a mouthful of air in manifest relief before his beard split in delight.

You bastard, Berry said under his breath. You smart son of a bitch.

'I was bloody worried for a minute or two, though,' Guto confessed to him outside. 'Couldn't see a thing for those flaming lights. I thought, Christ, what if he's not there? What if he was pissing up my leg all the time?'

The reporters had shuffled off to the Plas Meurig for the next two party Press conferences. They were almost in carnival mood. Berry had watched amazed as Bill Sykes had shaken Guto by the hand and Ray Wheeler had patted him on the shoulder. Suddenly they love the guy, Berry thought. He turned it all around.

The merchant banker from London – the guy who'd bought the farm and a bruised nose – had raised a hand to Guto, politely rebuffed the exhortations from the Press to elaborate further on the story and slid into the Mercedes waiting on a double yellow line outside the Drovers'.

'I confess,' said Guto, 'that I am developing a certain respect for the English. He came up to me, you know, after the *Western Mail* ran that piece. No hard feelings, old chap, all this, buys me a drink. Well, both a bit pissed, we were, see, when it happened, and he knew the damage it could do. So he says, look, boy, I'll come along and make a public statement if you like.'

'What can I say, Evans? You blew them away.'

Guto grinned evilly, 'I did, though, didn't I?' He glanced around to make sure the reporters were out of sight, then he leapt up and punched the air. 'Oh boy, thank you English! Thank you, God!'

'You asshole,' Berry said. 'You . . .'

He fell silent. Around the corner came a hearse driven by a man with a bald head who nodded at Guto as he passed. Apart from the bald man, the hearse was empty.

'Gone to fetch your mate,' Guto said.

Berry nodded. 'How far's the crematorium from here?'

Guto took off his Plaid Cymru rosette and put in it a pocket of his jacket. He was wearing the black tie he'd borrowed from Dai Death. 'Not far,' he said. 'We can walk.'

CHAPTER XLII

THE funeral service for Giles Robert Freeman was pathetic-ally brief. A throwaway affair, Berry Morelli thought, compared with Old Winstone's London send-off.

The entire business took place in the new Pontmeurig crematorium, the first the town had ever had, Guto explained. Built because, when attempting to extend the local cemetery, the council had hit a massive shelf of hard rock which meant that any future graves would have had to be dug with dynamite.

At the end of a wooded lane behind the hospital, the new crematorium looked, from the outside, like a small factory with two discreet steel chimneys hardly hidden by recently-planted trees, especially in December.

The chapel inside was maybe a third full, mainly due to the Press contingent. Reporters had filed in, fresh from the Conservative, Simon Gallier's conference, as the organ drone began. Only a handful of people had been in place when Guto and Berry had arrived. Berry didn't recognise any of them at first, although a young woman in a black suit and gold earrings looked vaguely familiar.

The minister had begun the service before Berry realised that another woman, sitting in the front row two or three yards from the coffin must be Claire Freeman.

He'd met Claire maybe a couple of times, never spoken much with her. She was the quiet type.

Now he was staggered by how different she looked. And it wasn't only her hair, which he remembered as blonde and was now almost black.

He wondered if poor old Giles would recognise her. And then wondered why that thought had come to him.

The coffin of pale pine sat on a plinth covered in black velvet. Would it slide away when the moment came, or just slowly sink? Berry looked at the coffin and tried to banish the image of Giles with his empurpled eye and his hands clawing at the black books.

Not meant to be there, the English.

Giles would be here for ever now, filtered into the Welsh air through the steel chimneys.

But why not a mellow grey stone in a corner of the churchyard at Y Groes, where wild flowers grew and the air was soft with summer even when it wasn't summer?

The minister was a young guy with what Berry now recognised as a local accent. Each word was enunciated in that rounded, robust Welsh way which still didn't cover up the obvious fact that the minister didn't know a damn thing about Giles. When you listened to the words, rather than the music of the words, you realised it was just a bunch of platitudinous crap which could have applied, Berry thought, to some John Doe they'd pulled out of the river.

There was just one hymn. An English hymn that Berry had never heard before. As the congregation sang, with little gusto, he read the words on the flimsy service sheet they'd been handed.

> *Love is kind and suffers long*
> *Love is meek and knows no wrong.*

What did this have to say about Giles Freeman? Anything at all?

Berry began to feel angry. Was this how it ended? They just signed the guy out, quick as they could, and drew a neat line underneath. Would they give him a plaque somewhere: Giles Freeman, immigrant, didn't last long?

He looked over at Claire. She wore a plain, black dress and no jewellery apart from a heavy Celtic cross around her neck. Over the back of her chair was slung a faded, green waxed jacket, the kind Giles used to wear. It didn't seem like a tribute.

Claire's blonde hair, the couple times he'd met her, had always been neatly trimmed, cut close to the skull. Her new dark hair was longer and wilder. And Berry thought she seemed taller somehow, maybe the way she carried herself.

Although she wore no make-up that he could detect, she had with her a glamour he didn't recall.

Each time he looked at Claire he noticed that the other woman, in the black suit and the earrings, seemed to be looking at her too. He remembered where he'd seen this woman now. In the street last night. The one he'd wondered if she was a whore. He felt bad about that now; she didn't strike him that way at all today.

'Who's that?' he whispered to Guto. 'Woman in the earrings.'

Guto looked at him suspiciously. 'It's Bethan,' he whispered back. 'Bethan McQueen.'

'Ah,' said Berry. The schoolteacher referred to earlier by Chief Inspector Gwyn Arthur Jones.

As the congregation sank down after the hymn, he heard the sound of stiletto heels on the chequered tiles at the entrance, and then a slim woman of sixty or so came in, followed by a harassed-looking man tucking the end of his tie inside his jacket. There was a black smudge on his forehead. They sat across the aisle from Berry. The woman did not look at the man. But, after a short while, she too began to look hard at Claire Freeman, as if there was something there she couldn't quite believe.

Berry tried to work out if anyone was with Claire and came to the conclusion that the people nearest her just happened to be occupying those seats.

She was alone, and she didn't look as though she cared.

He searched her face for tearstains, any signs of grief. The face was without expression but calm and womanly and strong.

And sexy? That dark glamour?

Jesus Christ, Morelli. He felt uncomfortable, ashamed. He wanted to be out of here, and then he felt ashamed about that too. Ashamed at the relief he felt at the end, five minutes later, as the coffin drifted away below his eyeline, the machinery working smooth, silent magic under the velvet-covered plinth.

Giles had gone.

Without a sound. Without a word in his memory.

He looked at Guto and saw that Guto was looking at the woman in the gold earrings, Bethan McQueen, who was looking at where the coffin had been and was pale.

Outside, amid the leafless trees, she joined them.

'That's it then.' Guto said. 'That's the lot. Don't mess about, do they, the English?'

'They mess about as much as anybody,' Berry said. 'That's what's so . . .'

'I feel very empty,' Bethan McQueen was saying. 'It wasn't a funeral, it was . . .'

'Waste disposal,' Berry said. He kicked morosely at the ornamental light-green, crystalline gravel around the crematorium building.

'Bethan, this is Morelli. He was a friend of Giles Freeman.' Guto turned to Berry. 'Bethan was teaching him Welsh.'

'Without great success, though, I am afraid,' Bethan said, solemnly shaking hands with Berry.

Reporters came out in a bunch, Charlie Firth taking out one of his thin cigars, Ray Wheeler saying, '. . . down the pub and give the poor sod a decent wake, eh?'

The sixtyish couple hung around the doorway, apparently waiting for someone. The woman pointed at the man's forehead and he took out a handkerchief and wiped away the black mark.

'What did you mean,' Bethan said to Berry Morelli, 'by waste disposal?'

'I wouldn't mind so much, but the bloody thing was serviced a fortnight ago,' George Hardy said. 'I don't suppose you happened to notice a Volvo garage in the town.'

'You fool.' Elinor's features were pinched with contempt. 'Is it likely?'

'Suppose not. I wish she'd come out. Get this over.'

'All you've ever wanted, George, is to get things over.'

Claire did come out then. She was with the minister. They shook hands and then spoke briefly in Welsh. The minister went back into the crematorium, Claire approached her parents.

'I wondered if you would come,' she said.

The sky had darkened, with a warning of rain on the gathering wind.

'Hello, Claire,' said George. 'We had a dreadful journey and then the car broke down two miles from here and we had to be towed in. You look marvellous, doesn't she Elinor?'

George always came out with the wrong things, or the right things in the wrong order. But what were the right things, in this situation? How were you supposed to approach a daughter who had deliberately kept you in the dark about the sudden death of her husband?

And who was not the daughter you remembered.

'Yes,' Elinor said. 'She looks . . . well.'

Claire kissed her father and looked calmly at her mother.

Elinor could stand it no longer. 'Oh, Claire . . . ' Face crumbling, though the muscles were fighting it. 'Why?' She was furious with herself for this.

Claire stepped back. The wind caught her dark hair, which seemed three times as long and dense as Elinor remembered it.

'I wrote to you,' she said. 'The letter's probably waiting for you at home.'

'Why didn't you *phone*?' Elinor's eyes were glassy with frozen tears. 'I learned about it in the *newspaper*, for God's sake!'

Claire said, 'I'm sorry. I find this difficult to explain, but I could not invite you here. If you were going to come it had to be your decision.'

She's so remote from us, Elinor thought. Look at her, with her shaggy mane and her faraway eyes.

'How do you feel, darling?' George was saying. 'Are you all right?'

Claire smiled with dignity and composure.

'I am adjusting,' she said.

'We should offer our condolences to Claire, I guess.'

'I think you'll find,' Bethan said, 'that she doesn't need your condolences.' She turned her back on the chapel entrance. 'I have to go. I'm sorry.'

Berry watched her walk away down the gravel path. 'I think I need to talk to her.'

'I don't think so,' Guto said.

'She was the one found Giles, right?'

246

'Listen, Morelli, leave her alone, she's had problems.'

'*Giles* had problems.'

'I know, but she cannot help you. Her husband died, see, a few months ago, of leukaemia. She has not come to terms with that. Her nerves are not good, they've taken her off work.'

Plaid's bearded hard-man seemed oddly ill-at-ease, Berry thought.

'I've known her a long time. Fond of her, see.'

Clearly, Berry thought.

Plaid's General Secretary appeared at Guto's elbow. Away from the TV lights, he'd taken off his tinted glasses. 'You have twenty minutes to get some lunch, Guto, then we're off to Eglwys Fawr.'

'Eglwys Fawr?' Guto was dismayed. 'That's practically North Wales. We really have to start by canvassing the barbarians?'

'Work North to South of the constituency, I thought. Then back again.'

'You are the boss,' Guto conceded. 'See you tonight, Morelli?'

'Sure, but I may have to barter over the bill. Or maybe tell the tabloid boys how much you're charging.'

'You wouldn't . . .'

'Try me.'

Guto scowled at him and followed the General Secretary down the crematorium drive. Claire Freeman and the older couple walked past Berry; none of the three even looked at him.

At the bottom of the drive Guto turned and called back, 'Remember what I said about Bethan, Morelli. I don't know what you want here, but she can't help you, OK?'

Berry was suddenly alone on the ludicrous green gravel in front of the modern disposal plant that ate Giles Freeman.

A line of Bob Dylan's went through his head, something about pitying the poor immigrant, who wishes he'd stayed at home.

He tried to analyse how he felt. Whether he was out of his

mind or there was something happening here. He couldn't get a handle on any of it. All too . . . Words like amorphous, nebulous and numinous came into his head. Crazy stuff.

Rain began to tumble on him, and he ran down the drive and back into the town.

CHAPTER XLIII

THIS, Elinor thought, frozen into silence, could *not* be happening.

The ghastly little pointed spire loomed up in the centre of the windscreen and she almost screamed in revulsion.

'Rather pretty, really,' George said, and Elinor shrivelled him into the back seat with a blowlamp glare.

Claire drove the Land-Rover like a man, spinning the huge utility steering wheel, dark hair bouncing as she tossed the big vehicle through the gears. As though she were a farm girl who'd been driving Land-Rovers and tractors most of her life, Elinor thought in dismay.

It was, of course, all George's fault.

When the garage in Pontmeurig had said it would take a day, perhaps two, to get the parts, he ought to have told them to forget it and had the vehicle towed to the nearest Volvo dealer, no matter how far away that was.

But not George.

Not compliant, feeble George.

Elinor and Claire had been drinking dreadful instant coffee in some dismal teashop, saying stiff, formal things to each other when George had returned from the garage with the bad news.

'Problem is, there's nowhere to stay in this town,' he'd said. 'By-election, you see.'

And then, without even looking at Elinor, he'd turned automatically to his daughter and said . . .

Actually asked her, without even thinking . . .

'Don't suppose there's any chance of you putting us up for the night, is there, Claire?'

248

Elinor had wanted to pour her coffee over his head.

But she could not help noticing that, for the first time, Claire had appeared discomfited. 'I'm not sure that would be wise.'

Elinor was damn sure it wouldn't be wise, having long ago sworn never to set foot in that abominable house again.

'Well unless you can lend us a tent,' George said with a silly laugh, avoiding his wife's blazing gaze, 'I don't know quite what we're going to do. The garage chappie said Aberystwyth was about the nearest place we could hope to get in, and apparently several of the hotels there are closed for the winter. Bloody inconvenient.'

'It's absurd,' Elinor said.

And then Claire had said, 'Look, if it's only for one night, perhaps—'

'No!' She couldn't stop herself.

'I was thinking of the *Tafarn*,' Claire said. 'The village inn.'

And now the Land-Rover was rattling down from the hills, out of the forestry, Elinor next to Claire in the front, George in the back. Claire had told them she'd acquired the second-hand farm vehicle from someone called Dilwyn, in exchange for Giles's car. Which Elinor thought was a disgusting thing to do within a few days of his death, as well as a disturbing indication that Claire was now committed to living in a place where a Land-Rover was considered a sensible mode of transport.

A grey squirrel shot out of the hedge, apparently intent on hurling itself under their wheels. Claire ignored it.

'Look out!' Elinor yelled, but Claire neither braked nor swerved.

'You've run over it!'

'Perhaps.' Claire didn't even look in the mirror.

Elinor was profoundly shocked. 'What's happened to you, Claire? What's *happened* to you?'

'Don't be ridiculous, mother.' Claire tossed her ragged black mane. 'They're vermin.'

Elinor was hunched in the corner, well away from her daughter, wrapping her arms around herself, shivering inside.

Claire spun the wheel as they rolled out of the trees and

past the sign that said simply, Y Groes. The lumbering vehicle went across the river bridge with only inches to spare either side. The inn lay before them, and above it reared the church, its squat tower massive from this angle, its weather vane pricking a pale halo in the cloudy sky.

'Stopping raining, anyway,' George observed from the back seat.

CHAPTER XLIV

IT took Berry all of twenty minutes to find out where Bethan McQueen lived.

First off, he went into the Welsh Pizza House and ordered a plain cheese and tomato from an English guy who wore a white plastic apron. On the apron a drooling red dragon brandished a knife and fork. The pizza was crap, but the guy thought Bethan McQueen might be the girl who lived over the bookstore.

Hampton's bookshop had a window display featuring the new Ordnance Survey maps, local travel guides and a handful of books – in both English and Welsh – about the history of Wales. Most prominently displayed was a paperback with a man's face superimposed over a map of Wales. The face looked thoughtful and ended in a beard with a forked tip. The book was called *Glyndwr, The Last Prince*. It was by a Dr D.G. Evans.

'Naw,' Berry said aloud. 'Couldn't be.'

He went in out of the rain.

'Dreadful weather,' said an elderly man, looking up from a copy of the *Spectator* spread before him on the counter.

'Could be worse, I guess,' Berry said.

'It *was* worse a few nights ago. The river almost burst its banks.'

Berry picked up the Glyndwr paperback and turned it over and saw another bearded face in a black and white photograph on the back.

'Holy shit,' he said.

'Sold seven copies in the past couple of days,' the elderly man told him proudly. 'Mostly to journalists more interested in the author than the subject.'

Berry put the paperback on the counter with a ten pound note. 'Guess that makes it eight.'

'Actually, they're remainders,' the bookseller confessed. 'Touch of inspiration, though I say it myself. As soon as I heard Plaid'd picked him as the candidate, I rang the publishers and offered to do a deal for however many copies they had left. They were only too pleased, only having managed to get rid of a couple of thousand.'

'When'd it come out?'

'Five years ago? Six? Not much interest, you see, outside Wales, in Owain Glyndwr.' He wheezed out a laugh. 'Actually, not much interest *inside* Wales until now. But that's business. You have to seize the moment. If he wins I'll doubtless flog the lot, if he doesn't I'll still have made a reasonable profit.'

Berry said, 'Listen, can I ask you . . . Does Bethan McQueen live here?'

'Ah.' The bookseller folded the paperback into a brown paper bag and handed Berry his change. 'The lovely and intriguing Mrs McQueen.' He pointed to the ceiling. 'Up there.'

'Intriguing?'

'Oh well.' He smiled ruefully. 'Beautiful widow living quietly and discreetly. Never any visitors . . . Well, this chap' – he pointed to the Glyndwr books – 'on occasion, but never for very long. I'm a terrible old gossip, as you may have gathered, so pay no heed to a thing I say. There's a short alley next to the shop door. Just inside that you'll find another door in a recess. Ring the bell. I don't know if she's in.'

'Thanks.' Berry stepped out into the rain and then dodged into the alleyway. The door in the recess was plain, no glass, and painted some indiscernible colour. He pressed the bell-push and waited, not able to tell if it was working.

Until the door opened and Bethan McQueen stood there in white jeans and a turquoise sweater of soft wool.

'Mr Morelli.'

'Hi,' Berry said, suddenly lost for words. 'I, ah . . . I have this feeling we should talk.'

'About Giles Freeman?'

'And maybe other things.'

Bethan McQueen said, 'Did you tell Guto you were coming?'

'Sure did.'

'And what did he say?'

'I don't recall the exact words. But he seemed to be indicating that if I bothered you I could expect to have him clean the street with my ass.'

Bethan McQueen turned on a small, impish smile. 'You had better come up,' she said, 'while he's safely out of town.'

'Tea? Or coffee.'

'Tea, please. No milk.'

'I'm glad you said that, I don't think I have any milk. Do you like it strong?'

'Like crude oil,' Berry said. While she made the tea he took in the apartment. It looked temporary, like a storage room for furniture that was destined for someplace else. There was a big sofa with a design involving peacocks. He sat in one of a pair of great fireside chairs with loose covers in a floral print. Too big for the room, like the enormous Welsh dresser in honeyed pine. The dresser was empty save for a few books.

As Bethan returned with a tray, two white cups with saucers on it, and biscuits, there came a hoarse crackle from outside and then a tannoyed voice announced:

'THIS IS SIMON GALLIER, YOUR CONSERVATIVE CANDIDATE. I SHALL BE AT THE MEMORIAL HALL AT SEVEN-THIRTY TONIGHT WITH MY SPECIAL GUEST, THE SECRETARY OF STATE FOR TRADE AND INDUSTRY, THE RIGHT HONOURABLE JOHN GORE. I HOPE TO SEE YOU THERE AND WE WILL BOTH WELCOME YOUR QUESTIONS ON LOCAL AND NATIONAL ISSUES.'

Then the same message – presumably – was repeated, in Welsh.

'He's English, this Gallier,' Berry said, taking a cup and saucer. 'But he's learned Welsh, right?'

'I believe' – Bethan perched on an arm of the sofa – 'that he has been on some sort of crash course. Two weeks' work at a residential centre. Very intensive.'

'Like, they wake you up in the middle of the night, flash a light in your face and make you answer personal questions in Welsh?'

Bethan smiled.

'That the kind of course you had Giles on?'

Bethan's smile became a frown. 'Don't think me rude.' She looked him hard in the eyes. 'But who exactly are you?'

Simon Gallier's speaker-van made a return trip up the street. 'DON'T FORGET. SEVEN-THIRTY AT THE MEMORIAL HALL. AND MAKE THOSE QUESTIONS TOUGH ONES!'

'That's a tough one,' Berry said.

'You do not know who you are?'

He drank some tea.

'Who do people *think* you are?' she asked.

It was the strongest tea he'd ever been served. It had to be at least a six tea-bag pot.

'I'm sorry,' he said. 'I'm not helping the situation am I? I, ah . . . I'm a reporter. I work for an American news agency in London. Giles was my friend. Originally, what happened was this guy we both respected – dead now – he told me to dissuade Giles from throwing everything up and moving to Wales. So I came out here with Giles – early in the fall this was – to look at his cottage. And there was . . . something there I didn't take to, OK? Now Giles is dead. That's it. That's everything. Basically.'

This was what reporters were supposed to be able to do, reduce the Bible to a paragraph.

And edit all the meaning out of it.

Bethan McQueen drank her tea slowly, watching him.

'Giles was my friend too,' she said eventually. 'I tried to teach him Welsh, and I failed. It was a disaster. I came to feel that the lessons were doing him harm. When I learned about his . . . tumour, it was as if I had personally, you know . . .'

'Finished him off?'

'Yes.'

'That's crazy, Beth.'

'Bethan.'

'Sorry.'

'No, *I'm* sorry. My husband called me Beth. I am being stupid.'

'If we're getting into self-flagellation here,' Berry said. 'Most likely, *I* killed him. I failed to persuade him not to come here. Didn't hardly try. If he'd been in London maybe he'd have gotten some medical attention instead of pushing himself like he did, to move out here in record time, commuting to and fro, all that.'

'I don't think that is what you're saying, is it?' Bethan said.

'I'm sorry . . .?'

'You said you think you might have killed him because you failed to persuade him not to come here. You are implying he died because he came to Y Groes.'

'Well, no, I . . .'

'That is not what you were implying?'

'I . . . Shit, I don't know.' Berry rubbed his eyes, drank more tea. She was forcing him to say things he hadn't even put into thoughts.

'Look, give me your cup,' Bethan said. 'I should not have tried to poison you.'

'What?'

'Nobody can drink tea as strong as that. Except for me when I am feeling beaten, which is most of the time at present.'

Berry held out his cup. 'It was wonderful tea. I mean that. Seriously.'

'You are joking. I'll make some fresh.'

'Listen, forget the tea. Siddown. Please.'

Bethan put her cup and saucer on the floor and sat down on the sofa. She reached forward and flipped the switch on the side of an archaic three-bar electric fire.

'This is kinda hard,' Berry said. 'It's like we're walking around each other, keeping a distance. Like suspicious dogs. Trying to provoke each other into snapping or something.

Listen, how about we go for dinner tonight? Always presuming there's some place other than the Welsh Pizza House where we can actually *get* some dinner.'

'I'm sorry. I mean, I really *am* sorry. I have to go to Simon Gallier's meeting. In my role as Guto's secret agent. I have to report back.'

Berry thought about this. 'Well, would you mind if I tagged along? I have to file some kind of piece to the agency tomorrow. I do need to see this guy Gallier in action.'

'All right.'

'Good. Maybe we can figure out how to approach this thing. Always assuming there's something that needs to be approached.'

'Mr Morelli, I've lived with this for so long that I don't know who to trust any more.'

'Berry, for Christ's sake.'

'Bury?'

'As in strawberry. My name.'

'Oh.'

They stood up. Bethan straightened her sweater.

'I would love to say you can trust me,' Berry said. 'Only I'm not sure I can trust myself. I'm notoriously neurotic.'

She faced him from the other side of the monster sofa with the brilliant peacock fans on it.

She said, 'Do you believe Giles died because he came to Y Groes?'

'I . . .'

'It's important. Do you believe it?'

Berry shook his head. 'Also, I'm indecisive.'

'Well I believe that Robin . . .'

'Robin?'

'My husband. I believe Y Groes killed Robin. I hate that village, Mr Morelli. I'd like to see the church fall down and every stone of every building smashed and pounded into the ground.'

THE NIGHTBIRD

CHAPTER XLV

ENGLAND

S HE'D been absolutely determined not to do this. A clean
break was the only way. They simply didn't need the
hassle of each other any more.

The problem was she'd got rather pissed on the plane –
private plane owned by the company, no expense spared when
you were working with these people, lots of Champagne, none
of this Sangria nonsense – and the thought of ferrying all her
luggage out to Daddy's place had been too tedious.

Besides, the Spanish resort where they'd been shooting –
two days for about six seconds – had been a sort of hot Bognor,
the kind of location which dictated at least an hour in the
shower absolutely as soon as one reached civilisation.

So Miranda let herself into Morelli's flat and made straight
for the immersion heater. It was supposed to be one of those
rapid ones, but she decided to give it twenty-five minutes,
because an hour in the shower was a long time for Morelli's
primitive cistern to cope with.

She picked up the mail and put it on his desk. No point in
trying to pretend she hadn't been here – Miranda would have
been the first to agree that her personal ambience was not the
easiest to dispel.

OK then.

She switched on every heater she could find, flung her case
into the middle of the floor and stripped off most of her clothes.
Sometimes feeling rather cold could be quite a luxury.

Miranda hated Spain. On the other hand, she did rather
enjoy doing commercials. So many well-known serious actors
were doing them these days that people tended to think that
if you were in one you must be a rather respected figure too.

She wandered into the bedroom. Duvet still thrown back.
He obviously hadn't returned from Wales. What an utter

259

plonker he was. Always worrying about the effect he might be having on the great cosmic scheme of things, or the effect he ought to be having. 'Taking responsibility, kid,' was how he'd put it, explaining that you shouldn't eat meat if you weren't prepared to kill your own.

Morelli was a mass of conflicting neuroses. How could anyone be the young Al Pacino on the outside and mid-period Woody Allen underneath?

Miranda marched into the bathroom and ran the shower. She gave it a couple of minutes to heat up and was about to step in when the phone bleeped.

She decided to go ahead regardless, but remembered then how annoying a telephone could be when one was showering – the shower never quite managing to drown out the bleeps. So she decided to unplug the thing. But, of course, curiosity won in the end and she picked it up and affected a Deep South sort of voice.

'Thiyus iyus the Morelli res'dence.'

A man's voice, educated, not young, said: 'Oh, is that *Mrs* Morelli?'

'It most certainly isn't!' snapped Miranda, reverting to type.

'Oh dear. Well, would it be possible to speak to Mr Morelli? I'm afraid this is about the seventeenth time I've tried over the past two days.'

'I regret to have to tell you,' Miranda said, 'that he's in Wales. Please don't ask me why.'

'Wales, eh?'

'Wales.'

'Well, would you happen to know precisely where in Wales he's gone?'

'Somewhere full of grim mountains and dead sheep, I expect,' said Miranda, beginning to feel rather chilly standing there in the altogether. 'Would you like to leave a message?'

'Look, if I'm barking up the wrong tree, cut me off or something . . .'

Don't tempt me.

'. . . but it wouldn't be a village called Y Groes, would it?'

'Called what? They all sound the same to me.'

'Y Groes. Spelt I-Grows.'

'Oh, well, look, I believe he has spoken of some such place, yes. But I really couldn't be certain.'

'Ah. Do you know if he's staying at the inn there?'

'I can't honestly say where he's staying. Look, can I take a message?' Over her shoulder, Miranda could hear the beckoning patter of the hot water.

'You see, it was about Y Groes that I wanted to speak to him. Are you a friend of his?'

'Friend, ex-lover, confidante – and highly qualified to pass on messages.' Come on, you old fool, spit it out.

'Perhaps I should explain . . .'

Must you?

'My name's Peters.'

'I'm writing it down.'

'Canon Alex Peters.'

This has to be a first, Miranda thought morosely. I'm standing here tit-and-bum naked, talking to a vicar.

'I conducted the funeral service for Winstone Thorpe. Perhaps your, er, friend mentioned him.'

Miranda barely managed to suppress a groan.

'You see, I was chatting to your friend after the funeral, and he told me how poor Winstone had begged him to discourage young Giles Freeman from making his home in Wales. Of course, I was born and brought up in South Wales and I'm afraid I was rather dismissive about the whole thing. Nonsense, I said. Lovely place, lovely people.'

Get on with it! Miranda was grinding her teeth.

'Then, you see, I read about Giles's death, and it said he'd been living at Y Groes, and immediately I thought about Martin Coulson and this awful man Ellis Jenkins.'

'I really think I should leave a message for Berry to ring you when he gets back,' Miranda said, goose pimples on her arms now.

'You see, I didn't know until I read about Giles's death that we were talking about Y Groes. Which, of course, is where Martin died so tragically a couple of years ago. Do you know the case I'm referring to?'

'I don't think so, but—'

'Died in the church. Twenty-five years old. Dreadful. And then Jenkins refusing to have him in his churchyard. Caused quite a stir in church circles. So I thought I ought to pass this on to Berry Morelli, as he'd seemed rather anxious, a little unsure of what he ought to do.'

'Oh, he *always* seems anxious . . .'

'It's probably of absolutely no relevance. Though I confess to being rather curious about where Giles Freeman was eventually buried.'

'Well, I'm afraid I really can't help you there,' Miranda said. 'Look, I'll get Berry to ring you, shall I? What's the number?'

Canon Alex Peters gave her a number. 'I'm at Woodstock, near Oxford. In retirement. Not much else to think about, you see. As I say, probably nothing, but if he should happen to ring you from Wales, pass on my number, would you?'

'Oh, I will,' Miranda said. And then, just a tiny bit curious herself by now. 'Look Mr, er – Canon—'

'Peters. Alex Peters.'

'Of course, I wrote it down. Listen, I shall probably regret asking this, but why wouldn't they let this chap be buried in the churchyard?'

'Ah, well . . .'

'Yes?'

'Well, because he was English, my dear.'

When she got back to the shower it was lukewarm.

Miranda shrieked in rage and frustration.

'God, Morelli,' she rasped through her teeth, groping for his bathrobe and discovering he'd taken it with him. 'Wherever you are, I hope you're really *suffering* for this.'

CHAPTER XLVI

WALES

ELINOR said, 'I hate this room.'

She didn't hate any particular part of the room. She didn't hate the Victorian bed. She didn't hate the deeply recessed window, or the low-beamed ceiling. Or even its size – rather cramped, with that enormous wardrobe.

'I suppose,' said George Hardy, with heavy resignation, 'that I'm supposed to ask you why you hate the room.'

Still wearing her funeral dress, Elinor sat on a corner of the bed, glazed gaze fixed on the window through which she could see, in the late-afternoon light, the rooftops of the cottages opposite the inn, the winter-browned oak woods on the edge of the village and the misting hills beyond.

She was wondering if all this – the car breaking down, having to come here – was fate's fumbling attempt to heal the cuts she and Claire had inflicted on each other.

Wasn't working, though, was it? Anyone could see the wounds had only widened.

'I don't *know* why I hate it,' Elinor said.

George said, 'I think I shall ask that fellow if I can use his phone, give the garage a ring in Pontmeurig.' George pronounced it Pontmoorig. 'Make sure the parts will be here tomorrow.'

Elinor, distant, still staring out of the window, said, 'Should have had it towed away. Back to England, if necessary. We could have taken a taxi.'

George didn't bother to reply.

Elinor stood up and turned back the covers of the bed to see if the sheets were clean. Unfortunately, they had the look of being freshly-laundered. She sat down again, on the edge of the bed.

As she sat down this time, the bed shifted and a floorboard creaked.

'Better ring the office too,' George said. 'Get them to stall any clients.'

'We won't be here for ever, George.'

'Can't count on anything these days.' Tidy George unpacked two clean shirts and hung them in the wardrobe. 'Good job you're so efficient,' he said brightly. 'Enough clothes here to last the week out.'

Elinor was determined not to rise to this bait.

'Handling it awfully well, though, isn't she?' George said.

'What?'

'Claire. I was quite surprised.'

And relieved no doubt, Elinor thought. He could never deal with women's tears. Blubbing, he'd called it once. Only once – she'd almost had his eyes out.

'No, she's a tough girl,' George said admiringly. 'What d'you think of her new hairstyle? Quite fetching, I thought. I'd almost forgotten what her natural colour looked like.'

'George,' Elinor dug her nails into the bedspread. 'Go and make your phone calls.'

The floorboard creaked again as she stood up.

That night must have been an encouraging one for Simon Gallier, Conservative Parliamentary Candidate for Glanmeurig.

There weren't enough chairs in the Memorial Hall in Pont; groups of people were blocking the firedoors and clustered in the passageway to the lavatories.

Novelty value, Berry Morelli thought. It was obviously a real night out for many members of the audience. Most of the men wore suits and ties.

He was standing under the platform, searching the crowd for Bethan McQueen and failing to spot her. Feeling a hand on his shoulder, he turned expectantly.

'We're down here, mate,' Ray Wheeler said. 'One space left on the Press table.'

'Oh. Sure. Thanks.' Berry allowed himself to be steered to a chair between Shirley Gillies and Bill Sykes.

'Mind boggles, eh?' Sykes grated. 'Bet old Johnny Gore's

never pulled a bigger crowd since his wedding. Oh, sorry John, didn't see you there.'

'Evening, Bill,' said the Secretary of State for Trade and Industry, leaning across the Press table and then whispering, 'Afraid I'm going to be a trifle boring tonight. Don't want to outshine the boy.'

'Poor old Johnny,' said Sykes, as the Minister hefted his considerable bulk up the three wooden steps to the platform. 'Couldn't outshine a ten-watt bulb.'

'I was wondering,' Berry said. 'what Ole Winstone would've made of all this. Think he'd've come?'

'Not a hope,' said Bill Sykes. 'You wouldn't have got Winstone back to Wales for a lorryload of Glenfiddich.'

It struck Berry that you could get a hell of a lot of Glenfiddich on a lorry. More than enough to make a cynical old hack overcome his prejudices. He made a mental note to raise this with Sykes when the speeches were over.

There were a few cheers as Simon Gallier stepped onto the platform. He was built like a front-row rugby player, had prematurely greying hair and a shambling, untrimmed moustache like, Berry thought, a badly made yardbrush.

Gallier made a tough, rousing speech, full of commitment to Wales and the language, a few Welsh phrases scattered strategically around. When he threw these in, there were odd noises of appreciation. English immigrants, Berry thought. Token Welsh wouldn't cut much ice with the locals.

His perception surprised him. He must be getting the measure of this strange, mixed society.

The Secretary of State for Trade and Industry was indeed, even by comparison with Gallier, extremely predictable. Almost as boring as the questions people asked afterwards. Berry suspected most of the questioners were plants. These guys were preaching to the converted. No opposition here – except, he thought, amused, for Bethan sitting somewhere back there discreetly absorbing it all for Guto's benefit. Mata Hari.

'One of Johnny's better efforts, I thought,' grunted Sykes as the minister sat down for the last time.

'Oh, Berry,' a voice breathed in his ear.

As Gallier's applause died, Berry turned to find Shirley Gillies contemplating him, a bijou smile dimpling her plump, downy features. She said, 'You must be getting really fed up, stuck in the Drovers' all night.' She dipped her eyelashes. 'I was wondering . . . why don't you wander back to the Plas Meurig for a couple of drinks before turning in?'

The implication was clear.

He couldn't believe it; she was genuinely turned on by all this shit. Wow. Was there a name for a person who was erotically stimulated by the cut and thrust – with the emphasis on thrust – of party politics?

'Thing is, ah, I arranged to see someone later,' he said, trying to sound regretful. 'Thanks, though, Shirley.'

'Oh, right, OK,' said Shirley. 'Just a thought.'

It was going to be somebody's lucky night. Maybe even Bill Sykes's, depending how legless the alternatives were around midnight.

As they stood up, the hall clearing, people talking in bunches, Berry said to Sykes, 'When you said Winstone wouldn't come back to Wales, you meant because of the bad time he had covering that story in the sixties, the murder of the two farmers?'

'Ha!' Bill Sykes snapped a rubber band around his notebook. 'Winstone never covered that story. He wasn't even born then. Indeed, that's the whole point.'

'Huh?'

'Now *there's* a mystery for you, old boy. Remind me to tell you about it sometime, eh?' Bill began to rub his knees. 'Not good for the joints, these damn chairs.'

'Hey, come on, Bill, t—'

Tell me now, he'd been about to say, but there was a hand on his shoulder again and this time, to his relief – relief and a frisson of something more interesting – the hand belonged to Bethan.

She was wearing her white raincoat, Guto's beautiful spy.

'Can we be seen talking?' Berry said out of the corner of his mouth. 'Or should I leave a message in the dead-letter drop?'

'Actually, this is probably the one place we are safe,' Bethan said. 'If Guto sees us together one of us will need to seek asylum in England.'

'Right. Ah . . .' Good a time as any. 'I was gonna ask. Guto – Guto and you . . .?'

'He thinks I need to be protected,' Bethan said.

'By him.'

'Of course. He thinks living alone is not good for me. He thinks I am in danger of having a nervous breakdown.'

'What do you think?'

'I think a nervous breakdown would be quite a relief,' Bethan said softly. 'Come on, let's go.'

It was George who made the discovery, just as they were getting ready for bed.

'That's it!' he announced, sitting on a corner of the bed, flinging down a sock. 'I'm going to find out what's causing it.'

He's drunk too much, Elinor thought. 'It's only a loose floorboard,' she said.

'Getting on my nerves.'

Elinor had more to worry about than a creak. It had been a most unsatisfactory evening.

She'd been almost hopeful at the start – Claire turning up at the inn at around seven, joining them for dinner. Roast lamb, of course. All the Welsh seemed to be able to cook was lamb. George enjoyed it.

There'd been nobody else dining at the inn, theirs the only table with a cloth. The little white-haired licensee had served them himself, reasonably courteously. An opportune time, Elinor had judged, to raise the issue of what was to happen now.

'Why don't you come and stay with us for a while, give yourself time to think things out?'

Claire had told her nothing needed to be thought out and then said, 'We'll never agree about this, mother, you must surely have realised that.'

George had said, 'Let the girl get over it in her own way.' And Elinor had found herself wondering if, for Claire, there was really anything to get over. It was clear their marriage had not been as well founded as she'd imagined.

'I shall come and visit you, of course,' Claire said. 'Sometimes.'

'I should hope so,' her father said in his jocular way, his second cigarette burning away in an ashtray by his elbow.

'Knowing how much you would dislike coming to my grandfather's house.'

Elinor had felt something coiling and uncoiling in her stomach. *Tell me I've got it wrong. Tell me you aren't going to stay here . . .*

'Let's just enjoy our meal, shall we?' Claire had said.

Later, in the bar, everyone had greeted Claire in Welsh, switching to English when they saw she was not alone. She'd introduced them to her 'friends', a thin man with horrible teeth and a couple, he bearded and hefty, she red-faced with little beady eyes and an awful gappy Welsh smile. All were appallingly friendly to Elinor and George, who was persuaded to play darts and allowed to win.

Not Elinor's sort of evening.

'Hey, look at this—' George had the floorboard up.

'Put the bloody thing back, for God's sake, George—'

'No, look—' He appeared ludicrously unattractive, sprawled on the floor, hair awry, white belly slopping out of his underpants, arm down a hole in the floor.

'Some kind of book, I think. Hang on . . . Here it comes.'

George brought it into the light. 'Probably a valuable first edition or something. Oh . . .'

The light from the centre of the ceiling fell on an ordinary stiff-backed notebook from W.H. Smith.

'Can't win 'em all,' said George. He stamped on the floor-board. 'Least I've stopped the damn squeak.'

'What is it?' Elinor said, in bed now, wearing a long-sleeved pale-blue nightdress.

George opened the book. 'Sir Robert Meredydd,' he read. 'Thirteen forty-nine to fourteen twenty-one. Can't be *his* note-book, anyway, it's written in Biro. Couple of diagrams, rough sort of plan, pages of unintelligible scrawl. Doesn't look very interesting. Why do you suppose it was under the floorboard?'

'I don't know. And I don't care.'

'Probably a bloody treasure map.' George laughed and tossed the book on to his bedside table. 'Remind me to give it to that chap Griffiths in the morning.'

'I wish it was morning now,' Elinor said.

'I don't, I'm bloody tired.'

'You're drunk.'

'What, on three pints and a Scotch?'

'There's an awful tension in here. In the air. Can't you feel it?'

'Only the tension in my bladder,' George said coarsely, pulling on his overcoat. 'Excuse me.'

As he stumped off to the bathroom across the landing – nothing en-suite in this place – Elinor pulled the quilt around her shoulders and picked up the notebook to take her mind off how much she hated this room. The book was not particularly dusty, obviously hadn't been down there long.

It fell open at the reference to Sir Robert Meredydd and Elinor saw that the date 1421 had been underlined twice and an exclamation mark added.

She looked at the diagrams. One appeared to be a rough map of the village with a circle marking the church, shading denoting woodland and a dotted line going off the page and marked 'trackway'.

Half the book was empty. The last note said something like 'Check Mornington.'

Elinor put the book back on the table, on George's side.

She'd hated those people in the bar tonight. Most of all she'd hated the way they and Claire had exchanged greetings in Welsh, Claire seeming quite at home with the language.

Elinor hated the sound of Welsh. Nasty, whining, guttural. If they could all speak English, why *didn't* they?

Her father had never once spoken Welsh to them at home. Yet had turned his back on them, returned to the so-called land of his fathers – and then, apparently, had spoken little else.

There was something rancid in the air.

When George returned they would have to put out the light, and the room would be lit from the window, which had no curtains and was divided into eight square panes. And the room would be one with the silent village and the night.

CHAPTER XLVII

SHADOWS clung to the alleyway along the side of the Memorial Hall. It was lit only by a tin-shaded yellow bulb on the corner of the building. Berry walked close to Bethan. He liked walking close to Bethan, though he wasn't too sure who was protecting whom.

Neurotic chemistry.

They came out on the parking lot below the castle. Any place else, Berry thought, they'd have had floodlights around a ruined castle this big. Made a feature of it. In Pontmeurig they seemed to treat their medieval monument like some shabby industrial relic, hiding it with modern buildings, parking cars and trucks as close as they could get to its ramparts.

Plenty cars here tonight, as many as in the daytime.

'Business has never been so good,' Bethan said, as they crossed the road to Hampton's Bookshop, 'The licensees are hoping that whoever wins the by-election will die very soon so they can have another one.'

'Where's Guto's meeting tonight?'

'Y Groes,' Bethan said quickly and pulled her keys from her bag.

'What time's he get back?'

'Alun's driving, so he'll have a few drinks afterwards. Half-eleven, twelve.'

'Gives us a couple hours to talk before he comes looking for your report.'

'He won't tonight. Close the door behind you.'

Bethan led the way upstairs, flicking lights on. In the flat she switched on a single reading lamp with an orange shade, went to plug in the kettle. 'How long you lived here?' Berry said.

'Only a few months. After Robin died, I went to work in a school in Swansea, but then they offered me the head teacher's job in Y Groes.'

'Hold on,' Berry said. 'I thought you were at Y Groes before.'

'Yes, but not working there.' Bethan came through from the kitchen in jeans and sweater, coat over her arm. She threw it in an armchair, sat on an arm of the sofa. 'I'll start at the beginning, shall I?'

'OK.'

She told him she'd been born in Aberystwyth, where her parents still lived. Went to college in Swansea, came back to teach at the primary school in Pontmeurig then at a bigger school in Aber. Met Robin McQueen, a geologist from Durham, working at the British Geological Survey Centre just south of the town. When they married they'd been delighted to be able to rent a terraced cottage in Y Groes, even though it would be a fifty-mile round trip to work each day for both of them.

'It all seemed so perfect,' Bethan said. 'Robin was like Giles – overwhelmed by the setting and the countryside and the beauty of the village itself. The extra driving seemed a small price to pay.'

'How long were you there, before—?'

Her eyelids dropped 'Under a year.'

'Listen, you don't have to—'

'There is very little to say. He complained increasingly of feeling tired. Put it down to the travelling and the stress. The stress, he— The survey team were being told to investigate Mid-Wales to find areas where the rocks were suitable for burying nuclear waste. Robin, of course, was fiercely *anti*-nuclear. He considered resigning. But then we would have been forced to leave the area – nothing else round here for a geologist. Then, worst of all, he found two prime nuclear-dumping sites in the Nearly Mountains, five miles from Y Groes, can you imagine that?'

'Awkward.'

'So he was tired and under terrible stress and he flew into a rage if I suggested he should see a doctor. And then—'

The kettle puffed and shrilled. Bethan got up. Berry followed her into the tiny kitchen.

'And then he *did* see a doctor,' she said dully. 'And of course it was too late.' She poured boiling water into a brown teapot. 'Far too late.'

Bethan pushed the fingers of both hands through her black hair. 'We had not quite two weeks,' she said.

'Jesus,' Berry said softly.

'My neighbour at the time, Mrs Bronwen Dafis, told me one day – being helpful, very nice, very understanding – that Robin would be dead before the weekend.'

'She was medically qualified, huh?'

'It emerged that she had followed a corpse candle from the church to our door.'

'Followed a *what*?'

'In rural Wales,' Bethan said, 'there are many signs and portents signifying death. The corpse candle is said to be a tiny light which floats a few feet above the ground. Identifying the house of a person who will soon die. Or perhaps someone will see his own corpse candle, trailing behind him along the lane.'

'People believe that?'

'That is the very least of what some people believe. There is something, also unique to Wales, I imagine, called the *teuli* or *toili*. The phantom funeral. A funeral procession may be seen carrying a coffin or pushing the coffin on a bier or a cart. Perhaps you are in some lonely place at night or twilight, and the cortège passes right through you.'

'Legends. Folklore. Country bullshit, right?'

'Of course.' Bethan poured two teas. 'Strong enough?'

'Fine. These stories . . . must scare the crap out of kids.'

'Except,' Bethan said, 'in Y Groes.'

'Why'd I have a feeling you were gonna say that?'

They carried the mugs back into the living room. Bethan put on the electric fire. They sat, one on each arm of the peacock sofa.

'All this furniture from the cottage?'

Bethan nodded and told him how, heartbroken, she'd at

first put the furniture in store and taken a job, any job, in Swansea – in spite of the entreaties of her neighbours, several of whom had seriously urged her not to leave.

'Obviously, they wanted me to stay because I was a Welsh-speaker and they needed younger blood. The young people leave this area in their hundreds, to find work. And because, well, that is what young people do, they leave their roots behind. So you have many villages which are full of old people. And immigrants.'

'Ah.'

'But not Y Groes. It is perhaps the only village in Wales where everyone is Welsh. And Welsh speaking.'

'Everyone? What about the Welsh people who bring their wives and husbands who happen not to be Welsh—?'

It hit him.

'Aw, hey, come on . . .'

Bethan shrugged.

Half asleep, Elinor thought at first, as anyone would, that it must be the wind.

And then she heard the unmistakable beat of wings.

The bed shifted as she sat up.

'What was that? What *was* it?'

George grunted.

'Did you hear it? George, did you *hear* it?'

A clear, cold night outside. A quarter moon in the top-left square of the deepset window.

Elinor shivered in her cotton nightdress.

'I was asleep,' George complained. 'For God's sake, I was *asleep*.'

'It's stopped,' Elinor said. 'It was a bird, I think.'

'Owl, probably.'

'Owls don't peck at windows.'

'I wouldn't know. I'm not an ornithologist.' George wrenched at the blankets, turned over.

'Stopped now.' Elinor spoke faintly and sank back on the pillow.

'Go to sleep,' George mumbled. 'We'll be away from here tomorrow, God willing.'

Eyes wide open, she wondered how much influence God might exert in a place like this. She was no more a theologian than George was an ornithologist. But she was a woman and he was a depressingly unresponsive man. There were things that he would never begin to understand.

She lay on her back looking up at the beamed ceiling, only white bars visible, found by the sparse moonlight.

'George,' she said after a while, unmoving in the bed.

'What?'

And came out with it at last. 'I think she's pregnant.'

George turned over towards her. 'What on earth makes you say that?'

'Oh, you probably wouldn't understand, but I can feel it about her somehow – the way she moves, her colouring, her skin tone. Not much more than a month perhaps, but it's there.'

'Oh dear. That *would* be difficult, especially in a place like this. How would she support a child? She's a freelance. No maternity leave for a freelance.'

'I'm probably wrong,' Elinor said, sorry now that she'd blurted out what was on her mind. She'd always had cause to regret confiding her deeper feelings to bluff, shallow, well-meaning George.

'Hope you are,' George said. 'Although I'd quite like to be a grandad one day. Completes the picture.'

Within minutes he was snoring. Always make the best of things, that was George. Elinor turned on to her side and after a while began to drift unhappily towards the blurred frontier of sleep.

Was pulled back by that hideous noise again.

The measured, sharp taps on the windowpane, the convulsion of wings.

Rolling over in her lonely terror, she saw the shadow of the nightbird against the moon-tinted glass.

In a flat, cold silence, as if the sound of the world had been switched off, it brandished its dark wings at her, a spasm of black foreboding.

And vanished.

She turned to face the wall. And did not sleep again, nor look at the window, until morning came in a sickly pink mist.

CHAPTER XLVIII

BERRY came down to breakfast and heard voices from the sitting room next door.

'Bethan has been here since seven,' explained Mrs Evans, setting down his three kinds of toast. 'Been following the Tory campaign, she has. Well, I never realised this electioneering was so complicated.'

Ten minutes later, as she carried his plates away, he heard her open the sitting room door. 'I'm taking your tea and coffee into the dining room. It's not friendly to leave Mr Morelli on his own.'

Guto's reply was unintelligible but audibly grumpy. He shambled in a couple of minutes later wearing a torn sweatshirt with something in Welsh printed on the front and a lot of exclamation marks. 'Morning, Morelli,' he said without enthusiasm.

'Bad night?'

'Don't even fucking ask,' said Guto, reversing a dining chair and sitting down with his legs astride the seat and his chin on his hands over the backrest.

Bethan followed him in, contrastingly elegant in black, with the big gold earrings. 'Guto has decided his meeting in Y Groes was not a success,' she said carefully.

Mrs Evans returned with matching tea and coffee pots in some ornate kind of china, put the coffee pot on the table in front of Guto. 'I've told you about sitting like that, you'll ruin that chair.'

'Oh, Mam, not this morning, for Chr— Not this morning, please.'

Mrs Evans put down the teapot. '*Two* black tea drinkers?' She said. 'There's coincidence. Strong or weak?'

'I like mine strong*ish*,' Bethan said. 'I am afraid *he* likes it so it corrodes the spoon.'

Guto threw her a penetrating look which said, And how the hell do you know that?

'Berry was at the Conservative meeting last night,' Bethan said quickly, pouring tea. 'They served tea afterwards,' she lied. 'He was complaining about the Tory tea, how weak it was. This is lovely, Mrs Evans.'

Guto's look said, Oh, *Berry*, now, is it?

'Anything else you want,' Mrs Evans said, scurrying off, 'I'll be in the kitchen.'

'Yes, yes, thank you, Mam,' Guto said irritably.

'So what went wrong?' Berry lit a cigarette.

'I truly cannot fathom it, Morelli,' Guto said. 'You know Y Groes, you've been there?'

Berry nodded.

'Not a soul in that village does not speak Welsh, am I right, Bethan?'

'You're right,' she said. 'And you are remembering that when Gwynfor won his by-election to become the first Plaid MP, back then, it was said he had one hundred per cent support in the Welsh-speaking communities of Carmarthenshire – in Llanybydder and Rhydcymerau.'

'Right,' Guto said bitterly. 'Of all the places, this was the one I was the least worried about. Didn't even think about what I was going to say in advance. I'd march into the school hall to universal cheers. Hard man of the nationalists, hero of the hour.'

He rocked backwards and forwards on the dining chair. 'You know how many were there? Nineteen. Nineteen fucking people!'

Berry reckoned Simon Gallier must have pulled nearly four hundred. OK, Guto's meeting was in a village, but, shit . . .

'Another notable chapter in the annals of apathy, it was,' Guto said, 'And worse still – get this – most of the nineteen were from farms and hamlets a few miles away. I should say there were fewer than five actual residents of Y Groes. And they were the people who knew me, come out of politeness – Aled from the pub, Dilwyn Dafis, Dewi Fon. What is it we learn from this, eh? What do we fucking *learn* here?'

'Maybe the meeting wasn't publicised enough,' Berry said.

'Bollocks. Nothing happens in these villages that everybody doesn't know about. Apathy, it is. Typical of this area. Makes you sick.'

He looked despondently at the floor. Bethan looked at Berry. The look indicated she could maybe explain this, and apathy was not the word she would use.

'Look, I have to go,' Bethan said.

'And I have to change, for my Press conference,' Guto said. 'Jesus, what if the hacks have heard about it?'

'Any of them there?' Berry asked.

'No. And with only twenty-one people in the bloody room, I can be sure of that, at least. But they'll have heard, see. Word travels fast. I tell you, if it goes on like this, I'm finished, man.'

'It won't, Guto,' Bethan said. 'Believe me. It is not like other places, that village. I know this. And you have over a week, yet.' She squeezed his arm.

Berry thought, He's worried about this getting out and he just told the entire story to a reporter.

He didn't know whether to be flattered or insulted that neither Guto nor Bethan seemed to consider him a real journalist.

When Guto, reluctantly be-suited, had left for the Drovers', Berry wedged himself into the telephone alcove of Mrs Evans's china-choked sitting room and called American Newsnet, collect.

'I was beginning to think,' Addison Walls said, 'that the telephone system had not yet been extended to Wales.' He sounded like he had a cold.

'It got here at the weekend,' Berry said. 'Just nobody could figure out how to connect the wires. So, how much you want me to file?'

'I don't want you to file a thing,' Addison Walls said. 'I read every damn word printed about that by-election and, as I predicted, it's all shit and of purely domestic interest. So what I'm lookin' for is you back here by tonight, yeah?'

'Ah, I don't think I can do that,' Berry said.

There was a long pause during which Berry could hear Addison trying to breathe.

'I hear you correctly? I said I needed you back here by tonight, and you said—'

'I said I didn't think I could make it. Like, you know, my car broke down.'

'You drive a pile of crap, Morelli, whadda you expect? So take a train. If there's no trains, take a bus. Fuck it, grab a cab, but get your ass back here by tonight, OK?'

'Addison, listen,' Berry said. 'How about I take a couple days vacation—'

'Nearly December, Morelli. You took all your vacation.'

'OK, I'll take some of next year's.'

'Morelli, Goddamn it—' He heard Addison Walls blow his nose. 'Listen, we're up to the eyes here. Paul went sick, I can't see the top a my desk for fuckin' influenza remedies that don't fuckin' work. You know what, Morelli, you've become a real weird guy. So, listen, you don't show up tomorrow, I am not gonna be all that worried. Give me an opportunity to test out my new shredder on your contract.'

'Addison, hey, come on . . . Just two days is all I'm asking.'

'You getting the general direction of my thinking, Morelli?'

'Yeah.' Berry felt some perverse kind of euphoria filling up his head. 'Yeah, I think I'm finally piecing things together.'

'Good,' Addison Walls said, and he hung up.

The sun was out, pale but definitely out, and the street sparkled after an overnight frost. Berry could see the broken denture of the castle walls, a sign pointing to the Welsh Pizza House – lousy name, lousy pizzas. Feeling suddenly very strange, very different, he began to walk up the street. Saw Guto's mom coming back from the shop with a teeming basket over her arm and a headscarf over her perm. Felt a crazy kind of affection for Guto's mom.

Guto too. He'd make the right kind of MP. Always be in

trouble, always say the wrong things to the wrong people. Berry liked that.

But how much of a chance did Guto really have? Why didn't Y Groes want him? Heart of the Welsh-speaking heartland.

He could get back to London in four, five hours. He could spend most of today here and still get back to London by tonight. Maybe come back next weekend, see how things were going.

Sure. No problem.

At the top of the street, past Hampton's Bookshop but before you got to the bridge, there was a teashop which also sold Welsh crafts. Mainly lovespoons, which were made of wood and were intricately carved and came in a variety of sizes. Berry wondered what they had to do with love. Maybe he'd ask Bethan, who ought, by now, to be waiting in there. An arrangement they'd made last night.

They'd talked until eleven-thirty, then Berry had said he ought to go because Guto would be home and Mrs Evans would want to get to bed. He hadn't *wanted* to go. Christ, no.

As he approached the teashop, he could see her sitting in the window, black hair tumbling into a black cowl-neck woollen sweater.

She'd told him last night how she'd done this dumb thing, gone to the education department and suggested they close down the village school. How she felt the school had been corrupting generations of kids. She'd found it hard to explain why she thought this. Said he'd need to meet the other teacher to understand.

Berry had told her about breaking into the judge's house that day with Giles. He'd told her about the study, the deep, dark atmosphere of hate.

'Yes,' she'd said. 'Yes.'

He hadn't told her about the room whispering, *sice . . . sice . . .* because he wasn't even sure that had happened.

The education department had told Bethan to take two or three weeks off. They figured she had to be nuts, trying to get her own school shut down, maybe heading for a breakdown.

I think a nervous breakdown would be quite a relief.

He walked across the road to the teashop. She had her back to him, talking to someone maybe. He caught a flash of gold earring as she tossed her hair back. No way could this woman be insane, but then, who was he to judge?

CHAPTER XLIX

INSIDE the teashop it was very dim, all the furniture stained as dark as the lovespoons on the walls. Which was why, from outside, you could only see the person sitting in the window. Why he hadn't seen the other two people at Bethan's table.

It was the older couple who'd been at Giles's funeral. The guy with white hair, yellow at the front, and deep lines down both cheeks. The woman thin-faced, harsh hair rinsed an uneasy auburn, looking like copper wire.

'Berry, this is Claire's mother and father.'

'Oh.' Somehow, he'd thought they must have been relations of Giles, rather than Claire. 'Hi,' he said, pulling out a chair.

Bethan introduced him as a friend and colleague of Giles's, down here for the election. 'Mr and Mrs Hardy had to spend the night at the *Tafarn* at Y Groes. They are having problems with their car.'

'But we're getting it back this morning,' George Hardy said. 'That's why we're here. Claire dropped us off.'

Berry turned to the woman. He'd heard her muttering 'Thank God,' when her husband talked about getting the car back.

'You don't like it here?'

'Not really our sort of place, I'm afraid,' Elinor Hardy said, tight-voiced.

'Not being *snobbish* or anything,' George assured Bethan. 'Good *God*, no. Wonderful place for a quiet summer holiday. Just that at this time of year it seems a little cold and remote and it's not quite what we're used to. Certainly never had to wait two days before to get what seemed quite a simple problem with the cam belt seen to.'

'We didn't get much sleep, I'm afraid,' Elinor said. The skin under her eyes was blue, Berry saw, and it wasn't cosmetic. She was fingering her coffee cup nervously. He wondered why Claire had put them in a teashop and just left them.

'Bloody bed kept creaking,' George said. 'Had to get down on my hands and knees and mess about with a loose floorboard underneath to stop it. Good God, I'd forgotten – Elinor, why didn't you remind me?'

From an inside pocket of his overcoat he pulled a slim, red, hard-backed notebook. 'Found it under the damned floorboard. Meant to give it to the manager chap this morning.'

'Unlikely to have been his anyway,' Elinor said.

'Suppose not. Must belong to somebody, though, and he'd be better placed than us to find out who, obviously.'

Bethan said, 'You found it under the floorboard in the bedroom? Can I see?'

George passed her the book. 'Keep it, if it's of any interest. Odd little hand-drawn maps of the village, that sort of thing. Probably mean more to you than me.'

'Thank you.' Bethan made no attempt to look at the notebook, slipping it into her bag.

'If you find any treasure, send us a few bob, won't you.' Ignoring his wife's withering glance, George laughed and coughed and pulled out his cigarettes. 'Don't mind, do you? Only things that seem to *stop* me coughing these days.'

A waitress appeared, glum girl of about seventeen. Bethan said 'Can I order you more coffee?'

Elinor grimaced.

'Just one pot of tea, then.' Bethan told the girl, '*Un te, plis.*' Pointed at Berry. '*Dim laeth.*'

Berry saw the woman flinch when Bethan spoke Welsh. She was in some state.

The hell with tact. He said, 'I hear that Claire . . . she has this amazing aptitude for the Welsh language.'

Elinor said, tonelessly, 'Has she?'

George Hardy looked at his watch, stood up, cigarette in hand. 'Think I'd better pop round the corner to the garage, see how they're getting on with it. Have to stand over these chaps sometimes. Nice to meet you, Miss . . . er. Yes.'

When he'd gone, squeezing his overcoated bulk past the racks of lovespoons, his wife just came apart.

She leaned across the table, seized Bethan's wrist. 'Look, I don't know anything about you, but please will you help me?'

'Of course.' Bethan was startled. 'If I can.'

'I'm sorry, I don't usually behave like this. But I don't *know* anybody here, do you see?' Berry saw her eyes fill up. She let go of Bethan's wrist, pulled a paper napkin from a wooden bowl. 'Pen.'

Berry handed her his.

'I want to give you my telephone number.' She began to write erratically on the napkin, talking as fast and jerkily as her wrist was moving. 'Want you to promise to ring me. If anything happens. You see Claire, don't you? Of course you do. Teaching her . . . that language.'

Bethan said, 'I—' Berry's eyes said, Don't contradict her, let her talk.

'Something's happened to her. She's not the same.'

'No,' Bethan said.

'You can tell that, can't you? You've only known her a short time, but you can see it.'

'Yes.'

'I won't say—' Elinor put down the pen, folded the napkin; Bethan took it. 'I won't say we were ever terribly close. Dreadful admission, but I have to be frank. Have to.'

She looked defiantly from Bethan to Berry and back to Bethan.

'Often felt closer to Giles. He would tell me things she concealed. And now he's dead. And we weren't told. Weren't invited to the funeral, you know.'

'That's awful,' Bethan said.

'She said,' Elinor pulled another napkin from the bowl, dabbed her eyes. 'She says she wrote to us, but she couldn't invite us here. We had to decide. For ourselves.' She blew her nose, crumpled the napkin in her hand. 'Never saw a letter. Read about it in the paper. Suppose she didn't tell us because . . . when my father died . . . we were about to leave for a holiday and I didn't tell *her*. None of us went to his funeral. I didn't want *her* going, didn't want her anywhere near him again.'

'Oh,' said Bethan. 'Of course. You're the judge's daughter.'

'He was a bastard. I think that's the first time I've ever used that word.'

'Why?' Berry asked gently. 'Why was he a bastard?'

'You don't want to know all that. No time, anyway. George'll be back soon. With the car.'

'You said you didn't want him near her again. I remember Giles telling me specifically that Claire never met her grandfather.'

'She didn't *remember* meeting him. We were once foolish enough to bring her here. As a small child. He . . . went off with her. I thought . . . that he wasn't going to bring her back.'

Bethan said, 'Went off?'

'I don't know where they went.'

'To the woods? To the church?'

'Does it matter? Please, all I want . . . Just ring me sometimes. Tell me how she is and if . . . You see, I think she might be expecting a baby. Perhaps that's why she's changed. I pray that's all it is.'

'Not the best time to have a kid,' Berry said. He felt very sorry for the woman. Obviously wasn't able to confide in her husband. Something not right when she had to pour it all out to strangers in a café.

Elinor Hardy straightened up, threw the crumpled napkin in the ashtray with two of George's cigarette butts. 'You must think me a very stupid, hysterical woman.'

'No,' Berry said. 'All the people you could've told this to, we're the ones least likely to think that.'

'I'll be better when I'm out of here. I know it's your country, but I don't like it here. Feel vulnerable.'

. . . *not meant to be here, the English* . . .

'Car goes wrong and you're suddenly stranded. Strange language, different attitudes. Birds pecking at your window in the night.'

Bethan's expression did not change at all, but Berry felt she was suddenly freezing up inside.

'Birds?' Casually. Hiding it.

'Pecking . . . tapping on the window. Kept waking me up in the night. Wasn't an owl, I saw it. Or I may have dreamt it, I don't know. I'm in a terrible state. I've got to get out of here, it's gloomy. I'll go and find George. Look, you will ring me, won't you?'

'I'll ring you before the weekend,' Bethan promised.

'Thank you. I don't even know your name.'

'Bethan. Bethan McQueen. Mrs Hardy, you *are* leaving today, aren't you?'

'Oh, yes,' Elinor said. 'Count on it.'

When she'd gone, Bethan rose silently, paid the girl, collected her bag and her white raincoat from the table. She walked out of the café and along the street, Berry following. She didn't speak. They came to the bridge and Bethan crossed the road and walked back towards the town, on the castle side. The frost had melted now, but the sun had gone in.

When they reached the castle car park, Bethan said, 'Your car or mine?'

Berry unlocked the Sprite. They got in. Berry started the engine. Not easy. Blue smoke enclouded the Sprite, which now had a cough worse than George Hardy's. Berry backed it round, pointed it at the road.

'Where we going?'

'Turn left,' Bethan said. 'Across the bridge. Keep going. You'll see a sign pointing over the Nearly Mountains to Y Groes.'

'I know it.'

'Pass it,' Bethan said. 'Keep straight on.'

'But where are we going?'

'Christ knows,' Bethan said. 'Somewhere where nobody has ever thought they've seen the bird of death.'

CHAPTER L

EVERY second farm they passed seemed to have a political poster pasted to a gate or a placard sticking out of a leafless hedgerow. Berry counted seven for Gallier (Con), three for Evans (Plaid) and two each for Labour and the Liberal Democrats.

'Could be worse,' he observed. 'All over the world, farmers are notoriously conservative.'

She didn't reply. She was sitting as upright as was possible in a bucket seat full of holes and patches.

At least the Sprite was responding, losing its bronchitis now they were into open country. He'd been getting a touch paranoid about that, having told Addison Walls his car had broken down and therefore been half-expecting it to do just that.

Superstition. Everywhere, superstition.

Five miles now into the hills north-west of Pontmeurig, and disillusion was setting in. At first he'd been stimulated by all that 'your car or mine' stuff on the castle parking lot. Now the space between them was a good deal wider than the gap between the bucket seats, and he didn't know why.

She said suddenly,

'Death fascinates the Welsh.'

The first time she'd spoken since they passed the sign to Y Groes.

'Corpses and coffins and funerals.'

'Signs and portents,' Berry said.

'You see these farms. Each one an island. Farmers never visit their neighbours. But when one of them dies, people will come from miles around to his funeral. All the roads to the chapel lined with cars and Land-Rovers for half a mile in each direction. On the day of a big funeral, the traffic police send for reinforcements.'

'Bethan, what is the bird of death?'

285

She didn't reply.

'Where are we headed?'

'Keep driving,' she said.

After a few miles they came to a T-junction, Aberystwyth to the right, Machynlleth to the left.

'Make a right here?'

She pointed to the left. 'Quickest way out of the constituency.'

Sure enough, after a couple more miles there were no more political posters. The landscape became rougher and a lighter, more faded shade of green. Kind of like the Nearly Mountains, snow on the high ground giving the crags a 3-D outline.

Presently, they drove down into a pleasant town, with a wide main street and a Gothic clock tower.

'This is the town that ought to have been the capital of Wales,' she said. 'Perhaps the earliest centre of Welsh civilisation.'

We had the sociology, Berry thought, now we get the history lesson. What is this, a school outing?

'But that's not why we're here,' she said.

'So why are we here?'

'Because at the top of this street is the best restaurant in this part of Wales,' Bethan said. 'Vegetarian meals a speciality. Park anywhere along here.'

Berry grinned. A long, slow Italian grin.

'No. No! No! No!'

'I'm sorry. My wife is rather distraught.'

'Nooooooo!'

'We lost our son-in-law, you see.'

Elinor strode out then, straight through a patch of oil, ruining her sensible pigskin walking shoes.

'Is there no chance for later today?' George pleaded.

'What can I do,' the mechanic said, 'if they send me the wrong parts. Look, I will show you a copy of the order we dictated to them over the phone—'

'Never mind, I believe you,' George said. 'It's just bloody inconvenient.'

'Quite an old Volvo, see.'

'Volvos last for ever,' said George, affronted.

Some minutes later he caught up with Elinor.

'It's really not my fault, you know.'

'It's never your fault.'

'Look, what we'll do—'

'I won't go back there. I'll sleep on a park bench first.'

'Dammit, there isn't a park. Nor any benches. But what I was about to say . . . We've got a few hours. We'll have lunch at that Plas Moorig place and see if they can't find us a room. Any room. How about that? Please . . .'

Over lunch, Bethan said, 'I want not to think about it. Just for a while.'

'OK. Fine.'

'Tell me about you.'

'Oh, shit.'

Bethan started on her fresh salmon salad. 'What is that stuff?'

'It's a vegetarian canelloni.'

'I know *that*, but what is it?'

'Well, it's got spinach and stuff inside.' He sampled a segment. 'It's OK.'

'For Wales.'

'No, it's real good. Jesus, you Celts are so touchy.'

He'd taken off his jacket, revealing a green sweatshirt probably older than Guto's, if less torn. In black Gothic lettering across the chest it said, AMERICAN WEREWOLF IN LONDON.

'You haven't told me about you,' Bethan said. 'You just said, "Oh shit," and then we were sidetracked by the food.'

'OK. I'm from New York originally, but I was brought up and educated in seven different states on account of my dad kept moving to further his career until it wouldn't go any further and he decided it was time he became a power and influence in the land.'

'What did he do? What was his job?'

'I just love it when people say that. I hate it when they say, hey, you related to Mario Morelli?'

'Who is Mario Morelli?'

'He's my dad, the bastard.'

'I had gathered that.'

'OK, Mario Morelli is maybe America's number one TV anchor man, known coast to coast. A household name, like that – what's that stuff you put down the john?'

'Harpic? Toilet Duck?'

'Yeah, he's a real toilet duck. Only the great American public doesn't want to know that on account of he has this mature elegance and charms the matrons with his dazzling Italian smile.'

He told her about Mario Morelli's role in the Irangate cover-up. He told her how his conscience wouldn't let him sit on this information when it seemed they were going to get away with it.

'Like, I don't want to come over as this big idealist. But when your dad's a national hero and you know what kind of asshole he really is . . . OK, in the end, it made no difference. Most of it came out. And Mario Morelli came out of it as this caring patriot. He did it for his country, all this shit. Cue for selfish, radical un-American activist son to leave town. Or leave country in this case. So I came to England and I find England's suddenly become a place where it's cool to make a million overnight and they're looking up to America as this big, successful younger brother who *got it right*, for Chrissake. That's about it. My vegetarian cannelloni's getting cold.'

He ate some cannelloni, then he said, 'One thing I kinda like about Wales is that it's just about the most obscure country in Western Europe, now even Belgium has the EC, but it doesn't seem to look up to anybody.'

'Wrong,' Bethan said. 'Wrong, wrong, wrong.'

'Wrong, huh?'

'You've only been exposed to people like Guto, who are the most vocal but not typical. For most of this century Welsh people have been looking up to anybody prepared to notice they're even there. Especially the English.'

'You're talking as a nationalist. It's an outdated concept.'

'How else can we defend what is ours? The English wanted more water for Liverpool and Birmingham, so they came into

Wales and flooded our valleys. Whole Welsh villages at the bottom of English reservoirs. And the humble Welsh people went to work for the English water boards and said how good they were and how well they looked after their employees.'

'Sure, yeah, but—'

'I know, that was years ago. But they are doing it again. Only this time they're flooding us with people and they're drowning our language and our culture.'

Berry put his fork down. 'You know,' he said. 'You're beautiful when you're defending your culture.'

'Sir, with my hand on my heart, I can tell you that even if you were prepared to sleep standing up in the third floor broom-cupboard, I would not be able to accommodate you.'

The proprietor of the Plas Meurig Hotel (two-star) was a short, plump Englishman in a double-breasted fawn-coloured suit which matched the walls of the hotel lobby.

'I'm prepared to pay over the odds, if necessary,' George said.

'Sir, I've turned away Conservative members of Parliament who are prepared to pay *well* over the odds. I've turned away a senior editor from Independent Television News with a chequebook as thick as the New Testament. I swear if I could get an extension block put up in five days, I'd call in the builders now and apply for planning permission later. I could be making a fortune. But I am utterly full and there's nothing I can do about it.'

'Well, where else would you recommend?'

'In this town, to be quite honest, there's nowhere I'd actually *recommend*. But I seriously don't believe there's anywhere you'd get in anyway.'

'Let's not be stupid about this,' George said to Elinor outside. 'It's going to be a damn cold night. I think we should ring Claire.'

At the top of the wide street, on the same side as the restaurant, was a very old building with flags protruding from its deep grey stonework.

Bethan said, 'This is where Owain Glyndwr convened the first Welsh parliament in 1403. By that time he was in control of most of Wales – the nearest we ever came to ruling ourselves.'

Inside, there was a tourist reception area with books about Wales and about Owain Glyndwr, including Guto's paperback.

'I bought one, you know,' Berry said. 'Still in the car.'

'It's really very good,' Bethan said. 'You should make time to read it.'

They saw a replica of Glyndwr's parliament table, pictures of the man himself, one of him sitting solemnly in state. The only real distinctive thing about him, Berry reckoned, was the fork in his beard, like somebody had tried to cleave his head apart from underneath.

'Hold on,' he said, as they emerged onto the street. 'I just realised who this guy is. He's Owen Glendower, from Shakespeare. Henry the Fourth Part One or Part Two, I can't remember. The point being—'

'Part One, I think,' Bethan said.

'The point being that Owen Glendower was a horse's ass. Pompous, full of shit—'

'The point being,' Bethan snapped, 'that Shakespeare was biased. The real Owain was a fairly modest, cultured man who studied law in London, had many English friends and would never have gone to war with England if he hadn't been faced with a completely untenable—'

'OK, OK .' Berry held up his hands. Few other people were in sight on the wide, cold street. Bethan was facing him on the pavement, small lips tight, fists clenched by her sides. This was not about the rights and wrongs of Welsh nationalism or whether Owain Glyndwr was full of shit.

Her fists unclenched. She looked small and alone and without hope.

'I think,' she said slowly. 'I think I am ready now to have my nervous breakdown.'

CHAPTER LI

THE Rhos Tafol Hotel was a white-painted former farmhouse about six miles west of Machynlleth. It overlooked the placid Dyfi estuary, beyond which mountains lay back, pink and gold in the last light of the last day in November.

The Rhos Tafol dated back to the seventeenth century and had a suite with a four-poster bed. OK, a *reproduction* four-poster. But four posts were four posts.

Tenderly, he kissed a small, pale left breast. 'How would you feel,' he said, 'about *another* nervous breakdown?'

The sky over the inn was like bronze tinfoil, the cottages around it coloured ochre and sepia and clustered together like chocolates.

Yes, it was beautiful. She had to agree. It cast its spell.

And inside the beauty it was only a village, only houses with front doors and gardens and electric cookers and televisions. It could not harm her.

This was because, before leaving Pontmeurig in the Land-Rover, Elinor had taken two valium.

Claire steered them casually, one-handed, over the bridge. 'You never know, having to come back here – it might be destiny.'

Destiny, Elinor thought. Dessss-tinnny. Fated to see it like this, in what passed for sunset. To understand why they were all so attracted to it.

'Or it might simply be incompetence and inefficiency,' George growled, trying to hold a match to his cigarette as they jolted to a halt in front of the inn. 'Can't for the life of me understand how they managed to send the wrong damn parts.'

Destiny and fate and beauty, Elinor thought, drifting. I shall leave tomorrow and still look back with a degree of hatred.

'Perhaps we should have taken it to Dilwyn's,' Claire was saying. 'Dilwyn is very good at improvising.'

'Don't want a Mickey Mouse job,' George said, opening his door, peering out. 'Don't know why you can't have a proper car, Claire. Hell of a way to the ground from these things.'

'You said that yesterday,' Elinor said, opening her own door, putting a foot into the air, giggling.

'Mother, wait . . .'

But she fell into the gravel. She was crying when Claire went to help her to her feet. 'Don't mind me, darling,' she said miserably, clutching her handbag to her chest.

Night came and they did not leave the reproduction four-poster bed, did not go down to dinner.

She clung to him for hours.

He woke intermittently, hearing voices from the bar below. Mainly voices speaking Welsh. Local people, farmers. He and Bethan must be the only guests.

It occurred to him that in only a few hours' time he was going to be out of a job. He could, of course, steal quietly out of bed and drive like hell through the night, reaching London by dawn, just time to shower and shave and change and present himself at Addison's desk by nine-fifteen. Then again . . . He hugged Bethan tightly. She moaned softly. Her body was slick with her own sweat, nothing to do with the sex. He hoped she was sweating out all the pain.

He slept.

Woke again. No noise from the bar now. Bethan stirring in his arms, mumbling, 'Which of us is sweating?'

'Don't wish to be ungallant,' he said, 'But I think it's you. I also think' – licking moisture from her shoulder – 'I also think I love you. Is this premature?'

'You don't know what you are saying.'

'Do too.'

'We've talked so much, you think you've known me for a long time, but it was only yesterday. What I think—'

'Don't care what you think. No, yes I do. I care.'

'I think having so much to talk over, things we'd never told anyone . . . that is a great stimulant.'

'Like Welsh lovespoons,' Berry said.

She kissed him. 'What are you talking about?'

'Those lovespoons. The long wooden ones. Aren't they some kind of Celtic dildo?'

For maybe a couple of seconds, because they'd pulled the curtains around the bed and it was too dark to see her face, he had the impression she thought he was serious.

Then a small hand closed around his balls.

'No, hey . . . I didn't mean it . . . Bethan, geddoff . . . I'll never . . . Bethan!'

After a third, rather more languorous nervous breakdown, she said, 'I have *got* to have a shower.'

'OK.'

'Alone! You stay and read Guto's book. It is the least you can do for him now.'

'Because I went off with his woman?'

'I am *not* his woman!'

'Well, he obviously—'

'Shut up and read the book.'

He looked at his watch on the floor by the bed. It was three-fifteen in the morning. They'd been in bed since about four-thirty yesterday afternoon.

Hell, he'd left all his stuff at Mrs Evans's. What was she going to think? More of a problem, what was Guto going to think?

As they'd had no cases – and not wishing to make anything *too* obvious – they'd carried everything they could find out of the Sprite's trunk. Bags full of useless stuff lay under the window, on top of them the two books – Guto's *Glyndwr* and the red notebook George Hardy had given Bethan.

Berry switched on a bedside lamp with pictures of Tudor houses on the shade. He heard the rush of the shower. He began to read, the way journalists read official documents when they have only twenty minutes to extract the essence.

She was right about Glyndwr. He was an articulate, educated guy who'd probably had no ambitions to rule an independent Wales. This had been a lost cause since the last official Prince of Wales, Llywelyn, had bought it in the thirteenth century. All the same, people in Wales – where there seemed less of a social gap between the peasants and the landowning classes – felt they were getting a raw deal from the English king, Henry IV. And Owain Glyndwr had been pushed into confrontation when some of his own land was snatched by one of Henry's powerful supporters, one Reginald de Grey, who seemed to have had it in for Glyndwr in a big way.

Guto's style was straightforward, fluid and readable – and maybe as biased as Shakespeare in its way. But Berry was prepared to give him the benefit of the doubt as he read the enthusiastic account of Glyndwr's rebellion which, at one stage, had put almost the whole of Wales under his control. Guto implied that a Wales under Glyndwr and his parliament would have come closer than anywhere else in Europe to some kind of medieval democracy. It was an appealing theory.

The book was fairly dismissive about Glyndwr's reputation as a wielder of supernatural forces – a side of him which had certainly caught Shakespeare's imagination. The only lines Berry could remember from Henry IV were Glendower claiming,

I can call spirits from the vasty deep.

Oh, sure, somebody had replied, or words to that effect. But are they really gonna show up when you do call for them?

Dr D.G. Evans quoted Shakespeare some more, Glendower boasting,

> *. . . at my birth*
> *The front of heaven was full of fiery shapes.*
> *The goats ran from the mountains, and the herds*
> *Were strangely clamourous to the frightened field.*
> *These signs have mark'd me extraordinary;*
> *And all the courses of my life do show*
> *I am not in the roll of common men.*

There had been claims, Guto wrote, that Glyndwr had been trained in Druidic magic and could alter the weather – a couple of his victories were put down to this ability. All crap, Guto said: the English view of the Welsh as wildmen from the mountains who, having no military sophistication, needed to put their faith in magic.

None the less, Guto conceded, all this stuff added to Glyndwr's charisma, put him alongside King Arthur as the great Celtic hero who never really died and one day would return to free his people from oppression.

Prophecies. Signs and portents and prophecies.

Bethan came out of the bathroom, a big towel around her. She looked wonderful, black hair all tangled, skin aglow in the warm light of the Tudor lamp.

'Feel better?' He tossed the book on the bed, rose and filled the electric kettle sitting there with tea and coffee and biscuits and soft drinks. One worthwhile extra that inns had picked up from the motel trade.

Bethan sat on the edge of the bed, towelling her hair.

'What happened to him? Glyndwr.'

'He retired, defeated.' Bethan said through the towel.

'Checked in at a retirement home for aged rebels, huh?'

'By the early 1400s, he was losing ground,' Bethan said patiently. 'It all fell apart and Owain just disappeared. He had a daughter near Hereford and one story suggests he went to live with her.'

'In England?'

'I am afraid so. But at least he could still see the Welsh hills.'

'Sad.'

'All Welsh history is sad.'

'Jesus, how would the Welsh survive without self-pity?'

'Unfair,' Bethan said. 'But tonight, I am prepared to excuse you.'

'Bethan . . .' He hesitated. 'Is this the first time since . . .?'

'Robin. Yes.'

'How do you feel about that?'

She put the towel down. Faced him across the bed. Her

eyes were brown and luminous in the lamplight. 'Glad,' she said. 'I have tried to feel bad but I don't. I wish we could stay here for a very long time.'

Pouring boiling water on four teabags – it wasn't a very big pot – he thought, I don't have a job to go to, neither does she.

'We can stay here a while,' he said. 'Buy a change of clothes.' He ran a hand across his chin. 'Razor. Toothpaste.'

'No,' she said. 'We can't. You know we can't.'

'Maybe we're both chasing shadows.'

Bethan said, 'You wanted to know about the bird of death.'

'Right now I can do without the bird of death.'

She said in a rush, 'The bird of death is supposed to come at night and tap on your window. It's an omen, like the *cannwyll gorff* and the *toili*, the phantom funeral. Sometimes it flutters its wings. At night, this – unnatural. Sometimes . . .' Bethan clutched the towel around her breasts. 'Sometimes it has no wings at all.'

'Why couldn't Claire's mom have simply been disturbed by an owl?'

'Oh, Berry,' Bethan said in exasperation. 'I am not saying she actually *saw* anything. It's what she *believes* she saw or heard or whatever. Yes, you're right, it's all nonsense. These things don't even exist – except, somehow, in the minds of people living in Y Groes.'

'I didn't say that. I never said it was nonsense.'

'Meaning?'

'Meaning I'm prepared to believe there's something essentially weird about the place.' He poured tea, passed her a cup. Gave the pot a stir and then poured a murkier brew for himself. 'We're talking about this now?'

'Yes.'

'OK, let's lay it all on the table and push it around. Robin died suddenly. Giles too. Suddenly, but natural causes. Who else?'

'Dilwyn Dafis, who runs the local garage. He had an English wife, a young secretary. He met her on holiday. Within a year or so of coming to Y Groes, she was dead. Breast cancer, I think, and it spread very rapidly.'

'That's three.'

'A couple of years ago, the Church in Wales sent a young Englishman as curate to ap Siencyn. I don't know much about this, but he had some sort of fall in the church. Broke his neck.'

'Four. Three natural causes, one accident.'

'And a suicide.' She told him about a child leading her to a body hanging from a tree by the riverbank.

'*You* found him?'

She nodded, lowered her heavy eyelids. With one small breast exposed, she looked like a creation of one of those Italian painters Berry didn't know enough about. Botticelli, maybe. No, too slim for Botticelli, hair too dark. Aura too sad.

'You had a bad time,' he said. Understatement.

'And then there was another one, about the same time as the suicide.'

She reached down for the red notebook. 'This is his, I'm sure. He was a historian of some sort. He came to the school once. He was writing a book about relations between Wales and England in the late medieval period, had some theory involving Y Groes. He wouldn't tell *me* about it, a little Welsh schoolteacher. He was a very pompous man. Nobody really liked him and yet they humoured him, let him stay at the *Tafarn.*'

'Could they stop him?'

'The *Tafarn* does not provide overnight accommodation. They have a dining room for local functions, but no bed and breakfast.'

'What about Claire's mom and dad? They stayed there.'

'Only, presumably, because Claire requested it. And yet Aled gave this man – that's Aled the landlord there – he gave this man Ingley a room. An unpleasant, prying English academic. That is curious, don't you think?'

'And he died, this guy?'

'A heart attack, they said. Found dead in bed.'

'Police called in?'

'No need.' Bethan riffled the pages of the red notebook.

'The local GP, Dr Wyn, examined him, said he knew of his heart condition and signed a death certificate.'

'Why'd this guy conceal his notebook under the floorboards?'

Bethan shook her head.

'How do you know it was his?'

She opened the notebook. 'Little maps of the village, rough plans of the church. Very detailed notes on a late-medieval tomb. Pages of references to different textbooks. Addresses. And look at it.' She passed him the book. 'It's quite new. The pages are a little dusty but not in the least yellow. It obviously had not been under the floor very long.'

Berry sighed. 'Problem about all this – you got half a dozen deaths. OK, all premature. But all of them *explained*. No mystery here. Nothing you could tell the cops.'

He dropped the red notebook on top of the Glyndwr paperback. 'Paranoia, Bethan. That's what they'd say. And what about Claire? She's English; nothing happened to her.'

'You heard what her mother said. She was taken to see her grandfather as a small child. He disappeared with her. We don't know what happened then. All I know is that while Giles was desperately struggling with basic Welsh, Claire was mastering the grammar and pronunciation at a speed I could not believe. And there are other things. *You've* seen the changes, her mother's seen it. It's uncanny. Eerie.'

'True,' he conceded. Reached across the bed, pulled her into his arms. 'But what the hell can we do about it?'

'I'm only relieved,' she said, wet hair against his chest, 'that her parents managed to get away before . . .'

CHAPTER LII

DID George *know* she was on valium?

She thought he must. How could anyone be expected to cope with reality as dismal as this without a little something to place a distance between one and it?

George did not, of course, need anything himself. Some sedative side of his mind seemed to be turned on automatically whenever life threatened to cross the pain threshold.

He certainly enjoyed his dinner again.

The little licensee had gone to great pains to make sure they were comfortable, lighting a log fire in the dining room where they ate alone. Serving lamb which George said was more tender and succulent than any he'd had before, even in the most expensive restaurants.

She had no opinion on this, did not remember tasting it.

The wine, though, she drank some of that, quite a lot in fact.

'Steady on, Elinor,' George had said, predictably, at one point.

At which she'd poured more.

'Another bottle, Mr Hardy?' The little landlord, dapper at George's elbow.

'Oh, I don't think—'

'Yes please,' she'd said to the landlord.

Thinking of the combined sedative punch of valium and alcohol and deciding she needed to be entirely out of her head if she was to sleep the night through.

'When's Claire coming?' Pushing her plate away.

'She isn't.' George lighting a cigarette, blue smoke everywhere. 'She's picking me up first thing, then we can get the car back. Won't take them more than half an hour once they've got the parts. So I told Claire not to bother coming over, we'd be having an early night.'

'An early night?' Elinor croaking a mirthless laugh as a log collapsed in the fireplace. 'Bit late for that now.'

'Have some coffee.'

'Don't want coffee, thank you. The Welsh can't make proper coffee. Nescafe and Maxwell House are all one ever gets in Wales.'

'Actually, what I didn't want—' George leaning across the table, voice lowered, '—was another night in that awful bar, all this bonhomie.'

'Oh, I hate it too, George. I shall drink here.'

'Please, Elinor . . . We'll be away tomorrow.'

'You bet your miserable life we will. If we have to flag down a long-distance lorry driver and show him my drooping tits.'

'Elinor!' Through his teeth. '. . . God's sake.'

'Perhaps I'd've been better off with a lorry driver, what do think George? Common people have fun.'

'Are you coming?' Getting to his feet, taking his cigarette with him.

'Did you ever imagine, George, that the day would come when you'd want to get me to bed only to save embarrassment?'

'Yes,' George said brutally.

She awoke thinking the night was over.

A reasonable mistake to make. There was a brightness beyond the curtains, before which all the furniture in the bedroom was blackly silhouetted.

But her watch showed 3.55 a.m.

Elinor, in a white nightdress, slid her feet into her wooden Scholls, made her way unsteadily to the door, turning the handle slowly because, for once, her husband was sleeping quietly, no snoring.

At least the radiators in this place worked efficiently. It must be a freezing night outside, but the atmosphere in the bedroom was close, almost stuffy. Same on the landing outside.

She locked herself in the bathroom, two doors away, used the lavatory. She was disappointed but not surprised that the combination of drink and valium had failed to take her all the way to the daylight. Washing her hands afterwards, she could not bear to look into the mirror over the basin, knowing how raddled she must look, still in last night's make-up for the first time in thirty-odd years.

She had no headache, but was certainly on the way down from wherever she'd been, despising herself utterly.

Why had they come? What had she been trying to prove?

Come to pay their last respects to their good and upright son-in-law. And to be at their daughter's side in her hour of need.

300

A joke. Claire had not needed them for years and would never need them now.

She bent her head over the sink, turned on taps again. Feebly splashed water on her face, left great lipstick smears on the towel wiping it off.

This time she did look up into the mirror. And in her sick clown's face she saw her father's eyes.

'Your fault,' she hissed. 'All this. I hope your soul is rotting.'

Her father's eyes did not flicker.

She turned away, pulled back the bolt and switched off the bathroom light, thankful for one thing: at least they had not set foot in his house. Not that Claire had invited them. Not once.

When she returned to their room, George was lying on his side, face to the wall. 'Mmmmmmmph,' he said.

At home they had twin beds. Next year, she decided, she would move into a separate room.

How far off morning?

The watch said 4.21.

But the light through the curtains was brighter. It could not be long.

She stood by the window; her hand moved to lift up the curtain . . . and pulled back. Suppose that bird was there again?

Beyond the drawn curtains it grew brighter still, blue-white like constant lightning.

'Errrrmph.' George rolled over.

Elinor forced herself to pull back the curtain a little, and she looked down into the village street.

The street was blue with cold.

Radiantly blue. A mat of frost the colour of a midsummer sky was rolling out over the river-bridge towards the inn.

Along this chilly carpet a figure moved.

He had a long overcoat of grey, falling to the frosted road, and a wide-brimmed hat which shadowed his downcast face. He moved like a column of smoke, hands deep in the folds of his coat.

She could not see his feet or hear his footsteps, only a sharp, brittle sound, perhaps the frost itself. He left long, shallow tracks behind him but, as she watched, the marks in the frost healed over and the bright blue ground shone savagely cold and mockingly untrodden.

The figure advanced towards the door of the inn, and with each of his steps the temperature dropped around Elinor, as if the radiators were shutting down in great shudders. Her body began to quake, her teeth to chatter, and the fingers holding back the curtain were numbed.

Reaching the door of the inn, the visitor paused, the cold rising from him like steam, brought a hand out of his pocket as if to knock.

It was not a hand but the yellow, twisted, horny talon of a bird of prey.

'Shut up! Stop that screaming, you stupid, bloody drunken bitch!'

Her body arched at the waist, her neck extended as if she were trying to vomit.

'Are you totally insane, woman? Shut up! Do you hear me, you bitch?'

On his feet now, between her and the window, George grabbed her by the shoulders and threw her down on the bed. 'Stop it!'

She looked up into her husband's bulging, sleep-swollen eyes.

Hands clenched around her bony shoulders, he lifted her from the bed then slammed her down again.

And again.

This time her skull crashed sickeningly into the headboard of Victorian mahogany.

George's eyes were opaque.

He smashed her down again, lifted her up, smashed her down, a rhythmic motion, grunting 'Stop it.'

Stop it.

Stop it.

Stop it.

PART EIGHT

THE RED BOOK
OF INGLEY

CHAPTER LIII

THEY watched each other over the breakfast table, different people now. She wore yesterday's black cowl-neck sweater and the big gold earrings; his sweatshirt still identified him as an American werewolf in London. But they were different people.

The Rhos Tafol's dining room overlooked the estuary, shining cobalt in the chill morning. There were perhaps twenty tables in the room, all stripped bare except for the one where they sat, by the window.

December.

'We could just walk away from it.' Berry spread marmalade on dry toast.

Bethan looked down into her boiled egg. He loved the fall of her eyelids; it was what put him in mind of the women in Renaissance paintings.

'Or not,' Berry said.

They'd lain and talked about it until the dawn streaked the Dyfi. She'd told him about Claire in the river Meurig, washing away the English. And about Claire's photos; the tree that vanished, whatever that meant.

He'd told her about old Winstone – whatever *that* meant.

Also about Miranda. Who was funny and diverting but belonged to the person he used to be before last night.

'So.' Crunching toast.

Bethan said. 'When I came back from Swansea to be head teacher – less than six months ago, I can't believe it – I thought I was going to change everything. Let some light into the place. It was pretty hard to do, coming back.'

'I don't know how you could.'

'The way I rationalised it, it was going to be a kind of memorial to Robin. Modernising the school, changing the outlook of the children. It was a mission. But—'

'—You didn't realise what you were taking on.'

305

'I was *very* determined. Nothing left to lose. Ready to fight centuries of tradition. And Buddug.'

'Buddug's this other teacher.'

'The name Buddug,' Bethan said, stirring the tea in the pot to make it blacker, 'is Welsh for Boudicca, or Boadicea.'

'The hard-nosed broad who took on the Romans,' he remembered. 'Drove this chariot with long knives sticking out the wheels, relieving whole legions of their genitalia.'

'I had never thought of it quite like that, but the way you depict it, it does seem horrifyingly plausible, yes.'

'She's like that, this Buddug?'

'She's worse,' Bethan said.

'And what you're saying is you think you might accomplish now what you couldn't when you came back from Swansea?'

'I am not alone this time,' Bethan said, and his heart took off.

'C'mon, honey.' She turned over, coughed. 'One more time for Berry.' She turned over again, caught.

'She is very old,' Bethan said.

'We don't discuss her age. It upsets her. When I'm in London, this guy checks her over every few weeks. You can still get the parts, if you know where to look.'

He followed the estuary back towards Machynlleth. 'I like it here. I like feeling close to the sea. You wouldn't care to stay another night, think about things some more?'

'I told you last night, I should *like* to stay here a very long time.' She sighed. 'Keep driving, Morelli.'

'One point,' Berry said, pushing the Sprite into the town, towards the Gothic clock tower. 'You're a nationalist, right? Guto's a nationalist. This Buddug and all the people in Y Groes, they're nationalists too.'

'Why, then, did Guto go down like the proverbial lead balloon?'

'Precisely.'

'You have to live in Wales a long time to work it out,' Bethan said. 'And just when you think you've understood the way it is . . .'

She ran the fingers of both hands through her hair, as if to untangle her thoughts.

'You see . . . There are different kinds of Welsh nationalism. There is Plaid Cymru, which envisages a self-governing Wales with its own economic structure – an independent, bilingual state within the European Community. And there is another sort which you might compare with the National Front, the Ku Klux Klan, yes?'

'Extreme right wing.'

'Except they would not think of themselves like that. They are protecting their heritage, they feel the same things we all feel from time to time, but—' She sighed again. 'I'm afraid there are some people for whom being Welsh is more important than being human.'

'And – let me guess here – this type of person sees Plaid as a half-baked outfit which no longer represents the views of the real old Welsh nation, right?'

'Yes. Exactly. *Da iawn*.'

'Huh?'

'Very good. In moments of exultation, I revert to my first language.'

'So that's what it was,' Berry said, remembering moments of last night.

Driving south in worsening weather, Berry wondered why neither of them had put a name to what they were up against. Six deaths. Accident, suicide and natural causes. All English people, no other connecting factor. They couldn't be talking murder. Not as the law saw it.

'Bethan,' he said. 'Can we discuss what happened to Giles?'

Sparse sleet stung the screen.

'*Listen* to me now,' she said, as if this had been building up inside for some while. 'There is one thing I haven't told you.'

Above the whine of the wind in the Sprite's soft top, she revealed to him the truth about Giles's 'fall' in the castle car park in Pont. Why they'd kept quiet about it.

'Giles himself was particularly anxious people should

307

believe it was a fall. I think he was embarrassed. Does that make sense to you?'

'I guess it does. Say the two guys are arrested, there's a court case. And then everybody working with Giles in London knows he got beat up on. In his beloved Wales. Yeah, I can buy that. No way would he want that out, the poor sucker.'

Bethan squeezed his hand on the wheel. 'I am so relieved. I was worried you would think we covered it up to protect ourselves.'

'Guto, yes. You, no. So who were they, these guys?'

'Just yobs. Troublemakers. Guto threw one in the castle ditch. I would know them again. We all would.'

'If it came out,' Berry wondered, 'is there any way we could use it to turn the heat on this thing? This guy, Inspector Jones—'

'Gwyn Arthur.'

'Yeah. Seemed approachable.'

'He is a nice man. But Giles did not die as a result of the attack. What could Gwyn Arthur really do now?'

'If only there'd been an inquest . . .'

'But what would it reveal? The medical evidence says he had an enormous tumour. What I would ask is, why did he *develop* the tumour? Why did Robin develop leukaemia? Why did the hiker hang himself by the river? Why did the professor . . . ? It's not something an inquest can go into, is it?'

'Paranoid delusions, Beth. Bethan. Listen, this may seem a distinctly American way of looking at things, and I apologise in advance, but is there anybody we could *beat* the truth out of?'

'Not my style,' Bethan said.

'Naw, me neither.'

'I am glad to hear it. But, look, there *are* still people we can talk to. I know . . . Why don't you stop at the next phone box.'

'We aren't gonna see any dead people, are we?' Berry was uncomfortable. He hated these places.

'Don't be a wimp. They cannot harm you.'

He shuddered. 'Bad enough seeing those pictures of Giles.'

'I know,' Bethan said quietly. 'I was there when they were taken.'

'Jesus, I'm sorry.' He kissed the top of her head. 'Forgive me?'

'I shall think about it,' she said.

'Bethan! is that you?'

'Hello, Dai. Where are you?'

'In the embalming room, come on through.'

Berry felt his legs giving way.

'Only kidding,' the bald man said, pushing through the purple curtains. 'Oh, I'm sorry, Bethan, I thought you had Guto with you. Bugger won't go within a mile of the embalming room, see.' He chuckled.

Bethan said, 'This is Berry Morelli. He and Guto have a similar attitude to death.'

Dai shook hands with Berry. The undertaker's hand was mercifully dry, no traces of embalming fluid. 'Morelli. Italian, is it? You want to go to that pizza place next door, show the buggers how to do it properly.'

Berry shook his head. 'No way you can teach an Englishman to make a pizza.'

'This could be true,' Dai said. 'The trouble with an Englishman, however, is he doesn't believe there is anything he cannot do. Come through to the office.'

The office looked out over a cleanly swept, white-walled yard. Over the top of the end wall they could see a segment of Pontmeurig castle.

There were four hard chairs with purple velvet seats and a desk. It had a phone on it and a diary, four brass coffin handles and a thickset man with crinkly grey hair.

Bethan said, 'Berry, this is Idwal Pugh. He is the mayor of Pontmeurig.'

'Hi, Mayor,' Berry said, shaking Idwal's hand. 'Berry Morelli. Don't get up.'

'I can never quite bring myself to sit on a chair in here,' Idwal Pugh said, short legs dangling over the side of the desk. 'Don't want to feel I'm here on business, see.'

'One day,' said Dai, 'we'll bring you in feet first, you bugger. Now, Bethan . . .'

'This is difficult,' Bethan said. 'And in confidence, please.'

'Of course,' Dai said. 'Sit down. I have told Big Gladys to make some tea.'

'Idwal, you remember that night at the Drovers' . . . Well, of course you do.'

'Oh *that* night,' Idwal said. 'I told you, we should have gone to—' He looked at Berry in alarm. 'Not police, this chap, is he?'

'He's a friend of Giles,' Bethan said. 'And of mine. No, he's not police.'

'Only, I thought, with this, you know—'

'Idwal, relax,' Dai said. 'I am not so short of work that I *want* you to have a stroke.'

'And we were talking,' Bethan said, 'that night, before the trouble, about Y Groes, if you remember. Dai was annoyed that Giles Freeman had managed to secure a house there when he could not. And you said—'

'I suppose I said I would not want to live there myself.'

'Correct,' Bethan said. 'You said, I think, that it was ungodly. Why did you say that?'

'What are you getting at here, Bethan?'

'Just tell me why you said that.'

'Well, I suppose . . . I'm a chapel man, see. Always been a chapel man.'

'Yes, and the only chapel in Y Groes is Dilwyn Dafis's garage before it was converted.'

'Well, see, it isn't just that . . .' Idwal began to fill his pipe. 'This is only my own thoughts, Bethan.'

'Yes, fine. Go on.'

'Well, this is a non-conformist area. Every village has at least one chapel.'

'At least,' Bethan said.

'But I remember, when I was a youngster, my dad telling me how they almost had to have a missionary expedition to take the Chapel to Y Groes. Known as Y Groesfan then, the crossing place. And the only village without a chapel. Only the other side of the Nearly Mountains, but it might have been some pagan place in Africa, the way they campaigned and raised the money.'

310

'Who campaigned?' Berry asked.

'Ah, well, see, this is the point. There was a farmer – I forget his name – who moved up towards Eglwys Fawr for a bigger farm and became a convert to the Chapel. And he still kept a field in Y Groesfan, on the edge of the village there. And he said, I will give this field for a chapel to be built there, and everybody began to raise money, in Eglwys, in Pont, in chapels down as far as Lampeter and Cardigan. It became a . . . how do you say it in English . . . ?'

'*Cause célèbre?*' said Berry.

'Exactly. A *cause célèbre*. Everybody gave money for the new chapel in Y Groesfan. And I am asking myself why. What was there in the history of this village that everybody should instinctively put their hands in their pockets to raise the money for a chapel, when there was no demand from the inhabitants. No demand whatsoever, even though many doors were knocked upon and Bibles proffered.'

'But surely, it's a *church* village?'

'Pah!' said Idwal, puffing contemptuously on his pipe.

'So they raised the money and they built the chapel,' Bethan said. 'What happened then?'

'Oh, it went very well for a time. Like, as I say, a missionary conquest of some pagan place in Africa. People travelled from miles around to attend services at the new chapel. Like a pilgrimage, see. The first motorcoach outings from Pont were to Y Groes – they'd got the name changed now, as well, to reflect its new status. The Cross. Oh, it was wonderful, for a while.'

'And what happened?' said Berry.

Idwal shrugged. 'Some say it was the war. Or that it was like everything that burns so bright. Soon extinguished. But myself, I think there is something in that place that needs to be cleaned out before the Lord can enter in. It seems to me . . .'

There was a loud tap on the office door, and it was shouldered open by a large girl whose hair was streaked in gold and purple like the curtains in the chapel of rest. She was carrying a tea tray.

'Thank you, Gladys,' Dai said.

'Will you be going over to Y Groes, Mr Williams, because you've another appointment at twelve. Do you want me to put them off?'

'I'm not going anywhere, girl. Why would you think that?'

'Well, no, I just thought, with the murder. Put it down here, shall I? If Mr Pugh will move his legs.'

'Murder?' Berry said.

'Oh hell, Gladys,' Dai said. 'Murder is a different thing altogether. Police do their own fetching and carrying with a murder.'

'Only they've found something else now, Jane was telling me from the café. More police cars gone chasing up the Nearly Mountains.'

'Bloody tragic,' Dai said, and it was not clear whether he was talking about the death or the fact that, because it was murder, he had not been called in to remove the body.

'Poor girl,' Idwal said. 'First she loses her husband, and now . . .' He shook his head.

'No,' Bethan whispered. 'Oh, please, no—'

'Oh, Christ,' Dai said. 'I thought you knew – I thought that was why you were asking all this?'

CHAPTER LIV

THE police car pulled in behind Gwyn Arthur's fraying Fiesta. Detective Sergeant Neil Probert got out and looked down to where his chief was standing, at the bottom of a steep bank, about twenty yards from the road.

Probert, the Divisional natty dresser, was clearly hoping Gwyn Arthur would climb up and join him at the roadside. But when the Chief stood his ground, Probert wove a delicate path down the bank, hitching up his smart trousers at the waist.

'Thinking of joining the Masons, are we, Neil?' inquired Gwyn Arthur. 'Come on man, the mud's all frozen!'

'Except for that bit,' he added with malicious relish as

Probert squelched to a halt in a patch of boggy ground, where all the ice had been melted by the heat from the Volvo's engine.

The big blue car had gone down the bank and into a tangle of thorn bushes. Three police officers were cutting and tearing the bushes away for the benefit of a female Home Office pathologist who was rather attractive – certainly the best thing they could hope to encounter on a December morning in the Nearly Mountains.

'I spoke to the garage, sir,' Probert said, squeezing brackish water from the bottoms of his trousers. 'He picked up his car at just after nine-thirty. Appeared quiet and precoccupied but not otherwise agitated. Inquired at the garage about a hardware shop and they directed him to Theo Davies, where he bought twenty feet of rubber pipe.'

'Not dissimilar, I take it,' said Gwyn Arthur, 'to the hose we see here affixed to the exhaust pipe.'

'Indeed, sir,' Probert said.

'In that case, Neil, it looks like a wrap.'

'Yes, sir.'

'Would you like to have a look at him, in case anything occurs to you?'

'No thank you, sir.'

'He doesn't look bad. Pink and healthy. Kind it is, to a corpse, carbon monoxide.'

'So I understand, sir.'

Gwyn Arthur nodded. 'All that remains, it seems to me, is for Mollie to furnish Forensic with a few traces of blood of the appropriate group.'

'Hang on, Gwyn, I'm not even in the bloody car yet,' the pathologist called across, and Gwyn Arthur smiled at her.

'Just a point, Neil. Did anyone see him arrive at the garage?'

'Yes, sir. He was in a blue Land-Rover driven by a young female. Assumed to be his daughter.'

Gwyn Arthur nodded. Shortly after the discovery of her mother's body, the back of its head a mess, he'd spent ten minutes talking to Mrs Claire Freeman. Obviously in shock, but remarkably coherent, Mrs Freeman had told of picking up her father, as pre-arranged, at eight-fifteen and driving him to Pontmeurig. It had been agreed that Mr Hardy would return with the car to collect his wife. His manner, as described by his daughter, was in no way suspicious. Indeed, he had several times expressed the hope that the car would be ready to collect so that he could take Mrs Hardy home.

'If you find a pen, Mollie—'

'I know, I know . . .'

In a plastic sack at Gwyn Arthur's feet was an AA book, found on the passenger seat, partly under the dead man's head. Across the yellow cover of the book had been scrawled,

I'm so sorry. I do not know why it happened. I loved her really.

That poor girl.

In thirty years of police work, Gwyn Arthur had several times encountered people around whom tragedies grew like black flowers. This was definitely the worst case – compounded by her being stranded in a remote village in a strange country.

He thought fleetingly of the death of Giles Freeman, of the American who had come to the station with his undisclosed suspicions. Undoubtedly, there was more to this than any of them realised, but the details were likely to be deeply private, and what good would come of digging it over now? It was a wrap. He had a result. Murder and suicide, a common-or-garden domestic. Leave it be.

Chief Inspector Gwyn Arthur Jones: firm believer in compassionate policing.

'Oh, and BBC Wales have been on, sir. I think they might be sending a crew across from Carmarthen.'

'Get back to Mike from the car, tell him to phone and tell them they'll get more excitement out of the by-election.'

Gwyn Arthur jammed his hat over his ears, picked up the plastic bag containing the AA book and followed Probert up the bank.

'Tell him to give them a quote from me,' he said. 'Say we

aren't looking for anyone else in connection with the incident at this time.'

Within the hour, reporters and crews from both BBC Wales and its independent counterpart arrived in Y Groes. Neither attempted to interview Claire. They had no luck with any of the villagers either, in that all those approached refused to give an interview through the medium of English. The licensee of *Tafarn Y Groes*, Aled Gruffydd, sounding very tired and nervous, said a few words to the reporter from Radio Cymru, the BBC's Welsh language radio station. Translated, it came down to, 'This is a terrible tragedy, and we do not want to make things any worse. Just let it go, will you?'

Max Canavan, of the *Sun*, was the only reporter who attempted to talk to the woman who had lost her husband and her parents in separate tragedies within a week. The door of the judge's house was opened to him by a huge, bearded man who informed the reporter in a conversational tone that if he did not leave the village immediately he would not leave it with his arms unbroken.

Deprived thus of a story which might have opened with 'Tragic widow Claire Freeman spoke last night of her grief and horror . . .' the national newspapers ignored what was, after all, only a domestic incident.

CHAPTER LV

So overgrown were the walls of the house with some sort of evergreen creeper that its gabled attic windows looked like the eyes of a hairy sheepdog under pointed ears.

Frightfully Gothic. Even when they retired, she thought, some clergymen just had to find a typical vicarage to hole up in.

She parked the Porsche proudly in the driveway. It was only a secondhand one, with two substantial dents on its left haunch which she'd refused to let them repair. But it looked even better for that. Miranda liked her cars – and her men, come to that – to convey an impression of having been around.

This Canon Peters clearly had been around. He wore a crumpled cream suit, and his clerical collar, if indeed he was wearing one, was hidden behind a beard like those supplied with the more superior Father Christmas outfits.

'My dear,' he said, flinging back the door. He had to be over eighty and yet he was looking at her, Miranda noticed, with the eyes of a man who thought that if he played his cards right he might be in with a chance here.

'*Ex*-lover, eh?' Canon Peters said. 'What can the boy be thinking of? And a Porsche too! Two visions to break an old man's heart. Come through, my dear.'

Phew—! He hadn't been like this on the phone.

Miranda followed the old clergyman along a dim hall and then into a big warmly toned room, its walls painted the creamy colour of his suit.

'Drove Triumph Spitfires for years,' he was saying. 'Now the sods have taken away my licence. Bloody eyesight test.'

'Didn't seem to me that your eyes were terribly deficient,' Miranda said.

'Fiddled the test, if you ask me. Thought I was too old for a sports car. Bloody bureaucrats. Like a drink?'

'Perhaps not,' said Miranda who had once had her own licence taken away, as a result of a mere couple of double gins. Well, perhaps three.

'Suppose I'd think twice too, if I had a Porsche. Coppers love a Porsche.'

'They do indeed. Now, Canon Peters—'

'Alex, please. Sit down, my dear.' He brought himself a whisky and sat next to her on the chintzy sofa, an arm flung across its back behind her. 'I didn't really expect you to come.'

Miranda was surprised too. When the Canon had phoned, she'd been lying on Morelli's bed watching morning television – some awful ex-MP who thought he was God's gift – and feeling somewhat at a loose end. She'd traded in her Golf for the Porsche the previous day, the result of a particularly

gratifying bank statement, and was trying to think of somewhere moderately exciting to exercise it.

But Wales?

Alex was saying, 'I can see you're hooked on this thing
already.' On a coffee table he had a six-speaker ghetto-blaster
of the most overt kind.

'Let me play you what I recorded from the radio. I listen
to Radio Wales every morning, sentimental old sod.'

He pressed the 'play' key. 'Missed the first bit, I'm afraid.
By the time I realised it was significant, damn thing was half
over.'

*. . . was found brutally beaten to death in a bedroom at the
village inn. Mr and Mrs Hardy had been forced to spend the
night at the inn after their car broke down. The couple, who
were from Gloucestershire, were in the area to attend the
funeral of their son-in-law, who died suddenly last week. Mr
Hardy, who was sixty-four, was found dead later this
morning in his car in a remote area about three miles from the
village. Police said they were not looking for a third person
in connection with the incident.*

'There,' said Alex, switching off the ghetto-blaster. 'I think
we can take it, don't you, that these two people were Giles
Freeman's in-laws?'

'It certainly looks that way. Gosh.'

'Did you try to contact your friend Morelli?'

'Oh yes,' Miranda said. 'In fact that's partly why I'm here.'

After the Canon's call she'd rung American Newsnet to
enquire if they had a number for Berry Morelli in Wales and
been told that Berry Morelli, as of this morning, was no longer
working for the agency.

'What?'

'He fired himself,' Addison Walls had said.

'Is he still in Wales?'

'Your guess is good as . . . No, hell, he's there all right,
the weirdo bastard.'

'But what's he *doing* there?

'Listen, lady, if I knew that . . .'

So, in the end, what had really done it for Miranda was the thought that she might be *missing* something.

That what Morelli had been rambling on about was not, in fact, the purest load of old whatsit, but something rather extraordinary – *and she wasn't part of it.*

This, and having no actual work in prospect for at least a month.

And owning a Porsche for the first time in her life and having nothing exciting to do with it.

Miranda's plan was to milk the Canon and drive across to Wales with whatever goodies he had to offer – and a lot of tyre-squealing on the bends.

'Martin,' she said. 'You mentioned somebody called Martin. Who died.'

'Poor Martin, yes. Super chap in his way.'

'So what happened to him?'

'Sure you won't have a drink?'

'After you tell me what happened to this Martin.'

'You're a hard woman,' Alex said, and he recalled how he'd met Martin Coulson some time after his retirement, while doing a spot of part-time lecturing at a Welsh theological college.

Coulson had been a student there, an Englishman, though you wouldn't have thought it, Alex said, to hear the boy speak Welsh.

'I'm no expert, mind. I was brought up in the Rhondda and left there at seventeen. My own Welsh is rudimentary to say the least. But my colleagues were enormously impressed by this young man's dedication. Actually, what it was was an obsession which lasted throughout his time at college. And his achievement was publicly recognised when he was declared Welsh Learner of the Year at the National Eisteddfod.'

'What an accolade,' Miranda said dryly.

'And after he was ordained he was keen to work in a Welsh-speaking parish. So the bishop decided it was time Y Groes had a curate. I think, actually, he was getting rather worried about Ellis Jenkins, the vicar there. Jenkins had been very well known as a poet, writing in English and then increasingly in Welsh and getting his work published under the name Elias ap Siencyn – ap Siencyn being the Welsh version of Jenkins. Anyway, the reason they were worried about him was that his work was becoming . . . shall I say, a little esoteric. And yet somehow strident. Rather extreme in an anti-English way.'

'Loony Welsh Nationalist vicar?'

'Lots of them about, my dear. Never read R.S. Thomas?'

'I've never even read *Dylan* Thomas,' said Miranda shamelessly.

Alex Peters made no comment on this. Miranda had taken note that the author's name which seemed to occur more often than any other on his own bookshelves was Ed McBain.

'Of course, Ellis Jenkins didn't want a curate, but he had no choice in the matter. So Martin, all enthusiasm, fluent in Welsh goes off to Y Groes, and within three months . . . he's dead.'

Miranda waited while Canon Alex Peters filtered whisky through his beard.

'The inquest returned a verdict of misadventure, although I was not convinced.'

'You thought he'd been murdered?'

'Oh, good Lord no, I thought he'd committed suicide.'

'Oh,' said Miranda, disappointed.

'He came to see me. Must have been about three weeks after going to Y Groes to take up his curacy. In a terrible state. Thin, hollow-eyed. Obviously hadn't been eating properly, or sleeping much, I would have said. We had a long discussion. I wanted him to stay the night but he refused. You might think, my dear, that we're all bumbling, stoical chaps, but I can tell you, a clergyman in the throes of emotional crisis is a dreadful sight to behold.'

'Was he a poof?' asked Miranda, this being the only emotional problem she could imagine the average clergyman having to come to terms with.

'Oh, nothing like that. Nothing *sexual*. No, quite simply, the much-lauded Welsh Learner of the Year had got up in the pulpit for the first time, about to deliver his maiden sermon to the assembled villagers of Y Groes – and believe me that parish is one of the few left in Britain that still pulls 'em in on a Sunday. So there he is in the pulpit, fully prepared, rehearsed – and he can't do it. Won't come out.'

'How d'you mean?'

Alex Peters threw up his arms.

'He finds he simply can't preach in Welsh!'

'I don't understand,' said Miranda.

'Neither did he. This man was good. I mean *very* good – one chap at the college told me he sometimes thought Martin Coulson's Welsh was more correct than his own, and he'd lived all his life in Lampeter. And yet whenever he got up in the pulpit at Y Groes, he was completely tongue-tied. And not only that, he found he was increasingly unable to speak Welsh to the villagers he met socially or in the street. I'll always remember what he said to me that afternoon. He said, "You know Alex, when I'm in Y Groes – as soon as I get out of the car – I feel like a damned Englishman again." '

Miranda thought to herself that Martin Coulson must merely have come to his senses after wasting all that time learning a language that was about as much use in the civilised world as Egyptian hieroglyphics. The best thing he could have done was get on the first available train to London.

'I didn't know how to advise him,' Alex Peters said. 'I wondered whether Ellis Jenkins was intimidating him in some way. I suggested he take a few days' holiday and think things over, but he insisted on going back. It's always been a source of great regret to me that I didn't go with him for a day or two – how much help I'd have been, with no Welsh to speak of, is debatable. But, as one gets older, these things prey on one's mind.'

'I gather he went back then.'

'Afraid so. I phoned him once or twice to find out how he was getting on. "Fine," he said. "What about the Welsh?" I said. "Done any preaching?" "Not yet," he said, "but I'm working up to it."

'So what happens next is Jenkins abruptly decides to take a holiday. Never been known before. So, off he goes to North

Wales on the Saturday, and the following day Martin ascends the steps of the pulpit, looks out over the congregation, opens his mouth to deliver the opening words he's presumably spent all night preparing – and has the most appalling nosebleed. I leave you to imagine the scene. Blood all over the pulpit, Martin backing off down the steps and rushing out. Service abandoned in disarray. All this came out at the inquest.'

'How horrid,' Miranda said.

'Next day they find the boy unconscious on the floor of the church. Cracked open his head on the pointed corner of some tomb. Rushed to hospital. Five days in a coma, then gone.'

'Why did they decide it was an accident?'

'Well, he'd had quite a lot to drink, apparently, and he wasn't used to it. There *was* evidence that he was very depressed. That from me, of course – Jenkins was away at the time of the Martin's death, and he was being rather vague and bland about the whole business. And there was no suicide note, and so the feeling was that he must simply have had too much to drink, wandered into the church in the dark, tripped and bashed his head on the tomb. The idea of somebody deliberately smashing his head into the stone didn't appeal.'

'But you thought—' Miranda was finding this rather distressing now. No fun any more.

'I suppose I had the idea of him kneeling there and being suddenly overcome with despair and throwing back his head and – crunch. Sorry, my dear, but you did ask. *Now* can I get you a drink?'

'Yes please,' she said. 'Just a tiny one. Lots of soda.'

Forty minutes later she was roaring westwards – though very much in two minds now about the whole thing.

Thinking seriously about all this, what you had was not an intriguing mystery but something really rather squalid: the story of a grim, unpleasant place where people couldn't settle down and had become unhinged and killed themselves or each other out of sheer depression.

When she'd pressed him, Canon Peters had shrugged and

said he just felt there were certain places you ought to avoid if you possibly could.

'Yes, but *why* . . .?'

'Oh, I don't know, my dear. Why do some places, some people seem to attract tragedy? Is it isolation? In-breeding? Perhaps it's something endemic to the whole area. Why was Winstone Thorpe so bothered about Giles Freeman moving up there? I don't think we'll ever reach any kind of conclusion. But I had it on my conscience that I might have fobbed off young Morelli. And well, you know, after failing to save Martin . . .'

Miranda had been vaguely intrigued by this vicar person, Ellis Jenkins.

'Ah.' The Canon had looked sort of wry. 'I did meet him once, at a conference in Lampeter. Spindly chap, staring eyes. And the stories, of course.'

'What stories?'

'His obsession with the old Celtic church – back at the dawn of Christianity in Britain. And what came before it.'

'And what did come before it?'

'Oh, Druids and things. All tied in with his preoccupation with being Welsh and the Eisteddfod and the Bardic tradition.'

'Tedious,' Miranda said.

'Very, my dear.'

Miranda had graciously declined another drink and whatever else Canon Alex Peters might have had in mind. She hadn't even stopped for lunch at any of the rather-inviting Oxfordshire pubs. The tang of adventure in the air seemed to have dissipated, leaving her quite moody and almost oblivious of the fact that she was driving an actual Porsche.

Morelli was arguably the most uptight, paranoid, insecure person she'd ever been close to. Was he really the right person to be paddling about in this grotty little pool of death and misery?

Miranda prodded the Porsche, and it took the hint and whizzed her off towards the Welsh border.

CHAPTER LVI

BERRY found it disturbing the way his whole life had been dramatically condensed in just two days, his horizon reduced to a shadow.

Was this how it happened? Was this what it did to you? Drew you in, and before you knew it there was no place else to go, and the sky was slowly falling?

He was walking from the little square behind the castle, through the back streets to Guto's place to pick up his stuff, pay his bill, thank Mrs Evans.

And then what?

Not yet noon, but it was like the day had given up on Pontmeurig; the atmosphere had the fuzzy texture of dusk.

He thought about Giles, who, once he'd seen Y Groes, was sunk. Nothing else mattered but to escape to the place – a place where the future, for him, was an illusion.

He thought about the Hardy couple, how desperate she'd been to hightail it out of here and how everything had pushed them back in until, different people by now – they had to be different people – they'd destroyed each other.

Different people.

He'd come here two days ago just to clear his own mind, settle his obligations. Now – he could hardly believe how quickly and simply this had happened – *he had no reason to go back.* The link with London and, through London, with the States had been neatly severed.

And there was Bethan.

Looking at it objectively, he had to face this – Bethan was part of the trap.

Maybe they were part of each other's traps.

Through the front window he could see Mrs Evans inside, dusting plates – a job which, in this house, must be like painting Brooklyn Bridge – and she saw him and put down her duster and rushed to the door.

'Oh, Mr Morelli—' she wailed.

'Hey, listen, I'm real sorry about last night, only I got detained and—'

'You haven't seen Guto, have you?'

No he hadn't, thank God.

'Only he've gone off in a terrible mood again. Came home last night moaning about being betrayed and giving it all up, his – you know – the candidate's job. He doesn't mean it, mind, but he's terrible offended about somebody.'

A somebody with black hair and big gold earrings and eyelids you could die over.

'How, ah, how's his campaign going?'

'Oh dear, you haven't seen the paper?'

On the hallstand, among about a dozen plates, was a copy of that morning's *Western Mail*, folded around a story in which Conservative candidate Simon Gallier was suggesting that support for Plaid Cymru was rapidly falling away. He had based his conclusion on a Plaid public meeting in the totally Welsh-speaking community of Y Groes which, he claimed, had been attended by fewer than a dozen people.

'—And when he saw that, on top of everything, well—'

'I can imagine.'

He could also imagine how Bethan was going to feel about this. What a fucking mess.

'Can I pay you, Mrs Evans?'

'You aren't leaving, are you?' She looked disconsolate.

'I, ah, think it's for the best. That's three nights, yeah? One hundred and—'

'You only stayed two nights!'

'I shoulda been here last night too.'

'Go away with you, boy. Two nights, that's eighteen pounds exactly.'

He didn't want to screw things up further for Guto by telling Mrs Evans that even two nights, at the rates quoted by her son, would come out at seventy pounds. He made her take fifty, assuring her that all Americans had big expense accounts. Then he went to his room, shaved, changed out of the American Werewolf sweatshirt and into a thick fisherman's sweater because it wasn't getting any warmer out there.

Then he carried his bag downstairs, thanked Mrs Evans again, assuring her (oh, boy . . .) that things would surely work out for Guto, and took his stuff to the Sprite on the castle parking lot.

Loaded the bag into the boot, keeping an eye open for the Hard Man of the Nationalists. Guto was a guy with a lot to take out on somebody, and he sure as hell wasn't going to hit Simon Gallier if Berry Morelli was available.

He got into the car and sat there watching the alley next to Hampton's Bookshop over the road, waiting for Bethan to emerge.

They'd parted outside the funeral parlour, he to pay Mrs Evans, she to go home and change. They had said not one word to each other about Elinor and George Hardy.

After half an hour it was very cold in the car and he started the engine and the heater. She knew where he was. She'd come.

What if she didn't?

He looked across at the flat above the bookshop but could detect no movement. And yet she couldn't have gone anywhere because her Peugeot was right there, not fifteen yards away.

But what if she *had* gone away? What would he do if he never saw her again? If that part of the trap were suddenly to spring open?

He couldn't face it. He needed to be here now not for Winstone or Giles, who were beyond any help, but for Bethan. Accepting now that this was why he'd let his job slide away. This was how his life had condensed – around her. There was no way he could leave here without her. But there was no way she was going to leave until—

A blink of white in the alleyway, and she came out and walked quickly across the street to the car.

Berry closed his eyes and breathed out hard.

Bethan got into the car and slammed the door and they looked at each other.

And he said, 'I know. Drive, Morelli.'

The village had been called Y Groesfan, and this had interested Dr Thomas Ingley.

Y Groesfan meant 'the crossing place', suggesting a cross-roads. And yet no roads crossed in the village; it was a dead end.

What other kind of crossing could there be?

The origins of the village were unknown, but the church was the oldest in this part of Wales, and its site, the mound on which it was built, was prehistoric.

Most of the graves in the churchyard dated back no further than the 1700s, but the tomb of Sir Robert Meredydd in a small chapel to the left of the altar was late medieval.

Around the time of Owain Glyndwr. It was recorded that Glyndwr, as a young man, had been to Y Groesfan in the late summer of 1400 to 'pay homage'. This was only weeks before he was declared Prince of Wales following a meeting of his family and close friends at his house Glyndyfrdwy in north-east Wales.

All this Bethan had learned from the red notebook found under a floorboard by the late George Hardy.

'But why does it have to be relevant?' Berry asked.

They were heading east from the town now, towards Rhayader, close to the very centre of Wales, where the executive council of Plaid Cymru had met to decide on a candidate for the Glanmeurig by-election.

'The last two people to hold this notebook are dead,' Bethan said, the red book on her lap.

'That scare you?'

'Left here,' Bethan said. She pointed out of her window. 'That church is Ysbyty Cynfyn. See the big stones in the wall? They are prehistoric. The church is built inside a neolithic stone circle. It used to be a pagan place of worship; now it's Christian.'

'Like Y Groes?'

'Probably.'

'You want to stop?'

'No. Can we go to England, Berry?'

'We sure can,' he said, surprised. 'Any particular part? Hull? Truro?'

'Not far over the border. Herefordshire.'

'Any special reason for this?'

Bethan opened the red book. 'There's an address here. Near Monnington-on-Wye. Do you know the significance of Monnington? Did you get that far in Guto's book?'

'Uh-huh.' Berry shook his head.

'You can look out from there and see the hills of Wales.'

'I think I understand,' Berry said.

CHAPTER LVII

H E liked less and less having to go into the oak woods, particularly in winter. Without their foliage, the trees could look at you.

And into your soul.

He did not look at them, could not face them. As he walked, he stared at the ground. But he could see their roots like splayed hands, sometimes had to step over individual knobbled fingers.

Remembering being introduced to the woods as a boy, as they all had been. Taught honour and respect for the trees, fathers of the village itself.

And once, aged eighteen or thereabouts, bringing a girl into the woods one night in May and feeling afraid at the inferno of their passion.

Gwenllian. His wife now.

He told himself he was doing this for her. Ill she was now, most of the time. Did not want to cook, would go into no bedroom but their own, wept quietly in the afternoons.

Looking only at the ground, he almost bumped into the oaken gate.

Rheithordy.

Looked up then, and into the face of the rector.

Cried out, stifled it, embarrassed.

Ap Siencyn, in his cassock, standing at the gate, motionless, like one of the winter trees.

'Rector,' Aled said weakly.

Only the rector's hair moved. Even whiter than Aled's and longer, much longer, it streamed out on either side, unravelled by a little whingeing wind which the oaks had let through as a favour.

The rector spoke, his voice riding the wind like a bird.

'You are a coward, are you then, Aled?'

'Yes,' Aled confessed in shame. 'I am a coward.'

There was a long silence then, the wind cowed too.

'We shall have to leave, I know,' Aled said.

'Indeed?'

'We . . . I . . . There used to be this exhilaration. A delight in every day. Contentment, see. That was how it was.'

'And you do not think we have to justify it? Nothing to pay, Aled?'

'But why upon me? Me and Gwenllian, all the time?'

'Perhaps it is a test. A test which you appear to be on the point of failing.'

'But when there's no contentment left, only a dread—'

'It's winter, Aled. In winter, the bones are revealed. In winter we know where we are and what we are.'

Aled said, 'Death himself walked from these woods last night, and across the bridge and to the door of the inn.' The pitch of his voice rose. '*We heard him knocking, with his claw, a thin knocking . . .*'

The rector said mildly, 'You've known such things before.'

'It's changed,' Aled said. 'There is . . . something sick here now.'

The rector did not move yet seemed to rise a full two feet, and his white hair streamed out, although there was no wind now.

'How *dare* you!'

Aled shook his head and backed off, looking at the ground.

'You puny little man.' He was pointing at Aled now, with a thin black twig, like a wand.

'I'm sorry.'

'If you go from here you must go soon,' the rector said.

'Yes. There are relatives we can stay with. Over at Aber.'

'You must get out of our country.'

'Leave Wales?'

'And never return.'

'But what will we do?'

'No harm will come to you, I don't suppose,' the rector said. 'Unless you try to come back here.'

Meaningfully, he snapped the twig in half and tossed the pieces over the gate so that they landed at Aled's feet.

'It's building again, you see,' ap Siencyn said, deceptively gently. 'You must be aware of that. You must surely feel it growing beneath us and all around us.'

Oh yes, he could feel it. Almost see it sometimes, like forked lightning from the tip of the church tower.

'It's like the rising sun on a cloudless day,' the rector said. 'Always brighter in the winter. Rising clear. And those who do not rise with it, those not protected, will be blinded by the radiance.'

Aled thought, this man talks all the time in a kind of poetry. Perhaps it is a symptom of his madness.

But the parish owned the inn and many of the cottages and so he, in effect, was ap Siencyn's tenant. And in other ways, Aled knew, ap Siencyn had the power to do good and to do harm. He looked down at the two pieces of the twig at his feet and saw where his choice lay.

'Don't leave it too long, will you, Aled? Make your decision.'

'Yes,' Aled said. He walked back through the wood towards the road, and the oak trees watched him go.

CHAPTER LVIII

'I FELT it was right, see,' Guto said. 'Meant to happen. All my life, the disappointments, the frustrations – all foundations for it. I mean, Christ, I *needed* this.'

Dai Death said, 'Oh, come on, man. Not over yet, is it?'

'It is for me. I'll tell you when it ended . . . that meeting in Y Groes. I just can't convey to you, Dai, what it was like. Thinking, you know, have I come to the wrong bloody hall, or what? Another pint, is it?'

'Not for me. And not for you either. Finish that one and get a sandwich down you.'

'Bloody mother hen,' Guto grumbled.

Well, all right, he was drinking too much, he knew it. And in public. The party's General Secretary, Alun, had warned him about this – 'half the votes are women, never forget that' – as they drove across to Aber for a lunchtime conference with two other Plaid MPs. The other MPs had been encouraging. You could not really get an idea until the final week, they said. But Guto had followed campaigns where a candidate who'd been strongly tipped initially had dropped clean off the chart in the first few days.

By the weekend the results of the first opinion polls would be out. If they were half as bad as he expected, he'd be placed at least third . . .

'Bethan it is, though, really,' Dai said. 'Admit it.'

Guto glared resentfully at the undertaker through his pint glass. Then he put the glass down, fished out a cigarette, the anger blown over now, leaving him subdued.

'Aye, well, that too.'

And that also would have been so right, both of them gasping for fresh air – her with the trouble at school, him badly needing a legitimate outlet for frustrations which were threatening to turn destructive. Westminster, the bright lights – and what was so wrong with bright lights? He'd convinced himself – well, Christ, politics weren't everything – that when he won the election she would go with him.

When he won . . .

He could have bloody wept.

'Who *is* this Morelli?' Dai asked. 'Who is he *really*?'

'More to the point,' Guto said, '*where* is he?'

This was also what the girl in the Porsche wanted to know.

'Seen you on the telly, isn't it?' Mrs Evans said at once,

having watched the car pulling up outside the house and this exotic creature unwinding.

'Well, it's possible,' Miranda admitted modestly.

'It's the red hair. Wasn't you in . . . Oh, what's it called now, that detective thing on a Sunday night . . .?'

'Oh well, you know, I pop up here and there.' Miranda was hardly going to remind this little woman that her best-known television persona was the girl accosted in a back street by a leather-clad thug impressed by her shampoo. 'Anyway, I'm awfully sorry to bother you, but a journalist told me Berry Morelli was staying here.'

'Oh, Mr Morelli. Him you're looking for.'

'I am indeed.'

'Well, he've left, not two hours ago.'

'Do you know where he's gone?'

'Well, I never asked him, not wanting to pry, Miss—'

'Moore-Lacey. Miranda Moore-Lacey.'

'Oh, lovely. He'll be terrible sorry to have missed you. Let me see now . . . I wonder if my son . . . Perhaps he can tell you where Mr Morelli is. Do you know my son?'

'I'm afraid I don't know a soul here.'

'Well you can't miss Guto. Very distinctive, he is. Black beard and a big green rosette. Can't be far away, he've a meeting to do in town tonight. He'll be at the Memorial Hall by seven. Do you know where that is?'

'I'll find it,' Miranda said. 'Thank you very much.'

As she slid into the car, the first snowflakes landed on its bonnet and instantly evaporated.

Within ten minutes there were rather more of them and they were not evaporating quite so rapidly.

When they found Bryan Mortlake, he was splitting logs outside his house, a former lodge next to the main road. He did not stop splitting logs when they spoke to him, and he did not invite them in.

'Ingley,' he said, raising the axe. 'Nutcase,' he said, bringing it down.

The axe hit the log dead-centre and the two halves fell from the block. One rolled over Bethan's shoe.

'Safer to stand further back,' Mortlake said, looking and talking more like a retired colonel than a retired academic. Except retired colonels, in Berry's experience, were more polite.

He set up another log. 'Not still hanging around, is he?'

'He's dead,' Berry said.

'Oh? Well, he was still a nutcase.'

'You have many dealings with him?'

'Not when I could help it. Would you mind moving out of my light. Snow's forecast for tomorrow, did you know that?'

'Dr Mortlake,' Bethan said. 'Would you tell us what Dr Ingley came to see you about?'

Mortlake brought down the axe. There was a knot in the log, and it jammed. He looked at Bethan as if it was her fault then hit the axe handle with the flat of a hand to free it. Both log and axe tumbled off the block and Mortlake looked furious.

'Look, what's all this about?'

'We found your name and address in this.' Bethan pulled the red book from her raincoat. 'I am a schoolteacher in a village in West Wales, where Dr Ingley was doing some research. When he died, his notes were passed on to me. I'm writing a history of the village and I thought—'

Mortlake snatched the book and thumbed through it for about half a minute before handing it back with what Berry assumed to be a superior, academic sneer.

'Bilge,' Mortlake said.

'*What's* bilge?' Berry said. 'What's he saying here? That's all we want to know.'

'You a Welsh schoolteacher too?'

'I'm a friend of Mrs McQueen. You have a problem with that?'

'Look.' Mortlake hefted the axe and the log onto the chopping block and stood back panting. 'Did you ever meet the man?'

Berry put a foot on the log, hit the axe handle, freed it and gave it to Mortlake.

'No,' he said.

'He had a crackpot theory about Glyndwr. Who, you may

remember, was supposed to have ended his days a few miles from here, at Monnington.'

'We are going there next,' Bethan said.

'Can't see what good that will do you. None of it's proven. There's an unmarked stone in the churchyard there, which they say is Glyndwr's grave. I doubt that.'

Berry said, 'What was the crackpot theory?'

Mortlake threw down the axe. 'You know, half the foolish myths in British history begin like this. In my view, when someone cobbles together a lot of patent rubbish and then dies without publishing it, we should all be damned thankful and let it lie.'

'Dr Mortlake,' Bethan said. 'This is only a little village project. What harm can that do?'

'What d'you say the village is called?'

'Y Groes.'

'Never heard of it.'

'It's near Pontmeurig.'

'Oh, the by-election place.' Mortlake gave in. 'All right, there's a legend – I mean, when you're talking about Glyndwr, half of it's legend – and the story goes that some years after his death— No, actually, there are two different stories, one says it was after his death, the other says it was when he was dying. Both come to the same conclusion – that four patriotic Welshmen couldn't stand the thought of the old hero dying in exile, came across the border and took him home. Or carted his remains home, whichever version you prefer.'

Berry sensed Bethan's excitement.

'Ingley was convinced this was true,' Mortlake said. 'He maintained there was a place in Wales where all the heroes went to die or whatever, according to some ancient tradition. You see, it's complete nonsense – man was bonkers.'

'Did he say where the place was?' Bethan asked.

'Wouldn't tell me. Big secret. As if I really wanted to know.'

'What evidence did he have?'

'Oh, he claimed to have discovered the names of the four Welshmen who came for Glyndwr. He suspected there may have been some collaboration here with John Skydmore, of Monnington Court, who was Glyndwr's son-in-law. Which was why he came to me.'

'You helped him?'

'He left me the names. I said I'd look into it. Didn't bother, to be quite honest. I can tell a crank from fifty paces. And don't ask me for the list because I've probably thrown it away.'

'Well, thanks,' Berry said. 'We'll leave you to your logs.'

'Very good memory, though, as it happens.'

'I'm sorry?'

'My memory. Very good. If it's any use for your . . . village project . . . the four men were a farmer, a lawyer, a coachman and . . . a carpenter, yes. He was said to have made an ornate coffin, fit for a prince, as they say. And their names, d'you want their names? Very well . . .'

He leaned on his axe, pursed his lips. 'Vaughan – John Vaughan. Robert Morgan. William, or Gwilym Davies and—'

Mortlake paused triumphantly. He'd plucked all four straight out of his head.

'—Thomas Rhys.'

He beamed.

'Don't tell me,' Berry said. 'He was the lawyer.'

Mortlake, in a better temper now, picked up a big log with both hands and set it on the block. 'You know more than I do, sir,' he said.

Dusk now. A pair of black swans glided across the pond behind the church. It was cold and utterly still.

'He was right,' Berry said. 'Gonna snow.'

The sky was taut and shiny, like a well-beaten drum.

'Snow is for the Christmas cards,' Bethan said. 'You won't find a country person who likes it.'

'This is a wonderful place,' Berry said, putting an arm around her.

Like Y Groes, Monnington was a dead end. Like the immediate environs of Y Groes, the surrounding land was soft and peaceful. But although the church was in a secret place, approachable only by foot along a shaded green lane, the landscape around was opened out, mostly flat, the hills serene in the distance.

They found one small, unmarked stone close to the entrance of the church. There was nobody around to ask if this was the supposed grave of Owain Glyndwr.

'This is totally England,' Berry said. 'You know, this is more like the real old England than any place I ever went to. No cars, no ice-cream stalls, no parking lots, no information bureaux.'

'I wish I could interpret what we've learned,' Bethan said, pulling away and going back to the stone which might or might not be Glyndwr's.

'Did I gather by your reaction that the families of these four patriotic Welsh guys still live in Y Groes?'

'I can't be sure. Yes, there's a Dewi Vaughan. F – O – N, he spells it, the Welsh way – how they spell it now, rather than then, I should imagine. And yes, he's a carpenter. Like his father before him. Davies – Dafis. Several of those. Thomas Rhys, well—'

'Very weird,' Berry said. 'Judge Rhys feels he has to return to preserve the family tradition. He leaves his house to his granddaughter, his chosen heiress. She changes her name to Rhys. Her husband, who is irrelevent to all this –' His voice dropped, '– dies.'

'And she's possibly pregnant, don't forget.'

'So Giles has served his purpose,' Berry said. 'Jesus, I hate the thought of all this. Sorry, what'd you say then?'

'I said, if it is Giles's baby.'

'Hey, what—?'

'I don't *know*.' Bethan said desperately. Snatching up the hood of her raincoat so that he couldn't see her expression, she moved quickly away through the graveyard, a ghostly white lady in the dusk.

CHAPTER LIX

HE almost didn't wear a tie.

In fact, if the Plaid Cymru president had not been lined up to speak he thought he would have had difficulty persuading himself to go at all.

At seven o'clock he entered the Memorial Hall through the back door and peeped into the main hall from behind the stage, convinced he'd be looking at half-a-dozen people and about three hundred empty chairs.

To his surprise, there must have been over two hundred in the audience already.

A big turn-out for the humiliated hard-man.

He was still feeling depressed and cynical when he climbed on to the platform at the Memorial Hall and took his seat next to the party president, who was going through a patch of unprecedented popularity.

Celebrity night.

By the time they were ready to begin, there must have been nearly five hundred crammed in, and a full complement of Press. He got an encouraging smile from the plump lady from BBC Radio, who seemed to fancy him. But all the rest, he was sure, had come to watch the official public funeral of Guto Evans's election hopes.

Since the report in the *Western Mail*, he was convinced, people had actually been avoiding him in the street, out of embarrassment

Fuck 'em, he thought. You've got nothing left to lose, boy, so fuck 'em all.

And he did.

He came to his feet feeling like one of those athletes on steroids. Full up with something anyway, and it wasn't the drink, thanks to Dai Death.

Somebody asked him the old question about where he stood on Welsh terrorism, petrol bombs and the burning down of property to deter immigration. To his surprise, he didn't give the careful, strategic answer he'd spent hours working out. Instead, he lost his temper and heard himself saying how much the great Glyndwr would have despised the kind of pathetic little wankers who could only come out at night with paraffin cans.

Politics, he roared, was a game for adults, not spotty adolescents.

Aware that this must sound pretty heavy coming from a man who looked like a sawn-off version of Conan the Barbarian, he felt a surge of pure adrenalin, like red mercury racing up a thermometer. Or one of those fairground things you slammed with a mallet and, if you were strong enough, it rang the bell. For the first time since the London banker had performed the knocking over of the chair right on cue, Guto Evans, fuelled by rage and bitterness, was ringing bells.

For over forty-five minutes, he fended off hostile questioners with the ease of a nightclub bouncer ejecting tired drunks. He didn't care any more what he said to any of the bastards.

'Ladies and gentlemen,' the Plaid president, looking shell-shocked, said when Guto finally sat down. 'I think you have seen tonight an example of precisely why we selected Guto Evans to fight this by-election. And why Guto Evans, without any doubt, is going to be the next MP for Glanmeurig!'

And up in Eglwys Fawr, Guto thought cynically, as the audience responded with vigour, the Tories will be saying exactly the same thing about Simon Gallier.

On his way out, men he didn't know patted him on the shoulder, and three women kissed him.

Groupies, by God.

Unfortunately, not that young, the three women – in fact, not much younger than his mam, really.

But, bloody hell, *this* one was . . .

She had definitely come to the wrong place, dressed like that.

'Mr Evans, I wonder if I might have a word.'

'The night is yet young, darling,' Guto said, his system still flooded with that desperate, high-octane, who-gives-a-flying-fart-anyway adrenalin. 'Have as many as you like.'

They spent the night in a glossy new hotel on the edge of Hereford. Country inns were out as far as Bethan was concerned. No oak beams, no creaking floorboards, no 'character'.

This room was done out in calm and neutral pastel shades. And that included the telephone, the TV with video and satellite receiver, the bedside lamps with dimmer switches and all the envelopes and containers of stuff which nobody ever opened but which showed the management really cared.

Towel-swathed, Bethan came out of the shower into this hermetically-sealed haven, where Berry Morelli was sprawled across the pastel bed, trying to screw up the colour-coordination with his bright orange undershorts.

'Sooner or later,' he told the ceiling, 'you're gonna have to tell me whatever it is you haven't told me.'

She didn't look at him, went over to the dressing table and began to untangle her hair.

Facing his image in the mirror, she said, 'Did you read the same thing as me into those notes about the church and the tomb?'

Goddamn red book again.

'Could be,' he said. 'Sir Robert Meredydd. Died 1421. That would be within maybe a year or two of Owain Glyndwr. You're saying this Meredydd actually *is* Glyndwr? That these guys brought him back to Y Groes and secretly entombed him under a false name?'

'Well, there we are. Possible, isn't it? I have also thought of something else. Dewi Fon, the carpenter. Davies, the coachman? Dilwyn Dafis runs the garage at Y Groes. Repairs vehicles, does a bit of haulage. It's a very old business. I didn't realise quite how old.'

'That's wild,' said Berry. 'I mean, that is *wild*. You're suggesting this guy Dilwyn's ancestor built some kind of special funeral cart or horse-drawn bier or whatever they had in those days to fetch Glyndwr home. And five centuries later the family's still in the transport business. Who's the fourth man, the farmer?'

'Morgan. There is only one Morgan family in Y Groes, and Buddug is married to the head of the tribe.'

'The ball-slasher?'

Bethan nodded into the mirror, unsmiling. 'The Morgans have farmed there since . . . who can say?'

Berry said, 'Are we imagining all this?'

She said sharply, 'You mean am I imagining all this?'

He went over and put his hands on her shoulders, didn't try to dislodge the towel. She carried on combing out her hair as if his hands weren't there.

'Bethan, I'm taking a deep breath, OK? What makes you think that if Claire is pregnant we may not be talking about Giles's baby?'

She did not reply, went on combing her hair, although the tangles were long gone.

Through the mirror, he saw what looked like old tears burning to come out. She blinked them away.

He felt suddenly angry but said nothing – where was the use in pressurising her?

But then, abruptly, she put down the comb, wiped her hands on a pastel tissue and told his reflection, without preamble, why she'd gone to Swansea after Robin's death.

When she'd finishing talking, he went over to the window and looked down to where sporadic night traffic was circumventing the construction site for some new road.

He really wanted to believe her.

But how much of this could you take? Things getting weirder by the minute.

'Stupid of me,' she said. 'I did not want to tell you, but you pushed.'

He turned back and started towards her.

'No,' she said.

He sat down on the bed, put his hands over his face and rubbed his eyes in slow circular movements.

He said, 'And it really couldn't have been his, Robin's?'

'No.'

'Bethan, I don't only want to believe you. I *need* to believe you.'

'That is not good enough,' she said.

sice . . . sice . . . sice . . . the air said. Tissue-thin-pages whispering.

Bethan tossed her head back, stared at the ceiling. The chasm between them was about a hundred miles wide.

You and me, the Gypsy said, *we in same shit. One day you find out.*

What Bethan had told him was that approximately three weeks after Robin's death, she had discovered she was expecting a baby. Because she knew in her own mind that this could not be Robin's child, she had moved to Swansea where no one knew her. And where the pregnancy had been terminated.

'I did not kill my baby,' she emphasised quite calmly. 'I killed *its* baby.'

'It?'

'The village. Y Groes.'

Oh, Christ.

He had no idea how to follow this up. Either she'd tell him or she wouldn't. His lips kept forming questions, but the questions never made it. Only one.

'How could you go back?' he asked. He'd asked her that before.

'How could I not go back?' she replied.

'And do you work with Morelli?' the Bearded Welsh Extremist asked. Every few seconds somebody on the way out would slap him on the back and say something jolly in Welsh.

'You have got to be joking,' said Miranda.

'Well what do you want him for?'

'I don't actually *want* him,' Miranda said frankly – no point in trying to bullshit a politician; they were all far too good at it not to spot it coming from someone else. 'I just want to pass on some information which might help him.'

'I see,' said the BWE, whose name she couldn't remember, except that it sounded vaguely insulting. 'Well, I don't know where Morelli has gone but I do know who he is with.' His eyes were smouldering, she thought, in rather a dark and brooding way, like some sort of Celtic Heathcliff. 'Tell me,' he said, 'have you anywhere to stay?'

'Well, I have,' Miranda told him. 'But it isn't much of a place.'

'Oh, well, good accommodation is hard to find with this election on.'

'You're telling *me*. I wound up at some faded Victorian dive called the Plas something or other.'

His eyes stopped in mid-smoulder and widened. 'The Plas Meurig? You managed to get a room at the Plas Meurig?'

'I realise there's got to be a better hotel somewhere, but I *was* in rather a hurry.'

He appeared to be regarding her with a certain respect, on top of the usual naked lust. But before she could capitalise on this, an efficient-looking man with tinted glasses and a clip-board slid between them. 'Guto,' he said. 'Problems, I'm afraid. Tomorrow night's meeting with the farmers' unions. Bit of a mix-up over the hall at Cefn Mynach. Liberal Democrats have got it, so I'm afraid . . . Look, I did try for an alternative venue to Y Groes, but it's central for the farmers.'

'No way, Alun,' snarled Guto. 'I wouldn't go back there if the alternative was a bloody sheep-shed in the Nearly Mountains.'

Miranda thought, *Y Groes* . . .

Lowering his voice, this Alun said, 'Come on, Guto. We should see it as a challenge. We can build on tonight's success, regain our position. You're acquiring an enviable reputation for turning the tables.'

'Aye, and the Press will show up in force when they find out,' said Guto. 'No, forget it, postpone it.'

'We can't postpone it. We'll come across as unreliable. Look, I shall make sure there's a good crowd this time. We can even take most of one with us. Come on man, you did well tonight.'

'Alun,' the Extremist said. 'I am getting a bad feeling about this.'

Oh my God, Miranda thought. Not another one.

CHAPTER LX

BERRY Morelli slept uneasily. Bethan did not sleep at all. Outside, even in Herefordshire now, it was snowing lightly but consistently.

They had not touched one another.

The room had caught an amber glow from the road-construction site below. And in this false warmth Bethan was remembering a close summer evening, a bitter argument with Robin, who was always tired and fractious but insisted it was nothing physical. She remembered storming out, nerves like bare wires, and being soothed at once as the air settled around her, as comforting as soft arms.

It did this sometimes, the village. Was absorbed through the skin like some exotic balm. The soporific scents of wild flowers on a breeze like a kiss. Your churning emotions massaged as you walked down the deserted street, past the *Tafarn*, the church tower soaring from its grassy mound, venerably beneficent.

Robin raging alone inside their terraced cottage at the top of the street, while Bethan was wafted away on the silky, cushioned wings of the evening.

She remembered the air lifting her gently over the stile to the meadow that sloped to the river, trees making a last shadow-lattice on the deepening green.

Remembered yielding her body gratefully to the soft grass, letting the breezes play in the folds of her summer dress. There seemed to be several breezes, all of them warm, making subtle ripples and swirls and eddies.

And she had fallen asleep and dreamed a child's dream of the *Tylwyth Teg*, the beautiful fairy folk.

Awoken in the moistness of the night, the dampness of the grass, the cold wetness between her legs, the bittersweet tang of betrayal, a lingering faraway regret.

And no memory at all of what had happened.

Of what,
Or who.

'Guto,' she said. 'Git-toe. It really is a super name.'

'Thank you,' Guto said dubiously. He was trying not to be charmed by this creature who, only minutes earlier, had been chanting git-toe, git-toe through clenched teeth, in concert with the rhythm of her loins.

What also filled him with a certain perverse delight was the thought that, in order to bonk this terribly English English-woman, he had actually infiltrated Simon Gallier's fortress, the Plas Meurig, and was about to spend a night within the hallowed portals free of charge.

Whatever the result, it had certainly been an experience, this by-election.

'You might as well tell me,' he said. 'How the hell did you manage to persuade them to let you have a room? And not just any room, for heaven's sake . . .'

He was looking up suspiciously at an ornate Victorian ceiling across which misshapen plaster cherubs frolicked amid gross moulded foliage.

'Isn't it so utterly tasteless?' said Miranda and giggled, a sound which reminded Guto of the tinkling door chimes in Pontmeurig's new health food shop which he'd entered for the first time during this afternoon's canvassing.

'It might be tasteless,' he said. 'But it's probably the best room they've got.'

An awful thought had crept up on him. They wouldn't, would they?

'Hah!' Miranda sprang up in the bed, wobbling deliciously. 'I know what you're worried about!'

'What am I worried about?'

'You think I've been planted, don't you? You think I'm an expensive bimbo hired by the opposition to discredit you. You think any second now the door's going to fly open and chaps will crowd in with popping flashbulbs. You do, don't you? Admit it!'

'Was a thought,' Guto mumbled gruffly.

'Hah!' Miranda shrieked and rolled about laughing. 'Oh, how utterly wonderful that would be!'

'Shut up, woman,' Guto hissed. 'Everybody'll know you've got somebody in here.'

'Oh, I love it when you call me "woman".'

'Well, come on, enlighten me. How *did* you get into a hotel that's been claiming to've been booked up solid for weeks?'

'I'm not going to tell. I have my methods.'

'Now look, I'll . . .'

'*Will* you, Guto? Will you really? Do you think you still have the strength? Well, in that case I'll tell you just a little. It all comes down to judicious use of that famous phrase, 'Do you know who I am?' which never works with the police these days but still tends to put hoteliers in the most awful tizz, especially in small-town snobby dumps like this. So don't worry any more, OK?'

'Who said I was worried?'

Miranda dug into the bedclothes. 'Oh dear, he's utterly flaked out, isn't he, poor little Welsh thing. All right, I'll give him half an hour to recover. And you can use the time to tell me all about this dreadful village where people go to die.'

'Y Groes?' Guto fell back into the pillows. 'I suppose I died there myself, in a metaphorical way. In the theatrical sense of presenting your famous one-man show and no bugger applauds.'

'Did you know a chap called Martin Coulson?'

'Met him the once. Briefly, like.'

'I was talking to this old vicar who believes Coulson committed suicide because he was brilliant at speaking Welsh but he couldn't get a word of it out in the pulpit. Does that make any sense to you?'

'Aye, I remember now – he spoke Welsh to me. I switched over to English pretty smartly, mind, when I realised how good he was.'

'Typical.'

'Well, I was brought up in the Valleys. Welsh is only my second language, see. You don't like to be put to shame in your own country by an Englishman.'

'Good heavens, no.'

'And you say this vicar thought he topped himself because he couldn't turn it on in the church?'

'That was what he said.'

'Sounds highly unlikely to me,' Guto said. 'Red hot, he was. And it's not an easy language to learn. This is what you wanted to tell Morelli?'

'More or less.' She told him how Berry Morelli had gone to Y Groes with Giles Freeman and returned feeling very funny, disturbed over some sort of dubious psychic experience. 'And when Freeman snuffed it suddenly, he got very upset. And now these other two people, Giles's in-laws . . . Well, gosh, it's even made me think. It's a lot of deaths, isn't it?'

'Probably more than you know,' Guto said. 'But it's all explained and, after all, they were—'

He'd been about to say they were all English, but stopped himself on the grounds that she could do a man a lot of damage, this one.

'Well, I'm going there tomorrow night,' he said.

'I heard.'

'So if you want to tag along, it'll be one more in the audience.'

'Super,' Miranda said. 'I look forward to it. Where do you think Morelli's gone? Will he be there tomorrow?'

'How should I know?'

'It's snowing again,' Miranda said, switching out the bedside light so they could see the white blobs buffeting the long window. 'Quite hard, too.'

'Berry, wake up. Please.'

He turned his head into the steam from a white cup of black tea.

'What's the time, Beth?'

'Nearly four-thirty. I'm sorry to wake you, but my thoughts are killing me.'

He sat up, took the cup. Waking wasn't so hard.

'Please can we talk. About everything.'

'We can try, kid,' Berry said. He'd called her Beth and he'd called her kid, and she hadn't reacted. She must be serious about this.

'OK,' he said. 'So what are we into here? One sentence. One word. Say it.'

Bethan said, 'Magic.'

'That's the word,' Berry said. 'That's the word we've been walking all around and poking at with the end of a stick on account of we don't like to touch it.'

'Perhaps there are two words,' Bethan said.

'And the other one,' Berry said, taking her hand, 'is black. Right?'

They sat on the edge of the bed in the overheated hotel room, holding hands and drinking tea and watching the snow fall, feeling more afraid now the word had escaped.

CHAPTER LXI

HOTEL staff had cleared most of the snow from the car park, but Berry had to dig out the Sprite, which coughed like hell and turned the air blue with acrid smoke.

'Could be pneumonia,' he said anxiously, driving into the centre of Hereford, where the early morning streets had a first-fall purity that would last maybe until the shops opened.

The snow had stopped soon after dawn, but the bloated sky suggested this was only an interim gesture of goodwill.

The city library was almost opposite the cathedral and at this hour they had no problem parking right outside. Waiting for the library to open, they wandered the cathedral grounds, an ancient island cut off from the city by a soft white sea.

Bethan said, 'If it snows again we may not make it back for days. We'll have problems anyway; it could be a lot worse in Wales.'

Berry thought it would be no bad thing if they didn't get back for weeks, but he said nothing.

On the way here, they'd talked about the baby.

He said it was the most insidious case of rape he'd ever heard of. 'Some bastard has to pay.'

Bethan thought this was unlikely. 'I'm sure, you see,' she told him, 'that when I was offered the head teacher's post – at the express request of the school governors, I've since discovered – it was expected that I would return very pregnant. And of course the baby would be looked after while I was at the school – very caring people in Y Groes. And the child would grow up like all the rest.'

'What would that mean?'

'I can't explain it very easily. They are children of Y Groes. Steeped in the Welsh traditions – traditions which no longer apply anywhere else, not to this extent anyway. Although the community is . . . clings, if you like, to its church, this church is different. There's an element in the religion of the village which is almost pre-Christian. It accepts all the eerie, psychic things – the *toili* and the *cannwyll gorff* and the bird of death – as part of life's fabric. All right, that's not unusual in itself, rural west Wales is riddled with superstition, but here it's a way of life.'

'But the church is Anglican,' Berry said now, under the massive spireless tower of Hereford Cathedral. 'Like this place.'

'Not so simple.' Bethan was wearing her pink woolly hat and a red scarf wound twice around her neck. 'The old Celtic church was the earliest form of Christianity in Britain and it probably absorbed many elements of paganism. Nobody knows for sure what its rituals were, or its dogma. I suppose we can say the two earliest known religious influences in Wales were the Celtic church and . . . what remained of Druidism, I imagine. Intermingled.'

'It says in Guto's book that it used to be suggested Owain Glyndwr had been trained in Druidic magic. Like, he was some kind of sorcerer who could alter the weather and—'

'—Call spirits from the Vasty Deep,' said Bethan. 'Yes. Obviously, Guto is deeply dismissive of all this. He wants Glyndwr to have been some sort of pragmatic early socialist with a deep commitment to democracy and the classless society.'

'What do *you* think?'

'I think Glyndwr was probably fumbling in the dark like the rest of us,' Bethan said, taking his arm. 'You need a thicker coat, Berry, you must be freezing.'

In the library they paused to glance through the morning papers. Over Ray Wheeler's story in the *Mirror* was the headline:

W — KERS!
GUTO BLASTS THE BOMBERS.

Bethan shook her head wryly. 'The things an election campaign can do to a person. Not three weeks ago he was saying that while he deplored the methods, he could fully understand the motives of anti-English terrorism.'

They went up some stairs, and Berry said to the guy in the reference section, 'We're interested in aspects of Welsh folklore. The, ah —'

'*Gorsedd Ddu,*' Bethan said.

'I don't think I've heard of that,' the guy said, and Bethan assured him this was not so surprising.

They spent more than an hour bent over a table, exploring maybe twenty books. At one stage Berry went down and moved the Sprite to avoid collecting a parking ticket. When he returned, Bethan announced that she was satisfied there was nothing to be learned here.

'This mean there's nothing actually documented on the, ah . . .?'

'*Gorsedd Ddu.* Probably not.'

Before they left the hotel Bethan had given him a very brief history of the Welsh bardic tradition. Of the Dark Age poets, of whom the best known was Taliesyn. And how, in the nineteenth century Edward Williams, who called himself Iolo Morgannwg – Iolo of Glamorgan – had identified himself as the Last Druid in Wales and set about single-handedly restoring the tradition. It was Iolo, an inventive antiquarian scholar not averse to forging ancient verse to prove his point, who established what was to become the National Eisteddfod of Wales – the annual gathering of poets and singers and cultural leaders honoured as 'bards'.

The inner circle of which was the *Gorsedd* – whose members appeared in white ceremonial costumes such as the Druids were believed to have worn.

'You mean it's all crap?' Berry had said, astonished. 'The great Welsh bardic tradition was *dreamed up* by this guy, bridging a cultural gap between the nineteenth century and the Dark Ages? It's all bullshit?'

'Well, let us say, ninety per cent bullshit. But it did fulfil a need in the Welsh people to . . . exalt their heritage, I suppose. It gave them this annual showcase for the language and the poetry. The Welsh love to show off.'

'And they conveniently forgot about the antisocial side of the Druids – like human sacrifices in the oak groves under the full moon, all that heavy ritual stuff?'

'Ah, now, some Celtic scholars say the Druids did not sacrifice people or even animals – that was just stories put about by the Romans. We only have people like Julius Caesar to rely on for concrete information about Druidism. But, yes, the organisers of the *eisteddfodau* have even forgotten that the Druids were pagan. It has always been a very God-fearing festival.'

They collected all the books together and took them back to the man in charge of the department.

'Nothing?' he said. 'Are you sure you've got it right about this *Gorsedd*, er—'

'*Ddu*,' Bethan said. 'It means black. The Black *Gorsedd*. Yes, but don't worry, there is nothing wrong with your books.'

'Oh, we do know that,' he said.

They sat a while in the car with the engine running, for heat.

'Where's that leave us?' Berry said.

No more snow had fallen and last night's was already being trampled into slush.

Bethan said, 'They talk about the *Gorsedd Ddu* in some places like you talk of bogeymen, to frighten the children. Eat your greens or the black bards will get you. Or the *Gwrach y rhibyn*.'

'What's that?'

'The *Gwrach*? A sort of Welsh death-hag. A monstrous woman with black teeth and leathery wings who's supposed to scare people to death and then steal away their immortal souls. She's a vengeful demon who preys on those who have sinned.'

'Jeez, what a country. What do the black bards do?'

'Well, the inference is that while the white bards—'

'—as invented by this Iolo guy—'

'I wish I hadn't told you that, now. Yes, the white bards, while they are amiable pacifists, the *Gorsedd Ddu* are supposed to have very real magical powers. They are stern and cold and . . . perhaps vindictive.'

'Question is,' Berry said, 'do they exist? This is the bottom line. And if they do, do they have any more of a solid foundation than the old guys at the eisteddfod or are we just looking at a bunch of fruitcakes?'

'And if they have—' Bethan leaned back in the ruptured bucket seat, the side windows and the screen all misted, blurred ghosts of people walking past. 'If they have foundation . . . powers . . . what can we do about it anyway?'

'Magic's not illegal any more. Not even black magic.'

'Killing people is.'

'How can we say that? Natural causes, accidents, suicide and, OK, a murder now. But it's solved.'

'Yes, it sounds silly. Utterly.'

'We're saying there's a – an atmosphere, whatever, generated here. Which causes outsiders – say, people not protected by the village or by this aura of Welshness, whatever that means – either to lose the will to live, to fail in what they most want to do—'

'Like Giles failing to learn Welsh – to be a part of something he so much admired—'

'Right. Or have their negative emotions take over. Lose

their normal resistance to unacceptable or downright brutal behaviour. Like ole George Hardy. Suburban solicitor beats wife to death. In short, go nuts.'

'Or,' Bethan said, 'if we try to explain the deaths from natural causes, to get into such a state that even their bodies stop fighting.'

'OK. Like the immune system breaks down or something of that order. My knowledge of these things is no more than the average hypochondriac. So they're exposed to diseases, tumours form that never would've, heart diseases worsen and, well, yeah—'

'I've always found it bitterly ironic,' Bethan said, bleakly, 'that Robin, who was so opposed to nuclear power, should die of a condition so often said to be induced by radiation escaping from nuclear installations.' She shook her head sadly. 'Radiation.'

'Was he happy in Y Groes? Was it like he'd imagined?'

'He – Oh, what does it matter now . . .' Bethan was twisting her scarf. 'The truth is we never really had much of a marriage in Y Groes. Almost as soon as we moved in, he began to be tired and irritable. The stress of the move and the travelling and having to search for nuclear dump-sites – that was what he put it down to. We used to go for walks together, along the river bank, up to the woods, and he would go so far and he just became . . . bone-tired, you know?' She turned away, stared hard at the people-shapes passing the misted car window. 'I'm going to cry.'

'Let's get outa here.' Berry flung the Sprite into gear, rubbing the windscreen clear, moving into a line of traffic on the one-way system out of town.

'We really *are* insane, aren't we?' Bethan was shouting at him. 'Tell me we're insane! Tell me we're imagining it all, fabricating something out of thin air to account for a lot of people's bad luck. Look, for God's sake, take me home, Morelli! Don't you have a job to go to?'

'No,' he said. 'And you don't want to go home. You know where we have to go.'

'No . . .' Bethan was shaking. That is, she was sitting there very still, but he knew she really was shaking inside. 'We can't.'

'How else?' He also was shouting now, against the gear-threshing of a big delivery van alongside them. 'How else we gonna find out one way or the other? How else, without we go in there and start kicking asses till we get some answers?'

'You don't know what it's like!' Bethan screamed.

A lorry's brakes hissed . . . *sssssssssssssssssssssiiiice!*

He turned into a stream of traffic crossing a wide bridge over the Wye.

'You came back, Beth. Nobody said you had to take that job. You'd killed its baby and you came back.'

Bethan wept, biting hard into her lower lip until blood came.

CHAPTER LXII

THE radio had described the road over the Nearly Mountains as 'passable with care'.

On the way to Pont, with his wife Gwenllian in the passenger seat, Aled had driven with considerable concentration, knowing of old what this road could do with a coat of snow on its back. On the return journey, alone now, his driving had been sloppy, his mind on other things, and he'd taken a corner too fast and ploughed the van into a snowdrift.

Digging himself out with the shovel he always kept in the back from November until May, Aled could see the tip of Y Groes's church tower, a light haze around it, wispy blue. While the sky above him, as he shovelled snow from around the van wheels, was thick as pastry.

He was going back. He had put Gwenllian, who did not understand these things, on the bus to Aber where her sister lived. But he was going back.

What alternative was there? He was the keeper, like his dad before him, of the most beautiful inn in the most beautiful place you would find anywhere. This was what he told himself.

He threw the spade in the back of the van. All around him the Nearly Mountains were tundra, no visible blade of grass. The slender creature about two hundred feet away was a fox, ears pricked, loping off when it saw him, black against the snow. Everything in black and white from up here, except the sky over Y Groes.

By the time he arrived back in the village – not yet ten o'clock – the sky had deepened to a lurid mauve, the colour pouring in from a circle in the clouds like a hole sawn in a sea of ice for Eskimos to fish. It was as if the church tower had stabbed out the hole.

In the village, the light scattering of snow had already melted. For the first time Aled did not like the fact that there was so little snow here while so much lay on the lower ground of Pontmeurig. For the first time it seemed less than healthy. The ochre and grey stone shone with moisture, like a film of sweat. The whitewashed buildings had a mauvish glow that made him think of the glow in the faces of people on radium treatment.

It's gone too far, Aled thought.

'Going to snow again, though,' Guto observed hopefully. 'Why don't we call it off now?'

He wasn't inclined to risk any journey which might so delay his return to Pontmeurig that it would be difficult to slip unseen up the stairs at the Plas Meurig and into Suite 2, where the woman at the centre of all his finest fantasies would be waiting in exquisitely expensive French knickers.

There had been a few amazing moments last night when the result of the Glanmeurig by-election had seemed a matter of little consequence.

'No way,' the General Secretary of Plaid Cymru pronounced. He glared at the sky through his tinted glasses – permanently rose-coloured, Guto thought – and then consulted his personal organiser. 'Saturday tomorrow, OK? Big day. And you have meetings scheduled all next week. This is a crucial one. We can't be seen to be avoiding discussions with the farming organisations. If *they* want to call it off, fine, but we cannot.'

'But, Alun, nobody will come! It'll be just like last time, and where does that leave us?'

Alun spread his hands. 'We're not dependent on the villagers, this time. It just happens to be a central venue. Farmers, this is, Guto. And tell me, what does every farmer have?'

'A bloody big chip on his shoulder,' said Guto.

'A four-wheel drive vehicle,' Alun said patiently. 'Enabling him to get to places otherwise inaccessible. Which is why they won't call it off. Deliberately – to see what you're made of. Fortunately, we also have two Land-Rovers at *our* disposal, one for you and me and one for Dai and Idwal and the boys from rent-a-supporter, so you will not be lonely this time. Anyway, it isn't going to snow that hard, according to the forecast. And you will come across as tough and dynamic and totally reliable.'

'Piss off,' said Guto.

'Will you be staying another night, Miss Moore-Lacey?'

Miranda was an inch or two taller than the proprietor of the Plas Meurig, but the way she looked at him made it seem like a couple of feet.

'Possibly,' she said.

His thin smile was barely perceptible on his plump face. 'Would it be possible for you to let us know by lunchtime, do you think?' Slightly less deference than yesterday, she thought. Might have to deal with that.

'I'll see,' she said airily and walked briskly through the hotel foyer to the front door, slinging her bag over her shoulder as a gesture of dismissal.

Outside the door she giggled, feeling almost light-hearted. Wondering how many points one was entitled to for a Neanderthal Welsh nationalist. Having woken her up at some ungodly hour for the purpose of giving her one for the road, Guto had slipped away before eight, confident of passing relatively unnoticed among all the Tories and Liberals milling around waiting for an early breakfast.

As she walked out to the Porsche, a man with one of those motorised things on his camera took about half-a-dozen photographs of her. Miranda waved gaily to him. Famous actress spotted in Wales. Hah!

All the main roads had been cleared of snow; the by-roads were not to be trusted, the radio said.

'We shall be all right then,' Bethan said. 'at least as far as Pontmeurig.'

Ahead of them, the mountains were pure white and flat as a child's collage.

'You ever break into a tomb?' Berry asked. 'Any idea how it's done? Jemmy? Jackhammer?'

Bethan began to worry about him. She wished she had not told him about the baby. He was unshaven, the blue-jawed tough-guy now, hair as black as her own falling over his forehead as he spun the wheel to ease his car between a snow-drift and the hedge on a steep incline. But there was a gleam of something unstable in his eyes. Something to prove – to himself, to his father. And to her now. Which she did not want.

'I'm not crazy,' Berry said.

Bethan said nothing.

'Just I hate secrets. Hate cover-ups.'

'So I've gathered,' Bethan said.

'Way I see it, if the big secret of that place is that Owain Glyndwr's body is there, and people somehow are dying so that secret can *stay* a secret, then it's time the whole thing was blown open. What we have to do is finish Ingley's work for him.'

'Ingley died,' Bethan said. They had come the roundabout way because of the snow and were entering the valley of the lead mine.

'We gotta blow it wide open. Let the historians and archaeologists in there. Be a find of national importance, right? Bring in the tourists. Let in some air.'

This morning the abandoned lead mine was bleakly beautiful, its jagged walls like some medieval fortress – the dereliction, all the scrappy bits, under humps of snow. In a place like this it would survive for ever, Bethan thought. Until its stones and the rocks were fused into one in the way the snow had united them today.

Wales has no future, the poet R.S. Thomas had written. No present. Only a past.

A past guarded with vengeful fury.

Somewhere around her stomach, Bethan felt a sense of insidious foreboding. Berry Morelli, like Ingley, like Giles in his way, had become ensnared.

'Berry,' she said. 'Please. Turn round. Let's go to an expert. Go to the University. Find some help.'

'No way,' Berry said. 'Academics don't take one look at a little red notebook and say, wow, let's get over there. They take years. Go to committees. Seek funding to establish official research projects. Only time they move fast is when it's clear that, if they don't, all the evidence is gonna disappear. I guess that is the kind of action we have to precipitate.'

'It won't let you, Berry.'

'It? *It* won't let me? Jesus.' The road widened out and he ground his foot and the accelerator into the floor.

'Listen,' Bethan said. 'How are we going to do this alone? Just two ordinary people. Two ordinary *scared* people.'

'All my life,' Berry said, 'it seems like I've been a scared person. Neurotic, wimpish.' UnAmerican, he thought. 'This is where it ends.'

Or you end, Bethan thought.

PART NINE

CELTIC NIGHT

CHAPTER LXIII

WHEN they made love that afternoon it was almost like a ceremony. This, in spite of the fact that it took place in the flat above Hampton's Bookshop, in Bethan's single bed, and to the banal cacophony of duelling speaker-vans, Tory and Labour, from the street.

A tender ritual, Berry thought. A parting ritual. But why should either of them be thinking like that?

They held each other and then he kissed her moist and beautiful eyelids as if for the last time.

'How about I go to Y Groes alone?' he said. 'Nobody there knows me. It makes sense.'

She surprised him. 'All right,' she said.

'OK.' He got up, pulled his jeans and fisherman's sweater from a chair.

'We'll go separately,' she said. 'You go in your car, I'll go in mine – if it will start after two days in the car park in this weather.'

'That's not what I meant.'

'It's the best you'll get.'

They dressed, went out to the kitchen. It was three-thirty. Soon the light would fade.

'Tea?' Bethan said.

'Let's go to that teashop by the bridge. I'll buy you a lovespoon.'

She smiled. 'I don't think I can look at another lovespoon after what you said about them. Hold on a minute, I'll be back.'

She went back into the bedroom and he heard her opening the wardrobe. She returned in seconds and said, 'It's snowing again. Try this for size.'

It was a fleece-lined flying jacket of brown leather, as worn by fighter pilots in the Second World War.

'Robin's?'

'It's the only thing of his I kept. He'd always wanted one. I bought it for him the Christmas before he died. It cost me almost a week's wages.'

Berry said, 'I can't.'

'Please . . .'

It was not a perfect fit, but it was close. Bethan adjusted the shoulders and arranged the huge, fleecy collar. 'It's to say all the things I haven't felt safe in saying. Well, not in English anyway.'

'You said them in Welsh?'

Bethan shrugged. 'Maybe. Come on, let's go.'

There was nobody else in the shop. They ordered a pot of tea, no milk. Sat down, but not in the window. Berry was still wearing Robin's flying jacket, which was kind of bulky and too warm in here, but he didn't feel he should take it off.

They looked at each other in silence for maybe half a minute, and then Berry said, getting down to business, 'You see any point in confronting Claire? I met her a couple times, but I can't say I know her well enough to raise something like this.'

'It might be worth talking to her,' Bethan said. 'There are things she ought to know by now. She's been brainwashed, of course.'

Literally, Berry thought remembering what she'd told him about Claire's head in the writhing Meurig.

'I would have to go alone,' Bethan told him.

'Why?'

'Because I doubt she'd speak English to you.'

'That far gone?'

'That far gone,' Bethan said. 'However, I should like to try someone else first. I have a feeling.'

'Someone in the village?'

Bethan was nodding as the teashop door was flung open and a young woman stood there and gazed at them. She was frowning at first, but then a slow, delighted smirk spread over her finely sculpted features.

She wore a bright yellow coat and a very short skirt. Her hair was vividly red.

'Oh my God,' she said, looking Berry up and down. 'Bloody Biggles flies again.'

Bethan thought she'd never seen anyone look so astonished – gobsmacked, Guto would have said – as Berry Morelli when the elegant red-haired girl walked over to their table and sat down.

'Ugh.' Inspecting the contents of their cups and wrinkling her nose. 'Not one black tea, but *two* black teas. If it wasn't so revolting it would be almost touching.'

Berry said, 'This, ah, this is Miranda. She's full of surprises. I guess this must be one of them.'

'Isn't he wonderful when he's embarrassed?' Miranda said, holding out a hand tipped with alarming sea-green nails. 'You must be Bethan. I've heard lots about you from Guto. Do stop squirming, Morelli.'

'And I a little about you,' Bethan said guardedly, shaking the hand.

'Now don't you worry your little Welsh head, darling,' Miranda said. 'I haven't come to take him away.' She was the kind of woman, Bethan thought, who, if she did plan to take him away, would be entirely confident that this would pose no long-term problem.

'Pardon me for asking, Miranda,' Berry said. 'But what the fuck are you doing here?'

'Gosh,' Miranda said. 'I think he's regaining his composure. All the same, not the most gracious welcome for someone who's come to assure him he may not be bonkers after all.'

'Coffee, Miranda?'

'No thank you, I can see the tin over the counter,' Miranda wrinkled her nose again. 'I'll come straight to the matter on which I've travelled hundreds of miles in appalling conditions. Have you by any chance heard of one Martin Coulson, former curate of this parish?'

'I didn't know that,' Bethan said. 'About the difficulty he had speaking Welsh.'

'Like you were saying about Giles.' Berry filled their cups

from the pot; Miranda winced at the colour of the tea. 'Inside that village the language becomes a total mystery to the English, no matter how well they were picking it up before. Like a barrier goes up.'

'It was very good of you to come and tell us,' Bethan said. 'Thank you.'

'How many coincidences can you take?' Berry shook his head. 'Clinches it, far as I'm concerned.'

'And what are you going to do about it?' Miranda demanded.

'The bottom line,' Berry said. He lit a cigarette, watched her through the smoke, wondering where she'd go from here.

'I think it's all rather exciting,' Miranda said, and they both looked at her, Berry with a rising dismay. He might have known she wouldn't have come all this way just to tell him about the death of an obscure country parson. She'd realised there was something intriguing going down and she wanted in.

'Listen, I realise it isn't my place to— But keep the hell out of this thing. Please.' Realising even as he spoke that this was just about the last way to persuade Miranda to back off.

'He's right,' Bethan told her seriously. 'It's not exciting. Just very sad and unpleasant.'

'Well, thanks for the warning.' Miranda smiled sweetly at them both, abruptly picked up her bag and sailed towards the door. 'I'll see you around, OK?'

She walked away down the street without looking back. Welsh snowflakes landing tentatively, with a hint of deference, in her angry red hair.

They cleared most of the snow from the Peugeot, chipped ice from the windscreen. 'It's terribly cold for December,' Bethan said, patting gloved hands together to remove the sticky snow. 'We rarely see much of this before New Year.'

It was coming down in wild spasms, the white-crusted castle looking almost picturesque against a sky like dense, billowing smoke.

'You're right, of course,' Berry said. 'One of us gets stuck, we at least have a second chance.'

The engine started at the fourth attempt. Bethan let it run, switched on the lights, pulled her pink woolly hat over her ears.

'OK,' she said. 'You follow me. When we get there, we park behind the school, out of sight.'

The equipment was in the Sprite, behind the seats. Early that afternoon they'd been to see Dai Death who, in turn, had consulted his friend, the local monumental mason, supplier of gravestones over an area stretching from Pont down to Lampeter. Dai had been suspicious, but he'd done it – for Bethan.

'But first,' Berry said. 'We go see this friend of yours.'

'I doubt I have any actual *friends* there,' Bethan said. 'This is just the one person I can think of who won't bar his door when he sees me coming.'

CHAPTER LXIV

U P IN the Nearly Mountains, headlights on, the snow was all there was. It came at the windscreen at first in harmless feathery clouds, like being in a pillow fight. Could send you to sleep, Berry thought.

The higher they climbed, the denser it became. Cold cobs, now, the size of table-tennis balls. The two small, red taillights of Bethan's Peugeot bobbed in the blizzard.

'Get me through this, baby, I'll buy you an overhaul,' he told the Sprite, pulling it down to second gear on a nasty incline, wheels whirring. Ice under this stuff up here.

At least the snow was a *natural* hazard.

we in same shit, you find out . . .

Like all his life had been propelling him into this. Leaving the US with his ass in a sling, so to speak. The disillusion of London and an England full of yuppies and video stores and American burger joints. Old Winstone dying on him. Giles.

All this he saw through the snow.

No family. No job. Now everything he had was out here in this cold, isolated graveyard of a region where people saw their own mortality gleaming in the darkness.

Everything he had amounted to a geriatric little car and – maybe – a woman who needed the kind of help he wasn't sure he had the balls to provide.

But if all his life was converging on this woman, it had to be worth walking into the graveyard, just hoping the Goddamn corpse candle wasn't shining for him.

For the first time since putting on Robin's flying jacket he went into a hopeless shivering fit, scared shitless.

Only five-thirty and Y Groes was midnight-still and midnight-dark.

Berry parked next to the Peugeot behind the school and got out, closing his driver's door just as quietly as he could, and looked around, disturbed.

'This is weird,' he said and wondered how many times he'd expressed that opinion in the past week.

But, yeah, it *was* weird. No snow falling any more, only a light covering on the ground, a passing nod to winter, an acknowledgement that the season was out there but wasn't permitted to enter without an invite.

'The blue hole,' Bethan said, taking off her woolly hat, shaking her hair; it was warm enough to do that. 'It might be quite natural. One of those places where the arrangement of the hills—'

'You believe that?'

'No,' she said. 'Not entirely.'

The sky was clear; you could even see stars, except for where the black tube of the church tower rose in the east. But only a few meagre lights in the houses. Power cut maybe.

He breathed out hard. 'Beth, listen, from now on, we have to start believing all this other stuff is real. The corpse candles, the bird of death, the whole cartload of shit. Because in this place it *is* real. We left the civilised world behind, we don't play by those rules any more.'

'I think I always did believe they were real,' she said.

'Beth, before we go in there, I just wanna say—'

Bethan put the pink hat back on. 'Save it. Please.'

'But if—'

'I know,' she said.

He looked far worse than she remembered. Perhaps it was the light from the oil lamp in the porch which yellowed his skin, made his eyes seem to bulge. His white hair was stiff, no spring to it, and his Lloyd George moustache misshapen and discoloured.

'Bethan.' Disappointment there, but no real surprise; even his voice sagged. 'Why do you have to do this to me?'

He didn't even seem to have noticed Berry Morelli standing behind her.

'You don't know why I've come yet,' Bethan said.

'Oh, I know, girl. I know all right. And I'll tell you, you didn't realise when you were lucky. Take your friend with you and get back to Pont. If you can still make it.'

'Still make it?'

'With the snow. That is all I mean.'

'No, it isn't all you mean,' Bethan said firmly. 'Let us in, Aled.'

'We open at seven.'

'Good. That leaves us plenty of time to talk.'

'Bethan, you don't want to do this. Too many people—'

'I'm allowed to do it. I'm Welsh.'

'But *he* isn't.' Aled didn't look at Berry.

'I'm not English either,' Berry said. 'And I'm not polite, so—'

'No.' Bethan put a hand on his arm.

But Aled sighed and stepped back then and held open the door from the inside. Bethan walked in and Berry followed, and Aled closed the door and bolted it, top and bottom. 'No lights,' he said, 'Snow brought down the power lines. Go through to the dining room where we can't be seen from the street.'

Through the dining room window, they could see a small yard and the church hill rising sheer beyond it, palely visible because of its light dusting of snow. Aled made them sit around a square dining table, one of only five in the room. Then he lit a candle in a glass holder on the table – the only source of light or heat; just dead ash and the husk of a log in the grate.

'For a schoolteacher,' Aled said, 'You don't learn anything, do you, girl?'

The convoy assembled at six on the castle car park. A Range Rover, a Daihatsu and a little Fiat Panda which was all Dai Death had been able to borrow from the garage at short notice.

Guto was furious when he saw who was piling into the six-seater Daihatsu.

'You said supporters,' he snarled at Alun, the General Secretary.

'It'll be fine,' Alun whispered back. 'A little adventure for them.'

'I hope there's a bloody pub there,' Charlie Firth was saying, getting into the back between ski-jacketed Shirley Gillies with her Uher tape-recorder on her knee, and 'Bill' Sykes in an ancient overcoat with a vicuna collar. Ray Wheeler was in the front with young Gary, Giles Freeman's replacement, and a farmer called Emlyn, who was driving.

It was still snowing, and there must have been four or five inches of it on the ground.

'Flaming cold,' Firth said.

'We'll just have to bunch together,' said Shirley. She was on her own tonight, TV news having been affected by a judiciously timed cameramen's dispute about overtime payments.

Idwal Roberts, tweed trousers stuffed into his wellingtons, looked at the Fiat Panda and then looked at Dai. 'You're sure this thing is four-wheel-drive?' Dai pointed to the appropriate lettering on the little car's rear door. Idwal looked unconvinced.

'I'm sorry, I've forgotten – which paper are you with?' Alun asked Miranda, who was looking startling in a huge lemon-coloured designer parka with lots of fake fur.

'*Gardening News*,' Guto told him.

Alun, seeming somehow less efficient in a leather flat-cap and without his tinted glasses, gazed up at the dark and tumbling sky. 'It was supposed to stop tonight.'

'You dickhead,' said Guto.

'Yes, yes,' Aled said, anguished. 'But there is no way anyone can ever prove it. And what good would it do anyway?'

Bethan began to feel sorry for him. He was worn and tired, his wife had left him . . .

'She will come back,' Aled said. 'When she is well again. When the winter is over.'

'A lot of it left to come,' Berry said.

'Yes.' Aled stared into the dead fireplace. 'I don't know, something has changed, gone wrong, isn't it?'

'Maybe it was always wrong,' Berry said.

'No. It was *not* wrong.' Aled's face was ragged in the candlelight. 'How could it be wrong? We were preserving that which was ours. A shrine, it was. Is.'

'Not "is",' Bethan said. 'You don't believe that now.'

'I don't know. Why are you asking me these things? There is nothing you can do, except to save yourselves. Perhaps.'

Berry said, 'How can it not be wrong if people are dying?'

Aled put his face into his hands, peered slowly over his fingertips. 'Ones and twos,' he said. 'That was all it ever was. It was so strong, see. They could not withstand the exposure to it. Some of them simply went away. Fine. But over the years, some . . . Ones and twos, that was all.'

Bethan's pity evaporated. 'Ones and twos? What does that mean, Aled? Minor casualties?' Hands curled into fists, pressing hard into the tabletop. 'Expendable English people, like Martin Coulson and— and—'

'Yes, yes— I was so sorry. He was a good man, Robin. A fine man. And I did try to talk you out of it, the cottage, once. Do you remember that day? But they see this place and there is no stopping them. Seduced, they are. You know that.' Eyes wide, full of futile pleading.

Bethan said quietly, 'The *Gorsedd Ddu*.'

'No. I will not talk about that.'

'Ap Siencyn then.'

'If you know, why do you ask me?'

Bethan hadn't known. Not for certain. 'And the others?'

'Judge Rhys?' Berry leaned into the candlelight.

'Yes, Judge Rhys, and now—'

'Morgan?' Bethan demanded. 'Buddug? Dilwyn? Glyn Harri?'

'Yes, yes, yes! And the rest are scattered all over Wales, I don't know how many, I only run a pub. Oh, God, what have I done?'

'Ap Siencyn,' Bethan said. 'Tell us about him.'

'What is there to tell that you do not know? The minister, he is, and the *dyn hysbys*.'

'What's that?' Berry said.

'The wise man,' Bethan said. 'The conjuror. The wizard. Most villages used to have one. Someone who knew about curing illnesses and helping sick animals and—'

'Like a shaman?'

'I suppose.'

'He cure people?'

'Some people,' Aled said.

'And what about the others?'

'We do not ask,' Aled said. 'It has been a good place to live.'

'Where does the *Gorsedd* meet?' Berry demanded.

Aled screamed out, 'What are you trying to do to me?'

And the candle went out, as if someone had blown on it.

CHAPTER LXV

THE first vehicle in the Plaid Cymru convoy drew up to find the village school in darkness.

'What the hell—?' Alun jumped down from the Land-Rover and strode to the school door.

'What did I tell you?' Guto roared after him.

Miranda stepped down into half an inch of snow. 'So this is Y Groes.' She paced about, kicking at the thin white dust with the tip of her boot. 'It's almost warm here, isn't that odd?'

'I can't understand it,' Alun was saying, walking round the building, looking into windows. 'I was talking to the FUW not two hours ago. They said it was definitely on. I said, 'Look, if there is any change, get back to me.' I gave them the mobile phone number, everything.'

'Oh, gave them the mobile phone number, did you?' Guto leaned against the bonnet of the Land-Rover and started to laugh.

'What's wrong?' Alun was affronted.

Headlights hit them, the Daihatsu crunched to a stop, and presently Bill Sykes wandered over, his long overcoat flapping. 'Are we here, old boy?'

'We seem to have a problem, Bill,' Alun said.

'The problem is Alun,' Guto told him. 'He is a city boy. Alun, do you have your mobile phone on you?'

'It's in the Land-Rover.'

'Well, if you go and get it, I think you will find the words "No Service" emblazoned across its little screen.'

'No way. That phone functions everywhere around here. It's the best there is.'

'Dickhead,' said Guto. 'They haven't even got television in Y Groes.'

'You're kidding.'

Guto stepped back and held open the door of the Land-

Rover for his colleague. When Alun emerged, the five reporters were clustered around the Plaid candidate in the beam of the Land-Rover's headlights. They turned to face the General Secretary, all looking quite amused.

'Right,' Alun said briskly. 'I don't know why it's been called off, but it obviously has. Well . . . As you can see, it's stopped snowing, so I don't think we'll have any problems getting back. I think the least I can do is buy you boys a couple of drinks. The pub is just over the bridge.'

There was a small cheer.

'You're a gentleman,' said Ray Wheeler, of the *Mirror*. 'A nationalist and a gentleman.'

Dai and Idwal arrived in the Fiat Panda, and Guto explained the problem. 'I'm not having a drink,' Dai said. 'Bad enough getting here as it is.'

'Well, have an orange juice,' said Guto, as Miranda appeared at his shoulder, frowning.

'I've just had a peep round the back,' she said. 'Morelli's car is there, parked very discreetly under some trees. And another car, a Peugeot, I think.'

'Bethan's car?' said Dai sharply. 'They came to see me earlier, wanted to know about—' He looked across the village to the church hill. 'Oh, bloody hell.'

They knew Aled was shaking because the table was shaking.

'Go,' he said. 'All right? Go from here.'

Berry found his lighter, relit the candle.

'Draught,' he said.

'Remember what you said when we got here?' Bethan asked him.

'OK. Not draught.'

The candle flared and Aled's white face flared behind it. 'Can you not feel it, man?'

Berry didn't know what he was supposed to be feeling. He looked around the room and out the window. It was still not snowing. There were still no lights.

'The snow will melt before morning,' Aled said.

'No chance. You shoulda seen it on the mountains.'

'The village is generating its own heat,' Bethan said. 'Is that what you're saying?'

'Bethan, I once told you, see, this village makes demands.'

'I remember.'

'Demands, you know – sacrifices.'

'You did not say anything about sacrifice.'

'The old Druids, see,' Aled said. 'They did not sacrifice each other, their – you know, virgins, kids. None of that nonsense.'

History lessons, Berry thought. Wales is all about history lessons.

'But I've heard it said they used to sacrifice their enemies,' Aled said. 'Their prisoners. A life's a life, see, isn't it? Blood is blood.'

He stood up. 'That is the finish. You have had enough from me.'

Bethan was too shocked to speak.

Aled picked up the candle and they followed him out of the dining room and through to the bar, where he unbolted the oak front door.

'Opening time soon,' he said. 'And you won't want to see the Morgans, will you?'

'One more thing,' Berry said in the doorway.

'No. No more things.'

'You have a flashlight I could borrow?'

Aled did not reply but went behind the bar and fumbled about and then presented a long black torch to Berry.

'Rubber,' he said morosely. 'Bounces, see.'

The crescent moon was curling from the tower like a candle flame. A huge, symbolic corpse candle, Bethan thought.

The smell in the December air was a little like the summer night smell of wild flowers, but heavier, sweet with decay, as though the flowers had sprouted unnaturally from the dead earth, like bodies in rotting shrouds thrusting their hands through the grave dirt. The ground, with its thin veneer of

371

snow, had a blueish, sometimes purplish tint, like the cheeks of the newly-dead.

Bethan felt sick. She felt Y Groes closing around her, bloated with blood, greasy with human fat.

'I want to leave,' she said. 'Now.'

'Not till we take a look at the church.'

'I will not go in there.'

'I'll go in then.'

'Did you realise what he was saying just now? About sacrifices?'

'I'll think about it later. Right now, I need to see that tomb.'

Bethan cried out, 'What good will it do now?'

She stood at the top of the deserted street, her back to the bridge, white raincoat drawing in the unnatural incandescence of the night so that it turned mauve.

Irradiated, Berry thought. He felt love and fear, and he almost gave in, hurried her back over the bridge to the cars. Foot down, out of here.

Then they heard voices from the other side of the bridge and he took her arm and pulled her into the alley between the *Tafarn* and the electricity sub-station which tonight had no electricity to dispense.

Laughter.

'. . . hey Shirl, you can't be cold now.'

'No, but it's awfully dark – Whoops!'

'Shit,' Berry whispered. 'What the hell are *they* doing here?'

'Guto,' Bethan whispered back. 'I can hear Guto's voice, and isn't that—?'

'Christ,' Berry said. 'It's Miranda.'

The bunch of people crossed the bridge and they heard a banging on the pub door and Dai's voice. 'Come on then, Aled. It's gone seven.'

'And don't tell us the beer pumps don't work,' shouted an English voice. 'Won't affect the Optics.'

The snow in the street seemed to sweat, and there was a kind of liquid hum in the air, as if the dead sub-station was a church organ and there was a hidden choir somewhere poised to sing out into the night.

Voice thick with growing nausea, Berry said, 'What's the Welsh for *fee fi fo fum* . . .?'

CHAPTER LXVI

A LED did not like this.

Every Friday night was more or less the same, summer or winter. By seven-fifteen, Glyn Harri would have come in, or maybe Dilwyn. Morgan, with or without Buddug, around eight.

These were the constants.

Others were regulars, not bound to a time: Dewi Morus, Mair and Idris Huws, Meirion, Dr Wyn. And then the occasionals, who included the rector.

Tonight, gone eight now, and none of them had arrived.

There was no precedent for this.

Nearly a dozen people in the bar, but none of them locals and half of them English. Reporters. Loud people, practised drinkers.

'What's that stuff?'

Man in an expensive suit, well-cut to hide his beer-gut. Late forties, going unconcernedly to seed. Leaning over the bar by the spluttering Tilley lamp, pointing to the bottle of Welsh Chwisgi.

'Whisky,' Aled said. 'Like any other. Blended over in Brecon.'

'Welsh whisky? You're bloody joking.'

'Try some,' Aled said neutrally.

'Is it cheap? It should be.'

'Cheaper than some. Dearer than others. There is also the Prince of Wales twelve-year-old malt. What you might call Wales's answer to Chivas Regal.'

'Stone me. Better just give us a single then, Alec. No soda. Got to savour this one. Bloody Welsh whisky, Ray! One for you? Make it two then, Alec.'

'We'll have the bottle,' Alun, of Plaid, said generously. 'Put it on my tab.'

Aled brought the bottle of Prince of Wales twelve-year-old malt over to the cluster of tables. A brass oil-lamp hung from a great brown beam above them. A log fire blazed.

'Isn't this cosy?' a woman said. The chubby one, not the glamorous red-haired one.

Shirley Gillies had had two gin and limes very rapidly.

'Yeh, if you like the rustic bit,' Gary Willis said, looking uncomfortable. 'Not very into the primitive, personally.'

'Trouble with you, Gary, is you have no soul,' Shirley said. 'A nice body, but no soul. I think it's rather wonderful; all the power lines down, the mobile phones useless.'

'And in a pub!' said Ray Wheeler.

'I told you,' Alun whispered to Guto. 'I told you it would be an adventure for them.'

'You know,' Ray said. 'This reminds me in a way of poor old Winstone Thorpe.'

'Winstone's Welsh Experience,' said Charlie Firth. 'Miserable landlady, every bugger speaking Welsh, all the pubs closed 'cause it's Sunday, and only Jack Beddall to talk to.'

Bill Sykes leaned into the lamplight. 'You know I really think it's time I scotched this one for good.'

'Better than Welshing it,' said Charlie Firth. 'Although actually, this stuff's not bad. I reckon what it is, somebody bought a case of Glenfiddich and switched the labels.'

'Sod off, Englishman,' Guto said. 'One of my mates, it is, makes this. But I shall pass on the compliment.'

'Go on, Bill,' Ray Wheeler topped up Sykes's glass with twelve-year-old Welsh malt. 'Winstone Thorpe.'

'Well . . . I suppose he told you he'd been sent out on a story about two Welsh farmers who'd been shot by their housekeeper.'

'Back in the sixties,' said Ray.

'Definitely not in the sixties, old boy. Long, long before that. And he only had Jack Beddall on the story because Beddall's been dead twenty years.'

'Oh, wonderful!' Shirley Gillies finished her drink. 'A mystery story. Can I have one of those?'

'On top of gin, Shirley?' Gary passed over the Prince of Wales bottle, two-thirds empty already.

'It *did* happen. The shooting. One of those peculiar rural *ménage-à-trois* situations. The housekeeper was an English girl who innocently answered an advert and found herself sharing a bed with two hairy yokels smelling of sheepshit. Most distasteful.'

'Oh, I don't know . . .' Shirley giggled and looked across at Guto, who had an arm discreetly around Miranda's waist. Shirley spotted the arm and looked disappointed.

'Anyway, the girl inevitably got pregnant and the farmers, being unable to decide which of them was the father, resolved the argument by throwing her out.'

'Typical,' Charlie Firth said.

'Only, when she left, she took their shotgun with her and returned that night and re-plastered the bedroom wall with the pair of them.'

'Heavy,' said Gary Willis.

'Quite a controversial court case in its day,' said Bill Sykes. 'She got off very lightly, perhaps because of the baby. I can't remember whether Winstone was actually born in the prison hospital or whether she was out by then, but he certainly—'

'You're joking!' Ray Wheeler put down his glass in astonishment.

'Hated the Welsh all his life,' said Sykes. 'Had it instilled into him at his mother's knee that no self-respecting English person should ever venture over Offa's Dyke. Been recycling the story as a sort of parable ever since.'

'Just a minute,' Miranda said. 'Where exactly did all this happen?'

'Oh, somewhere up North. Snowdonia way, I imagine. I think I was the only one he ever told, but he didn't go into details, even with me.'

'You mean this Winstone never actually came around here?'

'He never went to Wales in his life,' said Sykes. 'And he warned everyone else to stay out as well. Very fond of his mother, Winstone was. So now you know. I was sworn to silence, but it can't do any harm now, can it?'

'I can hardly believe it,' Miranda said in a low voice to Guto. 'Just wait till I tell Morelli. The only reason he got dragged into all this was old Winstone and his Cassandra routine.'

'I'm confused,' Guto said. 'And I think I would prefer to stay confused.'

Dai Death, who had no interest in any of this, was at the bar, quizzing Aled about Bethan.

'I don't know where they went,' Aled said. 'But if you find them, get her out of here. This is no joke.'

'I don't know whether I should be asking you this, Aled, but why would they want to go up to the church with two crowbars and a hydraulic jack?'

Aled was silent, but Dai could tell this had cut him like splinters from a suddenly shattered bottle.

Eventually, Aled said slowly, 'I shall have to tell them. If they don't already know.'

'Tell who? What?'

'But I will not.'

Unseasonal sweat shining on his head, rivulets rolling into his silver sideburns, Dai said, 'I am finding it hard to work out who is mad here.'

'Assume that everyone you meet is mad,' Aled said.

Shirley had taken off her ski-jacket and unbuttoned her blouse to a dangerous extent. Charlie and Ray were taking an interest, but it was clear Shirley wanted Gary Willis.

It was very hot in the bar, the log fire superfluous in its inglenook. 'Alec,' Charlie Firth called out. 'We'll have another bottle of that Welsh Scotch.'

Aled brought the whisky and went over to the window, high in the wall behind the journalists.

Where were they?

There were few lights visible in the cottages across the street, but there was a glow about the cottages themselves and a milky layer in the air. Premature snowdrops poked out of a tub under the window. He was sure they had not been there this morning.

'Can we move the table back from the fire,' the plump

woman was saying. Half stripped, she was. 'Too hot even for me.'

He wanted to tell them to drink up and go.

In fact – the realisation flared around him, underfired with a simmering fear – he wanted to go with them.

But if they did not go, he knew he could not stay and watch it happen, as he knew it must.

CHAPTER LXVII

Medieval, perpendicular. Two-tiered, pyramidal, timber-framed bellchamber . . .

The church was a giant monolith in its circular graveyard; its spire always seemed to be outlined against the brightest part of the sky, from wherever you were standing.

From the churchyard, you looked up and the whole edifice seemed to be swinging towards you, like a massive pendulum suspended from the moon itself.

'I can't,' Bethan said. 'I don't think I've ever liked old churches, even in the daylight, and I'm frightened of what this one has become. I'm sorry.'

Berry had it worked out. She was saying this because she didn't want *him* to go in there. If he thought she was the one who was most scared he'd maybe back off, seek help.

No way.

He took out his car keys. 'Listen, how about you go fetch the Sprite. The gear's in back. Give me time to check things out – might not even be open.' It was only a couple hundred yards to the cars, and there was plenty light.

She accepted the keys reluctantly.

'Listen, any problems, just blast on the horn, OK? Bring Guto and the guys outa the pub.'

He tried out Aled's flashlight. The beam was strong and white and threw a mist into the air. He hurriedly directed it downwards, and it lit up a grave, and Bethan drew in a sharp breath.

On the gravestone was carved,

Dyma fedd Thomas Rhys . . .

Berry tried a shrug. 'We had to be standing by *somebody's* grave.'

He tried to ignore the smell, which was as if the grave had been opened.

A lot of whisky had been drunk. Alun, of Plaid, was looking at his watch. Miranda had fallen asleep on Guto's shoulder. Guto was endeavouring to give Bill Sykes a true insight into the philosophy of Welsh Nationalism, while Charlie and Ray were sharing a cold meat pie.

Gary Willis had gone to the gents, and Shirley Gillies had followed him out of the bar.

At the bar itself, the Tilley lamp had spluttered out and been replaced with a couple of candles in ashtrays.

'Quiet in here, though, tonight,' Dai said to Aled. 'Where are all the locals then?'

Aled shook his head, said nothing.

'Funny buggers here,' Idwal Pugh said. 'Won't share a *Tafarn* with outsiders, see.'

'Rubbish, man.' Dai scowled. 'They have never been known for that. I've been in here of a lunchtime, an English chap walks in and everybody in the place stops speaking Welsh immediately, out of courtesy. Very hospitable people. Unusually hospitable.'

'Where are they then?' Idwal said. 'Most places, if there's a power cut, no telly—'

'They have no tellies here anyway. No reception, see.'

'Well, radio then. Not even a proper light to read a book by. What would they do but go to the pub? No, you are naïve about this, Dai.'

'What I want to know,' Dai said, 'is what Bethan and that American fellow are up to.'

'Get them out,' Aled said suddenly. 'Get them all out, Dai, for Christ's sake.'

Behind him the telephone rang, and everyone looked up.

Dai said, 'Don't imagine the phone to be working in a power cut. You forget it makes no difference.'

Aled said, '*Y Groes pedwar, pedwar, chwech.*'

'Aled, is that you?'

'Yes it is.'

'Aled, it's Gwyn Arthur from the police station. I'm ringing you myself because the roads are blocked all over the place and we've had to pull the cars off. Otherwise someone would have come out to see you.'

'Snow's bad over there, then?'

'Worst for ten years. Aled, Aber police have been on the line, and I am afraid I have bad news. Very bad news. You should sit down if you can.'

'Let's go for a walk,' Shirley said, and she grabbed Gary Willis's hand.

Gary thought, Ah, what the hell – and allowed her to pull him to the pub door.

The problem was, he was getting married in a couple of months and was trying to develop a new and disciplined attitude when faced with the sexual opportunities which, ironically, had seemed to come his way quite often since his engagement.

On the other hand, Shirley, by all accounts, knew the score. Had a husband somewhere and a very discreet, adult approach to this sort of thing. She was also considerably older than Gary, and so, he reasoned, it would be a sort of social service on his part.

Yeh, what the hell. They stepped out into the blue and purple night.

'Isn't it just amazingly . . . you know, not cold.' Shirley had left her ski-jacket in the bar.

'Bit odd, really,' Gary said. 'Considering the conditions when we were coming over the mountains.'

'I quite fancy coming over the mountains,' Shirley said,

grabbing hold of his tie and leading him into the street like a showman with a dancing bear.

She let him go when they reached the bridge, the river burbling below. Soft snow sat lightly and inoffensively on the top of the parapet. Shirley made a snowball and threw it at Gary. It hit him on the cheek and felt like candyfloss. Gary gathered up a handful of snow and advanced on Shirley who screamed delightedly.

Gary plunged the handful of snow down the front of Shirley's blouse. 'You swine.' She cackled and pulled his hand back down. 'Now you'll have to get it all out.'

'So I will,' Gary said.

By the time they'd made their inebriated way to the far side of the bridge the blouse was off, Shirley waving it at Gary like a football supporter's scarf. Gary managed to grab a sleeve and the blouse tore neatly in half, leaving them looking down at their respective fragments and laughing helplessly.

Gary, sweating, pulled off his jacket and hung it over the bridge parapet.

They might have been on a beach in August.

Shirley unfastened her bra, took it off and twirled it around her head as she bounced off towards the woods. Gary thought she couldn't half move for her size.

'Slow down, Shirl, you'll have no energy left.'

'Ho ho.' Shirley gurgled. 'We'll see about that, baby.'

Running past the school lane, she let her skirt fall to her ankles and stepped out of it and kicked it away with the tip of a patent-leather boot.

She reached the edge of the woods and stood panting, wearing only her boots, a pair of pink briefs and a silver necklace, her back to an enormous oak tree, a ludicrous grin on her face.

Just for a moment, as he stood at the edge of the wood, fumbling with his belt, the total madness of the situation was fully apparent to Gary Willis.

He saw the oak tree, heavy with snow. He looked up at the iceberg hills, stark in the starry night. He looked across the bridge to the village, feeble glows from behind the drawn curtains of Christmas card cottages with snow on their roofs.

He looked at Shirley and saw the sweat freezing rapidly on her grinning face, the skin of her exposed body blue and mottled. And he thought, *it isn't warm at all, it just seems warm to us.*

And then the moment passed, and nothing was clear any more.

CHAPTER LXVIII

BERRY walked into the nave, footsteps on stone.

Tock, tock, tock.

Outside, it had been unseasonally, ridiculously warm. Inside the church it was winter again. When he switched off the torch, the light was ice-blue from through the Gothic windows on either side and livid through the long window at the top of the nave, beyond the altar.

He was glad Bethan was not with him, but that didn't make him feel any better about being here.

He walked up the aisle towards the altar.

Tock, tock, tock,

tock, tock,

tock.

The churches of his several childhoods, in different States, had mostly been newish buildings masquerading as places as old as this. His dad had been a lapsed Catholic, his mom a Presbyterian. And so religion, to him, had been something pointless that people argued about.

Here, tonight – shining the torch on his watch he discovered it was not yet nine o'clock – he was aware for maybe the first time of the awful power of something venerated. Like the Welsh Language in Judge Rhys's study, only there was ritual worship involved here, and many centuries of it.

Whatever it was reverberated off the stones in the walls, was filtered through the mortuary light from the windows, lay rich and musky on the air.

And it didn't want him here.

Fuck you, he wanted to say, to make a stand, be defiant. But his full range of flip obscenities would seem pathetically peevish and infantile, and about as effectual as throwing stones at a tank.

'Help me,' he said, to his surprise, and the walls immediately laughed off the words.

mee, hee, heee . . .

He switched on the torch with a thunderous clack-ack-ack, and the monstrous shadows leapt out, rearing up then settling back just on the periphery of the beam so he would know they were there, and waiting.

He drew breath and the rich air seemed to enter his lungs in staccato bursts, like something that was planning to come out as a sob. It was thick, sour-milk air, like in the judge's study, only here it had a great auditorium to waft around in and ferment.

Berry found the tomb. There was only one. It was in a small chapel to the left of the altar. A chapel of its own.

It was three feet high and five or six feet long, as long as the stone figure of the knight laid out on top, hands together, praying.

The knight wore armour and its face was worn, the expression on it blurred by the years. But the essence of this remained, and it had nothing reassuring to say. Berry thought the face might at one time have had a beard, but he could not tell if the beard was cleft.

He didn't like to look too hard at it, felt it was looking back.

There was kind of a plaque thing on the side of the tomb, with lettering. But this was in Latin and maybe Welsh too, and he couldn't make it out.

Meredydd, the guy's name, it had said in Ingley's book.

Owain Glyndwr, I presume, was what he'd figured he'd say on approaching the tomb. Let the stiff inside know it was dealing with a wisecracking, smart-assed American who was in no mood for any spooky tricks, OK?

Only the words wouldn't come out.

He thought that if anything spooky happened in this place, there would be little question of how he'd react. He would piss himself, throw up, something of that order.

The years had not blurred a very ancient, sneering cruelty in the face of this knight that belied the supplication of his hands.

Berry didn't like him one bit and he had a sensation, like a cold vibration in the air over the knight's eyes, that the feeling was mutual.

He put out a finger, touched the effigy's eyes, one then the other. The way the centuries had worn the stone you couldn't be sure whether the eyes were closed or wide open. Berry felt exposed, observed, and was unable to rid himself of the notion that somebody was standing behind him in the cold chapel, perhaps the knight himself, a great sword raised in both hands over his head.

He tried to clear his mind of all such thoughts and made himself go through the motions of checking out the structure of the tomb, as Ingley must have done.

Before he died.

For Chrissake . . .

The body of the tomb was constructed out of stone blocks, each about ten inches by six, three rows of them supporting the top slab and the effigy.

He laid the torch down on the knight's stone-armoured breast, up against the praying hands with their chipped knuckles.

Then he turned his back on the tomb, fitted his fingers under the edge of the slab, closed his eyes, counted down from three . . . and heaved.

To his secret horror, the slab moved just enough to show him that with the equipment and perhaps a little help he could get inside.

The thought chilled his stomach.

OK. Calm down.

He knew he had to go fetch the stuff from the car, and whatever was in there he had to let out. And let some air into this place.

An act of desecration.

Sure. No problem.

Berry emerged from the chapel of the tomb holding the rubber flashlight confidently in front of him. The flashlight immediately went out.

He froze.

And the sour milk air clotted around him and clogged his head. He felt dizzy and sat down on some pew on the edge of the nave, and then found he could not move. His thoughts congealed; his senses seemed to be setting like concrete.

Then, after a while – could have been hours, minutes or only seconds – there were ribbons of light.

And the light came now not from the windows on either side or the long window behind the altar, but from above. It descended in a cold white ray, making dust-motes scintillate in the air, and he had the idea it must be the moon and the pillars and buttresses of stone were like trees on either side and the air was pungent now with brackish scents and the residue of woodsmoke.

As the walls of the nave closed in, he looked up into the night sky and on the boundary of his vision a black figure eased out of the mist.

CHAPTER LXIX

BETHAN parked the Sprite in the shadow of the lych gate and sat there for a minute or two, making her mind up.

Then she got out, slammed the door – you had to slam it or it would not stay shut – and walked back down the lane to the *Tafarn*.

What she was remembering was Martin Coulson, the curate, who had fallen and smashed his head on the tomb of Sir Robert Meredydd. And this had happened in broad daylight.

The image came to her of Berry Morelli face-down on the stone-flagged floor, unmoving, a river of dark blood flowing down the aisle. She began to run.

By the time she reached the door of the pub, the perspiration was out around her eyes; she felt clammy, wanting to shed her hat and her raincoat.

But she remembered how Owain Glyndwr, it was said, could bring about rapid changes in the weather to confound his enemies. Even Shakespeare's satire seemed to reflect this. Bethan, having studied Henry IV at college, knew all Glendower's overblown speeches, heard them echoing as she ran,

> *Three times hath Henry Bolingbroke made head*
> *Against my power; thrice from the banks of Wye*
> *And sandy-bottomed Severn have I sent him*
> *Bootless home and weather-beaten back.*

So Bethan took off nothing.

From the *Tafarn*'s ill-lit interior came sounds of merriment. Guto's voice, and the rest were English accents.

Inside the doorway she almost bumped into a stooping figure emerging from the gents' lavatory.

'Bethan! Where the hell have you been? You look all of a tizz.'

'Oh, Dai.' It came out as a long sigh.

'You look as if you need a drink, girl. Come and—'

'No, no, no.' Bethan wiped sweat from her eyes, smearing what remained of her make-up. 'You must help me, Dai. First, you have to get all those people out of there.'

'Oh hell.' Dai Death looked exasperated. 'This is what Aled was saying before he stopped talking altogether. Everybody's gone mad tonight. Anyway, they won't go. The road is blocked at the Pont end and God knows what it's like over the Nearly Mountains. The council's out with the snowploughs and they're waiting for some clearance from—'

'Dai, get them out, I do not care how. Tell Guto—'

'They're all bloody pissed, girl! They don't care whether they get home or not.'

'God.' Bethan was almost frantic. 'Then can you and Idwal get up to the church and help Berry?'

'Why, what's he doing?'

Bethan wiped her eyes again and clasped her hands in front of her, squeezing the fingers. And told him very slowly and very precisely that Berry Morelli was trying to break into a tomb which was believed to contain the mortal remains of Owain Glyndwr.

Dai looked sorrowful. She did not think he believed what she had said, only that she was insane.

'My job, Bethan,' he said, 'is to put them in, not get them out.'

'I wish this was all a joke, Dai. I really wish it was a joke.'

Dai put a calming hand on her shoulder. 'All right. All right. I will go. I'll bring Idwal. A good chapel boy. We'll both go. All right?'

Bethan nodded, sagging in the doorway. The heat was awful.

Aled washed glasses and watched the English drink.

The General Secretary of Plaid Cymru appeared at the bar. 'Did they say when the ploughs would be through?'

Aled shook his head.

'Where's Emlyn gone, the driver? He said he was going to see some friends, but he hasn't come back. We need a good driver now, more than ever, for these chaps.'

Aled shook his head, rinsed a glass, held it up in the candlelight, stood it on a shelf behind him.

'Any use, do you think, if I talk to the police?'

Aled made no reply. His hands moved mechanically, rinsing the glasses, holding them to the weak light, putting each one carefully on the shelf.

'I can't understand it. Why is the weather so bad in Pontmeurig when here it's so incredibly mild? I've never known anything like this . . . Oh, sorry, am I in your way?'

Charlie Firth had appeared unsteadily at his shoulder, holding the plate which had held the cold meat pie he'd shared with Ray Wheeler. The plate slithered from his fingers onto the slop-mat on the bartop.

'I feel sick,' Charlie said.

He said it loudly enough to turn heads. Ray Wheeler's head anyway. And Guto's. Miranda's head was still on Guto's shoulder, shifting occasionally in sleep.

'The way I see it,' Charlie said. 'It was either that Welsh whisky or the meat pie. I'm betting on the pie.'

Aled washed another glass, rinsed it, held it to the candle. 'You listening to me, Alec?'

Aled turned his back on Charlie Firth and put the glass on the shelf behind him.

'You tried to poison me once. I said it'd never happen again.'

'What are you talking about?' Alun said.

'*You* tried to poison me,' Charlie Firth said, stabbing Alun in the chest with a rigid forefinger. 'You're Welsh, aren't you?'

'And you, I'm afraid, are legless, my friend,' Alun said jovially. 'Go and sit down. We'll get you back soon, don't worry.'

'Come on, mate,' Ray Wheeler said. 'I had half that pie, and I don't feel sick.'

Aled washed another glass, impassive.

Charlie reached across the bar, snatched it from his hand and hurled it at the nearest wall. Nobody saw it connect; the light was too weak.

Aled said nothing but walked out through the door to the kitchen.

'That's it then.' Guto hauled Miranda to her feet in the manner of a man well used to removing comatose companions from bars. 'This looks like another of those scenes I need to avoid.'

'Don't know what's come over him,' Bill Sykes said. He'd removed his overcoat and his jacket, was sitting in shirt sleeves and a paisley waistcoat. Nobody had commented on the disappearance of Shirley Gillies and young Gary.

'The Welsh.' Charlie Firth's face was swollen with contempt, as if he were accumulating a mouthful of spit. Behind him, Guto eased Miranda into the doorway, half-dragging her; she was dead weight. He motioned with his head to Alun, who mouthed, 'We can't leave them here.'

'We bloody can,' Guto shouted.

'Where have you gone, Alec, you little Welsh twat?' Charlie Firth was roaring.

Alun dodged behind him to the door, shouting to Ray and Bill, 'We'll find Emlyn for you. The driver. Send him back.'

Outside, he found Guto on the bench to the left of the porch, with Miranda in his arms. 'Come on, come on,' Guto was whispering urgently.

'Yes, yes, I'm here,' Alun said, searching his pockets for the Land-Rover keys. And then he realised Guto was talking to Miranda, her head cradled in the crook of his arm, blue snowlight washing over her classically English autocratic face.

Guto stared up at him, panic in his eyes. 'Alun, I – I can't bloody wake her, can I?'

CHAPTER LXX

THE white moon, sickle-sharp, overhung the glade. The fat trees crouched, entangling their aged, twisted branches like the antlers of stags.

Groundmist was waist-high and looked as thick as candlegrease. The trees were in a silent semi-circle within the mist. He tried to count them and could not.

Not because there were too many of them, but because his brain was working too slowly for counting, like a clockwork mechanism winding down. Also the trees were somehow indistinct, embedded in the groundmist. They were one. An old entity. A fusion of consciousness, of now and of then.

More than trees. They had strong, vibrant thoughts and the thoughts had sounds which came from far away, as if windborne. One was as high as a flute or a lamb's bleat. Another sombre and quivering like the lower octaves of a harmonium. They could have been male or female. And they were orchestrated together, one voice, which could have been speaking in no other language but Welsh.

The mist cleared a little, although it did not evaporate as much as soak into the ground, leaving solid patches like mould, like fungus.

Around an altar.

Which was not an altar of stone, as artists imagine, but of wood, the trunk of an immensely thick oak tree, split in half as if by lightning, hewn out down its centre to form a shallow cradle, almost a coffin.

sice, he heard.

Wind in the trees, air-brakes of an articulated-lorry, bellows, a freezer door opening and closing.

siiiiiiiiiiiice.

There formed in the hollow of the altar, in the cradle, in the coffin, a satin-white woman with flowing red hair through which tendrils of mist drifted and curled.

The trees encircled her, their knobbled branches bowed. Stood there in the moonlight – so much light from such a slender moon – and watched her dying like an October butterfly.

Hunched on a stool in the dark beside the kitchen stove, his head in his hands, Aled wept savage tears, while the crazy-drunk reporter banged his fist on the bartop and screamed abuse at the Welsh nation.

Aled was not weeping for the Welsh nation.

He was weeping because it was the end of everything.

'. . . *on to the line at Aber station. Some sort of dizzy spell, perhaps . . . no, nothing anyone could do . . . So sorry, we are, Aled, sorry I have to tell you like this, too, but the weather . . .*'

'Come out, you little twat! No sodding guts, any of you. Come out, I want a bleeding drink!'

A shattering. Glasses, newly-rinsed.

The most beautiful pub in the most beautiful village in . . .

Aled howled aloud at the night, at the village, at the heat, at the snow, at the *Gorsedd*.

'*What time?*'

'*Not long after seven. Apparently, she just disappeared, went out alone . . . must have been confused, see, they said . . .*'

Seven o'clock.

'*Bethan, why do you have to do this to me . . .?*'

He came slowly to his feet.

'I'm helping myself, Alec, all right?'

'Don't be a pillock, Charlie.' Another English voice.

'Yeah, well, this way I *know* I'm not being bleeding poisoned. All right, Alec? That make sense to you?'

More glasses smashing.

But Aled's fingers were no longer shaking as he lit a candle, set it on a saucer and, holding the candle before him, went out of the kitchen the back way, through the scullery and into a stone-walled storeroom with no windows.

The storeroom had a long, narrow, metal cupboard, which was padlocked.

Aled put the candle on an old worktable, his hands flat on the cool metal cupboard door. Hesitated there a moment. And then felt about on the ledge above the storeroom door, where the key lay in grease and dust.

He undid the padlock, left it hanging from the lock as he felt inside the cupboard and found what he'd come for.

Guto and Alun lifted Miranda, all legs, into the back seat of the Range Rover.

'This is folly, Guto. Isn't there supposed to be a doctor here in the village?'

'Are you going to drive, or shall I?'

'Let me at least knock on a few doors first, get word to Emlyn to come and pick up the other reporters. Will take me no more than two minutes. We brought them here, after all.'

'Stuff the party image,' Guto shouted, loud enough to have awoken Miranda from any normal slumber. 'For God's sake, look at the place! You'll knock and knock and no bugger will answer!'

Few of the cottages even showed the glow of candlelight or

an oil-lamp now, and yet there was somehow a sense of silent, listening people behind every door.

'I mean, is this flaming normal? Atmosphere is as if there's been a nuclear alert.'

'Yes. It's strange.'

'So get moving, man. We have to get her to the hospital in Pont. And anyway—' Guto got in the back, lifting Miranda's head onto his knee, '—I wouldn't trust the bastard doctor here, and don't ask me why.'

Alun climbed into the driver's seat, Guto saying, 'In fact I wouldn't trust any bastard in Y Groes. Don't worry, Emlyn'll go back for them when he's ready.'

The elderly Range Rover clattered into life, was rapidly reversed by Alun into the alleyway by the useless electricity sub-station, wheels spinning in the thin skim of snow. Guto looking over at the hills, made majestic by the snow, thinking, Oh God, don't let us get stuck up there.

'Jesus,' he said, a hand on Miranda's cheek. 'She's not even warm. Heat. Put the heat on.'

'You're joking, it's—'

'Put the bugger on full blast, man!' He smoothed Miranda's icy brow. 'She can't – I mean, people can't just die, just like that, can they?'

'So who is she really?' Alun steered the Range Rover across the bridge. 'Not a journalist, then.'

Guto's hand moved over Miranda's throat, searching for a pulse, not knowing where it was supposed to be.

'Does it matter?' He felt his voice beginning to crack. Oh, Jesus, how abruptly, and with what brutality, life was coming at him these days. Despair to euphoria to an even deeper despair.

Alun braked hard.

'Strewth, man, you'll have her on the floor.'

'What is this?' Alun said.

'Whatever it is, sod it.'

'No, something odd here, Guto. A jacket over the wall. And – trousers. No, a skirt. It's a skirt.'

'Bloody hell, Alun, were you never young? Step on it!'

'In the middle of the road, Guto? A skirt discarded in the middle of the road?'

He swung the Range Rover off the road and into the entrance to the track that led into the woods, drove up it until it became too narrow for a vehicle.

Where he braked hard again and the engine stalled. And the headlights illuminated a wondrously ghastly tableau.

'God,' Alun whispered in horror, and in awe.

He seemed uncertain, at first, about what to do. Then, efficient as ever, he calmly opened the driver's door, leaned out and was copiously sick in the snow.

Grabbing up a handful of unsoiled snow, he washed around his mouth, rubbed some into his eyes and sat back and closed them, reaching out with his right hand to pull the door shut.

At the very instant it slammed into place, Guto thought he was aware of a distant blast, someone shooting at a rabbit in the winter hills.

Hesitantly, he lifted up Miranda's head, leaned across the back of Alun's seat, looked out through the windscreen and sat down very quickly.

'Jesus,' he said.

Alun sat up, put the Range Rover into reverse and looked constantly over his shoulder until they were back on the road and the headlights no longer lit a recumbent, erotic sculpture in marble, two figures coitally entwined, utterly still, frozen together for ever.

'It's a nightmare, Guto,' Alun said. 'It has got to be a nightmare.'

Yes. Of course. Sure. A nightmare. A dream from which you had to free yourself. The difference was that, in a dream, when that thought came to you, the realisation that you were in fact dreaming would wake you up at once.

This was the difference.

He tried to speak, to scream at the circle of black, malevolent trees under the white moon. He tried to scream out, you are not here, you are someplace else, this is a church for Chrissake . . .

These lines only came to him as vague things, nothing so solid as words.

Sice, the mist said, blown from the bellows. The mist had risen to cover the altar, but it may have been a mist inside his own head because this was how it was in dreams.

siiiiiiiiiiiiiiiiiiice!

'*Sais*,' Giles Freeman hissed, a sad spectre staggering out of the mist in a torn and soaking suit, with a bulging black eye. 'Means English. Often used in a derogatory way, like the Scots say Sassenach. Satisfied now?'

A string somewhere was pulled. A big door opened and closed. Thunk. Breath came back to Berry Morelli, air blasting down a wind-tunnel.

'DIM SAIS!,' he cried out, stumbling out into the nave, arms waving. DYDWY DDIM YN SAIS, YOU BASTARDS!'

'We never said you was, man,' Dai Death said calmly. 'Come on out now.'

Bethan, waiting by the lych gate, saw Dai Williams and Idwal Pugh leaving the church with Berry Morelli, he gesturing at them, as if arguing. He was all right. He was not lying by the tomb, leaking dark blood over the stone flags.

Bethan's relief was stifled by the realisation that nothing had changed. The air still was fetid, the moonstreaked sky bulging over Y Groes like the skin of a rotting plum.

She did not go to him but slipped back through the lych gate and hurried a little way along the road until she saw a track winding between the silhouettes of two giant sycamores.

CHAPTER LXXI

AROUND the timber-framed porch for several yards in all directions, the snow was as pink as birthday-cake icing and this had nothing to do with the strawberry sky.

When they dragged his body out, Charlie Firth seemed to have a hole in him the size of a grapefruit. As if he'd been punched by a fist in a boxing glove and the glove had gone through him.

Bill and Ray dragged him out on the off chance that he was still alive.

He wasn't.

The mistake he'd made had been to laugh when Aled had emerged from the back room holding out the double-barrelled twelve-bore shotgun and hoarsely ordering them all to leave his inn. Charlie had made some reference to Old Winstone's mother and a shotgun and that she, being English, at least had the nerve to use it.

Ray Wheeler remembered Aled's hollowed-out face in the wan ambience of the candle, by then not much more than a wick floating in an ashtray full of liquid wax. He thought he remembered a glaze of tears in the licensee's eyes as he poked the gun barrel under Charlie Firth's ribcage.

Ray certainly remembered Aled reloading the twelve-bore from a box of cartridges on the bartop, Sykes shakily saying something on the lines of, Now look, old boy, no need for this, surely? The banalities people came out with when something utterly appalling had occurred.

Blood and obscene bits of tissue had been slurping out of Charlie all the way to the door and Bill was relieved to leave him in the snow. He and Ray, liberally spattered with pieces of their colleague, backed away from the body, looking for some cover in case the mad landlord should come charging out after them.

They hid in the car park at the side of the inn, behind the Daihatsu. 'So where's everybody gone?' Ray said. 'It's like bloody High Noon. What the fuck's wrong with this place?'

Bill Sykes ran in a crouch – how he thought that would make him less of a target for a man with a twelve-bore Ray couldn't fathom – across the road to the only cottage with some sort of light burning inside. He heard Bill hammering at the cottage door hard enough to take all the skin off his knuckles and then enunciating in his polite and formal Old Telegraph way, 'Hello, excuse me, but would it be possible to use your phone?'

There was no response at all from within, where a single small, yellow light never wavered. Not even an invitation to go away.

'I need to telephone the police,' Bill said loudly into the woodwork.

To nil response.

'Well, could *you* perhaps telephone the police? Tell them to come at once. Please. Just dial nine nine nine. Think you could do that?'

The cottage was silent. The air was still. The burgeoning sky seemed to have sucked warm blood out of the snow.

'Oh, bollocks to this,' Ray yelled. 'Let's get the fuck out of here.'

In thirty years of journalism, in Africa, South America, he'd never known a place, an atmosphere, quite so unearthly. He climbed into the Daihatsu, fumbled around and almost wept with relief when he discovered the key in the ignition. Obviously nobody worried about teenage joyriders on the loose in a place as remote as this.

Bill climbed in the other side. 'Ever driven one of these things, old boy?'

'No,' Ray said, through his teeth. 'But I reckon this is one of those occasions when I could master the controls of a bloody Jumbo Jet if need be.' He leaned forward to turn the key in the the ignition, feeling distaste as a patch of Charlie's blood on his shirt was pulled against his chest.

Bill said, 'What about Shirley and young whatsisname?'

'I reckon they've gone,' said Ray, with more confidence than he felt. 'The Range Rover's gone, hasn't it? The Plaid bunch.'

'True. Well, off you go then, Ray. Probably the only way we'll get to alert the constabulary.'

'I don't know what the hell kind of story we're going to do on all this, do you?'

'Least of my worries, old boy. Least of my worries.'

After a hiccupy start, they got over the bridge and on to the road that took them out of Y Groes. There was only one and, at first, the going was easy enough. It was not snowing and the stuff on the road was impacted, no problem for four-wheel-drive.

They came soon to a signpost. Pontmeurig one way, Aberystwyth the other. 'Doesn't say how far Aberystwyth is, Ray. I think we should stick to what we know.'

'Yeah, OK.' Ray steered the Daihatsu, headlights full on, into the hills. Where it soon became quite clear that Y Groes had got off incredibly lightly as far as the weather was concerned.

As the road rose up, they could see the church tower behind them under a sky so rosy it seemed like some sort of ominous false dawn. But before midnight?

Above and around them, however, the night was darker than Welsh slate, and then the snow began to come at them like a fusilade of golf-balls, through which they first saw the figure at the side of the road.

'Reckon this poor bugger's broken down?' Ray slowed the Daihatsu. 'Or got his motor jammed in a drift?'

Bill Sykes was wary. 'Nobody we, er, know, is it? Better be a bit careful here, Ray.'

'Bill, it looks like an old woman.'

The figure lifted a stick to stop them. They made out a long skirt and a ragged shawl tossed in the snowstorm.

Ray opened his window, got a faceful of blizzard. 'Yeah, OK, luv. Can you make it over here, I don't want to get stuck in the ditch.'

Advancing on the vehicle, the bundle of old clothes grew larger absorbing the snow on either side, issuing bits of shawl and ragged, stormblown hair.

'Bloody walking jumble sale,' Ray said out of the side of his mouth.

'Don't you think it's a bit odd,' Bill said. 'This old girl out on a night like this? And don't you think—?'

'Yeh, I—'

The snow blasting in on Ray had suddenly become black and polluted with the smell of smoke and motor oil and also the four-day-old corpses in a makeshift charnel house he'd once been compelled to investigate in the Middle East.

He started to close his window, but the black snow was already filling the Daihatsu, and Ray went rigid with shock as he experienced a sensation of teeth on his chest and a slimy, probing tongue and a nuzzling and a guzzling at his bloodied shirtfront.

It was over in seconds and he was left with a heap of foul-smelling snow in his lap. When the appalling face came up in the windscreen, neither he nor Bill was able to speak; Ray's foot sprang off the clutch, and the Daihatsu spurted suicidally away into the white night.

Hearing a rustling sound and a crackling, Ray shot one final gut-shrivelling glance to the side and saw the creature hovering over the snow, kept aloft by her flapping shawl, or perhaps, he thought, delirious with fear, as the Daihatsu smashed through a barbed-wire fence, perhaps she had little wings.

'You said yourself this was a God-forsaken place. You said something had to get cleaned out before Christ could get in.'

'It's still the House of God, Morelli,' Idwal said. 'And I'm no grave-robber.'

'Think of it as an exhumation,' Berry said.

'I will think of it not at all.'

'Dai?'

'Come away, Morelli. Leave it. It'll do no good.'

Directly under the tower, the moon arching like a spotlit ballerina from its weather vane, Berry could see their faces very clearly. Idwal's was sombre, unmoving. Dai's disturbed and anxious.

He tried another angle. 'How much you know about this place? Why's it on a mound? Would I be right in thinking that in the old days, way back before there was a village, the oak wood covered all of this ground?'

'I don't know,' Idwal said heavily.

'And I don't care,' Dai said.

'So that maybe even before there was a mound – when's that, medieval, or earlier? – this was a place of worship. Sacred grove, whatever.'

'What happened to you in there?' Idwal asked him, with obvious reluctance.

Worst of it, he couldn't remember. Only that when they'd come up to him in the church, he'd been momentarily surprised to find it *was* a church and that when he looked up he couldn't see the moon.

'What does any of this matter?' said Dai.

'Of course it matters, you dumb bastards. People are dying.'

'I cannot believe any of this.' Dai walked off a couple of paces.

Sweltering in Robin's flying jacket, his whole body quivering with the need to do something, the stifling urgency of the situation, Berry looked up at the sky and it seemed like a great balloon, full of blood. He felt that soon the point of the church tower would spear the balloon and there'd be a never-ending gory deluge over Y Groes.

Alun had suggested to Guto that when they reached Pontmeurig Cottage Hospital, he should be the one to carry Miranda in.

'May still be able to keep you out of this whole business.'

'Oh, aye? And which of us will tell the cops about the bodies in the wood?'

'You are right, of course.' Alun sighed. 'This whole campaign has been jinxed. For us, that is. Why could none of this have happened to Gallier?'

The snow had started where the oak woods ended and the conifers began their stiff, sporadic ascent of the Nearly Mountains. It had been fluffy and mild at first, innocent as dandelion clocks, before the hedges had solidified into frozen walls, like the Cresta run, the snowflakes gaining weight and bumping the screen; if it had not been for the four-wheel-drive they would have got no further.

They were perhaps two miles out of Y Groes when Guto thought he heard Miranda moan. His heart lurched.

'Come on then, love.' He raised her head up in the crook of his arm.

'Want me to stop, is it, Guto?'

'No, no . . . Keep going, man.'

Despite all the snow, it was far darker up here than in Y Groes. Guto wound down his window to give her some air and was shocked, after the clammy heat of the village, at the chill which rushed in with a stinging blast of snow.

'Come on, darlin', please . . .' He couldn't see her eyes, but his fingertips told him they were still shut. Shielding her from the blast with his right shoulder, he wound the window back up with his left hand, thinking, Oh, Jesus, what does a death-rattle sound like?

The Range Rover suddenly crunched to a stop; a creak of brakes and a hopeless sigh from Alun. Guto looked up and saw in the headlights a sheer wall of white, over half as high as their vehicle.

'I'm no expert,' Alun said, 'but I estimate it would take ten men until breakfast time to dig us through that.'

Guto lowered his bearded face to kiss Miranda's stiffening, stone-cold brow.

CHAPTER LXXII

PAST the iron gate now, to where the judge's house sat grey and gaunt and self-righteous in the sick, florid night. All its windows darkened, except for one. And Bethan knew which one that was.

The light in the study was too small and weak to be the big brass oil-lamp. She approached it warily. She had to know precisely who was in the house.

She slid from tree to tree across the snowy lawn, eyes always on the window. And then, reaching the side-hedge, she edged along it towards the house, camouflaged, she hoped, by her long, white mac.

The study window was set so high in the wall that she was able to slip into a crouch beneath it, moving up slowly to peer through a corner.

All the bookshelves were in deep shadow except for a small

circle of heavy volumes above the great oaken desk at the far end of the room opposite the window. On the desk were two wooden candlesticks with inch-thick red candles in them, alight.

A book was splayed open upon the desk. Claire was not looking at it.

Her eyes were closed but, had they been open, their gaze would have been directed on Bethan.

Who gasped and sank down to the lawn.

In her memory, the old Claire's face had seemed small and round, the brisk, blonde hair fluffed around it. Now, under the tangled dark hair, the face had narrowed, the lips tightened, the lines deepened either side of the mouth. Severity.

Bethan wanted to run back to the hedge and away.

But she carried on under the window to the front door. It had been her intention to beat hard on the knocker to indicate she was in no mood for evasion. However, the door was ajar.

It opened without a creak and Bethan found her way into the living room, all in darkness, a gleam where the moon picked out the handle of a copper kettle in the inglenook.

There was no fire in the grate, nothing of the mellow warmth she'd found in here on the night of the first Welsh lesson.

Poor Giles.

Bethan shivered, not only at the memory of a dead, snarling Giles spreadeagled on the study floor but because the temperature in here was many degrees below the death-bearing mildness of the night outside.

This, she realised, was the reality. The heat outside, which did not melt snow, was something else.

Tightening the belt of her raincoat, she went through the open door to the inner hall, ducking her head although she was small enough to go under the beams. To her right were the stairs. To her left, a flickering under the door, was the—

Come in, Bethan.

She was sure not a word had been spoken aloud.

Yet she went in.

'We need to move fast,' Berry said. 'They're gonna know we're here.'

'Moving as fast as I can, man. You have the chisel?'

Berry patted a pocket of Robin's flying jacket. 'Fix the light first.'

Dai was wedging the torch roughly into the bottom of a centuries-old rood screen so that the beam was directed onto the tomb.

Distantly, they could hear Idwal Pugh pacing around outside. He would not come in.

Dai looked curiously at Berry. 'How do you know that?'

'Know what?'

'That they will know we are here.'

Berry shrugged. 'Shit, I dunno.'

The gipsy, he was thinking. She would know. Where are you tonight, lady? He grinned. He wasn't scared any more.

He thought, *Jesus Christ, I'm not scared any more.*

Dim Sais. Dydwy ddim yn Sais.

Where had that come from? He didn't know a word of Welsh, apart from *sice* itself and *da iawn*.

Weird, weird, weird.

Berry placed the chisel under the lip of the tomb, avoiding the eyes of the knight because this was just some old stone box, OK? Dai handed him the mallet and he struck the head of the chisel.

Thud-ud-ud.

Felt something crumble, give way.

He stopped. 'Where's Bethan?'

'Outside, with Idwal, I should think. She didn't want to come in, either. Morelli . . .?'

'Yeah?'

'This thing with Bethan and you. Nothing serious there?'

'What's that mean?'

'You know what it means, man, you know the way it has been for her.'

'Yeah.' Berry hit the chisel again. They heard fragments of loose stone fall a few inches inside the tomb. A flat kind of chink as a piece struck something and did not bounce off; rather the substance it had fallen on simply crumbled.

Dust to dust.

The torchlight flickered.

'She's not for you, boy.'

'You don't think so, huh?' Berry left the chisel jammed under the lid of the tomb. Dai fitted the end of one of the crowbars into what was now a half-inch gap alongside it.

The torchlight flickered.

Berry's eyes met the smooth, years-worn orbs of the knight's eyes.

They were open now. He knew those eyes were open.

'I think maybe we aren't gonna need the jack after all,' Berry said.

Bethan said, 'I've come to talk about trees.'

Miss Rhys, the judge's granddaughter, was bolt upright in the judge's high-backed Gothic chair, her face made harsh by candlelight which ought to have softened it. Bethan stood on the old rug, where the dead Giles had lain, both feet on the dragon's head.

Claire said, 'My tree or yours?'

'You found your tree,' Bethan said. 'I want to find mine.'

'Why?'

'I want to chop it down,' Bethan said simply.

Claire Rhys looked at her with contempt.

'Well?' Bethan did not move.

'Have you asked Buddug?'

'If I had been five days in the desert, I wouldn't ask Buddug for a cup of water.'

'Go away,' Claire said. 'Go and ask Buddug.'

Bethan moved towards the desk, intending to knock a candlestick over in her face.

'Come any closer,' Claire said calmly, 'and I shall have to harm you.'

Bethan stopped. The room had grown very cold, she thought, under the influence of its mistress's displeasure.

She said, 'What have you become?'

Claire smiled. 'You never really met my grandfather, did you?'

Bethan said nothing.

'I've discovered, to my shame, that he was rather a weak man. He knew he had to return here, that he could not break the chain. So he left my grandmother and my mother in England and he came back. He came back alone.'

Bethan was momentarily puzzled. Then she felt nearly ill.

'He ought, of course, to have brought them with him.'

The village, Aled had said, demanded sacrifices.

'But he was weak, as I say. He left them and he returned alone.'

. . . the old Druids, see, they did not sacrifice each other, their . . . you know, virgins, kids. None of that nonsense. But I've heard it said they used to sacrifice their enemies.

'You brought Giles as your little sacrifice,' Bethan said, her voice like dust.

'And also atoned for Thomas Rhys,' Claire said. 'Don't forget that. I had to complete what he could not.'

She meant her parents. She'd given her parents in sacrifice to Y Groes and to whatever lay in the tomb and whatever it represented.

He was only English, Sali Dafis had said.

'You were very stupid,' Claire said. 'You and your child could have belonged here. You could have lived in the warmth, at the heart of our heritage and watched it spread and grow and flourish like a lovely garden.'

'Once the weeds had been killed,' Bethan said.

'Your words.'

'And Glyndwr will rise again, like the legends say, springing from his tomb with his army behind him to free Wales from the oppressor.'

Miss Rhys spread her hands. 'We are not naïve. Glyndwr is dead and buried.'

They had both crowbars wedged under the lip of the tomb, the effigy on top slightly askew now.

The torch flickered.

Dai stood back. 'I think we are there.'

'How you figure we should play it? Slide it?'

'If we both get this end,' Dai said, 'we can lift it and then swing it to one side. Are you prepared then, Morelli?'

'For?'

'For whatever is . . . there. Spent most of my life with stiffs, see.' Dai said. 'You were a bit jumpy back at the depot, if I remember rightly.'

'These are old bones. Old bones aren't the same.'

Dai smiled, the torchlight glancing off his bald skull. 'And you reckon it's old Owain Glyndwr in here? Well, tell me, Morelli, how will you know?'

'Be more obvious if it isn't.'

'You mean if it's empty.'

'Is what I mean.' Berry stood at the head of the tomb, hands grasping the stone lip an inch or so from the eroded cheeks of the knight. 'OK, Dai? We gonna count down from five and then lift and swing? Four, three, two, one—'

The torch went out.

Berry heard the grating thump of falling masonry. An icy, numbing pain bolted up his arm.

When the torch came on again, Dai was holding it. Berry looked down and couldn't see the end of his own left hand beyond the lip of the tomb, beyond the smirk of ages on the face of the knight. He was in agony, knew his wrist was broken, maybe his arm too. And, worst than that, he was trapped.

Dai was walking off into the nave. 'I'm sorry, Morelli,' he said over his shoulder. 'But a man has to make sacrifices if he wants to retire to paradise.'

It was all shatteringly clear to Bethan now.

'And Dilwyn's wife? A harmless little typist from the South-East?'

Miss Rhys stood up. 'We've spoken enough, Bethan. Time you left, I think.'

'It doesn't bear thinking about. How can you live with it?'

'In comparison to what the English have done to the Welsh over the centuries, it's really rather a small thing, wouldn't you say? I should have thought that you, as a teacher—'

'But I don't have to live with it,' Bethan said. 'I can tell whoever I choose. Beginning with the police.'

'Bethan, I used to be in journalism.' Claire said wearily. 'I learned a lot about the police and the law. What it amounts to in this case is that the police don't believe in magic and even if they did, no offences have been committed under the *English* legal system. Now go away and dwell upon your future.'

When she calmly blew out both red candles, Bethan's nerve went; she scrabbled for the door handle and got out, feeling her way along the walls, through the hall, into the living room where the moon glanced off shiny things, and out into the blood-washed night.

She had to find Berry, get him away from that church, if Dai and Idwal had not persuaded him already to forget the fantasy of dislodging a tradition cemented through centuries.

She came out of the gateway, between the sycamores, looked up and down the country lane over the sweating snow. The Sprite was still parked where she'd left it. She looked in the back and saw that the hydraulic jack and crowbars were missing. Berry had gone to desecrate the tomb.

Trembling with anxiety, Bethan ran through the lych-gate into the circular graveyard where the atmosphere was close and clinging and the sky was low, red and juicy. She could see across the village – still no power down there, houses lit by glow-worms – to the Nearly Mountains, hard and bright with ice.

Bethan stopped and stiffened as a hand clawed her shoulder, spun her around.

Buddug seemed to tower over her, bulky in a dark dufflecoat, her big face as red as the sky.

'A question you have for me, is it, little bitch?'

CHAPTER LXXIII

THEY would come for him in time, he knew that.

It was not dark. The light from the sky leaked in from the long window, crimson.

He was too weary now to endure the pain of struggle, wanting to lay his head down on the tomb in exhaustion. But the only part of the tomb his head could reach was the head of the effigy, his eyes looking into its eyes, its lips . . . He turned away in revulsion and the movement dragged on his trapped arm and the pain made his whole body blaze.

He'd looked and felt around for something to wedge under the slab, next to his arm. Something he could lean on, hard enough perhaps to make some space to pull the arm out.

But Dai had taken away the jack and both crowbars and even Robin's flying jacket which Berry had hung over the rood screen while they worked on the tomb.

'Scumbag!' he screamed, and the walls threw it back at him with scorn. '. . . bag, ag, ag.'

The stone knight shifted, settled on Berry's arm; he thought he could hear his bones splintering, getting ground into powder. From the other side of the church wall, he heard the movement in the snow which he'd earlier assumed was Idwal Pugh.

'Idwal! Help me, willya!'

The cry was out before he could stop it.

No way could it be Idwal out there. No way could it have been Idwal first time around, when he and Dai were busy with the crowbars. Idwal had been dismissed or was dead or was a party to the betrayal.

Which was not a betrayal of him so much as of Bethan.

Was there anybody left in these parts who had not at some time betrayed Bethan?

He wept for Bethan and because of the pain, because he was trapped. Because, sooner or later, they were going to come for him.

Bethan looked up into the split veins and the venom. Black eyes and yellow, twisted teeth.

'*Gwrach*,' Bethan spat.

Buddug did not move at first, but something leapt behind her black pebble eyes. And then her enormous turkey-killer's hands came up with incredible speed and lifted Bethan off her feet and hurled her into the church wall.

Bethan's head cracked against the stone and bounced off, and Buddug whirled and brutally slapped her, with bewildering force, across the face so that her head spun away so hard and so fast she thought her neck was breaking.

'The first thing we learn at school,' Buddug said, not even panting with the exertion, 'is to be polite to our elders.'

Bethan fell in a heap to the soft snow and sat there, half-stunned, her back to the wall, feeling the blood running freely from her nose or her mouth. Her glasses had gone.

'And the next thing we learn –' Buddug bent down and dragged her to her feet, tearing her white mac at the shoulders '– is to stand up when we are spoken to.'

Bethan lolled, feeling her eyes glazing.

'Don't you go to sleep!' Buddug hit her again with a hand that felt as sharp and heavy as a wood-axe.

Buddug hissed, 'You killed our baby.'

Bethan tried to speak. Saw Buddug's hand raised again and shrank back against the wall.

'We like them to be pure-bred if possible,' Buddug said. 'Dilwyn's was a mistake. The child has to work harder, see, because of its mother.'

'You're sick,' Bethan whispered through swollen lips. 'Go on, hit me again. What more can you do?'

'Idwal!' They heard from inside the church, a weak and despairing cry. 'Help me, willya!'

Bethan's heart sagged in her limp body. Buddug's lumpen features cracked with glee.

'They say he loves you, the American,' Buddug said. 'Do you love him?'

Bethan desperately shook her head.

'You will not miss him, then, when he is gone. They will leave him tonight to see how much he can do to himself and then, in the morning—'

Bethan rocked her head from side to side to shut this out.

Buddug pinched Bethan's cheeks together to make her look at her. '*And then, in the morning—*'

'What are they doing to him?'

'No matter,' Buddug said, ignoring the question. 'He will be long gone by then. He will know that soon.'

The knight smiled a victor's smile with reddened lips.

From outside Berry heard the sound of scuffling, heard talking in Welsh, a voice cry out in pain.

He recognised the voice at once.

'Bastard!' Berry screamed at the Goddamn knight, his control gone. 'Motherfucker!' All the words that had seemed so pathetic, still seemed pathetic.

He pushed the fingers of his left hand as far as they would go into the gap between the slab and the walls of the tomb, rammed the arm in so that both arms were parallel under the knight's dead weight.

He waited two minutes like that, conserving his strength. Then he wrenched hard on the trapped arm and simultaneously heaved upwards with the good left arm.

The knight shifted and he felt an appalling weight on the left arm. The good arm.

He cried to the rafters in his agony and passed out with the pain.

When the long, bitter cry came through the church wall, Bethan pushed Buddug aside and made a rush for the corner of the building and the doorway.

Or intended to.

She'd moved less than a couple of feet when one of Buddug's great hands caught her by the throat and squeezed on her windpipe. She is going to kill me, Bethan thought. Like the ducks, like the chickens in the farmyard.

'We do not walk away when we are being spoken to,' Buddug said and squeezed harder.

All was quiet within the church.

'Will not be long, now,' Buddug said.

'Why are you doing this?'

'Do not make yourself ridiculous,' Buddug said.

Bethan thought of the *Gorsedd Ddu*, who judged the traitors and the cowards.

She thought, we must hear each other's agony and hopelessness before we die.

'*Dewch*,' Buddug said, taking Bethan's arm. Come.

'No.'

With little effort, Buddug twisted the arm until Bethan, gritting her teeth, felt the bones begin to crack.

Sobbing, she nodded and Buddug propelled her across the churchyard to the top of the steps.

A meagre light appeared.

He opened his eyes and saw both arms under the stone, and there was no pain now, but he could not move at all.

And beyond the chapel, visible through the lattice of the rood screen, the little light, like a taper.

The light did not move. It seemed to cast no ambience. Like the light through a keyhole, something on the other side of the dark.

Berry felt no pain, only sorrow and profound misery.

CHAPTER LXXIV

WHEN the blizzard eased a little, Guto and Alun left the Range Rover with its nose in the snowdrift and walked away in different directions.

Alun's mission was to climb to the top of the nearest hill with his mobile phone to see if he could get a signal and, if he could, to send for the police. And the ambulance.

Which was too late now, anyway. Snow matting his beard and freezing there, coming over the tops of his wellingtons with every step, Guto looked down on the Range Rover. Left with its sidelights on and its engine running to keep the heater going, quite pointlessly, for Miranda Moore-Lacey.

Guto didn't have a mission other than to walk. He should have stayed in the heat, laid Miranda's body out in the snow. At the thought of this, he rammed his hands bitterly down into the pockets of his presentable Parliamentary candidate's overcoat and ploughed on.

Years since he'd walked the Nearly Mountains, and that had been in decent weather; he hadn't the faintest idea where the hell he was.

However, reaching the crest of a ridge he found he was looking back towards Y Groes where the sky still was streaked with this unhealthy red, shining out like the bars of an electric fire in a darkened room. An electric fire in the dark always conveyed a sense of illness to Guto; his mam used to leave one in his bedroom when he was sick. Years ago this was, but the impression remained.

He wanted a drink. He wanted several drinks. He wanted to get blind pissed and forget the wasted years between being a sick kid in a overheated bedroom and a big, arrogant, macho politician with a hard line in rhetoric and a posh English chick in French knickers.

Stupid to think that he could make all those years worthwhile at a stroke. The rock band that almost got to make a record, the book that almost sold five hundred copies. The posh English chick in French knickers who almost survived two whole days of being Guto Evans's woman.

He glared down at the village of Y Groes with savage loathing, vowed to avenge Miranda in some way and knew he wouldn't because he'd always be too pissed to function in any more meaningful way than punching the odd wealthy immigrant. And in just over a week's time he'd be a member of the biggest political group in Wales: the FPCC – the Failed Plaid Candidates' Club.

Overtired, overstressed, overweight, Guto staggered on through the snow and the self-pity, hard to decide which was denser. The endless snow seemed to symbolise both his past and his future. As soon as he crunched a narrow path, the sides fell in.

Looking down at his plodding wellies, he did not notice the shadowy figure walking up the hill towards him until it was upon him.

'*Noswaith dda*, Guto.'

Guto did not recognise the man. That the man recognised him was no surprise; people usually did these days.

'You live near here?' Guto asked him. 'You have a phone?'

'I've come from there.' The man gestured towards Y Groes. Guto couldn't see him too clearly; he seemed to be wearing leather gear, like a biker.

'Poor bugger,' Guto said, in no mood for diplomacy. 'They let you out, is it?'

Guto felt the leather-clad man was smiling. 'They let me out,' he agreed.

'Good,' Guto said.

The snow stopped, the air was still for a time. Guto looked at his watch, feeling this was significant. It was 12.05 a.m.

Something companionable about the stranger. Something odd, too. Something odd about the leathers he was wearing, and what would a biker be doing in the Nearly Mountains at midnight in a blizzard? Guto glanced at the man but could not see him clearly; there was a haze about him.

They stood together on a snowy hummock, as though they

were having the same hallucination, looking down towards Y Groes. Guto noticed that the sky over the village had lost its red bars, as if someone had unplugged the electric fire. The sky over Y Groes was just like the sky everywhere else: charcoal grey and heavy with suppressed snow.

'No time to waste, Guto,' his companion said and clapped him briskly on the back.'

'You're right,' Guto said. 'Thanks. *Diolch yn fawr.*'

He turned away, tramped off down the hill back towards the Range Rover. When he turned around, the man had gone, but there was a kind of heat below his left shoulder where the hand briefly had touched him.

He almost bumped into Alun, who had come over the rise, his mobile phone in his gloved hand. 'Who were you talking to?'

'Some bloke,' Guto said.

'I got through,' said Alun. 'Gwyn Arthur Jones is sending to Carmarthen for the police helicopter. They say we should go back to Y Groes and wait.'

'OK.' Guto got in the front of the Land-Rover with Alun, not wanting to look at what lay on the rear seat.

Alun reversed the Range Rover for almost half a mile until they came to a sign indicating a lay-by and he was able to make a three-point turn and they went back towards Y Groes, as Guto always knew they would.

'God, I feel sick,' Miranda said in his ear, inducing icy palpitations down his spine. 'What time is it?'

Snow swirled around the Fiat Panda, tucked into the side of the inn. 'What have I become?' Dai Death said. 'Tell me that.'

'What have you always been, man? A covetous bugger.' Idwal Pugh sat in the driver's seat, where he'd been for the past hour, trying to get the car radio to work. 'Pontmeurig was not good enough. No, you had to find your paradise. Look at it. You call this paradise?'

'I didn't believe it. And then I did.' Anguished, Dai pummelled his knees.

'I told you,' Idwal said. 'I warned you not to go in there.'

'And then – was as if I was seeing everything through different eyes. I just dropped the bloody stone on his arm. I did that! Me! How is it I could do that? How?'

'You tell me.'

'Seems like a dream to me now. Maybe it was a dream. Come back with me, Idwal.'

'I will not.'

'See, I go back there afterwards—'

'You told me.'

'—when the snow has started and the fever has gone from my head. And I go back into the church, see—'

'Yes, yes. But *where* have they taken him?'

'—Bloody tomb open, bloody statue thing in pieces, shattered.'

'But what was in it, Dai? Did you look?'

'Oh, Jesus,' Dai wailed. 'Don't go asking me that.'

A question you have for me, is it, little bitch?'

'I don't want to know,' Bethan said, and knew immediately this was the wrong thing to say.

Buddug smiled horribly.

As a wind blew out of nowhere, she forced Bethan down the river bank to the edge of the water. Bethan looked up. Even without her glasses she could see the church tower had lost its grip on the moon, which seemed to be swimming away in a churning sea of cloud.

'Look, Buddug! Look at the sky!'

'It will pass,' Buddug said. The wind had seized her ragged hair, making it writhe like serpents. She was the *Gwrach y Rhibyn*. The death hag. She pulled Bethan into the shelter of the bridge. 'I will tell you how it was,' she hissed into Bethan's face, with a gush of vile breath.

'No!'

'We all came to see. A beautiful summer night, it was, the sun going down. And you in your white summer dress. Like a bride.'

413

'And my husband already dying.' Bethan tried to turn he head away and Buddug seized her cheeks between thumb and forefinger.

'Indeed, perhaps that was the very night he *began* to die,' Buddug said, the muscular fingers of her other hand caressing the bruised skin on Bethan's neck with dreadful tenderness.

'No . . .' Bethan closed her eyes, felt and smelled Buddug' warm, putrid breath, began to cough.

'You closed them that night, too . . .' Bethan jerked both eyes open, looking into Buddug's yellow teeth, the black gaps between them, the breath pumped through those gaps like poison gas.

'You did not care,' Buddug said dreamily. 'You were in thrall to the night and the sweet smells and the old magic. And as you lay with your legs spread . . .' A heavy gust of wind came through the bridge, with a surge of snow.

'*Gwrach!*' Bethan screamed through the wind. '*Gwrach! Gwrach! Gwrach!*'

Buddug had both her butcher's hands around Bethan' throat now, holding her at arm's length and looking from side to side, down at the river then up at the church and th heaving sky, with the sudden realisation that something funda mental had altered. 'What have you done, bitch? What have you done to the night?'

'*Gwrach!*'

'You are . . . *cachu*.' Buddug's eyes burning red like coals.

Bethan felt a thumb going up into her larynx, its nail pro bing like a knife. She felt the skin parting, her throat constrict ing, tongue out, eyes popping.

'And when I can see in your eyes that your time is upon you,' Buddug told her. 'I shall tell to you the name of th father of your child.'

Bethan felt herself rising above the horror of the night and th hag's slaughterhouse hands and graveyard breath. Rising into the Wales of her childhood, low tide at Ynyslas, a fire of driftwood on her birthday, the view from Constitution Hill a sunset over the last ice lolly of the day. She heard lines of poetry: Gwenallt, Dic Jones the bard and finally, sonorously, in English, the haunted cleric, R.S. Thomas:

> *to live in Wales is to be conscious*
> *At dusk of the spilled blood*
> *That went to the making of the wild sky*

Between the snowflakes, she felt the hot splashes of blood on her face, opening her eyes at the deafening blast, Buddug's hands still around her throat but no grip in them any more.

And Buddug, no head to speak of, most of it in fragments down the front of Bethan's torn once-white raincoat.

NOS DA

CHAPTER LXXV

THE other side of midnight people began to emerge from their homes in coats and scarves, carrying lamps and torches, all very muted, hardly saying a word to each other. Like survivors of some bombing raid. Mair Huws, from the Post Office, and Eirlys Hywels silently helped Bethan take off what remained of the raincoat and wrapped her in an old tapestry cape, leaving the bloody mac draped over the bridge, dripping into the river.

Aled was crouching alone just inside the alley between the inn and the sub-station where the wind could not reach him. By the light of his torch, propped up against a brick, he was slipping another cartridge into his shotgun.

'What are you looking at? He stood up and pointed the twelve-bore vaguely around him. In fact, nobody was looking at him except Berry Morelli, smoking a cigarette, one sleeve of his flying jacket flapping empty.

'Well, Aled. What can I say? You blew her head off. Dump the gun now?'

Aled shook his head. 'To the rectory I have to go.'

'Hey now, Aled,' Berry said. 'Think about this. Just take—'

'What is there to think about?' Standing with the gun hanging loose in his limp hands, white hair bedraggled, Aled put on a stark smile. 'Mass-murderer I am now, isn't it?'

'When we explain to the cops—' Berry said, but Aled shook his head.

'Explain. Explain this?' He chuckled sourly. 'Where do you begin? No, what I am doing is giving you an easy explanation, isn't it?'

Berry said, 'Grief-stricken madman goes on the rampage with shotgun.'

Aled smiled ruefully. ' You are a little ahead of me, boy.'

Berry looked at the little white-haired mass-killer and saw some kind of flawed hero.

'Go on, you bugger,' Aled said. 'Leave me be. Go to your woman.'

'Why'd you do all this, Aled? There's nothing gonna bring her back.'

Aled said, 'Listen man, an accident. I have no reason to think otherwise. I blame no one for that. I—' He patted his jacket pocket, spare cartridges rattled. 'I don't want the third degree, Morelli. Don't know why I turned away. Been coming on a long time probably.'

'One more question, OK?'

Aled sighed. 'I ought to shoot you as well, you nosy bugger.'

'The tomb. Unless Glyndwr had curly horns—'

'Morelli, it never mattered what was in that tomb. The *Gorsedd Ddu* has *always* looked after this place, long before Glyndwr. *Y Groesfan*, the crossing place, where the warriors and heroes and the men of magic came to die. People have lived here half-aware of this for centuries. What they brought back, the four, was – I don't know – the *spirit* of Glyndwr, isn't it? Or something. How do you say it in English – the essence?'

Which they corrupted, Berry thought. They took the magic, and they wove that into the tapestry of this place. He thought of what he and Bethan had learned in the library over at Hereford yesterday. The impression they'd formed of the latter Druids as purveyors of a degraded version of the Celtic religion.

This was the tradition continued by the *Gorsedd Ddu*.

'Can of worms,' Berry said, thinking of graveyard worms, grown fat on the dead. 'How could folks live with all that?'

'Ah, Morelli, you will never understand. It's powerful, see. It works. What else in Wales is truly powerful these days, other than our traditions?' Aled's top teeth vanished into his snowy moustache. 'Excuse me, I am going to take the air.'

'No way I can talk you out of this?'

'Not unless you have a bigger gun,' Aled said. Berry watched him walk away across the bridge into the snow.

He discovered Bethan was at his elbow, wrapped in some kind of Welsh rug.

'He's gone to kill ap Siencyn,' Berry said. 'I don't see him coming back.'

She gripped his only visible arm.

'No,' Berry said. 'He know's where he's at. I think.'

'Just goes on, doesn't it?' Her voice was hoarse and fractured; she kept massaging her throat. 'On and on.'

'Something ended here tonight. You must feel that.'

'Nothing truly ends with guns,' Bethan said.

Berry shrugged, which hurt his broken arm. 'How do you feel now?'

'How do I look?'

Bruises besmirched most of her face. The skin was purple and swollen around both eyes. Her lip was twisted and her cheeks blotched with blood, some of it her own.

'You look wonderful,' he said.

'Your poor arm. Is it very painful?'

'Not like in the church. Christ, I don't think I ever felt more – you know – than when I was lying with both arms jammed in the Goddam tomb and there's this candle drifting towards me across–'

Bethan looked up sharply.

'Don't panic,' Berry said. 'It was Aled. The dissident. His, ah, wife died.'

'Gwenllian?'

'Accident in Aber. What pushed him over the edge, I guess. Sign that when something goes real bad, it ceases to discriminate between the English and the Welsh.'

'Or traitors and the cowards,' Bethan said.

'I liked him. Whatever happened here tonight, whatever lifted, it was in some way all down to him. Not me or you. *He* did it.'

He licked his forefinger and rubbed a blood-fleck off her nose. 'What happens in the church, Aled puts down the candle and he levers up the slab so I can get my arms out, and then we kick the slab clean off the tomb and smash the shit outa the fucking effigy. He does most of that; I'm hurting too much.'

Bethan said slowly, 'So you know now what was in the tomb.'

'Yeah.'

'Do I have to ask?'

'Bones,' Berry said. 'Bones. Like you'd expect. Only *not* what you'd expect. Soon as the air got inside they more or less crumbled away. But, yeah, we saw what it was.'

'And?'

'Aled figured it for a ram.'

'A ram? As in . . . sheep?'

'Yeah. Make what you want outa that. Me, I don't want to think too hard about it. I lost enough sleep already.'

The rotors of the police helicopter were heard, a distant drone and then a clatter. And with the clatter a searchlight beam swept the village.

'Best place to land, I think,' Chief Inspector Gwyn Arthur Jones said, 'is the school playground. What do you think, Neil?'

Sergeant Neil Probert only grunted. Flying at night through intermittent snow, he'd been terrified most of the way. Even the pilot did not look exactly happy. He'd made them wait an hour until the snow had eased, before deciding it was safe to make the trip at all.

Neil had not spoken since the searchlight had picked up the Daihatsu on its side at the bottom of a gulley, and Gwyn Arthur had ordered the pilot to go in low enough to ascertain that they were both dead, the two men who'd been flung out into the snow. They could not have been anything *but* dead.

'Tell you one thing, Guv,' said the pilot now, a Cockney called Bob Gorner. 'You won't catch me doing this number again.'

'Ah, worst of it is over, man,' Gwyn Arthur said scornfully. 'Right now, come on, let's go round the village once again before we land.'

There was still apparently no power in Y Groes. Plenty of little glimmerings, though, candles, lamps. Far more than you'd expect after midnight even in a town the size of Pont. Something was up, Gwyn Arthur thought. No question.

The police helicopter circled over the pub – lots of wispy little lights around there – and then over the church and back again towards the river.

'OK, take her in then, Bob. No wait – what's that?' Gwyn Arthur leaned forward in his seat.

Neil Probert, feeling queasy, didn't move, just closed his eyes and muttered, 'Where?'

'By there . . . See it? Figure scurrying along the bank. Could've been a child. Gone now. Under the bridge, maybe?'

'Want me to go round again, Guv?'

'Yes, one last time, then we'll land.'

Neil Probert groaned.

When the searchlight beam had passed over, Sali Dafis came out from under the bridge, small and lithe, elfin in a black tracksuit. The air was temporarily still, a break between snow salvos.

The body of the big woman still lay on the bank, headless. Partially covered in snow, in various shades of pink and a kind of crimson which was close to black.

Sali looked down at the body, then up at the church tower, then down at the body again, and finally up at the bridge, to her left, where her *nain*, Mrs Bronwen Dafis, had appeared.

Old Mrs Dafis leaned over the bridge parapet and watched Sali silently.

Sali crouched beside the body in the snow. She began to brush away some of the soft, white snow, and then the hard pink snow. Finally the ice-blood around Buddug's neck.

She glanced up again at the bridge, and Mrs Bronwen Dafis nodded.

So did the woman now standing next to her, the younger one. Whose face, the girl could tell, even from this distance, was equal in its severity.

Sali plunged her small, white hand into the gore.

Rheithordy.

The gate was open.

But no light shone from the house, not a candle-glimmer.

He knew where the rectory was, though, could sense its bulk, although there was no feeling of a building about it.

Sometimes it was a building, and sometimes it was just a part of the woods, the oak trees crowding the lawn almost shouldering the rectory itself, as if feeding sap to their brothers in its frame.

Aled walked to the front door of the rectory and the snow went with him, flurrying around his body. He felt a sudden power – *he* was bringing the snow. He was the bad-weather man.

The door was unlocked. He turned the knob and it opened and the smell came out at him, mouldy, brackish, the smell of the oak woods in decay, only ten times as strong as it would have been in the wood itself.

'Rector!' Aled's voice was harder and colder than the snow that came with him.

What did he know of ap Siencyn? Who *was* the man? The latest in an ancient line which sometimes has been interrupted but never for long because the wrong men would not last in this parish – if they were Welsh they would move away, if English . . .

'Rector!'

Poking the gun before him, Aled entered the hall, scattering snow.

He kicked open the doors, one by one, saw still rooms tinged with snowlight through steep, multi-paned windows.

No firelight, no candles.

He knew, then.

Abruptly he turned and stalked out of the rectory into the night, where they were assembled around the entrance.

Snarling, breathing in spurts, Aled crouched and blasted both barrels into the night and into the company of ancient oaks gathered before him on the rectory lawn.

There were four shots; he had obviously reloaded.

Groups of people stood in the snow outside the *Tafarn*. Nobody spoke.

Bethan watched the faces of the people and saw a complexity of human emotions, from shock and bewilderment, through tired acceptance, to a kind of relief.

Among the people conspicuous by their absence were the mechanic Dilwyn Dafis; his mother Mrs Bronwyn Dafis, the seer; skeletal Glyn Harri, the village historian. And bluff, bearded Morgan Morgan, farmer, and husband of the late Buddug.

Bethan wondered for whom the *cannwyll gorff* shone now.

'Over?' Berry wondered.

The police helicopter was almost overhead. The villagers began to drift away, many into the *Tafarn*.

Bethan said, 'You won't tell Guto, will you?'

'Huh?'

She said, 'That there was a ram in the tomb.'

'I don't understand. And where the hell *is* Guto?'

'Probably in the bar with Miranda celebrating his victory in the by-election.'

'Jesus, how long was I *in* that church?'

Bethan would have smiled but her facial muscles weren't up to it. 'He believes he had a vision in the Nearly Mountains. There is a folk-tale about the Abbot of Valle Crucis in North Wales. How one morning on the Berwyn Mountain the abbot is approached by a figure out of the mist which turns out to be Owain Glyndwr. And Owain says, Good Morrow, Abbot, you are out early, something like this. And the Abbot says, No, you are out a hundred years *too* early. And Owain vanishes, never to be seen again.'

'Until he runs into Guto on the Nearly Mountains?'

'Guto is not laughing about this. He claims there was a miracle, which he won't talk about. But . . . Well, he is now convinced he will win the by-election.'

'Who knows?' Berry said. 'Maybe we did let something else outa the tomb. The whole point – the whole secret of this – is not what actually happened but what you *believe* happened. Hey, am I getting mystical, or becoming Welsh, or what?'

Bethan pulled him into the shelter of the *Tafarn* porch. Through the door they could see a lot of people quietly drinking, helping themselves; no landlord any more. The atmosphere was like an overcrowded hospital in wartime, full of assorted casualties, people looking around wondering what happened and who was left alive.

Wind-blown snow hit the porch in a cloud. Berry stared at it, expressionless. Bethan said, 'What are you thinking?'

'Trying to figure out what happens now,' Berry said. 'Apart from getting my arm fixed. Sitting around waiting till I can drive again. Watching the bruises heal on your face.'

'And then you'll go back. To London?' Keeping her expression as neutral as she could, given the condition of her face.

He shook his head.

'To America?'

'No way. I got no roots left anyplace. Maybe I should stick around awhile until something suggests itself.' He tried to hold her eyes. 'Maybe I should learn Welsh.'

Bethan flung an arm around his neck and kissed him, which hurt them both quite a lot. 'Start with this . . . *Fi'n caru ti.*'

'Tea? Hold on, I got it. You're saying "I'd like a black tea, no sugar . . ."'

They smiled stupidly at each other. 'Yuk, how utterly nauseating,' Miranda said, coming out of the bar, sipping a vodka and lime. 'How is it that other people in love are so unbearable?'

She stood with them on the porch, red hair a little awry, but otherwise as elegant and unruffled as ever. 'That bastard Guto,' she said.

'What'd he do now?'

'He's dismissed me,' Miranda said petulantly. 'Until after the election. He thinks I won't be good for his image. How ungrateful can you get? Besides, he's awfully funny in bed. I mean, what am *I* going to do until after the election?'

Miranda took a big, sulky sip from her vodka and lime. It seemed to Berry that Guto had a point here.

'Well,' he said thoughtfully, watching Bethan out of the corner of an eye, his spirits suddenly up higher than the helicopter. 'I can get you a ten-inch lovespoon, but you got to buy your own batteries.'

'This the last time, guv?'

'One final look. No hang on, listen, you hear that? Can you cut the engine a second?'

'It's a bleeding helicopter, guv, not an Austin Metro.'

'Sorry, Bob, stupid of me. It's just I thought I heard . . . well, a shot. Never mind. Look, there's the child, do you see her?'

'Where?' said Neil Probert, eyes closed.

'Wake up, you dozy bugger. What do you make of that?'

'Sorry, Sir.' Neil leaned over Gwyn Arthur's shoulder. The searchlight had picked up the small girl on the main street.

'Skipping along, see. Not a care in the world, as if she's going home from school. And *what* bloody time is it?'

'One twenty-five, Sir.'

The child looked up at the helicopter, directly into the searchlight's glare, and even from this distance they could tell she was grinning.

'Kids,' said Gwyn Arthur, forgetting for a moment that he was investigating at least one suspicious death. 'What are the bloody parents doing? And what's that all over her face? Toffee?'

The child skipped gaily up the street. 'Oh Christ . . .' said Neil Probert. 'Who's this?'

'Jesus . . .' Gwyn Arthur breathed. 'Get us down, Bob.'

The man with the shotgun was stalking the child along the street.

'Get the fucking thing down!'

'Yeh, yeh, got to be the field, though.'

'Can't you get any closer?'

The man was perhaps three yards behind the girl. He raised the gun to his shoulder.

'Sod the fucking field!' Gwyn Arthur screamed. 'Go in.'

The pilot glanced wildly from side to side, judging distances, road levels. 'Gonna damage it, guv.'

'So it's damaged . . . Go in!'

They were so low now, churning up the night, that the man's white hair was blown on end. He went into a crouch, the gun aimed at the back of the child's head.

'Hit him in the fucking whatsits – land on him or something.'

The girl stopped.

She turned round.

The man's hair and his clothes were quivering in the swirling air.

He lowered the gun.

The girl's hair was unmoving in the rotor-driven maelstrom. She stood quite still in the spotlight, staring at the man.

The man stood there for long, long seconds before sinking slowly to his knees in the snow and fumbling with the shotgun and something else.

'What's—?' Neil said.

'A twig,' Gwyn Arthur said, suddenly calm. 'Pen. Pencil. I don't know. But he's fitting it under the trigger guard.'

Aled rose from his knees, the shotgun upright on the ground, its barrel tucked under his chin. The child watched him lift a foot, bring it down the side of the gun to where the twig, pencil, whatever protruded from the trigger guard.

Neil Probert turned away.

'OK,' Gwyn Arthur said quietly. 'Pull back. Land in the schoolyard. Don't scare her any more.'

The star burst of blood and brains covered a very wide area of the snowy street.

Bob Gorner said, 'She ain't scared, guv. Tell you that for nuffink.'

The child had turned her back on the mess and was skipping back up the road, past the *Tafarn*, towards the cottages, to where two women were waiting. They each took one of the child's hands.

'She's in shock.' Gwyn Arthur said uncertainly.

But Neil Probert knew what the pilot meant. He sank back, closed his eyes, the sweat cooling on his brow.

Bob killed the searchlight and took the chopper into an arc towards the school.

None of them spoke.

For a moment it seemed the child had thrown a shadow ten times her size across the snow. A monstrous shadow, with the illusion of small, hard wings flapping at its shoulders.

PHIL RICKMAN

The Chalice

£5.99

Glastonbury is considered by many to be 'the holiest earth in England', for here, it is said, lies the Holy Grail, and this West Country town has always been a centre of pilgrimage full of mystics and healers, poets and artists. Many local people resent the intrusion, and hostility continually bubbles beneath the surface . . . as does an ancient pagan magic. Glastonbury Tor, the mysterious conical hill once the site of Druid rituals, has an awesome history of unexplained phenomena.

The magical Tor has been a lifelong obsession for Diane Ffitch – to the disdain of the locals, who know her as 'Lady Loony'. But, as the mystical atmosphere of the place becomes soured by bitterness, violence and death, Diane is convinced she is being warned of impending disaster. Her closest friend, Juanita, is sceptical; and while the writer Joe Powys just *might* understand, he's determined to stay well clear of Glastonbury, where he knows the veil is thin and the forces of light and darkness now shine with equal intensity.

But with the supernatural beginning to seep through the cracks, someone must face up to the worst of all possibilities: the existence of an anti-Grail – the Dark Chalice.

'I emerged shell-shocked and still completely involved with the story, I was going round in a daze'
Barbara Erskine

PHIL RICKMAN

December

£5.99

December has the shortest days, the darkest nights . . .

On the night of 8 December 1980, John Lennon was murdered in New York. Meanwhile, in a recording studio built into the ruins of the medieval abbey of Ystrad Ddu, four musicians – brought together because of their psychic sensitivities – were attempting to finish an album. As it turned out, they were all so emotionally damaged by the events of that unholy night that they burned the tapes instead . . . or thought they had.

Now, years later, Dave and Simon and Tom and Moira have been lured, cajoled, virtually blackmailed into returning to complete their almost forgotten masterpiece . . . along with Tom's despairing wife Shelley, his disadvantaged daughter Vanessa, Weasel the roadie, Prof Levin the alcoholic recording engineer. All of them back to the abbey.

In December, naturally.

'No one writes better than Phil Rickman of the shadow-frontier between the supernatural and the real world'
Bernard Cornwell